BOOK 2 IN THE SHADOW SWORD SERIES

# THE
# LAST SEER KING

## S.J. HARTLAND

Dark Blade Publishing

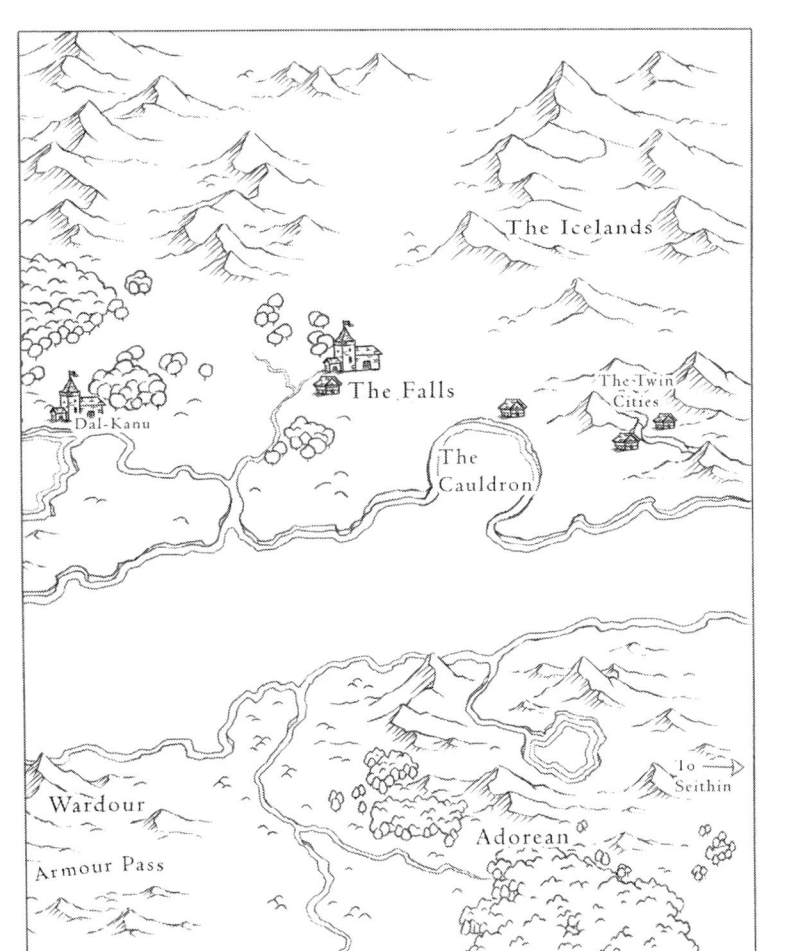

The Icelands

The Falls

Dal-Kanu

The Twin
Cities

The
Cauldron

Wardour

Armour Pass

Adorean

To
Seithin

# DANNON

The chaos that followed the battle should please him. The disorder, the promise of rich spoils. Broken lands, broken lords, broken authority were all grist for the Varee.

Instead, the silence sank into him, a beast of a thing that pawed his neck with unease as the clanging, pealing iron and the screams of men ebbed away.

Not even a breeze stirred through the pile of ash from a pyre where a young warrior Dannon never knew had died before the fighting erupted.

Only death surrounded him. Beneath its pall, the world had become quiet and still: the forest, drenched with shadows, the castle rooted in stone on the edge of the sea, its towers spiking the heat-hazed sapphire sky.

The eye of the storm was upon this battlefield, lost moments when time eddied between combat's fury and its miserable aftermath… so familiar to a Varee war captain.

Hidden on the edge of green-black trees, armed riders at his back, Dannon gripped his horse's reins, his disquiet caged in his tensed hands. He could not forget that crash of metal on stone as guards flung the gates back and Isles warriors fell upon the king's forces, breaking Cathmor's line. How panicked men had trampled flags flat, abandoning their war engines to flee into the trees.

Barely an hour ago, Icemen had chased them down until the dead strewn through the forest outnumbered the dead upon the blood-churned field. Now the battle was done. A kingdom's fate had turned. And he was here to pick at the broken realm's bones.

A woman's cry ripped apart the emptiness. She dropped to her knees beside a body in the tangle of severed limbs and shattered bone littered between the forest and the castle. More figures, pitifully waiflike, emerged from the castle gates to drift among the slain. Carts for the wounded rattled from Tide's End.

A soldier wearing Isles livery, a dented helmet under his arm, whistled callously as he ordered dull-eyed captives to hurl their weapons onto a pile of iron. The breeze carried laughter that was shrill with relief.

An Isles victory then. Dannon shouldn't care. No. He couldn't *afford* to care.

"Sweep up those who fled," Dannon told his companions. "Avoid the paths—they will. They're displaced now, on the run and vulnerable. Be quick before whoever has command at Tide's End chases them down."

Leather scraped as well-trained warriors on horseback slipped away through the trees. There was only an indolent murmur of waves against the castle's base.

The afternoon sun warmed Dannon's face and slanted harsh light upon the naked rigging of the majestic Isles fleet at anchor. A wind finally awakened, breaking apart the heat, creaking through the ships. Its gusts carried a fresh, clean scent of fading summer.

A strange place this city with its ramparts and castle towers looming high above droning, white-tipped waves. A place where a man like him could never belong. Not just because of the Isles' unfamiliar expanse of sky and sea or its relentless, draining heat, but because of this land's rules, its fealties. The very conduct of life. All contrary to the code of the wild lands beyond the gorge.

Dannon laughed softly to himself. *Morose man.* That's what his wife had always called him when he was lost in reflection. "Life is serious enough without the weight of your heavy thoughts," she'd tease. "Come back to me, oh, Dannon the Deep and Distant."

"Dannon the Deep and Dashing," he'd reply, wriggling his brows so that she giggled.

A branch snapped. Dannon turned fast. Pain shot through his shoulders as metal jaws ripped him off his horse. Trees, sky whirled. He hit the ground hard, winded, his spine jarred.

The steel teeth bruised as they were torn away. Someone dragged him to his knees. Dizzy, disoriented, Dannon tried to focus on a weathered face and dirty brown hair tied in a thong. When he recognised who stood over him, sword drawn, his belly churned in disbelief.

"Volker? What is this? I ordered you to track down fleeing soldiers. The aftermath of battle is the perfect hunting ground for slavers."

The man ripped Dannon's sword from its shoulder holster and tossed it into the bushes. He dragged his tongue nervously over his thin lips. "Just stay still, Captain. Nice and still."

Dannon started to rise. Volker jabbed his sword hilt into Dannon's temple. He dropped in a huddle, moaning.

"Still, I said." Volker waved his sword. "On your knees. Cross your ankles. Lace your fingers together on your head. Do as I say, or I'll hit you again."

Reluctantly, Dannon obeyed. His gashed temple dripped blood. A slow anger moved from his breast into his limbs. Volker had attacked him with a man-catcher. Even padded, its dangerous jaws could break bones. The Varee used it—rarely—to snatch armoured warriors from their horses.

"What's this about? If I've wronged you somehow, we can talk about it."

"Talk, talk, talk." Volker dragged a grubby hand through hair lank with oil and sweat. "No more clever talk from you, Captain." He groped for rope in his belt.

Dannon swayed on his knees. "How dare you attack me!" His fury burst up to cover his fear. "What do you want?"

Volker scuffed his boot on the grass and glanced into the trees.

Was his captor expecting someone? At the thought he had more enemies, a chill nipped along Dannon's backbone.

"Suppose there's no harm in you knowing," Volker said. "I'm meant to kill you. Our oh-so-brave leader thinks you're too clever, too dangerous. He won't tolerate rivals." His sly grin spread. "But I'm not going to kill you. Not when you're worth a fortune."

Dannon briefly shut his eyes, struggling to take that in. He knew the overlord resented him, but Conroy had broken every Varee code by coming after him.

"A battlefield is indeed the best place for slavers to scoop up merchandise. You're right there. But none of the warriors we capture today will be worth half as much as you."

"What?" Dannon groped at the pouch in his belt. The poison within was a last resort, a painful death, but a long while ago, he'd resolved never to be captured alive again.

Volker pricked Dannon's wrist with the sword tip. "Touch that pouch, and I'll cut your fingers off. You think I'm going to let you kill yourself with mord's breath? There's no easy way out for you, Captain."

Dannon tongued his dry lips. "What—what do you intend to do with me?"

"When it's dark, I'm going to take you back to the Mountains. Turn you in for the bounty." Volker whistled. "It's huge. Who'd think a lousy Cahirean was worth so much?"

"You snake." Dannon fisted his hands. "You swore a blood oath to the Varee, to our god." He seized a furious breath. "To me. We don't turn on our own."

"We do if the reward is rich enough." Volker's eyes gleamed with lust for wealth. "And it's rich. So rich, the others whisper about how no host captain ever had such a price on his head. I had to act before they found the courage to betray you."

"You're Varee. Our loyalty to each other keeps us strong."

"Our?" Volker sneered. "You're Cahirean scum. Prey, like any other prey. Why shouldn't I profit from turning you in? Word is the Lord of Vraymorg or even the king's sheriffs will pay very well for your body—proof of death and all that—but they'll pay more for a living Varee war captain to execute. A warning to the rest of us."

"There's a Varee expression about blood money. That it can only be spent fast or not at all."

Volker jeered. "There's another Varee saying too. That we dance with steel until we dance on a gibbet. You're going to dance on a rope, Dannon." He stepped closer, dangling a cord from his fingers. "Don't be stupid. Either I take you in alive, or you cause trouble and I take you in dead."

"The king's sheriffs, you say—" Dannon reached for his anger. "Which king, though?"

"What?"

Dannon jerked up. He smashed his head into Volker's chin. The man stumbled, recovered, and slashed with steel. Still finding his balance, Dannon only just sucked in his belly. The blade sliced his tunic, missing muscle by a hair's breadth.

"Scum." Fading sun glinted wickedly on metal as Volker thrust again. "You're going to die like your scum father. Grovelling. On your knees."

Dannon flinched clear then backed up, his hands raised defensively. Volker was on him once more, bellowing and swinging.

Air parted Dannon's hair as he ducked. Staying low, he tackled Volker's legs. The man crashed down, his breath whooshing out as he hit the ground. Still dizzy, Dannon clambered up as fast as he could. He drove his heel into the fallen man's wrist. Volker screamed. His fingers fell away from the sword.

Dannon stood over him, panting. Volker's shriek and the flash of sunlight on the blade stirred up a childhood memory of swirling dust, drumming hooves, and the clash of iron.

He remembered his father's knees hitting the dirt, a stain spreading beneath his fingers as he clutched at his belly. He remembered screaming, his high-pitched cry swallowed by the tumult as men grabbed his shoulders to hold him back. "My father wasn't scum. He died fighting. Trying to save me."

The man on the ground sneered. "Your father begged for his life. He offered anything, even you, to save his miserable hide."

"No!"

"You're as pitiful as he was. He died on his knees, blubbering like a baby."

"You're lying."

Volker's lips peeled back from blackened teeth. His eyes were cold and full of contempt. "Your father, that Cahirean coward, begged—right before I cut off his head."

Shock numbed him. When it fell away, it left a hollow place inside. "You. It was you—" Dannon could not continue. This snake had not only killed his father but also defiled his memory with lies. That memory was all Dannon had of him, all he had of his other life. Now, this treacherous piece of filth, a man who had offered his blood oath, had betrayed him. For such a worthless reason as monetary gain.

Dannon's rage exploded. His head spun with it, his body taut with the need for violent release. He yanked Volker up by his tunic to punch his face. Again and again, he struck.

One blow shattered a cheekbone. Another drove into Volker's nose with a satisfying crunch. As he pounded flesh to pulp, Dannon's knuckles grew slippery with blood.

He realised he was shouting. Sounds at first. Then words. Slowly, they penetrated his shut-down mind. "He never begged. He was honourable and brave, and you took him from me."

"He was as worthless as you," Volker wheezed. "Just Cahirean filth."

"I am Varee," Dannon yelled. "I have to be. I have to belong."

The words hit him. He dropped a sagging Volker. Blankly, he

stared, not seeing the bleeding man, only hearing his own voice fade away into the murmur of the waves. *I have to be. I have to belong.*

Groaning, Dannon pressed his torn knuckles into his cheeks. Everyone needed to find a place somewhere. To believe in something. Without the Varee, he had nothing. No one. At even the thought of such loneliness, a pit opened in his gut.

He retrieved Volker's sword. Part of his mind again closed off as he lifted the blade.

Volker struggled to his knees. "No." He scrambled back. "No."

Dannon thrust. Once. The sword speared flesh then ribs. Blood spurted in a bright fountain, crimson against the shadowy trees. Volker dropped on the grass, limbs sprawled. More blood spilled from his slack mouth. His eyes glazed.

Dannon wiped the blade on the dead man's tunic. "I am my father's son," he told the corpse. "I know who I am. I belong." Digging his nails into his palms, he pushed aside the doubt.

"I belong," he said and turned away.

# VAL ARQUES

"**H**e's alive. Get him into a cart and back to the castle." Worried voices swelled and receded like the tide. Irritating hands lifted him.

He tried to tell them to let him lie there on the quiet battlefield, to let him slip away from the pain into a comforting blackness, but he couldn't make a sound.

Wheels rattled over stones. Vraymorg drifted into that ether on the edge of consciousness, unable to measure time passing.

"The wound is ugly," a man said.

"Do what you can for him. Send for me if there is any change."

More hands groped his body, holding his shoulders as someone cut off his clothing.

"Kaell's sword." He snatched at an arm. "I need it. Don't—clean—it." Then his fingers fell away, and he plunged into welcome emptiness.

He woke to black night besieging the glow from a candle beside his bed. Curved stone surrounded him. It might have been his chamber at Vraymorg but for the salty tang and the sheen of moonlight through windows, oddly bright as though reflected up from a velvet sea.

Vraymorg lay completely still, listening to droning waves as his sluggish thoughts stirred. A battle. Yes, he remembered that. He remembered the fire. Kaell. *Oh gods, Kaell.*

*The sword. Where is the sword?*

He peered about then sighed in relief. The blade lay upon a chest, moonlight striking its gleaming length. It seemed hardly different to his sword. Except, knowing part of Fortitude's wicked secret, he could scarcely bear to look at it.

Vraymorg sat up. Pain slammed into him. He clutched at his gut, breathing hard, teeth clenched as he pushed to his feet. He took one staggering step then another. The sword was a handbreadth away. All he had to do was reach out and take it.

Muscles in his back cramped with reluctance. His skin damp and hot, he released a breath to draw down his shoulders and curled his fingers about the hilt. The blade pulsed as if alive. With a cry of horror, he flung it down. Oh gods, he could not do this.

*Coward.* The word thumped in his skull. *Coward. How many times did you fail him? Do this as a final act of fatherhood. Trust Arn had told him the truth, that this magic would work.*

He bent, bit back a scream at the rip of fire across his gut, and emptied his mind. That was the only way he could sweep up that blade and lurch to the door.

Outside, a man slumped on a stool looked up sharply. "My lord, what are you—" Ewen broke off, his gaze on the bloody sword. Slowly, he lifted his eyes to his lord's face. "What are you doing with Kaell's blade?"

Vraymorg braced a shoulder against the wall. "Where's the girl's room? Azenor's."

"She's dead." Ewen started to rise. "Just now. The physician went to fetch her brothers."

"Where's her room?"

"At the end of the passage. Val, whatever you intend, don't do it."

"You don't know what I intend."

"Don't do it. Please."

Vraymorg pushed off the wall unsteadily. "I have to do this," he muttered. "Alone."

He left the man staring after him as he staggered along the

darkened corridor. Air dense with frangipani and the first hint of rain whipped flames in sconces. From deep below, drums beat out a primal rhythm. Voices and laughter floated from afar like the remnants of a dream. A celebration. It belonged to another world.

*This tower, though...* Vraymorg realised he knew it. In these passages, he had played hide-and-seek with his brother. In the hall below, he had wed Finya and carried her up winding stairs to the wedding-night bedchamber. Nervous. Eager. In love in a heady, hopeful way he had never felt since.

*Tide's End.* That they brought him here surely meant an Isles victory. Though unlikely, it had to be. Beyond that, he had no clue what had happened. Answers must wait until daylight.

He groped along the wall to the farthest chamber, a short distance, but for him a dizzy, endless nightmare. His gut burned, his legs shaky. At the door to Azenor's room, Vraymorg summoned feeble strength and pushed inside.

The ocean's comforting rumble, its briny breath, hit him like the pain. Insistent. Unlocking memories. Some welcome, some not.

His mother's room. Here, she had laughed, loved, and sobbed with all the furious passion of an Isles woman. From this window, she had leaned to encourage her young sons learning to lunge and parry in the courtyard, crying out in dismay when a blow put one on his knees.

Sadness throbbed inside him. Time had stolen so much. He could not lose Kaell too. Whatever the price, Vraymorg would pay it to save him.

Vraymorg stumbled to the girl upon the bed. Moonlight through an open window struck her tumble of dark hair. He paused to study Azenor's face. Surely she could not be dead, not with that sheen of light on her skin. Not this girl. How alive she had seemed in the Mountains. How fierce. The physician must have made a mistake.

He leaned forward, his hand close to her nose and mouth. No breath warmed his palm.

"I'm sorry," he whispered. "I wish I could save you too. Perhaps you're at peace now. How can I know? I only know I have to save Kaell. I've failed him too often, and I can't do it again." He sighed. "Arn says I can bring him back. That this sword stained with Kaell's blood can revive him."

A thread of his mother's jasmine-and-sandalwood perfume swirled around him, as elusive as a sharp-footed bladesman. Her laugh echoed. Shapes, shadows, the past, and present entwined in an eerie fog. Fever blurred his reality.

Perhaps this was a fever dream, too, nothing more. Perhaps he was still in his bed, unable to move, imagining this room. Imagining what he was about to do.

Nausea pushed up into his throat. Vraymorg propped a hand against the pillow. The sword's ugly glint urged him on. A cursed sword. The proper blade for a cursed man.

Deliberately, he lifted his gaze to the night sky, to clouds edged with ivory starlight. He could not look at her, or he would hesitate and turn away.

*Think only of Arn's message: This will save Kaell.* He pressed his lips to the bloody sword. Then he bent and kissed her.

The room, the roar of the sea, the murk creeping from the corners all circled him, closing, closing, closing. His breath froze in his lungs. An odour rose up. Not jasmine. Not even the sea's brine. A rotten stench, so thick it hazed.

Choking, spluttering, Vraymorg staggered to the door. The hinges shrieked an accusation. As though in a dream, he reeled into the passage, sweat pouring down his back, tears staining his cheeks.

As he reached a corner, the nape of his neck prickled. He turned.

Along the corridor, a man watched him. Not Ewen. A stranger.

For a long moment, he and the man stared at each other as though a cord tethered their gazes. Then, without saying a word, the figure slipped into Azenor's room.

The strangeness of that moment lingered. It meant something. But Vraymorg had no strength left to wonder at it. He collapsed where he was, the sword sliding from his hand. A different nightmare closed about him.

# HEATH

Heath tapped fingers against his empty scabbard. How long must he be trapped in this airless hall, his hairline damp, his pants uncomfortably plastered to his thighs?

If only Velleran were here. This was his elder brother's domain—the world of courtiers and polite, empty talk. Velleran would smile and simper, then later, in their chambers, sneer at those who had preened at his flattery.

Impatiently, Heath swept a look down the long chamber at his new allies. Strangers for the most part, they clustered in a riot of colour about a platform where Gendrick Caelan sat straight-backed on a cushioned chair. Isles lords and ladies, their perfumed bodies adorned in flowing fustian cloaks, their sheer gowns of silk so fine they might have been dyed spiderwebs.

Stunted shadows dappled the tiled floor. Sunlight struck rounded pillars fluted to the roof and fell upon the casket behind the platform. In this heat, they had best surrender the fallen Lord Hatton to the sea and his gods quickly.

Heath swiped sweat from his temple. A tedious business, victory. It was all very well, winning and all that, but he had plots to weave and lordlings to deceive. One duty to complete. To abduct Aric Caelan.

The object of his *quest*—how noble and worthy that word made his devious schemes sound—stood with his uncle at Gendrick's shoulder as, one by one, defeated lords from the Falls, the Plains, or the Downs knelt with a rustle of cloth and squeak of leather boots to kiss the new king's ringed fingers.

Each muttered an oath. Meaningless, surely. Loyalty belonged to family. The rest was merely a matter of convenience and gain. To the Ice lords, one Telorian king was much like another, just so long as the sovereign left them alone in their distant caverns.

Idly, he watched Gendrick. With curling black hair and etched cheekbones, the new king looked as much a son of the Isles as his brother. Gendrick, though, possessed a bitterness Aric did not. Tortured lines forced his mouth into a permanent scowl, and his stare was clouded with cynicism. His was a hard face, in fact, for a careful man whose expression did not change regardless of whether an Isles warrior or a repentant traitor knelt before him.

*Except…* Heath edged closer. Every time the king glanced at Aric, a flicker of disgust flashed in his eyes. His mouth slitted, and his cheeks sucked in with resentment. Heath's scalp tingled pleasurably. Gendrick hated his brother. Hatred, Heath could use.

The ranks of traitors and loyal noblemen and women thinned. Heath strode out. As he slid to one knee, curious looks burned his back. *An Ice lord at Tide's End? Where were his fangs? Shouldn't he wear a black hood and carry a grimoire?*

When the king thrust out his hand, Heath dutifully pressed his lips to the cold topaz ring. "We must talk," he said softly, "about how you repay the Icelands for helping you take the throne."

Gendrick's hand froze in midair. He gave a curt nod. "Come to my chambers."

Heath straightened. He began to turn, when the hall's metal doors flew back with a resounding clang. Men and women whipped about. One or two voices rose, strident in objection, then died to murmurs.

Every sound stripped from the hall. Every sound but one. In the quiet, it was magnified—an echo of footsteps on tiles as someone walked unhurried through the columns towards the king.

Guards levelled spears to block the intruder. At last able to see who had entered, Heath arched a brow. He knew his would not be the only backbone to stiffen with disbelief.

For in a hall where the ghosts of Isles lords surely paced, in a castle built by a Caelan king as a symbol of Telorian defiance, an enemy had dared to come. Openly, brazenly. An elegant blond figure richly attired in garments of the finest samite and flanked by tall, equally fair companions.

*Archanin. It has to be. So the rumours of an alliance are true.*

Gendrick's shameless audacity astonished even him. Ghouls had slain thousands in the Mountains and Downs, and the new king received their god here, publicly.

"Let him through," Gendrick said.

The guards lowered their spears. Space opened before Archanin and his attendants as the crowd flinched back. With a complacent smile, the ghoul god advanced on the king. He did not bow.

Gendrick leaned towards the newcomer. "Archanin."

Their suspicions confirmed, the gathering hissed. Guards moved in, ready to settle any disorder.

"I have come"—the ghoul god paid no attention to the disturbance—"to offer my commiserations at your father's death and to congratulate you, Gendrick, on your elevation to king of all of Telor." He paused. "It is customary, is it not, to offer a new king a gift? I formally give to you, King Gendrick, a fortress upon the borders. The Fern Castle."

A cry rose from the Mountains men within the hall. Over the growing chaos of mutinous voices, a guard clanged his spear into the tiles and bellowed for silence.

Heath wondered what Vraymorg's reaction would be when he heard about the careless surrender of a Mountains castle. From the little he knew of the man lying wounded in a chamber above his head, he expected scorn. A hot, sharp blast of it. Vraymorg's anger caged by a porous layer of control was part of why this lord fascinated him.

A now-familiar yearning tortured him. How could he entice Vraymorg to the Icelands? Trickery, perhaps. Or simply take advantage of the chaos, seize Vraymorg forcibly, and dump him at Myranthe's elegant feet like a dutiful brother.

*Duty.*

Heath scoffed at his self-deception. He might pretend his preoccupation with Vraymorg was about duty, but it was about a complicated web of need and longing too uncomfortable to examine. That in itself was unlike him. He liked to understand his every motivation, exhausting though it was to have this endless internal battle play out in his head.

"I thank you," Gendrick said to Archanin, a sliver of sarcasm in his tone. "I accept your gift as a sign of a new friendship between our people."

The crowd watched with horrified fascination. Heath shook his head, aware admiration tempered his shock. After one day as king, Gendrick had stirred up dissent.

"This ceremony is done." The king's uncle, Tomasin Caelan, glanced uneasily about the chamber as though discerning the ugly mood. "Let us adjourn to the feasting hall. I, for one, have a dry throat."

Relieved laughter broke out. Men and women drifted off, heads bent close to whisper. Others lingered, darting stormy glances at Gendrick. The king remained where he was. He called a guard to him. The guard listened then nodded. He approached Heath.

"My lord," he said, "the king bids me show you to his chambers."

Heath followed.

Gendrick let him wait. A snub, perhaps, to put an uppity Ice lord in his lowly place or to allow time to stoke his imagination so that he would nervously wonder which of his misdeeds Gendrick was about to expose.

Even aware of the king's manipulation, Heath stalked back and forth outside Gendrick's chambers. More than once, he brushed his hand over the worn leather of his empty scabbard. Without a sword's weight against his hip, his body felt unbalanced, unclad even.

While he paced, he considered ways to abduct both Aric and Vraymorg. Some of his plots were devious. Others were plain reckless. In his current restless mood, he favoured the reckless.

Pausing by a table, he reached for a wine jug. It slipped through his fingers, clattering to the floor. Wine ran into cracks between tiles. Heath stared at the spreading stain beneath the rocking jug. Then he stared at his hand. It shook.

He squeezed a fist, surprised at his weak grip. *Weariness. That's it. Must be.* Only two days ago, he had commanded his men in a bloody tumult, an exhausting dance of steel and nerves. That alone was enough to make any man unsteady.

The doors to Gendrick's rooms opened. The ghoul god swept through, his brisk steps hinting at displeasure. At Archanin's aura of power and menace, Heath's arms prickled, but he resisted the urge to step back.

Archanin stopped. He passed blue eyes over him. "Who are you?"

"That's a difficult question to answer. Do you mean my name? My position? What I am? What I do?" Heath sighed with dramatic effect.

"I see." Disinterested, the gaze shifted away. "A fool."

As Archanin strode off, Heath laughed, his earlier awe gone. *Perhaps I should have grovelled.*

Distracted, Heath took a moment to realise a guard had summoned him twice into the new king's presence.

Glaring sunlight lit the vaulted, long room beyond the doors. The walls were white, the floor tiled. Heath trod on a large mosaic of a servant tipping water into a tub while a heavy-breasted woman bathed. Red bougainvillea in pots curled up fluted columns. Wide, low windows opened onto a balcony overlooking the sea. Sheer curtains billowed at doors flung back to let in the salty breeze.

Despite the couches with fluffed cushions, the writing tables, and the tall-backed chairs, Heath found it uncomfortably sparse, as though the streaming light and the fresh gusts off the ocean rid Tide's End of every accumulated memory and emotion. So unlike the Icelands, where the closed-in caverns breathed with the past and all its trapped pain and struggle.

Gendrick turned from contemplating the sea below a window. *A blue expanse of nothing,* Heath thought. *Ugh.*

He swept a bow adept enough to impress even Velleran. Not that he'd ever bend his knee to his elder brother. Velleran's head was swollen already. "Your Grace."

Gendrick preened. That boded well. Heath could manipulate a vain man.

"Damadar, have you heard of the Sword Brotherhood?"

Heath curved an eyebrow. Not quite the greeting he'd expected. "I recall a phrase in an old poem about men rising up in a brotherhood of swords. Why?"

"My new ally just warned me about them. Archanin believes with my ascension to the throne, a time of prophecy is upon us." Gendrick snorted a laugh. "My new ally is also upset his changeling Kaell died in that fire. He thinks I should have stopped it."

"Very unreasonable," Heath said. "Speaking of new allies—"

"Yes, yes." Gendrick swept a hand through air. "I understand Cathmor made certain promises in return for your father's support."

"There's a matter of land. And I'm supposed to wed some child."

"Cathmor's widowed cousin. I must do something with the girl, but should I give an heiress to you?" Gendrick paused. "Can I trust you, Damadar? You wisely decided to fight for your rightful king, but a man who betrays one liege lord can betray another."

Heath spread his arms in a bid to appear guileless. "I assure you, Your Grace, I can be entirely trusted to serve my family's best interests. My sister, Judith, even calls me predictable. She also says I'm arrogant, irritating, and too fond of my own voice."

"Clearly a woman of insight, your sister," Gendrick said. "But back to betrayal?"

"Such a joyous word. It so effortlessly tumbles off the tongue." Heath pushed damp sleeves away from his wrists. "With my father's consent, I betrayed Cathmor only because he refused to surrender something my family badly desires."

"Oh?" Gendrick covered a yawn. "What might that be? Some remote castle on the border? Trade concessions? Gold?"

"No." Heath had Gendrick's measure, but what he said next still carried risk. "He refused to give me your brother."

A stillness saturated the other man. In the absence of words, Heath heard a creak of hulls and caught a flash of colour as a sail unfurled. A seagull's caw carried from the breakwaters.

Slowly, Gendrick's hand fell away from his mouth. "My brother." He slid Heath an insulting sneer. "You want Aric for what... use?"

"Use," Heath echoed. *Delightful.* "You misunderstand, Your Grace. Nothing carnal."

"Carnal covers all manner of motives," Gendrick said. "So tell me, Heath Damadar. Why do the lords of the Ice desire my brother?"

"It's simple really." Heath halted for dramatic effect. He often did the same in a fire dance, his sword suspended above a fallen opponent, waiting for the breathless crowd to urge him on. "We would like to kill Aric. If you have no objections."

The king rocked back. "You're serious."

"Entirely serious." Unusual for him. Rather uncomfortable.

As he submitted to another gruelling look, Heath plucked his sticky tunic off his breast. For all the Iceland's frosts and scourging winds, the Twin Cities felt very dear.

"It's a strange thing," Gendrick mused. "But I have no objections at all. Though perhaps you'll tell me why you would like to kill Aric—and how?"

"Gladly, Your Grace. My sister Myranthe believes she's uncovered knowledge of how to restore death riders. She intends to drive a knife into Aric's breast. Do tell me if anything I say concerns you."

Gendrick lifted his shoulders. His stare held upon Heath. "Nothing concerns me—yet. What do I care about death riders? As for Aric..." He dug ringed fingers into his jaw. "I was raised to be king. My brother was raised to go to war. That is all."

That was all. Not to outshine the heir. A younger son should succeed, but only so the glory reflected on his brother. Be clever but not brilliant so the rightful successor did not pale in comparison.

Even as a second son, Heath understood Gendrick's resentment at being his father's firstborn then being presented with a brother just that bit braver and more charming.

He hadn't expected Gendrick to be so jealous of Aric. *Useful.*

"It breeds discontent if a king suffers rivals to his throne." Gendrick sniffed. "A younger brother, especially one with Caelan blood, can become a focus for the disaffected, for rebellion."

"Indeed," Heath said. "Stability, order. These matter. Popular is not a good quality for a leader."

"Aric doesn't have what it takes to rule," Gendrick muttered to himself. "No one sees what he's really like. Not quite the handsome, gallant prince they think. Huh." He broke off with an uneasy look at Heath. "I—I only mean I was raised for this. To rule. Aric wasn't. He's good at waving a sword about, but kingship is about hard decisions."

"Save us from heroes," Heath said, pretending not to notice

Gendrick's discomfort at what he had admitted. "Their only purpose is to die in battle. They're useless in peace. In fact, they get in the way. If I had such a brother…" He let the sentence hang.

Gendrick twitched a smile. Or at least, Heath thought it *might* have been a smile. He wondered if with practise before a mirror, he could duplicate that same sardonic edge to his grin.

"Yet, sadly." The king sighed heavily. "You cannot have Aric."

Just like that. Heath thought he had been suitably persuasive, stroked this man's vanity, played to his fears. *Ah well, it would be rather dull if Gendrick just threw his brother in a sack and handed him over.* "May I ask why not, Your Grace?"

Gendrick's smile was radiantly benign. But Heath sensed a sick satisfaction beneath it. "I already promised my brother to another." He waved a hand to accent the words. "A small price for peace." That smile corrupted the edges of his mouth. "A very small price."

Heath's steps dragged as he trudged from the hall onto the sea walk. White-tipped waves murmured. The sun's last light rimmed the horizon with dusted orange. Gulls circled.

He paused by a waist-high wall to order his thoughts. *Why should Archanin talk of a sword brotherhood? The stuff of Icelands legends.*

Waves rolled in then retreated, their motion mesmerising. Time flowed, its measure only in the first shimmer of stars clustering in the slow rising purple-hued darkness.

*Why drop that jug?* Heath knuckled the wind-blunted stone, his grip strong now. *Exhaustion, surely. Too long away from home.*

A woman wearing a priestess's robes, her grey hair tied in an austere bun, passed him. She nodded. Heath watched her toddle along the path towards the castle. *What is her name? Anne? Anna? Ainge.*

He had just turned back towards the sea when a woman screamed. The sound cut off sharply. Heath spun. He could see no one.

"My lord." A guardsman stood before him.

"Did you hear that?" Heath squinted into the gloom gathering below the castle walls. "I thought I heard a woman cry out."

"I did not pass anyone just now, my lord."

"Hmm." Perhaps he imagined that cry. Or it was a wretched seagull, so noisy with their incessant squawking. Heath considered the guardsman irritably. "Well, what do you want?"

"The lady Judith has returned. There's trouble, though. You bid me watch her—"

"What's she done?"

The man looked at his feet.

Heath sighed. "What's she done?"

The guard raised his head. "My lady ordered me to help carry him off. They're hiding him until dark then intend to sneak him out the postern gate. She bid me stay silent, but my duty is to you—" The man grimaced. "My lord, there's something you should know."

⁂

From outside the walls, the towers of Tide's End shadowed the tangle of trees, their canopy a dark smudge against the violet sky. Steam rose from damp grass. Storm clouds stalked the rising moons. Heath longed for rain, how it fractured the heat, released the muggy scents of gardenia and pepperbush, and at last stirred up a breeze.

Back against the discovered cart, ankles crossed, he watched the postern gate.

Judith was the first conspirator through. She drew up hard. "Oh," she said.

He tilted his head and considered her, saying nothing. A powerful weapon, silence.

"Heath," she began then broke off as Dillon appeared, dragging a gagged and bound man. At the sight of Heath, Dillon, too, said only, "Oh."

Heath folded his arms. "What have you done?"

Judith drew her top lip over her bottom. "It's not what you think."

"I think you've abducted this man."

"All right. It's exactly what you think." She sounded unrepentant.

He sighed. "At any other time, I couldn't care less if you snatch up fifty Isles captains and sneak them out postern gates. I'd even help. But someone is bound to miss this one. And by someone, I mean Aric Caelan."

"No one noticed a thing, Heath. Don't forget I learnt from the best—you."

"Oh, soothing flattery? No doubt you learnt that from me as well?"

"You always say keep it simple. So we did. Just carried him out of the infirmary as he slept. Nothing surreptitious."

"Dillon?" Heath edged up a brow. "How did my darling sister rope you into her mischief?"

Dillon shrugged. "She asked."

"She asked." Heath looked from one to the other in disbelief. "You both know what we're here for, don't you? We attract enough attention as it is."

Judith plucked at his sleeve. "If we burned the place to ash, no one would raise an eyebrow. Tide's End is chaotic. Carts rumble in and out, carrying the dead and wounded at all hours. Strangers everywhere. Servants, lords, soldiers, officials, priestesses all milling about."

Heath pushed off the cart and approached the captive. Pairas glared.

"If you behave," Heath said, "I'll remove the gag. Nod if you understand."

Pairas nodded curtly. The moment the gag came off, he swung

on Judith. "You crushed my ankle, you Icelands witch."

Judith slapped his cheek. Heath laughed. The man had become a dangerous distraction. He should have buried his blade in Pairas's heart in Tide's End months ago.

"It's time you understood your place." Judith tilted her chin haughtily. "Slave."

"Slave?" Pairas echoed, bewildered. Heath laughed harder.

She gestured to Dillon. "Get him into the cart."

"Take your hands off me." Pairas struggled. "I'm no slave. I was born in the Isles."

"And it seems you'll die in the Icelands." Heath kicked a wheel impatiently. "What's done is done. Judith can't sneak you back in. Get in the cart."

"I can't," Pairas muttered. "They broke my ankle."

Heath looked at the blood-soaked bandage then flicked up his brows at his cousin.

Dillon said, "We don't have shackles. Can't have him running off."

"I suppose she asked?" He turned to Pairas. "My captain is skilled, and unless he doesn't like you, he probably only bruised that ankle. If you're a good boy, he won't hurt you again."

Pairas bristled. "Don't talk down to me."

Heath laughed in his face. "Why? Because you're king of the sand dunes? Judith is right. You must understand your place."

At Heath's nod, Dillon struck Pairas across the mouth. The man fell against the cart. "Still too cowardly to hit me yourself, Damadar?"

Heath twisted a grin. "Sadly, my sweet sister weaved a spell that means I can only look on as others enjoy hurting you."

"What?"

"Don't you worry about it. It's a problem for the only apparent grown-up here."

With Dillon's help, Heath hoisted Pairas into the cart and freed his hands.

"I'll see to my chest." Judith hastened away. "Where is that driver?"

Dillon wandered after her. Pairas rose to his elbows. Sweat pooled on his brow. He was hurting but determined to hide it. *Proud fool.*

Heath passed him a waterskin. "Water. Drink."

"Is that a command?" Pairas snatched the skin. "There's no point ransoming me. My father won't care."

"Ransom? Judith has not quite confided in me—she must think I'll disapprove—but I imagine she intends to make you part of her household. She has other slaves."

The Isles captain grew very still. "What will be my duties?"

Heath put his back to the cart. Pairas was her mess. Not his business to explain.

"Damadar, please. I can't—I can't ask her. Let me know what I face."

Faint compassion stirred within Heath. If it were him, he, too, would beg to know, to understand, to meet his fate straight on.

"I heard slaves work your fields, that you blind them so they can't run."

"I doubt my sister snatched you to till her fields."

"Then what?"

Heath pondered what was kinder. *Ignorance?* No, he would pay Pairas the courtesy of offering what a warrior deserved—the truth. He swept a suggestive gaze up and down the man's body. Pairas flushed, first with embarrassment, then with anger.

"Well, you did ask," Heath said. "And you liked her well enough before."

"I liked a woman in a tavern. A warm, strikingly beautiful, unusual woman."

"Well then."

"That woman wasn't real."

"You made her think she was that woman."

Puzzlement replaced Pairas's anger. "There are hundreds of men like me."

"Yes, warriors just as courageous and splendidly stupid. She likes your spirit." *Was that it?* A memory niggled—Judith's words when he asked her why she wanted him to spare Pairas. *"He reminds me of someone."*

"My spirit…" The fire in Pairas's dark eyes died. "I think Blackstone ground any spirit from me." He laughed hollowly. "Why did you leave me to her, Damadar? The whip. The knife. That might have been honest enough. What I expected. But Blackstone—"

"There's a price for defiance." Heath's tone softened. "We, all of us, must pay that price if we choose that path." The words weren't for Pairas anymore. Heath played a dangerous game. He must be prepared for the consequences if he failed.

Pairas dropped his head into his hands. "This can't be happening. When Isles soldiers found me, I thought I was safe."

Judith returned, snapping instructions at a man dragging a trunk.

"Judith, I had hoped for your help here," Heath said.

"I can't hide him at Tide's End. I'll wait at the Bay of Wrecks. Arrange passage by ship to the Icelands. You may need to get our other target away quickly."

*Target. Or targets?* Heath swung her up into the cart. "Behave." He shook his finger at Pairas as he replaced the gag. "You, too, behave."

Pairas glared.

The cart rattled away into gathering gloom. Heath stared after it, an odd roiling in his gut as though his sister had slipped away with the cart. Everything was slipping away. Everything was changing.

He put his hands on his belly button to hold in an ache of loss. That yearning to lose himself in contest rekindled, a need to embrace the exhilaration of fear.

The dusk closed in. Its dewy sweetness reminded him of another evening before the battle, of a field on the edge of the king's camp. Stamping feet had turned its grass to dust as bored men hewed with swords. Heath had matched strokes with a warrior or two with fancy footwork, until he tired of their dance and put them in the dirt.

One evening, he had lingered to watch Vraymorg sweep and cut with steel against other Mountains men, gaping at the man's precise bladework and his bewilderingly quick feet.

The memory heightened his ache. How ecstatic it would be to fight Vraymorg in the fire halls. Heath didn't expect to lose. But to slay a worthy opponent, even to spare him and demand that this proud lord beg for his life, would be more satisfying than arousal and its release.

Perhaps he could get everything he wanted. The castle was in disarray, displaced men and women everywhere. However, the twisted plan unfolding in his mind was far from what Judith might call simple. He required Aric's cooperation. Aric's *unwilling* cooperation, at least.

# VAL ARQUES

C reeping dawn brought form to shapes and shadows. He lay in a soft bed in that same octagonal chamber of stone. Silken arras hung upon the stone walls, and thick rugs covered the floor beneath wooden chests and tables. Still a lord's room. Not a prison.

So he was right—an Isles victory. Relief tore through him, only to vanish as he remembered the last time he had awoken, how he'd crept to Azenor's room. Yet, if it saved Kaell—

Vraymorg flung off a silk sheet, desperate to return to that room. But when he tried to rise, pain lanced his bandaged groin. Groaning, he fell back, his breath laboured, his useless body impossibly weak. Curse it. He always revived quickly after killing blows. But recuperating from a lesser wound meant days and days of pain.

The fresh scent of a rising sea floated through open windows. Above its roar, he grew aware of a man's rumbling snores from a shadowed corner.

Aric slept in a chair, his long legs stretched before him. He stirred. "You're awake."

"Hard to sleep with your snoring. Though I'm glad to see you alive, Aric." He squinted at the other man's bruised cheeks and the cut on his lip. "If not quite unscathed."

"It's nothing." Aric touched his fingertips to a bruise. "Cathmor's torturer sought to reshape my face in her own image. Are you in pain? Shall I call the physician?"

"I've taken wounds before," Vraymorg retorted gruffly.

The ache was not nearly as agonising as it had been the last time he had woken. Somehow, his body broken and feeble, he had managed to stumble from the room. *Unless that was a fever dream... No, no. Let it be real. Then Kaell might really be alive.* "How long was I out?"

"Two days. I think you might have been delirious. The first night, your servant—Ewen, is it?—found you in a pool of blood in the passage."

*No dream then.* A dizzying hope entwined with his guilt. He had to get to Kaell. Again, he tried to rise. Pain cut into him, an angry crease across his midriff. Someone had struck him down in battle, someone quick and angry. His head throbbed. The battle blurred in some recess of his mind.

The door swung inwards. Heath Damadar peered inside.

"He's awake," Aric called tersely.

Heath padded across the room, barefoot and likely naked beneath a loosely belted cloak. "Vraymorg, I am pleased you're with us again." The Ice lord's smile was wide and disarming. "Forgive my lack of attire. In this heat, I understand why Isles folk sleep naked. I even managed to nod off last night until I heard a dreadful noise."

"Probably Aric snoring."

Aric paid him no heed. He was staring at Heath with thinly disguised contempt. "What do you want? I thought you had diverting company."

"The lovely lass you set upon me? Thank you, Aric. I was suitably diverted. Until this godsforsaken din outside my bedchamber."

"Din? My snoring isn't that bad." Aric's grin didn't reach his eyes.

Vraymorg glanced from one man to the other. At Heath's

appearance, Aric had tensed like a drawn-back bowstring.

"Din." Heath patted his mouth. "Men with heavy steps trying to creep about, muttering about fetching you. Some of the Falls' prisoners tried to escape. Your guards want to beat them to death as punishment."

"Curse it." Aric surged to his feet and rushed from the room.

Heath took the chair. "Very intense, that one. Much more interesting than I remember."

"He doesn't seem to like you."

"I wouldn't say that. He sent me a nice present last night. Dark-haired little thing, breasts you wouldn't believe." Heath mimed with his hands.

Vraymorg looked through the man's mock-edged humour. It hid something, but what? Heath Damadar remained a mystery to him. He might possess the same graceful movement as Judith, the same dark-brown hair; even the same teasing tone. But he had little of Judith's warmth. Instead, lazy words and a lazy smile only masked his sharp wit.

"He wanted you distracted and out of the way, then."

"He wanted to keep me away from you, Vraymorg."

Cold crept along his neck. "Why would that be?"

"He's oddly protective of you." Heath sat back. "Enough about grumpy Isles princes. All the fish they eat makes them ill-tempered. Do you want to know what's going on? Ah, such drama. A fascinating brouhaha of mayhem. What do you remember?"

Vraymorg rubbed his stubbled chin. "The flames. Kaell." The words tasted ashen in his mouth. *What if the sword's magic didn't work?* He glanced about in alarm. "My sword."

Heath's smile seemed a little too familiar. "That blue-bladed Seithin thing? It was beside you where you collapsed the other night. No idea why you were wandering feverishly about the castle, waving a weapon. It's there." Heath nodded towards the chamber's back. "Unpleasantly bloody. The boy's blood, I think."

Vraymorg snatched at a memory. "You gave me a sword as the fighting started."

"You carelessly lost yours. Flung it down then later insisted we retrieve it."

"That was Kaell's sword. I've never liked it much."

"You liked the one I gave you rather too well. I'm glad I fought with you, Vraymorg. Steel in your hands, and you're a beast unleashed. Do you ever lose control? There's an old tale about Serravan warriors surrendering to an otherworldly fury if in peril."

"I don't lose control," Vraymorg said coldly.

"No." Heath's gaze hung on Vraymorg's face. "I don't suppose you do."

"Why does everything you say sound like a challenge?"

"Part of my charm. We can discuss me instead of the battle if you prefer. I'm content either way. If it comes down to it, I'm more interesting."

"The battle is hazy." Vraymorg ignored his companion's nonsense. "I remember calling my men to me then you shouting to men of the Ice. The king's forces outnumbered us. Until Isles warriors arrived. So we won the day?"

"The day was ours, yes."

"And the king?"

Heath cast him a curious look. "Cathmor is dead. A good thing too. Only way you get a new king is to finish off the old one."

Vraymorg's tongue thickened in his mouth. "Who?" he whispered. "Who killed him?"

Heath hesitated then said, "You did, my lord."

Vraymorg turned his head to hide his expression. First, he had put aside his vow to Devarsi. Then he'd killed her descendant. "I remember Janak shunting men aside to come at me. Others seized my arms from behind as he struck at me."

"You can thank Janak for your wounds. Then thank Gendrick Caelan for running Janak through with steel. He racked up quite a count once he joined the fun. For all his many faults, let no one say the salt-head's timing is not excellent."

"And Aric?"

"I told my captain to cut Aric free as soon as fighting broke out. Good thing too. The king had ordered Caelmarsh to kill Aric if the battle turned against him."

"Your cousin struck down Caelmarsh?"

"If only," Heath said. "Then I could have put his head on a platter and presented it to Judith. She likes that sort of dramatic gesture, says it makes her feel gooey inside. No, Caelmarsh sent a minion to kill Aric. Dillon struck down the minion, of course, but the former Downs lord is in the wind. A pity. I really wanted to carve him up."

"You're much too fond of your own voice, Damadar. Just tell me what's going on."

"You sound like Judith. She says I'm not nearly as amusing as I think." Heath sighed. "Very well, my Lord of Brevity. The lords of the Falls and Plains offered their oaths to Gendrick. Their men surrendered. Isles warriors are still chasing down those who fled."

"Wait." Vraymorg flung up a hand. "To Gendrick?"

"Lord Hatton is dead," Heath said. "An arrow pierced his neck in battle."

So his eldest son, Gendrick, had become the king. "Who else fell?"

"Your servant Ewen is dealing with the Mountains' dead and wounded. He says they must be buried in your cursed hills."

Vraymorg nodded. Mountains warriors believed the gods would not find them otherwise.

"The lords of Telor met while you lazily kept to your bed. Some needed a little prodding to elect Gendrick king. I hoped a few might prove rebellious and give us the spectacle of a beheading or two, but no. Turns out beneath a bit of bluster, they're submissive mice."

"The peace may not hold," Vraymorg cautioned. "Too many noble families profited under Cathmor and will not readily embrace an Isles prince, even Roaran's descendant."

"The mice will be sensible. Gendrick has my father's support.

And yours, I assume, my lord. Though, why turn on Cathmor? I never thought of you as a likely ally." That cool intelligence flickered in eyes mirroring his sister's, a rich, dark brown that hid far too much. "What did Aric call you? The king's man."

*The king's man. But which king?* Vraymorg held back a wild laugh. *Do not trust me yet, my young lord of the Ice. If I read her intentions right, Rozenn of Cahir is plotting to put my son upon the throne. If I can betray one king, I can betray another.*

The door banged open. Aric returned.

"All is well?" Heath said.

Aric sank onto a stool. "For now." He glanced at Heath then looked away.

Again, Vraymorg sensed Aric's mistrust. "Aric, your father—"

"I can't talk about him." Aric pressed his palms into his thighs as he rose then strode to the window. He stood staring out, shoulders hunched, gripping the sill with stiff hands.

"Fair's fair, Vraymorg." Heath offered that deceptive smile. "I told you all my nasty misdeeds. Tell me yours. Begin with the bit about how you are an Isles prince."

Vraymorg glared at Aric's back. That explained Heath's comment about the Serravan.

"I didn't mean to betray your confidence, Vraymorg," Aric muttered without turning. "It slipped out in the heat of everything."

A shutter banged in a breeze fragrant with lavender. Vraymorg remembered his mother's perfume in Azenor's room, how it had corrupted to a base stench.

*What have I done? What if Arn lied?* Gods help him, he couldn't turn back now. He had to find Kaell—if he lived. *Dare I hope he does? Could I casually ask after Azenor?*

He managed a shrug. "Centuries ago, a sorcerer cursed me." He couldn't say any more, especially about a sunlit room where a nineteen-year-old Val Arques Caelan wept in despair. "Blood magic. You're no stranger to that, Damadar."

It came out sharper than Vraymorg had intended. An accusation.

Heath's mouth knotted in a grimace. "I assure you, my lord. The Damadars are not nearly as dark and dangerous as our reputation."

# KAELL

Kaell was dead. He had to be, even though he had no clear idea what that might be like. Darkness maybe, a twilight haze like a dream, then something new and strange. Perhaps the afterlife was a wonderful place beyond the Enarae, where his lord, when he, too, died, would find him.

But familiar sensations poured into him. Groping hands that pulled him towards wakefulness. The aroma of candlewax. The sight of dawn's pink flush beyond a window. Cloth rubbing his skin. Even the weight of his head on a downy pillow.

"What... what..." Kaell stammered. His thoughts hammered to beats as quick as the steps in a swordfight. Tower room. *A tower beyond the Enarae?*

No, there were two men in the room, their hands upon him. The smell of tanned leather clung to their garments.

Kaell sat up abruptly. The men reeled, astonished. Then they grabbed him and dragged him from the bed. Dazed, unable to understand where he was, Kaell struggled. His body did not obey him as fast as it should. "Let go of me. Who are you?"

"Shhh," one said. "No one's going to hurt you. You're meant to be asleep."

"I'm not asleep. I'm dead. I must be dead."

The man laughed. "The physician thought so too. Turns out, he was wrong, girl."

*Girl?* He struggled to understand. *What girl? Where?* Kaell's panicked gaze slid down. He wore a shift, his feet bare. No, not *his* feet.

At Kaell's cry of disbelief, the man clamped a palm over his mouth. Kaell bit him. His attacker staggered, wringing his hand. "Little cow. Grab her."

The second man seized Kaell's shoulders. He twisted free. The other came at Kaell, bellowing. Kaell weaved, the simple movement awkward. His attacker's momentum hurled the man into his companion. The two strangers sprawled against the bed.

Kaell stumbled for the door, tripping over his own feet, surprised at his clumsy gait and how light his body seemed. Catching a reflection in a mirror draped by a crumpled gown, he rocked to a halt.

*Azenor Caelan. Here?* He glanced behind, looking for the woman in the mirror. But there was only one figure. Only him.

A shudder ran cold through him. Impossible. Not only was he not dead, not only was his body not his, but he was trapped in the form of the woman who had betrayed him.

Shocked, he could only stare. The face was not his. The black hair not his. He tore his hands over Azenor's womanly hips, to thighs, then—gods—to breasts.

Sounds broke through his turmoil—footsteps as the two men came at him. Kaell took one last look at the mirror. Then as best he could in this strange, unresponsive form, he fled the room.

# VAL ARQUES

The physician's poppy juice confined him to his bed, unable to search for Kaell. Drowsy, his limbs heavy, he tossed in a fitful sleep through the night, at last falling into a dream that dissolved to nothing more than a vague sense of unease as someone shook him awake.

Aric stooped over the bed. "I need your help."

"What?" Vraymorg battled to remember where he was. Early-morning light broke up shadows in the tower room. Beyond curtained windows, birds chirped. "What's happened?"

"Azenor." Aric lowered his voice. "Damadar took her."

Vraymorg struggled upright, grunting at a dull ache. *It wasn't Azenor. Not if the magic worked.* "I don't understand. Ewen, he said—"

Aric spluttered a sound. "That useless physician. He swore she stopped breathing, called us all to her bedside." His laugh splintered into bitterness. "She was asleep. *Asleep.* The man was drunk, no doubt. Gendrick wants him whipped for incompetence."

*Not dead.* Alarm locked up Vraymorg's body. Maybe he'd made a mistake when he leaned over her. *Gods help me, if she wasn't dead, what have I done? Or, or... was it Kaell?* That would mean Damadar had unwittingly taken Kaell.

"He's holding her at the Fern Castle," Aric said. "I'm to come alone to the shore below Tide's End at dusk, in return for her life." He covered his face with his palms. "It's just like before when the ghouls took her. I can't lose her again, Vraymorg. Not again."

*Azenor. Kaell. The Fern Castle. What's happening here?* The world had tilted while he slept. Vraymorg rolled awkwardly to his feet. "I'll gather some men."

"You can't. Heath has spies everywhere. They'll alert him if too many riders leave the castle. I don't know who to trust. Will you help me?"

Vraymorg stared at a pulse throbbing in Aric's neck. His sleep-hazed thoughts knitted too slowly. If Heath held Kaell, thinking it was Azenor, he had to get to the boy.

"Your brother. Surely Gendrick can force Heath to give Azenor back."

"Heath says if I tell Gendrick, he'll kill her. He has informers everywhere. His cursed Ice men are even guarding her rooms so no one learns she's missing. You're wounded, but there's no one else I can trust to help me rescue her."

"I can ride. Fight, if I have to. Where's our scheming Ice lord now?"

"Asleep. He's fond of a certain dark-haired lass I persuaded to slip something into his wine last night. He'll wake later than he intends."

"Still, the moment he wakes and finds us gone, he'll come after us."

"Let him come." Aric bared his teeth. "All that matters is Azenor. Once she's safe, let him do his worst."

# ARIC

Typ he gate sergeant hoisted a lantern to their faces. "Castle's locked down. No one goes in or out without permission." Aric threw back his hood. "Let me pass. Make haste."

The light bobbed as the man dipped his head. "Forgive me, my prince." He turned to signal to sentries.

As the portcullis creaked up, Aric glanced uneasily at the few early risers. Fog steaming off a rolling, murmuring ocean blurred their shapes. Odours of stale beer and woodsmoke drenched the courtyard.

"Say nothing about seeing us," Aric bid the sergeant. "Have my men returned?"

"Not yet, my prince."

At his side, Vraymorg edged up a brow. "They're hunting Caelmarsh?"

"They're hunting the Lord of the Henge. The Henge is part of the Isles, but Sherrin Cross forgot that somehow. A time in irons will help his memory."

The portcullis struck the roof. Aric urged the horse through the gatehouse. With the walls at his back, unease twisted his gut. Did he do the right thing? Would Heath keep his word?

No longer able to contain his nerves, he stirred the horse to a gallop. Hooves pounding, Vraymorg's horse kept pace. They thundered past the king's camp, the remains of canvas and smashed metal blackened against the rutted earth. A fox padded across a grave's piled dirt. The stench of soot and decaying food overpowered scents of forest and sea.

*That's what war stinks of. Rotting flesh and fire. Lies.*

Like misshapen gods, Cathmor's siege engines stood tall against the dawn. He and Vraymorg left the trebuchets behind as the woods closed in, a deepening well of trunks, budding branches, vines, and rambling bushes. When the path meandered through tangled undergrowth, Aric slowed. Hearing Vraymorg's harsh breaths, Aric realised he, too, was panting. He reined in the horse so his companion drew alongside him. "Sorry. I forgot your wounds."

"It's all right. I know you're in a hurry to find Azenor. And we will. I swear it."

Aric flushed with guilt. This man selflessly helped him, and his reward would be betrayal. Yet he must pay Damadar's price. The gods had offered a second chance to save Azenor, to prove himself. He could not fail her again. "I'm sorry… about Kaell."

"Yes," Vraymorg said.

"I wish—"

The man threw up a gloved hand. "I don't want to talk about Kaell."

*I can't.* Vraymorg didn't need to say it. The words sat behind his shuttered eyes, in the tight lines about his mouth.

They rode in silence as the lightening sky crowned the dark-green trees. The mist lifted. A breeze herded clouds. When Aric breathed out, droplets hung in the air.

He thought of Kaell shackled to that stake, alone with his thoughts. He remembered Blackstone's foul breath and foul taunts in her torturer's tent as she waved a knife. *"Your fault he'll burn. Though the fire's quick. You'll die slower."*

Again, he dug his heels into the horse's flank, determined to drive away the past. Vraymorg matched his canter, uncomplaining. Aric stole a look at him. What was he like, this warrior he had uncovered in dusty books, the only Telorian to win the famed Wardorian Contest of Swords? Except he had no right to curiosity, not of a man he intended to betray.

When hard sunlight streaked through trees, they crossed a bridge above a river of sleek, deep water, its banks verdant with ferns.

"I remember this bridge." Vraymorg's laugh held an unexpected carefree note. "My brother Karolus and I stole away from lessons to see it built. We climbed down to the rocks to throw stones in the water. I must have been ten."

Aric blurted, "There's so much I want to know. About you. About your life. Everything."

"I told you my name."

"And?" Dying leaves crackled as a snake slithered off the bridge.

Vraymorg peered up through latticed branches. "It's midday. How far to this castle? I've travelled there from the Mountains but not from the Isles."

"We passed a burnt stump a bit back. That was well over halfway when I attended Lord Brucean's wedding at the Fern Castle. So you won't say more?"

"I don't think I owe you anything, Aric Caelan. Certainly not explanations to satisfy your curiosity."

Aric shrugged. "It's a long ride."

The echo of their hoofbeats drifted off into the trees. With indignant squawks, birds took flight from shaking bows. Paws displaced twigs.

Vraymorg sighed heavily. "I was born after the Wardorian emperor known as the Mazart conquered Telor. My father was Lord of Avanti. Still young. 'Still foolish,' my mother always said. I remember her perfume, her laugh, how she'd stand on the cliff in storms, face turned to the wind and roaring sea."

His gaze softened as it fell in the distance. In that moment, Aric, too, was a child at Tide's End, watching a woman laughing as rain whipped hair about her face.

"I grew up beneath that shadow of defeat. Even so, life was good. I wed a girl I'd loved since childhood. Odd though it sounds, I was content. Until—" Vraymorg broke off. His face was tight and grim.

"Until my reputation as a bladesman reached the Mazart," he said flatly. "He invited me to compete in the prestigious Contest of Swords. I was nineteen. My life, that life, ended at nineteen."

"Your father *let* you go to Wardour?"

His voice sharp, defensive, Vraymorg muttered, "He had no choice."

"So you went unwillingly to Wardour. And the sorcerer... killed you?"

Vraymorg strangled the reins with his hands. He dropped his eyes to his wrists then tore them away.

*Knife cuts. Had this man, a warrior—*

"No." Vraymorg shook his head. "No. I can't speak of this."

"I'll admit I am curious about you," Aric said. "Damadar is too. There's something odd in the way he looks at you. It makes me think if others knew who you were, they'd try to use you."

"I can take care of myself." Vraymorg spurred his horse forward.

Aric considered his rigid back. *If only that were true.*

# HEATH

Smug with triumph, Heath braced his palms on the parapet and listened to the grinding portcullis. So close now. Every piece in place.

An unsuspecting Aric had been manipulated into betraying Vraymorg, into leaving the castle and the protection of his warriors. Heath's men waited, ready to pounce.

A door thumped along the wall walk. Dillon hurried to him. "I've been searching for you. There's trouble. She's gone."

"Of course she's gone. We took her."

"No, we don't have her."

"If that's a joke, I'm not laughing."

At his threatening tone, Dillon rocked back a step. "I sent two men to get Azenor. They swear she fought them off."

"The fools are drunk."

"My lord, there's no sign of the girl."

Heath clenched his hands at his side. "Find her. Before Aric learns I don't have her. Be discreet. I don't want questions."

"Yes, my lord. To the other matter, I've men camped outside the walls, ready to ride for the Fern Castle. Each knows to keep his mouth shut."

"How many?"

"Forty."

"Forty is enough to scoop up two stray lordlings," Heath muttered, his elated mood partly restored. "The castle is deserted, after all."

# KAELL

Trees dipped in the wind. Branches grated like a clash of vambraces on the battlefield. Thin sunlight threaded leaves, a speckled path of ivory through shadows.

Kaell did not know how he'd reached the forest. The past few hours had dissolved into a disoriented blur. He only knew he must not stop, that he had to escape what he had seen in that mirror.

Careless of where he headed, he forced his awkward body to run, his gait like a lumbering drunk's. His balance, the way his weight transferred from foot to foot, even something as small as how his soles brushed the ground weren't right. His legs were apart from him. Even her skin was a cloak, a costume he could not strip off.

Everything was familiar but also changed. The sky was the same blue but seen through different eyes. Trailing grass was brushed with different fingers. Shockingly new, but not.

A flower's rubbery stem, the creamy texture of petals drew an odd response from his body. A prickle. A heat. The fragrance stirred a memory, but not his own.

He had been dead. Now he lived. That wasn't right. Kaell took a shuddering breath and ran from this place, from this truth. But his fear and shock shadowed him, feeding the churn of panic in his belly.

*How is this possible? Her body. Azenor's. And what of my lord?* Kaell's last memory before he had awoken was the fire, the smoke, the comforting press of Vraymorg's arms. His lord speaking words Kaell had yearned to hear. *"I love you like a son."*

His lord had said those precious words then plunged a sword into his gut to do this. *This.* Kaell pulled up hard. Uncomfortable anger flared through him. His lord's final words pounded in his head. *"One thing I can do for you, Kaell. Save you."*

*Save? This is saving?* He had asked Vraymorg for death. He'd trusted him. Instead, the man he loved like a father had forced his spirit into a woman's form.

A sob choked off his breath. He swept up a branch, his knuckles whitening about the gnarled wood. With a bitter cry, he thrashed a trunk again and again to drive away his fury, to still his thoughts with a relentless rhythm. Sweat beaded on his brow. *No, her brow.* Perspiration ran down the hollow of her throat where Kaell had trailed his fingers, down between breasts he'd cupped in his hands. He'd kissed these lips.

The branch slipped from his bleeding fingers. Kaell could not move on or go back. He stood dazed, caught in a bewildering spell of sheer disbelief. Sweet alyssum blazed about him, the honeyed perfume impossibly lovely, his shredding mind grasping that scent, like the scent of Azenor's skin that night they'd made love.

A torrent of misery swept away his anger. Kaell sank to his knees. He began to weep, wracking, anguished sobs in a voice that wasn't his. To hear Azenor crying made no sense to him, nor did the soft, womanly cheeks wet by his tears, the tears of a man who did not know what to do next.

# ARIC

Fields of wilting wheat rimmed yet more forest. The castle loomed ahead, its fat keep spiralling against a rocky cliff blotted by delicate ferns. Across a wide but dry moat, white walls rose from a hill beside a waterfall.

Aric had always thought the Fern Castle beautiful, but now, its towers seemed sinister, as if they had absorbed his guilt. The shadow thrown by its keep groped rather than lengthened. Rustling leaves menaced. No bird sang. Cloying scents of rotting earth and sickeningly sweet dying daisies pricked his nostrils.

Dismounting beside Vraymorg, Aric stared up at the deserted walls, the wide-flung gates, and raised portcullis. "If I did not know better, I would think it abandoned."

"Inviting, isn't it?"

"You suspect a trap?"

"Heath Damadar has a subtle mind. Traps are just his thing. We should wait for dusk."

"We need to get inside now. Before Damadar discovers I'm not at Tide's End."

Vraymorg chewed his lip. "All right. But not through the gates."

They took rope from their saddlebags and clambered down a steep track to the moat.

Late sun blazed off white stone. Both men darted to the base of a jutting tower. No horns blasted. No one shouted. The waterfall misting their faces thundered into a pool. But a heavy, foreboding quiet enshrouded the castle.

Aric hurled the rope at wall crenulations above his head. It soared then thudded to the earth. He threw again. This time, its loop caught a merlon. He tugged to make sure it held then wiped his palms on his pants, grasped the rope, braced his feet against the wall, and climbed.

Vraymorg soon joined him on the guard walk. His tunic was spotted with blood from a reopened wound.

"Are you—?"

"I'm all right."

Aric glanced below into an empty courtyard. The faintest breeze stirred weeds. An overpowering perfume rambled from a vine that was purple with passion fruit.

"What if you're wrong?" Vraymorg asked. "What if he isn't holding her here?"

"I'm not wrong." Aric turned to head for a door to a tower.

Vraymorg grabbed his shoulder. "Wait. No one on the guard walk. The gates are open. Damadar is clever. He might suspect you'd guess about this place. Maybe it's a trap for you."

"You wait." Aric shrugged off his grip. "I'm going to save my sister." He stormed along the walk towards the tower, hearing Vraymorg curse.

"This is reckless," the man muttered, following Aric down the stairs.

The tower opened into a dying herb garden, sharp with camphoric rosemary, opposite the keep. Aric crept through sunlight to stairs leading up to a splintered door. He pushed it wide, aware of Vraymorg's careful steps at his back.

The high-roofed hall was dark and still. It smelled of dust. Unlit torches stood erect in sconces above overturned benches and tables. Stains discoloured the stone floor. Cold ashes were piled in an enormous hearth. Even though ghouls had sacked the castle only days ago, a forgotten, eerie atmosphere needled the back of his neck.

Aric remembered Brucean's wedding. The fire had blazed cheerfully. Ale had flowed while guests in bright tunics and gowns shouted with laughter. In the gallery above, fiddlers had played as he drank wine with Aiden.

Later, while coals smoked and men snored, he'd kissed Aiden by the fire, unlacing his shirt so he could slide his hands over warm, bare skin.

It didn't feel like the same room.

On the threshold, Aric paused, unable to take that final step. It was his last chance to warn Vraymorg. *Should I? Can I even trust Damadar to return Azenor?*

The gloom and his guilt suffocated him. A rat scuttled inside a wall. A rising wind whistled through towers, rattling loose shutters.

No, he couldn't risk his sister's life. Not after he had failed to save her from Archanin. He had to see this through.

Shoulders hunched, Aric stalked inside. Vraymorg drew his sword and followed.

A laugh echoed through the hall. Aric froze.

"This is interesting." A male voice carried from above. "I didn't expect visitors."

"Who's there?" Vraymorg whipped up his blade.

A shape darted through a patch of sunlight near the doorway into blackness beside the walls. "Who's there? Why, all of us."

Torches flared. Light blazed from the gallery. Along its length, blond archers nocked bolts. Fear turned Aric's belly. They weren't Ice men. Defiantly, he slid his sword from its scabbard, but his lungs contracted. What good was a blade when the enemy was beyond steel's reach?

"Put it down, or we'll shoot."

"Take cover," Aric shouted to Vraymorg as he started for the stairs. A quarrel smacked into his shoulder. He spun and nearly fell. A second bolt skimmed his thigh.

Aric staggered, shocked, dully hearing Vraymorg yell his name as he collapsed. The sounds and scents of Brucean's wedding feast enfolded him. Men and women thumped their feet or shouted toasts. A guest snatched Aric's sword and threw him down.

*Aiden?* He was rougher than Aric remembered. Too rough. He sank into darkness.

⁓∾⦂∿⁓

"Aric." Vraymorg's voice drew him back to wakefulness.

He was lying on his back on stone, his shoulder aflame.

"Be still," Vraymorg said. "I'll get that bolt out."

Pain overtook his body as iron and wood ripped through muscle. He blacked out. When he came to again, Vraymorg knelt at his side, strapping Aric's wound with torn cloth.

"What's happened?" Aric croaked. "I don't understand. Who attacked us?"

"Ghouls," Vraymorg said. "Didn't Heath's men find this castle deserted? Well, it's not. We're prisoners. They took our weapons. No, keep your hand clamped on that thigh."

Aric blinked into irritating torchlight. *Where is Damadar?*

Resolute footsteps clattered over stone. A figure stood over him. Aric squinted.

"No." Panic flared through him. "No. It's not possible. Where's Azenor? She's meant to be here. Ice men brought her."

Archanin laughed. "Do you see any Ice men?" He swept an arm towards armed figures moving in to encircle the two men.

Aric stared in bewilderment, unable to make sense of either Archanin's words or his presence with a host of ghouls. "I don't understand."

Heath had told Aric he was holding Azenor at this castle. In return for his sister, Aric had only to bring Vraymorg here, take him captive if the chance arose, and surrender him to the Ice lord. Simple.

Except there were no Ice men and no signs of Heath. Unless Heath had lied. Or Archanin and his ghouls had killed Heath's men.

"Where's Azenor?" Aric demanded. "What did you do with her?"

"I don't have her. A pity. Lord Brucean's bedchamber is perfect for loving reunions."

His meaning sank in. Anger burst up in Aric, a fire in his breast and limbs. He sprang at Archanin. Ghouls grabbed him and threw him down. Grunting in pain, he rolled to his knees, his hands and clothing sticky with blood.

"My, my, princeling." Archanin fingered his gashed cheek. "Such violence. Who is this with you?"

Aric glanced at Vraymorg. His companion had his head down, his unruly dark hair hiding his face.

"Get the other one up." Archanin snapped his fingers. "Let me look at him." Helplessly, Aric watched ghouls hurl Vraymorg to his feet and take hold of his shoulders. The ghoul god stilled. "I know you."

Vraymorg said nothing.

"Impossible..." Archanin drew closer. "Kaell's lord. I killed you."

"Your knife turned on a rib."

"Is that so?" Archanin groped beneath the man's tunic. "No wound. How? I stabbed you in the heart. Why aren't you dead?"

*Dead.* Aric stared at Vraymorg. *Does that mean this man cannot be killed?* It hadn't quite hit him until then what living for centuries meant.

"Your knife turned on a rib."

"You think you can lie to a god?"

Vraymorg did not reply. But for a stubborn press of his lips, he might have been made of stone.

"The man without fear. I remember you very well." Archanin brushed the back of his hand down Vraymorg's cheek. "This is a pleasing turn of events. I expected to win the Mountains through storm. But now I have its lord… Secure him and bring me the Isles prince."

Ghouls shoved Vraymorg against a pillar and bound him to it with rope. Others came for Aric.

He scrambled back, his knees slipping in his own smeared blood. "My brother. You're his ally. We're allies."

The ghouls paused and looked to their lord.

Archanin smiled. "Your brother didn't tell you? Of course he didn't."

"Tell me what?"

Archanin's laugh was pitiless. "Gendrick and I are indeed allies. Under one clause of our agreement—or contract, shall we call it?— I get the Downs if I deliver Cahir and its queen. Under another clause, I get you."

"What?"

"I asked for a hostage to ensure he did all he promised in return for my support. Your loving brother offered you, to do with as I like. Just so long as you disappeared."

"No." Aric recoiled. "No. He wouldn't."

"He would. He did." Archanin gestured. "Take him."

Ghouls seized him. He broke free, trying to rise. They grasped his ankles and arms. Aric writhed. A fist pounded his midriff. His breath huffed out.

Memory hurled him back to moonlight gleaming upon stone, to a ghoul hitting him as Azenor screamed his name. All those months ago, he'd believed his only option was to do as they said and kill Kaell. But what if he had sought Kaell's help instead? Would their fates be different? Or perhaps his always led here, to this deserted castle.

His captors roped his wrists and threw him down. Archanin crouched, his gaze on Vraymorg as he pressed hard on Aric's bloody shoulder. Aric bit back a scream.

"So tell me, my Lord of Vraymorg." Archanin dug fingers into Aric's wound. "What sort of man cannot be killed by a knife?"

"Let him go," Vraymorg hissed through clenched teeth. "He's hurt."

"How sad." Archanin pulled Aric against him. "Tell your story, Vraymorg. Quickly now. I have a realm to win. An army to summon from beyond the Enarae."

"Stop it." Vraymorg strained against the ropes. "He's done you no harm. I'm Lord of the Mountains. I hunted your kind, hunted *you*. Hurt me. I killed Kaell. Not the flames. Me."

"Did you, my lord?" Archanin's tone held no anger, only mild interest. "To deny me Kaell, perhaps? You and I will talk about that soon. But first, since you still refuse to answer my questions—"

His hot, sweet breath misted Aric's throat. Archanin's wet tongue lapped his skin. Aric had time only to register a single jolt of fear before his captor sank his teeth into his flesh. Then his skull exploded in agony.

# VAL ARQUES

"Let him go. Curse you, let him go!" Vraymorg wrenched at the ropes until blood from deep cuts trickled down his arms. His anger about what Aric had done to Kaell fell away. It all seemed so long ago, so meaningless. "I'll tell you whatever you want. Just stop hurting him."

Unhurried, Archanin lifted his head. He discarded Aric, rose, and pressed his palms into the pillar beside Vraymorg's shoulders. "You'll satisfy my curiosity?"

Vraymorg threw Aric a despairing glance. Sprawled, skin cadaverous, blood soaking his tunic, the Isles man was very still.

"You murdered him. You foul monster."

"He's alive. Just. It won't take much to finish him. But I'm more interested in you. Back in that dreadful Mountains fortress, I killed you. Why aren't you dead?"

"You drove a knife into my heart, if that's what you mean." He did not bother to disguise his scorn. "But I can't be killed. Not that way."

"Not that way? Which way then?"

Vraymorg shrugged, sullen. "I don't know."

"Don't know or won't say?" Archanin nudged Aric with a boot.

"I don't know!" Vraymorg shouted.

"So what are you? Some whelp of Khir's? Did my godly brother seduce your mother?"

"My father was Lord of the Isles, not a god. A sorcerer cursed me."

"How?"

Vraymorg blinked in surprise. No one ever cared how. The few who knew his secret had other questions. What is it like to live forever? Is it lonely? Does it hurt to die?

Briefly, he shut his eyes. His gut clenched. Perspiration wet his armpits. It broke out on his thighs, at the back of his neck, on his hairline. He could not tell this story. "I don't remember," he muttered. "It was too long ago."

Archanin's breath stirred a strand of Vraymorg's hair. "I think you do. But we'll have plenty of time to talk about that. Just you and I. What did this sorcerer want of you?"

*Want.* Vraymorg's back ground against the pillar. "No," he said. "No." He could not think of that sorcerer. Nor of a sunlit room where he had wept while butterflies flounced beyond the window bars.

"So stubborn. But such a prize." Archanin's laugh stalked the dusty hall. "I can drain your blood, let you recover, and kill you again. My own cow to milk."

The other ghouls sniggered. Vraymorg tore uselessly at his bonds. Better to be dead.

"Perhaps you did kill Kaell. Why? For duty or love? I begin to think there's a wonderful ruthlessness about you."

Vraymorg blanked his expression. This monster must never learn the truth, that Kaell might be alive. To protect the boy, he had to focus Archanin's wrath on him.

"I let Kaell burn," he said. "To save him from you."

Instead of rising to anger, Archanin smiled. "When I have you somewhere secure, we'll talk about how I might punish you. About those scars on your wrists. About what makes you afraid." He paused. "Do you remember our conversation? About fear?" He smoothed a lock of his captive's hair between his fingers. Vraymorg wrenched his head aside.

"Lovely things must be kept immured from the world." Archanin dropped a hand to Vraymorg's thigh. "For my use alone." At his proprietorial fondling, the ghouls sniggered again.

Vraymorg drove his teeth into his bottom lip. Sweat plastered his tunic to his body. "You'll get nothing from me but defiance."

"Is that what you think?"

"I know the truth about you," Vraymorg blurted, the words bitter. "I know you're not as you seem."

Archanin drew very still. He considered his captive with low-lidded eyes. Then he shrugged. "It hardly matters. You won't be telling anyone." To his companions, he said, "As soon as it's dark, we leave. I did not intend to remain here this long. Though—" He brushed his hand over Vraymorg's arm. "It proved fortuitous."

"Yes, lord." A ghoul gestured at the captives. "And these two?"

"I should not like to insult Gendrick by refusing his gift. As for this rather extraordinary creature—bring him too. He'll make a pleasing distraction while I take this land in blood and storm. Prepare them both for travel."

Archanin moved off. Ghouls milled in a bustle of heels rapping stone, laughter, thuds, thumps, and scrapes.

"Aric," Vraymorg called, "can you hear me?"

The Isles warrior lay in pooling blood, his limbs contorted. He groaned.

"Aric, get up. You must get up."

"I'm sorry. He threatened to hurt her."

*The Three protect us. Did his wounds scramble his wits?* "Aric, listen to me. Find the strength to get up. We must escape."

In a whisper-thin rasp, Aric said, "Can't move."

Then he would see this man die. Maybe not here. Not yet. In some foul den where Archanin took them both. How many men must he watch die? No, he had to get free.

Again, Vraymorg strained and twisted against the cords,

careless of how they sliced his arms. Footsteps tramped closer. A ghoul dangled shackles from his hand. "No trouble, or I'll make you bleed."

A thrum vibrated through the dusty air. The ghoul staggered, an arrow in his back. Across the room, another screamed and spun downwards. Like black sheets of rain, arrows hissed from the gallery. They clattered to the floor or tore through flesh and bone. Ghouls whipped out weapons and scattered to every corner of the darkening hall. With deafening yells, armed men streamed through the doors.

Vraymorg's strained senses blurred. Shapes flashed past. Shrieks, cries, clanking metal all twisted into an uproar. Blood sprayed his face as a man fell against him then stumbled away, cursing. Torchlight flashed on slashing steel.

The stench of blood and the nauseating terror of violent death muddied the hot air. Metal sang, crashed, chinked, rang. A storm of sounds. Then nothing.

"He's here, my lord."

Dizzy with shock, Vraymorg could only stare as Heath Damadar strode towards him, a bloody sword gripped in his gloved fingers. "Unharmed, I hope, Dillon."

Fragmented parts of his mind jammed together. *Aric. Is Aric safe? Azenor. Does Heath have her? In this very castle? Might Kaell really be here?*

"Aric? Is he..." Vraymorg's voice trailed off. *Dead.* He couldn't say it.

Heath breathed fast, stirred up. Blood trickled from his gashed temple. He stepped sideways so Vraymorg could see a man bent over the Isles prince.

"This is a mess." Heath turned his head. "Physician, tell me he'll live."

"This man is very weak from blood loss, my lord."

"Will he survive a journey?"

"I think so, my lord."

Heath braced a gloved hand against the pillar. "What is going on, Vraymorg? This castle was deserted."

Bewildered, Vraymorg could not answer him. His thoughts spinning, he watched Heath's men collect weapons and support wounded companions outside. Others threw headless ghouls into a corner. Too few. Most must have fled.

"Archanin." Vraymorg forced out words. "He was here."

"The ghoul god? Well, he's not anymore." Heath flicked sweat-matted hair off his brow. From blood spreading upon his torn tunic, he had taken a wound but didn't care. His every gesture was taut with controlled intent, his intelligent eyes sharp.

Vraymorg realised he only now saw Heath Damadar clearly, that the fight, the struggle, had exposed the warrior beneath the prattling nonsense and charming pretence. This was at last Rolland Damadar's second son uncovered, the fire dancer.

"Release me, curse you." The cord burned his bloodied wrists. "These ropes are tight."

Heath cut him free and passed him a waterskin. Vraymorg drank deeply, desperate to know if this man held Azenor—Kaell— in this forsaken place.

At Heath's gesture, men carried Aric outside. Others dragged branches into the hall, tossing them onto benches piled near ghoul corpses. "What are you doing?"

"Burning the dead."

"And burning the castle down too? This is a Mountains castle. I want it intact."

Heath waved an arm at the door. "Best step outside, my lord. I've a carriage waiting."

Vraymorg passed a hand over his damp brow.

"My lord, I must insist." There was steel in Heath's tone.

Head swimming, needing air, Vraymorg took a step. To his surprise, he staggered then nearly fell.

Heath grabbed his arm. "You're in shock. It hits a man like that."

Vraymorg brushed off the other man's grip and lurched through the doors. Dusk swept more mist in. It rolled from the forest, the air surprisingly cool. A feverish sweat, though, wet the nape of his neck. He reached for the wall too late. The ground swept up towards him as he fell.

Heath hauled him to his knees. "Do not be so proud. Let me help you."

"What's wrong with me? This isn't shock."

The Ice lord supported him to a carriage. "No questions now. Please get in."

This man's too-confident manner niggled at him. Vraymorg knew he must not get into that carriage, that he had to regain control of his body. He managed to stand.

Heath was watching him. "You're very strong. It usually takes effect at once."

*The water. Curse it, the water.* Vraymorg groaned. "You poisoned me. Why?"

"Don't be so dramatic. You'll sleep, nothing more. Not yet."

"Whatever you intend," he hissed, "I'll fight you with every sinew in my body."

A silence fell about them. Heath regarded him intently. "I know you will, my lord. I realised very quickly you're too dangerous to toy with. Please stop fighting. It's pointless."

"What are you up to? Why burn this castle? Where's Aric?" *And Azenor?*

Heath offered a careless shrug. "The story will be Cathmor's men set the fire. Led by that traitor, Sherrin Cross."

*Story?* Vraymorg leaned against the carriage. "I don't understand."

"They fled the battle and hid here. When you and Aric tracked them down, Sherrin killed you both then burned your bodies in the castle. That's what I'll tell Gendrick and his new council of lords."

"Why tell them this?"

"So they don't look for you or Aric."

Dread chilled his spine. Not at Heath's words so much as his matter-of-fact tone. This man didn't fear Vraymorg or the king.

No longer able to stand, he slid his back down the carriage, groaning at the strain of holding back sleep. "Aric is hurt. You must get him back to Tide's End, or he'll die."

"My physician understands if he fails to keep Aric alive, it will be his head. I only hope my sister, Myranthe, has some foul-stinking potion to cure a ghoul bite." Heath sighed heavily. "Please get in the carriage before you pass out."

Vraymorg rubbed his eyes. "What is all this about? What do you want?"

"What do I want?" Heath grinned. "Barrels of Cahirean wine. That Isles lass from last night in my bed. Oh, not what you mean?"

*Not badly wounded, then?* Even upon his death bed, Heath's tongue would surely be the last part to stop working. The return of his mocking tone, though, was disconcerting.

"You know what I mean." His head lolled against the door.

"A serious talk, my lord? Very well. At first, we wanted only Aric. We scoured Telor for a warrior, the right warrior. In the end, I was sorry it was him. I liked him, you see."

"We?" Vraymorg struggled to focus.

"Judith and I. She has many talents. You're intimately familiar with some. In this instance, she and I were sent to combine our skills to find a bladesman. Our saucy sister—that's what I call Myranthe—waits in her lair for the fruits of our laborious search."

Vraymorg spilled a crazed laugh. He could think of only one reason why an Icelands sorceress would hunt warriors. "You want to restore death riders. You dangerous fool. You're not the first, and you won't be the last. It can't be done. The same sorcerer who cursed me destroyed them. The knowledge is gone. No one knows how to make a death rider."

Heath shook his head. "Myranthe found some writings left by another Icelands sorceress from Roaran's reign."

"Then why aren't death riders among us, delivering justice to kinslayers, punishing the wicked? Gods, man. I didn't take you for a fool." All so senseless, and he was so wretchedly tired.

"There is one among us... somewhere." Heath's smug tone was as irritating as an itch Vraymorg could not reach. If only their oh-so-righteous god punished conceited, self-satisfied Ice lords.

"And soon there will be three—as in the past. The knowledge is no longer lost."

*Three.* Vraymorg could count. He didn't like what it meant. "You hunted Aric." *Then hunted me?*

"'Hunt' sounds crude. I'm far subtler than that. Yes, we sought Aric. Until he holed up behind his father's strong walls. So I asked Cathmor to give him to me as a spoil of battle. He didn't seem to want to. That meant the king had to fall."

"Then what? When Aric bid me help save his sister, that played into your hands?"

"My lord, really. I'm never careless enough to leave anything to chance."

What had Aric said? *"I'm sorry. He threatened to hurt her."* There was a shift in his mind, a click as he put the facts together. Those words. Aric's manner around Heath. Vraymorg groaned. "I've been a fool. Aric brought me here deliberately."

"Go on." Heath grinned encouragement.

"You told Aric to bring me to you in return for his sister."

"Very good." Heath nodded. "This castle was empty. I swear it. The perfect luring spot."

"Aric was meant to overpower me. Take me prisoner."

"Something like that. Of course he didn't realise we intended to abduct him also. Do you think some fool singer will one day find poetic words about how betrayal breeds betrayal and weave them into a sentimental song that makes you weep when you're drunk?"

"Azenor. What have you done with her?"

Heath frowned. "The strange thing is Azenor escaped me. She ran away."

*Ran away.* Nervous excitement tore through him. Perhaps the magic had really worked. "What do you mean?" Vraymorg swallowed. "Do you know where she is now?"

"Haven't the foggiest." Heath shrugged. "Turns out, I didn't need her. I have dutifully collected Aric and swept up a warrior Myranthe will badly want to prod and poke. Val Arques Caelan. That's what Aric called you. I spent last night studying manuscripts Aric carefully collected in his library."

"Pity you didn't choke on the dust."

"Delightful." Heath's smile widened. "Myranthe will weep with joy when I dump you at her feet, Val. I can call you that, can't I? Now I'll return to Tide's End, tell a sad story of your unfortunate deaths, and no one will wonder what really happened to you both."

Vraymorg's mind blanked. Heath's plan was flawless. Unless he found a hole in it, he'd wake a captive in the Icelands, unable to get to Kaell.

At Heath's gesture, guards bundled him into the carriage. An unconscious Aric was slumped on the bench opposite, beside the physician. Dillon climbed in and rearranged Vraymorg's limbs into a comfortable position.

Heath touched his hand to his brow. "A pleasant journey to the Bay of Wrecks, my lord. Judith expects you. I'll come look after you once I've told my story, supported the new king, and all that. Dillon, don't forget to give Val a little of that potion every few hours. Just watch for muscle twitches and scowls, and you'll know when. I'm sure he'll give you little trouble."

He, in fact, intended to give big trouble. *Too hard. Too sleepy.* Vraymorg tried to rally his strength. It couldn't be the end. Someone would come after them, to stop Heath.

As he fought sleep, he reheard Heath's words. *A sorceress from Roaran's reign… A death rider already among us.* He remembered Arn in his tent, eyes fever bright, and his awe as he spoke of his new lord, the man he'd betrayed Archanin to serve.

"Damadar," he croaked.

Heath leaned in. "Val Arques, I wish it was not like this. From everything I've read, from everything I've seen, you are remarkable. But you and I must both serve the gods."

"This death rider, who is it?"

Heath's expression did not change, but the faintest flicker shadowed his eyes.

Vraymorg laughed. "You don't control him, do you? Maybe you don't even know where he is. That's why you're afraid. Something went wrong. Who is this rogue death rider?"

"I don't—" Heath ran his tongue over his lips. "All right, my lord, since you're so clever, work it out." He shoved his hands to his hips, the familiar swagger back in his manner.

"How should I know who this death rider is?"

"Here's a clue," Heath said. "A king of Telor. A powerful king murdered by a man who had loved him. Think about that, Val. Dream about it, even."

At last, Vraymorg surrendered to sleep. He knew who he'd see in his nightmares.

# KAELL

H e returned to the walls of Tide's End and stood on the forest's edge, staring up, clad only in a shift. The king's army had gone. From the charred tents, the churned earth, and the mordant scent of death, a battle had raged in the field.

Kaell assumed Cathmor had won. He didn't really care.

Despite the wind off the sea, its whine through towers, its beat against walls, the stillness of this place enclosed him. He was aware of it, but it did not penetrate his mind.

Kings and battles—those no longer mattered. All that mattered was whether his lord was within this castle. Except Kaell could not walk into *her* home. He could not find the guile to pretend to be the woman who had betrayed him. Not when he wanted to peel off this skin, to be rid of her.

His gaze held on Tide's End. There were no answers there. No comfort. Nothing. He turned away. He could go to the Mountains. The battle decided, that was where his lord would end up.

He began to walk. Time moved about him, a meaningless drifting that could not touch him. On and on, he plodded, stopping only to drink at streams, nibble at mushrooms growing in fallen logs, or fall into an exhausted sleep. The air grew colder. The land slanted into foothills. Kaell tracked the Mountains road but rarely used it. A few travellers passed in the distance.

Once, a man attacked him as he slept. With his wrists pinned, the odour of unwashed flesh stale in his mouth, an unfamiliar fear beat within him, an awareness of his new vulnerability. This woman's body exposed him to dangers Kaell had never considered before. Alarmed, roused to violence, he groped for a rock and smashed it against his assailant's head.

Blood trickled from the stranger's temple. Kaell stared at it. He smelled it. The scent was like a blow. He scrambled to his feet, hands flung up to drive back hunger.

Gods help him. How was this possible? The ghoul part of him survived, even in Azenor's body. It was a sick joke, surely, a punishment the gods had meted out because he'd failed them.

His bloodlines must be bound to his spirit and not to his flesh. Maybe the Quisnaf view about the nature of men and women was right—that each had an amorphous, eternal soul and who he was, even who he had been, was attached to that.

The odour of wet iron was overpowering him. Palms damp, his mouth full of saliva, Kaell dragged his tongue over his lips, already able to taste this man's blood.

The image was so clear, how he would kneel beside the prone figure, how his teeth would break skin. The texture of blood would be thick in his mouth, warm down his throat. He tensed his muscles to pounce. A thought ambushed him. Just one thought. Of his lord.

Kaell could feel Vraymorg's calloused fingers press into his shoulder. His lord's voice echoed in his mind. "A warrior bonded to Khir must only ever kill ghouls."

Shocked by his weakness, he reeled away. How could he forget that oath to the gods? An oath made in blood, no less. Whatever he'd become, he would not kill to satisfy some sick, bestial need.

Trembling, Kaell ground a fist against his thigh, snatching at anger to fight down the hunger. If he killed that man, it would be Vraymorg's fault. His lord had two chances to stop him from becoming a monster. In the Mountains, he'd come into Kaell's cell with a sword. Then in the Isles, Vraymorg could have let him burn, could have let this end.

Kaell threw back his head and yelled. His cries swept towards the trees then died away until nothing remained to suggest a tormented figure stood here.

That night in the Mountains, he hacked at Azenor's hair with the stranger's knife. Kaell watched dark locks fall at his feet and felt nothing.

He tore off the clothes he had stolen from his attacker, lay down, and considered this body. Dispassionately, he explored with her hands. She was leaner than he remembered, but her skin was still as soft as a child's, the cropped hair just as silken.

Kaell held her hand before his eyes. It seemed so small and unblemished compared to his own. He could not accept that it belonged to him.

He fell back, staring up at starlight sprinkling leaves, and plotted how to be free of Azenor. Magic? Death? At last, he cradled his head on his hands, seeking the emptiness of sleep.

As he neared the Mountains fortress, Kaell imagined the words he would say to Vraymorg. *Did you try to find me? Did you? Or did you just leave me like this? Alone?*

He gave up. Once before his lord, his pain would burst out in a simple cry of "Why?"

Vraymorg had been the one immovable thing that made sense. A rock. A beacon. Always there. But now, even that was gone. The world had become untrustworthy and bleak. Kaell had nothing to hold on to or hope for. Except the truth… maybe.

His thoughts in turmoil, he crossed a wooden bridge above the icy blue waters of the Great Digger into a town he recognised. Rushbridge seemed impossibly peaceful, an eternity away from the disorder in the

Isles. Water gurgled over polished river stones. The last of summer's wildflowers dipped and bobbed in a fragment of breeze.

Mesmerised by the remote beauty, Kaell's mind stilled for the first time since he had fled Tide's End. A memory nagged. Faint at first, a shimmer. Then he remembered a stranger bending over him in that room at Tide's End. Yes, surely it had happened. A man with dark-blue eyes had kissed his lips and whispered, "I promised to awaken you with a kiss."

Kaell shook his head. Maybe he'd dreamt it. He couldn't trust his memories. He couldn't trust anything or anyone.

Cloak and cowl up to cover Azenor's hair, he walked into the town as a bell began to toll. At the sound, so like the one in the well tower at Vraymorg, misery kicked in Kaell's breast. He longed to wind back time to a past where he might be on his way home to his lord without dread and anger so intertwined he could no longer separate one from the other.

*What if none of this had happened? The ghoul attack. Archanin... Azenor.* He could not forget that night on the Isle of the Gods, how Azenor's hair was like streaming midnight, her skin warm and scented of blossoms, how she drew him down to the ground. Her lips—

Kaell dragged hands down her face, groaning. It hurt to think of her. *Why does it still hurt?*

Rushbridge was little more than a cluster of houses with pens for goats and hens built against their earthen walls. A stray dog with mangy fur padded the dirt streets. Pigs squealed as Kaell passed.

The townsfolk crowded into the only square, standing around a man hammering a notice to a pole. Sun beat on his dark, glossy hair. A frieze cloak swung from his broad shoulders. A few paces away, a bridled horse waited. *A messenger from the Isles?*

Curiosity nipped at Kaell's detachment. Despite the signs that Cathmor's army dispersed, surely the king's monster trebuchet had breached Tide's End.

Eager now to read the notice, Kaell shouldered into the jostling throng. Voices pealed about him, some low, some excited. He heard "Gendrick Caelan? Who's that?" Laughter followed as someone replied, "Some useless salt-head. They're all the same."

The messenger edged back. Townsfolk pushed forward to study the notice. A few turned to tell illiterate neighbours what it said. One man shook his head. A woman wearing a yellow bonnet wailed. Others muttered.

Kaell could not breach the knot of people. "What does it say?" he begged a stranger.

The man scarcely glanced at him. He shoved an embroidered, heart-shaped chaplet onto his head. "It lists those killed. One death will hit these lands hard."

Kaell started to ask who that was, but the stranger moved away. *Do they mean* my *death? Or—* His heart skipped in alarm. Desperate, he pushed towards the notice.

An arrow thumped into the post. Hoofbeats drummed the ground like thunder, a terrifying rumbling, a portent of death. Kaell whirled. Instinctive fear rolled up his backbone.

A boy ran into the square, shouting, "Raiders!"

For a heartbeat, time slowed around Kaell, a bubble cutting him off from the coming tumult. Then it exploded, sweeping him up into a hurtling, scrambling mob. Horses charged around him. Hooves kicked. Leather scraped. Metal flashed.

The speed of the attack surprised even him. The chaos. The maelstrom of bodies and iron, the cries of terror, ringing steel, and sizzling arrows. Horsemen fanned out everywhere, whooping men who knocked villagers off their feet, threw torches on thatched roofs, or cut down those who snatched up weapons.

A rider thrust out a gauntleted arm to knock Kaell over. He jumped back, a swordsman's move, but this body took a heartbeat longer than it should have to react. As another raider rode in from behind, Kaell spun. He registered not only a delay between thought and movement but also his weakness after so many days with little food and sleep.

Bracing, he let the rider come before flinching aside at the last minute. The horseman tore past then wheeled his horse. Kaell summoned his remaining strength and leapt at him. Her muscles did not respond as fast as his own, but he still caught a flash of an astonished face as he smashed into the raider and dragged him into the dirt.

Kaell sprang up, grasped the man by the shirt, and punched him. The blow landed awkwardly, but with ghoul strength behind it, he knocked the raider out cold.

He grabbed the man's sword. The first rider dismounted. His face half-hidden by a helm, he strode right at Kaell, long steel in a gloved hand. His bright-blue tunic and garish scarlet cape looked ridiculous amid the fighting.

Kaell spluttered a crazed laugh at the bizarre scene—he in a clumsy, untrained body waving a blade about against a warrior dressed as a parrot.

"Girl, put the sword up before you get hurt," the man commanded.

Kaell still laughed as smoke spiralled high above. Sparks from burning houses blew about him.

The raider lowered his blade. "Eloise." His voice was breathy.

"Back off." Kaell waved the sword.

The man stood stunned. Then he shook his head as if to clear it. "No. You're not her. Of course you're not." He raised his weapon and came at Kaell again.

Kaell cut at the man's legs, momentarily disconcerted by the sword's heavy, slow drag. The raider rushed a parry. Kaell pulled back his arm to thrust.

Pain burst through his back. The blow from behind knocked him to one knee. Some part of his dazed mind registered a whir of air as a blade swung. Everything slowed.

The scarlet-caped raider whipped up a hand, his mouth forming, "No."

Kaell's face smashed into the ground. He toppled into darkness.

# HEATH

Like a slumbering beast, the Icelands market twitched in the hour before dawn. Wind puffed through enormous rock caverns, stirring leather belts, gloves, whips, and scabbards hanging for sale in timber-and-canvas stalls. A chime tinkled at the entrance to a wealthier merchant's silken tent, where armed retainers stood guard. Poorer traders slept on bedrolls in their stores, knives in their fists.

Hood up, Heath moved from shadow to shadow with a fire dancer's sure-footed stealth. Even so, a man stepped out, his lantern's flare glinting on his drawn blade. A watcher's silver brooch clasped his cloak.

"My lord Damadar." The man sheathed his sword.

"There's no lord here," Heath hissed as he shouldered by. *Too long away, and I've grown soft. Once, I would've slit his throat to shut him up.*

He slipped through stalls and tents, deeper into the warren of greed within the mountains. Over centuries, the markets had become a city in themselves. Every dawn, carts rumbled in with exotic fruits from Adorean and grains from lush Downs valleys. Some brought weapons, jewellery, leatherwork, fur cloaks, and expensive soap from Quisnaf.

Others carried highly profitable goods of a different kind. The infamous Icelands slave markets had flourished for a thousand years, and only one Telorian king had tried to stop it.

Heath wondered why Roaran Caelan had bothered. Six centuries ago, his laws had simply forced the slavers into the mountain's blackest depths.

Shoving a sleeve to his nose, Heath hurried through a low-roofed passage. In the slave caverns beyond, the stench was no better, but a thin stream of air at least stirred the stink.

He passed crevices cut into the rock walls, enclosed by iron bars. He heard rustling then a moan. A pale hand stretched towards him.

The cells might contain one wretched inhabitant or ten, depending on a captive's value. Best to be worth a lot, Heath had decided a long time ago. Or nothing, which brought a quick death. Anything in between meant misery.

In a cobbled square, torchlight etched a timber platform. A tunnelled wind clanked chains, carrying a drifting mutter or cry as sleepers fled nightmares that paled beside what waited when they woke. A vile place this market, a place only for the lost or forgotten.

Or the mislaid.

Heath entered a forest of creaking metal poles with branches of long, low-hanging chains. Guarded by the sharpest watchers, slavers manacled captives worth gold. They were kept close to huge braziers offering warmth and some light.

Heath's gaze fell on a young man huddled with his head cushioned on his arms, his dark hair thick with dried blood. A soldier from the look of him. Swept up after the battle.

He looked peaceful, as if sleep offered an escape from the misery life had become for anyone who fought for the wrong king. The man's badge of a scarlet heart and crown adorning a tattered tunic marked him as a Plains man.

Heath paused then grinned. *A Plains man? Hardly.* But given the price on this Isles lord's head, no wonder he'd sought a disguise.

Smiling, Heath walked on. Surely the gods had again winked at him. He often sensed their approval in a fire dance; their delight when his sword smote to deliver another offering. A man who was beloved by his gods—now that was a man truly blessed.

On the edge of his vision, movement blurred. An armed watcher stepped from the murk.

Heath spread his empty hands. "The slave master expects me."

The watcher levelled his blade. *Clearly a trusting sort.* Heath liked him already.

"Lose the sword in your belt," the man snarled. "Or you don't see the slave master."

"No, I don't think so." Heath shrugged carelessly. "I feel naked without a sword. And seeing me naked stirs up envy. Envy leads to bloodshed. For that, I need my sword."

The watcher squinted. "What are you babbling about?"

"Being naked. Didn't you follow? *I* understood what I said."

More watchers circled. Maybe. The caverns muted sounds, and watchers moved like ghosts. Then a whistle shrilled. A grey-haired man hobbled into the light, his garments simple leather over a wool tunic. His escort, a surly young man armed with both sword and knife, followed. The watcher stepped back. The others melted away—if they'd been there at all.

The newcomer bowed. With receding hair and stooped shoulders, he looked anything but a villainous king of sorts. Yet the man had held power in these caverns for as long as Heath could remember.

His escort's hair was an unruly dark brown beneath a cap. A sapphire ring on his thumb caught the light as his hands moved restlessly over the hilt of a short Adorean sword scabbarded at his waist. A useless blade. Heath would easily knock it aside unless this man's lunge and thrust proved as deep as a stallion in heat.

"My lord," the slave master said, "you came."

*Of course I came,* Heath thought. *You have something I want. Actually two things now, but I'll play my hand carefully.*

At the word "lord," the slave master's companion grunted in surprise. Heath laughed shortly. He'd arrogantly assumed everyone knew him from the fire halls.

"Who's a lord?" Chains jangled as a wrinkled prisoner sat up, as though a highborn visitor could only be there to free him. A watcher appeared to kick the old man.

"The withered fool is lettered." The slave master shrugged. "Come this way."

His escort blocked Heath. "He's armed."

"Heath Damadar means me no harm." The slave master's lips peeled back from a gap-toothed smile.

"Come for your cut, Damadar?" the guard sneered.

"Not at all." *Who exactly is this insolent worm?* Heath liked worms, especially rude ones. It felt so satisfying cutting them up. "My family's agent has that in hand."

"Ten percent each month." The slave master's greasy smile did not fade. "It is high."

"Is the price of protection ever high?" Heath returned exactly that smile.

His smile died. "True, oh true."

"You have something to show me. Come, come. I have little time."

The slave master beckoned. "Follow me." He led Heath towards a young man snoring away despite the discomfort of ankle shackles.

Heath kicked the sleeper's legs. "Hello, Pup."

The captive grunted. "Go away, big foot. I'm tired."

"Tired, are you? Wait until the whip tears up those impressive shoulders and you can't lie down for a week."

The man opened one eye. "I know that voice."

Heath dragged him to his knees—no easy task, as the prisoner was as tall and heavy as him. "Pup's been very foolish." He shook his head sadly. "I should leave you here to rot."

"Rot, brother? Never that. They'd easily sell me. For a good price too. You ask the slave master there. I'm young to begin with—"

"Young and stupid."

"Good with a blade."

"Dangerous."

"Lettered."

"Debatable."

"Nice teeth."

Heath laughed. "You've got me now. So what price to free my brother?" He raised his brows at the slave master.

The man's oily smile reappeared. "No price, my lord. Only your continued goodwill."

"And what price if I want Griffin to… disappear?"

"Disappear?" Griffin spluttered in disbelief. "What? You wouldn't."

*No sense of humour, Pup.* Even the high-and-mighty Velleran would enjoy the joke.

Heath ruffled Griffin's dirty hair. "With the cost of the war, we're low on gold. Velleran thinks one younger brother is enough to keep in the style to which I've become accustomed. So I'll pretend I didn't see you. Don't worry. With those teeth, you'll find a nice home, Pup."

Griffin slapped his hand away. "This better be your usual nonsense."

Heath tossed a jangling purse to the slave master's companion.

"Heath." Griffin drawled the word. "What's the money for? To free me or make me disappear?"

Heath was sorely tempted to continue teasing. "Ah, cut him free. I'm fond of the fool. And keep the gold. A thank-you for keeping the fool safe."

The slave master nodded at the shadows. A watcher stepped out to unlock the shackles. As Griffin staggered up, brazier light shone upon his bruised cheeks.

"I was reluctant to believe he was your brother at first. A lot of men say they are who they aren't," the slave master mused. "But this one—"

"Had good teeth?"

The man flashed his rancid smile. "Had a certain arrogance, shall we say."

"You did the right thing, fetching me. As I'm here, I need a word." Heath drew him aside, away from his escort and the watchers.

The slave master leaned in. He rubbed his hands. "Is there some other way I can serve you, my lord?"

"There is." Heath patted another purse of coins in his belt. "The black-haired prisoner pretending to be a Plains man." He pointed back. "I'll wager he's from the Isles."

"Who can say? Perhaps a younger son thought dead? So many men lost, either killed in battle or hiding throughout Telor."

The man really didn't know who he held. *Good gods.* "Where did you scoop him up?"

"Stone Bridge, drunk on Venivan wine. He passed out in an alley and woke in chains."

"My, my." Heath scratched his cheek. "The king will not take kindly to slavers simply abducting folk off the streets." Rules existed to keep the trade "far back"—the Icelands expression for anything untoward. Scouring the area around a battlefield and picking off the powerless was one thing—

"The king has other concerns. Ghouls in Dal-Kanu? Unheard of. That's what happens when a precious salt-head takes the throne."

"Nothing precious about Gendrick," Heath corrected. "The king makes use of his ghouls, I'm told. Makes use of us all. Even I have a purpose—the king intends to give me a wife." That morsel of gossip would be common news soon, but he would flatter the slave master with a confidence.

"The rumour is the dead king's cousin."

"The rumour is right. A widow, thank the gods. But to business." Heath shook the purse. "Silver. Enough for the Isles warrior—and your new escort. I take it you're not yet fond of him?" He arched a brow. "Unless he's a nephew or something."

"Even a nephew"—the slave master eyed the purse—"can be bought for the right price."

"I'll remember that."

"However, he is not my nephew. Nor am I fond of him. You may have him."

"Of course you won't tell him that." Heath tossed the purse. "Just send him and the Isles man to me. The usual arrangement. Ask for my cousin, Dillon."

"A hard man, that one. I wonder if even cousins have a price?"

*Dillon, what have you done? Upset our slave master? Very careless.* "Maybe they do. But Dillon is useful."

"You will let me know, my lord, the moment you no longer find him so?"

Beyond the caverns, Heath paused, his spirits bright. He'd retrieved not only his brother but also a traitor the king sought to punish. Plus he'd procured a worm to cut up in the fire halls, a distraction to ease his yearning. The man he desired above all others to fight, to defeat, was not yet his to play with. Until then, Heath must make do with worms.

"Why have we stopped?" Despite the mild night, Griffin shivered in Heath's cloak.

"Waiting."

Dillon stepped out of the darkness. "Good to see you, Pup." He squeezed Griffin's shoulder. "No trouble, then?"

"Trouble for you," Heath said. "The slave master asked if I'd consider selling you out."

Dillon shrugged. "I'll keep clear. Thank you for the warning."

"What'd you do?" Griffin asked.

"Took a lot of money off the old fool at cards."

"You cheated?"

"Not at all. In fact, one of his minions tried to rob me. It all ended messily—bloody."

They moved into the city's tangle of stone-and-timber houses, of temples, bathhouses, and taverns. In its squares, bronzed trees shed leaves. In its crooked alleys men and women of the night, their perfumed bodies draped in silk, called down to customers.

According to the tax collectors, two hundred thousand people worked, slept, loved, argued, and bustled about the cobbled streets and torchlit passages of the famed caverns of the Damadar "left" city. More if they counted slaves. But no one did. Anyone far back was invisible.

The crisp night blurred the city's sounds to a hum. A thin breeze carried scents of honeysuckle and spice, of smoke from dying cooking fires. Heath enjoyed these nights on autumn's cusp, when cool air invited sleep but without the chill furs did not banish. Pleasant after the tormenting Isles heat he'd left behind ten days ago.

In his lavish chamber at Tide's End, he'd sweated and tossed in a too-soft bed, the damp air swollen with heat. Only near dawn did he fall into an exhausted sleep, waking bleary-eyed and dull-witted.

At the city's curtain wall, Dillon led them along a lane beneath the walk. Sentries strode overhead, watching for fires from the defensive towers built from the Twin Cities to the sea. Where the wall met a tower, he unlocked an iron door to a chasm.

Heath remembered the tutor who had explained why the ravine splitting the cities made them impregnable. Grizzled, shortsighted, the man had moist palms that stained parchment as he turned pages in books, his voice so soft his student had to lean to hear. Should an enemy take one city, he'd said, the defenders fell back to the other, flooded the channel, and rained arrows at the attackers from the round towers along the ravine's length.

Dillon moved off to keep watch. Heath dropped his hands to his hips. "All right, Griffin, what can you tell me? I must say it's disappointing to find you in the far-back caverns."

"Disgusting place." Griffin shuddered. "I need a bath, Heath."

"You wouldn't believe how often I heard that in the Isles. The fools bathe daily. I've a theory it washes away their sense of humour. Now what of the Sword Brotherhood?"

Griffin shuffled his feet. "Can we do this later? I'm covered in fleas."

"Let's do it now, Pup."

Griffin scratched behind his ear. Heath stepped back. Who knew what bloodsucking, tiny fiends crawled in those caverns? Actually bloodsucking fiends stalked the caverns on two legs too. One, he called "sister."

"I put the story about in the taverns that I was a Cahirean mercenary seeking word of a sword brotherhood. Some muttered about old rhymes. That's all. Then it went wrong."

"Dangerous times, brother." Heath heaved a despondent sigh. "So nothing then." He was certain the myths held a forgotten truth. Myranthe certainly believed them. Archanin did too. Why else question Gendrick about such a brotherhood?

"Well..." Griffin scratched again.

"Well?" Heath encouraged.

"Not certain how reliable this is." His brother covered a yawn with his palm. "I overheard two watchers whispering about the Father-Keeper sneaking about late, hood up."

"The Father-Keeper?" Heath echoed doubtfully. A lettered scholar could have nothing to do with sword brotherhoods.

"Ask him what he's up to." Griffin shifted his weight impatiently. "He's a mouse. He'll easily frighten and spill all his secrets."

"Maybe. I must think."

"Excellent. You think. I'll bathe."

"One moment, flea-ridden one. How did you end up chained to a pole?"

"Oh that." His voice held a blush. "I asked too many questions in the far-back taverns. Kept to the Cahirean silver-sword story. They jumped me outside in the dark."

"What a gift they'd think you. A young bladesman alone in a strange city. Worse, blundering about alone in the far-back caverns, where no one sees anything."

"I told them my name. That man with the slave master called me a liar."

"And then he hit you. Well, someone bruised your cheek."

"That was earlier. There was a fight—"

Heath threw up a hand. "Stop now. It's too much for my delicate ears. You can explain it all to Myranthe—the fight, the pole, all of it. She's cast spells trying to find you."

"No, no, no. Not Myranthe," Griffin pleaded. "She'll scold me until my ears fall off."

Somewhere away in the dark, Dillon laughed.

"Or tell Velleran." Though their elder brother wouldn't scold Griffin, just look disappointed. "He needs to know."

"Not that, please. I beg you. Take me back to the caverns," Griffin muttered. "Chain me to the pole again. Now, Heath."

# KAELL

Kaell staggered at the end of a rope tied to a saddle. Blood from his torn wrists soaked the coarse fibres, its metallic scent sharp. His legs had long ago fallen into an unconscious rhythm. If only his thoughts could do the same. Then he might escape the flurry of doubt and dread.

He no longer cared where his captors took him. His mind snagged on that notice in the town. *What if I never have a chance to ask why? What if it said—*

*No.* He refused to think that. His lord was the best bladesman Kaell ever knew. That man, that bladesman, could not die in battle.

Low branches choked by brown leaves crushed against him as he plodded on. A cool autumn wind hunted through trees. Summer, though, lingered in the perfumes of loamy earth, honey, and moss. When Kaell stumbled, his knee flattened bluebells.

His captor patiently reined in his horse until he rose. "Walk on."

The man was not at all what Kaell had expected of a brutish slaver. His blue shirt and scarlet cloak were as ridiculously garish as his companions' garments, but his heavy-lidded eyes held intelligence. Their hazel colour was common to Cahir, just like the nut-brown of his cropped hair. Paler stubble pelted a strong jaw and grim unsmiling mouth that matched the straight lines of the man's sun-darkened face.

That face pricked at Kaell's memory. A tournament field. A man with a staff bending down to help him rise. No, the strand of memory receded.

He looked away from his captor's back to the straggling line of captives from the town. Some held children by the hand or carried them in stiff arms as they shuffled along the track between the forest and a wide river, its surface sleek with swirling currents. Many bowed their heads, their will to fight dented by the two-day march and slap of leather across shoulders.

Every muscle in Kaell's legs and back ached at the physical toil of this journey. But for all his exhaustion, his bewilderment at what unfolded, he held his resentment within, a secret flame carefully stoked while he awaited his chance to escape. A distraction or careless moment was all it would take.

"Dannon." A girl with gleaming black hair called out as she ran across a bridge ahead, a bow and quiver over her shoulder. The bridge jutted from the bank to an island, where a palisade ringed timber huts on stilts, no doubt a defence against melted snow bloating the spring river. "Dannon, you're back."

With an impatient sigh, Kaell's captor raised a hand. His shirt came up, exposing a hilt in his belt. It was far from fancy, just iron and thread. A sword revealed a lot about a warrior's character. A hard man, this. Despite the illusion of his garments, he was not especially vain or flamboyant.

"Walk on." Dannon tugged the rope.

Kaell hadn't realised he'd slowed. Dragging breath through his teeth, he stumbled over the bridge towards the village.

Guards at the palisade grinned at Dannon. "Captain. A good hunt. Word is you dared cross the gorge."

*Captain?* Kaell reassessed the man. *Not just a slaver then, but a leader of sorts.*

"A village near Vraymorg."

Kaell pressed his lips together so tight, they hurt. His lord would answer this outrage with steel. *If he still lives.* Grief tore up his gut.

"Move." Dannon glanced back.

Unaware his steps had slowed again, Kaell glowered but walked on.

A loose ring of timber houses spread across the field before him. The fortified island was flat except for a hill overlooking a firepit that rent the grassland like a blackened sword slash.

In the midst of the houses, a crowd milled about the returning raiders. Some called out to riders or slapped backs. Their voices blended to a swill, their swirling green or indigo gowns and tunics a cacophony of colour.

The air was dense with scents of roasting meat, pepper, horseflesh, and mud. But even unshed, the odour of blood overpowered all else. An ugly reminder of what he was.

As the Varee forced their captives into a staked enclosure, a man's slurred shouts carried from a hut. Some turned towards the hut with disgusted mutters. The girl with the bow started forward. A boy held her back.

"He'll not lay a hand on her again, Shahven," she said. "Not ever."

"You're right. It's time someone stopped him. That *I* stopped him."

"No, don't." She grabbed the boy's arm.

He threw her grip off and ran into the hut.

Kaell paused to stare.

The captain leaned from the saddle. "Walk on, girl."

Reluctantly he did, his gaze flicking from the gates to the river. If he were to escape, the bid must be before they thrust him behind that staked enclosure. He twisted his hands. One jerk, and the ropes would come off. *Then the bridge or the riverbank? Fight or swim?*

Guards pulled the gates shut behind the last prisoner. Glaring light at his back shadowed the captive's face, but given his cloak of black and grey, Vraymorg's colours, Kaell must know him.

"Move." A raider curled his whip about the man's leg.

The prisoner stomped on with exaggerated tardiness. Kaell mentally acknowledged the tiny act of defiance before his thoughts turned again to escape.

"The host captain suspects that one is quite a prize," a raider told a villager. "We took him by surprise, found him with a girl— in the act." He rattled a salacious laugh. "Naked, he still snatched up a sword. He'll regret that hour of passion a long while."

"Who is he?"

"A Vraymorg warrior. Won't give a name. Dannon will trick it out of him. See, they're taking him to the mage's hut."

Raiders dragged the captive to a timber hut. This time, Kaell glimpsed his face. Aalart Hillborn. He hoped the Vraymorg guardsman didn't prove stubborn and force the Varee to hurt him.

"Water," he begged, aware everyone was watching Aalart. "My throat is parched."

Dannon bent to pass a skin. Kaell tore his hands free, grabbed the man's foot, and tossed him from the saddle. The horse reared up, kicking. Unable to grab its reins, Kaell backed away and ran at the bridge.

Shouts broke out. Guards surged from the gate. Villagers spun to gape. Those raiders still mounted rounded their horses, whooping at the prospect of a chase. They swept forward in a storm of dust to block him.

Cut off from the bridge, Kaell whirled, his muscles at last reacting faster, and bolted towards the far riverbank. Leather creaked as his pursuers closed in quickly.

An arrow twanged. It tore past his shoulder so close the air shimmered. The dark-haired girl with the bow stepped into his path, bowstring drawn back. "Stop," she shouted. "Or this goes into your knee."

Kaell shuddered to a halt. He threw a desperate look at the men running at him, at the horsemen circling, cracking their whips on puffing dirt, their grins wide. He gestured surrender.

They moved in at once. Kaell fisted his hands to control his fear. *Stay calm.* Now came his next plan—one they would never expect from an outsider.

Men grabbed his arms.

"Lost something?" one smirked at the captain.

Dannon said nothing. Tight-jawed, he brushed dirt from his tunic. "Take her to the stone."

They marched Kaell towards the enclosure. Villagers parted to let the warriors through. A few shook their heads. Others chuckled, enjoying the spectacle. But instead of forcing him in with the others, his captors thrust his wrists into manacles anchored to a weathered rock.

Kaell tugged at chains thicker than those he'd broken to escape Archanin. Panic roared up. "What are you doing? Free me. You can't do this." He wrenched at his restraints. Iron only scraped on rock.

Forcing down his alarm with slow breaths, he peered about, an odd curiosity beneath his fear. Kaell knew stories of the Varee. No one knew who they really were, where they came from, or how they survived beyond the gorge.

At first glance, the village resembled others in the Mountains. Ranks of stilt huts stretched along the river inside the defensive timber wall. Villagers bustled about a stone building that might be a storeroom. A covered burrow beneath a mound was likely another.

Women carried wood to the firepit. Others took buckets of water to the prisoners. An axe thudded. A withered man wearing a bone necklace waved a carved stick at the sky as if entreating the gods. Barefoot, naked from the waist up, his atonal wailing was like a screeching wind. His toothless grin reminded Kaell of a skull.

A stout man with sweat-stained trousers marked a book as he counted captives in the enclosure. The boy who'd comforted the archer approached him with determined steps.

"How're they hanging, Shahven?" The stout man sucked in his flabby belly. "I see you grew some at last. Dealt with your father, did you?"

The boy looked uncomfortable. "I don't want to talk about him."

"Surprised your sister hasn't cut his throat while he sleeps. Fierce, that one."

Shahven's gaze shifted to Kaell. "Paul, I'll buy her."

"Who? The dark-haired lass?"

"I—yes. Her."

Kaell laughed aloud to hide his disquiet. No one was going to buy him.

"What are you offering, Shahven?"

"I own a cow," the boy said in a serious tone. "Four pieces of gold—"

Paul chuckled. Taking the boy by the elbow, he walked him to Kaell. "You're Varee-born, Shahven. You know how much young women fetch?"

Kaell slitted his eyes to show his contempt. Nothing. For he had a bloody surprise planned. Too bad—for them. They shouldn't have brought him to their village.

Shahven bit his lip. "She's trouble, though. Tried to run. That lowers her worth."

"You'll bring her to heel? How? You don't have the stomach for cruelty."

"I—" Shahven glanced at Kaell then down. "You're right. My wits have fled."

Paul sighed. "I suspect, though, she is indeed trouble. The sooner she's in the Icelands, the better, I'm thinking."

They moved away.

# DANNON

**W**ith wisped hair and tattooed skin hanging off his ribs in folds, the mage looked like a creature of nightmares. The eerie chatter of the old man's bone necklace always chilled Dannon's spine. The rattle of death.

He forced his thoughts to their captive. "Still nothing to say?"

Bound to a chair, defenceless, the Vraymorg warrior did not reply. He followed the mage's every move with low-lidded eyes.

Dannon sighed. A long, unpleasant night lay ahead. A pity. The prisoner could be no older than twenty, with curling, brown hair that invited a lover's touch. "Begin."

The mage whipped a poker from the fire and turned with a deceptively benevolent smile. The captive jerked back, struggling hard against the ropes.

"He's afraid," the mage said. "This one will break quickly."

"Where's the fun in that?" Mark the Mad and Merry One replied. He leaned over the prisoner. "Tell us who you are."

Dannon had yet to see Mark's merry side. Varee names were often ironic. Bodrin the Tearful was a man who never cried. Charlotte the Meek, a bold archer. Sometimes, though, they reflected a shameful truth. Like Dannon Bloodtaker.

He leaned a shoulder to the wall, aware of a dull weariness. It was in his fingers as they drilled against his belt, in the lock of his muscles. But it was of the spirit rather than flesh.

So often Dannon had watched the mage at work in his foul hut, gagging at the odours of ferrous blood and fear and the cloying potions and ointments, as thick as incense.

Yet he kept his mind apart from what was unfolding, an observer caught on the edge of this life—a warrior likely to die for the Varee but always an outsider.

An ache tore up his breast. *Why am I here?* This question often troubled him. And yet, his restless yearning, his need for more, did not have a name. He only knew he was drifting, waiting, hungering to find a purpose beyond fighting, killing, and growing rich.

Once, that had been enough. Now even sacking a village across the gorge—a reckless venture he dared not attempt while the former Lord of Vraymorg lived—offered nothing.

*What do I want... Love?*

The word was a wind whispering through a chasm, a fading memory of childhood. Like the passion-fruit vine his mother had planted to hide their home's bracken walls, left to wither when she died. The word was his wife's grave, their unborn daughter buried with her. A smothering grief. Cold.

Despite the violence about to unfold, his thoughts would not turn from the girl, a girl who was so out of place in that town of mud and dirt. How haughty, how fearless her glare had been as she swept steel. Was that what intrigued him? Her defiance she did not bother to mask? Or did he simply, shallowly, find her likeness to his dead wife too alluring?

"Eloise," he'd blurted in that town, sounding like a grief-stricken fool, not a warrior and host captain of nearly thirty-five.

A hesitant hand tapped the door. At Dannon's call of "come," Shahven scurried in, a guilty flush on his face. *Now what has he been up to?*

"Shahven. Good." The mage waved the red tip at the prisoner. "Perhaps you can save this stubborn man pain. Do you want to save him pain, Shahven?"

The mage's usual game. Shahven's appearance was always the first move.

Dannon looked away. The fire's glow threw shapes upon the walls. They jigged as though an unseen puppeteer jerked their strings.

If he shut his eyes, he could see the fire in his father's house. He could see his father's chair near the hearth, his father's hands on the arms, the tips of his resting fingers rough, the skin calloused where a sword hilt had rubbed and rubbed.

He could remember the leathery scents that clung to his father's clothes, the odour of oil as he polished his sword. He recalled every detail except his father's face.

"I would save him pain, yes," Shahven said.

The mage puffed slow breaths on the bound man's cheek. "Such a gentle child. It hurts him to see another suffer, you see."

The captive swung his head towards Shahven. "Don't look at him." The mage swept the poker back and forth. "Not when I'm about to burn your eyes out."

"No." Shahven jolted in alarm. "Let me talk to him, convince him to be reasonable."

The Vraymorg man pressed his back into the chair, his stare locked on the red tip.

"So stubborn." The mage shook his head. Without warning, he jabbed the poker at the prisoner's breast. As the man screamed and thrashed, Mark held the chair, grinning.

Dannon winced. *Why invite pain? Pride? Or because his name revealed too much?*

"Stop, stop." Shahven grabbed the mage's arm. "Let me talk to him."

"You have a kind heart." With a glance to Dannon for a sign, the mage tossed the poker back into the fire. "Very well. Talk to him. But when I return, I take his eyes."

The mage led Mark out. Dannon pushed off the wall to stir the embers with the poker. The prisoner watched him, his teeth clamped into his lip against the pain, wary rather than afraid.

"Can I—?"

At Dannon's nod, Shahven rushed to wet a cloth and dab at the man's burn.

"It hurts, I know," the boy said as the captive groaned. "I could not bear to watch. Don't make me watch them take your eyes."

"I've heard about the Varee," the man wheezed. "Blind, I'm less valuable." He had the lyric tone of those Mountains-born. Dannon suspected who he was. He just needed a name to be certain.

Shahven held a cup to the prisoner's lips. "A false hope. Is your name worth your sight?"

"I can't tell them." Sweat streamed off his brow. His sodden tunic clung to his perspiring body. Once he talked, Dannon would ask the mage to soothe the man's burns with lotions.

He pushed the poker deeper into the fire and rose. "The mage will be back soon."

Shahven glanced up. "Can you delay him? Dannon?"

The captive's head shot up. His lips pulled back into a snarl.

"Dannon," Shahven said. "The mage."

"He is not known for his patience. He will take this man's eyes."

Shahven sat back on his heels, his worried look upon the prisoner. "Tell me your name," he begged. "Please. In my dreams, I hear the screams of men the mage has blinded. I'd save you that. I never want to smell burning flesh again."

The man tore his narrowed gaze from Dannon. "By my gods, I wish I could tell you, boy."

"Please. For me. So I need not see you suffer. Your name can't mean that much."

A log rolled into a spray of sparks. Confused, the captive stared at the tears welling in Shahven's eyes. He sighed. "I suppose it's just a name. I'm Aalart."

Shahven covered the captive's hand with his own. "Thank you, Aalart." He arched his brows at Dannon.

"You've done well, Shahven. I know enough," Dannon said.

Aalart jerked his head around. "You don't know anything, slaver."

"I now know who and what you are."

"A lie."

Dannon gripped the chair as he bent over the man. "You fought well. You're a warrior."

Aalart's head drooped. "I should never have been taken."

"Any warrior can be overwhelmed by greater numbers. As to who you are…" Dannon sighed impatiently. *Why didn't my men notice?* "You tried to rip a badge off your tunic."

Aalart sneered. "That doesn't mean a thing."

"A captain's badge, perhaps?"

No word from Aalart, only a flicker of his tongue over lips.

Dannon straightened, crossed to the door, and flung it back. The mage thumped his stick as he entered, an inane smile upon his lips. Mark trailed behind.

"My master," Shahven said, "you have salve for his burn?"

"In a moment, Shahven." The mage was looking at Dannon.

Dannon said, "His name is Aalart Hillborn."

The prisoner glared at him with hatred.

Mad Mark whistled. "You're certain, Host Captain?"

"That's the remains of a badge on his shoulder. This is Aalart Hillborn, one of the new lord of Vraymorg's captains." Dannon nodded slowly to himself. "Rare to catch a captain alone, outside Vraymorg's walls. We're fortunate."

"Too fortunate?" Mark twisted Aalart's ear. "Is he a spy for the Vraymorg whelp?"

"I think not. He fought hard, intending to force us to kill him, not take him alive."

"Hillborn." The mage scratched his grubby, bristled chin. "A lord's son, then."

"The boy's worth money." Mark patted the captive's shoulder. "I like him better already."

"How did you—" Aalart stammered in disbelief.

Dannon turned away. So little betrayed so much. A name. A ripped tunic. How could he know? They all asked that. And why, they wondered later, did they need to confide in a child to save him from watching their torture?

Trickery wasn't part of it. Dannon's wits cut as sharply as his blade. As for Shahven, the boy was entirely sincere. He really did only wish to save others pain.

# KAELL

Kaell tugged at the chains. No one cared. He cursed. No one heard—not above the laughter, the smashing glass, or the firepit's roar. The wind scattered sparks into darkness and drove smoky clouds across a bloated moon. Its nip chilled his skin.

Slouched about tables, thrusting wine cups at slaves to fill, the Varee indulged in a feast as excessive as their garments. Women flirted with warriors. Drunken men squabbled, reeling to their feet with drawn knives and threats before breaking into laughter. Giddy children darted about, playing games. More slaves turned a fresh-slaughtered cow on a spit.

Rage roiled up in Kaell. The brutes not only served Archanin but took pleasure in enslaving others. And he could do nothing but watch their disgusting celebration.

He heaved at his shackles again as guards dragged captives one by one before a platform where five men sprawled in padded chairs behind a table. Dannon sat with them, his aloof gaze falling beyond the fire into the empty night.

"It's no good," a young voice said. "Those chains are thick. We've had to hold rogue ghouls here once or twice."

Shahven wore what Kaell guessed were his best garments, a silken shirt likely blood red in daylight, polished boots, and flared pants. A knife poked from a sash about his slender waist.

Kaell tugged at iron again. "I have to try."

"Can I—" The boy hesitated. "Can I sit? I'll explain what's happening."

"I think it's clear what's happening." Kaell's outrage churned. The law banned slavery. But here, beyond the reach of lords and kings, it flourished.

"No doubt it seems strange to an outsider." Shahven sat cross-legged. "But the trade is ancient among the Varee."

"Ancient or not, I won't be sold like cattle. Or for a cow, for that matter."

Shahven's shoulders shot up. "You heard that. I'm sorry."

Kaell sighed. *This boy is how old? Sixteen?* "So what *is* happening?"

A drunken cheer rose from the Varee. A stick-legged boy ran from guards, only to fall face-first into the dirt. Guards swooped him up and dumped him on his knees.

"Tonight the catch is collared—the centuries-old slang for it," Shahven said. "As children, my sister Natasha and I always played this game when raiders returned with captives. We'd sit on the steps to our hut, guessing what collars would fit around which necks."

"Gold for the most valuable," Kaell suggested. "Iron or bronze for the rest."

"For the most part, collars are iron, plain and modest. But the necks of those the slave master judges will fetch a high price, or those to be ransomed, are adorned in silver. We make no distinction except in worth. Gold is gold. And more gold is better than less gold."

"The slave master," Kaell said. "That fat man with the book."

"The Little King of Coins, they call him. Paul's tongue makes buyers think they've a bargain even if he cheats them. He's too fat for a horse—his excuse for not riding with the warrior host. Still, they hoist him onto a poor beast to go to the Icelands markets."

"Who's he?" Kaell pointed to the bone-necklace man.

"The mage. I'm apprenticed to him. He's teaching me the old ways of magic and healing."

The mage jiggled behind a man in the most prominent seat on the platform. Firelight illuminated the symbols cut onto the magic man's stick.

"And them?"

"The overlord and his council. Our fiercest—some might say most vicious—warriors."

Kaell watched the procession of captives to the platform. As Paul extolled each one's worth, the overlord yawned and gulped wine.

"We keep a few to work the fields, tend to horses and in the kitchens, fetch water, clean chamber pots, cook, mop out mud after the floods," Shahven explained.

"All tasks beneath the Varee." Kaell snorted in disgust. This world beyond the gorge proved unpleasant indeed.

Guards pulled a child from a woman's arms and dumped her before the council. At the small boy's distressing cries, Kaell shifted uneasily. "What will happen to the child?"

"We raise him as Varee. He's young enough to forget his other life."

The boy's mother wept. Kaell squeezed a link of chain in his fist. This was wrong. No wonder his lord had taught him to hate slavers. He heard another echo of Vraymorg's voice. "No one has the right to do what they will with another's body."

"I will take her." A warrior with plaited hair rose from a fur-covered bench. He shook a purse at Paul. "Twenty pieces of silver. More than fair."

"What will you do with her?" a companion mocked. "It's different with women to goats."

"Not even a goat would go near you," the warrior retorted, tossing the purse at Paul.

The slave master caught it and peered inside. He nodded at the overlord.

"Done. The next?"

Guards dragged Aalart forward. Laughter and voices died away. Men and women swung their legs around benches, elbows on tables, to watch. A mutter broke out here and there, then the voices faded until only the crackle of flames carried in the night.

"His family will no doubt pay," Paul began. "You know his particulars?"

"Once they pay, do we send a fighting man back to the Lord of Vraymorg?" The overlord's tone dripped with sarcasm.

"We'll have his oath not to take up arms against us," suggested an older man at his side.

"Oaths can be broken. Sell him."

"The overlord is called Conroy, Wolf of the Mountains," Shahven whispered. "Pig of the Mountains, more like. Beside him is Robert with the Blood of Lions."

Kaell scoffed. The man had earned the name in his distant youth, no doubt. The grey-haired Robert looked as worn and useless as a buckled blade.

Kaell's eyes strayed to the host captain. Even among warriors, his stillness, the breadth of his muscular shoulders, and the proud tilt of his head set him apart.

Dannon leaned to whisper to the overlord. Conroy scowled. "Very well." He raised his voice. "My captain of the host wants him held. He intends to make this man fight for us."

"A risk," murmured a bearded man nearest Kaell and Shahven.

"The host captain will break him," another said. "He'll have him forget his own mother."

"To the stone." Conroy waved his hand.

"I cannot tell if Dannon is pleased or not." Shahven shook his head. "He always shows little emotion, whether it is fear, joy, or pleasure."

Guards dragged a struggling Aalart to the stone, chained him, then released Kaell and forced him to his knees before the platform. A silence closed about the field.

The overlord leaned forward. His companions fidgeted. A woman carrying a pot stopped. Within the quiet, a chord of excitement played. Their expectation, how they feasted, laughed, and took pleasure in a ceremony of misery all raised Kaell's hackles. He and the captured villagers were nothing to them. Just merchandise to be sold.

Flames flickered like chattering tongues. For all their warmth, Kaell shivered. What if his knowledge about Varee law proved wrong? How would he escape then? Panic beat up, tightening his throat. He seized a breath, concentrating on his inhalation and exhalation.

"We know nothing about her." Dannon sounded gruff, his expression guarded.

"I'm told she fought with steel in that village," the overlord said. "Then caused more trouble here."

"She has the look of the Isles with that raven hair," Robert said. "Except her skill with the sword suggests she could be Quisnaf."

"Sell her in the Icelands." Conroy sat back. "If she's Quisnaf, she's too dangerous."

Guards grabbed Kaell's arms. He tore free, clambered up, and shouted: "I demand the right to fight for my freedom."

A hush fell over the watchers. It held for a moment, deep and full, resonating like a low melody. Then a tide of shocked voices rippled through the crowd. Dannon scowled.

"Do not be stupid, girl." Conroy flapped a hand. Guards seized Kaell again.

"I have the right," Kaell cried. "I understand your laws."

Chains jangled as Aalart strained against the shackles. "I demand to fight too."

Paul laughed. "You missed your chance, Captain, so shut up."

"But I have not," Kaell said. "When first before the council, a captive may challenge the Varee champion to win their freedom."

"Silence, fool girl." Conroy shot to his feet and stabbed a finger at Kaell. "Are you asking to die? A challenge is a fight to the death."

Kaell poked his chin up. "I know this."

"I forbid it. You are not Varee. Take her."

The mage stepped out. "She is within her rights."

Conroy rocked forward as if to menace him. "I said no."

"She invoked the law," the mage stated mildly. "An old law though it is."

"She will surely die. Dead, she is worthless."

"Nevertheless"—the mage rattled his stick—"it is the law. Though it is not worded quite as she thinks."

Kaell frowned. "What do you mean?"

The old man's skull grin appeared. "The law says you can fight not to be enslaved."

"It is the same thing, surely."

The mage shook his head. "You fight to prove your worth to the Varee host."

Conroy smiled viciously. "You may withdraw your demand."

Kaell shrugged off his irritation. True, he had misunderstood. *But so what?*

"I have nowhere to go," he said, the weight of the words upon him even as he admitted it. His lord could be dead. Kaell did not know where he belonged then. Or what his life meant without Vraymorg. "Here is as good as anywhere. My demand stands."

A clamour broke out, a burst of startled laughter then muttering. Conroy sat down hard, gripping the chair arms. "You foolishly invoke our laws. So be it. What weapon do you choose?"

At the sly edge to his tone, Kaell sensed a trap. "The sword."

The overlord tried to hide his smile. At his nod, two men hurried off.

Dannon considered Kaell. "Who would you fight?"

"Your best bladesman. It means nothing to defeat anyone less."

"A good answer."

Men returned with a sword. They bore it as they might a casket, one holding the guard and the other the tip. Firelight and moonlight glinted off gleaming steel and an embossed hilt. They dropped the sword at Kaell's feet then stepped back, grinning.

The council members stilled. So did the Varee watching intently from tables or crowding near the platform. Even enclosed captives craned to see over taller heads, sensing the strangeness of what unfolded.

Kaell closed his fingers around tattered threads. Guessing the trick, he slowly hoisted the blade. Heavy, yes, heavier than any ordinary sword. Impossible for a woman to easily lift with untrained muscles. But not for a woman with a warrior's knowledge and ghoul blood.

With a cold laugh, he swished steel through air. For less than a heartbeat, there was a delay between his will and the action. If that happened while he was fighting, he was dead.

"Impossible." Conroy rounded on the men who'd brought the blade. "It is the wrong weapon. You were to bring the ceremonial blade, the one used for challenges."

"That is it," one stammered. "I swear it."

"So it is," Dannon said, rising. With elaborate attention, he unclasped his cloak and laid it over his chair. A scabbard angled from his belt, his hilt within easy reach of his fingers.

The mage passed him a goblet. Steam rose from its contents. Dannon drained it fast. With a steady hand, he placed the goblet on the table. He grew very still, very composed, his focus far from this field and his opponent. Then he blinked, let his sword arm fall to his side, and jumped off the platform. As he strode towards Kaell, sword swinging at his hip, the Varee sighed as though knowing how this familiar ritual ended.

"So you are the best bladesman?" This close, Kaell caught the otherworldly gleam in Dannon's eyes, not like a battle spell where a warrior cut himself off from what befell him but a calm acceptance. *Of duty? Or of an inevitable victory?*

"I am not certain. My real skill is with the bow. However, this unpleasant task falls to me."

"I've heard them call you Dannon."

"My Varee name is Dannon Bloodtaker."

"Perhaps I'll take yours, Bloodtaker." Kaell levelled the sword. He could hear Dannon's blood pounding like axe blows. That uncomfortable hunger stirred. How might this warrior's blood taste? Hot. Rich. All he needed to do was throw the host captain down and rip his teeth across his throat.

"I shall no doubt spill yours." Dannon's sigh sounded sad. "I am sorry for it. You are reckless, but your spirit reminds me of someone I once deeply cared about." He drew his blade, his eyes hazy, as if he were drugged. But as his fingers curled about the weapon's hilt, he roared and slashed at Kaell's head, a lethal blow meant to kill.

There was an instant, a tiny sliver of time, when Kaell almost let Dannon strike him down. But his hand instinctively whipped the sword up. Steel scraped, the sound unnaturally loud in the taut hush.

Scoffing at his opponent's surprise, Kaell riposted, this untrained body now responding much faster. The Varee warrior flinched then stabbed with swift jabs—high, low, then high again. Kaell met each with drilled steel, giving up little ground.

The rhythm broke for a splinter of a second. Kaell thrust. Dannon recoiled as he blocked, his face a mask. Kaell pursued like a vengeful spirit, hewing and smashing with fire-lit steel.

The Varee captain relentlessly defended then changed his tempo to take over the attack. Kaell parried hard then countered, the stroke quick enough—his ghoul strength masking this form's flaws. But he had to consciously command the action rather than rely on his muscles' practised memory.

Dannon gave no quarter, his stokes as brutal as he might deliver to a man. Kaell recognised this was no warrior who cruelly toyed with opponents. His false attacks might be slippery, his combinations clever, yet his intent was direct. Kill. Kill quickly.

*Why bother to defend, to attack, to go through the motions?* Kaell needed only to lower his blade. His misery would end. But something stopped him. Perhaps pride. Perhaps refusal to so easily surrender his life to any opponent. Or perhaps the desperate hope his lord wasn't dead.

The crowd roused, their murmurs becoming shouts as though shocked the fight had not ended quickly. Onlookers surged forward to ring the combatants.

On the edge of his awareness, Kaell glimpsed the archer pushing through the mob. Bowstring drawn back, she loosed an arrow. As it came towards him, he sighed out a relieved breath. *At last. No more struggle.* But the missile only skimmed his arm. Kaell staggered.

So the gods willed he must live a little longer. He banished the pain and blood to a corner of his mind. A distraction, nothing more.

"Stop," Dannon hissed. "You dishonour me, Natasha." He waited until Kaell had steadied then struck at him with whirring metal.

Kaell swept his blade back and forth to deflect strike after savage strike. Sweat trickled down his back. The sword's weight tore at muscles tiring quickly despite his inhuman strength.

With a cry to rally his will, Kaell surged into Dannon's attack. Their blades caught. The Varee captain forced Kaell's heavy sword lower. Sweat poured into Kaell's eyes, his aching arms ready to give. Still Dannon pressed, his expression lacking elation or anticipation.

Kaell collapsed to his knees. Shoulders burning, screaming muscles ready to snap, he strained to hold the weapon above his head. He could just let it fall. It would be so easy.

Ripping the sword clear, he rolled. The captain's blade smacked the ground. With a shout of frustration, Dannon whirled and came at him. Kaell scrambled up, blocked a thrust, answered with a quick and deceptive feint.

Like any good bladesman, Dannon sensed rather than saw the danger from that last-second disengage. He jumped back. Kaell's sword followed him, his stroke deep and his body's force behind it.

Iron just missed the man's hip but speared his thigh. Dannon skidded to one knee. Kaell kicked at his head. The host captain plunged back, his weapon slewing across grass. Onlookers gasped. A muttering ran through the crowd like wildfire then fell away into a stunned silence.

Conroy surged to his feet. Warriors moved in, ready to rush Kaell. The Varee leader waved them back. "Now, girl," he shouted. "Do it."

Kaell stood over the fallen man. He poked steel to his throat.

Sprawled in slippery grass, bleeding, Dannon panted, "Finish it. Curse you, finish it. Don't taunt me."

Kaell hardly took in the words. He could smell Dannon's blood. At its scent, at the sight of it, the compulsion to feed, to surrender to this lustful hunger consumed him, the ghoul part of him roaring up. That part of Kaell needed to kill, to impale this man, and drink him dry.

The part trained by his lord to weigh the consequences, to think six steps ahead, was a quiet voice within. Weak at first, struggling against temptation. Then that voice grew stronger. *Hold on. Do not become what Archanin wants.*

Kaell stepped back and let the sword wilt. Battle fever disappeared. In its wake, weariness wore into him, his arms and shoulders aching.

"Who was your master?" Dannon begged, rising to an elbow. "Tell me. A master surely trained you. You did not fall into this."

"What are you doing, girl?" Conroy yelled. "A challenge is to the death. Kill him. Blood must soak the ground, or you'll displease the gods."

Kaell stared at him, astonished that the Varee overlord wanted him to slay the captain.

Dannon dragged in a sharp, outraged breath. He staggered upright, shouting, "You want me dead, butcher? Will you do it yourself or send another assassin?"

More murmurs rose up from those watching. Robert grabbed Conroy's arm. "What's he talking about? You sent someone to kill him?"

"He's a liar," Conroy said. "I should have shut his filthy Cahirean mouth years ago." He tore out his blade and stormed down the stairs, shouldering men and women aside. "The gods demand blood. If this fool girl won't give it to them, then I will."

Kaell backed up. Onlookers cleared a space about the two men.

Conroy spat at Dannon. "You're scum. Hardly worth killing."

"Why don't you try?" Dannon drew a knife.

Conroy thrust at him, his sword a blur. Its tip speared Dannon's shoulder. To Kaell's shock, Dannon grasped the blade with one gloved hand and drove it deeper into his own flesh.

Conroy's eyes stretched. He lunged to wrench his weapon free. His opponent grabbed him, wrestled him about, and pressed an arm to his windpipe. Bellowing in anger, Dannon slashed the overlord's throat. Blood pumped over his hands and garments, a dark spout against the moonlit sky.

Its scent prickled Kaell's nostrils. In the darkness of desire, he could almost feel a part of him breaking off inside. The beast. The ghoul. Straining for release.

*No. No. Keep it back. Fight it.* Perspiration poured off his arms. He dragged in slow breaths. The monster subsided. Slowly.

Dannon dropped the overlord's corpse. He ripped the blade from his shoulder and faced them all, a palm clamped over his wound. "Blood is spilled!" he cried. "That is an end to it. Unless anyone else has a quarrel with me?"

Silence. Every eye dwelled upon Dannon, upon his stained knife.

The mage's necklace rattled as he thumped his stick on the platform. "Our new overlord has spoken. Let all be at peace."

A few muted cheers lifted. One or two warriors came forward to slap Dannon's back.

Dannon turned to Kaell. "What do you call yourself?"

"Kate." As good a name as any. Close enough to his own to disguise a slip.

"Will you give your oath, Kate? Will you swear loyalty to the Varee and to our gods?"

"I—" The words choked in his throat. He could not put aside Khir. The god of battles had guided him his whole life. But he had no choice. Reluctantly, nausea pushing up his throat, Kaell spat out, "I do."

"Then I will ride with you, Kate," Dannon said. "You are now part of the Varee host."

# DANNON

"Never thought I'd see anyone take you down." Patrick swigged wine from a skin. He leaned a shoulder against the door to Dannon's hut, the firepit's shimmer an orange cloud at his back. "A girl, of all people. Picked up that sword like a stick. Strong. Quick too."

Dannon slid his tunic off his wounded shoulder. Blood flaked from its folds. Weariness collapsed his every muscle.

He wanted the solitude of his bed and time to decipher flurrying thoughts. What had just happened? He had never sought to be overlord. "No doubt trained from a young age under a blade master."

"I know men who've carried a blade a lifetime only half as fast." Patrick wiped his wet mouth on a sleeve. "Colla, for one. Lumbers like a bear. Thinks like one too. Slow and mean. I wonder who she really is? Can't trust someone you don't know." He tilted his head to drain the wineskin. His brushed-back hair gleamed in candlelight as if waxed. "That's better." Patrick burped then stretched his lips into his usual lupine smile.

"You won't ride with her?" Dannon unbuckled his weapons belt. "Come, don't tell me you don't want a blade like that with you, rather than against you?"

"Oh, I'll ride with her. Or ride her, if she lets me." Patrick leered. "Though I prefer to be the only one with a sword when I'm with a woman."

"You're a pig," Dannon said.

Patrick only grinned at the insult. "She not only got through your defences but under your skin, I see."

"No. I just don't like the way you talk about women." Kate's scorn and her skill with the blade intrigued him; that was all. For one mad moment in that village, he had thought the girl waving a sword at him was Eloise. Alive once more.

Dutifully he had tied that girl's hands and brought her back. His wilder side had wanted to throw her over his saddle and ride off. But Dannon had locked that part away long ago. Rash men died young. Careful men did not.

What might have become of them had he surrendered to instinct? What if, for once, he had put aside reason?

Patrick offered a playful bow. "If you've decided to become defender of her nebulous honour, I'll leave Kate to you. I wish no dispute with the Bloodtaker."

"The Bloodtaker is wounded," Dannon reminded him with an uneasy chuckle. Patrick was ambitious. He'd challenge him one day. But not yet—probably.

"Injured or not, you're still fast with the blade, Dannon. Too accurate with a bow too. But you're hard to kill because you're so cursed clever. I think that brute Conroy forgot that."

Dannon didn't feel clever. Just bone weary, belly sick from his wounds, and sore. He hoped the wood witch arrived soon with her potions and poppy juice. And her soft hands.

Heat stirred in his groin. Juliette had even softer lips he'd kissed more than once. Not that she belonged to him. Juliette came and went unquestioned, healing those in need, the Varee, villagers, even Vraymorg soldiers.

Dannon sought nothing, only gladly opened his arms when she came to his bed. Of late, though, he knew from her quiet, secret smile Juliette was thinking of someone else. Ah well. He did not stoop to jealousy. Only curiosity.

"Is it true what you said?" Patrick watched him. "About Conroy trying to kill you?"

"It's true." Dannon peeled off pants stiff with blood. The seeping thigh wound was a skilful cut. Any deeper, and Kate would have crippled him. Then, sniffing weakness, Patrick or another would have challenged him in a fight to the death. That was how the Varee won power.

"I knew he was ruthless. But that goes against the code. What happened?"

"A story for another time." Dannon's head spun with all that had unfolded.

"I'll hold you to that." Patrick fingered a silver charm strung about his neck. "About this Kate. What if she's Quisnaf? Or a Sister of Cyrah? A spy. Can we trust her?"

Dannon shrugged.

"The mage wants you to use the brew."

"No," Dannon said. "It's cruel."

"The mage said you'd say that. He said to tell you if you don't, he'll have her killed."

*Kill something so fascinating and dangerous?* The careful part of Dannon whispered, *Take no chances.* The wild, hidden part screamed no. Instinct and reason. Always at war within him. "I'll question her. Tonight."

Patrick snorted. He preferred a simple solution. Kill the problem, and it disappeared. He would make a good host captain—except he was Varee-born.

*A frustrating tradition,* Dannon thought as he sank onto a stool. The ancient writings described how the first host captain had ridden with the Varee. Generations of mages had argued over those words. Ridden *with* them. The host captain was an outsider. Like Dannon.

Patrick could aspire to overlord but not host captain. A pity.

His mind was not devious, so Dannon guessed he could manage him, just as he had "managed" Conroy. A cruel man that. Sentimental. He would gut a rival for a perceived slight but sob over a dead dog.

"Find Kate and send her to me," Dannon said. "I'll question her. Question, that's all."

Patrick clicked his tongue against his front teeth. "The mage will be displeased about the brew. What's your problem? You drink it nearly every night."

He drank the brew because it was too late for him. He yearned for its promise of emptiness, its gift of sweet, sweet oblivion. It offered an escape from his own wretched thoughts. His own wretched dreams. Yes, his dreams most of all.

# KAELL

"Will you run?" Dannon asked. Candlelight and pain smudged his face. Moonlight blurred the outlines of a room deceptively large because it held so little. A few stools. An iron-framed bed laden with furs. Rugs covering the planked floor. Cut logs piled near the hearth. Beeswax candles upon a cedar table bleached the night's stiff, black curtain.

The space was the man's domain, yet he was not at rest in it. Instead, Dannon tapped the table, his tension betrayed not by this drumming but by the rigid control of every other part of his body, his emotion permitted to escape only in the extremity of his fingertips.

"Will you run?" he asked again.

Their gazes locked. Held. In the mountains after midnight, in cold that stank of nothing but memories, every pop from the blackening fire, every dog's bark lay exposed in the quiet.

His voice low, Kaell said, "I hate everything you stand for. You're slavers, murderers. You serve a creature you call a god but I call a monster."

"You just offered your oath to that monster. Are you so false?"

"I'm not false." Except, he was. To protect himself, he had put aside the god he'd bent his knee to his entire life. *If I should die, would Khir forsake me now?*

Dannon's gaze held steady. Candlelight glinted in one eye, his other bruised by shadows. "Do you remember what you said? 'I have nowhere to go.' Do you remember that?"

"I remember." In that moment, that awful moment when he'd imagined his lord might really be dead, it had rung true. He threw out his arms. "Did you hear what I said? I despise you. When they tore that boy from that poor woman's arms, I wanted to grab a sword and kill you all."

"The boy will be all right," Dannon said stiffly.

"He belongs with his mother. Not with you."

Dannon smoothed a fold in his tunic with his palm. A single ring circled his third finger, his arms empty of gold or silver. "You don't understand. In time, you will."

"I don't want to understand. I want no part of this—or you. You may as well throw me in the same foul hole as Aalart."

"Aalart?" Dannon looked up sharply. "You called him by name. You know him?"

*Careless.* "How can I? Why did you summon me?"

Dannon's gaze held on Kaell's face for a moment longer. He sighed. "The mage wants you questioned. He doesn't trust you."

Kaell's lips curved into a sneer. "So you're to question me?"

Dannon poured wine into two glasses and passed one to Kaell.

"Get me drunk, so I spill all my secrets?" With a contemptuous huff, Kaell took the glass. "I have no secrets." Only the one that would get him killed. A bonded warrior would not survive a day in a Varee village.

"All women have secrets," Dannon said. "Yours, I suspect, are far from ordinary. Let's start with how you learnt to fight so well. Are you a Sister of Cyrah? Or Quisnaf?"

"Quisnaf?" Kaell snorted. "Do I talk like I'm from Quisnaf?"

"You speak like someone Mountains-born. But you fight like a Quisnaf warrior."

A man with a slave's iron ring about his neck appeared at the door. "My lord, if I may?"

At Dannon's nod, he carried a tray inside and laid bowls of soup, cheese, fruit, and bread upon the table. Then he picked up a spoon to taste the first dish.

"What—what are you doing?" Dannon spluttered.

Eyes downcast, the man muttered, "The previous overlord feared poison."

Dannon grunted in disgust. "There's no need. Just go."

The man bowed and left.

Kaell coughed a bemused laugh. "What was that about?"

"I inherited everything owned by the man I killed."

"Even slaves, it seems."

"I never kept—" His shoulders hunched. "Will you—you must be hungry."

"Not so much." *At least, not for food.* Kaell carried his cup to a stool and sat. Desperate to thrust down that other craving, he gulped wine. Its peppery black-currant fragrance threw him back to winter nights by the fire at Vraymorg, listening to his lord's stories, laughing or arguing, feeling he belonged.

The wine soured in his mouth. He belonged nowhere. Archanin had taken that from him.

"I won't share your bed, if that's what this is about." Kaell twisted the glass, the wine crimson in candlelight. As crimson as blood. Heart knocking against his ribs, Kaell looked away from a pulsing, pumping vein in Dannon's throat.

The image was there, clear in his mind—of how he would bite into that vein, sighing with pleasure at that first resistance of flesh, the pungent scent, then the smooth, thick texture of blood coating his tongue. Maybe Dannon would moan, try to push him off and thrash, only for his violent spasms to die away, his breath fading.

They were alone. No guards waited outside the door. He could spring at this man and surrender to lust. Be done with denial and guilt. Become the monster he barely held back. Or he could hold on to himself just a little bit longer. *Until when exactly? Why?*

"That's not what this is about." Dannon sat opposite. "I assume you've been told where to sleep?"

"They found me a room off the long hall."

Dannon rolled his cup in his palm. "Though, if you were to stay here tonight, it would protect you."

"Oh?"

"If others thought we are lovers, then not even the mage could question you without my permission. Under Varee law, the only way for another to take you is to challenge me."

"Ha. I thought Varee women had more rights."

"You need to earn those rights, Kate. Earn our trust." Dannon leaned towards him. "The mage wants you interrogated. This way, I can save you from that. Think it through."

Kaell shoved back the stool. He rose to stalk the room, cup in hand. "I don't know why you would wish to save me. But all right. If it means I'm left alone, if you give me your word *you'll* leave me alone, I'll stay."

Dannon arched a brow. "The word of a slaver and killer?"

Kaell paused by the bed to brush his fingers over a fur rug then a scabbard, its etched leather well-worn. A quiver of arrows and a beautifully crafted bow lay near it. Dannon's sword might be simple, but his bow was exceptional. An archer by choice then. A bladesman second.

He considered the austere room. Surely a Varee host captain possessed both power and wealth. Yet apart from Dannon's weapons and a single book on a table, the room held no ornaments. Nothing to make it comfortable. No bowls, cushions, or wall hangings. It was as if this man did not really live here, only passed through on his way elsewhere.

"By Cyrah, you look like her," Dannon blurted, his voice cracking.

Kaell's hand stilled on the bow. A memory stole through his mind of that Mountains village, of Dannon drawing still in surprise then calling out a woman's name. "Like who?"

"Someone from the past." Dannon's voice was soft. He shook himself. "Yes, the past. And the past should stay locked away where it cannot hurt us."

From his words, from the subtle way Dannon commanded a sword, from the cauldron of uncovered meaning in the room, Kaell suspected a complicated nature warred within this man. A man who chose bloodshed. But a man who'd loved? Who had been loved?

Kaell dropped the bow and sat on the edge of the bed. "Let me leave. I'll only bring trouble down upon your head."

Dannon sat forward on the stool. "Is someone after you, Kate? Tell me. I can help."

"You don't know me. Why would you want to help me?"

"I know what it's like to think you're alone, how a pit opens in your gut." He pushed to his feet and sighed. "Take the bed. It's too soft for me as it is. Stay tonight in this hut, and word will spread you're under my protection. The Varee are terrible gossips."

"I can look after myself," Kaell muttered.

"I used to think the same." Dannon smiled sadly. "Now I know no one is safe. For the gods are cruel. They let you glimpse happiness then take it away so they can watch us squirm. I try to ignore them in the hope they ignore me in turn." He tossed Kaell a blanket. "We'll talk in the morning."

When early light forced back the hut's shadows, Dannon shook Kaell awake. He said, "Come outside."

Kaell blinked off sleep. "Why?"

"I have something for you."

Puzzled, Kaell rose, threw a rug over his shoulders, and followed Dannon from the hut to the palisade gate. A plaid of grey and pink tapered into paper-thin clouds. The air was crisp, the village hushed. Frost crunched beneath his soles.

As sunlight struck the walls, very new and very pure, he saw a groom holding a saddled horse. At his side, a guard watched over a woman shielding a boy with crossed arms.

The woman from the fire ceremony. The child so cruelly torn from her. Kaell's breath wavered. He glared at Dannon. "What is this?"

"A gesture. How you interpret it is up to you."

"What?"

"Her plight, her son's plight clearly disturbs you. I'm letting them go."

Kaell's throat tightened. "Is this some game?"

"You're wrong to think we're only slavers, Kate. Only killers. That isn't all we are. All we can be." He swallowed. "All *I* can be."

Kaell crinkled his toes against the damp, chill grass, his mouth dry. "There's no catch?"

"I give you my word they'll go free. My word means something."

He stared at Dannon, at first puzzled, then with a slow-curdling resentment.

*No, no, no.* The word repeated senselessly in his skull, a useless railing against Dannon's cleverness. Kaell had intended to break his word, to leave. To find his lord.

Scarcely aware of frost numbing his feet or the cool draught lifting his fringe, Kaell looked at the woman. Her cheeks were tear-stained, her hair tousled. She clasped the boy tightly to her. He looked at the child. His small hand clutched his mother's leg.

"My word means something too." Kaell could manage no more than a whisper.

Again Dannon's searching gaze dwelled on Kaell's face. "Go back inside, Kate. It's cold."

# HEATH

**H**ood up, a torch of burning pitch in her hand, Myranthe stalked through the ice caverns towards mischief. Heath knew it. His sister's plots outnumbered the kill notches on his sword. He admired her wickedness—usually. Why, if she schemed to turn every prince in Dal-Kanu into a toad, he'd even cheer. But a furtive midnight journey deep into the mountains hinted that her machinations interfered with his.

With his fire-dancer's stealth, he trailed Myranthe through hushed passages of stone, the echo of her quick, precise steps like hammer blows. The walls pressed close. The scent of damp earth was as thick as molasses. But after the diminishing, endless skies of the Isles, Heath found comfort even in the icy draughts tonguing his neck.

It was always cold in the Damadar caverns. The dead chill magnified every sound: the *tap, tap, tap* of Myranthe's heels. The swish of his cloak against his leather boots. The whip of flames smoking in ostentatious wall cressets.

Then her footsteps died. Myranthe stood at the one door Heath did not want her to approach. Hesitantly, slowly, she flattened her palm against its iron. A hum rose from her throat. A pleased growl.

*Forget that door*, he willed. *Forget him. Leave.*

The flame in her hand fizzed. Myranthe disappeared into a pool of shadows, her shape etched by the copper glow from torches farther along the passage. Sweat moistened Heath's hairline, his breath stalled. Time stretched and stretched.

At last, Myranthe snatched up a new brand and walked on.

He sighed in relief. A tussle of their wills had been deferred— for now. But his sister was not stupid. Far from it, curse her. She knew his captive's value. Sooner or later, she would make a play for him.

The game. That was the spice that seasoned life in these caverns. The subtle struggle for power, the danger. Uncovering secrets. Tonight, the game meant unmasking Myranthe's plots.

Heath quickened his pace to follow her into a sloping tunnel where cobwebs clung to empty sconces. Stale air layered his skin like grime.

He didn't recognise the passage. This buried city had secrets. He knew some. The brother-keepers, guardians of the past in their musty library, knew others. But not all. No one knew every passage snaking through the Twin Cities, whether they spiralled into gloomy, windowless antrums within stone, to ancient, hidden places with brackish, black pools, or just led nowhere.

The tunnel opened into a chamber as imposing as a temple. An avenue of carved pillars, round and worn, shot up to a high vaulted roof. His boots scuffed tiles warmed by springs deep in the earth. Even the walls looked sculpted instead of rough cut from rock. Beyond the pillars, at an iron-ribbed door green with age, Myranthe's steps faltered. Caught in torchlight, she rocked on her toes as if on the edge of flight.

Heath's scalp tingled with unease. That door frightened her.

Shoulders braced, Myranthe pricked a finger with her knife and smeared blood on the door. It creaked open. With only a flicker of hesitation, she pushed inside.

An odd fluttering wisped between Heath's shoulders as he crept after her. A foreboding atmosphere clung to this threshold as if an ethereal, menacing presence waited beyond. He folded his fingers around his knife. *Turn back. Leave the mysterious mumbo jumbo to sorceresses.*

But part of him wanted to embrace the fear, to revel in the thrill pricking his spine as he stared it down. Afraid, he was alive. He fisted a hand to still the recurring tremor. *Yes. Alive.*

Heath took a determined step inside. Two torches burned near the door, their smoke acrid, but beyond their cheerless circles of light, the chamber disappeared into blackness. Beside faded murals on rock, rotting cloth hung in strips. Soggy chunks of plaster from the domed ceiling spilled in ugly piles. Washed-out rugs chewed by mice partly covered grubby, sloping flagstone as cracked as the cobwebbed walls. The papery air stank of dust.

"You shouldn't be here." Myranthe moved out of the murk, her hood thrown back. Light from a candle she carried on a holder streaked her flowing dark-brown hair an autumnal red.

Heath leaned a shoulder to the wall, his arms folded over a silk shirt beneath his fur-lined cloak. His tone careless to hide his disquiet, he asked, "Why? Did I interrupt something?"

"You always choose the right moment."

"So women tell me in bed. It's part of my charm."

"You're as charming as an icicle and as useless. Why are you here?"

"Sweetness, I found the door to this frightening place wide-open. On a three-moon night, no less. Careless that, Myranthe. Anyone could walk in, someone without my charm even."

"Anyone did. Why are you here, Heath?"

He could not hold back a shiver. "Where is 'here,' exactly?"

Myranthe's gaze dwelled on his face, her expression unreadable in the poor light. But her nails skittering on her belt betrayed her excitement. "Let me show you."

She led him to a slab of stone, the only thing in this chamber of whispers and shadows. Dust lay thick on its surface. Red flakes from rusting metal chains covered centuries-old, etched patterns.

*An altar.* Gooseflesh rose on Heath's arms.

"So this is where they made death riders?" His voice was not quite steady.

"Can you feel it?" Myranthe threw out her arms. "The power of this room?"

Heath shoved a sleeved arm to his nose. "I smell rank air. Delightful."

"The sorceress stood here. She bound the warrior thus." Myranthe swept her palm over the rusted shackles. "Come closer. Look."

"And soil my fine garments?" He brushed cobwebs from his brocade cloak.

Myranthe raised her candle to his face. She had a disconcerting way of exposing his thoughts, of violating the secret places within. "Anyone might think you vain, brother. The artful stubble. Your body always exquisitely adorned, tunics crisp and clean, boots polished, a silver brooch fastening your cloak."

"I am vain. So what?"

"Your true vanity, Heath, is of the mind, your belief in your superior wit. Yes, you're arrogant. Though that is not a flaw for a fire dancer. Nor for a Damadar."

He clasped a hand to his breast. "You always see into me, Myranthe."

"I see into a lot of people," she said, unsmiling. Turning, she poked her light at three containers in an alcove cut into the rock wall near the altar, their glass stained brown. Two were empty. Reverently, Myranthe carried the third to him.

"It's his." Her voice was breathless with awe. "*His.*"

The container held a heart, raw and bloody. Heath recoiled a step. He swallowed. "Why is it still bloody?"

"Does it disturb you?" Myranthe touched fingertips to the glass. "A spell keeps it from ever decaying or changing, despite the passage of centuries. As if our ancestor had just torn it from his chest."

"This entire place disturbs me."

Myranthe peered about slowly. "I find the power in this room enlivening. Malignant, yes, but never frightening."

"Perhaps to you." Heath's scalp crept. He badly wanted to flee. But something about the chamber anchored his feet to the stone floor.

Myranthe replaced the container. "The door can only be opened on a three-moon night. And only by a sorceress. Mother first brought me here as a child."

"For a picnic, perhaps," Heath muttered.

"She showed me his heart. I wanted to destroy it because he betrayed our gods."

"Of course you did."

"But Mother held the container to her breast. Lovingly. 'You would destroy something so beautiful simply because you don't control him?' she said in that irritating, whispering voice of hers. 'He will return. Perhaps it will be you, daughter, who places the collar of ice about his neck.'"

Heath rocked back a step. "You really do mean *him*, don't you?"

Myranthe did not seem to hear. Her expression distant, wistful, she said, "As a child, I used to lie awake, the candle guttering by the bed, dreaming of death riders storming out to deliver our god's justice. I imagined his return, what he might look like, even how he grew afraid when I held up the ice collar."

"No one has seen Roaran Caelan for centuries."

She shivered with pleasure. "It will be me, Heath. Who can resist this wondrous vision? Everything I've desired, mine. The seer on his knees, humbled. Our family powerful and unassailable. How heady to succeed where every other sorcerer and sorceress failed."

"That old rhyme—" He blenched.

"Yes, that old rhyme." Myranthe spread her arms, chanting:

*"When ancient swords rise up again,*
*In cells called brotherhoods of men,*

*Then he who to our god is sworn,*
*Though fled and free, will here be drawn,*
*And lead them with his will kept tight*
*By a slave's collar made of ice."*

She began to laugh. Heath thought he heard others laughing also and glimpsed flitting shapes through the chamber's shadows as rancid breath steamed his neck.

"What's here?" He trembled. "I sense something."

"The guardians of this chamber. The collar's guardians."

"The collar." Fear clogged his throat. "It's here then. Ready to enslave him."

Myranthe reached for a silver box in the alcove and slid back its lid.

Heath edged nearer. In the satin lining, a coiled collar glistened as pale as stardust. But for all its glimmer, he did not want to touch it—or even look at it.

"It will never tarnish or break or melt," Myranthe whispered. "Not until I place it around his lovely neck. Roaran Caelan will kneel, and I will enslave him, return him to our gods." With an elated sigh, she shut the lid.

"I think I've seen enough." Heath laughed nervously. "This place is uncomfortable. Even I feel something dark and strange here. And I have none of your gifts, Myranthe."

"Dark and strange." Myranthe nodded. "You are right. Because we live in darkness in the Icelands and magic is of the dark. Those who think otherwise—those who shy away from the darkness—are cowards." She blinked and fixed a look on him. "You followed me, Heath. Why?"

"To say goodbye." An excuse, though it was also true enough. "Dillon and I leave before dawn so we can catch the tide at the Cauldron."

"What?"

Heath grinned, snatching at something ordinary like the prospect of a journey to banish his unease. The heart, the vicious collar—he knew what must happen, but to be so close to such dangerous magic unsettled him. Arms spread, he pivoted. "Well, what do you think?"

"About what? Why must you choose a roundabout route with words?"

"Oh, she who is lost in her own enchanted world." Heath sighed heavily. "Here I am, trying to say farewell. I am finely attired, ready to be sacrificed—"

Myranthe abruptly turned her back.

"On the altar of wedlock," Heath finished carefully. *What was that about?*

With a relieved laugh, she faced him. "Poor boy. The things we do for family."

Heath frowned. The atmosphere of this awful chamber clearly unnerved him. He imagined undercurrents that weren't there.

"And while I do my bit for family, I insist you do not play with my possessions. In the heat of one of your tantrums, you surrendered a valuable prisoner to your beloved brother. So repeat after me: I, Myranthe, wicked sister of Heath, shall not play with his captives."

She looked at him blandly.

"No playing, Myranthe. No tormenting. No touching. Nothing."

"In your absence, who will have the key?" she asked with an ingenuous batting of eyelids. "The one you keep close so I cannot enter that chamber. Or do you intend to let him starve?"

Heath touched the key on its leather cord at his neck. "I'm not going to tell you. He's nothing to do with you, Myranthe."

"Judith. Judith will have the key." Myranthe tilted her head speculatively. "Why does this man absorb you? You don't want him in your bed, do you?"

"No." He batted air to dismiss her words. "It's not that. It's nothing I can explain. In truth, I don't yet know what it is."

"Shall I tell you? It goes beyond your need to know enlivening fear again after years of vanquishing every challenger. Oh, does my insight into your character surprise you, Heath? I know you better than you know yourself."

The key's weight burned his breast. He coughed a startled laugh. "I thought it was that. I thought he fascinated me because he's Val Arques Caelan, the only Telorian bladesman to win the Wardorian Contest of Swords. What would it be like to defeat a man like that?"

"But it's no longer just about the challenge, is it?"

"I don't know when it changed, Myranthe. When it—" *Corrupted? When it became about need?* "Now I don't think I want to understand."

"I could tell you."

"No. Don't." Heath forced down his hunched shoulders, desperate to escape her penetrating gaze. "Well, time is as fleeting for a traveller as pleasure for a man about to wed. I must away to do my bit for Damadar honour."

"And Damadar power."

"And Damadar coffers." He started for the door.

"Upon the throne sits Caelan king… when ancient swords rise again," Myranthe said. "It will be me, Heath. I'll trap Roaran Caelan and place that collar of ice at his throat."

"Sword brotherhoods and collars of ice. As a child, I trembled at the stories. A time of myth and change is indeed upon us." Hand on the door, he paused. "Remember. No playing with my possessions."

Myranthe had already turned away. He wondered if she even heard him.

# KAELL

As Dannon recovered from his wounds, he became Kaell's guide to the Varee village.

He showed Kaell the long timber hall with its roof thatched with reeds, the brick oven house where women queued to bake their bread, and the stone-walled armoury which housed swords and bows. In the forge, a bare-chested, heavy-shouldered blacksmith, his hair thick with soot, shaped iron. In the yard outside the tannery, a man scraped hair from skins upon a line.

Fences around gardens kept out the hissing geese. Wherever he and Dannon walked, Kaell could hear a miller's waterwheel slapping water and the blows from a carpenter's hammer that stirred up barking dogs.

"The river floods in spring," Dannon said to explain the stilt huts. "Even so, this island is safer than the old village. A lord of Vraymorg came in storm and burned that one down."

Kaell knew a prickle of interest. "Why?"

"Vengeance. Because the Varee cruelly executed a bonded warrior. Long ago. I had the story from an old man in the village whose grandfather used to talk about it."

Kaell badly wanted to press him for more, but it could be

dangerous to show too much interest in bonded warriors and Mountains lords.

"I'll introduce you to the weapons master." Dannon gestured towards a field where men and a handful of women bouted with blunted swords. "You'll start training tomorrow." He paused, frowning. "I assume you'd rather ride with the Varee host than be assigned other duties in the village?"

Kaell hesitated, unwilling to take up the sword for the Varee. But he had never been trained for anything else.

The last month of summer passed. The rhythms of his new life seeped into Kaell. For a warrior, it offered routine at least in the hours of mind-numbing drilling with swords. And a familiar discipline overlaid every aspect of fighting.

But at night, the fire roared, and too much wine and laughter flowed. The decadence of the feasts was shocking to a man from the grim, ascetic fortress of Vraymorg. More than once, Kaell had stumbled upon couples in the darkness, their garments dishevelled, their bodies moving together in a slow rhythm.

At their soft moans, at the sight of moist, naked skin, there was an awakening, an urging, then a gathering of heat inside him. He wondered about the release found in uninhibited pleasure. But it could not be for him. Not in her body.

Sometimes, he would sit at one of the feasting tables, listening to Dannon argue with the older councillor called Robert. As they disagreed about sieges and battles, using spoons or cups to represent soldiers, castles, tunnels, and trebuchets, his thoughts broke free of their miserable rut, and the warmth of their talk, so familiar, comforted him.

"I taught you better than that," Robert said when Dannon insisted the legendary Cahirean fortress of Isamasalle could be taken inside two weeks by blocking its wells and forcing the thirsty garrison to surrender.

"Why?" Dannon said. "What have I said that is wrong?"

"You never take a fortress you can't hold."

"Who said I wanted to hold it?" Dannon asked.

One afternoon, Kaell came upon Dannon alone by the river, his gaze turned inward. Reluctant to intrude on this man's solitude, he turned to leave.

"Kate," Dannon called. "Come and look at this."

Kaell joined him at the water's edge. Dannon crouched beside a long-stemmed flower, its petals a brilliant red. "It's a river orchid," he said. "It flowers only once each year."

"It's beautiful." As the bud unfolded, the orchid's spidery bloom released a scent like witch hazel.

"Many superstitions are attached to these orchids," Dannon said. "That to come upon one flowering is a portent of death. There's even a famous Cahirean commander who decided the sight of one blooming was a message from the gods to attack his enemies."

"Did he triumph, this Cahirean commander?"

"Oh yes." Dannon touched his fingertips to a petal. "But it had nothing to do with luck or gods. Battles are won by clever, prepared men. Not by pious men."

"You don't think the gods care what happens to us?"

"I know they don't," Dannon said.

At dusk the next day, he again sought Dannon by the river.

Kaell's need for company surprised him, as though he was so lost and lonely, he clung to the only man who had shown him kindness. *A slaver and killer.* He laughed to himself at the words.

"This is a surprise." Dannon looked pleased.

Kaell fell in beside him. For a long while, they walked in silence beside the river. At last, Kaell said, "A pebble for your thoughts."

His companion raised an eyebrow. "A pebble? My thoughts are worth far less than that."

"Lofty, are they?"

"Only kings and queens may aspire to lofty thoughts. I can aspire only to clever thoughts."

"About what?"

"I shall not surrender my answer for nothing. You offered a pebble. Well, where is it?"

Kaell scooped up a smooth stone. He found himself grinning as he handed it over.

"All right." Dannon nodded. "A pebble's worth of the nonsense in my head. I was thinking about the Ice Rider."

"The Damadar lord from centuries ago?"

Dannon stopped and turned to consider Kaell. "Well, well," he said softly. "Yes, that Ice Rider. No one seems to remember him these days."

"The Wardorians call him the Cold Conqueror. There's an old poem about him. It's in Wardorian but beautiful in its way. I like stories of the past…" Kaell's voice trailed off. A clear image flashed in his mind of talking about an infamous siege with Aric as they climbed up to a cave in the Isles. He remembered the brief moment of warmth between them, the promise of friendship.

A pang of loss shuddered through him. Drunken Varee around the firepit muttered about the new Isles king, Gendrick. But no one spoke of Aric.

Dannon was watching him. "You're lettered?"

Kaell scuffed his toe over grass.

"You read Wardorian. That sort of education is denied to most women, to most men in Telor too. Kate, if you're Quisnaf, you have nothing to fear from me. You might even find I'm—" He stopped and looked away.

"I'm not Quisnaf," Kaell said sharply. He slid Dannon a puzzled look, curious what he'd been about to say. "You know, the Ice Rider's legend is proof the gods indeed set our fates."

"You mean the storm that delayed the Wardorian fleet so the Ice Rider had time to march his army to the Cauldron and stop the invaders landing? No. That was luck."

"Or maybe the Icelands god Ghani-Jai favoured his devout subject. Is this the sort of thing you often ponder?"

Dannon's eyes hazed as he peered across the river. "When I was young, when she wasn't correcting my parries or my lunges, my mother told me stories of battles and wars, of grim heroes and heroines, of villains and fools."

Kaell had grown up on similar stories, had hungered for them. "Then—" He thought it through. "She was a warrior?"

"Something like that."

That night, fed up with his own miserable company, Kaell sank onto a bench near Dannon and Robert. A silver jug sat on the table between them. When Dannon refilled his cup, Kaell held his out.

"You don't want this, Kate." Dannon whipped the jug away.

Robert gripped his arm. "Dannon. Let her drink. The mage—"

"I don't care what the mage said."

Kaell heard how Dannon slurred the words. He peered harder at the Varee overlord. Even in distorted light from lanterns swinging from poles, he could see Dannon's pupils were distended, his focus unsteady.

Robert withdrew his hand. He sat back, his narrowed gaze upon Dannon. "How much have you drunk?" he asked quietly.

"Enough."

"You need your wits about you, man. Dal-Kanu is a viper's nest."

"Dal-Kanu?" Kaell echoed in surprise. "You're leaving?" He was unprepared for the wrench of loneliness that tore through his body. *Where did that come from? Why?*

"I am summoned." Dannon knotted his hands on the table, his

shoulders hunched. "I've been expecting it. In truth, it took longer than anticipated. I must go to Dal-Kanu and bend my knee to my god. A new overlord pledges his life and blood to Archanin."

"His blood?" Kaell echoed with distaste.

"My blood now belongs to Archanin. Should I betray him, only he can take it."

"It sounds horrific." Kaell remembered kneeling before Archanin in that abysmal prison in the Waste Mountains, spitting out sickening words. Would Dannon offer his oath without a second thought? Or would the words choke in his throat also?

"Be careful how you go, friend," Robert said. "Do not give Archanin cause to doubt you."

Dannon's knuckles strained. "Why should he doubt me?"

"You know why." A look passed between them. Robert was the first to look away. He sighed. "I thought when you wed my daughter, you would be safe, that you might embrace this life with your heart and not only your head."

"I have," Dannon protested.

Robert made a disbelieving sound.

Kaell leaned back into shadows. His companions had forgotten him. Even the sounds of laughter and chatter from Varee warriors drinking at other tables faded into the distance.

"I've tried," Dannon muttered. "But since her death—" He shook his head. "It's as if I'm not real. Eloise died, but I became the shade. An echo. Drifting. Waiting for life to start again. For something to bring me to life again."

"Something in your dreams?" Robert stared over Dannon's head into the glowing fire. "These dreams are evil, Dannon. They'll be the end of you."

# DANNON

D annon knelt on cracked stone, fear creeping at his neck. He could neither see nor hear the ghoul lords gathered in this ruin with its rows of torches in once-majestic sconces, age-tarnished walls, and eddying stillness. But their eyes fell upon him.

Above the collapsed roof, the first stars winked in a measureless sky. Moonbeams spilled through blackened beams onto a tangle of dust and weeds and cobwebs, its frosted light eerie. The only sounds were his breaths, too loud, and a sweep of cloth over flagstones as Archanin walked unhurried towards him.

"A new overlord"—Archanin's voice was softly seductive—"must pledge his life to me. Will you offer that blood oath, Cahirean?"

Head down, eyes fixed on the grimy floor, Dannon stammered, "I-I can do that."

He must. The need to belong ached in him like a wound. Without the Varee, he was nothing. A man adrift. Alone. The thought hollowed out his breast.

The ghoul god pressed a jewel-hilted knife into Dannon's hand. Noise stirred, a mutter, a ghoul lord shifting his weight, a sail of yellow flame rippling in wind. Beneath it all, Dannon's panicked heart bayed, beating, beating, beating.

He was a man who dreamt of warriors carrying ancient steel, who heard another lord calling to him. He was an imposter. Surely, this god would know.

But Archanin, for all he was, did not see into Dannon's false heart. "Repeat these words: 'I pledge my life, my blood to my lord, Archanin, God of Seithin.'"

"I pledge my life, my blood to my lord, Archanin, God of Seithin."

"Soon god of this world also."

"Soon god of this world also."

The ghoul lords edged closer. Torchlight glinted on golden hair and chiselled faces. They were tall and slender, their cold loveliness like the beauty of marble. Dannon recognised Raggamirron and the Lady Yama—Archanin's favourites—as well as the grasping, conniving Tarthalan, his face scarred by a bonded warrior's blade centuries ago.

"You all are witnesses to his oath." Archanin addressed them. "If our new overlord ever proves untrue, then every drop of his treacherous blood belongs to me."

"We bear witness," they chanted. "He is yours."

At Archanin's nod, Dannon ripped steel across his wrist. Even though he'd braced for it, the sharp pain stunned him briefly. He detached his mind just as he did when he killed. He could strike a man down in battle and feel nothing. Yet, he badly wanted to. To feel. To believe. He wished he could believe in Archanin.

The tension dissolved. Freed from ceremony and tradition, the ghoul nobles broke apart, all speaking at once. One slapped his thigh and laughed at a shared joke. Tarthalan whispered to Yama, his hand at her waist. She playfully pulled free and wagged a finger.

Dannon could only stare as his blood slowly dropped to the floor. It seemed unreal. Like his life. A pale echo of his dreams. Who he was supposed to be, how he was supposed to live, was just beyond his grasp. It was there, if he could only understand the message.

"Leave us," Archanin said.

The hall emptied in a clatter of boots and a door's distant creak. Dannon's blood silently ebbed into cracks. The wind rustled dead leaves against walls. He lifted his eyes to Archanin's.

The ghoul god's gaze was long and hard. "Do I bind you close or kill you?"

Dannon swallowed, his throat rough.

Archanin crouched. He grasped Dannon's jaw, that heavy stare still upon him.

"What is it about you that disturbs me?" Archanin's fingertips moved to Dannon's mouth. Dannon's surprise fell away to longing. The Varee embraced the pleasures of the flesh enthusiastically, but never had he experienced a god's touch.

Archanin bent his head. At his kiss, Dannon moaned softly. A current of ecstatic fire rippled through him. But his god only gripped Dannon's hair to turn his head, his tongue lapping his throat.

"You would feed on me?" Dannon whispered. "To bind me to you?" To show him his place. To humiliate him. "Your bite will kill me."

"Your blood oath saves you. You shall not die. I have upon occasion offered my new overlord a gift and taken him into my bed. But you, I will bind to me another way."

"You are my god," Dannon said. "You may do with me as you wish."

Archanin laughed. "A proud man like you does not surrender his will. Even in your eyes, I see how you resent kneeling to anyone."

"No, my lord—argh..." he cried as Archanin bit into a vein. The hall, the dust, the moonbeams disintegrated as though slashed by swords. Colours and shapes exploded then bled away into darkness.

The coldness of stone snatched him back to the hall. Dannon woke on the floor. Listless, he ached everywhere as though recovering from a winter fever.

Archanin stood a short distance away, staring through a broken window, his expression remote.

"Am I dead?"

The ghoul god didn't look at him. "Not nearly. You are strong, Cahirean."

Dannon peered up at rotting beams stark against the sky. Opaque starlight drifted down. A branch in the invading forest tapped against a shattered turret. Beneath the candlewax, the air smelled metallic. "What is this place?"

"A ruin." Archanin turned. "For now. Gendrick Caelan gifted this shell on the edge of Dal-Kanu to me. He mocks me with this offering. But it shall become my first temple. Others will follow. When I take this land, and I *shall* take it, I will even raise up a temple in the Isles, so glorious Roaran Caelan will stir in wonder in his unmarked grave."

How he loathed Roaran, his hatred naked in his voice every time Archanin spoke the seer king's name.

Archanin swept his palm down a crumbling pillar. "Can one despise the dead, do you think?"

"Yes. Or at least resent them."

"Because they abandon us? Because they leave?"

"Yes."

A hush buttressed like shadows against the broken walls. Archanin sighed. "You are a strange man. Come." He reached to help him up.

At the touch of his fingers on Dannon's arm, that current rippled again. "Where?"

"The king holds a feast in my honour," Archanin said. "To celebrate the formal alliance between us. You will attend me. You have more to learn this night, overlord."

With his embroidered sleeves, the gold threads in his tunic, and the etched glass goblet on the table before him, Gendrick could not be mistaken for anything but a king.

"Our new ruler is not so handsome as his dead brother," Archanin confided to Dannon from his seat at Gendrick's side. "Still, his is a suitably noble face. A pity he's a snake."

Dannon glanced from Gendrick to the long feasting hall at the Castle of the Lake. A few guests raised dark Isles eyes from their trenchers to meet his, perhaps wondering at this man standing at the ghoul's shoulder like a servant.

"I am thirsty." Archanin shoved a goblet at him.

His head still swimming from the temple bloodletting, Dannon bit back indignant pride. He cut his wrist over the goblet, wincing at the pain.

"Enough." Archanin snatched the cup from him. "I do not wish you to keel over."

"Who is he?" Gendrick stared with interest. "Your personal server?"

The ghoul god waved a dismissive hand. "He is a host captain who killed his overlord and now takes his place. Such is the way with the Varee."

"Barbaric," Gendrick said with no note of censure, only curiosity. His look held for a moment on Dannon as though he wondered what use he could make of a killer.

"Merely tradition," Archanin corrected. "As it is tradition that a new overlord must open his veins to pledge his life and loyalty to me."

"Perhaps I should do the same." Gendrick stroked his bristled chin. "Demand my subjects not only bend those stiff necks but spill blood for me. That'll rile the complacent fools up."

He leaned to Archanin. "Look at them, my fine lords and ladies. So beautiful. Yet how they whine. An endless tide of complaints. Wolf's-heads, Your Grace. Deserters, Your Grace. Lawless men. The roads are not safe, Your Grace. Do something, Your Grace."

Archanin laughed softly. "Every ruler endures the burden of ruling."

"The seas are filled with pirates, Your Grace," Gendrick continued, his tone bitter. "The fields full of peasants who refuse to plough the soil, the towns with merchants who cry poor and will not pay taxes. Fix it, Your Grace. So we may grow fat and rich."

He snatched up his cup and drank. "My sheriffs track the wolf's-heads. Isles ships—my ships—chase the pirates. I send men to persuade the merchants to find extra coins in their purses. Still, they whine. Even these new men I raised to the nobility. Greedy fools who hold out their hands for more land, more favours. Always more."

A man on Gendrick's left interrupted his conversation with a woman of middle years, her auburn hair coifed beneath a net. "What ails you now?" he asked impatiently.

From his fine attire and his place beside the king, Dannon guessed the man must be Tomasin Caelan.

"Do you know, uncle?" Gendrick gulped more wine. "I begin to think Aric laughs at me from beyond the grave."

"This castle is said to creep with ghosts," Tomasin replied with no apparent irony.

"No, no, no. My brother's ghost does not stir. I mean the burden of kingship. Aric has the better deal of it. He is at peace, after all, away from rapacious lords and simpering ladies."

"The weight of a crown is heavy," Tomasin replied in a serious manner.

Gendrick smothered a yawn. "Yes, yes. So you always say."

"You prepared to rule all your life. Kingship—"

"You haven't seen my high priestess, have you, Archanin?" Gendrick rudely turned his back. "I seem to have misplaced her. First, my sister vanishes, then my brother's captain, heir to that pirate rock in the sea. Now Aingear."

"What do I want with withered priestesses—" Archanin broke off at a horn's blast.

Like everyone else, Dannon looked towards the doors.

Archanin leaned towards the king. "I saw no performers outside. No actors preparing to delight us with a bawdy farce. No singers. You've planned something special tonight?"

Gendrick's smile was thin and cruel. "I think you'll enjoy this."

The doors flew back. Guards shoved a man into the hall. His lank, dark hair fell untidily onto bowed shoulders. Soiled tunic and pants and a tattered cloak hung loosely on a diminished body.

A woman jumped up with an anguished cry. The man at her side pulled her down.

*Her brother?* Dannon wondered. *Husband? A lover?*

The prisoner glanced at her as guards brought him through the tables. In his wake, a murmur picked up then died away.

"I wondered what became of him," Tomasin muttered as guards threw the captive down before the king. "Three weeks rotting below is a long time."

"Not nearly long enough." Gendrick rose, pressed both hands into the table, and leaned towards the newcomer. "These past weeks, we've seen many traitors dragged before us."

"A stream of them," cried a bold lord, heavy of shoulder and heavy with wine. "But if they beg nicely, you pardon the fools."

Gendrick scoffed. "I pardon those who admit their crime, beg for mercy, and pledge their loyalty."

*Those who could pay.* Dannon hid a grin.

"What is a king if he cannot be merciful?" Gendrick said.

*Poorer,* thought Dannon.

A woman smiled. "You are too good, Your Grace."

The king's gaze briefly settled on her. She was a striking woman with ample bosom and a thick, lush sweep of black hair.

Gendrick stabbed a finger at the prisoner. "Sherrin Cross, look at me."

The prisoner slowly lifted dull eyes to the king.

"Traitor," the bold Isles lord bellowed. "You turned against your king and lord. You!"

"Traitor," another cried. Others took up the call until voices and stamping feet rolled together in outrage. "No mercy, Your Grace."

"Silence!" the steward yelled.

"Always an uproar at these feasts," Archanin confided to Dannon. "Once a lord beat a magician who stole his purse as part of his act. Few nights pass without some Isles noble taking offence at the recently pardoned sitting at the same table."

"A Cahirean poet once wrote, 'Jealousy, thy name is noble,'" Dannon replied.

Archanin raised his well-shaped brows. "Again, you surprise me."

"Silence." The steward thumped a lance into the floor. Voices hushed. In the quiet, a woman sobbed. Glances swung to her, some sympathetic, others hostile.

"Who is she?" Dannon asked.

"Isabelle of the Henge." Archanin shrugged. "Can the sister be blamed for the brother's crimes? Traitor's blood is traitor's blood. Still, she is wed to one of the king's fiercest allies, so she must be forgiven."

"Sherrin Cross, formerly of the Henge." Gendrick's powerful voice echoed.

*Useful for a king,* Dannon thought. *Or an actor.* That night, Gendrick was surely both.

"You betrayed your true sovereign to fight against the Isles. Why?"

"I have no words for you," Sherrin croaked. A man chained in darkness had little use for his voice. Dannon knew that better than most.

"Nothing in your defence?" Gendrick rounded the tables to stand over Sherrin. "Nothing to explain why you murdered my brother, a man you called friend?"

"I did not kill Prince Aric." Sherrin tried to rise, but a guard pushed him down. "Who started this lie? For that is what it is. A hideous lie. I admit to the rest, but not that."

"You are a traitor and a murderer," Gendrick said.

Sherrin turned up a lip in contempt.

*A pity he must die,* Dannon thought. By all accounts, Cross wielded a blade expertly. He could use a swordsman, traitor or not—especially traitors, in fact. Their need to seek redemption often drew out loyalty or foolhardy bravery.

"Your father and brother betrayed me," Sherrin said. "They broke their promises."

Disapproving voices swelled into a chorus of hisses.

"My father and Aric betrayed you?" Gendrick straightened to his full, menacing height. "My brother, murdered by you. My father who died protecting the Isles against men who came to smash our walls—against men like you."

"Scum traitor," a man spat towards the prisoner. "No forgiveness."

Voices broke out again, sharp with hatred. Feet stamped to a chant of "traitor, traitor, traitor."

Gendrick threw up his palm. Into a bristling hush, he said, "I found it in my heart to show mercy to others who took the king's part against us. Lords some, warriors. Widows who pleaded they took no part in their husband's misdeeds."

*Rich widows, of course.* Dannon wondered if he had become too cynical. Surely not. The world was as it appeared. Shallow and greedy.

"But you." Gendrick shook his head sadly. "You fought beside my brother, beside me, countless times. That you should turn on us—"

"Death," a woman screamed. "The noose."

"The block," another said. Others surged up to hiss and shout. Sherrin dropped his head.

"My brother trusted and loved you," Gendrick said. "When he went after you to bring you to justice, you killed him then burned his body in the Fern Castle to hide your foul crime."

"I did not kill Aric," Sherrin said through gritted teeth. "How many times do I have to say it? To you, to your questioners. I was never at the Fern Castle. It's lies. Yet because of these lies, you condemn me. I demand the right to combat, *Your Grace*."

Another hush shrouded the room. Accusations on hold, guests awaited the king's ruling. Dannon wondered if Gendrick might let his champion carve up this man. Even a bladesman like Cross could not win after weeks chained below.

He glanced at Isabelle. She sat forward, watching the king fearfully.

"Traitors have no right to trial by combat," Gendrick said.

"So the block then," Sherrin sneered.

"No. Your death shall be a lesson to show the harsh price of treason."

Isabelle dropped her head. Her shoulders shook. Dannon realised she'd heard these words before, that she knew exactly what the king would say next.

"Not the block," Gendrick said. "For this traitor—the blood house."

<hr />

"We live in strange times." Gendrick reached for a carafe. Lamps spilled muted light onto a feasting hall now empty of guests. Servants had cleared away plates and goblets. Only a handful of guards stood discreetly at the back.

"A Varee killer with a price on his head in my hall yet not in chains." The king poured wine. "Archanin tells me you now lead his people."

"Some of them, Your Grace."

Gendrick sipped wine. "I trust Sherrin does not die quickly, Archanin. Of course, once dead, I will wish to display his body. Or whatever parts of it remain."

"Where did you find Cross, Your Grace?" Dannon asked. If he betrayed a king, he would at once take a ship beyond the Ice Sea. Or did this man's vengeance reach even that far?

"Heath Damadar sent him in chains as a gift. He scooped the fool up in the slave markets."

"Damadar." Archanin thumped his glass down on the stained tablecloth. "I misjudged him, it seems. I let his prattle deceive me when, by all accounts, he is a clever man."

Gendrick drained his cup. "Too cursed clever, if you ask me. He'll trip on his plots sooner or later. And nearly a traitor himself—until he switched sides."

"Hmm." Archanin frowned into the distance.

"I scolded him for attacking you in that castle, Archanin, but he shrugged it off as a mistake. Mistake. Huh. Nothing that man does is without reason. Do you know, he tried to bargain with Cathmor for my brother's body? Then he dared suggest I might like to hand Aric over to him. Just like that. Hand him over."

"Whatever for?" Archanin drummed his fingers on the table. "Sorcery?"

"Death riders," Dannon said, remembering a legend his mother had told him. "That's one reason for wanting a warrior's body."

Gendrick shot him a surprised glance. "Another clever man, I see. Indeed. Heath told me some nonsense about his sister's plans to restore them."

"Myranthe Damadar is powerful." Archanin's thoughtful gaze lingered on Dannon. "You interest me, Cahirean. You know all manner of nonsense."

Dannon did not know how to reply to that. He sensed if he became too interesting, his god might also think him too dangerous and kill him.

"As for this Ice lord," Archanin said, "his insistence that he only came to that border castle to capture Sherrin Cross always bothered me. Damadar was up to something. And his untimely violence cost me a number of warriors as well as an intriguing prisoner. That handsome creature, Vraymorg."

"What does it matter?" Gendrick flicked his wrist. "He's dead. Burned, along with Aric."

Again Archanin said nothing, only beat his fingers on the table.

The king throttled his goblet with a knuckled hand. "They are dead, aren't they?"

"They are both dead," Archanin said, "according to this Ice lord."

"Why should Damadar lie?"

"Your brother was dying, certainly, but that Mountains lord with Caelan blood? I left him in robust health."

*Caelan blood?* Dannon blinked in surprise. *How? The man was Mountains-born.* At least, he had always assumed so. Clearly, he didn't know enough about the last Lord of Vraymorg.

Gendrick flapped a hand. "Yes, yes, you told me many strange things about Vraymorg. That he has Caelan blood. Impossible. That you stabbed him in the heart, but he didn't die. Even more impossible. Now you want me to believe Damadar took him—for what purpose?"

*A man who did not die?*

Archanin laughed. "Surely an Isles man is familiar with every pleasure of both the intellect and the flesh. Your hedonistic pursuits are what I like about Tide's End."

"I just wed Damadar to Cathmor's cousin, and I assure you he enthusiastically bedded the girl."

Archanin poured more wine. "If desire isn't Heath's motivation, he no doubt procured this man for his sister."

"Another death rider?"

"Or something much simpler. Myranthe's dark magic will be frighteningly powerful with the aid of this man's Caelan blood."

Gendrick dropped his voice. "Mind who you share these tales with. Stories of immortal lords with old Caelan blood will unsettle the feeble-minded."

"Superstition already runs riot, Gendrick. Cultists gather in your cities, insisting Roaran Caelan will return to save them all. 'Though fled and free, will here be drawn,' the rhyme goes. Others whisper of the rise of a brotherhood of swords."

"That old Icelands myth again." Gendrick snorted. "Bah. A tale for children."

"Still," Archanin said, "much about the Icelands is unsettling. It is a bastion of Seithin magic. I wonder why you do not move against these haughty Damadars."

"Aha." Gendrick pounced with a stabbing finger. "You fear Myranthe. You want me to rid you of her threat. While I do that, what will you do, Archanin? Hmm?" He sat back, arms folded. "It seems to me only one of us upholds his promises. Give me what I asked for."

Dannon drew in a breath. *What else does Gendrick want?* He was the first king since Roaran to rule all of Telor. Surely such unbridled power was enough.

Yet even as the thought formed, a raw ache ground through him. How hollow such power must be. Lonely. He would give it up, give up so much more, to never be alone.

"My warriors ended that uprising on the Downs," Archanin said mildly. "They dealt with rioters in Dal-Kanu. Talk grows that the king of Wardour builds a fleet so he can attack Telor before you cement your grip on the throne. You cannot hold this land without me."

"You promised me—"

"I promised you Cahir and its queen, and you shall have them both."

Into the silence, Gendrick steadily drank wine. Archanin again tapped his fingers.

"Your Grace..." Dannon's bewildered thoughts tumbled too fast. *The Lord of Vraymorg, a man of Caelan blood who could not die. A sword brotherhood. A sharp-witted Ice lord.* "If Heath Damadar did indeed snatch Vraymorg, then—" He wet his lips.

"Then?" Gendrick reached for the jug to refill his cup.

"What if Cross didn't kill your brother? What if this Ice lord took him also? If I secretly abducted someone, I might do as Damadar did—set a fire and accuse another of killing them."

"Good gods." Gendrick shuddered. "I don't like this at all. I hired a Quisnaf blood sniffer to search for my sister. I'll get her to hunt down Aric too. Then kill him."

Dannon felt Archanin's stare on him again, weighing.

"Let me comfort you there," the ghoul god said to Gendrick. "Your brother was close to death. No one could make use of him or even save him."

"So you say." Gendrick snatched up a goblet and drained it so fast, wine spilled onto his chin. "I begin to think I will only feel comforted if the blood sniffer shows me Aric's body."

With heavy steps, Dannon followed Archanin from the smoky hall into a long corridor. The night swept about him with its scents, sweet and indolent, its breath pleasantly cool. Candle flames fanned in sconces beside woven hangings.

At the sight of Archanin, resplendent in black leather boots, dark-blue tunic, and long cloak, guards shrank back. The boldest stared after them, but even they dropped their eyes if his lord turned his fair head.

"And the only thing I like about Dal-Kanu," Archanin said with a soft laugh, "is that they all rightfully fear me." He paused to smooth his hair. "As you do not."

"I—"

"No, don't bother to deny it. Do you know what I glimpse behind your stare when you kneel to me, Dannon?"

"No."

"Nothing." Archanin walked on. "Raggamirron insists that emptiness made you a good host captain and will make you a good overlord. I, on the other hand, wonder what it hides."

"Do you mean to kill me?"

His lord stopped abruptly and turned. He laughed scornfully. "You don't care, do you? I could take my blade and cut your throat, and you would offer me that same cryptic gaze."

"I would care," Dannon said. "I am fonder of life than you think."

Archanin's stare held on Dannon. "How is it you quote poetry and know about old Icelands' legends? Who was your father?"

"A mercenary from Cahir, my lord. Of no particular birth."

"Your mother then? Was she nobly born?"

"No," Dannon said. "She was no one." The lie caught in his throat. "Though both my parents were lettered. As a boy, I was always reading, always eager to hear stories. When Robert took me in, he recognised my interest in history and language and nurtured it."

A child giggled. A barefoot girl of no more than ten or eleven, hair loose, her gown as thin as undergarments, tiptoed down steps ahead. "You can't hide, Alecc," she called. "I'm coming to find you."

As she disappeared, a boy peered below. Seeing the stairs empty, he clattered after her.

Archanin sniffed. He stilled, frowning. "Now that is interesting. His blood is decidedly not what it should be at all." He stabbed a finger. "Bring me that boy."

Dannon stepped out to catch the child's sleeve. He brought him struggling to Archanin.

"You're the Cahirean brat," the ghoul god said. "Alecc, they call you. Word is Gendrick won't give you back to your witch of a mother. Not until she agrees to wed him."

"Don't you dare speak of her like that. You know nothing, whoever you are."

"Here's something I know, brat. I smell your Caelan blood. Who's your father?"

Alecc curled a lip. He drove a booted heel into Dannon's foot and wriggled free.

"You keep away from me!" he cried. "I know who my father is, and you won't want trouble with him." Quick as a hare, he scampered off. "Miranda, where are you?"

"Miranda?" Dannon raised his brows.

"One of Gendrick's hostages." Archanin shrugged with disinterest. "Not every recalcitrant lord can be bribed with land or titles."

He led Dannon into a courtyard beneath a sky of mottled slate. Moonlight threaded wafer-thin clouds. A well bucket creaked in the wind. Banners slapped air. After unlocking the postern gate, Archanin trod through a damp passage beneath the castle walls into Dal-Kanu.

Such a sprawling, ugly place, the famed City of Kings. A mess of grimy alleys and jostling, rude crowds, of markets and stalls, taverns and temples. And all caged within pressing stone so Dannon could not escape Dal-Kanu's odours of rotting food scraps and mud.

The sharp tang from pine forests at least drowned the stink of offal as they hurried through dark streets. Sounds swirled, indistinct, as though the slumbering city breathed.

A building of hewn stone loomed ahead, its windowless, grey mass needling the sky, its shadow blotting an already-murky square.

Guards swung open brass doors to admit them to a high-roofed entrance chamber where a multitude of candles poked at the gloom. It smelled of beeswax and dust.

Raggamirron offered a short bow to his lord then turned to Dannon. "Captain. No, overlord now, isn't it? You finally killed that brute Conroy."

"Yes." His ruthlessness still surprised him. Yet, had it really been impulsive? Maybe from the moment Volker had told him Conroy had ordered his murder, he intended revenge.

Archanin pushed past Raggamirron into a long passage glowing with yellow light. "The king keeps his promise?"

"See for yourself." With a grim smile, Raggamirron followed him.

Archanin summoned Dannon. "Witness the future, overlord.

The king obliges by sending me his enemies. The Varee shall do the same. Before you return to the Mountains, we shall discuss a quota, a percentage of your captives set aside for me."

The corridor led them past miserable, dark cells. It was dry and warm, though, as if the nipping autumn wind could no more assault the stone walls as the candlelight could the blackness.

Raggamirron grasped a torch and swung it towards a cell. Dannon gaped in horror as prisoners flinched or flung their arms up to shield their eyes. Dirty, their clothes rags, their names no doubt forgotten, they huddled in straw, weeping or staring at nothing.

"We have nearly four hundred now." Raggamirron walked onto another cell. "Enough so we do not have to bleed them so often."

"Until the king runs out of traitors to throw to us," Archanin said.

Raggamirron shrugged. "Then he shall throw us thieves and murderers. Soon, we'll build houses like this all over Telor."

Dannon paused at bars. A young man wearing a tattered soldier's uniform staggered up. He curled his thin fingers about iron. "Help me," he pleaded.

At the stench of unwashed flesh and the sight of the prisoner's gashed arms, Dannon reeled a step.

"Help me."

"I can do nothing."

"Then you're as much a monster as them." The man spat at him.

Dannon wiped his cheek. He stumbled after Archanin and Raggamirron, his heart and the man's words echoing in his eardrums.

They took the stairs to a room where wood was piled beside hearths. Rugs covered timber-laid floors.

Archanin sat back in a cushioned chair. "Gendrick Caelan is a vain fool," he told Raggamirron. "He has agreed to give me the Downs if I send an army of ghouls to Isamasalle to drag Rozenn of Cahir back to his bed."

"This is a distraction. When will we take this land, my lord? Your real army, an army the size of which has never been seen since the days of Seithin, gathers beyond the Enarae, waiting for you to bring them to Telor. I long for the return of the days when every land submitted to our rule."

"There is an obstacle. Someone works against me in the Enarae, prevents me uncovering the secrets of the Hawkwood. Only when they are known can I bring so large an army through the gateway. Only then will Telor become the new Seithin."

*The Hawkwood.* The name sparked a memory, but when Dannon reached for the thread, it frayed at once.

"You need a seer," Raggamirron said quietly.

Archanin laughed bitterly. "I need a man who has been dead for many centuries. I need my enemy's help."

They fell into other talk, paying Dannon no heed. He was glad of it. A host captain learnt how to wear a mask, but a war of emotions raged inside him. Shock. Confusion. Outrage.

This place was a slaughterhouse. It was far, far from the world beyond the gorge where the Varee willingly offered blood to feed their ghoul protectors.

"Gendrick condemns a traitor to this place," Archanin was saying. "An Isles lord who sided with the king."

"A traitor, indeed."

"Dangerous because even as they cursed him, some admired him. This man is loved still. I shall feed upon him myself. I find I have a taste for Isles blood."

"As you wish." Raggamirron shrugged.

"Put him with my priestess. When the temple is built, move them both there."

"As you wish."

Archanin turned to Dannon. "There is one other I desire to bring to this place. You will deliver him. A gift from a new overlord to his god."

"Yes, my lord. Who is this man?"

"This pretender in the Mountains. The son."

*The son?* For a moment, Dannon didn't understand. "You mean Philip? The new lord of the Mountains?"

"I do." Archanin smiled faintly. "All this talk about the former lord of Vraymorg has roused my appetite for Caelan blood. I'm curious to know if that runs in Philip's veins too. Bring him to me. If I cannot have this man, Vraymorg, the son will have to do."

"I'll find a way to get to him." That promise was easier said than achieved. Philip was safe behind fortress walls. Either he must be drawn out or—

"My priestess." Archanin stroked his lip again. "I neglect her." He rose, beckoning to Dannon with a curled finger. "Come. You have more to learn tonight."

Dannon dipped his head. "I am yours to command, my lord."

# AINGEAR

She had a fire, candles, a bucket, water for washing, a cot with blankets, and books. If she asked for herbs or roots, ghouls brought them. An imprisoned priestess couldn't ask for more. Only freedom… or death.

From Archanin's smug expression as he strode into her prison, he did not bring either. Just more demands—and a stranger. A man, with unremarkable brown hair and hazel eyes, Aingear would not notice in a crowd.

Her book in her clenched hand, she rose. "What do you want now?"

"A potion," Archanin said.

Aingear took a quivering breath, battling frustrated anger in vain. She hurled the book at the wall. "I can't stand it. I can't. Kill me or release me."

The stranger took a step as if to comfort her then drew up, his expression blanked.

Calmly, Archanin said, "Whatever for? You have all you need here. Light, clothes, food. Every strange herb and strange everything you desire."

"When the king hears—"

"The king will not. He thinks you disappeared. Poof. Magic.

Speaking of magic, you're going to brew me up a potion, priestess."
Archanin kept his distance. Wisely. She'd once raked his face with
her nails—and found it satisfying, even though it didn't hurt him.
A prisoner, helpless and alone, she had to strike out any way she
could.

"For what purpose?"

"I must induce a vision. Someone seeks me, tries to discern my
intentions. The truth of that whispers through the Enarae. A man
or woman with powerful magic is piercing its veil with apparent
ease and blocking my sight."

Aingear shrugged. "Perhaps Khir. Or the Quisnaf goddess Cyrah."

He shook his head. "I sense when my brothers and sisters move
within the Enarae. This is different. Someone human. I must know
their purpose."

Aingear dropped her head to hide her expression. She, too,
glimpsed someone in the Enarae. Felt their power. Except she
knew exactly who it was.

At a bird's distant caw, she remembered another night at Tide's
End when a raven had settled in a crevice below Aric's window. A
warm wind had rippled over a rolling ocean beneath a dusky satin
sky while the castle slumbered ahead of battle.

A man with blue eyes had come to her on the sea path. The
wonder of it, of him, still resonated like a dark, compelling phrase
of music she could not help but hum again and again.

"Surely a god does not need a mere priestess to mix a potion to
put you in a trance," she said, her tone carefully bland.

"Magic has different rhythms." Archanin waved a hand. "I use
the power of what surrounds us to enchant, to cloud minds, even
to fling wicked priestesses about if they so deserve. But I am no
seer. And the Enarae is the domain of seers."

He searched her face. Slowly, he blinked. Then again. His brows
arched in astonishment, a flicker of growing awareness in his eyes.
In a low voice, he said, "You know."

"No."

"You cunning old woman. You know who it is. Tell me."

Fear tore through her. She must keep her secrets. *His* secrets. "I am a prisoner," she stammered. "Powerless. What could I know?"

"A high priestess of the Isles gods? Tell me what your gods show you." He menaced with a step towards her. "Answer me, or I'll throw you into the cells below."

"No." Aingear clamped a palm over her mouth. "No. Please."

"My lord," the stranger said, "is this necessary? Surely she knows nothing."

The ghoul god whipped about with a glare. "You forget your place, Dannon. Stand there and say nothing." He spun back to Aingear. "Tell me, or I'll throw you below to be milked for years. You know what happens there, don't you, priestess? You hear the screams."

"I cannot tell you what I don't know."

"Fetch Raggamirron," Archanin said. "Tell him to prepare a place in the cells."

"No," Aingear rasped. *Not that, anything but that.* "Stop. You're right. There is someone. I've sensed them too."

"I need a name."

"I didn't understand, you see. Why would he come to me? After all I've done."

"Who acts against me?"

"No, no. I can't."

"Below. You'll live in filth and pain."

Aingear could picture those cells. Sometimes, she heard sounds so horrible, she cowered on the bed. To lie in squalor with no hope of rescue or even death was a horrendous fate. She could not face it. But how could she give *him* up to his enemy?

"Even if I tell you—" Her voice shook. "You won't believe it."

"Who?" Archanin demanded. "Tell me who?"

She drew in a ragged, despairing breath. She must trust he was as powerful as Archanin. That he even knew she would betray him and protected himself.

"Your last chance. Tell me at once, or you go below."

"Roaran Caelan," she cried. "There. You have it. Roaran came to me."

Silence. It sat only upon this room. Amidst a tapestry of birdsong, distant wheels rumbled over cobblestones.

Over the weeks in this prison, Aingear had come to terms with the truth. The sheer enormity of it. That he lived changed everything. Everything.

"A ghost," she whispered to herself. "A phantom, I thought. But he stood there, flesh, not spirit, the breeze stirring his hair. He looked at the castle, his eyes sorrowful. Legend says Roaran has blue eyes. Oh, not true. For they are the darkest of blues, like the sea beneath a stormy sky. And such torment in them."

Archanin began to laugh.

She could not hold back the words. "I glimpsed a shape at his back, a shadow—"

Still Archanin laughed.

"Power, such power. It flowed off him. Oh, by The Three—" She clamped a hand over her mouth. She had killed so many, executed them as cultists.

"You're lying," Archanin said. "It must be a lie."

"It is no lie."

He whirled away, his back to her. Muscles strained against his beautiful garments as though his body caged a writhing pain. "Could it be true? It would explain so much. All that I glimpsed in the Enarae would at last make sense."

"I saw him. I talked with him. Roaran Caelan."

"I believed him to be dead. Who or what is he to defy death? Is he that powerful?"

Aingear laughed coldly. "You are afraid," she jeered. "You're afraid of him."

Very slowly, Archanin turned back. "Afraid? You misunderstand, priestess. I am elated. I thought Roaran was lost to me. He is not. At long last, I will not only have terrible vengeance against the man who imprisoned me for centuries, but he will tell me the secrets of the Hawkwood. Then I will take this land."

# DANNON

Dannon lay on his back beneath soughing trees. Frost sheathed grass. Autumn fell upon the Mountains with bitter winds to sweep rusty leaves against trunks and rid polished-charcoal skies of all but moonlight. Despite the cold, he wouldn't risk a fire. It was dangerous enough for a hunted man to be so close to the fortress of Vraymorg, alone.

He rested his head on his arm and watched silver moonbeams flitting through dying foliage. Gnarled branches creaked a tune, their rhythm out of step with his heart.

The horror of the blood house had shaken him. A grisly place of nightmares. And this god he knelt to… a god who imprisoned helpless men and women in such filth. Archanin sickened him. But Dannon wasn't ready to face what his disgust meant. He needed the Varee and their fallen god. Without them, what was he?

As for the rest… that was all too strange. The last Lord of Vraymorg had Caelan blood and could not be killed by steel. Dannon shifted his hips restlessly. *Impossible.*

If not a prisoner in the Icelands, Vraymorg was surely dead. No doubt there were those who mourned him, who might care what befell him, but Dannon wasn't one of them.

He quietened his thoughts, listening to a song in the wind as he curled and waited for sleep. His fingertips brushed a wildflower's stem, rubbery and moist, the petals creamy like his wife's skin. Like Kate's skin. *Stop. Don't do that.* Kate wasn't Eloise. She intrigued him, nothing more. Desire left a man like him vulnerable.

If only in that shadowy place beyond wakefulness, Eloise waited. Perhaps she might smile as he pushed her against the wall, his weight on her, his lips on that lovely mouth. He imagined how it softened beneath his, how her hands fell to his hips to hold him close, thigh to thigh. Except when he tried to picture her face, it was Kate's.

"She reminds me of you, Eloise," he whispered. "She fascinates me because I cannot grasp her. And you know yourself how I must understand everything, peel back the layers until it makes sense." He laughed softly. "Kate, she calls herself. I doubt that's her name. I doubt she's even Telorian. Quisnaf, maybe."

A bush quivered. The trees rustled. He stared into the solace of darkness. The wind murmured. It touched his hair as if Eloise had brushed her palm over his scalp as she passed by into the night. Strangely comforted, he sighed and fell asleep.

In his dreams, neither Eloise nor Kate came to him. Instead, an old vision stalked him. Dannon rocked his head, trying to keep it back. On it rolled. On and on, pulling him down into the ward of a ruined castle ringed by two dry moats. Twin moons prowled above towers. Wind moaned through cracked stonework. He could taste its salt on his tongue, feel its steamy breath on his neck.

A voice said his name. With both dread and expectation, he turned to peer across the desolate courtyard of dirt and weeds. Strange warriors in old-fashioned garments, wearing steel at their waists, beckoned him.

He jerked awake, his mouth dry. At first, he couldn't understand where he was or why his heart echoed in his skull. Then he remembered the dream. *No, no. Not again. Why this dream? Always this dream.* Even the mage didn't know what it meant.

Dannon clambered to his feet, fed up, sick of doubts and questions and this senseless, repetitive vision. Words burst from him, uncontrolled. "What do you want from me?" he shouted into the darkling forest. "What do you want? Just leave me alone."

He stared at the pewter sky, at dawn's rose tints scattered upon silhouetted peaks far away. A paw turned a leaf. His horse snorted. The first notes of a bird's song shrilled. The stillness of the coming morning entombed him. He was alone with this burden, his need to understand.

In a voice now soft with despair, he whispered to the fading night, "Tell me. Please. What am I supposed to do?" Then in a tone even softer, the words a yearning, he breathed, "Who am I? Tell me who I am?"

Dannon rode over the bridge just ahead of the Venivan. That was what the Varee called the trader. No one knew his real name. No one asked.

Twice a year, he crossed the gorge, reins looped through fat fingers, his creaking cart laden with silks, furs, spices, wines, pewter jugs, silver brooches and rings, exotic birds with rainbow feathers chirping in cages, and all manner of bows, swords, and knives. He passed unhindered because he sold more than goods. The Venivan sold information.

"All quiet?" Dannon asked a sentry.

"Patrick led a raiding party to the Downs. Took that girl like you told him to. Is that the Venivan I hear? One day, his cart will sink the bridge."

"We need a new bridge anyway."

Axles squeaked at his back as Dannon rode in. A few villagers raised a hand in greeting then forgot him as they rushed to the trader, their voices an excited babble.

The Venivan jumped down to unload. "Patience, patience. I've brought many fine items this time."

By day's end, he would sell everything. The Venivan haggled with a tongue as smooth as Paul's. The man never sold flesh, though, recognising the Varee accepted no rivals.

Dannon left his horse with a slave and limped into his hut. With a weary sigh, he sank into a chair, still troubled by what he'd seen in Dal-Kanu. It stirred up doubt. And he didn't want doubt. He wanted his life to be simple.

Robert appeared at the door. Dannon's gloomy mood lifted. He waved his friend inside.

The councillor's knees creaked as he sat. "Archanin didn't kill you, then?"

Dannon laughed. "That's not to say he won't."

"Gods are capricious. Who's to say what they won't do?"

"Or ask. Archanin bid me bring him a present."

Robert raised a brow. "Beyond the usual blood offering? Something special?"

"Something tricky. He wants this new pup at Vraymorg."

The man gripped the chair arms. "Surely he jests? Not even you can get to Philip."

"I'll think of a way."

"Why not just storm the most impregnable fortress in Telor? Maybe Philip will get such a shock, he'll surrender."

Dannon grinned. He enjoyed Robert's dour humour. "Will you take wine?" At a nod, he rose and filled two cups. "So what have I missed?"

"Patrick took Kate raiding." Robert accepted a cup. "Why you suggested it, I have no idea. Every chance, she'll run off. There's the usual squabbling. Two half-wits came to blows over Rolland's daughter, Cassie. One of the new slaves fled. Didn't get far. He'll be whipped." He looked hard at Dannon. "About the girl—"

"Yes?"

Robert paused to drain his cup, then in a careful voice, he said, "Has she been in your bed?"

Dannon braced his hands against his thighs. "No, not yet."

"Get it done, Dannon."

"Just like that? Does Kate get a say?"

"The council is uneasy about her. They agree with the mage about using the brew. Bind her to you and to us quickly, and maybe they won't insist. You can be engaging when you choose. Do it. Seduce her, make her fall in love with you."

"How can you say that? Eloise was your daughter."

"And dead now for more than ten years. This is about duty, Dannon. Do whatever it takes, just so long as the council is assured we can trust her."

"I'll get it done, as you put it." Uncomfortable, he changed the topic. "How fares my young prisoner?"

"Rotting nicely in the storeroom." Tongue to teeth, Robert clucked. "He's too old, my friend. You can't turn his loyalties, no matter how long you lock him up."

"He'll break," Dannon said. "It's lonely in that storeroom. Each of us, even Aalart Hillborn, fears being alone."

At dusk the Venivan laboured up the steps, puffing as he accepted a seat and a cup of wine.

"The stairs too much for you, old man?" Dannon remembered his first glimpse of the trader, that contrast of bright hair and sun-darkened skin. Dannon was twelve, a captive in irons, gaping at the strangeness of this place. The Venivan still looked exactly the same.

"I'm an old dog indeed." The man gulped wine. "Old enough to know there's trouble."

He swept his hard, blue eyes to his host's. "Two armed riders followed me across the gorge. Picked them up near Vraymorg. Lost them in the night."

"Sent by the new lord, Philip?"

"Maybe." He wiped his mouth on his sleeve. "Except riders tailed me last time I crossed the gorge too. I'm thinking the old lord, the dead one, set them on me, and the son follows his lead."

Dannon nodded slowly. "They want to track us through you."

"Or they're just suspicious." The Venivan shrugged. "I've crossed the gorge twice a year for three decades. Someone's bound to wonder why I'm not dead or a Varee prisoner."

Dannon kneaded tight muscles in his neck with his fingers. If acting on Philip's orders, the riders might take the merchant to Vraymorg for questioning. That could be his way in.

"I heard you just returned from Dal-Kanu," the Venivan said.

"An unpleasant city. Crowded. Stinks of mud."

"Word spreads about Archanin's blood house. The first of many, I understand."

Dannon fought a shudder. To be imprisoned in a foul hole without hope was worse than dying. He was not willing, however, to paw over his disquiet about that appalling place. "And you? Robert says you've come from Tide's End."

The trader ventured everywhere but back to Veniva. Dannon assumed he had enemies there but had never asked. One thing he'd learnt in the Mountains: say little and don't appear eager to know, then others perversely wanted to confide.

"And the Icelands," the Venivan said. "The only place in Telor not in turmoil, what with the Damadars ruling with their iron fists." He gulped more wine. "Or is that ice fists?"

"In Dal-Kanu, they call Gendrick Caelan the usurper," Dannon said. "There have been riots. Ghoul warriors put them down."

"Word is your god promised the new king a queen."

"Your sources are remarkable."

The Venivan touched his nose. "Word is Archanin intends to march a ghoul army into Cahir to drag Queen Rozenn back to Telor and to Gendrick's marriage bed."

"So Archanin said." Dannon thought back. "There was a boy at Dal-Kanu. Gendrick refuses to give him back to Rozenn or something."

"I heard talk of this. Rozenn sent her son to Cathmor to be fostered. When Gendrick seized Dal-Kanu, he scooped Alecc up as a hostage. Smart what his brother Aric did. Send ships to take Dal-Kanu while Cathmor's soldiers invested Tide's End."

Dannon shrugged, only interested in threats against the Varee. That meant the lords of Vraymorg, not distant Dal-Kanu.

"Talking of kings. Strange whispers in the Mountains." The Venivan helped himself to more wine. "Mutterings about an ancient king returned."

Dannon laughed. *Superstitious nonsense.* He was a man without gods, believing in steel and his wits. Yet... he was also a man tormented by strange dreams. "Ancient kings returned? Do you mean these cultists and their foolish nonsense?" He tapped his temple. "Surely they all drink hill brew and dance around naked."

"Then you won't care to hear a rumour sweeping the Damadar twin cities?"

"That's too far off to concern me." He shrugged. "What's that expression? May the Icelands turn to frost and snow, the Damadars be buried in their caverns, and the keepers—"

"Drown in ink." The Venivan shaped a brow. "You quote King Dace—"

"Angry the haughty Damadars refused to send soldiers to fight Alecc of Adorean." The Icelands may turn to frost and snow. Dannon's father had said that to dismiss trivialities.

He had a sudden clear memory of his mother laughingly calling her husband a silly old sod for quoting long-dead kings, then reaching for her sword. "The Icelands will turn to frost and snow many times before Dannon remembers to step back before he parries."

She had started for the door, only to pause and glance over her shoulder. "What are you waiting for, boy? An invitation from the gods?" Yet his mother's god, alien to Telor, was as cruel as any other.

He shook off the past. It was as seductive as old stories. A refuge. "These rumours?"

"Very strange stuff." The Venivan balanced the cup in his palm. "There's talk in the far-back caverns of a sword brotherhood returned."

Dannon jolted. He remembered Archanin's warning, how Gendrick had dismissed the rumours as fairy tales. His belly clenched. It could not be connected to his dream and the stern-eyed men wearing archaic armour.

"There's rumours about a lost death rider drawn back to the Ice halls." The trader sniffed. "Probably nonsense."

"There are no death riders. Not anymore. Perhaps they never existed." Dannon rose and took a bag of coins from a chest. "I heard talk of Dal-Kanu soldiers at Vraymorg." He tossed the bag.

The Venivan caught it. "You have solid sources, too, overlord. Soldiers arrived from Dal-Kanu, protecting a Quisnaf woman. A witch of sorts, sent by Gendrick to sniff out his sister. If she's alive. No one but the king thinks she is, mind you."

Dannon's shoulder ached as he sat. "About these men following you. They may well grab you when you return. Question you. Harshly." He could not hold back another shudder. The cells below the Mountains fortress were a place of nightmares. His nightmares.

The man tutted. "Such foolishness. I am a simple trader."

"Have they seen your face?"

"No. I keep the hood up."

"Then stay a few days with us, Venivan." A plan took shape in his mind. Though dangerous, it could come off. "Let me take your place. I need a way into Vraymorg."

"A way in? They'll take you in, all right. Right into the cells. Don't forget there's a price upon your head."

"A price to tempt a man?" A price to tempt Volker, at least. Anger tightened his shoulders. He had always watched his back, but his companions could still succumb to the lure of blood money.

"To tempt some men, yes."

"I want them to learn who I am," Dannon said. "I'm counting on it."

It had been a long while since he had chosen such a reckless plan. If it went wrong, Philip's interrogators would torture and hang him. But what better way to get close to Philip than be invited, roughly, into the lord's lair?

The Venivan shook his head. "Count on them throwing you into a deep hole and leaving you to rot. I'll need compensation, just in case you don't return my wagon."

"How much?" Dannon asked.

⁕

Dannon escorted the Venivan to a guest hut then ambled along the riverbank, wondering what an overlord really did. Settle squabbles, listen to gossip. Nothing, apparently.

He paused to watch a flock of birds dip and soar. The air clenched like a fist, heavy and breathless. Thunderheads blackened the horizon. The forest across the river was a wall of silent green. Everything waited for the first autumn storm to break. Everything lay still. Except for his churning thoughts.

*Who is Kate? Can I trust her? Why do I even care?* Dannon chewed his lip. He wanted life and his place in it to be straightforward. Not dizzyingly tilted by a girl he hardly knew. No. The uncertainty, his restless seeking for answers, had started before Kate. It had started with the dreams.

A woman giggled. She slid her hands about his waist.

Dannon sighed inwardly. "Natasha."

"Our fearless leader alone beside the river. Hoping to find a stray lass?"

*No, just solitude.* Dannon pulled away gently as he turned. "Natasha—"

She launched at him, arms about his neck, dragging his head down for her kiss. He kept his lips stubbornly closed, aware of the archer's strength in her upper arms as she pinned him to her.

"What's wrong with you?" she breathed. "Kiss me back."

Thigh pressed to his, her nipples taut against his chest, she groped at his buttocks, knotting their torsos together.

"What are you doing?"

"You want me." Natasha covered his mouth with hers again, one hand holding his hips, the other rubbing between his legs. His body responded before his mind caught up.

"No." The word burst from him more gruffly than he'd intended.

"Don't pretend you don't like it," she murmured through her kiss. "You liked it the night of that feast. How you writhed and moaned beneath me."

"Stop. Just stop."

She pulled back, staring at him in surprise. Thunder growled. In the unlikely, late warmth, Dannon's tunic stuck to his back.

"Stop?" Natasha arched a brow. "That's not what you said that night. 'Yes, that,' you moaned. 'That. Touch me there, Natasha. Oh gods, Natasha.'"

"Natasha—"

"Why so cold now, Dannon? Is it this Kate? I saw her go into your hut before you went to Dal-Kanu. Does she do this?" She nipped his lip with her teeth. "Or this?" She stroked his groin.

"This can't happen again. I'm too old for you. You're not even nineteen."

"And Kate? Is she old enough?"

"This is nonsense—"

Natasha scrunched his tunic in her fist, her face as hard as sun-dried clay. "First that healer, Juliette. Now her. Kate." She spat the name. "She doesn't even want you. Everyone can see it. Except you."

"Natasha. You're a beautiful girl. It's just—"

"It's just what?" She backed away, palms raised. "Don't you do that."

"Calm down."

"Oh, calm down? How dare you tell me to calm down! How dare you spurn me for some girl who's not even Varee." Her voice rose to a shout. "She's nothing. I hope she dies. I hope in the next raid, Felix Hillborn takes her prisoner. That he hangs her."

"You don't mean that."

"I hope he hangs you, too, Cahirean. I hate you. I wish you were dead. You—an outsider—reject me? I won't forget this insult."

With a flick of hair, she whirled and stomped off. He watched her go, uneasy. Natasha had a temper. Everyone knew that. She also knew how to stubbornly stoke resentment.

Anger boiled over. Resentment did not. It simmered. It twisted. It festered. Like a wound. Dannon would have to watch her.

Hooves clattered over the bridge. A few Varee emerged from huts as Patrick led riders through the gates. Dannon clambered up from the bank to meet them, his gait awkward.

*Curse this shoulder.* Juliette had warned him he wouldn't swing a sword properly for months, but he'd hoped she was exaggerating in that way healers did.

He remembered Juliette's last visit, how she'd smiled to herself as she collected her bandages and ointments. He had no need to ask where she was going next. To her new lover.

No matter. He, too, desired another.

Dannon drew up sharply, surprised at the admission. Kate intrigued him. He liked being around her. But desire—that was dangerous. It meant a surrender of control. It opened up a man. Weakened him.

Patrick dismounted and came forward, grinning.

"No trouble?"

"Nah. Though a couple of villagers grew balls. Farmers in some hole along the river met us armed with pitchforks. Said they weren't going to pay anymore."

"And?"

"I set the girl on them."

"Oh." Dannon sought Kate dismounting among the other warriors. Once she was outside the palisade, he had half expected her to flee.

"A test." Patrick watched his face. "Just like you were testing her by insisting we take her with us—to see if she'd run."

"And?" Dannon waited. "Did Kate pass your test?"

Patrick shrugged. "She wounded two, quick and not so bloody. The rest crumbled. So much for defiance." He patted a purse in his belt. "I made them pay extra. For the trouble."

"She didn't try to slip away?"

"Aw, Dannon. When we're so charming?" Patrick laughed then sobered at once. "There was one odd thing." With a glance over his shoulder, he drew Dannon aside. "Heard talk in a village about a man asking after a dark-haired lass with a Mountains accent who swings a sword well."

"That's a little too specific. I wonder what he wants with Kate. Who is this man?"

"No name, just what he looked like. Salt-head with black hair. Handsome, the women said. Very blue eyes."

"Sure he's a salt-head? Never heard of blue eyes in the Isles." Dannon nibbled his bottom lip. "Keep an ear open next time you ride out."

Patrick slapped his shoulder. "So how was it? The bloodletting and all."

"Nothing to it," Dannon lied. "I bent my knee, said a few words, spilled blood."

When Patrick moved off to tend to his horse, Dannon called to Kate. She left her horse with a slave and joined him.

"I've a task for you," he said.

She brushed dirt from her tunic. "What task?"

He didn't answer at once, only smiled.

"Don't play games."

"Very well. I need your help to abduct the Lord of Vraymorg."

"Cursed drums." Philip pressed his palms into the windowsill. "These cursed Mountains with their cursed thieves, their cursed petty lords, and their cursed petty demands."

"Kept me awake," the king's envoy muttered. "The drums."

His wrists bound, two men holding his shoulders, Dannon considered the envoy with displeasure. The man had wavy grey hair and sandy eyebrows framing eyes so guileless, he must surely be sly. Too much ale or rich food padded his formless cheekbones.

Philip, though, looked every bit a trained soldier. Leanly muscled, he moved with a restless intensity. Even among friends—and one enemy—he wore steel at his hip. He had his father's black burnished hair, dark eyes, and long legs. The same material but a different mould. Philip lacked the former Mountains lord's striking beauty.

"My hair is thinner and all because of these cursed hills." Philip leaned on his elbows. "Where's the witch?"

"In her tent, being witchy." The envoy covered a yawn.

"She is welcome to a chamber in the castle," Philip said stiffly.

"Trust me, my lord." The man unfolded a smug smile. "Her company leaves a lot to be desired. She has the social graces of a toad."

*And you would know,* Dannon thought. *About toads, that is.*

"She can't be that bad, surely."

"You'll not have had much experience with the Quisnaf, my lord. Rude-tongued and single-minded. All about duty. Her idea of polite conversation will be to jab you with steel."

"I shall take your word for it, shall I? Given your experience with Quisnaf witches?"

The man's simpering manner returned. Perhaps he didn't realise Philip mocked him.

"What are you grinning at?" Philip turned to glower at Dannon. "Do you feel neglected? Believe me, young man, I'll get to you soon enough."

At the "young man," Dannon hid another smile. Philip was far younger than him.

The new Mountains lord faced the envoy. "You can tell the king I am too busy to attend him in Dal-Kanu at present. Take him my list of new sheriffs. That will appease him."

"I'm sure that will thrill him. Only the king is anxious to see this proclamation the last Lord of Vraymorg left with a servant naming you his son and heir—"

"I'm as surprised as Cathmor, believe me."

"The king also wishes to learn how you'll settle with the Varee. Given their god is his ally, he desires an accord between you."

Philip slapped the sill. "These scum attacked a town under my protection. I must answer this with force."

"That won't please him at all." The envoy patted his plump mouth. "Perhaps in these difficult times, it is best to let bygones be bygones."

"Bygones?" Philip spluttered. "The Varee are slavers, murderers. No, I shall settle with them. And soon."

*Settle.* Dannon considered Philip with interest. *Maybe this new lord has some of his father's iron after all.*

A door banged. A young soldier entered in a rush and fell to one knee.

"Oh, get up, Torin," Philip snapped. "I am not my father."

"But you are my lord, my lord," Torin said.

"Did your tongue trip on that?" the man holding Dannon muttered.

Philip gestured. "This is the trader we arrested crossing the gorge from Varee lands. Take a good look. I suspect he's not who he says."

Torin rocked back, agape. Dannon flashed the young soldier a grin. Reputation meant everything in the Mountains.

"Well," Philip barked. "You fought the Varee more than once, Torin. Do you know him? Is he Varee? He has a bladesman's shoulders."

Dannon had an archer's shoulders. But that wasn't their business.

"A bladesman's arrogance too." The man at Dannon's back laughed without warmth. "Objected to us taking hold of him like he was some lord."

Torin backed up another step. He spluttered, "My lord, it's him."

"Who?"

"It's the Bloodtaker himself." Torin's voice shook. "Dannon, they call him. He's their war leader." He carved a warding in the air with his fingers. "They say he's cut down a thousand men with the sword. More with the bow."

"Rubbish," Philip said.

"It's true, my lord. They say his arrows never miss and you won't ever see them coming. Afterwards, he rips the arrow from your flesh with his teeth, boils up your bones, and drinks your blood. It's said he pledged his body to demons. That he can't be killed."

*That's new. Can't be killed?* Dannon could only imagine what he might do with eternity. An eternity of fighting. Of drinking the mage's brew to escape dreams. *How wearisome... how lonely.*

The perfume of jasmine from a vine at the window stirred a memory of the rambling creeper outside the hut Dannon had shared with Eloise. The fragrance of the white star-shaped flowers had overpowered the night air. With thin fingers, Eloise had touched those blooms placed in a vase beside their bed. For a few moments, her face softened, the pain forgotten.

"Their scent reminds me of my childhood," she wheezed. "Of long days when my friend Beatrice and I collected mushrooms in the pine forests, careful never to go too far in and lose our way. Of lying with Beatrice beneath shady trees, the breeze warm on our legs and falling asleep in the wildflowers. Idyllic, Dannon, those carefree summers." She squeezed his hand. "I wish you had come too. But you always had your nose in a book."

"I wish it, too," he said, forcing a smile as she sighed and lay back on the pillows.

In Philip's castle, in this grim room of stone, however, there were no wildflowers or carefree summers. It was autumn. His season. The melancholy, toneless months matched his mood.

Dannon's gaze passed to the windows. Dusk settled with a hazy blotch of blood orange, a jagged stitch of colour below building storm clouds. The air smelled of rain. Somewhere faraway, thunder rumbled, unless it was just Philip's cursed drums.

Aware the stunned silence had held too long, he glanced at his captors' expressions. Philip seemed shocked but elated. Torin looked frightened. Of the two men gripping his shoulders, one sniffed. But the second glared with hatred.

"Good gods," Philip said. "It hardly seems possible. But why pose as a trader?"

"To gain access to this castle or to you," the steely-eyed man said.

"You may be right, Felix. He guessed we'd arrest the Venivan."

*Aalart's brother, Felix Hillborn?* Dannon's heart knocked against his ribs. That explained the man's vicious scowl. Dannon thought he knew what Felix would like to do to him.

The envoy rubbed his hands. "How delicious that I should be here when such a notorious outlaw falls into your custody. How soon before you hang him?"

"Surely you're anxious to return to Dal-Kanu?" Philip said, his tone faintly sardonic.

The envoy smiled insincerely. "I might stay while you interrogate this villain. You do intend to be a little rough, yes?"

"We intend to be *very* rough," Felix corrected.

"What happened to letting bygones be bygones?" Dannon raised his brows at the envoy, his careless manner masking his tension.

"Such bad weather." The man fluttered a wrist. "So sad I could not deliver the king's decree about peace before they hanged you. I've never seen an execution. Is it terribly shocking? I've never seen a man tortured, either. Perhaps I'll be sick."

"Stay if you must," Philip said. "But I advise you to back away so his blood does not splatter your clothing."

"Blood?" The envoy trembled. "Oh, how thrilling." Nevertheless, he retreated to a corner as men hustled Dannon into a chair, his bound hands at his back.

Dannon raised his eyes to Philip. "Do you plan to splatter my blood yourself?" For all his light tone, fear knotted his belly. If his plan went wrong, they would do more than splatter his blood.

"You speak only when the lord speaks to you," snapped the second man holding his shoulders. He had deep-set eyes below thinning hair swept back from a moist forehead.

"Let him warm up his tongue as he pleases, Hugh," Philip said coldly. "He'll use that tongue to either talk or scream." He looked at Felix. "Did you search him?"

"We took a knife and sword off him."

Philip braced his hands on the chair arms to lean over his prisoner.

"You're a thorn in many breasts, Dannon. How could you expect to pass yourself off as this Venivan? I heard you're sharp-witted, but perhaps you're reckless as well."

"I am both." Dannon yawned, trying hard to keep up the cavalier pretence. His heart clamoured in his breast, and sweat dampened his neck—the neck they'd stretch if he wasn't as sharp-witted as legend would have it. "Best get on with the torture bit. I should warn you, I have a high tolerance for pain."

Felix jeered. "All the better, brute. Talk, or don't talk. Either way, you bleed."

"Did you attack Rushbridge?" Philip asked.

"I was there."

"Do you have my brother?" Felix growled.

"You mean, did your brother return to me? Aalart has long been my eyes and ears here."

After an ugly silence, Felix struck Dannon across the mouth. "You lying snake! You abducted him."

Dannon tasted blood as he tongued his split lip. This lord hit harder than Mark the Mad and Merry One. If he didn't escape, he was in for a lot of pain. "'Abduct' means unlawfully taking hold of someone. Aalart came willingly. He is no prisoner."

"Don't waste time with lies." Hugh menaced with clenched fists. The young lord had a reputation for violence. Dannon knew villagers averted their eyes when he rode past.

Philip's scouring gaze hung on Dannon's face. "The Varee never dared breach the gorge before. Why now?"

"You know why."

The man's knuckles whitened on the chair arms. His warm breaths fanned Dannon's face. "Because you feared my father and you don't fear me?"

"You're untested."

"And that attack is a test? You'll see my answer, wolf's-head, as you rot in an unpleasant hole awaiting execution. I will hit back and forcefully."

"How do you intend to execute me? I'm sincerely interested."

"You buy and sell flesh. You kill unlawfully." Philip straightened. "The noose."

"You know what the Varee say." Dannon worked at the cords. "That we dance with steel until we dance on a gibbet."

"Where is my brother?" Felix repeated evenly. Dannon admired the man's control. He must be boiling inside, desperate to learn where Aalart was. Wondering, just wondering if Aalart really could be a spy. Doubt was a very curious thing. It niggled away, impervious to reason.

"With me. But he's no prisoner."

"You're lying." Felix's tone remained steady. "Where do you hold him?"

The ropes loosened. Carefully, his expression neutral, Dannon groped at a painful stitch on his forearm. "I can tell you where Aalart is. But he's there willingly."

Felix gripped the chair as if to stop himself from erupting to violence. "I want to know where your village is, its defences, how many warriors are within."

"Why stop there? How about if they made love to their wives last night?"

"Just the village's location. That and the truth about Aalart," Philip said.

"You don't want the truth." Dannon laughed scornfully. "Aalart told us when to attack Rushbridge. He betrayed you. And not for the first time."

A storm of anger built on Felix's face. He struck Dannon hard. The blows spun his head back and forth. This man could indeed teach Mark a few tricks.

"You're not sure I'm lying. That's why you're so angry." Dannon spat blood, sliding the tiny blade hidden under his skin through broken stitches. Fear swooped in his gut. If he let it take him over, he was lost.

"You really are just scum," Philip said. "From your reputation, I thought you might be something more."

To Felix, he said, "My father at times left difficult prisoners with you. Make this brute tell you where the Varee villages are, what sort of defences they have."

Felix did not smile. "I know how to make a man talk. I also know how to make a man scream. He's going to do both." He gestured to Hugh. "Prepare a cell below. Find me knives, hooks. Start a fire."

"You're bleeding." Philip's stare dropped to Dannon's tunic.

Dannon sprang up, the knife gripped in his bloody fingers. He slashed at Felix's arm. The man reeled, gasping in pain.

Philip went for his sword, but Dannon knocked his hand aside. He pulled the young lord against him, the knife to his throat. The others tensed. "Move, and I kill him."

"You wouldn't dare," Felix hissed. "Drop the knife, fool. Do you think you get to walk out? From the most heavily fortified castle in Telor? Armed with that tiny thing?"

"That's the plan," Dannon said, though it wasn't even close. He had counted on Philip surrendering him to an interrogator—just one interrogator—right away. He'd intended to overpower the interrogator then find and abduct the castle lord quietly.

"Felix," Philip yelled, "take him. It doesn't matter about me."

Dannon yanked his prisoner's head back and edged the blade across Philip's throat. Blood oozed along a thin cut.

"Stop." Felix flung up his hands.

"You." Dannon nodded at Torin. "Bind your lord's wrists."

"No—no, I," the young soldier stammered. "I won't."

"Think," Dannon said. "I only need a hostage to get clear. But if I can't use Philip as that, then I'll kill him and take my chances."

Torin slid a frightened gaze to Felix. The man stared with loathing at Dannon. From the laboured rise and fall of his chest, Dannon guessed Felix wanted to rip off his head with his hands, Philip be damned.

"Do as he says," the man muttered at last. "Keeping our lord safe is our only concern."

Reluctantly, Torin bound his lord's hands and stepped back. Dannon tore Philip's blade from its scabbard, tossed aside the knife, and thrust the sword tip to his captive's back. He forced the young lord to the door. Philip bucked.

Dannon pricked him with steel. "Settle down. I don't intend to hurt you unless I have to."

"How do we know you won't kill him?" Felix demanded.

"I'll certainly kill him if you follow." He groped for the door then pulled Philip outside.

A guard spun.

"If you want your lord safe, go inside," Dannon told him. "Felix will explain."

The guard looked to his lord.

"Do it," Philip said.

Dannon shoved his prisoner along the passage. Only half the lamps were lit, their smoke spilling scents of oil and smoke. Beneath the fumes, rain pricked. He absorbed the castle's sounds of ringing steel and footsteps, seeking anything out of place as he nudged Philip up a curved stairwell.

"Where are you going?" the man protested. "You can't get out up there."

"Just walk."

At a landing, he pushed Philip into an empty bedchamber. From the glare of late sunlight vanishing beneath thunderheads, he guessed the room overlooked the gorge. Dannon pulled Philip to the window. One look below, and he sighed in relief.

On a ridge above the gorge, Kate slouched on a hay cart's bench. She wore Aalart's cloak, hood up, its captain's badge restored to the shoulder.

He whistled. She raised a hand then urged two bullocks forward until the cart was right below the window. Dannon poked steel into Philip's back. "Jump."

"No. Kill me here, because I'm not going anywhere."

*His father's iron, indeed.* With an impatient sigh, Dannon slugged him in the jaw. He caught the man, grunting at the effort of hoisting his deadweight up and over the sill. For a nervous heartbeat or two, he feared he'd calculated wrong before Philip plunged safely into showering hay.

Once Kate had dragged their captive clear, Dannon jumped, rolling as he landed. Spluttering, coughing, he swiped hay from his mouth and drew Philip against him, a shield against the counterattack he knew was building above. Already, men crowded at the window. More appeared at the parapet overhead, archers among them.

"Don't shoot," Felix called out. "You'll hit our lord."

"I warned you," Dannon shouted up. "If you followed, I'd kill him."

"Let him go," Felix said. "You're free. Leave him behind."

"Aalart." Dannon let his voice carry. "You take him. I'll drive."

Kate clambered back. Grasping a knife with the distinctive Hillborn crest on its carved handle, she crouched beside Philip. The man groaned, his dazed eyes blinking open.

Dannon wasn't sure what happened next. He knew Kate stiffened. Then her face twisted in dismay. First her breaths, then her voice shattered as she stared at Philip.

"No," she said. "No, no, no."

"Kate?"

"It isn't him. Oh gods, what does that mean? I thought you meant abduct him. Him. That I could at last see him, talk to him. Is he dead? Really dead? No. He can't be. He just can't."

"This is the new Lord of Vraymorg. The son. Archanin wants him. I told you that."

"You only said we were to abduct the Lord of Vraymorg. I thought... I thought—"

With a defiant yell, Philip grabbed Kate's arm. He wrestled for the knife in a tangle of limbs. Then Philip gasped and jerked. He fell against Kate. They froze like that, clasped together—Philip limp, Kate rigid with shock.

Across the gorge, jagged light flashed between peaks. Thunder cracked. A whoosh of wind banked leaves against the cart's wooden wheels. Beneath sodden clouds, the land darkened. A fat, hot raindrop struck Dannon's eyelid, snapping him from his stunned torpor. "What have you done?"

She stared at him blankly over Philip's head.

"Kate—"

With a muted sob, she pushed the man away. His body fell back, a blade in his breast.

"No," Felix screamed. An arrow tore into the hay.

"Kate!" Dannon dived. He hit her hard, his momentum driving them both over the side. More arrows flew, a thick pelt of death striking the cart and ground.

"Take them," Felix bellowed. "Open the gates. I want them alive."

Dannon held Kate to him as they crouched behind the cart. "Give me Aalart's cloak. We can use this."

Dazed, her movements mechanical, she took off the garment. Dannon bobbed up to toss it into the cart then ducked as another storm of arrows whirred.

"What have I done?" Her voice shook. "Oh gods. Why did he struggle?"

He had no time to think about Philip, about any of it, not with archers above and soldiers set to burst out the gates. "We have to go. Now, Kate."

"It wasn't him." She dropped her head into her hands. "Where is he? Please, Dannon, tell me where he is."

"There's no time."

"I killed him. His son. He fell onto the knife. Khir help me, I didn't want to hurt him."

Dannon grasped her wrists. "It's gone wrong, but we have to go."

She tore free. On hands and knees, she beat a fist against the ground. Her cries echoed up the gorge. Other sounds gathered, too: rushing feet, rattling steel as a portcullis rose, Felix shouting orders. An arrow splattered mud near Dannon's boot. Shapes formed in the twilight.

Dannon hauled Kate to the sheer incline of the great gorge. Its rubble fell away into darkness. Arms about her waist, he stepped off.

Wind rushed in his hair. The dusk and storm around them were a blur. He hit the hard slope with a jarring thump. Dannon lost hold of Kate, only to bump into her as he flailed, trying to control his falling body. He could not. He could only let himself go.

As he tumbled, stones rending and bruising his palms and buttocks and ripping his pants, his heels skidded to break his speed. He clawed at roots. All the while, he could think only of Kate's expression, that flat, miserable emptiness in her eyes when she had stared at Philip's body.

Lights bobbed on the slope, a yellow tail coming down and down the gorge. There were shouts followed by an urgent bustle. "Find them. Don't let them escape."

"Kate." Leaves crackled against Dannon's cheek as he moved. His arms and shoulders ached, his chest aflame. He bit back a groan. "Are you hurt?"

"No."

Dannon pushed unsteadily to his feet. At a wave of pain, he bent over, dry heaving. "Patrick's waiting at the bridge. Follow the gorge," he panted. "I'll lead Felix and his men the other way."

"Why would you do that? I can't let you do that for me."

He groped for her arm. "I need you to be safe." At the idea of Felix capturing and harming her, coldness settled in his belly.

Kate did not answer. He couldn't see her face in the darkness. But he heard her breaths. Sharp. Quick. Uncertain.

"I'm not leaving you to be captured and killed," she said. "We go together."

Dannon found Kate slumped on the grassy bank overlooking the firepit, a flagon rocking beside her. She said nothing when he sat, the distance between them set by the barrier of her drawn-up knees and frozen stare.

Jaw tight from holding in accusations, his ribs bruised from the fall, Dannon watched sparks jig across the night sky in a skirling wind that nipped through his tunic to his bones.

Mutton crackled on a spit. Drunken men and women whirled about the fire in a bizarre but familiar dance, their shrieks of laughter wild and abandoned.

"To Philip," a man cried, clashing his wine cup against his companion's. "May he rot in the Enarae."

Dannon pushed down his repulsion at the celebration of a young man's death. On another night like this, he, too, had drunkenly cheered the demise of an enemy—the former Lord of Vraymorg.

Dannon twisted his ring. That feast had been unlike any other, an orgy of wine and laughter—and yes, sex, where he'd succumbed to Natasha's kisses.

"You said nothing the whole way back," he said softly. "Then you went straight to the armoury and tore it up. Made a mess, throwing things about."

Kate shrugged.

"Why?"

Silence.

"Because of this man, Philip? You knew him?"

"No."

*Then why gape in horror at Philip? Why thump the ground and yell?* "You recognised him."

"No."

"Kate—"

"Dannon." Her voice was sharp.

"I'll ask this once. Just once. However you answer, I'll accept it, and we won't speak of it again."

"Then ask," she snapped.

"Did you kill Philip deliberately? To spare him becoming Archanin's prisoner? Was it kindness? I could understand that."

Slowly, she unlocked her arms from about her knees and stretched out her legs. "He fell onto the blade when we struggled. I'm sorry he's dead."

Dannon leaned back on his elbows. He could hear a couple in the nearby shadows thrown by the hill, the low sounds they uttered. He closed his eyes, remembering the first night Eloise had drawn him away from a feast. When she pulled him down into the grass, he'd been so eager. An eager clumsy boy.

He remembered the softness of her slightly parted lips and how he had marvelled at the touch of her skin as his hand slid over her body. When she'd undressed him with confident fingers and trailed kisses down his belly, he had thrown his head back, thinking he could die in that moment and be content.

Dannon snapped his eyes open as a spark flew into the grass. He watched it so he didn't stare at Kate's nipples through the thin fabric of her shirt. He knew how her breasts might feel in his palms, the weight of them, the texture of her skin beneath his thumb.

*What's wrong with me?* She was clearly hurting. But they had come close to capture and inglorious death, and the need for the reassurance of pleasure, a reminder of what it meant to be alive, flared in him.

Life was uncertain, after all, and the callous gods shaped the paths of men and women from pain. They would come close to death again, and soon.

The silence knotted with tension. The quiet between them had become complicated—by his desire. Yes, that. The gods had prepared a trap, setting him up to care, and he could not stop himself from walking into it.

"And what you said?" His voice sounded hoarse. He willed her not to notice his voice or the erection straining against his pants.

"What did I say?"

"You looked at Philip, and you blurted, 'It's not him.' Not who, Kate?"

She did not answer.

"Not the previous Lord of Vraymorg? Is that who you meant?"

"Don't. I can't talk about this." Grief tore up her voice.

His duty was to march her to the mage's hut and question her. But he didn't move. Instead, he wanted only to stroke her hair, to comfort her with helpless words. *It's all right. Tell me why you hurt. I want to understand. Not as your overlord. Just me, Dannon. It will stay between us, whatever you tell me. I swear it.* "I thought you'd come up this hill to grieve for Philip. But I was wrong. It's him. Vraymorg."

"Yes," she said flatly. "Yes, I came here because of him."

Dannon's tongue thickened as he swallowed. "What was between you? Is he your liege lord or a lover or what? I need to know, Kate."

"Who needs to know? The Varee overlord? Or Dannon. The man who seeks solitude by the river and pauses to admire an orchid in bloom?" Sweat beaded her brow, her face a screwed-up mess of despair and anger. All for a dead man. A memory. Except—

*I don't think he's dead.* He nearly said it. *This man you love. I think someone covered up his abduction with lies.*

The night grew colder. Only a chink of moonlight bled through squalling clouds. Dannon looked away from her at the flames dancing shapes on the hill. The village closed about him, stifling. *Or is it this world's rigid expectations? Do this. Be this. Believe this.*

When he glanced back at Kate, she stared beyond the village. Beyond him.

Abruptly, he rose. He could no longer be there, his body taking over with need, his mind detaching from that need, forcing away thoughts he must dwell on later. *Let her keep her secrets. For now.*

Dannon drank wine and rocked a chair on one leg, a foot braced against the hut wall. In a holder on the veranda beside him, a candle burned down. Its flame stood upright.

Idly he brushed a hand through a moonbeam, just as he might snatch at dust motes dancing in sunlight. Easier to touch moonbeams than understand Kate. Beneath her sorrow, he sensed anger. Not a remote sort of anger. Intimate. Focused. Yet anger hadn't taken her up that hillside. That was grief.

"Dannon?"

The chair nearly tilted over. "Kate." His voice, his heart, uneven.

She appeared on the rim of pooling candlelight, etched against the night, shifting her weight from foot to foot. "It's not what you think."

Dannon gripped his cup's baked clay, the rest of him still. A trick he had learnt as a child when the Varee questioned him—to push all his emotion into his fingers so his body and expression revealed nothing. "You don't know what I think."

Kate dropped her hands helplessly to her side. "You think he was my lover. He wasn't."

"Then who was he? Why do you weep for him? A lord of Vraymorg, no less."

"I can't tell you. But I swear it's nothing that threatens you or the Varee."

She didn't trust him. He couldn't blame her for that. So much distance lay between them, an endless expanse of what was not said.

Kate sat on the steps. "They're bringing Aalart out."

Dannon sat straighter, tension in his shoulders. Again, she called his prisoner by name.

Thoughtful, he watched guards flank Aalart to a table. Clothes ripped, feet black with dirt, his dark hair knotted and unwashed, the man no longer bothered to struggle as the guards shoved him down onto a bench and plonked a cup of ale and a trencher before him.

"Tomorrow, he shall be fed nothing, so he wonders if I intend to starve him," Dannon said as Aalart snatched up a leg of mutton. "Then I shall lay out a feast once more. There can be no patterns, no certainties."

"You won't easily break him, Dannon. This is a captain, no less. Vraymorg warriors take pride in their courage. He will hold on to that."

*Vraymorg warriors take pride...* She wept over the castle's former lord, knew Aalart by name, but the Varee had never heard of a bladeswoman like Kate at the castle.

"I know how it can be done."

"How?" She turned to face him.

Dannon tipped the chair back onto two legs, peering up through cobwebbed clouds. The sky domed, frighteningly endless. Firelight, candlelight, and a moon's gleam hewed the darkness with too many moods.

*She could understand,* he thought, wondering at his need to confide. *I know she could.* But this story, his story, was too raw. To tell it meant breaching his mind, stepping into a private, intimate recess of memory, part of him concealed where not even duty intruded.

"I know," he said quietly, "because it was done to me."

"What?"

"I'm not Varee-born."

"Oh?"

"My mother was—" No. That secret was dangerous. "From far away. My father, a Cahirean silver sword, a mercenary." That first. The rest of his father's identity had stayed with him. Not even the beatings, the whip on his back, the sleepless nights when his belly rumbled drew out that truth. Only because they did not know the right questions to ask.

"One year, saffron merchants hired my father to guard them and their wares. I'd just turned twelve, at last old enough to go with him. In the gorge between Cahir and Telor, the Varee attacked."

Dannon remembered clouded dust, a horse's screams, and the odour of blood. A fat merchant fell to his knees, guts spilling between clutching fingers, sobbing the name of a woman. His father had hacked at two raiders, shouting his defiance. Dannon had shouted too. Wild with battle fever—the term learnt later— he'd ridden at armed men, whirling a useless child's sword. They had fallen in about him, whooping.

"A man knocked me from the saddle, a giant—that's how he seemed to me—with ringlets of black hair and a weathered face. I fell hard, winded, then scrambled to my knees in time to see a brute cut down my father. The blade cleaved his back open so he sank first to his knees then onto bloody ground. I knew he was dead. Not because of that stroke, but because of a wrenching in my gut, a shattering in my mind.

"Shocked, disbelieving, I tried to crawl to him, but they grabbed me. I did not sob. Not then. Not while they watched, their curiosity cruel and morbid. The boy who did not cry, they called me. I heard them muttering about how old I might be and how I used a sword so well."

"How did you?"

He smiled, thinking back on his mother instructing him on balance, distance, which edge to use for which parry, how to watch another's feet, their eyes, to understand when they might attack. "I first picked up a wooden sword at five. I was too young to understand tactics, the language of blades, but I drilled parries, beats, disengages, and footwork, so even by the age of twelve, my hand moved instinctively when I held a weapon."

Kate listened in silence. A curious sympathy flowed between them, one Dannon rarely reached even with men he fought beside.

"The Varee brought me here. I fought them, cursed them. With every blow I tried to land, every object I snatched up to hurl, they only looked more pleased."

"And then their host captain set about—"

"Breaking me down. To nothing. Stripping away my past."

"The way you're attempting to break this man now?"

"I was a boy. Alone. My father slain, my mother dead of a winter fever when I was ten. The Varee took everything from me then gave it back. A place among their warriors, a wife. It will be harder with Aalart. His loyalties are set. I must convince him that other life is lost."

"Why bother?"

Dannon rocked the chair. "By tradition, our host captain cannot be Varee-born. If I can win Aalart, he'll bring different skills, old knowledge. Our warriors fight with passion and strength. Imagine that ferocity but with the discipline castle weapons masters teach."

Pausing, he looked right at Kate. "You fight with that discipline. Who was your master?"

That sympathy of minds, of experience still bound them. But the moment, if it existed at all, faded as the mage appeared through smoke, carrying a silver tray.

"Two goblets." Dannon could not keep the anger from his voice. "The mage will not let this rest."

The mage bowed. He offered first Dannon then Kate a goblet.

"What is it?"

"An escape," the old man said. "From your thoughts. From yourself."

Kate eagerly took the cup.

"Do not drink," Dannon said.

"Why not? You drink it. I've seen you."

"I wish I never had." How heady that first sip had been. It had hurled a twelve-year-old boy into dreams—wondrous, welcome dreams—that freed him from his windowless prison.

In those visions, his father had mussed his hair, the touch as real as the cool, smooth iron beneath his fingers when his mother closed his grip around the hilt of her sword. How he wanted to hold onto those dreams. How desperate he had been to drink again and again.

But the wine also did the unexpected. It awoke locked-up knowledge. Not a memory, more a compulsion hidden within him. For the first time, Dannon had dreamt of that desolate castle and the warriors carrying blue-steel blades. Now, even when he was sober, they haunted his sleep, their presence a meaningless urging. To do what, to be who or what?

Kate put the goblet to her lips. Dannon rose from the chair to stop her. The mage held up a hand. In the flickering light, his eyes were glassy and hard.

She took a sip. For a heartbeat, nothing happened. Then she slumped against the steps, her arms stretched to embrace someone unseen. Her lips soundlessly carved words.

The mage turned his weird eyes on Dannon. "You tried to interfere. Even when the council ordered me to do this. Do you choose this woman over your duty, over the Varee?"

"No. Of course not. I will always put my duty to the Varee first. But she isn't hiding anything." At a flare of impatience, he sent a candle flying from its holder. "You promised me answers. You promised the wine would unlock the truth. What does it mean? The warriors in my dreams?"

"The wine frees many things, Dannon. Longing. Desire. The past."

"I need to know."

"A time of change is upon us." The mage shifted his gaze to the darkness. "The meaning in your visions will be revealed. But you should not be so eager, Dannon. No, you should be afraid. If the truth means you are dangerous to us, I will surrender you to Archanin myself."

"You've known me since I was a boy, old man. I will not turn on the Varee."

"I know nothing of you, Cahirean," the mage said. "I fear these dreams are not of the Varee or our gods. I sense other gods seeking you."

"I have no gods," Dannon said.

# KAELL

Time passed because it must. Very soon after the night he sat on the hillside with Dannon, mourning his lord, autumn winds stripped trees bare and puddled red leaves over the forest floor. The air emptied of summer's honey and blossom, its perfume pungent and earthy as cold, slanted rain turned fields of wildflowers to mud.

The passage of seasons, though, did nothing to soothe Kaell's bitterness. Grief and uncomfortable anger wore him down to emptiness. The days were grim, a blur of villages, pounding hooves, flames, and screams. He held back his arm so he wounded or disarmed but never killed. At night, he drained the mage's silver jug so he didn't weep in his dreams.

Sometimes, he woke thinking he lay in his bed at Vraymorg, and the tread of steps to his door were his lord's as he came to scold him for oversleeping. In those deluded moments, he was happy. Then the truth piled onto him. His lord was dead. His old life was gone.

Small things, unlikely things, reminded him of the man he loved like a father. Kaell might hear a laugh or glimpse the shape of a man's back, and his breath died. Him. It was him. Then misery crushed his heart. Not his lord. Never him again.

One autumn afternoon, he took a skinful of the mage's brew into the underground burrow to find Shahven, a lantern at his feet, marking pages in a book as he took stock of barrels. It was a dim place that smelled of turned soil, sharp cloves, and rosemary. The earth walls were tightly packed, the roof buttressed by wood. Along one side, large barrels were stacked in frames. Sacks, jars, and glass vials sat in rows.

"Kate?" Shahven turned with a warm smile. "What brings you here?"

Kaell smiled back. "I'm exploring. Away from prying eyes. Though probably someone is watching the entrance to make sure I return and see where I go next."

"It's just that they don't know you. It won't be forever."

"I suppose not." Kaell wandered between the barrels, his hand trailing over the worked wood and iron. He took a swig from his skin, seeking that soft blurring in his mind. But it took many cups of wine now to bring him comfort. "So much wine."

"Not just wine." Shahven nodded towards barrels at the far end. "That's for our ghoul masters when they visit. Used to be Raggamirron came once a month. But with our god in Dal-Kanu, busy building his temple, it's not very often now." He shrugged.

"Do you mean—"

"Blood. The mage mixes it with wine and herbs to keep it fresh. He hasn't taught me how yet." Shahven thrust a book into his pocket. "I'm done. Very dull taking inventory." He looked at Kaell. "You coming? It's black as pitch without the lantern."

Kaell stole another look at the far barrels. "I'll only be a minute." Surely no one would miss a cup or two of blood if he crept back to the burrow later. It would be easier than swimming the river as he'd done to find a beast in the forest to drain.

Shahven scooped up the light and disappeared. Kaell memorised the chamber's dimensions. When he returned, he could not risk a candle.

A shape at the entrance blocked the glaring afternoon sun. Recognising Natasha, Kaell nodded curtly and started to push past. He didn't see the knife, only a blur as she thrust at him. Kaell jumped back, thankful his body responded at once now. Steel scraped the wall.

Grasping her wrist, he tore the blade from her and flung it back into the burrow. "You want me dead, Natasha?" Kaell heaved, exasperated. "Because of Dannon? I'm not interested in him." He let her go.

She stood breathing hard. "Liar," she spat. "Do you think I'm blind? That I don't know you sleep in his bed? Everything was different before you came. Why do you stay? No one would care if you left."

*No one would care...* He turned the words over in his mind, surprised to realise she was wrong. Dannon would care. Kaell laughed to himself. A slaver and killer, his friend. Their relationship had crept up on him so that he'd only seen it in pieces—until now.

"If you stay," Natasha said, "I'm going to kill you. First you, then him."

Kaell shouldered past. "Do your worst, Natasha. I don't really care."

It was not until he rode out beside Patrick the next day that he thought about how her fingers curled about her bow and her lips lifted off her teeth as she stared after him.

# VAL ARQUES

At a rattle of bolts, Val lifted his head off his knees. A brazier flared, casting a silhouette upon rock walls. Timid footsteps rang on stone as though the intruder feared disturbing—what? The rats? The dead? Not even spirits haunted the dank-walled prison. It held only him.

"Who are you?" his disused voice ground out. "What do you want?"

Water slapped iron as a woman dropped a bucket and basket beside him.

Through light-dazzled eyes, he stared. Her face lush, all plump lips and round cheeks, she was not quite pretty but not plain. Thick red hair tumbled loose and long, glinting in the brazier's dancing light.

"You're to wash, my lord."

He scraped up a laugh. "There's no lord here. It's just Val." To the world, Vraymorg was a dead man. He was no longer that man. No longer Lord of the Mountains. No one.

"Yes, my lord. You're to wash. Or—" Her gaze passed to his wrist shackled to the only other thing in the hole—a rock. *The* rock. Given their close tethering, he had grown fond of it. A pillow for his head. A brace for his aching back. An ear for his complaints.

"Or?"

"Or I bathe you. I was bid do that if you cannot manage."

"Why? Why now?"

Fire sparked on copper in her hair as she bent her head. "I was told not to talk to you," she whispered. "Please. I don't want to get in trouble."

"With who?" Val cleared his throat. "With Heath?"

"Please. I can't." She bit her lip. "I'm sorry. That he chained you up, I mean."

His smile cracked his lips. "Why? Is it your fault?"

"Of course not. But this is a foul place."

"What? All this opulence? Foul?" He glanced at the stark windowless walls of stone, at cobwebbed sconces and torches Val guessed had sat unused for decades.

The cavernous chamber had a slab floor so warm, it must be heated from below. It was empty of all but dust and grime, the brazier that burned down fast on the rare occasion it was lit, the rock… and him. A vast space for one prisoner. Diminishing. So he keenly felt his solitude.

"A palace, is it? Has anyone come to your palace? Before me?"

Val managed a soft laugh. "I'm not left to starve, if that's what you mean. Some poor boy scuttles in every day or so, drops a bowl of distasteful porridge and a cup of water as near as he dares, takes the slop bucket, then scuttles out."

"Scuttles? He'd be afraid then."

"Of me?"

The woman nodded. "I was told to beware of you too."

*Beware?* Val jangled his shackled wrist. Heath had carefully snapped on his pretty bracelet then turned the key. Hours trying to work the band off did nothing but pass the time. "You think I'll lunge at you?" The chain was so short he couldn't straighten, let alone leap.

She shook her head. "No, I don't think you'll hurt me. It's your tongue I'm to beware of."

"A weapon, is it?"

"They told me you'll get into my head with soft, clever words."

*If only.* Soft, clever words would catch in his rough, dry throat. "If I promise not to fill your head with evil words, will you answer a question?"

"I must hear the question first."

A guarded response, that. "Can you tell me anything of what goes on beyond these walls?"

She darted her eyes away from him, licking her lips.

"I need to know if someone close to me lives, if there's word of—her. Azenor Caelan."

"I'm sorry." Still, she didn't look at him. "I am forbidden to speak."

"Aric Caelan, then," Val pressed. "He was badly hurt. Does he live?"

"I don't know."

*Or can't or won't say?*

The woman reached into the basket. "I've brought food, water. A little wine."

"My, my, fancy. Is it a celebration? My birthday, perhaps?"

She lifted her head. "Is it your birthday?"

"A joke." Val had no clue about the date, even if it was day or night. By his rough calculation, he had spent two months chained to the rock but couldn't be sure.

"Ah, soft words." Smiling, she wrinkled her nose. "I'll bathe you first if you don't mind."

Val laughed. His body's odour no longer made him gag. "I suppose you better. Or I'll do it myself—if you find a key and let me loose?" He curved an eyebrow.

"I was told you'd ask that."

"By the same person who warned you about my soft tongue?"

She nodded. "My mistress."

*Now who might that be? Not Judith.* She would never leave him in such a place. It had to be Myranthe, the sorceress Heath had thrown at him. *What were his words? "She'll weep to see you." I'll weep if I see her. Tears of anger.* "Mistress, huh? I thought I was Heath's special prisoner."

The woman shot a worried look at the door. Voices carried in empty caverns.

"You are." As she dipped cloth into the water, steam rose in mist as soft as his supposedly charming tongue. "But he's not—" Another careful glance. "Here. Not for three weeks."

"Where is he?"

"Dal-Kanu." The woman took a knife from the basket. "So my mistress took this chance to send me to see how you fare."

"So Heath's in Dal-Kanu." Val wondered what she intended to do with the knife. "And he left me here—" *To rot? To become better acquainted with the rock? Oh enough, Val.*

The woman shivered. "They call that lump the Breaking Stone."

"I can't pretend I don't understand why."

"It's centuries old. In the distant past, the Damadars chained captives here to... well, to break. It's said in the chaos after King Roaran's murder, the sound of weeping carried into the passages, day and night. Warriors, fearless in battle, lords or princes who commanded thousands of men, begging to be set free. Left alone here and broken." She shrugged. "Of course, some were just left to starve."

*Where are their ghosts?* Val slid a glance at the unformed darkness. He could do with company, but he preferred it wasn't the dead.

"The Damadar prince everyone calls the Ice Rider deemed this place too cruel. He shut it up. It's not been used for centuries."

"Until me."

"Yes, until you, my lord. Can you stand?"

"You mean, can I slouch?" Val straightened as far as the chain allowed, his back bent.

Light flashed on the knife's blade. He jerked back, his palm scraping rough stone.

"I mean you no harm, my lord." The woman slipped the knife beneath his tunic, its metal cold on his breast. Carefully, she cut away cloth. Next, she ripped off his pants.

The rags were stiff with dirt, and Val was glad to be rid of them. Just so long as she clothed him again.

He squeezed his eyes shut as she washed him. The cloth on his skin and the occasional brush of her fingertips were not erotic but pleasurable.

The woman dabbed at his wrist twice then stopped abruptly.

Val snapped his eyes open. Even in the flickering light, he knew what she stared at, a frown between her brows. With no bracelets or sleeves to hide the white scars, he could only pull his hand away. An ache burned in his chest, half shame and half defiance. Only another who had faced the same misery and powerlessness could understand why he had done that.

"Sit again." Her voice softened with pity. He didn't ask for pity—and didn't want it.

Val bit his lip hard enough to draw blood and dropped, only to surge up, spluttering as she emptied the bucket over his head. "The bath was good—until the last."

"Lice crawling in your hair. Anyway, you'll dry soon enough. Hot springs warm these lower caverns." She passed him wine. "An apology for the drenching, my lord."

"Hmm." Val took the cup. "What's your name?"

"Evelyn."

"I like that name. It's beautiful."

"Soft words." Evelyn smiled. "Drink. It's not poisoned. No point when they can just leave you to starve."

Val sniffed the wine. He took a sip. Then another. Then a mouthful.

Evelyn looked down quickly, but not before he thought he saw her smirk. No, he was mistaken. A trick of the light.

He swilled robust plum and spice flavours in his mouth. It tasted impossibly good. The last time he had drunk wine was in the king's camp when they invested, or almost invested, Tide's End, while sitting with Judith.

He remembered her lazy smile, how she'd put down her glass with deliberate care to slide a hand along his thigh. Just the promise of her touch on his groin roused him, her fingertips only thickening his erection. He could even taste Judith's tongue in his mouth, tanged with a remnant of berries, and feel her breath on his cheek as her hand circled, stroking—

*By The Three, what's in that wine?* Surely, he still breathed in Judith's perfume, knew the burn of her caress on his skin. Reluctantly, Val shook off the past. Dwelling on what he couldn't have was useless. He had to concentrate on one thing—finding a way to Kaell.

Evelyn bent to repack the basket, careful to avoid looking at him. He knew a ridiculous flush of gratitude. His arousal was obvious.

"I'll leave water." She placed a carafe beside him.

"Thank you. But you left me more—hmm, vulnerable than when you came."

"I'll ask my mistress if I can bring a blanket tomorrow. Fresh clothes." As if compelled, she lifted her eyes. His body was hard with muscle, forever unchanged, and often drew admiring gasps from women. Even so, her appreciative gaze struck him as bold for a servant. Then Evelyn picked up the basket, the iron bucket, the discarded rags, and walked off, smiling.

Rising heat dried the grungy stone. Val stamped his feet. The brazier burned out, its gift of light cruelly transient. Shadows pooled below the door. Night? Bringing what? Another day. Then another night. He'd lost so much time in this foul hole when he must find Kaell. *Curse Heath Damadar.*

He bit back anger. It had done him no good in those first weeks alone in the darkness. For days, he had raged at the walls, cursed, and wrestled with the chain. It had changed nothing. He was powerless.

Right now, he could not get to Kaell. He had to accept this or go mad. With a sigh, Val sank back to the rock, his hand trapped uncomfortably above his head.

Judith's perfume lingered, delicate in his nostrils. Maybe Evelyn might return with more of that wondrous wine that brought waking dreams. Such tiny things made life bearable. Wine. Clothes.

Finding the warm floor soothing, Val shut his drooping eyes. He didn't realise he slept until his arm prickled. Drowsily, he wrung his hand until blood flowed back to it, then he drifted off again.

Footsteps forced their way into his dreams. He imagined someone bent over him, that he felt a prick of pain, but he only sighed and nestled his head against the crook of his arm.

A while later, a sound grated. Val jerked his head up. Light flooded through the door. The clatter of booted feet moving quickly echoed like a blacksmith's blows. With a puff of dust, torches flared to life. A lantern weaved. Blinking, Val shaded his eyes.

The footsteps stopped. A man stood over him, his face shadowed. But Val knew him.

"Heath." He seethed briefly then forced back his anger—a useless waste of strength that put him at a disadvantage. "And I hoped to sleep without nightmares. I heard you were in Dal-Kanu, bending and scraping to new kings."

"Bending and scraping to my new wife." Heath dropped to his haunches with a contented sigh. He passed his eyes slowly but keenly over Val. "You look as sleepy as a kitten. I clearly left you much too comfortable."

"Not at all. I'm rotting away nicely."

"Hardly that." Heath barked a laugh. "You appear your usual grumpy self but otherwise in excellent shape. No wonder you swing a sword as you do. Nothing but muscle. But surely I left you clothed?" He flicked up a brow. "Now who has been playing with you?"

Val hurled off sleep. He needed his wits around this man. "You're the game player. You're the one who dragged me in here and gave me this lovely trinket." He jiggled the shackle.

"Now I think of it, iron isn't your colour. Black, perhaps. To match your mood."

"My mood?" Val spluttered. "Cursed way to leave a man, Damadar. Chained like a dog. I can't straighten. But if I sit too long, my arm withers. For what offence?"

"It's called the Breaking Stone for good reason. Did I tell you the name? The stories this rock could tell."

"I'm sure I'm in good company." Again, Val searched for absent ghosts.

"Only the best break on this stone." Heath stood and kicked the rock listlessly. "Or don't break, apparently. Do you know, Val, you disappoint me. After more than two months, I expected a sobbing, cowering wretch. Not mad, though. That would never do."

"Oh, I'm mad."

"At me? How sad, given I kept you safe from all manner of nastiness outside. Anyway, not that kind of mad. Witless." Heath tapped his temple. "I did hope you might be a wee bit lonely. Begging me to stay and chat. And yet, here you are, just irritable and freshly scrubbed up. Have I told you about my new wife?"

"I demand to see your father. Take me to Rolland. Or at least carry a message to him. I can raise a ransom for my freedom if that's what this nonsense is about."

"My father considers you too dangerous to ransom, even if money was the way to his heart, Val. Come to think of it, does he have a heart? Myranthe doesn't. Or if she does, it's like a prune."

"What do you want from me?" Val threw at Heath in exasperation. He was tired of games, tired of ghosts who weren't there, the ache in his arm that was. Tired of Heath's mockery. "Do you intend to just leave me here? Until I sob? Beg? I am not an easy man. I can't always hold my tongue, hide my contempt. I know I have enemies. But what did I ever do to you?"

"I'm not your enemy, sweet boy." Heath scratched stubble on his chin. "Far from it. I'm your only friend in this treacherous place."

Val considered that stubble, Heath's dusty boots, the tousled dark-brown hair, and creased garments. "I see it now," he said sarcastically. "You do care."

"Of course. I just said as much."

"In your usual mocking tone."

"Mockery is something of a habit," Heath said. "Why is my affection suddenly apparent?"

"I'd guess you just rode in from Dal-Kanu, and the first person you rush to see is me. I'm touched."

"With my sneaky siblings, I had to make sure you were still kept tight." Heath offered that easy smile of his. A little too smug, always. Except it never seemed to trip him up.

"Is it time, then?"

"For what, sweet boy?" Crouching again, Heath fisted Val's hair to wrench his head back. "You're very cryptic tonight."

"Time for your sorceress sister—your words—to find her knives and strap me down."

"Hmm." The thoughtful look returned.

"What does *hmm* mean?"

Heath let go of Val's hair, rose, and stretched. "*Hmm* means no knives for you. Though what fun it could have been. I'd have held your hand. Would you have screamed for me?"

"What?" He sounded disappointed. How badly he must want out of this hole, away from this rock. *The* rock, he corrected. *Still this nonsense, Val? Yet, what else do I have but nonsense? Oh wait, I have Heath.*

"Myranthe, my saucy sister, was so very angry at me. The relief to be in Dal-Kanu."

Val's head pounded. Heath always brought on some sort of ache. In his head, his heart. "Maybe she'll strap *you* down," he threw back. "Maybe you'll scream for *me*."

Heath's expression brightened. "That's better. I like it when you're bitter. I get a tingle all over."

"Now I understand. I'm kept here for you alone. Well, that was a lecherous gaze before."

"Ah, more tingles. We go beyond bitter. We deliver blows to my very core."

Val shook his arm. He had tingles too. "Cut me free, and I promise more than blows."

"I'd like nothing better than to cross swords with you, Val. But apparently, we can't always have what we want. I tell Judith that all the time."

Val made an exasperated noise.

Heath rubbed his temples. "You might take pleasure in knowing that Myranthe is of a like mind to you. She recently delivered me not quite a vicious blow but a hefty slap."

Despite his dislike, Val leaned closer. "Why?"

"Because of you." Heath laughed. Val had heard that same sound echo in his dreams ever since this man forced a sleeping draught on him and shoved him into a carriage. "Here, I was all bloated with pride. Not only had I dumped Aric Caelan at her feet like a dutiful puppy but delivered her a lovely surprise. You."

Again, his gaze swept up and down. For all Val's words, he recognised Heath's look. One bladesman assessing another, seeking weaknesses, rating strength.

"Myranthe was a tad upset Aric was close to death. Well, what could I do? Did I ask him to allow some god to bite him? She huffed and puffed and carried on. I thought my offering of a Caelan-born bladesman might appease her. Especially if Aric foolishly let himself die."

"So Aric isn't dead?" Val struggled up and shook his arm to life. It stung. He peered harder. Blood crusted a long cut on his forearm. It was straight like a wound from a knife.

"One story at a time." Heath teased with a jabbing finger. "This is about you." He paused. "You. Val Arques Caelan. The man I long to fight in the fire halls. Of course I never lose. In the end, I'd kill you."

"Is that what you think?"

"There's a mood and rhythm to a fire dance. You don't know its steps. Yes, I'd kill you. Though…" He frowned as if surprised. "If you begged me, I'd spare your life. That's a compliment, by the way. I never spare anyone. But none of the men I've killed are you."

Val curled his lips into a sneer. "You are surely the most conceited creature in creation."

"Conceit is only one of my many fine qualities."

"Where's Azenor Caelan?"

"This again?" Heath threw up his arms. "I don't have her. I never had her. I told you that. Now can I finish about Myranthe? I promise you'll like the end of this story."

"It's all just rambling nonsense," Val muttered.

"It takes a certain skill to ramble, Val."

"It takes little skill to turn around and walk out. Leave me to rot in peace."

"Not until I finish. Now, where was I? You wouldn't wake up and impress Myranthe with your bad temper, and we had to impress Myranthe, because she's very scary."

"Blah, blah, blah," Val said.

"So my cousin and I—you'll remember Dillon—hurled you onto Myranthe's bench, rid you of a few garments, told her the 'true' Caelan-blood bit. Both parents with Caelan blood. Rare, given that the priests and priestesses frown upon it. Myranthe cheered up then." Heath's laugh rattled around in Val's brain. "'A bladesman, you say, Heath? He certainly looks like a bladesman. Clever boy, Heath.' Until—"

"You let slip about how I'm dead."

"Now I never thought it a problem. But then, what do I know?

Myranthe sorted me out. She put her hands all over you—probably not necessary—then threw a nasty tantrum, shouting about other magic tainting you. Seems you're useless to her. I'm useless, too, by the way. Then that slap. And another to make sure I realised what a worthless creature I am."

"So here I am, chained like a dog, because you made a mistake."

Heath clamped a hand over his heart. "And guilty I feel about it too."

"Not a bit, I'd say."

"You're beginning to know me very well. The problem is my half brother Velleran wandered in to hear the Caelan-blood bit and became very excited. So I threw you in here to keep you out of everyone else's clutches."

"So I should be grateful?"

"Myranthe and the high-and-wishes-he-was-mighty Velleran plot something to do with you. That's never good." His gaze lingered. "For the moment, you're still mine, but I sense a struggle coming. Myranthe will try to take you sooner or later. Either on her own part or for Velleran. I only wonder if her scheme will be straightforward or deliciously devious."

"Your sister surely can't be any crueller than you."

Heath burst out laughing, genuinely amused. "Val, really. You think because Judith is so warm and I'm so charming, you know what my family is about. You don't. This"—he waved his arm—"is a kindness. It most certainly kept you out of sight, if not quite out of mind."

"I'd settle with *you* being out of sight."

"Ha." Heath glanced at the torches. "I'll let them burn out. The brazier too. Just a small gesture. I mean, I am very fond of you. Who else trades words with me as you do?" He began to walk away. Halfway to the door, he stopped and turned. "Who did clean you up? I left strict instructions about your care. Or lack of care."

"A servant girl." Val slid his spine down the rock. "Came with hot water, food, and wine."

Heath grinned. "I've got it now. A servant girl with coppery hair, perhaps? And you said I'm the game player?"

Smiling, he strode away. Val heard his laugh echoing down the passage even after the door clanked shut.

# KAELL

Kaell thumped his cup onto the ale-stained plank, spun a coin at the tavern keeper, and shouted, "Wine."

"Steady up, Kate," a Varee warrior named Tullan called from a table at the back of the shabby dirt-floor room. "You'll show up Patrick. One sip, and he's snoring in his chair."

At his companions' gusty laughter, other patrons glanced up then at once looked away. The hard men were easy to pin as Varee. Like beasts at rest, they sprawled around a table, their woollen cloaks rank, kill notches in the belts strapped about garish tunics.

A buzzing began in Kaell's ears. He clutched the plank. How had he come to this? To call these outlaws allies? If his lord knew—*No. Do not think of him. Drink. Forget.* Kaell slapped his palm against wood. "Bring me wine."

Cool, pine-scented air accompanied glaring sunlight as the only door opened. A raven-haired man, sword at his hip, sauntered inside. A man too finely attired to belong in this kings-forsaken hole.

A man with blue eyes.

Kaell's arms prickled. It must be him. The stranger tracking the Varee from town to town, asking dangerous questions about Azenor.

Kaell glanced at Patrick. The Varee man nodded.

The newcomer leaned his elbows on the plank so close to Kaell, he caught the soapy scent of his hair and skin beneath the room's fetid swill of sweat, unwashed flesh, and stale beer. The stranger did not look at Kaell, only paid the tavern keeper for a cup of wine.

A drunk in a tattered uniform lurched up. A soldier, no doubt, scattered like the rest of Cathmor's army to the edges of civilisation like this Downs den. "Well, hello darling—"

"Go away." Kaell didn't bother to look up. He was fed up with invasive stares, innuendoes, and men who groped, patted, or touched him needlessly.

"A sweet, young girl like you shouldn't drink alone, not in a place like this."

"You think I'm sweet?" Kaell turned. He even smiled then, as sweetly as he could, and pressed against the man. What he didn't expect was the strange sensation. Not just the shocking bulge rubbing his hip, but a surprising sense of power. Unwanted power.

The soldier's eyes stretched. Not at Kaell's nearness—but at the knife prodding his groin. Hands raised, he backed up. If he were a dog, he would have shown his belly.

Kaell forgot him and considered the newcomer. Everything about him was elegant, from his embroidered tunic belted over his hips, his long legs to his glossy shoulder-length dark hair. Despite his relaxed pretence, he was edgy like a spring, his sword a shaved heartbeat from release.

And what a sword. A niello hilt and engraved pommel. The opposite of Dannon's unpretentious weapon. Hardly ornamental, though, given the blade's well-worn grip, the oiled leather scabbard, and the thick calluses between its owner's third and fourth fingers.

"You're a long way from the Isles." Kaell glanced from the sword to the clean, straight lines of the man's face. To those dark-blue eyes. No mistaking him as the one hunting Azenor. The moment he had walked into this place, those eyes had sealed this man's fate. He bit back guilt. *Why care about a stranger?*

"How do you know I'm from the Isles?" The man smiled. He might have been thirty-six or thirty-seven, a warrior in his prime. Except for that smile. It was old.

Kaell remembered Arn talking about those who had known too much sorrow too often. How it layered and layered, packed tightly so no peace settled between. Warriors all had that sort of smile, Arn had said. That sort of hard, weary look in their eyes.

Then it hit him. That look. His lord also had that look.

Kaell gulped wine. Desperately. To kill thoughts of Vraymorg. If only he had more of the mage's wondrous brew that let him forget not just who he was but *what* he had become.

Wiping his mouth with the back of his hand, he said, "You can always tell an Isles man."

The stranger leaned closer. "And how's that?"

"Aww, look at that. The pretty salt-head's in love with our Kate," Patrick jeered. A girl on his knee tongued his ear.

"Don't go bruising his handsome face now, Kate," Tullan said. His companions sniggered. Again, others carefully averted their gazes.

"They're all strutting peacocks." Kaell intended to goad the blue-eyed man into a fight. He wanted it done with, this stranger and all his unknown threat in the Varee's loving embrace. So he could forget him and drink the mage's brew until he passed out.

The stranger only laughed. He held up his cup to the tavern keeper. "I suppose we are. More wine."

"Don't like Isles men. Traitors, the lot of them." Kaell swiped at Azenor's crudely cropped hair. How strange it felt between his fingers, more unruly, thicker than his own.

"Don't like any men," Tullan muttered.

"She likes Dannon well enough," Patrick said, unsmiling.

"An overlord's not a man." Tullan bumped a woman carrying a jug as he barked laughter. Ale slopped onto straw, adding its odour to the scents of burnt meat and smoke.

A bull-necked man stomped up, another drunken fool in a den of them. "You, girl, watch your mouth."

"Treacherous salt-heads." Kaell wanted to hit something. Anyone. Lashing out dulled that razor of memory. Anger was far, far easier than sorrow. "Cowards, every one of them, the king included."

Red-faced, the man swung a fist. Though full of wine, he connected. Kaell staggered back, recovered, and rubbed his chin. "That it? I've seen dead men hit better."

Bellowing, the man balled his fists again. Kaell ducked the punch, grabbed his opponent's arms, and jammed his knee into the man's groin. The brute doubled over, rasping. Kaell hurled him into a bench. It smashed. His body crashed to the floor amidst the shards.

The tavern keeper growled, "Here, you."

"Got a problem?"

The man looked at Kaell and showed his palms.

Again, the door crashed inwards. A warrior called Rob, sweat streaming from his sun-leathered skin and bald head, rushed inside to whisper to Patrick.

"Kate." Patrick slid a meaningful look at the Isles stranger then the door. Still riled up, Kaell only half nodded, looking for someone else to hit. Every drinker kept their head down.

Patrick shoved the woman from his lap and led the Varee outside. Kaell forced his hands to unclench. With a disappointed sigh, he scooped up his cloak.

The stranger blocked his way. "What's the hurry? We only just started to trade insults."

"No."

"No, what? No, you don't like my face? No, it won't rain? No, the king doesn't have an heir because he's impotent? That's the rumour, anyway."

"Move aside, salt-head."

The man grasped his shoulder. Kaell stilled. This was his

chance. Just smile. Look right into the stranger's eyes and make up some lie to draw him outside.

At the thought he was capable of such deceit, Kaell flushed in shame. How low could he sink? So low he would entice a stranger to his death?

No. Whatever skin he wore, a stubborn, hot-tempered, brave, fierce, complicated man had raised him to know right and wrong. That code made him who he was. He couldn't discard it because it was inconvenient or dangerous or because it didn't fit with the role he currently played.

He couldn't abandon it because he grieved for a man who abandoned him by dying.

Kaell shrugged off the stranger's firm grip. "Let me pass." He dropped his tone. "And don't follow me outside if you want to stay free. In fact, just stop following me anywhere. Whoever you think I am, I'm not."

"Follow you? I'm only after a little conversation."

Kaell gripped his sword hilt. "Listen, fool. I'm doing you a favour. Keep far away, or you'll find yourself in a slave market."

The Isles man stood his ground, smiling. Then in a low voice, he said, "Your companions want you to bring me to them. You should do it."

"What?"

The door crashed open. Soldiers streamed inside. Their badges and dark-blue woollen cloaks marked them as king's men.

His body tight with alarm, Kaell tried to slip past. Soldiers shoved him back. "Get over there," one ordered as his companions blocked the doors. "All of you, against the wall."

Grumbling, the tavern's occupants lined up. Kaell nibbled his lip. *What could these soldiers want here?*

The bull-necked man staggered to his feet. "King's men don't tell me what to do." He spat at the ground. "This is a long way from Dal-Kanu." Two soldiers hurled him into line.

"You don't mean us, do you, sweetheart?" said a black-eyed

woman. She stood hands on her hips, breasts spilling from her low-cut gown.

"You too," the soldier said. "Move. And you." He pushed the tavern keeper.

"This is your fault," Kaell muttered as the stranger backed up beside him. "I would be gone if you hadn't delayed me."

"Why, what do they want?"

"How should I know?" Kaell kicked the wall. If they learnt he rode with the Varee, they would hang him. Someone might tell, to save their own skin.

The soldiers parted for a young woman. Her hair showered in gold and red strands onto a tunic over pants tucked into boots of soft leather.

The Isles man started. "Quisnaf," he whispered.

Kaell blinked. *Here?* He knew of the Quisnaf—who didn't?— but he'd never expected to meet one. They rarely left their city of caves. Everyone said that. And few men travelled there willingly.

The woman swept the room with a blue-eyed stare. "What a den of scum. I suspect we're wasting our time here." She breathed in deeply. Her bored expression changed to one of surprise. "And yet, what is that I smell? Someone in this room has very curious blood."

"Blood sniffer," the stranger muttered to Kaell. Hand to his sword hilt, he peered about as though seeking a way out. "Too dangerous. She'll know at once."

*Know what?* "What's a blood sniffer?"

"Shut up." A soldier pushed Kaell against the wall.

Kaell thrust off his hand.

The soldier grinned. "Big sword for a woman. Lot of attitude too. What might you be?" He called over his shoulder, "Kandra, one here causing trouble. Maybe for a reason."

"I'll get to them, Waterman."

"And if she doesn't, I will." Leering, the soldier groped at Kaell's breast.

That same fear he'd felt in the Mountains when a stranger attacked him swooped into his stomach. Such power in this body. With a smile or a touch, he could draw a man outside to his death. But such vulnerability too. A different sort of threat.

The soldier turned away. Kaell went for his sword.

The Isles man grasped his wrist. "Eleven soldiers," he whispered. "More outside."

Kaell dropped his hand. Curse it, the man was right. Even with his ghoul strength, he would need a distraction to escape.

Kandra paused before a reed-thin, stooped man, shrugged, and moved to Kaell.

"This is the one." Waterman appeared eagerly at her shoulder. Another dog. "Tried to run."

"I was scared," Kaell muttered. He slouched, attempting to appear harmless.

Kandra sniffed. Her sneer fell away, her eyes wide with astonishment. She drew in another deep breath. "By Cyrah, what are you? No? Never mind. A discussion for later." She gestured. "Arrest her. There's Caelan blood there."

For a second or two, Kaell stared at the Quisnaf woman, not understanding.

Then panic seized him. He bolted, only to hit a barrier of soldiers. They grabbed his arms. Bucking, thrashing, he threw them off. Others leapt in, knocked him to the floor, and subdued him with their bodies, knees, and elbows.

The soldiers yanked him to his feet. Held by the shoulders, Kaell struggled uselessly as Kandra tore his sword from him.

"Very curious," she said, smiling. "All of it, your blood, your sword. You wouldn't be a Sister of Cyrah, would you? Though that doesn't explain the Caelan bit."

The Isles man inched back. Kandra swung on him. "Where are you going? I want to have a long look at you, handsome."

The stranger offered a careless shrug. "Thank you for the compliment, but I'm no one."

"He's just some stray salt-head," the tavern keeper jeered.

Kandra arched a brow. "I'm seeking stray salt-heads. Disarm him."

"Thank you so much." The man glared at the tavern keeper.

Waterman grinned as he tore the stranger's blade from his belt. He whistled. "Look at that. Seithin steel."

The guards turned to see. Kaell threw a punch. A soldier plunged back. More rushed him. Kicking, cursing, writhing, he fought his way to the door.

A man tackled his legs. He crashed facedown. Soldiers piled onto him, pinning him to the ground. One slammed his skull against a table leg. Dazed, Kaell could not resist as they hauled him up. He slumped, his head lolling, as six men held him.

"Be a little careful." Kandra covered a yawn with a palm. "Given the king will wish to talk to that one."

She turned to the blue-eyed stranger. "As for you. Your Caelan blood is overpowering, even from a distance. And there's something else that puzzles me. Who are you? No, wrong question. *What* are you?"

*Caelan blood?* Startled, Kaell stared at the stranger. *How? Why is such a man here?*

"Not talkative? We'll see if that changes in Tide's End."

"Tide's End?" the stranger echoed warily.

"That frightens you?"

"The salt air dries my skin." He brushed a hand over stubble. "Not particularly attractive."

"Caelan blood and a sense of humour. The king will badly want to meet you." Kandra nodded at Waterman.

Sword drawn, the soldier started forward. The Isles man moved fast. He grabbed Waterman, whipped him about, and squeezed his throat with an arm. Choking, gasping, Waterman dropped his sword to break his attacker's hold. His assailant shoved him, sending him sprawling, then swooped on the blade.

Sword extended, the Isles man backed up, watchful. The hard

gleam in his eyes, Kaell recognised as clearly as he recognised the bladesman's stance. A will to not only defend his person but to kill.

Two soldiers sprang at him with naked steel. Their target swept aside both thrust and cut, his parries sharp and deceptively effortless. At a lunge from the side, he crashed his blade down, whirling in time to block a swinging blow at his head.

"I want him alive!" the Quisnaf woman screamed. "Alive!"

The third soldier jabbed at his legs. The Isles bladesman captured the sword near his hilt in a circular bind and wrenched it from the man's hands. Open-mouthed, the soldier froze long enough for the stranger to swat him into a wall with an arm.

Kaell tensed, ready to break free if his captors dropped him to help. But they held back, trained, he guessed, to know they would get in each other's way in the confined space.

Grinning now, the Isles bladesman rounded on the last two. As he extended his sword, his shadow fell on the wall. Kaell blinked in shock. The shadow was too large. The wrong shape. Not a man's shadow but a monster writhing.

He rubbed his eyes. That blow to his head had rattled his wits and his vision. Why, he even imagined a chill descended on the tavern.

A soldier attacked, thrusting low to wound. The Isles warrior blocked, his body twisted sideways to make a smaller target. With his empty hand, he tore a cup off the plank and smashed it into the man's skull. The soldier staggered then dropped to his knees. Uncertain, the last one circled.

"Stop!" the woman cried. "Leave him to me."

The soldier edged back. The Isles man turned. She stood between him and the door.

"Get out of my way," he said.

Kandra did not move. In a voice dark and low, she said, "I saw that shadow. I know what you are now. It's not possible. He destroyed you, all of you. Yet I smell it in you." Closing her eyes, she breathed deeply as though to compose herself.

The stranger frowned. He looked from the woman to the door. Blade levelled, his weight distributed for either attack or defence, he fell back a step.

Kandra opened her eyes. Lifting a hand, palm outward, she chanted in a language Kaell had never heard before. The man froze, his stare widening with surprise. Then an unseen force slammed him back. He hit a wall hard and slumped, limbs splayed. He did not move.

Kaell bucked. *Khir help me, what is she? What power does she possess?* He'd only ever seen Archanin use that sort of magic.

Waterman stumbled to the fallen man. He kicked his ribs. "Good hunting," he smirked. "Wouldn't expect anything in a hole like this."

"But all sorts of things crawl out of holes." Kandra smiled benignly at Kaell as he struggled. That smile was all he saw before a hilt smashed into his skull.

A jolt jarred his shoulders, dragging him up through a shallow dream. Groaning, his neck aching, Kaell lifted his head off steel bars. He was in a cage on the back of a cart. It creaked along a road flanked by trees with low-hanging branches. Autumn sunlight crept through red leaves, its glare fading as it slunk into shadows.

"Awake at last." An armed man on horseback passed a flask inside.

His throat as dry as clay, Kaell took it but did not drink. "Suppose it'll make me sleepy."

"Suppose you'll find out." Whistling, the rider moved on.

"It won't make you sleep." On the far side of the cage, the Isles man slouched over his drawn-up knees. Dried blood matted his hair. "Blood sniffer wants us alert for questioning."

At the iron shackling the stranger's wrists and ankles, Kaell bristled with ridiculous resentment. They had restrained this man but not him. No one feared him in this body, the threat in him invisible. His skill with a sword meant less than his silken hair and the curves beneath his clothes.

*Except... think it through.* To be misjudged, underestimated, offered a hidden advantage. Kaell sipped. He screwed up his nose. "Water. Disgusting. I need wine."

"I'm beginning to suspect what sort. Demon brew, from your tremor. Dangerous stuff."

"Not your concern, salt-head. World looks better that way."

"Better what way?"

"Through a glaze."

"I'm sorry you're hurting," the stranger said unexpectedly.

"What do you care?"

The man leaned his head against the bars, eyes closed. Sweat sheened his brow. He must have hit the wall hard.

"Your blade is Seithin steel," Kaell said. "She said you have Caelan blood."

The stranger did not reply. Kaell peered about, forming plans to escape then discarding them. Six or seven horsemen, all armed, flanked the cart. The iron bars were thick, though his ankles and wrists weren't fettered. When they stopped for the night—

He considered the bucket and the straw. No, their captors wouldn't let them out of the cage until they reached Tide's End. *What then?* "You called her a blood sniffer. What's that?"

With a weary sigh, the Isles man opened his eyes. "She can tell who you are from your blood. A rare talent, expensively bought. More so if the witch has other... abilities."

"Like magic? She certainly flung you around like you were made of rags. What did she mean about knowing what you were?"

The stranger's gaze drifted towards the forest and its bruised depths. "She meant a bladesman," he said distantly. "Just a bladesman."

"With Caelan blood," Kaell muttered. "And maybe something else, too, something they fear, given your shackles."

"Just a bladesman," the man muttered.

Back to the bars, Kaell studied him. Surprising the similarities between his lord and this stranger. The lips, maybe. The same gleaming black hair. But not those dark-blue eyes; no one in Telor had eyes that colour.

The cart jolted along the grooved track. Ebbing sunlight ran to and fro. The cart's wheels crackled through a sea of clustered orange. Flanking riders brushed aside stark branches, cursing when they rent cloth. There was no sign of the Quisnaf woman.

A shape flashed between trees. A twig snapped. Kaell pressed his face to the bars, his pulse aflame, as whooping riders waving blades surged from the woodlands.

For a stunned heartbeat, the defenders did nothing. Then they braced, weapons drawn.

The attackers smashed into them in a cacophony of noise and flashing steel, of threats, grunts, throbbing hooves, of arrows whipping through air. Swords clashed in a mighty pealing. A mess of figures, streaked light, and roiling colours surrounded the cart.

"Took their time." Kaell exhaled in relief. He wasn't sure Dannon would risk warriors to free him.

"Who?" The stranger sat straighter.

Kaell guiltily looked away. The fighting boded well for him but not this man.

The cart rocked to a halt. Loosed arrows zipped overhead. Iron clanked as men traded blows. A horseman thundered past.

The Isles man gripped the cage, yelling, "What's happening?"

The rider flinched as an arrow nipped by his shoulder. Clouding dirt swallowed him. Blades sang in a vicious, off-key chorus. Men cursed. Terrified horses whinnied. Dust whirled. More arrows whisked air. The driver screamed and dropped.

It fell quiet.

Steel clattered across the bars. Kaell jumped then swore as Rob appeared beside the cart, grinning. His scalp shone with sweat. Gore splashed his tunic. More armed Varee warriors stomped up, their clothes, faces, and hair blotted with blood, innards, and bone shards.

Patrick reined in. His face was gaunt, all cheekbones, his mouth a hard, pink-lipped slit. "Our glorious overlord sent us. Want out, girl?" At his nod, Rob crashed his sword down on the lock then kicked in the iron door.

Kaell crawled through then straightened, brushing straw from his pants.

Patrick's stare fell on the Isles man. "Your friend too shy to join us?"

"I'm content," the prisoner said. "Warm in the sun. Hay for my head. I've known worse."

Rob jabbed his blade through bars. "Out. Or I prick you like a pincushion."

"A kind invitation, but no thanks." Chains clanked as the man folded his arms.

Patrick dismounted. "Throw a spark on that hay."

At their cruel grins, Kaell winced. He could do nothing to help this man now, except stay silent about the Quisnaf woman's revelations. Caelan blood. That shadow. Khir only knew what the Varee would make of that.

Reluctantly, the Isles man crawled to the door. Rob hauled him out and dropped him at Patrick's feet like a hunting dog with prey.

"Handsome, isn't he?" Patrick whistled. "Worth a bit in the markets. Ever seen him before, Kate? Know why an Isles man— he's that, for sure—is asking about you?"

Kaell managed an indifferent shrug. "Don't think it's him."

"He'll tell us once we get him back to the village." Patrick's eyes were flint. "Then we'll sell him. A man like that will fetch gold."

"Moves like a bladesman," Tullan muttered. "Get a good price for a bladesman."

"Observant, aren't you?" the Isles man said. "Do I get a say in this?"

"You get a say in response to our questions," Patrick said.

"Talking of questions." He turned to Kaell. "Why'd king's soldiers arrest you, Kate?"

An easy lie. "Someone in that tavern told them I was Varee."

"Hmm." Patrick dropped beside the captive and fisted his hair. "Unusual eyes. Especially with that black Isles hair. The Quisnaf pay a lot for Isles warriors. More for handsome ones."

The stranger blenched. At the prospect of becoming a slave in Quisnaf? Or the humiliation of shackles and pawing buyers?

"Certainly looks like the description of the man following you, Kate."

"He's not."

Patrick considered his reflection in the knife. "You question him, Kate." He rose and tossed Kaell a knife. "Just don't cut his face. It's worth money."

"I'm not sure what I did to offend you." The stranger uselessly bucked against Rob's hold. "Meet a girl in a tavern, try to talk to her—"

"Follow her," Patrick said.

"I don't understand. What exactly are you accusing me of?"

Kaell crouched. Reluctantly, afraid for this man, he said, "Villagers in Ryol's Forge said a stranger with blue eyes was asking questions about me. Heard the same in a stinking village only fit for pigs."

"Dal Pig." Rob nudged Tullan. "Place of the pig. Do you get it?"

"You're a fool."

"Yeah, come from Dal Fool, you onion."

"What sort of insult is that?"

"Then someone's asking questions in King's Tomb." Kaell ignored their nonsense. "Salt-head with blue eyes. Big, glinting sword of Seithin steel in his belt."

"And then I take the big, glinting sword into that tavern." The man sighed. "You're right. Put a knife in me. I'm so stupid, I deserve it."

The stranger had admitted it. Just like that. Wasn't he afraid?

Why not bluster or bluff his way out of this? "So you *are* following me. Why? Just who are you?"

"Call me Big Sword," the man replied pleasantly.

"And when it's cut off?" Rob taunted. "What will we call you then?"

"Small Eunuch." Tullan slapped his thigh and bellowed laughter. The rest sniggered.

Kaell sat back on his heels. "Who are you?"

The stranger fixed his striking eyes on him. So softly that only Kaell heard, he said, "Someone who's been looking for you for a long while... Kaell."

Kaell's breath stalled. He went cold inside. *Who is this man?*

Patrick grabbed his shoulder. "What are you whispering about?"

"He's got a smooth Isles tongue, this one," Kaell said nervously. He thrust the knife tip up into the prisoner's jaw. "Maybe I should cut it out."

Patrick laughed nastily. "That's more like it, girl." He stepped back to address Rob. "Go scout ahead. We're on the edge of Vraymorg lands. Could be outriders."

"If you have any pity in you, kill me," the prisoner said quietly.

"What?"

"They're going to torture me, Kaell. Until I tell them who I am. And I can't do that."

"No, they won't. They're going to sell you."

"I'll hold out for a while. Maybe longer than most. But in the end, everyone breaks. They'll uncover my name. Then they'll pass me on to Archanin. He will not be merciful."

*Archanin.* Kaell remembered the shadow at the man's back in that tavern. Who or what was worth surrendering to a god? "Who are you?" he whispered.

"Tell them it was me." His smile was grim. "Tell them I wrestled the blade from you." The stranger began to mouth words under his breath.

Kaell shivered. Surely, that was the same language the Quisnaf blood sniffer had used. The knife shuddered in his grip. A force compelled his hand slowly forward. *What—what?* Desperately, Kaell fought to control the blade, even drop it. But he could not stop himself plunging the knife into the captive's throat.

The Isles man jerked. He collapsed cheek to grass. A red stain spread beneath him.

Kaell stared at his bloody hands, at the bloody knife. At the dead man. He could see Patrick turning, starting forward, his face white. His voice was a remote buzzing.

Hot, dizzy with shock, Kaell swayed.

*Oh gods. What have I done?* Unwillingly, he had again become a killer. Who he had been was gone, every code he had held ripped apart. At least his lord did not live to see his fall. Bad enough knowing he'd failed a dead man.

Patrick stood with his legs spread, a thumb dug into his belt. The wind lifted the edges of his fringe. "What happened? That was valuable merchandise you just killed."

"I didn't—" Kaell stammered. He scrambled for words to explain. "He did it."

"He stabbed himself? You fool girl. How did he get the knife off you?"

Kaell didn't correct him. Patrick would never believe him if he started babbling about magic. "I got too close. It happened fast."

"Gods." Patrick dragged his fingers through his oily hair. "You just cost us a fortune."

Kaell scrambled up. "I'm sorry. I can't be here. There's somewhere I've got to be."

"Wait up, girl." Patrick blocked him. "You're coming back to the village to explain to Dannon how you let a prisoner steal your knife and kill himself."

"I've a message to deliver for Dannon first. He says it's vital. You can check with him."

Patrick's narrow gaze hung on Kaell's face. Then he reluctantly moved aside. An edge to his tone, he said, "Oh well, if *Dannon* says it's vital."

Kaell managed to walk off slowly. The moment he hit the trees, he ran.

It was only a hut: timber walls with a timber floor and thatched roof. It sat in a patch of sunlight amid thick trees. Kaell staggered to the door. He rapped its wood.

Cloth rustled over boards. A young woman opened the door. "Who are you? What do you want?"

"Alyssa." Kaell folded to his knees before his childhood friend. "Alyssa. I don't know what to do. I don't know what's happening. Help me, Alyssa." He wrapped his arms around her leg and sobbed.

# VAL ARQUES

A boy brought more wine. Val remembered the slumber that caught him up after he drank Evelyn's gift. He put the cup on the floor. He looked at it. He thought about Evelyn's smirk.

Then Val snatched up the cup and drank, wanting only the release of dreams. Perhaps to see his wife and son, though their faces always fragmented like mist when he woke.

He leaned his head against the rock, submitting to that shadow world on oblivion's edge. Drifting. Did he hear Cathmor's scornful tone? Perhaps Telorian kings indeed haunted those who killed them. Was that Judith's laugh? Why did a pang of loneliness spear him at thoughts of her?

Loneliness. Helplessness. Despair. He could see a tower room where dust motes danced in sunlight as he beat his fists against the door. Where he choked on the sickening, cloying fragrance of roses and scented oil. Where a man with damp hands watched him.

"No." Lost in the past, he cowered from flaring torches. Men reached for him. Val went limp in their grips, not resisting; a nineteen-year-old bladesman forced into this room by guards who turned the key as they left.

The iron band at his wrist tore away. The remnants of the nightmare dissolved to a stone cavern, warm slabs of stone, and Ice men. Not Wardorians with knowing leers.

"What's happening?" he croaked.

Like the hard-eyed Wardorians, the guards did not answer. But this was not Wardour and he was no longer the young man who had sobbed bitterly in that sunlit room where the wind carried the sea's brine, gardenia, and heat. Whatever unfolded, he would face it unbowed.

A guard threw a blanket over his naked shoulders and hauled him up. Val swayed. The man took his arm. Prideful, he shook free. The unsmiling guard tapped a belted sword.

He nearly laughed in the man's face. Did they really imagine he would run without knowing his way out of these endless ice caverns? He may as well be in a desert of sand dunes.

Armed men escorted him outside into uncomfortably bright light. Val squinted and stumbled. They pulled him up and pushed him along a whitewashed passage. Torches puffed smoke and spilled opaque light in overlapping circles. Cool air nipped his neck. It smelled dead like winter but pleasant after the fetid prison.

The guards flanked him up spiralling stairs entombed by stone. A tower. Better that than deeper underground. No one spoke. The only sounds were their boots on the steps, a swish of a cloak as it brushed the wall, and his bare feet scuffing over cool, worn stone.

At the top, they shoved him through a door. A key turned. A bar dropped with a thump. It all happened very fast. Professionally. Without fuss.

Val shoved his back to the door and considered the small circular room. It held a fur-covered bed, a chair, and a carved dark-wooded chest. Rugs hung on more whitewashed stone walls, a shield against the cold. A shuttered window promised light. *Sunlight. At last.*

He padded across a deep rug and knelt beside the chest. The odour of camphor rose up as he threw back the lid. Within, he found candles and clean clothes—pants and a woollen tunic, which was embroidered with the Damadar sword and ice badge.

Just as Val finished dressing, a grate in the door slid open. A man peered in. "Step back from the door." The grate slammed shut. The key rattled.

A strongly built young man, cheeks flushed from cold, stomped inside. Given his Damask tunic and sword hilt of patterned silver, he was not a guardsman. He took a stance at the door as a woman swept in haughtily, her familiar auburn hair showering down her back. Her long woollen gown dragged over the rug.

Val edged up a brow. Of course. What had Heath said about games?

"I did wonder at Heath's laugh when I told him of the servant girl. Myranthe, is it?" About time she showed up. He, too, had a game to plot. "And which brother is this?" He gestured at the man. "Apparently, there are lots of you."

Myranthe fondly rested a hand on the young man's arm. "My brother Griffin."

What had he heard about the youngest Damadar? A decent swordsman. Humourless. Single-minded. Soldiers in Dal-Kanu sniggered that Griffin rarely let drink pass his lips and refused to succumb to a lover's charms in case fleshly pleasures diminished his skill.

"So. Do I call you Myranthe or Evelyn? Why the pretence?"

"I thought you enjoyed our game." Myranthe dug teeth into her lip, a gesture that clearly didn't just belong to her servant-girl guise. "An impromptu one, I admit."

"Oh?"

"I intended to send a servant with wine to put you to sleep so I could take a little of your Caelan blood for a spell. In the end, I brought the wine myself—once I'd manipulated a certain sibling into surrendering the key." She shrugged. "Curiosity, I suppose. Heath did warn me not to touch you. A lord of Telor he thinks he should chain to a rock."

In the better light, Val recognised she was at least thirty. Her face, though not pretty, was striking, dominated by those large, deceptively soft eyes, a full mouth, and a lush tangle of hair.

"The wine did bring sleep, thank you," he said stiffly, recalling the cut on his arm. He made no mention of the bath. "As to the rest: Heath says he's protecting me—from you."

She laughed aloud. "That's funny. When all he wants to do is kill you in a fire hall."

"You didn't hear, then. Heath says if I beg, he'll spare me."

Myranthe stilled, surprised.

"Heath never spares anyone," Griffin said.

"Griffin speaks the truth. For an intelligent man, my brother is surprisingly violent." Myranthe moved her eyes over Val slowly. "Well, well. His regard does make you singular. I suppose he chained you up so he could rescue you once you fell into despair."

"It's a tested method of breaking a man, Myranthe," Griffin instructed seriously. "Darkness. Solitude." He dragged gloved fingers through hair the same dark brown as his brother's.

There, the similarity ended. Heath had a subtle mouth and lazy eyes masking a wicked wit. This boy's open face hinted at frankness. Smooth-skinned, Griffin cropped his hair well above shoulders not quite as heavily muscled as Heath's. Still, he rocked on his toes with a swordsman's balance, as restless as a stirred snake. While Heath might wait out an enemy and study him— mock him—Griffin would rush in headfirst.

"Heath had no right to take hold of you." Myranthe addressed Val. "My devious brother took advantage of my"—she winced— "distraction. Velleran has now put you in my care."

"I doubt you rescued me from pity," Val said. "What do you— what does Velleran want of me?"

"What? No thank-you for freeing you from that hole?" Her eyes glittered with amusement.

Griffin rose to her defence. "She sent word to Velleran. Told him Heath was keeping you in a gruesome prison for no apparent reason."

*Sent word?* Either the Icelands heir wasn't here or—worse—he wasn't in the Twin Cities.

"Quite a storm of words came back," Myranthe said. "Velleran ordered Heath to surrender you. Heath is furious. This first round in the game to me."

Val swept an arm at the walls. "In this game, I'm still a prisoner. Just with a new gaoler."

Myranthe hesitated.

"Yes," Griffin said firmly. "Be glad about it."

The young man would not permit anyone to criticise her. Val wondered if she deserved such loyalty.

"Something funny?" Griffin shot at him.

"You remind me of someone."

He reddened, as if suspecting Val was mocking him. Well, with Heath for a brother…

"Griffin." Myranthe touched his arm. "I wish to talk alone with my guest. But make sure he's, hmm… secure first."

Griffin stepped in with a strap. Val reluctantly held out his wrists. Of course it couldn't be that easy. Myranthe wouldn't risk staying alone with an unbound man. No, to escape, he would have to be clever, to manipulate her as he suspected she intended to manipulate him.

"It's not quite a prison," Myranthe said when her brother took up guard outside.

"More games?" Val gestured in irritation. "A barred door. Shutters on the windows"—he nudged one open with a shoulder—"hiding, just as I thought, iron bars. No going that way."

Brow pressed to the bars, he snatched breaths to fight down his frustration. He needed to be out there, where Kaell was, somewhere. Alone maybe. Confused. Angry?

*Get Kaell's sword. Escape. Find a chink in the bonds between the Damadar siblings. If one even exists. Deceive.* Except subterfuge and artifice were not the usual way his mind worked. He was too straightforward. Too obvious. Scarcely able to control his anger, let alone use it strategically.

Myranthe joined him at the window. "Not 'this way'? Where would you go anyway?"

Snowcapped peaks blistered in ridges to the horizon above forested mountains and sinking valleys rutted with rivers. Only a remote castle's skeletal towers blotched a clear sky too brilliant to look at. The air smelled crisp and sharp with pine.

"Nowhere, it seems. How far up are we?"

"This is the highest tower. You misunderstood my question. Where would you go anyway, Val Arques Caelan?"

He smiled grimly. "You use that name to remind me that beyond these walls, the Lord of Vraymorg is dead. That I have nothing left."

"I wouldn't say that." She dragged another long look over him. An assessing look, but one that also held a trace of carnal awareness.

*Could I use that? What sort of man might attract a woman like this, a sorceress? A man who challenged her, perhaps.* "What do you intend to do with me?"

"Nothing. Today, at least. That's all the time we have, really, isn't it? Only today."

"And tomorrow?"

"Nothing."

"And after that?"

"Velleran has plans for you. You won't like them, but there's nothing you can do."

He thrust away the menace in her words. That only meant he had to be clever, sooner.

Still, Myranthe's gaze lingered. Unexpectedly, she said, "Griffin will bring you a knife. Take off that beard. It doesn't please me."

"I'm to please you?" *Time to rebel.* If he submitted, she would lose interest in him, both as an opponent and as... something else. "The beard stays."

"Do you know how childish you sound?" She was studying him

intently but dispassionately. "Perhaps you're not what they say you are." When he did not answer, she shrugged. "Take the beard off yourself. Or someone else will."

*Someone else can try.* He nearly said it. But he needed words that pierced like spears, not petty ripostes about beards. "And here you are, the mighty sorceress, arguing with a prisoner about a beard. But then perhaps you're not what they say, either."

Myranthe unfolded a slow smile. "That's better. Heath did warn me you're both irritable and stubborn. But…" She brushed the back of her hand over the bars. Such a small gesture, but he was certain she wanted him to know she was imagining touching him.

"But?"

"There's really no point to rebellion, is there? For I am exactly what they say I am, Val Arques Caelan. And here, in this chamber, you are less than what they say you are."

"There is to me. A point, I mean. And if you're implying that here in this chamber, I am what *you* say I am, then do your worst. Break me down if you can. But I won't submit to anything, not even removing the beard on my chin."

Her eyes flared as though she saw him properly for the first time. She nodded. "So you would turn even this into a game? If you seek to play, be warned, Val Arques Caelan. Make sure you first understand the rules."

# DANNON

"I never told you to deliver a message." Dannon shoved his hands to his hips. The air in his hut was thick, the walls close. "You lied. Why, Kate? And where did you go?"

Kate swung her boot repeatedly into a table leg. "Into the woods. I needed to think," she said sullenly. "I didn't realise I was a prisoner."

"To the woods near the fortress of Vraymorg?" Dannon could not keep the anger out of his voice. Her lies were transparent. She must think him a fool. "Is that what you mean?"

She glanced up sharply. "Why would you think that?"

"Because you knew him. Vraymorg. How?" Dannon had only ever thought of the former lord of Vraymorg as an opponent to defeat. Never someone who loved or was loved. Yet, he drew not only Kate's anger but her grief.

"This has nothing to do with him." She kicked the table again.

Dannon huffed out a breath. "It's dangerous for you to be alone near the fortress," he said irritably. "The new Mountains lord has doubled the patrols." And doubled the price on Dannon's head. "Felix Hillborn has made it his mission to destroy us."

"Probably because you hold his brother," Kate muttered. The thud of her boot against the table leg picked up again. She slid him a sideways glance. "You spend ages in that storeroom with Aalart. What do you do there?"

"Talk." He drove a palm through the air. "I want him to think of me as a friend."

The thumping stopped. Kate stared at him, a slight quiver to her lips. "So you use friendship to manipulate others?" Her hands fell lifelessly to her side. Voice hoarse, tight, she said, "Is that how you are with me too?"

Dannon's heart clenched in anger. "I have always been true with you. Even when you lie to me. Lie and lie and lie."

"So says the slaver and killer. The wolf's-head with a price on his head."

"Nothing between us has been false. At least on my part."

Kate's gaze hung on his face. Beneath the defiant, too-bright glitter, there was something vulnerable in her eyes. She dragged her hands to her face. "I want to believe you," she whispered. "I should like a friend. Just one friend, at least."

*Friend.* Could he settle for that? Friendship was deceptively simple. It was a balm, welcome and warm, but it possessed layers. Some ached like a wound. Some could not be put into words, only accepted.

His hip jolted the table as he sat down abruptly. He gripped the wooden edge to stop it rocking. "What happened out there? Patrick says the prisoner was shackled. No threat. How did he get hold of your knife?"

"I was careless and got too close," Kate said. "It won't happen again."

"Or did you let him take it? Because you knew him. Maybe someone from your past?"

She smiled coldly. "You're still fishing, Dannon. Just ask what you want to know. Of course I'll probably lie to you. Given how I lie and lie and lie."

"Very well. Who are you?"

"Kate."

Dannon sighed. "See? You force me to dance around you. I wish you could trust me."

She turned away. Muscles strained beneath her tunic as if her whole body tensed.

*Let me be that one friend.* Dannon nearly said it. *If you're Quisnaf, let me protect you. I have reason enough to protect a Quisnaf woman.*

"Stay here tonight," he said. "You'll be safe—from me."

"Safe to fall into wondrous dreams?"

Except dreams weren't safe. No, not at all. Not when men clad in outdated armour stalked him. Dead warriors. Calling him to them.

⁓

Sometime later, a banging on the door roused him from slumber. Dannon was up at once, sword in his hand, crossing the room to answer the summons. He flung the door back, allowing a burst of chill night air inside.

Robert stood on the porch, stamping his feet against the cold. He eyed Dannon's blade. "Forget the sword. Arm yourself instead with your wits."

"What's happened?" Dannon hammered.

"He's here, demanding your presence. You're summoned to the meeting hall."

"Who?"

Robert was already turning away, shoulders hunched beneath his cloak. "Archanin."

Alarm roiled in Dannon's gut. He'd known the reckoning was coming. In a way, he was glad it had finally arrived. Anticipation of pain was far worse than staring down the threat. "I'll be a moment."

"Make it a quick one."

Dannon retreated inside. He shut the door at his back, his

breaths sharp. Archanin would punish him for breaking his promise to deliver Philip. So be it. He deserved it.

He considered the young woman asleep on the bed. A shudder of dread ripped through him. The oh-so-dutiful mage would have already told Archanin all about Kate. A Quisnaf spy, he would call her. Archanin might find that far too interesting.

With quick steps, Dannon walked to the bed. He shook Kate roughly. "Get up."

"Wha-what?" She blinked, her eyes cloudy.

"You need to go," he said. "Archanin is here."

"Archanin." She sat up fast. "Here? No!"

In some part of his mind, he registered his instincts had been right—that she had reason to fear the ghoul god. "Get dressed." He shoved a cloak at her. "Go through the huts to the river. Swim. You can swim, can't you?"

Kate nodded as she scrambled off the bed. With fumbling fingers, she pulled on her boots. "When can I come back?"

"You can't, Kate. By now, the mage will have told Archanin all about you."

Kate snatched up her sword. At the door, she stopped and threw him a bewildered look. "You don't know, do you? About me?"

"All I know is what you've told me. Now go. Quickly."

She sank her teeth into her bottom lip. "Isn't it your duty to surrender me to him? Why aren't you?"

Dannon thought about the blood house in Dal-Kanu, the prisoners in squalid cells, and the man who had called him a monster. He thought about the yearning in Kate's eyes as she said, "I should like a friend. Just one friend, at least."

"I don't know," he said.


A RISING WIND whipped through eaves in the surrounding huts as Dannon crossed the hushed ward, his lamp held high. Clouds sped past two low bloated moons. A faint crackling carried from the firepit and its glowing embers.

Dannon stopped. He considered first the gate sentry then a hide strung over a rope in the tanner's yard. The line extended from a hook near the hall's exposed roof beams to a ground peg. After a quick glance about, he put his lamp's flame to the skin. He waited until it caught alight. Then he went to the hall.

Ghouls near a roaring fire in a hearth broke off their talk at his entrance. Their stares were cold. They always were.

A little apart, reclining in a cushioned chair, a jewelled goblet in his hand, was Archanin. A flustered slave hovered nearby with a jug. Raggamirron stood at the ghoul god's shoulder, his palm resting upon his sword pommel.

His face expressionless, Archanin turned his head to consider Dannon. He beckoned with a curled finger. His body tight, his heart a clenched fist, Dannon walked to him and dropped to one knee.

In the light from a lantern swinging from a ceiling hook, Archanin's blue eyes were almost translucent. A shiver stole down Dannon's back, even before his lord said in a deceptively calm voice, "You failed me."

Dannon kept his eyes lowered. He did not reply.

"I commanded you to bring me Philip. Instead, Philip is dead, and Felix Hillborn, no friend to me, rules the Mountains." Archanin's tone was even. But he squeezed the goblet with a white-knuckled hand.

"It was my fault and my fault alone," Dannon said. "I accept whatever punishment you choose."

"Even death?"

Dannon glanced up sharply. Alarm tore through him, tightening his lungs, enflaming his heart. "I—" he stammered. "Whatever is your will, my lord."

"My will," Archanin scoffed. He rose, moved behind Dannon, and grasped his head to bare his throat. A knife to a vein, he said,

"Did you kill him? Philip? Or… was it the girl?" He made a thin cut in Dannon's skin. "Your mage told me many interesting things about this young woman. You should have sent word about her at once."

"I did not wish to bother you with trivialities."

Archanin cut him again. Dannon clenched his teeth against the pain. "A great lord, an all-powerful god, has more to concern him than strays who end up in our ranks," he wheezed.

"Great lord. All-powerful god. Do you think to flatter me, Dannon?"

"I think only to save my life." Let Archanin believe him to be afraid and despise him.

Archanin drew back the blade. He rested his hand on Dannon's hair. "Give me the girl, and you may yet appease my displeasure. I'm told she is under your protection, yours to surrender. A Quisnaf spy, your mage believes. It troubles me that a spy is here, now."

"She's gone. Fled. I don't know where."

"Is that so?" Archanin returned to his seat. He closed his fingers about the knife, his narrowed eyes dwelling upon the man kneeling before him. "If you're lying, I'll slowly, agonisingly bleed you to death on the rack."

Cold sweat ran down Dannon's back. He glanced at Raggamirron, the voice of reason among Archanin's nobles. But rather than counsel his lord to be merciful, the ghoul showed only curiosity.

*Where are the sounds of alarm? The tanner's line should be ablaze by now.* Unless the fire went out before the flames reached the roof. The gods, after all, were malicious.

"Search his hut and then the village for this girl." Archanin snapped his fingers at a group of ghouls. He rose to kick Dannon hard so that he sprawled on the floor. "Whip him. Twenty lashes for failing to bring me Philip. Then another twenty for letting this girl flee."

"Fire!" The shout at last came from outside. "Fire!"

The hall erupted to chaos. Ghouls snatched at weapons, their voices a discordant swell as they ran for the doors. Somewhere above, timber creaked. Smoke filled the rafters.

"My lord, the roof's alight." Raggamirron pushed forward. "You must leave."

Archanin's cool gaze shifted again to Dannon. "A fortunate interruption. For you. But if you've deceived me in any way, I will have your blood." Unhurried, he swept up his cloak and strode to the door.

Dannon pushed to his feet. Smoke filled the hall. It was in his throat, its stink in his nostrils. Coughing, spluttering, he groped his way outside.

Villagers emerged from huts, many still in night shifts or hastily stuffing shirts into trousers.

"Get some water on those flames!" Dannon shouted. "Form a line from the river. Grab buckets, fill them, and pass them along."

But even as he took control, Dannon knew he wanted the hall to burn. Without proper accommodation for his entourage, Archanin would not linger.

A hall could be rebuilt. Its destruction meant nothing to him. Even the forty lashes that would soon scar his back meant nothing.

He was beginning to suspect what did.

# VAL ARQUES

The bar rose. Heath burst in. Hair damp, the scent of soap trailing behind him, he wore a kersey cloak over linen shirt and pants. Every bit the arrogant lord, with that same smug grin.

"Disappointing." He wagged his finger at Val. "You've had days to plot how you might leap at me from behind the door, overpower me, and run. Nothing like a good chase to stir up an appetite for dinner."

Slowly Val turned from the window and the mind-emptying landscape. The sky bled at dawn, the bleached sun faded to twilight then became violet night full of trilling bugs. Always the same pattern, always the same blotted sea of green and white that dulled his senses as much as that cavern.

Could a man drown in boredom? Maybe he should ask Heath?

"Did Myranthe send you to shave me?"

Heath tilted his head, amused. "Do you know, Val, I expected your greeting to be, 'You again, snake'? Not 'Did Myranthe send you to shave me?' Why? Do you want me to shave you?"

Val fingered his beard. "Your sister wants this off."

Heath tapped the knife at his belt. "What if my hand trembled? You unsettle me so. Though Myranthe is right—for once. You're too young to have a forest growing on your chin. Rarely see a beard on a man here unless he's a father's father."

*Young? Really?* Val raised an eyebrow.

Heath chuckled. "Talking of young, I heard you met Griffin. Pup has all the personality of a stone, don't you think?"

"Unlike you, he no doubt has other qualities. What do you want?"

"That's better. 'What do you want, fool?' was my next guess for your first words." Heath smoothed a fold in his tunic. "A little conversation. No one is as rude to me as you."

"I can't imagine why not."

"Delightful."

Val fingered the beard again. It itched, but even if it shrouded him from head to toe, he would still refuse to take it off. *Keep Myranthe's interest. Force a chink. Escape and find Kaell.* "I'm only interested in conversation about what Velleran intends to do with me. Or how you've convinced your father to ransom me."

Heath slumped into a chair. "How's the new prison?" He waved a hand. "Very nice, from what I can see. Tower cell and all. Who are you again? Must be someone important."

*Important? Not at all. A forgotten man.* "It's superior to the last," Val said carefully. "And I like having clothes. Why? Have you come to offer to take me back to the old one?"

Heath stroked stubble on his chin. "You miss it? I always thought darkness better suited to your character than all this clear white light."

"I miss the quiet," Val said. "It was quiet here, too, until a moment ago."

Heath leaned back with a contented sigh. "I can be quiet. Shall we just sit here silently and contemplate the meaning of love and life while it grows dark? Or perhaps discuss why two months of solitude below doesn't seem to have rattled you one bit."

Val laughed coldly. "Two months? Rainer Caelan imprisoned me for nearly two decades."

"Oh?" Heath arched a brow. "Why?"

"What's it to you? Idle curiosity?"

"My curiosity is never idle."

"Either tell me something useful about what's going on beyond these walls, or go away."

"What? You mean outside? Griffin's lurking somewhere. Myranthe, the little sneak getting in Velleran's ear, set him on me. I don't mean with the sword—I fancy my chances against Griffin with swords. No, he wants to throw words at me about not abducting stray lords and obeying Velleran until I'm so bored, I'll agree to anything."

"Delightful." Val used Heath's word sarcastically. "It's beyond me why no one cuts you down with steel the moment you start blithering."

Heath's grin reappeared. "There's that tingle again. I so hope you jab and weave with the sword the way you do with words."

"You should see my feint."

"Yes." Heath's searching look narrowed to Val's eyes. "There's that. I've asked myself: why hasn't Val Arques Caelan, once an Isles lordling, Serravan bladesman, taught all manner of nastiness, plotted his escape? Why is that, Val?"

"Perhaps I'm not quite as clever as you."

"You're certainly not as nasty. Or sarcastic. Quite a temper, though. How you ranted and raved when you woke in that cavern. Predictable, given you didn't like the shackles. Healthy, even. It's when you grew quiet, I wondered what you were up to. What dastardly deeds were you plotting as you stared out that window?"

"I was thinking about using your vigorous tongue as a rope."

"More tingles."

"You have a serious problem. Get your physician to fix you by lopping off your head."

"The tingles, the tingles." Heath lurched from the chair. "I just came to make sure you're safe. You are but a babe in arms when it comes to dealing with Myranthe."

"She seems much nicer than you."

"She's as sweet as limes." Heath frowned as he considered Val. "If you're going to take on Myranthe, Val, here's a tip, since you're not in her devious league."

"And you are?"

"Only through years of observation. Listen up. If she gets a whiff that you want something, she'll use it against you. So don't demand to see my father or ask what's happening in Dal-Kanu or the Isles."

"How can that hurt me?"

"You're so sweet. Let me be clearer. Nothing Myranthe does is by chance. You're in this tower because that's where she wants you. Next comes the game. She'll let you think you chose it and even made up the rules, but it's a wicked trick. Whatever game you think you're playing, that won't be it."

Val arched a brow. As if he could believe anything this man told him.

Heath sighed. "That's the best I can do, Val. I did try to keep you out of her paws, but she appealed to a higher power called Velleran. Now I can do nothing but leave you to my saucy sister."

He strode to the door and knocked on the wood. "But should you find you're losing the game, just send word, and I'll come and save you."

"Ha," Val said.

# KAELL

Sweat glued Kaell's tunic to his skin. Beads of it slid down his arms, his back, uncomfortable on slick thighs. At every cut of steel through air, every swipe with his weaving sword, his tearing muscles flamed. At every lunge, his aching limbs grew heavier and heavier.

In the two days since he had fled the Varee, this had become his routine. One shadow fight after another. Pain, he willingly embraced. The burning in his neck and shoulders, his wobbly legs were all a challenge. Another opponent to defeat.

White clover that defied early frosts brushed Kaell's ankles. Irritably, he waved away a bee humming near his ear, watching it meander off towards a log hut set in rambling forest. Set on the edge of a patch of grass wild with feathery dandelions and bright with autumn light, Alyssa's home was small but tightly built to withstand winter's vicious winds. Washing hung from a line strung across a small porch, though he wondered how it ever dried beneath the trees.

Alyssa appeared on the porch, wiping her floured hands on an apron. "Enough. You've been at it since dawn. And all day yesterday from the moment you arrived."

"It's never enough."

"Come and eat before Will gets home. Rest a bit. It'll be dusk soon."

Kaell swished air, the sword's doleful note satisfying. He lowered his arm. "For a bit."

Hens with clipped wings clucked indignantly as he followed Alyssa into the hut. Filtered light streamed into a small room furnished with a table and two chairs. Straw covered the planked floor. Cold ashes filled the fireplace. From a cot in the nearby bedchamber, Alyssa's baby girl giggled contentedly.

Kaell tugged off his damp gloves and slouched in a chair, his sword at his feet. Alyssa plonked a bowl of pottage on the table. When he reached for a wineskin, she slapped his hand away.

"No more, Kaell. I've had enough of this nonsense."

"There's too much in my head, Alyssa. I can't stand to think."

"You can't stand it? I can't stand seeing you hurt yourself like this."

Kaell grasped her hands. "It's all right. It's not the brew. Just wine."

"It's not all right. You need to pull yourself together, Kaell."

"I've killed two men. I didn't mean to, but it happened. I broke my oath."

Alyssa sighed. "Things change, Kaell. Vraymorg is dead. You're no longer a bonded warrior. Your oath means nothing."

"You're wrong."

"Am I? Ah, what's the point. I can't talk to you when you're like this. I'll get the cows in. If you're drunk when I return, you'll sleep with the chickens tonight." She stormed out.

Kaell slumped over the table, head on his knuckles. When he pictured the Isles man lying dead beside the cart, the man's face became Philip's. Kaell groaned. *What have I done?*

A floorboard creaked. Kaell glanced up. Every part of him stiffened. Except his heart. It smashed against his ribs.

The Isles man from the tavern stood in the doorway. He held a sword.

"You're dead." Kaell shakily rose then sat down hard.

"It depends on how you look at things." The man kicked Kaell's blade away. "Get up and walk outside."

"Why? Revenge, is it? You only have yourself to blame for the Varee taking you captive."

"Again, that's a matter of perspective. I thought I had a Quisnaf blood sniffer to blame." Grim faced, hard-eyed, the man waved his blade. "Up."

"I'll finish my meal first." Unhurried, Kaell spooned pottage into his mouth. He tried to rein in his spinning thoughts. How was it possible this man was here, alive?

The stranger nicked his arm with steel. "Or I knock you out and carry you."

Kaell put down the spoon. He glimpsed a flash of skirts at the door.

"Alyssa won't be pleased if we break things. I bring her enough trouble as it is."

The man shrugged. "Then outside."

"Outside," Kaell drawled the word, careful not to look at the woman creeping up behind the stranger, a black pot in in her hand. "Then what? What do you want with me?"

At her footstep, the man started to turn. Alyssa swung the pot at his head.

The stranger sank to the ground, his eyes shut. Alyssa dropped the pot. She shook. "Did I kill him? Please, no. I didn't know what to do."

Kaell seized her shoulders. "You did the right thing. He came for me. The gods only know why." Completely bewildered, he shook his head.

"Did you do something to him?"

"Why must I have done something?" Resentment flared up. How quick she was to judge. She didn't know what it was like to wake in a strange body, forsaken by the man he considered a father.

Kaell released her. He remembered how Alyssa recoiled when he had first turned up at her door. Or rather slunk up like a stray dog. Maimed. Sobbing a ridiculous story.

She hadn't believed him—not even when he told her tales of their childhood, of climbing into trees in the orchard to pelt apples at the blacksmith's sons, of setting up their "castle" in the ruined hunting lodge at the bottom of the gorge. It was only when his cheeks flushed as he spoke about a stolen kiss that she had touched her lips and stared in shock.

Alyssa glanced at the man. "Who is he?"

"A man I watched die. Khir help me, how is he here?"

"Because he didn't die. You were drunk. He wasn't as badly hurt as you thought."

Kaell grabbed the stranger's blade. His mind whirred, first with alarm—this man had tracked him here—then with relief. He hadn't killed again, intentionally or not.

"I really thought he was dead. Whoever he is."

"He's wellborn. Look at his clothes and boots. Soft leather." She fingered the man's cloak. "Kersey wool. What I'd do for a cloak like that for Will."

"Keep it then," Kaell said gruffly.

"I'm no thief," Alyssa said.

"Won't matter to him."

"No." Alyssa stamped her foot, just like she did whenever he'd tramped mud across her scrubbed hall at Vraymorg. At that unexpected memory, his breast ached. If only he could go back.

"We're not going to kill him, Kaell. That's not who I am. It's not who you are either."

Kaell threw up his arms. "I didn't say we should kill him. But we have to do something with him. He called me Kaell. And he knows about you. I must keep you safe."

"We'll tie him up and make him swear to leave us alone. Will has rope." She spun away.

He listened to her rummaging about. *What to do... What to*

*do…* This man wouldn't just go away because Alyssa poked him with her crochet needle.

When she returned with cord, Kaell bound the stranger to a chair. He grabbed a fistful of dark hair.

The man moaned.

"Why aren't you dead?"

The stranger said nothing. But Kaell was almost sure he smirked.

"I've brought you trouble, Alyssa," he muttered. "I'll fix this." Kaell glanced at the wineskin, wishing it held the mage's brew. He badly wanted that emptiness where not even guilt intruded. *Dannon understands. Dannon knows about the need to forget.*

Alyssa caught his arm. "No more drink."

Kaell pulled free. "Who are you? My mother?"

The stranger laughed.

Kaell pressed his palms into the chair's back. "I wouldn't laugh if I were you."

The man smiled but did not share the joke.

Alyssa filled a cup from a clay jug and put it to the stranger's lips. "I'm sorry I hit you so hard."

Kaell spluttered his annoyance. From her deferring tone, he half expected her to add, "My lord." *My lord, so sorry we tied you up. I know it's a bit inconvenient—my lord.*

He thrust a knife to the man's throat. "Who are you? What do you want?"

"I intend to tell you. But now is not the time." The stranger twisted his hands.

"How do you know my name?"

The baby began to cry. Alyssa turned for the second room. "It's all right," she said when Kaell started after her.

At a noise, he whipped around in time to see the stranger come off the chair fast, his hands free. He shouldered into Kaell, knocking him aside, and bolted for the door.

Kaell steadied, scooped up his sword, then rushed outside after the man.

"Kaell," the stranger goaded in a singsong voice from the trees. "Come and play, Kaell."

He whipped about. The forest sat hushed and still. Gripping his sword, Kaell shouted, "What do you want from me?"

"Come find me, and I'll tell you. You're warm. Warmer. No, cold."

Kaell pushed through shrubs, sword levelled. "Where are you? Show yourself."

Hearing a rustle, he pounced on stunted bushes. Leaves exploded into the gathering twilight as his sword cut and carved.

"Thank The Three you saved us from those dangerous bushes," the stranger mocked.

Kaell lunged at undergrowth. No one. He howled his frustration.

"Tricky that echo when wine soaks your wits."

At the faintest sound behind, cloth brushing waving grass, Kaell plunged into the trees. He hacked at saplings then drew up hard. *Think. Sniff him out. Listen. Use those ghoul senses.*

A blow swatted him to his hands and knees. Wheezing, he groped for his dropped blade. A shadow fell over him. The man loomed above, holding a long, thick bough.

"That's for being a drunken idiot," he said. "And this is for forcing me to come after you again."

He crashed wood down onto Kaell's skull.

The stranger hoisted him over his shoulder and carried him through the trees. Head throbbing, every step jolting his bruised body, Kaell couldn't find the strength to resist. He closed his eyes against the dizzying sweep of ground below.

At last, the stranger slung Kaell down beside a cart hitched to two horses.

"You don't need a hand, do you, dread lord?" someone said.

Half in shadow, a man leaned against the cart. "No? Good. I'm dreaming of a lovely lass called Diana."

The Isles man laughed. "Name like that, she'd be Quisnaf."

"Well, she's gone now. Right at the good part. Unless that's Diana with you? But if this is a dream, why are you here? Bad enough you're around so much when I'm awake."

"You could always leave," the stranger replied cheerfully.

"Where would I go?" The second man straightened. The last light fell on his face.

Kaell's breath ripped out. *No, no, no. Impossible. What happened here? First one dead man, now another.*

"Nicky, best say hello." Kaell's captor waved a hand. "Get all the nasty shocks out of the way. Well, some of them."

Nicky bowed elaborately. "Hello, lackwit. Why anyone ever let you near a sword, I don't know. Didn't you learn the first rule is never drop the stupid thing?"

Kaell could only stare. The last time he had seen Nicky was in those Varee caverns in the Waste Mountains, his chest punctured by a blade.

"I saw ghouls kill you," he spluttered. "How can you be alive? Who are you both? What do you want with me?"

"I want an apology," Nicky said. "Sorry, Nicky, for getting you killed."

"You were—dead then?"

Nicky wagged a finger. "Only partly dead, given who my lord is. So you can say, 'Sorry, Nicky, for getting you partly killed. Sorry, Nicky, that revolting ghouls drank your blood.' I told you not to surrender your sword."

Kaell could not take in such madness. He shot a look at the forest. He needed to run, to get far from two dead men and too much he couldn't understand.

"No, you don't." The Isles man thrust a boot to his chest. "Behave. We're not here to hurt you." He grabbed Kaell's wrists and tied them with vine.

Cursing, Kaell wrenched at the bonds then yelped, his skin aflame. Witch weed. But that meant—

The Isles man nodded. "I know exactly what you are and why witch weed hurts you."

*Who is this man?* Kaell shuddered, remembering the blood sniffer's shock and her awed whisper.

His captor stretched. "I broke my back carrying him. Help me get him in the cart."

"You're too delicate, dread lord. Just you rest. I'll do the heavy work." With a put-on grunt, Nicky took Kaell's arms. "Don't you have other slaves? Maybe you worked them to death."

Kaell broke into a frenzied writhing as the Isles man grabbed his legs. They must not get him into that cart. But with every jerk, twist, and kick, the witch weed burned.

The two men threw him into the cart and shackled his wrists to a length of chain fastened to its headboard. Kaell rose to his knees, tugging uselessly at thick iron.

The Isles man passed him a skin. "Water?"

"I want—"

"Wine? No."

Kaell groaned. "Kill me now."

"Let me," Nicky said. "Please, my lord."

"I don't understand what you want," Kaell seethed. "I don't know you. Why abduct me?"

The man did not answer. He climbed onto the driver's bench beside Nicky.

"Just lie back, sweetness." Nicky jigged the reins. "We've a bit of a journey ahead. I'll find a song just for you. About a stupid bladesman who dropped his sword."

"Someone cut off my ears," Kaell muttered.

Nicky chuckled. "I'd enjoy that far too much." He peered up at the sky. Faint stars glimmered through murmuring trees. "First moon will be up soon," he said to his companion. "Remember that old Isles song, Roaran? Women on the Rock sang it when we foolish men strapped on swords, ready to follow our betters to glory and death."

*Roaran.* Kaell stored the name. A pretentious name. The name of a dead king. Otherwise, it meant nothing to him.

He punched the cart's side. None of it made sense. He had to get free of them.

"Early moon and men look high," Roaran recited. "Pray it's not their time to die. But unquiet seas bring death and tears, and bladesmen answer, 'We'll show no fear.'"

"Oh, for the Isles, we'll shed our fear," Nicky broke into song, his voice carrying through soughing branches. "We'll dance with death and protect what's dear."

He sang as they followed a weed-tangled road winding higher into cloud-rimmed peaks. The splattered dregs of twilight seeped away. The moons burned, their glint eerily silvering shadows. Worn out by his struggle and disquiet, Kaell plunged into a dreamless sleep.

# VAL ARQUES

The dusk bird—that was what he called it. As twilight's purple veined the flotsam of day, as shadows lunged at valleys between endless, pallid mountains, the bird hopped along his sill to peck at mortar around the bars. Its brilliant blue fascinated him, its careening dance mesmerising.

His world had become very small. The sky. The snow. The door. A bright-blue bird, so tiny it would not fill his palm.

One morning, Val fingered the crumbling stonework the bird had broken up. After jiggling a bar loose, he squeezed his shoulders through the gap to peer around the tower.

The Twin Cities, a maze of stone buildings and paved streets, splayed into an embrace of mountains. A biting wind shook skeletal trees. An ice-blue river snaked below arched bridges and beyond the walls onto the flat wilderness.

Across a distance of several sword lengths, a second tower jutted into the hazy sky. A woman sat at its top window. Unruly white hair flowed about her stooped shoulders.

Val raised a hand, shouting, "Hello. Who are you?"

She only stared.

"I'm Val. Are you a prisoner too?"

Then in a voice waveringly thin, she said, "Are you my son?"

"Who are you?"

The woman turned away.

Wine arrived in a carafe, its fragrance of honey and melon the perfume of carefree Isles summers. *Thank you, Myranthe, but this game has played out already.*

If he drank it, he would surely lose himself in dreams as pleasant as the wine then wake to find another cut on his arm. He wondered exactly how much of his blood she needed.

Val filled a cup, swilled wine, then poured it through the bars. He set both cup and carafe on the table and lay upon the bed. *Setting the scene for a feint, Heath.*

He smiled at the thought. After days of solitude, he had begun to have conversations with the young Ice lord in his head. When he mulled over a plan to escape, he could hear Heath's gentle ridicule or amused encouragement. If he kicked the wall, Heath teased him about his bad temper. Even when he lost heart and curled on the bed, an imaginary Heath urged him to get up and outwit Myranthe.

The candle burned down then fizzed. Keys jangled. The bar rose. The door creaked. Footsteps trod towards the bed. A figure bent to listen to his deceptively slow breaths. Fingers grasped his wrist.

Val leapt up and shoved. Someone staggered back. Val swung his arm, felt it connect with muscle and bone then heard a thump. Stepping over a prone form, he rushed through the door—straight into guards. They grabbed his shoulders and marched him back inside.

A man rose off the floor. Torchlight from the stairwell spilled on leathery skin stretched over bony cheeks and straggly grey hair. "You didn't drink the wine," he scolded. From his tone, Val expected him to add, *Naughty boy.*

The man scooped up a knife. His foot crunched glass. "You smashed my vial. A pity."

Unhurried, he lit a new candle and held it to Val's face. His flat glare was like a snake sizing up a meal. "My lady only wanted a little blood. Though it seems you make a habit of disobedience. I believe she told you to shave off that hair."

"I've been busy," Val said.

"You've been recalcitrant." A colourless voice from a grey man. "I'll do my lady a favour. She likes to be obeyed. Hold him."

The grinning guards tightened their grips.

Val struggled—Heath would be disappointed if he wasn't disobedient—until a guard squeezed an arm around his throat. Forced to stillness, Val clenched his teeth as the grey man hacked at his beard.

"Butcher," he cursed at a careless nick.

The guards laughed.

The man snatched up the wine cup to catch blood from the convenient cut. He wiped a dirty sleeve over the wound and tapped Val's shaven cheek. "Drink the wine next time, boy."

Swearing, Val bucked. The guard choked his windpipe.

"I'd have bled you from the arm, nice and easy, as you slept. Now you'll have to clamp hard on that." He gestured. "Best not bleed out now, boy. My lady would be displeased."

He turned for the door. Smirking guards let Val go and backed out. As the lock shifted and the bar thumped down, Val pressed fingers to his neck.

*So much for escape, boy.* Though the attempt was about pride. About holding onto some sense of who he was. Pretending he wasn't helpless.

Until he learnt his way through the caverns, until he had Kaell's sword, until he had thick clothes to survive the cold, escape was probably useless.

# KAELL

Throbbing pain in his skull woke him. His mouth tasted stale. Moaning, Kaell sat up.

The cart still jolted along a dirt track, but now a florid tapestry of cinnabar and peach scorched the horizon. The last shards of night disappeared into dawn's soft sounds and scents.

"Sleeping sweetness is back with us." Nicky glanced over his shoulder. "With daylight, the road will get busy. Best keep him quiet. Here, take the reins."

He climbed back, cloth in his hand. Kaell recoiled. Nicky grabbed his jaw, stuffed a gag in his mouth, and tied it tight. At this further indignity, Kaell muffled a curse. *He'll pay,* he swore to himself. *Both of them will pay.*

As sunlight drowned the dawn, they reached lands protected by the mighty fortress of Vraymorg. The road bustled with merchants' covered wagons, and farmers pushing barrows or herding geese.

Armed men rode by, badges on shoulders. Kaell didn't recognise their heraldry. The victorious Isles king had raised too many new lords to greatness. Others fell low. Pitiful ragged beggars with blackened feet, haggard soldiers with torn uniforms, or dull-eyed peasants shuffled aside to let the cart through.

"How did Telor come to this?" Roaran's voice drummed with anger. "This was once my land. My people. This is why I must do what others will not, what they will think ruthless, repellent even."

Who dared say such words? And what if the ruthless act involved him? Kaell shivered. He drew knees to his belly, his skin damp and hot.

A group of armed riders approached. Their captain demanded to know about Kaell.

"Varee thief." Nicky flashed an easy smile. "Ganna lose her hand."

"Thought there was a truce with the Varee. Which lord deals out punishment?"

"The new Lord of Vraymorg wants this one. Felix Hillborn. It's personal."

The men rode on.

"No one cares anymore," Roaran said. "This land has lost its way."

Nicky only shrugged and picked up his song. "Oh, for the Isles, we'll shed our fear."

Kaell moaned through the gag. That dizzying ache in his head did not let up.

"Dread lord." Nicky nudged his companion. "Something up with your dread creature."

Roaran looked back. "Pull up," he said sharply. When the cart rolled to a stop, he clambered to Kaell and touched his brow, frowning.

"Roaran, you look very serious."

Roaran rested his hand in Kaell's hair. "That cursed Varee brew. I should have realised." He peered about. "We're near Old Forge. Nicky, run for Juliette. Bring her at once."

Nicky dropped the reins. "Bad then?"

"Juliette will know what to do. Meet me at the dead city."

The other man jumped down and straightened his sword belt. "Sure you can handle dread creature by yourself and all?"

Roaran offered him a look of mock hurt. "I am your dread lord."

"So you are. Very well, I'm for the lovely wood witch." He sighed heavily. "I'll smile charmingly at her, but she'll look right through me, as always. That lass, for all her skill, has no taste. Juliette only has eyes for you. Poor girl."

He took off into the trees, whistling the same Isles song.

# VAL ARQUES

Arms crossed, he held his eyes on the door, the centre of his world. Every distraction—food, servants with water for bathing, carafes of wine—came through that one threshold. More than once, he had considered ducking behind the door and clobbering whoever came through—Heath, with luck. What then? Run into guards again?

The grate slid. Griffin said, "Move into the centre of the room."

Val stubbornly stayed put.

Griffin walked in. Two guards followed. They threw Val against the wall, using their bodies to pin him when he struggled.

*Why bother?* Val imagined Heath's mocking words. *Because I'm stubborn*, he replied. *You said so. If I did as I'm told, no more tingles.*

Griffin hammered a fork-shaped iron band into the stone wall around Val's wrist. The guards stepped away. The ones who'd come the previous night had a vicious sense of humour at least. These hard-eyed Icemen were not amused.

Val tugged at the band fixing his wrist shoulder-high to the wall. "What is this?" he stormed.

"It's a trident." Griffin deftly tossed his hammer from hand to hand. "They're used in the fire games to catch a blade."

"If your sister wants my blood, tell her I have a thirst today."

Griffin's gaze was oddly sympathetic. "No wine. No blood. My sister wants words." He left, taking the guards with him.

Val watched the gaping door expectantly. *What are you waiting for?* it taunted. *I'm open. Run. Find Kaell. Explain.* He strained uselessly at the trident until his wrist bruised.

Myranthe took her time to appear. Brightly, she said, "Oh, there you are."

*Where else would I be? Exchanging nonsense or sword strokes with Heath in a torchlit hall perhaps? Rolling on a bed of fur with Judith. A pleasing image, that.*

"Is this necessary?" Val squeezed a fist. "I had no intention of hitting you with the chair or throwing you on the bed for a wild hour of passion."

She arched a brow. "Feeling feisty, are we?" Heath's mocking tone.

*Siblings indeed.* "A little riled up, yes. Griffin pinned me to a wall. After your minion visited last night."

"You were very naughty." Again, her tone was condescending and Heath-like. "I offered you the gift of sweet dreams. And you threw it—and my wine—away."

"Your wine smelled divine. Venivan? Tempting. Until I recalled I am apparently stubborn."

"So Heath says." She drew closer. "I'm pleased to see that unflattering growth gone. Though my minion made a mess. Hacked your neck too. Naughty Penn."

"Penn, is it? I call him the grey man."

"He is indeed grey now. Pen has served me since I was old enough to stir my first potion."

"Knew you in the womb, then? I hear wickedness is something we're born with."

"Hmm, you would trade words with me as you do with Heath? Amusing, but not the game I came for."

"So it's wild passion against the wall, then? Heath says I give him tingles. You too?"

Myranthe tapped fingertips on stone. Her eyes half closed as she studied his face. "Is that what women always want from you? I had no idea you thought you deserved to be so poorly used."

His skin heated. Val whipped his head aside. "You know nothing about me or what I think."

"Touched a wound, did I? You can't hide, Val Arques."

An uncomfortable feeling stirred. Women did want that from him. And he was willing to oblige them. *Why?*

"Maybe you think you're ruined already. You value yourself so little, it doesn't matter who enjoys your body." Still she watched him through low-lidded eyes, a voyeur to pain, savouring the way her barb went in and how it twisted around.

"You're wrong." He met her gaze, his chin tilted defiantly. Despite the belittling taunt, interest gleamed in her eyes. *Use it. If she wants games, make it a game of seduction.*

Myranthe smoothed her hair, only to drop her arm as if to hide a revealing gesture. "I came to talk. To offer a game we must play out fast before my brother Velleran returns and you become his concern and not mine."

"Why should I want to play any game of yours?" Val said gruffly. "What's in it for me?"

"I'll tell you what is going on beyond this room. In the Mountains. Or Dal-Kanu. Surely, you have questions. Think of one. The first that comes into your mind."

*Kaell. Where's Kaell?* "Why do you take my blood?"

"I'll answer at no cost. Caelan blood enhances magic."

"Cost?"

"Like anything else, information comes with a price."

"I have nothing to barter with."

"Not true." She drew nearer still, her perfume of sandalwood and violet tantalising, her lips slightly parted, her breath soft.

"The wall has certain advantages if you want to be quick. But if it's performance you're after, the bed is preferable."

Myranthe laughed coldly. "Your game is obvious, Val Arques. Choose another."

"Game?"

She wagged a finger in front of his face. "You caught my unguarded look in Heath's little hole and think you can use your obvious attractions to—what? Seduce me? Yes, I enjoyed touching you. I savoured the attraction for a moment then dismissed it. So do not make the mistake of thinking you can unsettle me."

"Maybe you unsettle me." He drew her into a rough embrace.

Their thighs pressed, her body warm against his, nipples erect through her flimsy gown. He was aware of a faint stirring in his groin, a longing to feel bare skin against bare skin that he noted with a jag of surprise then forced aside to ponder later. Hand on her hip to hold her against him, Val sought her lips.

Myranthe's mouth briefly softened beneath his. Then she pulled free. "A strong move in any game, Val Arques. I'll give you that. I even took pleasure in that kiss. But it won't win you anything. That game only hurts you. Let me show you how."

Her eyes emptied of all warmth. She stripped him with a dehumanising, indifferent gaze she might throw at a fine gown or gemstone for sale. "You're pretty to look at. Nice to touch. But offering your body wins you nothing but self-disgust. Now to matters not of the flesh. What do you want to know?"

Val shifted, again uncomfortable. He was accustomed to glares from men aware of his reputation with a sword and flirtatious glances from women. But her debasing stare exposed him in a manner a lord and bladesman never endured. It was an objective assessment of nothing beyond physical beauty, a slave on the block.

He thrust aside his unease. In these caverns, friendless, no longer a lord of Telor, seduction might be his *only* weapon. Even if it humiliated him. He forced an indifferent tone. "Again I say, what can I offer in return? You don't want my body, it seems. That's all I own in this dread place."

"I didn't say I don't want your body. But you're mistaken to think you own even that."

The Ice princess indeed. Ruthless. Unfeeling. Too clever. To match wits with Myranthe, he must measure every word, sift every gesture, seek out every hidden intention. "My obedience, then? I can't give you that. My blood?"

"Again, both I will take if I want. Really, Val Arques, you disappoint me. Surely you realise you have no power?"

"If I'm powerless, then what do you want?" She was right, curse her. He had nothing. Frustrated anger blazed beneath his skin. Unleashing a torrent of curses, Val tugged violently at the trident.

Myranthe nodded slowly. "All a feint, as Heath warned me. Not just the offer of your favours, but the controlled manner, the self-mocking humour too."

"To what end? What attack does my feint hide?" His shoulders slouched with resignation. This game had already passed him by, its rules known only to her. How could he hope to manipulate her when already outplayed?

"You're furious at your powerlessness—"

"I'm not powerless."

"You loathe any kind of shackle. When Griffin bound your hands a few nights ago, you endured it only because you had no choice. You don't like this, you certainly don't like me, and you're playing a long game with a clear goal—to escape. Maybe even take revenge."

"You're right." Val shrugged. "Of course you're right. What captive wouldn't do anything to escape. Except beg." This woman would despise a man who did that. "Except murder."

"You want me to think I'm safe alone with you? So there is no need for tridents. Now you take me for a fool. You'd make me your hostage."

"I would never take you for a fool. What do you want?" His voice frosted.

"What do I want?" Myranthe leaned forward. She brushed hair from his brow.

Val reluctantly tolerated it. They weren't lovers. Not friends.

She had no right to touch him—but she could do what she wanted with him. He was no fool, either. A sorceress answered to very few. Perhaps only the gods. Curse her. In this tower room, in her city, she was all-powerful, and he was defenceless.

"I want answers, Val Arques. To know things. Things I can make use of."

"Answers to what questions?" He glowered.

Myranthe smiled with genuine pleasure. "This is better. The thinly suppressed anger—this is honest, at last. So we can begin."

"The game? I don't know the rules."

"They're simple, Val Arques. It's like this. You know certain things I'd also like to know. So I'll barter question for question with you. Or answer for answer, if you like. An important question, one worth much to you or to me, for an important question. Something trivial for something small. Do you understand?"

"Ha. Then shall we play? But why this band at my wrist? We could sit at that table, you and I, and exchange answers."

"Is that a question? A wasted one, in my opinion."

"I suppose it is."

"So I will answer truthfully. I want you at a disadvantage, to feel trapped. You don't like constraints, do you?"

"No. And that answers your question. A wasted one, in my opinion."

Myranthe tapped a finger against her pursed lips. "You are right. Not the question I intended. It slipped out." She offered a more appreciative look. "Ask me something."

Val paused. The one question, the one burning in him, the one he was desperate to ask, he could not. *Is there word of Kaell?*

But Myranthe must never learn about Kaell. A bonded warrior had skills that could turn the fate of kingdoms, whatever his appearance. She could track down Kaell—use him for some game. "Aric Caelan. He's alive?"

"Yes."

Val waited. When she said nothing, he asked, "Is that it?"

"The game is new to you, so I will be generous. Aric is much recovered, though it took my considerable skills to keep him alive."

"Blood magic?"

Myranthe wagged a finger. "That's two questions."

"But I'm new at this."

"Oh, beloved deceiver. Thy tongue is dipped in honey, thy smile is warm, and thy words drip with gentle lies." Myranthe sighed dramatically.

"You quote the Damadar lord known as the Ice Rider."

"Very clever. You're clearly classically educated."

"Is that a question? Then yes. As son to an Isles lord, my tutors taught me not only history and languages but literature. Poetry. Aric's sister, Azenor. Is there word of her?"

"Three questions you owe me now. My last was a statement, not a question."

The toll of questions owed could hit one hundred for all he cared. He had to uncover where Kaell might be—without revealing the truth. Blanking his expression, he pressed, "Is there?"

Myranthe shrugged. "No word has reached us about Azenor since she disappeared. Gendrick, I understand, hired a Quisnaf blood sniffer to search for her, but even he fears she is dead. Do I get a question now? I've been patient—and generous."

Val slumped against the wall. No word of Azenor. It didn't mean anything. Kaell might have been careful or in hiding. *I'll find him. Make things right.* "What's your question?"

"Name the sorcerer who did… whatever he did to you. How?"

His heart slammed against a rib. "Ask something else."

"Play fair," Myranthe said. "Or the game stops and you learn nothing. His name?"

It had happened so long ago. Surely it couldn't hurt him anymore. "He took the title Mazart when he seized the Wardorian throne. 'Ruler of all,' it meant in the Seithin tongue. He conquered every land, including Telor. Destroyed your precious death riders. That's why you're curious? Because of your death riders?"

"I'm curious because of correspondence Heath found in Tide's End. A Duke of Avanti asking the Mazart for news of his son. Val Arques. The bladesman who won an infamous contest of swords… then disappeared."

"If you know so much already, it is another wasted question. I begin to think you're not so good at this game."

"Your wrists," Myranthe said. "Why?"

Silence. It howled about him. Then his body reacted before his mind could shut down the terror. His chest tight, his mouth dry, he groped at the wall near his hip. He trembled, the stone unsteady beneath his feet. "No." Val forced back the panic.

"Name your price." Her fingers drummed stone, their *tap, tap, tap* hypnotic. "What can I offer to draw an answer?"

"There's nothing."

The tapping stopped. Again, she stroked his hair as she might groom a pet. The gesture was small but infinitely suggestive. *I can do this,* her touch said. *I can do whatever I want to you.* "You have no power, Val Arques. You forget that. Nothing."

"Maybe I do. The power to deny you answers."

Myranthe's breath warmed his cheek. Her gaze held on his face. Then her expression shuttered. She took a deliberate step back as though to clamp down her eagerness.

"Very well," she muttered to herself. "I was wrong to think that will be easily surrendered. Your shield will only come down when I leave you nowhere to hide."

*Nowhere to hide.* The words sat between them with foreboding. No matter what she did or what she promised, he could not look within at that secret shame.

"I won't—" His gaze fell to his scarred wrists. *Lock it away. Tight. Bury it.*

Myranthe drifted the back of her hand down his cheek. "Know this, Val Arques. It is the secrets we hide from ourselves that give others power over us."

He shrank into the wall, pushing the meaning away before it

sank into his mind and corroded into doubt.

"Shall we continue? I'm feeling especially generous so take another question. Think carefully. I cannot promise to be in such a pleasant mood again."

"Where's my sword?" *Kaell's sword.*

"Heath has it. He collects things with sharp edges and soft curves. Come, is that it?"

"What will you do with Aric?"

"Still questions about a man who betrayed you. Not about your fate?" She smoothed his tunic at his breast. "I begin to suspect you care very little what happens to you, Val Arques Caelan. You're proving an intriguing man. Not at all what I expected."

When he made no reply, Myranthe dropped her hand. "Very well. If that's really what you want to know. The ceremony proceeds at the next three-moon night. Aric is precious to us, and we treated him with kindness, but it took time to restore his strength."

Val did not hide his disgust. "Took time to make him strong enough to murder."

"Hypocritical from an Isles man with gods so bloodthirsty, they demand sacrifices."

Val looked into her eyes. Empty of compassion. Hard. Speculative. *What was Heath's warning? Whatever game you think you're playing, that isn't it.*

His spine crept with unease.

"Next question?" Myranthe said sweetly.

# KAELL

Kaell hardly took in the rest of that hideous journey. His head pounding, his skin slick and hot, he only opened his eyes when the cart creaked through grainy red-stone walls. The dead city Roaran spoke of, surely.

The bones of its buildings sheathed what might have been cottages with tofts, barns for storing grain or animals, and a long house. The city's turrets reached into a cloudy sky, their sheer height bright with sunlight. Yet a shiver iced his neck. It was eerily quiet.

Wheels grated over ground-down cobblestones. Drawing up, Roaran climbed back to free Kaell, lift him, and carry him inside a crumbling tower. Too sick to resist, Kaell tried to focus, but he could not think beyond the pain in his skull.

The tower was a shell, dark-stoned and broken. Cobwebs glistened on walls breached by tree roots. Ivy entangled square pillars in a circular room beyond tarnished iron doors. Grime layered the slabbed floor. Moths fluttered on a vine strangling spilled blocks of stone.

For all its decay, the tower's tranquillity crept into Kaell as his captor laid him on a pallet a little away from a hearth. Cold ashes scattered in the fireplace, though a stack of wood waited, ready for the Mountains night.

Roaran crouched and tipped a waterskin to Kaell's lips. He waited patiently as Kaell drank. "It will be all right. Nicky's gone for a healer."

Moaning, Kaell shut his eyes against the assault in his skull. He heard Roaran rise, his steps on stone, then a creak. "We're well stocked. This storeroom is full."

"Word spreads of your return," a man replied in a low voice. "Others have magic in these lands. In their fires, mages glimpse a child, great lord."

*Great lord? Who is this Isles man?* The thought slipped away. Kaell wanted to sleep and feel nothing.

"They can't know," Roaran said sharply.

"They know you'll stop Archanin. That if you do not, he'll bleed this land for centuries."

Even through his fever, Archanin's name stirred wretched memories of that vile prison, Kaell's helplessness, and the ghoul god's soft, manipulative voice.

"Archanin's cult spreads," Roaran said. "His temple rises from a ruin. What sort of man is this Gendrick? A fool if he thinks he can control a god." He sighed. "Our position here?"

"We can hold this dead city for a time," the unseen man muttered, his voice muffled as if to disguise it. "The gates ground to dust centuries ago, but the walls are intact. I've set sentries."

"At dusk, I'll go to the walls and cast a spell to shield us behind a barrier. Before the Varee grow curious. Though as long as Archanin does not learn my name, we're safe."

*Spells.* Kaell trembled, unable to understand what a sorcerer wanted of him. Dizzily, he traced his captor through the afternoon glare.

Roaran stood at the foot of worn steps, staring up.

"I'm uncomfortable about this," the unseen man said. "About him. If he's not willing then…" His words died away into a tense silence.

"I'll persuade him." Roaran brushed a palm over a stairwell

spike. Flakes of rust snowed onto the slabbed floor.

"And if you can't?"

"Whatever it takes, no matter how long it takes, I'll make him see sense. If I flinch because this is hard, this land is lost."

"And what if holding him is just plain wrong?"

Roaran laughed bitterly. "Wrong? For too many centuries, I tussled with what's wrong and what is necessary. In the end, it comes down to what must happen."

Harnesses jangled. Nicky burst in with the healer Kaell knew from the Varee village. Juliette flung her shawl back, releasing a cascade of dark hair.

Roaran strode forward to take her hands. "Juliette, thank you for coming at once." He turned to Nicky. "You did well to find her quickly."

"It's been a while, Nicholas Saltman," the unseen man said. "Died lately, have you?"

Nicky whirled to the speaker. "Our spy. Stepping from the shadows into the main game. If you had the pleasure of the dread lord's lips locking on yours, you'd envy me my two deaths."

Kaell shifted restlessly. *Two deaths?* The more he heard, the more frightened he grew. These men, who talked so carelessly of death, still had not told him what they wanted of him.

Juliette looked to Roaran. "Do these two always carry on so?"

"Sadly, yes, like children. I try to keep them apart. Come this way." Roaran led her to Kaell.

At the sight of the wood witch, Kaell sighed in relief. She would take away his pain.

Juliette crouched. "Leave me, Ro. I'll examine Kate alone to preserve the poor girl's modesty. See to the children. They're about to come to blows."

"What did Nicky tell you?" Roaran said.

"What you suspect. Demon brew."

"And the rest?" Roaran looked edgy.

Juliette touched her brow, teasing. "Dread lord, the lands

beyond the gorge are full of whispers. That an age-old prophecy unfolds. That this girl is important."

*Important how?* Kaell squirmed on the pallet.

Juliette slid a hand beneath his tunic to his belly. "The best way to judge a fever."

Kaell groaned. "Your hands feel good," he whispered. Then at last, blissfully, he passed out.

⁓⧉⁓

When Kaell woke, Roaran and Juliette talked softly near the lit fire. Lamps burned. Moonbeams streaked through rotting shutters. Fluttering wings and a belligerent squawking carried from rooftop crenulations.

Kaell feigned sleep. In the darkness, he would slip away into the pine forests.

"It's as you thought," Juliette said. "Anyone accustomed to drinking demon brew suffers if it's withdrawn for more than a few days. There's something else at play here, though."

"Yes?"

"I'd suggest whatever she drank had been infused with crown of dreams. I know Dannon. He's clever. Careful when needs be. With an outsider, he'll take precautions."

No, Dannon had tried to stop Kaell drinking the brew. Carefully, Kaell shifted his head. The ache had dulled.

"And how is clever, careful Dannon?" Roaran tilted an eyebrow.

"Jealous?" Juliette punched his arm. "I've seen Dannon with this girl. Not like him to show his feelings, but you men are peculiar creatures, and there's something in how he looks at her that's different to even how he looks at me."

"So he is the Bloodtaker no longer? Just plain, lovesick Dannon?"

"Stop it." She laughed.

Kaell pushed aside the blanket. On elbows and knees, he crawled towards the door.

"And what is crown of dreams? I've never heard of it."

"You wouldn't, being a gentle Isles man. It's a vine with crown-shaped flowers. You boil its roots and mash them into a paste. The mage adds it to wine at ceremonies to bring visions. But take it too often, and you can't stop. Dannon can't."

"Why force it on our young guest?"

"Cut off the brew, and she'll reveal any secrets to get more."

A ridiculous need to defend Dannon rose up in Kaell. Dannon hadn't poisoned him. He'd let him go. Saved him from Archanin.

*A slaver and a killer.* A slaver and a killer who had become his friend.

"How do we cure this?"

"She'll come through it," Juliette said. "Sooner with my herbs."

Kaell dizzily tried to rise. When he couldn't, he again crawled.

"I'll fetch—" Juliette broke off with a tinkling laugh. "Dread lord—I sound like Nicky, but it is strangely appropriate—dread lord, your prisoner escapes."

"With all the speed and grace of a drunken tortoise." Roaran walked unhurriedly towards Kaell. "I'd best run fast, or he'll get away."

Kaell collapsed facedown. He didn't have the strength to get up, let alone fight.

With an indulgent shake of his head, Roaran slung Kaell over his shoulder.

"Let me go. What do you want of me?"

Juliette tugged at Roaran's arm. "Ro, what did you mean, '*He'll* get away'? *He*?"

"It's a strange tale, Juliette." Roaran lowered his prisoner back onto the pallet.

Exhausted, Kaell curled up. *Too hard to escape tonight. Tomorrow.*

"Once you force evil-tasting herbs down the turtle's throat so he has a restful sleep," Roaran said, "stay with me tonight, and I'll tell you all about it."

She smiled. "As long as you put the bickering children to bed first."

A woman's laugh, softly seductive, reached into his dreams. Firelight gyrated shadows on stone walls. The only sounds were its crackle, a distant tramp of feet, a faraway rustle of leaves—and that laugh.

Kaell peeled back the blankets and sorted his memories. An Isles man—a dead man—had brought him to a dead city. Juliette had banished his pain so he could sleep.

The laugh echoed again, sensually raw. Curious, Kaell crawled towards the sound. At first, he was aware only of flames licking blackened stone in the hearth. Then his gaze caught. Widened.

Before that fire, knees sunk into fur, a man and woman embraced as if bound together in stone. Sweat glistened on naked skin. The atmosphere ripened with desire. Kaell rubbed his eyes, thinking it a dream.

The woman laughed, that same throaty laugh that had woken him. "Slow, slow," she pleaded.

"As you wish." Her lover bent his head to lick her nipples. She moaned in pleasure, her skin flushed, her fingers clutching his damp, curling hair. "No. Faster, faster."

Laughing, he swung her around and down. The fire at their backs, its light fell on his face, catching a blue-gemmed glint in his eyes.

*Roaran.* Kaell recoiled. *An Isles man indeed.* Everyone knew they brazenly, unashamedly, bared their bodies publicly. Deeply uncomfortable, he staggered up and stumbled for the door.

The cool night air brushed against his face, pleasurable after the heavy, dangerous sensuality of the tower. Beyond a crumbling wall infested with crawling roots, moonlight tinted the leafy top of thick trunks. A forest. Safety.

A twig snapped. He spun. A figure came at him. Kaell ran, his gait unsteady. Footsteps pounded behind, then his pursuer crashed into him. Winded, he thrashed beneath a man's broad body, until his attacker gripped Kaell's hair to pull back his head and slam it into the ground.

They left him curled on the pallet. Kaell squinted into candlelight, his skull throbbing. Juliette knelt to tend to him. The camphor of herbs, the stringent odour of salves, and the milky vanilla of lotions from bottles and sachets were like a web about her.

Roaran watched her with a contented smile. He wore pants but nothing else. Firelight illuminated whorling tattoos on his muscular shoulders. A bladesman's shoulders.

"I remember when Nicky first carried me to you," he said to Juliette. "How you stitched a deep gash, calling me a crybaby every time I winced."

"He was," Juliette confided to Kaell. "Still is. Whenever he takes a wound, he declares it more painful than the last. Now, how does that feel? Your head should stop thumping soon. I added a little poppy juice to the potion so you'll sleep."

"It doesn't hurt as much," Kaell admitted. "Your hands are soothing."

Roaran mumbled an amused "Indeed."

Juliette smiled to herself as she stooped to pick up her concoctions.

"He's stronger, yes? I can talk with him?"

Juliette turned, dropping her hands to her hips. "If you mean torment, then no."

"I mean talk," Roaran said. "You forget, Juliette, this one is very, very precious to me."

"To all of us, Roaran." She walked away.

Warily, Kaell watched Roaran approach. For a long moment, the man regarded him steadily, saying nothing in a silence that never softened as it lengthened.

"I wish I could save you the struggle ahead," he said at last. "For your sake as well as mine, I wish I could walk away. Lose myself in Juliette's arms and forget about gods and duty." He shook his head as if surprised by doubt. "Except duty is all I have."

Kaell's eyelids drooped. So peaceful to be on the edge of sleep, knowing its comfort waited.

"You're exhausted," Roaran said. "Tomorrow. We'll talk then. You'll know it all, Kaell."

"Let him sleep, my love," Juliette called from the fireside. "Come back to bed."

Roaran turned slightly. "You don't hate me for what I must do? Now you know the truth?"

She rose and slid her hands around his waist. "I pity you. I could not do it. Come to bed."

"If only it were that easy," he muttered. "To bury pain in your kisses."

"Bury it," Kaell heard Juliette say as he gladly surrendered to sleep. "Bury it deep."

Back to a pillar, knees drawn towards his chest, Kaell listened to his captors' hushed voices, their laughter, their booted steps. Every sound was magnified in this forgotten place. His ghoul senses isolated water trickling over stones, even a wolf's distant howl.

Kaell considered the distance to the door. All he had to do was run.

"Dread lord, dread creature at last awakens." Nicky peered down expectantly as though Kaell might entertain them all with a jig. "Been back with us a while too. Listening, were you?"

"What do you expect? I need to learn who you really are and what you intend."

"Why, sweetness, you need only ask." The man swept a mock

bow. "Nicholas Saltman. Slave to the dread lord. Swordsman. Sometime singer."

"All-the-time fool," Kaell muttered. "And you sing badly."

"Let me tell you, boy, I come from a long line of singer swordsmen." He turned. "Didn't I say he was rude, Roaran?"

"Nicky, enough." Roaran was polishing a sword at a table of worn wood.

"Yes, Nicky," Kaell sneered.

Nicky wagged a finger. "I remember your silliness in that Varee cavern. Yes, Nicky. No, Nicky. Let me throw down my sword and get you killed, Nicky."

"Pity I missed the bit where ghouls left you alive while they fed."

"My, my. Someone should teach you manners."

"Nicky, leave him be." Roaran did not look up. Lamplight gleamed on blue-hued steel and an intricate niello hilt. A second Seithin blade. No one—no one—had two.

"Dread lord, may I please torment the prisoner a little longer?"

"No."

"I suppose you want to torment him yourself? Well, so long as I can watch." Nicky wandered off, humming. Next, he would start singing.

"No, I beg you, don't let him sing, dreadful lord," Kaell jeered to mask his growing alarm. "I'll tell you anything, just so long as he doesn't sing."

With an impatient "hmm," Roaran scraped back the chair and rose. The lamp's light etched his shadow on stone. Its shape billowed to wings.

Fine hairs rose along Kaell's arms. "Who are you?" he whispered.

"He means you, master of all," Nicky called from near the fire.

Roaran placed the sword carefully on the table. As he crossed the room, more misshapen shadows moved with him. Fear cut Kaell's breath. He recoiled against the pillar.

"You feel it, too, don't you?" Roaran stood before him. "The otherworld breathes and sighs tonight. The veil is thin."

"I don't know what you mean. There's nothing here." Kaell flung another desperate glance at the door. Could he make it? His strength had not fully returned.

"It's time we talked, Kaell."

Kaell staggered to his feet. "No, it's time I ran." He bolted for the entrance. Neither Nicky nor Roaran moved. He reached the doors and put a shoulder into them. They did not budge. He rattled the handle up and down. Still, the doors would not open.

For a few useless moments, he pushed, kicked, and hurled his weight against their bronze. Then the fight went out of him. He slid his back down the door and dropped his head into his hands.

Roaran sighed. "I didn't want you to suffer the indignity of more restraints, so I enspelled the tower. I'm sorry, but I can't have you running off. Kaell, please." He gestured to a chair.

Reluctantly, despair like a wound within him, Kaell rose, walked to the chair and sat. "What do you intend to do with me?" he asked wearily. "Kill me?"

Roaran returned to the table. He traced the sword's edge with a gloved finger. "Kill you?" he said. "Oh, Kaell. It's far worse than that."

Nicky chuckled. "That's funny, lord of all."

Roaran did not smile. "No," he said to Kaell. "Not kill you. This is where I tell you the truth."

# VAL ARQUES

A key jangled. Val rose and placed his wrist against the wall, like a trained dog. He just needed a tail to wag. "Woof," he said.

Griffin ignored the fool barking at him. "Move your hand. I broke up the wall there freeing you last time."

"You broke my finger too."

Unsmiling, Griffin hammered the trident into place. "You tried to seduce her. I heard you. Don't do it again."

"It's in the book of escape tactics for prisoners."

"There's a book? Oh, a joke. Ha, ha. Anyway, that won't work," Griffin said seriously. "Myranthe is very calculating in matters of the heart."

"She has a heart?"

Griffin shook his head. "You're remarkably carnal for a swordsman. Practise restraint. Purity strengthens a bladesman."

"Says who? Is there a book about it?"

"Another joke? It's well-known the best bladesmen rarely succumb to fleshly seductions."

"Really? Who?"

"It's what I read. Dace Caelan for one—"

Val leaned his head back and laughed heartily. "Now *you're* joking."

Indignant, Griffin squared his chin. "Dace walked beyond the Enarae to fight the dead. Through flames to show courage. Everyone knows a swordsman like that—"

"Oh, everyone knows," Val teased. Broken finger or not, he still liked Griffin. Though a hard young man, he was straightforward and lacked Heath's and Myranthe's cruelty.

"Everyone knows a swordsman tested by the dead lost their strength for a time if they sought sexual pleasure. It's in one of the old books the father-brother keeps."

"That's true enough," Val said. "Though it just made them careful. Dace could no more put aside temptations of the flesh than he could put aside a sword."

"I don't believe you."

"Believe what you like. Dace Caelan was my cousin. As king, he always had a guard at his door for the reasons you said. When he was… hmm… vulnerable."

"I forgot you were cousins." Griffin frowned. "And it wasn't just once?"

"What a sheltered life you've led. Dace was a young warrior and a young king. He liked women, and he liked men, and they certainly liked him."

Griffin scowled as he walked out. A good half hour later, Myranthe scowled as she walked in. A Damadar trait. The scowling. The games.

"Whatever did you say to Griffin?"

"Why, what's he done?"

"Let one of my women entice him into her bedchamber. Now how did you corrupt my brother?" She drew closer, smirking, as though they partnered in mischief.

He was strong enough to strangle her with one hand. But it was not in him to kill like that, whatever the provocation. "We talked of carnality. He thinks warriors need to be pure."

"He's always thought that, yes."

"I told him the truth about my cousin, Dace. That's all."

"Not so pure?" Myranthe drew back. "Such a relief. From the

stories, I always thought Dace Caelan a fascinating king. So much repressed rage. Talking of carnal—"

"Or not. Griffin showed me the error of my ways. I'd like to keep my fingers."

"Silly boy. He must have been eavesdropping. Then you have questions for me?"

"Just one." Val paused. He dragged in a slow breath. "What will it take for you to free me?"

"That is serious indeed. What do you think might buy your freedom?"

Val swallowed hard. *Not that. Do not ask.*

Myranthe strained a strand of his hair between her fingers. "Aric wishes to see you," she said.

Val tongued dry lips. "I have no wish to see him."

"You could be kind, Val Arques. The wrong he did you torments him."

"Let him stew in his guilt." Unconsciously, he clenched his shackled hand. Consciously, he opened it, trying to quieten his heart. *Let him stew.* Aric's betrayal kept him from Kaell.

"And let you stew in your resentment? I begin to understand you make a bad enemy." She didn't sound afraid, only curious. When he didn't answer, she said, "A piece of information reached me. About who a Quisnaf blood seeker found in some wretched Downs tavern. Agree to see Aric. That and answer one question, and I'll tell you what, or who, it was."

"Oh?" Val tried to hide his eagerness. "What do you want to know?"

"I want to know about Kaell," she said. "I want you to tell me what he really was."

# KAELL

The gloom deepened. Roaran lit candles. Their tiny flicker made no difference. Nor did the fire. Because it wasn't the darkness that oppressed his spirit. It was his disquiet.

*This is where I tell you the truth…*

Nicky banged the door as he stomped in. "They're coming, Roaran. The brotherhood. They say they're ready for the ritual."

"Soon."

"What ritual?" Kaell surrendered to panic. "I won't let you carve me up on some altar."

"I liked you better drunk," Nicky said. "You weren't so stupid. My lord said you're precious to him. You're precious to the brotherhood too."

"This isn't happening." Kaell kicked the chair leg. "I'm going to get free, and then I'm going to make you pay for abducting me."

Nicky grinned. "No, you're not. Because you're going to be—"

"Nicky, shut up," Roaran said quickly.

"What, because I'm going to be dead?" Kaell began to laugh. He didn't care about death. No. It was a relief. An end to struggle and doubt.

"You wish." Nicky stomped off.

"How did you make me stab you?" Kaell asked Roaran. "It was magic, wasn't it?"

Roaran sank into a chair opposite. "I'm sorry for that. But it was the surest way to escape them. A wound can incapacitate me for days, but death restores my strength quickly."

"Do you mean—" Kaell wet his lips. "You've… died before?"

Roaran briefly closed his eyes. He sighed heavily. With obvious reluctance, he said, "The first time, there was a man. Centuries ago."

*Centuries. Oh gods. That can't be true.*

"He sought to punish me. For turning my back on him. He had a knife. He took his time. Slow cuts. Shallow wounds. All the while, he watched my face." Roaran's tone was dead, as if he deliberately kept himself apart from the words. "It wasn't just the intimacy of my death Lucius sought. It was having power over me."

He looked into the darkness. For a long moment, he said nothing. Then he sighed again. "His captain grew impatient, demanded to know why it took so long to kill me. 'Such a death must be savoured,' Lucius replied.

"The captain sneered. 'What? To kill a king?' Lucius just smiled. I can't remember the room, the captain's name, but I remember that smile. How Lucius said very softly, 'No. To kill a friend.'"

"A king," Kaell echoed uneasily. "I don't understand—"

"Just spit it out," Nicky called from the stairs. "Your creature is too stupid and obviously knows nothing of Telorian history. Lucius of Cahir. Centuries ago. The clues are there."

"I know enough," Kaell snapped. "And I don't belong to anyone."

"You belong to the dread lord."

"Gods." He stared at them both. "I'm held captive by madmen. Just kill me."

"You keep asking that." Nicky rubbed a dagger on his shirt. "If only I could oblige. Maybe I can just tickle you a bit with my blade." He raised his brows at his lord.

Roaran shook his head. Face drawn, he leaned towards Kaell. A thin line of moisture darkened his hairline. "We have to talk, Kaell. You have to know it all. I owe you that."

Kaell twisted his hands, afraid. Not at Roaran's words but his hard, bleak expression. "You owe me nothing. I don't even know you."

"I made you."

Kaell went utterly still, like a bird trapped in a dog's mouth. His breath caught then released, its exhalation a thunderclap in the hush. "You think you're a god?" he blurted. "Mad. Both you and Singing Boy over there."

"No, not a god. Though I serve one. Reluctantly."

"We all serve the gods," Kaell scoffed.

"So we do." Roaran sat back with a sigh. "But I don't want to talk about gods. I want to talk about you, Kaell. You see, I know all of it. I have every answer. Everything you longed to understand about who you are, where you're from, about why the gods let Archanin take you prisoner, even why you're trapped in Azenor's body."

"I don't believe you," Kaell cried, grasping at defiance to hide his fear. It had to be a lie. "How can you know any of this? Who are you?"

"A servant of Ghani-Jai."

"Talk about round and round." Nicky spread his arms impatiently. "Just tell him, Roaran. No?" He stomped to Kaell and grabbed his jaw. "You should tremble, boy. A servant of Ghani-Jai is a death rider."

"What?" Kaell shuddered. "They don't exist. Not any longer."

"Then what's he? But even that isn't why four warriors are coming to bend their knees. They're here because the Mountains are full of whispers, and this one runs wild."

Kaell's stare held on Nicky's face. *Do not speak,* he willed. *Do not.*

"Do you know what it says, Kaell? It says: Our lord returns. Our king. Roaran Caelan."

The fire flared as though whipped by wind. A drumming in Kaell's ears drowned thought. Sweat broke out in his armpits. "It's not possible."

Nicky let Kaell go. He turned to Roaran, exasperated. "You tell him."

Roaran faced him. There was something sorrowful about his expression, something old. Something resigned.

Kaell shrank back into the chair. "No," he whispered. "No. I don't want to hear. I don't want to know."

Roaran said, "I am a death rider. And I am also Roaran Caelan."

The air was breathless, the silence palpable, as if the fire had died and the wind fallen silent. Kaell could not utter a sound or look away. His mind broke up beneath the struggle between sheer disbelief and the need to grasp at the impossible to explain this man.

"It's a lie," he croaked.

"And yet, am I not known as the king who does not lie?" Roaran pressed fingers to his temples, his face gaunt as though he endured hidden pain.

"No, no. It's too incredible."

"I've watched you since your lord brought you as a child to Vraymorg, Kaell," Roaran said. "I know everything about you."

Transfixed, Kaell tussled with the words. Slowly, they leached into him, tantalisingly seductive, reaching into his yearning to know who he really was.

"That's where your story starts," Roaran said. "With your lord. I'll tell you about it—if you want to hear it. About who you are, where you come from. Unless you're afraid."

The challenge snapped Kaell from his stupor. He poked out his chin. "I don't believe you know anything about me. I think you're mad. But I am not afraid to hear what you say."

The fire roared up, its crackle like wild laughter. A log clunked. Sparks showered into the coals. The past shimmered, a rich array of currents, of skirring shapes and blurred images.

Roaran smiled faintly as he stared into the fire. "Yes, you are," he said.

"This is how it begins." Roaran's gaze turned inward. "With the god Khir. He always comes in the deep of night when Caelan's Mountains fortress of Vraymorg slumbers and not even the moons shatter the murk."

Kaell could not hold back a shiver.

"Khir leads your lord below. To a passage long forbidden. To a door." Roaran looked into the distance. "Even when I was a captain of the Serravan, younger than you, none of us, masters or students, dared walk through it. Oh, we all knew of it. We whispered about it, wondered what it was like in that passage. Whether cobwebs clouded the walls or dust lay so thick, a man might drown in it. We knew of that door. But no, we'd never enter."

# VAL ARQUES

"With a word, Khir unlocks the door," Val told Myranthe.

Darkness, crisp and heavy with cold, shuttered the tower cell. A robed scribe Myranthe called a "brother-keeper" sat upon a stool outside the open door to take down Val's words.

"The brother-keepers protect our great library here in the ice caverns," she said in answer to his unspoken question. "They are guardians of knowledge, purveyors of truth."

Just as he must become a purveyor of truth—in return, he hoped, for the truth about Kaell's whereabouts. A risk telling her the story, but he had to take it.

"What is he like?" Myranthe pressed. "Khir?"

Val shut his eyes. "There is an unworldly beauty to his golden hair, his dark eyes, a shining."

"Roaran Caelan writes that in the caves of the Quisnaf, as King Rainer lay dying after defeating the demon, Khir came for his grandson's body. Roaran glimpsed, for a single moment, the god's true form. And Khir was hideous."

"I do not know what the truth about Khir is," Val said. "How strange you have writings by Roaran here, kept safe in this white prison."

"Only to you, a prison."

Khir led Val into the darkness. Its emptiness brushed with the rough prickle of sackcloth.

Except... was it empty? He saw nothing, heard nothing. No scent, pleasing or pungent, came to him. Nor could he touch or taste anything. The darkness had no form. Yet Val knew it existed. That it was just there.

Then the emptiness erupted to chaos, beautiful and terrible. It swirled with vibrant colour: dawn's rose, the dark-rimmed blue of dusk, the black opal night. A sun flared to an unforgiving crimson then dipped into slate. Sounds breathed around him, alive. A humming tide, a whir of blades, a languid flap of wings, a bee's drone. A child laughing.

At last, twisting shapes took form and became a deserted street beneath tall walls bulged with towers. So many towers. He knew at once where he must be.

A hot wind whipped up dirt. It fanned his face with scents of violet, powdery and hazy, and of jasmine entwining columns between unbroken rows of bougainvillea.

Buzzing flies, a scattered breeze through palm trees, even a sentry's cry from a watchtower, all seemed unnaturally loud. This city should have thousands of voices: merchants, soldiers, sorcerers and priestesses, young seamstresses, princes, armourers, smiths, children's giddy cries, even the soft whispers of young lovers. They were silent.

This city waited. It waited to die.

He walked to a square where boys in rags splashed in a stone fountain. In the shade of a nearby tree, old men sipped cool drinks.

"We may yet be saved," one said. "Our walls are high. If we can hold out—"

"How? Our ships burn. What is left of our tattered army falls back. Only the city guard walks the walls. Seithin will fall."

"With magic, then. The priests and priestesses meet. There is talk of a new spell."

His companion's laugh sounded cynical and defeated. "The Mazart has magic too."

Val walked on. Through stirred dirt and spidery daffodils, he smelled smoke. The sentries on the wall must glimpse across the desert a red shimmer on a glistening sea as the famed Seithin fleet burned and sank.

Seithin, the city of fountains, of temples, theatres, and libraries, the cradle of magic, light and dark. An invincible city. But it was about to fall to an invader for the first and last time.


THE WOMAN SANG OF LOVE. She folded freshly washed clothes on a shaded veranda. Palms in large painted pots sprayed green leaves. At her feet, a child played with a wooden toy.

Her simple task, her joy as she sang, railed against fate, resonating with hope that life might go on. Yet her song died on her lips when she saw Val. "I had a dream," she said. "I thought it only that. But now you are here, just as you came to me in the dream."

"Khir sent me for the boy," Val said.

A scorching wind scuttled from an alley. Sweat rolled down his arms. It trickled from his matted hair into his eyes.

The woman covered her face with her hands and whispered, "What will happen?"

"The Mazart's army is coming. The city will burn."

"There's talk of another spell, blood magic to destroy the invader."

"The city burns. All within perish."

Her breaths shattered into a sob. "My husband. The boy's father. He is a soldier. I have not had word from him for weeks. Is he dead?"

"I'm sorry. The gods reveal very little."

"In the dream, Khir commands me to give you my son—" Her voice failed. Swiping at tears, she crouched beside the barefoot, blond child. He smiled trustingly as she lifted him.

"What will happen to my son?"

"He'll survive. Grow to manhood. Beyond that, I do not know." Val took the boy from her. "What are you called?"

"Caolin." Her voice shook.

"And the boy?"

"Kaell."

As he walked away, he could hear her weeping. The child watched his mother over his shoulder. He beat his small fists against Val's chest.

# KAELL

"Caolin," Kaell's voice crept out. All of him was raw, breaking, his turmoil of loss and disbelief held tight inside, a dam that must soon release. "Archanin spoke the truth. I am named for her. What did she look like?"

"She was no older than twenty. Slender, not so tall, with hazel eyes and light-brown hair. There is something of her in you, though your hair and eyes must be like your father's."

"Who was he?"

Roaran shook his head. "Your lord might know."

Kaell laughed bitterly. "My lord is dead. Why did he do this to me, then go and die?"

"If you want the truth, Kaell, I know these answers too."

Kaell stared. When Roaran said nothing further, he shouted, "Then tell me! Tell me. I don't know anything, and it's destroying me."

Roaran leaned to poke a stick at the embers. "I promised you the truth. So here it is." He threw down the stick. "Your lord stabbed you with that sword because I sent a man to tell him it would save you."

"What?"

"Val would do anything, risk everything to save you. He loves you, Kaell. I knew it even if he couldn't admit it."

"I want to believe you. Just as I wanted so badly to believe him when he said he loved me like a son—" He looked away, his chest tight. "Even if that were so once, he can't love me now. I should be glad he's dead. If he learnt what I've done—"

"All of us can only ever hope to be forgiven," Roaran said quietly.

"I would forgive him," Kaell said. "I would forgive my lord anything if only he lived." His eyes felt gritty. "Why did he have to die? Why?"

The candle fizzed and guttered. In only the fire's glow, the pillar cast a shadow over Roaran's face. He tilted a new candle to the dying flame and settled it in soft wax. But in that short time, the meaning of all Roaran had said sank in. *Your lord stabbed you because I sent a man to tell him it would save you.*

*Roaran. He sent a man. Roaran did this.*

Hot, sharp anger roared up in Kaell. "I understand now. I'm trapped in her body because of *you*. All of this, Archanin, Azenor. All of it, you." He shot to his feet and ran at the door. Again, he put his shoulder into it, again and again, his rage exploding through his body. "You did this!" Kaell shouted. "You did this to me."

"Yes," Roaran said. "It had to be you, you see. You're Seithin-born. The last of the Seithin, in fact. That's why Archanin could make you like him. Only you, Kaell, could have both Seithin and ghoul blood."

Kaell shook his head fiercely. "I don't understand. How do I *still* have Seithin and ghoul blood?" He brushed a hand down his body. "I'm no longer me. I'm her."

"Bloodlines are not attached to our bodies, as you may think. They're who we are, part of that eternal essence that makes us unique…" Roaran's voice trailed away.

There was a silence. Then Roaran sighed. He rose and wandered in a tight circle near Kaell. "I didn't expect to have to do this alone. I thought he might be here. Your lord. It should be Val here now, telling you, 'Everything is all right. You're safe.'" His stare drifted far beyond the tower. "I possess the truth about you, Kaell. A compelling, huge truth. But I do not possess those tiny moments that bind two people together."

"Go away," Kaell muttered. "Just go away."

"I would comfort you if I could," Roaran said. "But you will only resent me, feel your loneliness more acutely with a substitute for the man you really want here. All I can do is show you the past, hope you understand."

Returning to the table, he picked up a knife and dragged its edge across his wrist. Dark, red drops fell on stone as he trod to Kaell.

Kaell recoiled, his back hard against the door.

"You need blood." Roaran pressed his wrist to Kaell's lips. "From now on, you'll drink mine."

Roaran's blood tasted sharp in Kaell's mouth. Just one mouthful, and a waking dream tore into him, a torrent of scents, colour, and sounds. He could not resist the storm of fragmented images, fragrances, tastes. He saw people and places he didn't know. Those he did. Seeing, hearing, feeling as Roaran did. For he was now Roaran and caught in his past.

HE IS IN A CAVE. He hears pattering rain and the whip of flames. Azenor's lips are wet on his naked body. Her fingers entangle his hair. Sensation after sensation ignites his desire. Damp skin. Soft caresses. Velvet kisses.

"Witch," Kaell moans. Her hand glides and strokes, arousing. She cries out as he thrusts, muscles flexed, a languid pleasure building, flooding, releasing.

Other memories crowd in, some terrible, some beautiful, all pieces of a dangerous story. Jumbled. Incomplete. Out of place.

"My lord," Nicky says. "Thom is a trap. Archanin will take the boy."

"This must happen. I saw it."

"A kiss, Azenor," he says as the moons fade above the Isle of the Gods. "I'll awaken this body with a kiss."

He is in a passageway in a castle, about to enter Azenor's room, when he glimpses Vraymorg. For a moment, they lock gazes. Then he turns away.

His shoulder touches a woman's as they lie in bed. A draught stirs a wisping curtain at the doors to a balcony. The tide murmurs on the distant reef. The wind carries a tang of brine. His body is hot, impossibly, pleasurably hot.

"Give me another child, Roaran," his queen says.

He tastes wine on her breath as she kisses him, breathing in the rich perfume of her hair, of creamy skin. He aches with loss. Guilt.

A hundred battles cascade into one. Kaell knows sharp pain and sees faces, an endless number of men who scream as his sword hacks, and hews, and kills.

"Rosette, my love," a warrior on his knees weeps. His blood splashes Kaell's face as he swings the blade.

"For Ghani-Jai," he shouts. Darkness rises at his back. Merciless and unrelenting. Powerful. Part of him. His sword slashes and cuts. Men shriek and die.

A cruel presence moves with him as he ploughs down bodies and severs limbs. Thrust, stab, sweep. Blood, more pain. A surge of pain, then strength.

Arn walks through a moonlit forest. "Shining," he whispers as he kneels. "My lord is silver like the night."

Kaell stands in a tent's shadow, his face hidden. Balanced on his toes, he is ready to rush out to save an unarmed boy from an assassin.

Nicky plucks at his sleeve. "Kaell is safe. An Isles captain came to Vraymorg's aid."

Flames fan hot. A ghoulish crowd jostles him as he watches himself at the stake.

"Step back, Vraymorg," a king shouts. An old man stands at the king's elbow, ghost-pale. "You wait, too, Roaran Caelan?" the spectre says, turning an eyeless gaze on him.

"Yes," he says. "Who do you wait for?"

"For my son," the ghost whispers. "His name is Cathmor. He dies today."

A man brushes his hair from his damp brow. The memory is impossibly clear. The hall in Dal-Kanu, shadows thrown by its pillars upon its tiled floor. Candles flicker in tall holders. The man kisses his mouth, even as the knife kisses his flesh. "It is a moment to hold on to, Roaran. To kill a king. To kill a friend."

He is in a chamber of ice, hands holding him down as he yells and thrashes. Iron bruises his ankles. Iron at his wrists. At his neck. All he knows is loneliness.

A woman chants, calling to her god. Candlelight flickers on a naked blade in her hand. The knife comes down...

THE LAST VISION WAVERED behind Kaell's eyelids: ice walls around a stone altar. The echo of Roaran's wretched scream set his teeth into a grimace.

Kaell choked back a sob. "What did you do to me?" he whispered, slumping to his knees. "Haven't you done enough?"

Roaran leaned a shoulder to a pillar, every bit the elegant prince. Too fine. Strikingly lovely. Like Archanin and just as dangerous.

They were alone. *Khir help me.* He did not want to be alone with this man.

"A seer's blood." Roaran sounded sorrowful. "It's different to drinking any other."

"What have you done?" Kaell cried. "I didn't want to see that. I didn't want to know."

"You glimpsed just a little of my story, Kaell. So you understand nothing happens without a reason. That it all led here, to a prophecy about a child born to defeat Archanin."

Parts of the vision slid into place. "How—" Kaell started in a ragged voice. "I know this. How can I know this?"

"The prophecy should be impossible." Roaran's gaze again slipped within. "A child with Seithin, ghoul, and Caelan blood. But the Seithin were destroyed or turned by Archanin into creatures like him."

"I don't want to hear any more," Kaell said. "Just leave me alone."

Roaran's eyes flared into blue fire. "Remember what Archanin said to you? That Khir made a mistake. He chose a Seithin boy as a bonded warrior. A child destined to free Archanin from my enchantments trapping him in that dread castle."

A shiver crept at Kaell's neck. "So he said."

"It had to seduce him, the thought of being free. So he didn't kill you. So that Archanin, too, made a mistake and gave you his blood. After all, why should he fear a prophecy that's impossible? No child can have Seithin, ghoul, and true Caelan blood."

Kaell rattled the door handle desperately. He sensed Roaran edged towards a terrible truth. "Stop," he whispered. "Just stop."

"Then came Azenor's part. We made use of the Isles priestess to bind you two together."

"Azenor. She let me think—"

"I understand more than you know."

"You can't know about betrayal—" Kaell broke off, astonished. Fragments of memory flashed. A woman with black eyes. Her caresses. Her laugh, cruel, punishing. "You can't give me another child. You're broken, Roaran. I despise you, husband."

Kaell growled. He would not feel sympathy. Not for a man who held him captive.

"You wanted answers," Roaran said patiently. "You begged your lord to tell you who you were, where you were from. Val stayed silent to protect you. Everything he did, always to protect you."

Kaell's throat thickened. His lord knew the truth about him but had said nothing. He no longer knew what to think about the man he loved as a father. The blur of anger and sorrow complicated everything.

"It was all for a reason, Kaell. Everything you suffered. You should find comfort in that."

"Comfort?" He glared.

Roaran took a step closer. He lifted his hand to Kaell's cheek but did not touch him. "I'm sorry you faced this alone. Azenor was meant to bring you to me. I even sent Nicky to find you both. Well, you know what happened. When you escaped to the Isles, I encouraged the high priestess to think her gods chose you as a sacrifice so she performed a binding ritual."

"Are you gloating? Your words disgust me."

"I'm not proud of this, Kaell. But it had to happen. Archanin. Azenor. Even Aric poisoning you so that you could not glimpse that ghoul ambush in a vision. Then later, convincing Val to stain your sword with your blood. A memory sword. Cursed, when you know its story. In the end, he did his part, but again, you eluded me. Until now. All is in place. Except—"

Roaran faltered. His stare flickered to the darkness at the room's corners.

Kaell would not look into that murk. He swallowed hard. "Except what?"

"The hardest part. Something I must now do."

"Say it." His voice sounded hoarse. "Just say it."

"The prophecy says a child born of Seithin blood, ghoul blood, and true Caelan blood will defeat Archanin, end his coming reign of blood."

"His coming reign? No, wait. A child? What's true Caelan blood?"

"A child of Caelan parents. Rare, because the gods forbid such unions. True Caelan blood is far too dangerous, far too useful to sorcerers and sorceresses. I know of only one man with that forbidden blood. He is destined to be hunted."

Kaell's heart belted his ribs. He thought he wanted the truth, that he could stare it down, but now he wanted only to run.

Roaran began to pace. "I'll say it plain."

"No." An awful suspicion burned through Kaell. "Don't say it at all."

Breathless air fanned. Flames crackled in the hearth. Smoke wisped. Roaran stopped his pacing. He lifted his eyes to Kaell's. He said: "I must ask you to have a child."

Kaell could not blink, could not breathe. The words crushed him to the door. If he looked away, if he moved, then that made it real. And what he heard couldn't be real.

"I won't touch you," Roaran said. "It's nothing like that. I simply need to take a piece of your soul and a piece of mine and create a child. You would carry that child. That's all."

"That's all?" Kaell spluttered. "You don't know what you're asking."

Roaran ripped taut fingers through his hair. "Please try to understand. You have ghoul and Seithin blood, now Azenor's Caelan blood. Add my Caelan blood, and that's true Caelan—as the prophecy demands."

"No, no, no, no. How could you think I'd agree to anything you want—the man who abducted me, who manipulated me."

"Everything I've done, Kaell. Everything you've suffered comes down to this. Turn away now, and it all means nothing. For both of us. I've hurt so many to save Telor. I can't flinch."

"Why tell me this?" Kaell shouted. "Use some potion, and I'll know nothing."

"I will never force you. Never. I know in time you'll understand what's at stake, what Archanin will do—not only to Telor but every land." Roaran lifted his shoulders in a helpless gesture. "Help me, Kaell. Help me destroy him."

*Everything you've suffered…*

The pain of that past year, his shame at Archanin's hands, Azenor's betrayal—all of it knotted in his mind then exploded in a cold, clear bolt of fury. All that misery because of some nonsense prophecy, to serve this man's purpose.

"I'll kill you." Seething, Kaell drove a fist into the door. "You first, Roaran Caelan. Then your grinning, singing fool. You'll pay for all you've done to me."

"I understand," Roaran said quietly. "It's too much to ask. Yet I have to ask it. I have to coldly put aside my misgivings about how hard this will be for you and think only of the greater good."

"Is that how you justify this? That you *have* to be cold? That it's somehow noble because it saves everyone?" Kaell edged every word with scorn. "You're holding me against my will. Even if I accept your argument about saving Telor, how can I agree now?"

Roaran fell back a step, as if to remove any threat in his presence. "It will be magic only, Kaell. I will not seek anything unseemly from you. Please. Think about it. You and I are both born to duty."

He walked away. Kaell stared after him, shocked by all that he had heard and what Roaran sought of him. Then he let out a yell and thumped the door with all his might.

The room fell to stillness. The fire burned low until it was no more than red-glowing embers. The wind moaned through cracks as if Roaran's absence freed it to wander where it chose.

Kaell tried the door again. It would not budge. He considered climbing to the windows, but Roaran had said the entire tower was enspelled. Frustrated and angry, he slid down again, back to the door, his hands clasping his knees.

He couldn't bear a child. The idea had no foundation, no shape, in his mind. He had no idea of what it might be like. And what happened after the birth? Did he help raise the child? Or did Roaran? No, he had to escape this man.

But no one escaped a death rider, at least, according to legend. They hunted down the guilty, no matter how far they ran.

*Death rider.* He trembled, unwilling to believe it. Yet Roaran's memories screamed the truth through his beleaguered mind. Ice walls.

Shackles. A woman's chants. A knife. Roaran, defenceless, mouthing a prayer to gods he did not believe in, whispering his queen's name.

Kaell gasped. *Was that pity? No. Please, no.* He had to hold on to his anger. It was all he had. Otherwise—what? Give in to someone who had abducted him, who was the cause of everything that happened to him?

As dawn breached the darkness, Nicky clattered down the stairs to poke at the ashen fire. "When did that go out? No wonder I dreamt I was in the Icelands. Though—" He grinned. "It wasn't all bad. There was this Ice lass—"

Kaell stirred on the pallet. He could hardly remember seeking the bed last night.

"You hungry, dread creature? Guess I'd best check with our dread lord about feeding you or whether he wants to serve you his blood again."

"I'm not hungry." Kaell wanted only to curl up, away from everything and everyone.

"Hope you had a long, hard think about what Roaran told you," Nicky said. "The good of the many and all that. I'd do it in a heartbeat if it meant bringing down a ghoul god."

"He took me prisoner," Kaell muttered. "Even if I might have agreed—"

"Your refusal will hurt him more than you. There's a song in that. Shall I sing to you?"

"Go screw a goat or something."

"There's that anger again. Best get it out, or it will poison you. Like it poisons him." Nicky walked away. Kaell heard a trapdoor thump and boots scrape a metal ladder.

Roaran wandered in, yawning. He combed his fingers through tangled hair. Warily, Kaell watched him, his backbone taut, his gut in turmoil.

"What are your plans for your dread creature today?" Nicky reappeared with a bowl.

Roaran slouched at the table, his face drawn. Unbidden, that same appalling memory flashed in Kaell's mind. Ice walls. Chains on an altar. Blood. Gasping, he shrank back.

"It takes a bit of getting used to," Roaran said quietly. "Being in my head."

Kaell drove his fist into the chair. "I don't want to be in your head."

"My memories will fade into dreams. The next time won't be as intense." He turned to Nicky. "Make him comfortable. I'm expecting guests and must remove the spell about this tower. Two nights from now, two moons will be full. I will rouse the brotherhood."

"I'll move the child from harm's way."

"Use a little of Juliette's potion. Needs be, I'll help."

"You're too delicate, Roaran. Caelan prince and all. Everyone knows their blood is thin."

Footsteps crossed the room, then Nicky waved a cup at Kaell. "The true believers come, dread creature. Best you go for a little sleep."

Kaell struggled hard as he shouted, "You keep away from me."

Nicky lifted his brows in delight. "Let's have a little tussle, then. I'm all restless caged up here."

Kaell wrenched his head away. He was still too weak to fight Nicky off.

Nicky grasped his jaw to trickle nectar into his mouth. "What shall we do to fill the time until you pass out? How about a song? I know a good one about fighting for the Isles."

Kaell moaned. "How long before I sleep?"

# VAL ARQUES

A horn pierced Val's sleep. Dawn's slumber shattered in a disharmony of drums, shouts, and cheers. He rose and stumbled to the door. "What's happening?"

The grille slid. A surly face appeared. "Not your concern. So shut up." The grille closed.

Val banged the wood. "What's going on? Is an enemy at the walls?"

A chair scraped then a second guard looked in. "You want me to come in there?"

"Just tell the fool," the first man said. "Then we can get back to our game."

"Keen, aren't you?" the guard called over his shoulder. "When you're winning." The man jeered at Val. "Who'd dare attack the Damadars? What with Lady Myranthe the most powerful sorceress in centuries. Our lord's back, that's all."

"What?"

"The Ice Lord himself. Rolland. He and the young lord, Velleran, travelled to the high lands to visit a healer of great renown. Both returned just now."

"Why a healer?" But the guard shut the grille.

Uneasy, Val pressed his back to the door. Kaell would have

found a rhyme in all this. "When the lord's away, the Damadars will play."

However, Rolland and Velleran's return did not bode well. Not if Velleran indeed had unpleasant plans for him.

The drums thumped into the dusk. As night gloved about the tower, the music of fiddles then ribald laughter and boastful cries drifted up from within the ice halls.

A boy brought food, but Val only picked at it. He prowled about the chamber, shoulders tense with apprehension.

The bolt rose. Griffin strode inside. A servant at his back set down an iron bucket of steaming water and laid garments, cloths, and soap on the bed.

"Clean up." Griffin leaned a shoulder to the wall. "My father wishes to see you."

"You're to help, are you? Or just watch?"

Shrugging, Griffin stomped outside.

Val disrobed and scrubbed, his thoughts disintegrating into anarchy. This was it. The Icelands lord summoned him to reveal his fate.

Now was the time for anger. That hard, bright fury that had carried him over those first weeks chained to the breaking stone. He needed it now to summon a haughty stare, to stiffen his spine. To demand they release him. But there was no fury. Only his twisting gut.

Clean and dried, he dressed in a lawn tunic and linen pants then pinned a black woollen cloak about his shoulders. *Garments worthy of a lord. A good sign or not?*

*No boots, though.* That limited his chances to escape. Thoughtful, he combed sleep-tousled hair then considered his stubble. *Too bad, Myranthe.* It stayed.

Griffin returned, nodded at Val's appearance, then held the

door wide. Boots or not, Val considered bolting to rile up Griffin—an entirely gratuitous romp through the ice caverns. He grinned to himself as guards marched him down the stairs. Heath, it seemed, had infected him.

Griffin strode behind, watchful. If Heath had been at his back, his hand on his sword hilt, Val might have teased him about his lack of trust to draw a retort. The younger Damadar, however, would only ignore him.

They took him through whitewashed passages, some so narrow, he choked on the guards' sweat and the fresh-bathed scent of Griffin's hair. In one cavernous room, lit by pitch, Val paused to stare at ice walls. Water dripped and pooled beside mats, low couches, and tables. More ice burned his soles. A guard shoved him on towards tall brass doors.

They stood open. At the sight of a vast hall within, Val's legs wobbled. He seized a breath—and prepared to learn his fate.

The pillared hall was fit for a king. Or a lord, as it happened. Val's toes sank into woollen rugs then brushed cool marble. Tapestries of battles and hunting scenes on desolate, white slopes draped the walls.

He passed his eyes over it all: the intricately carved screen that cut the long hall in two, the dark-wood chairs, the thick crisscrossed roof beams, the glowing fire in a hearth, the draped windows—to stop upon a gaunt, white-haired man in an imposing chair.

Footsteps died away. In the quiet, the man's breaths rattled. He narrowed unblinking, dark-brown eyes to an unyielding lance point on Val's face.

Myranthe sat nearby on a couch, her head bent over a book. Heath knelt to poke a metal bar at the fire. At his side, Judith lifted her shoulders in a gesture that said "What could I do?" then smiled.

Val grinned back. That one genuine smile comforted him. It even partially restored his self-belief.

A sturdy man of about thirty-five towered protectively at the older man's side. Velleran, surely. The Icelands heir wore a long-bladed sword in a careless manner suggesting it was always scabbarded at his waist. His hair, its light brown common to Adorean, curled softly to deceptively relaxed shoulders. His olive skin he had no doubt inherited from his Adorean mother as well. Velleran, the whispers went, could also inherit her brother's throne.

If he was prepared to fight for it.

Some men chose struggle and bloodshed for rich reward. Some did not. Did Velleran Damadar seek glory? Did men respect or even love him enough to die for him in battle? Val decided he didn't care. He cared only what this man chose to do with him.

Griffin pressed his shoulder. "Kneel."

Val bristled. *Woof. Should their dog run?* A merry old chase through unfamiliar ice caverns held wicked appeal. But he always told Kaell, "Pick your battles, boy." Deliberately without haste, he dropped to one knee.

"Father." Griffin bowed elegantly. "You asked to speak with our guest."

*Guest?* Val caught Heath's needling grin. *"Let's talk this out in a fire hall,"* that grin said. *"Just you and me, guest."*

Rolland's stare raked Val's face. He thought dark-brown eyes could not look cold. But this man's were glacial. "You are not what I expected, Vraymorg."

"Don't let the handsome face fool you." Heath threw down his poker and rose, dusting soot from his knees. "Val is a delightfully dangerous man."

"Obsession is dangerous, too, Heath." Myranthe did not look up from her book.

"I thought it overdue we talk." Rolland ignored them. "In my absence from the Twin Cities, things… happened. It is unfortunate my son treated you so poorly."

His apology was too late. "You didn't know Heath abducted me? Unlawfully?"

"Unlawful? I'd say opportunistic." Heath pressed his hands into Myranthe's shoulders.

Rolland gripped the chair arms. "Heath took you to serve our gods."

"This makes my abduction right?"

The Icelands lord waved away the objection. "Our gods demand we restore death riders. What is done in their name is lawful."

Val began to laugh. He couldn't help it. It was all too ridiculous. The breaking stone, the endless whitewashed walls, wine laced with potions, Myranthe's games, then this cold man and his dangerous brood. All for cruel gods who were not his.

Griffin struck him across the face. The punch spun Val back and down. He braced his arms against the floor so the impact only jarred his wrists.

"Stop." Velleran was at once beside his brother, grasping his shoulder. "You fool. I do not want him damaged." He glanced at the wooden screen.

Val pushed to his knees. *Odd words. And why that nervous look at the screen?*

"Do not mock gods you don't understand," Myranthe said quietly, still without looking up.

"What makes you think I don't understand your gods?"

She finally lifted her head. "Unlike your Isles gods, our god has real power. You should remember that, Val Arques Caelan."

He swiped at a bloody lip. Myranthe again had used his full name to show her power over him. *I know all about you, she meant. Nothing can be hidden.*

"Except Myranthe cannot sacrifice a man already corrupted by blood magic." Rolland's voice remained unsympathetic. "Our problem became what to do with a man we chained up—"

"Like a dog." Heath lifted a brow to Val. "That's how you put it."

"A lord of Telor, the Lord of the Mountains, no less, we made our enemy." Rolland clasped his hands together on a lap rug.

"It's Val Arques Caelan," Val corrected, his puzzled gaze on the screen. "As a forgotten man—" *Finely dressed, freshly bathed, but forgotten all the same.* "I am no longer custodian of the fortress Vraymorg and no longer entitled to that name."

"Did you feel neglected?" Heath tilted one brow. "I only chained you like a puppy to save you from my rapacious siblings."

"You smooth-tongued snake." Myranthe slapped off his hands. "You sought to break him for your own purposes, not save him."

"I could say the same. You made use of this man, also."

"My purpose is not secret. I use his Caelan blood in potions. What of it?"

"Strange way to take it. Scented wine, your hot hands all over his unclothed body."

Judith frowned. Then her detached gaze fell to the fire.

"Enough," Velleran commanded. Power resonated within the man's lyric tone.

Myranthe glared at Heath then returned to her book.

Telling, the stillness. Velleran did not demand respect; it was given.

"You brought this trouble upon us, Heath," Velleran said. "You acted without thinking. Reckless, as always. Fortunately for you, I've turned this to our advantage."

"Ransom me." Val held Velleran's light-eyed stare. "Once free, I can put aside the insult." The lie sounded sincere.

"If it were me, I'd come after Heath, after all of us," Velleran said.

"I'm not you."

Velleran smiled. A hard smile. "I am yet to understand what sort of man you might be, Val Arques Caelan. That makes you dangerous. In fact, my father thinks it safest to execute you."

"How will you do that?" His voice was steady. His heart was not. "Given I'm tricky to kill. I'm sure Heath and Myranthe told you all they know of me."

"Which is so very little." Heath sighed dramatically. "You blurt angry words when prodded, but otherwise, nothing real comes out. Though I do enjoy your bad temper. That sharp tongue. Judith likes your tongue, too, except she tells me it's not always so sharp."

"Shut up, Heath," Judith said.

Myranthe slammed her book shut. "Four Seithin temple knives will kill even a god. With a blood sacrifice, just one is enough."

"Will it be you then, Myranthe?" Val asked quietly. "Will you take up those four knives and drive them into me?"

"Your blood is far too valuable," she said. "If it were up to me, I would keep you imprisoned here so not only I but the Damadar sorcerers and sorceresses who come after me have use of you."

"I prefer the knives," Val said.

Myranthe's uncomfortable penetrating gaze held on him a moment. Her lips curved into a slow smile.

A knock at the door spared her any reply. The same robed scribe who had scribbled down his words from the other night entered, bowing low.

Velleran whirled. "Why are you here? I did not send for you."

"I sent for the brother-keeper," Myranthe said. "We are the holders of all knowledge, brother. This man is of Caelan's line. We must ensure his story is faithfully recorded."

"Leave." Velleran waved away the scribe, who bowed and backed out.

"Velleran." Myranthe pushed back her chair. "It is our duty. Think—"

He threw up a hand. "I said no. What happens here shall remain between us."

Rolland fitfully coughed up phlegm. Val remembered the guard's words about a healer. Was this man gravely ill? Unlikely compassion stirred in Val's breast.

"Father." Velleran tucked a blanket about the older man's chest.

"I'm all right." Rolland flapped a hand. "Let us finish this. As a lord of Telor, he deserves the truth." He blinked at Val, his eyes watery with pain. "I had you brought here as a gesture of respect. I imagine you are a man who likes to stare down his fate, no matter what it is."

"Then—what is my fate?"

Rolland leaned back. Heath again prodded embers. Myranthe closed the shutters against a rising wind. Judith hummed, her expression blank. No one looked at the screen. Yet Val's neck prickled. Someone watched.

Bluntly, dispassionately, Velleran said, "I intend to sell you."

"Sell?" A whir of troubling thoughts briefly overwhelmed him. Val glanced uneasily at the screen. "To whom?"

"A select, secret auction is underway. We invited a few parties to bid, those able and willing to pay well for such rare merchandise. A man with Caelan blood."

"You can't." Val shot up. "You have no right."

"And who will stop us, Val Arques?" Myranthe taunted. "That the king pronounced you dead means no awkward questions. In fact, it adds to your worth. Considerable as it is already, given how valuable your blood is to a sorcerer or sorceress. Though you'll find it unsettling to know some bidders have a purpose beyond magic."

"I have treated you as respectfully as I can, Vraymorg." Rolland pushed weakly to his feet. "The rest of this rather sordid business, I leave in my eldest son's hands."

He propped his shrunken body against the chair. "Until Velleran assesses the final bids, Myranthe will afford you every comfort possible as befitting a man of your rank—in return for a little of your blood for her potions. But scorn her kindness, and I'll throw you to my sons like meat to a pack of dogs."

A good way to describe Rolland Damadar's ill-assorted whelps.

"Every comfort," Val echoed dully as Griffin supported his father from the room. "I am not a man who ever craved comfort."

"I can always chain you to the rock again." Heath offered that slick smile of his. One dog eager to snap at the raw meat. "I promise to visit you often. You can be rude to me."

"Tempting. Can I also run you through with a sword?"

"Again with this rubbish?" Griffin snorted from the doorway.

"Enough. All of you," Velleran ordered. "Leave. Now."

Book in hand, Myranthe pushed back her chair and strode to the door. Judith rose to follow. She paused beside him. "Val—"

"Judith," Myranthe called. With a shrug, Judith trailed her outside.

Heath threw down the poker. As he passed Val, he said softly, "I'm sorry for it. I did try to keep you safe." He pulled the door shut at his back.

Val was alone with Velleran, his guards, and whoever hid behind that screen.

THERE WAS A SINGLE MOMENT empty of anything but the fear gathering inside him.

Then Velleran nodded. The guards pounced. Two grabbed Val's shoulders. A third tied his wrists and hurled the other end of the rope over a beam. Arms stretched above his head, Val tugged. Thick knots only seesawed over wood.

"Cut me free," he demanded, his panicked stare on the screen. "You have no right."

Velleran grabbed his jaw and turned it towards the light. "Fortunate. Griffin's lack of control shouldn't leave much of a bruise. Now stand still."

"Why? Who's behind that screen?"

Velleran flicked fluff off his captive's cloak. "Calm down. They only want to look at you."

"Who?"

"The final four bidders." Velleran scratched at his neck beneath his collar, disinterested. "They wish to see the merchandise is exactly as promised. Is it hot in here?" He turned to a guard. "Find a servant to dampen that fire. This room is stifling."

The guard briskly disappeared.

Val again wrenched at his restraints. He cursed.

"Just stay calm." Velleran strode to a cabinet and poured wine. "I understand you're indignant, that this is unpleasant. But it will not last long. No one will touch you. They only have the right to behold the goods at this stage."

A man in servant's robes stepped from behind the screen, head bowed as he scuttled to Velleran. "My lord, a request." The servant put a hand to his mouth.

Velleran listened, scowled, and snorted. "Entirely gratuitous. No."

The servant whispered again.

"Insist? Oh, very well." Velleran summoned a guard. "Strip him to the waist."

"No!" Outraged, Val writhed, heaving at the ropes.

The guard advanced. Dodging Val's kicks, he circled behind, unclasped his cloak, then tore off his tunic.

"Don't make such a fuss." Velleran drained his cup. "Surely a man who looks like you is used to unwanted attention. Indeed, my sister declares it astonishing you stayed free so long."

The guard stepped back. Val dropped his head, shaken by humiliation. To be unwillingly displayed—looked at—was more than uncomfortable. It was deeply unsettling. Almost unconsciously, his shoulders slouched towards his breast, to hide his physique from unwelcome eyes. But the rope held him in this position, wrists spaced, his body exposed to whoever observed from behind the screen.

Metal rapped against the door. Velleran frowned. "I said no disturbances."

"My lord," a man called from the passage. "It is important."

Velleran grunted, put down his cup, stalked to the door, and flung it back. "Well?"

A man stammered, "Apologies, my lord. A woman is at the gates. With a small escort of soldiers. She demands admittance."

"Demands?"

"She is very insistent, my lord."

Velleran shoved his fists to his hips. "Well, who is it?"

The servant dropped his voice. At whatever he said, Velleran visibly jolted. "There's no mistake?"

"No, my lord. Her insignia is on their banners."

Velleran scratched his chin. He faced the screen. "Unfortunately, honoured guests, I must draw this to a premature end. An urgent matter requires my attention. My sister will give you each a sample of the prisoner's blood."

At his nod, a guard cut Val free. Puzzled, Val stretched his shoulders and shook his wrists.

Behind the screen, whispering, shuffling, then muttered complaints broke out.

"My apologies." Velleran gracefully bowed to his unseen customers. "But as you see, the goods are as described." He spun back. "Return my guest to his room."

# HEATH

Heath rapped the door. He swayed—slightly. Five cups of wine was little enough for a man seasoned in decadence. Six, and he would pick a fight with a man. Seven, and he would pick a fight with a lot of men.

Judith edged the door open. She sighed heavily. "It's late."

"Only for some, Judith." Heath pushed unsteadily into the rock-walled room. It was low-roofed, snugly warm, and lit by firelight and candles smoking of beeswax. "The wine still flows below. Drunken fools are still groping young women or young men who won't look as pretty in the morning. Musicians are still assaulting my ears. Not to mention Griffin. He insisted on instructing me for a good half hour on how wine will make me slow, open to attack. Blah, blah, blah."

"Pup has a point."

"Indeed. I was in great danger tonight. All that wine and some fool of a fiddler swinging his bow around."

She closed the door behind him. "I'm not alone, Heath."

He sniffed. "The scented candles? I'm wounded, Judith. You never bring them out for me. Where is your scowling lover?" Or should he say, crippled lover? The description was mean, even for him.

Judith pulled a slipping nightgown back over her shoulder. "Asleep. And he doesn't scowl particularly." No, Pairas limped particularly. Because Dillon was particularly heavy-handed with a hammer.

Heath threw his cloak onto a table and sprawled in a chair by the fire. "What does he do then? No, don't answer that. I know. Everyone knows. Such frightening sounds from this room. It's too much for my delicate constitution."

"Heath." Judith impatiently flicked hair behind her ear. "Delighted as I am to see you—"

"If only you meant it, sister dear."

"But why must it be in the middle of the night?"

Because some fool of a fiddler had kept him awake? Wrong. It was his fool thoughts rattling around like a tune. "It's early, little Judith chick. Nearly dawn."

"You're in a mood. Go find someone to fight, Heath." She slid a look at the bedchamber.

"Did I interrupt something? So sorry."

"You're never sorry." Judith dropped her hands to her waist. "If you won't go away, tell me what's on your mind. Plots? Or just your usual nonsense?"

"My nonsense is never usual. No, I'm pondering what your scowling lover is up to."

"Pairas?"

"No, no. Your last scowling lover. The one Myranthe forbids you to go near."

"I'll go near Val if I want." Judith folded her arms. "It's you who shouldn't. You bring out the worst in him."

"He bites." Heath grinned fondly. "I dangle a little worm of an insult, and Val gobbles it up and then gives back as good as he gets—almost. He's not quite as witty as I am, but he does wound me at times. So Myranthe really did warn you off?"

Judith sat down stiffly. She shrugged.

"Told you she'd turn you into a toad or something?"

"Told me not to interfere," she muttered. "Anyway—"

"You had Pairas to play with. The male counterpart of you."

Judith broke up a startled laugh. "Whatever makes you say that?"

"You're both rather pretty." Heath swung his foot against the chair. "Both rather wanton."

"And you're both rather annoying and rather drunk. Please go away, Heath."

He leaned to touch her knee. "Do you miss him? Val, I mean. Any bold plans to rescue him? I know you're fond of our grumpy guest. And you have a kind heart. Perhaps you should be more like Myranthe. Calculating and cold."

"Perhaps you could be more like Velleran." She slapped his hand away. "Also calculating and cold. And not of a mind to wander the passages before dawn."

"I could never be as pretentious as Velleran. My lips would crack."

At her reluctant smile, Heath ached with loneliness. He missed her, missed the days when it was just him and Judith, hunting swordsmen. He missed, too, their shared confidences of childhood. *When did it change? With her new lover?*

"Heath." Judith yawned. "Will you go away? It's late."

And cold, even beside the fire. A sure sign dawn neared.

"I've been thinking about gods." He hiccupped, wondering if she had wine. "I have this idea they might look like Roaran Caelan. Myranthe—in a rare sharing but never caring moment—showed me an old parchment describing Roaran. Another Isles prince with curling raven hair. How dull. Blue eyes, though. You know she's obsessed with him. Roaran."

"Heath—"

"He's up to something."

"Roaran?"

"No, Val."

"You're really not going to leave, are you?" Judith sighed. "Very well. Let's talk about Val. I wouldn't be surprised if he was plotting something. He is a capable man."

"Yet he makes just one clumsy bid to overpower Myranthe's chief mischief-maker, Penn, only to run straight into guards and be marched back into his prison."

"Which means what?"

"That the serious bid is in the plotting stage. A longer game, shall we say?" Heath stroked his chin. "You tell me, Judith. You know him best. With you, he was not on his guard."

Her eyes misted. "No, not on his guard." The fire snapped and crackled. From the distant feasting hall, a fiddle's melody floated, lonely in the crisp predawn stillness.

"Perhaps you have something of his, Heath? He needs to get it before he escapes."

His mind clicked random incidents together. "Such a clever sister. All those questions Val asked about Kaell's sword. Even in Tide's End, his insistence it not be cleaned seemed odd."

"Kaell's sword?"

"That's it, Judith. We have his sword. And Val Arques Caelan wants it back."

"What's this about Val Arques?"

They both turned. Myranthe stood in the doorway.

"Look who's here, Judith," Heath said. "Our saucy sister. Or is that sneaky sister? Skulking about at dawn when all wicked sorceresses should be sleeping. Come inside, Myranthe." He sprang up and gestured. "Put your feet up and tell us all your guilty secrets."

"Why are we meeting here like this?"

"Who's meeting? I came to annoy Judith," Heath said. "And drink wine until the world makes more sense. Are you here to annoy Judith too? Or drink?"

"Velleran wants you." When Judith reached for her cloak, Myranthe added, "No, just Heath."

Heath stubbornly sat down. "Why?"

"He'll tell you himself." Myranthe rattled the door. "What are you waiting for? An invitation in gold ink?"

"Oh, very well." With a put-on sigh, Heath lurched to his feet.

"Sister. A moment." Arms folded, her tone determined, Judith blocked Myranthe's exit.

"Get out of my way. I've things to do."

"Not until you listen," Judith said. "Val did us no harm. But we treated him poorly. A lord of Telor, no less."

Myranthe curled up her top lip. "Why do you care? A night or two in this man's bed doesn't mean you know Val Arques."

"I don't *know* the stray dog on the street, but I can still pity it. Let me at least talk to Val."

"You'll do as you're told," Myranthe said tartly.

"I always do as I'm told." Judith turned her back to tilt a dying candle to a new wick.

Myranthe watched her with a tight frown. "This is unlike you, Judith, to question Velleran's decisions. Surely you can't think we should just let this man go?" She fluttered a wrist, scoffing. "A Serravan-trained bladesman with Caelan blood? It's astounding he stayed out of a sorcerer's clutches until now. Others will always seek to use him. Possess him."

"He could have found a place here," Heath said. "In time, I would break him down."

"I've seen captives broken in a day. It's simple. Find what they're afraid of. Use it."

"I said break down, not break." Heath whipped his sword half out then slammed it back into the scabbard. "If you hadn't interfered, I could make him love me, Myranthe. A man chained alone, in darkness, begins to long for anything other than the emptiness."

"Yes, yes. He begins to look forward to your visits. Your company. Your taunts, even. He'll beg you to stay. Even beat or torture him. Anything so he is not alone. But you forget—he is not yours to play with, Heath. You merely took advantage of Velleran's absence."

Heath grunted in disgust. "Velleran and his ships. He should be content to be Lord of the Ice. He will plunge us all into a costly war with Adorean if he seeks to take the throne."

"But if he succeeds, Heath." Myranthe rocked on her toes. "Think how powerful we will be. No longer beholden to Dal-Kanu. Not just lords, sovereigns. Feared. Respected."

Heath dragged ringed fingers through his hair. "Surely Velleran can fund his war another way. I agree with Judith. Val did us no wrong."

"You like him." Her tone turned sly. "Shall I tell you why he intrigues you?"

"No."

"Surely you want to understand your longing. Or… are you afraid?"

"Myranthe." Judith drew her gown tight. "Do not do this. I hate it when you're like this. You can wound us all too easily with words."

"And what about you, Myranthe?" Heath gripped his sword hilt so hard, his palm ached. "What sort of longing does he rouse in you?"

Blankly, she stared at him. "What did you say?"

"I asked what longing he roused in you. I asked if you, too, deceive yourself."

She looked away fast, smoothing her gown. "I want only to outwit him in our game. Because I need something from him. A story he does not wish to tell."

"Is that so?" He hid his surprise. Myranthe rarely misunderstood her own motives.

"Yes." She nodded to herself. "Yes. That's all. Though—" She wet her lips. "He is a striking creature. Defiant tonight as he heard his fate. What might it be like to play out this other game, the one I let him think he controls?"

Heath began to suspect what he had unwittingly awakened. His gut churned. He could not quite say why her words unsettled him.

"Velleran will grow impatient." She held the door, her expression again veiled.

"That's never good," Heath muttered as he brushed past. "He might do something sillier than usual." He paused to touch Judith's arm. Not in a gesture of support after Myranthe's belittling words. Judith was stronger than she seemed. No, it was a gesture of regret. He missed her.

"Heath." Myranthe curled a finger. He followed her into the corridor.

They walked without speaking, her raised shoulders the only hint she wrestled with her thoughts. Not a breath of air shifted within the predawn pall. But a chill off the stone slabs burrowed through Heath's boots and into his soles.

He tongued his furry mouth. A musty odour of spilled wine clung to his cloak. When he grew up, he'd drink less. Or when he grew old... though that wouldn't happen. Not now.

"You were right to challenge me," Myranthe said softly. "Indeed, I must thank you. If I did not examine this... hmm, need, shall I call it, then I might have known regret. Now I can cut it out and be done with him."

"Cut it out? You consider any softer feeling a pustule to be removed?"

"Isn't it? Never let obsession fester, Heath. Or do you not yet see it for that?"

"I know myself very well," Heath countered, defensive. "I know my every flaw. Every weakness, I've taken apart and examined. Every feeling."

Her face was partly shadowed. Passing torchlight lit coppery strands in her hair. "If you understand yourself so well, why deny what's wrong with you? Your hand trembles. You can't control it. You're deceiving yourself into pretending nothing's amiss."

Heath said nothing. He didn't look at her.

They reached the audience chamber.

Myranthe turned to leave. "I need not waste my time with this nonsense. She is a foolish woman to come here."

"She?"

"A silly, vain chit who Velleran will chew up and spit out. A needless distraction. I must prepare to trap the seer. The signs are clear. Roaran will be forced to return here. Soon."

The passage absorbed the sound of her steps as she walked off.

With a bemused "ha," Heath pushed through the doors. Dawn's first tentative rose spilled through chinks in velvet curtains onto the room's polished green-marble floor and columns.

Heath always thought of this high-roofed atrium as a chamber of echoes, far from intimate. Save for scattered benches and a cushioned lounge near the balcony where the idle could watch the symphonic beauty of sunsets across the valley, the room was bare.

At such an early hour, servants were yet to fling back shutters and let in the murmur of the stirring city beyond. Even so, from the mist clouded low and thick near doors, Heath knew the ground outside must crunch with frost.

His glance fell on Velleran's wife sitting straight-spined on a padded bench with a Quisnaf companion. Instead of her usual bored disdain, Pauli watched her husband with keen interest. Deceptively aloof guards waited a respectful distance away.

Velleran gripped the carved, wooden arms of a high-backed chair. Before him, a man and a woman stood like petitioners. Heath only just noted the woman's bright hair when she whirled with a hopeful gasp.

He blinked, completely astonished. *The Queen of Cahir. Here?*

"Heath Damadar. Thank Cyrah," Rozenn cried. "You'll understand." She rushed to seize his arm. "It's an outrage. Please persuade your brother to help me."

Still lost, Heath could only stammer, "What's happened?"

"How could you not know?" Rozenn dug her nails into his wrist. "That foul ghoul god attacked Cahir, seized my kingdom on behalf of Gendrick."

"What?" Heath exchanged a look with his brother. *Cahir.*

*Taken by Archanin. Its queen—here. Expecting what?*

"As I've explained, Your Grace," Velleran spoke with elaborate courtesy. "Very few ships risk sailing to the Cauldron in late autumn in case they are frozen in for winter. No news has reached us from Cahir, or even Telor, for a week now."

"Cahir is lost." Rozenn still groped Heath's arm. "An army of ghouls and Isles warriors overran Isamasalle. My protector, Tarvan Blackstone"—she gestured at the armed man—"helped me flee."

*An army of ghouls—and Isles warriors?* Heath rubbed his eyes. No sleep and too much wine were not helping him take this in.

Rozenn dropped her arms to her sides. "I am a queen without a kingdom. I must get it back. You will help me."

Velleran began to laugh. Heath knew that cool laugh. When he was a boy, it had meant his half brother was about to swat an irritating child aside. "And why should we do that?"

Rozenn faced him. "You must help, Velleran. The Icelands army can retake Cahir."

"And you will buy that army? With what?" No polite *Your Grace* this time. Not for powerless queens who had lost their thrones.

"Name your price," Rozenn hammered. "When I take back my kingdom, you'll have gold."

"No," Velleran said.

"What?"

"You have no gold. You have nothing but that pretty face. Do you think your beauty alone is enough to entice me to turn traitor? Gendrick Caelan is our liege lord. The Icelands will not betray our king. Especially a king powerful enough to seize Cahir. The answer is no."

"You cannot deny me." Rozenn stamped her foot. "There is no one else able to defy Gendrick, not with this fallen god at his side."

Alarmed, Blackstone turned towards her.

"No." Velleran's tone brokered nothing. "I will not stir to take back Cahir for you."

"Then that foul tyrant Gendrick wins. He already holds my son, Alecc. Now my kingdom."

Heath grimaced, incredulous. She couldn't really have thought Velleran would move an inch to help a queen of distant Cahir— and for gold she didn't have. Even if she was willing to offer more, even her body for a throne, nothing would move his calculating, cynical brother to act.

Velleran rose and stretched his shoulders. "You put me in an awkward position, Rozenn. I am loyal to my king. I know his mind, his heart. Again and again, he speaks of his love for you, of how he wants only an alliance through marriage."

"Love," Rozenn scoffed. "He wants to wed me to get Cahir. It was a mistake to come here. We will leave at once."

"No," Velleran said, condescendingly polite. "You will honour me by remaining as my guest—until I can send you to Gendrick so he may reunite you with your son."

"You can't." Palms raised, Rozenn backed up.

"What else can I do, little queen? It's my duty. Guards, take hold of Her Majesty. Gently."

"You will not," Blackstone shouted, whipping his blade out as he thrust her behind him.

Heath sighed. *Too early to spill blood. Such a mess on the marble.* He drew his sword.

A whirring cut the air. Blackstone groped at his breast. Between his fingers, a dark stain bloomed around a protruding knife. His blade clattered to the floor. For a heartbeat, he tottered. Then he folded.

Heath's startled gaze found Pauli. She was on her feet, fisting a second knife.

*A skilled throw,* he thought with reluctant admiration. But then, everyone knew how dangerous the Quisnaf were. If he were Velleran, he'd sleep in armour.

"Tarvan!" Rozenn fell to her knees beside the dead man. "You killed him."

"He dared draw steel in my husband's presence," Pauli said coolly.

Rozenn dragged a fist to her mouth to hold in her sobs.

"Oh good gods." Velleran winced in disgust. "I can't stand weeping. Heath, you take her. Arrest her escort. Put her somewhere comfortable until I can send her to Gendrick."

"I came to you for help, Velleran Damadar." Rozenn swiped at her tears. "And this is how you treat me. Like your enemy. I promise you, you'll rue this day."

Velleran sneered. "Because you'll curse me with a petty Cahirean spell? Be very careful who you threaten, my dear. Perhaps you haven't met my sister?"

"Your Grace." Heath stretched a hand to Rozenn. "If you would come with me."

Reluctantly, Rozenn rose. He placed his cloak about her trembling shoulders. She let him escort her from the chamber, her gait unsteady, her face ashen, her gaze on nothing.

That dawn chill still clung to stone in the corridor outside, its light smothering the torches' glows. The air breathed with woodsmoke and frost.

"Please." Rozenn drew up sharply. She grasped his hand. "Let me go. I'll give you whatever you want."

"I'm sorry for you, Your Grace. But you were foolish to come."

"There was nowhere else," she whispered. "Once—the Mountains. But not now."

Because Val was no longer lord. Heath remembered gossip in the king's camp about who had sired Rozenn's son. Surely not. He preferred the horned-demon story.

"I'll give you all I have. I'll give you—" Rozenn dragged her top lip over her bottom. "You can have me. Just let me go."

"Your Grace," Heath said roughly, "don't do that."

Rozenn pressed her hand to his breast. "Help me retake my throne and rule with me. I have no consort. Why not you? You're clever. Everyone says so. But as a younger son, you can never rule the Icelands. Put aside your wife, save me, and I will make you a king, Heath."

Gently, he took her wrist. "You are very beautiful, Rozenn. Entirely desirable. And if in Dal-Kanu, all those months ago, you had come to my room, I would have gladly made love to you. But not now, when you're desperate and don't know what you're doing."

"I'll tell you about the brotherhood." Her voice shrilled in desperation. "It is about to rise up. In the Mountains, the Isles, the Falls. In your caverns. The beginning of the end."

Heath stopped and turned. "I know about the brotherhood."

"You don't. You can't. No one does. Only him. The seer I see in my fire visions."

"I do," Heath said with a faint smile. "And tomorrow night, I even intend to hunt them down."

# VAL ARQUES

Val stalked the length of his tower cell. After a restless night tossing at nightmares then a restless day struggling with darkly uncomfortable imaginings, he could not banish his dread. Someone had hidden behind that screen, someone who wanted him for an unpleasant reason. The Quisnaf had long sought him, yes, but Velleran spoke of four final bids.

Pausing at the window, he gripped the bars. Daylight, thin and fleeting as winter neared, had already disappeared into a vast sea of darkness. In the face of the empty expanse, helpless despair nearly overwhelmed him. Not just bars, but this city, the land, and its extremes kept him from Kaell. The frost hardening the ground, the bone-stiffening cold—they were all foes to outwit.

He was running out of time. If Velleran sold him, the gods only knew how he would get to Kaell.

At the door's creak, Val turned sharply. A servant set a carafe on the table.

"There is a message." The young man shuffled his feet.

"Well, speak it then."

"My mistress says the wine is an offering of goodwill. She understands last night's events might prove troubling. She hopes to ease your distress a little."

The servant scampered off. The door shut. Val sniffed at the wine.

*Goodwill?* Myranthe wanted him unconscious so she could harvest his blood to present to prospective buyers or to concoct spells in her dark den. He assumed it was a den. Sorceresses always abided in gloomy holes filled with stinking potions, greasy lotions, and secrets.

Val considered the carafe. Tainted or not tainted—he didn't care. Let her take his blood. Tonight he wanted to escape himself. He drank a cup.

The Venivan wine was delicious, its fragrance the nectar of those last, lingering summer days in the Isles when a warm breeze rippled over an undulating sea. On a day like that, he had wed Finya, nervously vowing to protect her. Later, he'd awkwardly tried to undo her gown's copious buttons as his raven-haired wife giggled. Finya's joyous laugh sometimes filled his dreams. *If only I could picture her face...*

Time had locked away too much of his past. He couldn't remember their son's face, either, or the face of his cousin, Dace. But the feeling of how Dace's grin warmed like verdant spring after winter remained.

Yawning, Val undressed and stretched out on the bed. He had nothing else to do in this whitewashed room. Sleep came almost at once.

Light footsteps stole through his dreams. Soft fingers whispered down his cheeks to his lips. *Judith.* He smiled, rose to an elbow, and peeled back the blankets.

She dropped her cloak and lay beside him. In the darkness of his dream, her naked body was warm, her skin smooth. Her breasts pressed his chest. Her fingers knotted his hair. Pleasurable heat moved through him. Val put his hand on the nape of her neck to draw her close. Her mouth willingly opened beneath his, her tongue probing. He tasted wine mingled with the malt of her lips. She dropped her hand to his thigh, her rousing caress stealing higher.

"Judith," Val groaned as she stroked. Beneath her circling, rubbing touch, he grew urgently hard.

The woman pushed him down and straddled his hips. A maddening, wondrous, intoxicating spell fell about him; there was only moist skin, her moist mouth, that unbearable sweet need to touch, kiss, and feel. Still certain he was dreaming, he let his hands roam over her back and breasts, teasing nipples as she mounted him and arched her back.

"Judith," he moaned. "I've missed you."

# HEATH

The father-brother scuttled across the deserted square, as clandestine as a bull. Heath choked back a laugh as he crouched beside Dillon in an alley's murk deep in the caverns. A ménage of spice, blossom, and cold surrounded them.

Earlier in the night, silk-clad women, their hair swept up with combs, had called from balconies to passing men. In the window boxes of their houses, night-blooming winter orchids released fragrance. The perfume of pleasure.

Now only a watchman's steps echoed in the stillness.

"The old man's up to no good," Dillon muttered as they broke cover to follow. "Where might he be stalking to?"

"Can the father-brother stalk?" Heath mused. "He is a scholar. A record keeper. He scurries. To where? No one knows. Who knows anything in this life?"

Dillon did not reply. His boots crunched frost.

"I feel reflective tonight," Heath said airily. "Of a mind to think upon death, upon love, upon all manner of deep and even spiritual things. What do you think of that?"

"I think that captive in the tower unsettles you." Dillon waved the torch ahead. "I think you miss Judith, and this man fills some void."

"Dear Val. I enjoy our caustic conversation. Naughty of Velleran to want to send him away. Any idea who my brother's mysterious bidders are?"

Dillon grunted. "I've heard a few things. But I'm not saying. Especially to you when you're half in love with him."

"You're no fun tonight," Heath said. "Judgemental. There are different kinds of love, Dillon. There's desire. There's the love of friends. There's admiration."

His companion flung out a hand. "He's stopped. All your blither, and he nearly saw us."

"Blither? How unkind. Just what Myranthe would say."

"No, she'd call you a blithering lackwit."

"And turn me into a little bird, so my blither became a sweet tweeting."

"Shut up. I hate it when you're in this sort of temper."

"Distemper, you mean." When he got no response, Heath dropped to his haunches. "All right, I am chastened and focused. What is our stalking scholar doing?"

Beneath a blazing torch, the father-brother greeted a man with a back-slapping embrace. They whispered together, then the newcomer grabbed the torch and hurried down an alley. With a glance over his shoulder, the father-brother followed.

"Now that was a furtive look," Heath said.

Dillon doused their light. They slipped after the bobbing torch.

Their targets stopped at a door. Again, the father-brother peered about, shifting his weight. The door opened. The two men entered.

"Wait here," Dillon said. "Be silent. That means no blithering. I'll fetch the others."

Heath shoved his back to a stone wall. A restlessness tugged at him, a need to be elsewhere, saving Val from Myranthe's nasty game. Val was too straightforward to take on Myranthe but too stubborn to back down when outplayed.

He nibbled his lip, thinking about Dillon's words. *You're half in love with him.* That wasn't it. But something lay behind his complicated mess of yearning and need.

*Obsession?* Myranthe's word. Heath shifted uncomfortably.

He hadn't dared dwell on it before, let alone say it. Obsession. Dangerous, dangerous obsession. Obsession would distort his thinking, leave him vulnerable. It had to be cut out. A quick final severing.

Dillon returned with soldiers. Heath led them to an entrance cut into rock. At his nod, Dillon kicked in the door. In a spacious room, six startled faces turned. One or two of the men went for swords. The soldiers fanned out, threatening the strangers with blades until they all whipped up their hands.

The father-brother looked helplessly from the armed intruders to Heath. His lip quivered. "My lord," he stammered, "why are you here?"

"Where are the women?" Heath took in the surprisingly opulent room. Tongues of flame danced in the hearth. Rugs hung from walls and lay thick on the stone floor beneath chairs, tables, and chests. It was warm and comfortable, not quite his idea of a den of intrigue.

"Dillon." He threw his arms wide. "You promised me women, exotic creatures of rare beauty—and rare talents."

"There are no women here," said a stranger. He was young, very clean, and impeccably dressed, with an artfully shaped beard and fierce, dark eyes.

Heath sighed. No one was any fun tonight. No one understood him. Judith perhaps, but she was too busy pretending at love. Obsession or not, he would have to torment Val. He appreciated Heath's nonsense enough to snarl at least.

"No women." Heath stroked his shaven chin. Maybe he should grow a beard like that man's. His new wife might like it. She didn't seem to like much about him at the moment. "Only traitors."

"My lord, no." The father-brother burst forward. So eager to tell Heath lies, he would surely wring his hands. Soldiers pressed him back.

"But you meet in the dead of night, deep within the caverns. Surely plotting to overthrow kings or lords. Perhaps murder my brother."

"Not traitors," the father-brother insisted, his face stricken.

"Oh, I know," Heath said. "I'm only teasing you." He waited until the man flushed with relief, then he said, "You're a sword brotherhood."

A silence fell hard. The strangers exchanged uneasy glances. The bearded one lifted his chin. "What is this? A sword brotherhood?"

"A brotherhood of swords." Heath explained patiently. "Like that old poem. My sister reminded me of it. You'll have heard of her. Myranthe. The sorceress."

The nervous looks flew again. Myranthe had that effect. Hand-wringing would surely begin at any moment.

"The sorceress." The man tongued his cracked lips. "Then she knows. She's seen us."

"Seen it all," Heath lied. "When seed of ancient swords rise again, in cells they call brotherhoods of men. Something like that." He smiled broadly.

Still no one spoke. Every one of them stared at him in horror.

"Then we are discovered," a third man whispered.

"Oh gods." The father-brother dropped his head.

Heath sprawled in a cushioned chair with padded armrests. Legs crossed, he leaned back and smiled disarmingly. After all, he didn't want to take their heads. Only their secrets. "So, this brotherhood. Tell me all about it."

"Say nothing." The bearded man wiped damp hands on his pants. "He's bluffing. The sorceress has not seen anything."

"Dillon, kill someone. I don't care who."

Dillon brightened. He didn't like talk so much. But killing? Now that was straightforward.

"No, stop, stop." The bearded man stepped in front of Dillon. He shoved his hands in pockets, his breath quavering. "What do you want to know?"

"Why are you all here? Why is the furtive father-brother here?"

"You followed me." The father-brother groaned. "This is my fault."

"What is your purpose?" Heath said.

"We don't know it," the bearded man said.

"Dillon, kill a few of them."

"No, wait my lord." The father-brother threw up his palms. "We'll tell you the little we do know. Those of us gathered here are all descended from Serravan warriors. Dead warriors."

Dillon scowled at Heath. "What is this?" that scowl said. "What mess have you landed me in?"

"We all started to have dreams." The bearded man grew eager to make Heath understand. "As soon as Gendrick Caelan took the throne. 'Upon blood throne sits Caelan king,'" he recited. "That's the first line to that prophecy."

Heath's scalp crept. So it really was all about a silly, old rhyme. Collars of ice, lost seers, sword brotherhoods. Myranthe would be rapturous.

"The dreams drew us here. We're to wait until the seer transforms us with his spells." The father-brother fell to his knees, fingers cradled. "My lord, we don't plot against you. I swear it." He gulped. "What will you do, my lord? About us, I mean."

Heath grinned. "That's simple. See my cousin there? Not much family resemblance, true. He's not quite as appealing as me, but he's charming in his own way."

They all looked at the charming Dillon.

Maybe Heath should tell him to curtsey, twirl, or say something charming. He caught Dillon's scowl. *Or not.* "My charming cousin Dillon—you'll like him when you know him, truly—is going to join your brotherhood."

# KAELL

Kaell woke on a cot, caged behind iron beneath the stairs. At once, he surged up and gripped the bars. Pain shot through his hands. "What's this?" he bellowed. "Let me out."

"Witch weed infused in the metal." Juliette slouched on the steps level with his head. Dust motes danced in moonbeams spilling about her through ruptured walls.

With a groan, Kaell dragged hands down his face.

"Don't be afraid," Juliette said. "No one wants to hurt you. Especially Roaran. He'd spare you if he could. But he can't. If this doesn't happen, this land will bleed for centuries."

Kaell hunched his shoulders angrily. "He's a monster. Everything that happened to me, the way I am now, is all because he manipulated me."

Juliette shook her head. She looked sleepy and warm, her lovely hair tumbling about her shoulders. "You're wrong about Roaran. This isn't easy for him."

"Go away," Kaell muttered. "Just go away. I can't stand any of you."

"You sound like a rebellious child." She sighed deeply. "I thought you'd be different. I don't know… terribly noble. Given you were a warrior dedicated to Khir."

"Rebellious," Kaell spluttered. "I didn't ask for this, to become part of his plots." He dropped onto the bed. If only his lord were there, telling him it would be all right. The comforting thought briefly dazzled. Not to be alone. To be understood.

Kaell considered the cell. A few paces long and nearly as wide, it was close to the doors. Besides the cot, it held a clay water carafe, a bucket, neatly folded pants and tunic, and a tub of water. A high grate framed a moon in a deep-purple sky. "How long did I sleep?"

"Two days," Juliette said. "You're probably hungry. Nicky will bring you food. Blood, if you need it. You'll find clean garments and cloth for washing on the bed. There's a bigger tub in a back room." She giggled. "Roaran bathes daily. Nicky too. A little dirt, and they both cry like babies. What's the expression? Once an Isles man, always an Isles man."

"How long will I be kept here?" Kaell asked. "Until I agree?"

"Roaran will talk to you. But not tonight. Tonight, he must awaken the brotherhood."

"The brotherhood? I keep hearing that word. What is it?"

"You should bathe," Juliette said. "Things look brighter after a bath, I find."

Alone, Kaell disrobed and stepped into the tub. He scrubbed his skin hard, focusing on the task so he didn't have to face the turmoil within.

Just as he finished dressing, the tower doors crashed open. With a blast of wind, with a drag of red cloaks over the slab floor, three women stormed in. Candlelight glistened on their swords. Only a crack of thunder could have made their entrance more dramatic.

Kaell pressed closer to the bars as Roaran descended to the hall. Barefoot, he wore only a short dark-blue tunic and pants, the simple garments worn with an effortless elegance Kaell now associated with the Isles. "Greetings, sisters. Greetings, Ailis."

The tallest dropped to one knee. Like her companions, she wore loose pants tucked into calf boots and an unadorned, woollen tunic belted at the waist. Creamy skin and dark-red lips were at odds with her severe plait of long chestnut hair. "Your messenger sent word you have need of us. How may the Sisters of Cyrah aid you, Roaran Caelan, servant of the old gods?"

*Sisters of Cyrah.* Kaell shivered. His world, already tilted, already a dangerous, frightening place, shifted again. First a dead king. Now half-mythical warriors of a goddess.

Roaran grasped the woman's shoulder. "Rise, Ailis. I need both your sword and wit."

"Death rider." The youngest impatiently shifted her weight.

Ailis whirled. "You speak out of turn."

Roaran said, "Child, I cannot see you."

A memory nagged. Kaell's books taught that according to the Sisters' traditions, a stranger must only recognise the elder unless she permitted a younger sister to speak.

"She is Sloana." Ailis waved a hand. "She may speak, though her words will be nonsense."

"Sloana." Roaran arched a brow. "That means warrior."

Ailis shrugged. "She is our gift to you. Or our curse. An ill-disciplined child, as you see, who does not know her place."

"A child," Sloana tossed lank brown hair over her shoulder, her scowl insolent, "who won a contest of swords for the right to fight with you, seer."

Roaran circled his gift slowly, the assessment another tradition Kaell recognised. Roaran nodded. "She will do."

Sloana slapped her thigh, her square face red with excitement. She was thick-necked with shoulders that slumped with muscle. No doubt she could swing a sword. Though Kaell wondered if she would be slow, more bull than snake. Bladesmen must be lithe as well as strong. His lord had taught him how to stretch his limbs to stay graceful, to balance the bulk of muscles.

"Our warrior sisters wait outside the walls," Ailis said. "Tell us what you need, seer."

Roaran rubbed a stubbled chin. "I need you to bring me a man. Unharmed. He is Varee and will not come willingly. It will be dangerous."

She sniffed in contempt. "Dangerous? Against scum."

"Many scum," he corrected. "You cannot easily ambush the Varee, Ailis."

"You will bring a fog across their lands. We will take them by surprise."

Kaell edged as close as he could, intrigued. The third sister, her face hidden beneath a hood, looked his way. Beneath her stare, he froze, oddly unsettled.

Again, Roaran needled his temples. "It is a spell I have not cast for many centuries, but it is a sensible idea. Yes, I will bring fog across their lands."

"And we will deliver this man you seek." Ailis gestured to the hooded woman. "The old mother insisted upon journeying with us, seer. She brings a warning."

The third sister bent her head. Strands of dark-red hair wisped about a bony jaw. Without offering her name, she said, "Heed my words, seer. They are dire. Someone seeks you through the Enarae. I glimpse them often now, hear their incantations."

Roaran shrugged. "Many with magic move through the Enarae."

She threw back the hood. In daylight, her eyes might have been a washed-out Venivan blue. In the twilight, they seemed opaque. "You do not grasp my meaning... They know your name, seer. Your true name."

Wind blew the doors back. Leaves scuttled over stone in a furious dance. The creak of the well bucket seemed far away. Sloana rushed to shut the doors again, closing off the empty, abandoned whispers of the dead city.

"You're certain?" Roaran's voice was low, his shoulders up.

At their tense postures, Kaell's spine tingled with unease. More mystery.

"I am certain. They cast spells to find Roaran Caelan, son of Karolus, lord of the Isles, son of Marginet of Quisnaf, descendant of the sorceress Sorgaine."

"I felt a shift," Roaran said distantly. "A shadow on my mind as if the Enarae warns me of danger. Except I cannot drain my strength with a vision before I rouse the brotherhood."

"You must. Your name is known. You are in peril."

"Who?" Roaran braced a shoulder to a pillar. "Myranthe Damadar? Does she dream in her den of my return, of placing that collar of ice about my neck?" He laughed coldly. "I will never return. The Icelands is the one place I cannot go. I know that."

"You must uncover your enemy," the woman said. "They weave strong magic in a bid to trace you. They name you properly before the gods. They shall have power over you if you do not stop them. You cannot fall. If you do, seer, this land falls with you."

Roaran slumped onto the steps, Ailis and the hooded woman beside him. Unable to hear, Kaell could only puzzle at their gestures, at why the third sister scratched patterns in stone.

Sloana prowled about the chamber. Pausing by the cage, she stared guilelessly at Kaell. "I envy you. You will help him bring down a god."

Kaell backed up to the bed to escape her words. Everything he had lost, every foul thing that happened to him, was because of Roaran. For all his charm, he couldn't do what the seer king wanted.

Ailis rose. "Sloana," she called sharply. "Your lord did not bid you talk to his captives."

"Perhaps she can talk some sense into him." Roaran pushed to his feet.

Ailis gripped his arm in a salute. "If you are ready to cast your spells, we will ride to the Varee village and do them harm."

"Except him," Roaran said.

"The man who is lost, who seeks to find his way," the third woman muttered.

"We know him by reputation, my lord," Ailis said. "We will separate him in battle, capture him, and bring him to you. The rest we will take as slaves."

She glanced at Sloana. "The child will serve you well enough, Roaran Caelan."

"If she does not," her companion's voice was throaty, "take a whip to her."

"I would not dare."

"You?" Ailis scoffed. "You dared ride across our lands where no man will go. You dared challenge me with steel. Once, centuries ago, you fled a prison of ice. 'You cannot use me,' you told the gods. 'I will be free.' You will never waver, Roaran Caelan. I know you."

Kaell dropped his head into his hands, groaning. Roaran would not turn from his path.

Their footsteps faded as Roaran escorted them outside. A hush clung to the tower, with its cracked walls, its ivy-strangled pillars. A few candles licked at cold air.

Through the grate, Kaell heard Juliette talking quietly with Roaran outside. "You can and will persuade him. There is still time."

Kaell could not hear Roaran's reply. It fell quiet. He lay on his back, staring at the broken roof. A long while later, more voices carried. A man said, "You look ill."

"I wove a spell to bring mist," Roaran said. "Did you come to find me? From the look on your face, you have something on your mind."

A boot scraped stone. "Don't do this, my lord." The unseen man's voice was low and tight, distorted by the grid. Not Nicky's. The man Kaell had heard on that first night in the tower.

"I like this little enough because of him. But for your sake,

Roaran, I beg you to find another way. Even holding him against his will is wrong. Such an act must change you. You will be less than what you are."

"If I do nothing, Archanin wins," Roaran said.

"Put aside this prophecy. I love you too much to wish this burden on you."

Silence. Then Roaran said, "Burden, yes. Tell me who else can carry it?"

# DANNON

Aalart fell with a grunt, his blunted sword clunking on dirt. Dannon pulled him to his feet. "Keep better distance. You let me get too close."

Save for two bored guards, they were alone on the training field. Smoke rose from huts as dusk closed with rose shards about the half-deserted village. A handful of slaves tended to the firepit. Old men gossiped on verandas. Sentries guarded the bridge, watching for the return of the Varee host out plundering a merchant's caravan.

"It's meant to be a ruse." Aalart's grin always surprised Dannon with its warmth, how it altered his face so he seemed little more than a boy. "I'm inviting you in so I can pounce."

"'Look, look, I'm near so you can strike?'" Dannon raised a brow. "Not working, is it?"

"Because you don't react the way you should. Then just when I think my invitation failed, you attack."

"Catching you unbalanced, both on your feet and in your mind. Funny that." Dannon pressed the sword into his hand. "Again. And don't show me your intentions."

"Easier said than done. You don't fight right. You're tricky. Not—" Aalart stopped.

"Not honourable?" Dannon shook sweat from his fringe, unoffended. "There is no honourable, Aalart. There's only dead."

"There are rules," Aalart protested. "Bladesmen are more than brutes."

"Says who?" Dannon took guard, sword extended. "Again. Wear me down. I'm not at my full strength after that whipping. Forty lashes takes a toll. Don't play nice. Use it."

Aalart's eyes gleamed with the thrill of contest. He beat the blade. Dannon did nothing. The other man lunged. Dannon retreated, waiting for that single moment of broken rhythm. When it came, he changed speed and chased Aalart down hard. His opponent responded with rapid parries.

"Every time you use the blade, you give me information," Dannon instructed. "So don't do it unless it's necessary. Use your feet first. Distance, boy, distance."

"I prefer steel between us if it were you and me," a man said.

Dannon drew up, wincing as underused thigh muscles clenched. He clipped his blade to his belt.

Patrick grinned. "Don't let me stop you, Bloodtaker."

"We're done." Dannon gestured to the guards.

Aalart surrendered his weapon. "Back to the hole."

"For now."

The guards marched the prisoner off. Patrick shook his head. "It won't work. You'll have to cut his throat sooner or later. Do it sooner, I say, Dannon."

"The boy looks forward to our bouts."

"Next, he'll call you brother and embrace you—just before he stabs you in the heart. If you're serious about this, we'd best find the boy a wife. Nothing binds a man to the clan like a woman's bedazzling charms."

Just as they had bound him. A vivid, sweetly bitter memory formed in Dannon's mind—a woman's tinkling laugh as she pulled him down into a field of calamint and petals from shedding wild rose bushes, sunlight glinting on her unruly hair.

There had been sunlight, too, when Eloise died. A bright stream through open shutters, the air soft with blossom. His wife, their unborn child, and all that tied him to the Varee dead. *So why not leave? Why not?*

Grief tossed in his gut. Dannon shook off the past and retrieved his cloak. "You've been gone days. Archanin, surely, didn't want you to search that long for Kate. Any sign of her?"

"Not a thing."

A twig snapped. Dannon spun. Beneath night's new cloak, an eerie mist slunk across the river, wisping between trunks, thickening as it rolled towards them. Within, shadows ran to and fro.

Patrick patted his shoulder. "You're twitchy tonight. Fog, that's all. There's nothing—" An arrow thudded at his feet.

Dannon groped for his blade. Figures darted through mist. "Ambush," Dannon shouted. "The river. We're under attack."


A SMATTERING OF STARS GLOWED. Cicadas chirred. A paw disturbed leaves. Then nothing. The mist vanquished even the darkness, its cold, damp void drawing in every sound as it advanced.

A sentry at the palisade took up the cry. "Attack! Sound the alarm!" Men joined them from the village, waving torches, swords, or spears.

"Fall back," Dannon said. "They've archers."

"Where? Fog's too thick to make anything out."

Patrick stabbed his blade towards the dim woodland as he edged back into pallid moonlight. "There."

Shadows wedged between embracing trunks and boughs. Dannon could see nothing. "Someone fired at us." *Why aren't they still firing?* The moon offered clear, if distant, targets for enemy archers.

Patrick snatched up the arrow. He cursed. "The Sisters of Cyrah use this fletching."

Men stiffened, muttered, and peered uneasily into the pressing grey cloud. The moon at their backs frosted thatched roofs, its glow besieged by the expanding grey mass.

A panting sentry ran up, a fleck of ash on his face. "The bridge guards are missing."

"They're here." Dannon's neck prickled.

This was how Cyrah's warriors liked to attack. In blackest night, they would sweep in to stir terror then fade away. But it had been years since they had dared challenge the Varee.

"Should we go in there and kill them?" The sentry poked his blade at the trees.

"No." The mist crept ever closer to the bunched men.

Dannon roughly counted his companions. Too few. Most of his warriors were still tracking that Cahirean caravan through the gorge, hoping for rich pickings.

"Nicca." He called an archer to him. "Take some men and circle right. Get behind them, but don't go into the forest."

An owl hooted. Nervous men spun. Moonbeams glittered briefly on drawn steel before mist enfolded the tense men. At once, figures rushed from the trees.

"Smash through," Dannon yelled as he ran forward.

His men roared and charged into a line of attackers. Bodies, metal clashed as though parts of a beast had become one, then buckled, splintering into limbs, a torso, and a head. The night broke up into madness. Shouting. Cursing. Shrieking, clanging steel. A press of violent death.

Dannon broke through the line. Potential opponents slipped away. Startled, he whipped around seeking someone to fight. Two figures leapt at him, stabbing, not slashing. As he jumped back, he glimpsed their faces and long, pale braided hair. He knew who attacked them, but the sight of two women still unnerved him. For an instant, he baulked.

His hesitation gave them an obvious opening. Neither took it. Instead, they circled, jabbing. One yelled to someone behind.

Dannon whirled in time to block a low-thrusting spear.

A spray of blood and innards blinded him. He swiped his eyes. A man reeled into him then collapsed. A woman yanked her sword from his corpse. She ran past Dannon as if he did not exist, shouting as she ploughed into the melee.

More warriors streamed from the mist. Some dropped flaming torches onto tinder-dry grass. Flames roared up. Their light revealed a grotesque scene of writhing bodies caught in furious, ugly, straining dark knots. The night ran with screams, a pounding through the earth, and that stridor of metal. The scent of blood, sweat, and smoke was grease-thick.

Dannon's scalp prickled with dread. His men were outnumbered. And even more figures swooped from the trees, bellowing, firelight reflecting off their naked steel. Yet still only three engaged him. He swung at the closest. She blocked but didn't riposte. He hewed again into another heavy parry. More circling. More thrusts at his calves.

The third flanked to cut off his right. He half wheeled towards her. If all three came at him at once, he was dead.

They didn't. They dogged him. Driven back towards the fire, Dannon could only extend his sword into a wall of iron. The women worked in tandem, forcing him left along the line of flames, herding him away from the others.

Realising the blaze blocked his retreat, he jerked in alarm. They were separating him from his men. Desperate, Dannon struck out with rabid cuts, thrusts, sweeps. But he could not breach their combined defences.

A whip cracked. It whistled through air a heartbeat before it hit his shoulders. He yelped. Another crack. Pain burst across his thighs. It cut his breath, nearly knocked the sword from his hand. He staggered. In that split instant of distraction, steel pressed at his neck.

"We have him." A woman wrenched his blade off him. "Finish this."

A hilt cuffed him on the side of his head, putting him on his knees. Panting, dazed, Dannon struggled to grasp what had happened. His sword was gone. His gaze blurred on carnage.

There were too many dead men. Too many Sisters of Cyrah. He could only watch as the survivors surrendered, as women rounded up captives and prowled among the wounded. Across the fiery barrier, frantic villagers cried out to brothers, fathers, or sons.

Two warriors dragged him into the ring of prisoners. The dying fire crackled around them, leaving a line of blackened earth. The line was impossibly straight, as if someone had poured oil there earlier.

A gaunt-cheeked woman approached, attended by two armed companions. Mud splashed a long gown entirely out of place among pants, tunics, leather surcoats, and helms. The last licks of flame caught red glints in her plaited hair. "Show me."

To Dannon's surprise, her escort brought the woman to him. He lifted his head, his eyes slitted in anger as she inspected him. Wisps of hair strayed about her bony, lined face. It was too dark to see the colour of her eyes, but she held them intently upon him.

"Olinda, Priestess of Cyrah. I would speak with you." With a *thump, thump* of his stick, the mage walked barefoot through hot ash. Sweat glistened on the folds of loose skin on his bare chest and on his ugly skull-like head. His bone necklace rattled.

The closest women drew back, glowering. But none stopped the mage on his path to the priestess. Once he reached her, he bent his head to whisper. Puzzled, Dannon watched the two speak quietly together, a curious symmetry to the way each leaned towards the other.

He tried to guess what they said from gestures, from the way the mage clapped his stick into the ground. From the woman's sly smile as she lifted an arm to point—at him.

The mage turned. He looked right at Dannon. There was something stiff about his posture. A nearby captured warrior on his knees also lifted his head to gape at Dannon.

Then a drumming rumbled through the earth. The stillness erupted to chaos. Women gripped swords. They spun towards the bridge as dust clouded against the first moon. Dannon gasped in hope. The Varee host had returned.

A warrior rushed up to a woman near the priestess.

"How many?"

"At least sixty."

The priestess bristled with annoyance. "Leave the others. Bring him. He is the prize."

"No." Dannon jerked free. His captors groped at him, cursing. He swung his fists, twisted his body. Kicked. Thrashed. Broke free. They would not take him.

Riders leapt the smouldering fire. A few women turned to meet the challenge, but only a few. The rest slipped away like smoke.

"They'll escape to the river." Dannon grabbed a dropped sword and whirled to fight off his attackers. No one was there.

Varee warriors sprang off mounts to chase the sisters into the forest, slashing at long grass or scything branches, prowling the riverbank, swords drawn.

The mist retreated fast over the water. Moonlight winked through leaves. The night was again bright with starlight. No sign of the sisters. No sound of them. No bodies or wounded had been left behind.

Men regrouped near the blackened fire. Villagers searched among the dead and injured, wailing at the sight of a beloved face, calling for healers. Dark wings circled the carnage.

Focused on taking control of the disorder, Dannon didn't notice at once how warriors crowded about the mage, listening. Not until a man turned to scowl. Not until the mage jabbed a finger at him. With a single beat, his mind registered an unstated threat.

Two men stomped up then hesitated. One looked at Dannon's drawn blade and nibbled his lip. Villagers edged forward, sensing drama, isolating him in a press of curious onlookers.

The mage forced his way to the front. "Why do you hesitate? Arrest him."

*Arrest?* Astounded, Dannon tilted his chin defiantly. "On what charge?"

The mage's face was hard, his mouth set in a tight, pitiless line. "Their priestess declares a claim on you. She says I must not interfere because it is a matter for the gods, that they call you to serve them in an ancient brotherhood. But I know what this brotherhood is. It is intent on destroying us and our god."

Anger warred with Dannon's shock. Hisses, mutters, and glares heated his back.

"What? This is nonsense—" At a clout between his shoulder blades, Dannon's knees hit dirt.

"Take him," the mage said.

Men seized his arms. Others snatched his sword. Sneering, Patrick tore Dannon's pouch of mord's breath from his belt. He tipped it up and let the wind catch the powder.

"You'd trust their word?" Shahven shoved through the riled crowd. "The Sisters of Cyrah will say anything to destroy us."

"He's an outsider, boy," a man shouted. "It's him we can't trust."

Shahven spread his arms, pleading. "You know this man. You, Nicca. You, Warren." He confronted each warrior as he named them. "You, Patrick. You've all fought beside him, call him friend. Their priestess lies. She wants us to turn on our strongest fighter."

"The mage speaks the truth."

Heads turned.

Natasha stood at the front of the villagers. "It hurts me to admit it, but it's true. He plots against us. He and the woman who shares his bed. This Kate."

"Natasha," Dannon stammered, "what is this?"

She looked him right in the face. "Once, relaxed after our lovemaking, he boasted of how he's so clever and we're all so stupid, we don't see his schemes."

"Don't do this, Natasha."

"Where's his new lover now? Where's Kate? Run off to join her sisters, no doubt. That's how they knew to attack us when the host was away. She was their spy here."

A low mutter picked up then erupted to outraged shouts. Villagers fisted their hands or rattled spears. Dannon struggled in his captors' hold. He'd fought for these people, laughed with them, shared stories. Now they stared with loathing as though they'd never known him.

"Take him." The mage thumped his stick. The clunk jangled up Dannon's spine with foreboding.

"Wait." Robert stepped forward. "You cannot condemn a man merely on the word of the faithless Sisters of Cyrah."

"I shall not," the mage said. "I'll test what her words have unwittingly revealed."

"Test?" Robert said. "What does that mean?"

"It means I'll do what I should have when he first told me of his dreams."

Dannon dug fingernails into his palm. Those cursed nightmares.

"Dreams?" Patrick echoed.

Some in the crowd elbowed each other or whispered. Robert dropped his head. Natasha stood with her hands to her hips, sneering triumphantly.

"He told me of strange dreams, but I did not heed the danger," the mage said. "Now I'll uncover the truth. Learn if we have a traitor in our midst, a man sent to destroy us and our god."

"How?" Shahven scoffed. "You'll torture him? That will take many days, and information gained through agony is never reliable. You taught me that, old man."

"No." The mage's eyes glazed as if he already looked into the otherworld. "I shall follow him into his dreams."

# KAELL

He knew each man at the table. But not one would look at him. Not Torin, nor the silk merchant Giles, nor the arrow smith Dean. Not even Felix Hillborn.

"Torin." Kaell pressed as close to the bars as he dared. "Torin, please. You know this is wrong. Help me."

The young warrior kept his eyes steadfastly on his clasped hands. Giles swung a mud-splashed boot against the table leg. His short sword poked from beneath an impeccable cloak, his shoulder-length brown hair brushed and shining. Dean also pretended not to hear as he smoothed his canvas tunic with a calloused hand.

Early moonlight slinked through cobwebbed arrow slits into lamplight that slashed shadows, its sallow glow on their enraptured faces. Pitch and smoke swirled.

Feet bare, head uncovered, Roaran paced a tight line. He paused to squeeze Felix's shoulder. "No word of Aalart?"

"He is lost to me," Felix said bitterly. "Because of that man. Dannon."

"Aalart is no traitor. Things are seldom what they seem."

"I wish that were so, my lord. But I saw Aalart kill Philip."

Guiltily, Kaell dropped his head. He had to tell Felix the truth, to find the courage to speak shameful words. *I killed Philip. I killed your lord. His son. My lord's son.*

"I can't ask this of you, Felix," Roaran said. "With Philip dead, I need you to hold the fortress of Vraymorg."

"You must ask," Felix said. "Whoever I become will hold Vraymorg for you."

*Become?* Kaell shivered. What dark magic was unfolding here?

"The spell may not work on you." Roaran wearily rubbed his eyes. "The dreams called to Aalart."

"Felix." Kaell gripped the bars, careless of their burn. "Felix, you know me. Do you understand what he wants of me?"

The man still would not look at him. "I cannot help you, Kaell."

"What if this were you, Felix?" Kaell's voice cracked in despair. "What if he wanted you to have a child?"

Slowly, Felix lifted his eyes to Kaell's. His hard, cool expression held no compassion. "We each must play our parts. These men"—he swept a hand—"are sacrificing more than you."

"We're willing," Torin said. "We prepared our entire lives."

"My lord." Giles frowned. "One of us is missing."

"He'll come." Roaran carried four unlit candles in tall iron holders to the middle of the room. "This man seeks me, though he cannot yet name his longing."

He stripped. Torchlight struck sigils whorling across his naked shoulders, arms, and breast. Kaell's scalp crawled. In the treacherous light, their swirls and orbs writhed like tentacles. Roaran clasped his knife. Sweat glistened on the straining muscles in his back. He briefly closed his eyes.

Every one of them drew very still, watching.

Roaran seized a breath. His expression remote, his body tensed, he cut his palm. Wincing, teeth clenched, he squeezed his bleeding hand into a fist, opened it, then slowly circled, trailing blood after him. Mesmerised, Kaell's gaze dwelled on the four men as they sat cross-legged within the ring of blood, their expressions fierce with excitement.

One by one, Roaran lit the candles. As the fourth flamed, a gust of wind slammed the doors shut then at once died. The fleeting moonlight shrank away, leaving only the eerie flicker of candles and bulging shadows. Giles trembled. Torin looked entranced, a half smile on his lips.

Kaell could not tear his eyes from a drop of blood suspended on Roaran's palm. Time slowed. The crimson bead swelled then slowly, slowly dripped. With the force of metal striking an anvil, it hit the floor.

"They're here," Roaran said quietly.

Kaell hugged his body. "What's happening? Someone tell me what's happening."

"No, no." Dean shot to his feet. "I can't do this. I thought I could, but I can't. We've our own lives, all of us. Giles, you're a silk merchant. Rich, successful. Will you give that up?"

"My father prepared me for this," Giles said. "It is a duty of blood. Your courage must not fail you now, Dean. We all swore an oath."

"Torin," Dean pleaded, "you're only twenty. Too young to throw away your life."

"Does my youth," Torin's fervour brought out a stutter, "make me less w-willing to s-s-serve the gods?"

Dean dropped his head into his hands. "I have a wife."

"And I have a dying father who will have no heir," Felix said scornfully. "You will do this, Dean. You must."

Pale-lipped and shaken, Dean stood undecided. Then he knelt again.

Roaran passed each man a clay pot. An otherworldly scent eddied about the tower chamber. Translucent air thickened. The candle flames violently whipped then stood absolutely upright.

Kaell again pressed against the bars, curiosity dampening his fear.

Giles clutched his pot to his breast. "I remember the first dream. I was seventeen. My father sat me down, his tone heavy, his thick, black brows drawn down. 'We are called,' he said. 'We are legatees of duty.'"

Felix nodded. "Aalart told me of these wondrous visions. I'll admit I was envious."

"What we attempt here now started on a night in the Isles long ago," Roaran said. "I summoned not only the most courageous warriors of my time but warriors of the past. They pledged their lives to defeat a fallen god set to rise up, pledged to prepare their descendants."

"We are willing, my lord," Felix said.

Giles tilted his chin proudly. "Will our brothers also hear the call, my lord?"

"Once I begin the spell, it will awaken the brotherhoods across Telor."

They spoke no more, breath on hold, faces dazed. Kaell's arms tingled. The dreadful weight of the moment fell upon every one of them, participant or unwilling spectator.

Roaran closed his eyes. He looked every bit the warrior king of legend. Candlelight glowed on his blue-black hair, on his vicious sigils. Which bound this man to his god, Kaell wondered, and which bound him to his seer craft?

Again, Roaran took up the knife. His glassy stare fell beyond the tower. Face dark with resolve, his body braced, he exhaled slowly. With two quick strokes, he slashed his arms, two long cuts from the crook of his elbow to his wrist.

He gasped in pain, staggered, and collapsed to his knees as blood streamed from the gashes. For a moment, he bowed his head, his chest rising and falling as he drew in deep, slow breaths. Then he lifted his bleeding arms and chanted.

The words were like a dark song. It resonated deep within Kaell. Transfixed, he watched Roaran.

An earthy, pungent scent flared. As if etched by fire, the symbols on Roaran's skin lit up. Shadows rose from the ground, unformed, hulking masses.

Kaell reeled a step. What terrifying magic was this?

"Blood." Roaran gripped his thighs. "Blend it now."

The men exchanged frightened glances. They cut their palms over the pots.

The sounds of the dead city, the night with its rustlings and mewing, ebbed away. There was only Roaran's laboured gasps as blood pooled about him. For a heartbeat then another.

The stillness exploded. Wind crashed every shutter against stone. A whoosh of air flattened flames. Magic webbed Kaell's skin, its touch as brittle as a book's worn pages.

Torin cried out and fell in a huddle.

"I see my life and another's," Dean murmured, staring at nothing. "So many memories."

A disembodied laugh echoed in the room around them, seemingly from nowhere. Kaell shuddered. He knew that laugh.

"Archanin." Roaran staggered to his feet in alarm. He stared upon a particular spot as though seeing something the rest of them could not. "No, no."

Felix scrambled up. He grabbed the seer's shoulder. "What is it?"

Roaran groaned. He stretched out a hand to point at nothing. "The Enarae opens, needle-thin," he said. "Not part of my spell. I see Archanin surrounded by candles, his skin coated in blood. He's watching through the breach. His words fly as daggers." He screamed and slumped to the floor, his body jerking.

Kaell glanced around in panic.

That laugh came again, echoing all about them. "Die," Archanin's voice said. "Die."

Dean clawed at his neck. He strangled a sound as he dropped to the floor, convulsing. Then with an agonised scream, he stilled.

Giles groped at a wall. Blood rimmed his pupils.

"No!" Roaran struggled to his knees. "You won't win. I won't let you destroy them."

Kaell's ribs ached at the held-in tension, his breath gone. He could only watch as Roaran crawled to his knife and slashed his own breast. With another cry of pain, the seer smeared blood everywhere, shoulders, thighs, face, hair. He incanted a spell.

The air charged with sage and lemongrass. Archanin's laugh choked to a hiss of rage.

A shape rose at Torin's back. It slid into the warrior. Torin twitched. A lump rippled beneath his cheekbones. Another shadow enfolded Giles.

Roaran shouted. He closed a fist around air, as if enclosing Archanin's curse in his grip. When he opened his palm, a grey cloud rose from his hand. It floated towards the window.

Branches grappled at the tower's stone as the ugly magic in the ashen mist brushed past. A screech then a flutter of frenzied wings broke out as the cloud hit the trees. Then only a distant rustle marked its passage into nothing.

Kaell sucked in a shocked breath. Everything—Roaran, his power, that scent, the touch of the otherworld—was far beyond his understanding. In disbelief, he stared at Dean's body then at Felix as he pushed to his feet.

"It didn't work," Felix said, then in a louder voice, "It didn't work. Dean died for nothing."

"The spell worked, only not for you, Felix." Roaran swayed on his knees, his hair matted, his body streaked red. "I couldn't save Dean. I'm sorry. But the others…" He looked at Giles as the man rose unsteadily. He said, "Welcome, Gethin Maelstrom."

Torin dropped to one knee before the seer. In an assured voice with no trace of the young soldier's stutter, he said, "My lord and my king."

"Welcome, Cadan Tiernan." Roaran touched the man's hair. "My friend."

Gethin Maelstrom. A legendary warrior from the past.

Cadan Tiernan. A lord's youngest son who turned pirate, redeemed by his king, Roaran Caelan. Kaell knew this man's story, too, from his history books.

And with that, he understood.

Roaran's brotherhood was a brotherhood of the dead.

They huddled about the table, heads bent close. Their candle guttered as they talked. Roaran tilted a new one to the last blue spark. When goblets emptied, Juliette rose from her seat at the fire beside Nicky to pour wine.

Kaell sank onto the cot. He dropped his head into his hands. Magic. Prophecy. If only it were a bad dream he could wake from. Instead, his nightmare rolled on and on. He no longer knew how to flee fate, how to escape what he couldn't understand.

Near dawn, Felix sprang up. "Do not leave me out of this, my lord. It's my fight too."

Roaran tipped his chair onto one leg. Dark patches stained bandages on his arms. "The blood spell failed in your case. You are as you were, Felix. No warrior took you over."

"I can still serve you."

"Then hold the Mountains for me. Hold Vraymorg. It's more important than you know."

"Why?" Felix leaned, his palms flat on the table. "Why?"

"Because that's where it ends," Roaran said softly. "That's where every ghoul lord will be drawn when Archanin agrees to perform the Seithin gauntlet. That's where we'll strike."

Felix sat down hard, his face tight with fear. "There is only one reason why Archanin would permit the gauntlet. What have you done, Roaran? What *have* you done?"

Roaran closed his eyes. He looked ill and tired. "Every one of us must answer for his crimes. I must answer not only for what I've done, but what I intend to do."

"You don't expect to survive," Felix said. "Oh gods, Roaran. No. Not the gauntlet."

Cloth rustled as men shifted restlessly. In the tension, the fire's crackle seemed impossibly loud. The thump of a log rolling in the flames took Kaell back to the hall at Vraymorg, to a miserable, damp afternoon where he had sat reading near the hearth.

His book was a Wardorian tomb raider's account of his journey to the ruins of Seithin. The raider had told a story of finding a chamber where priests prepared captives for the Seithin gauntlet. Not a gauntlet in the usual sense. A ceremony far more vicious.

"My lord." Cadan reached across the table to touch Roaran's bandaged arm. "You know I trust and love you as I always did as your captain, but I don't like this at all. Is there no other way? Not just the gauntlet but—him." He looked at Kaell.

"What would you have me do?" Roaran said. "Turn back now?"

"Juliette?" Cadan called to the woman near the fire. "What do you say?"

"I say my lord should not hesitate." Her voice was fierce.

"You know of this, Saltman? What the prophecy requires?"

"I know." Nicky stared dismally into the fire. "My lord must do whatever it takes to destroy Archanin. The boy must agree to play his part. It's the gauntlet I can't accept."

Kaell sprang up. "I will not do this. Just let me go."

They all turned. Cadan settled a thoughtful look upon Kaell.

"Be brave, boy. It is for the greater good," Felix said pitilessly. "Let that give you comfort."

Grey light filtered through rotting shutters and the broken roof. A bird's clear shrill accompanied the dewy dawn. At last the group about the table broke up.

"I will hold Vraymorg until you come, my king." Felix clasped Roaran's shoulders.

"Be careful, Felix," Roaran said. "Archanin knew I intended to raise the brotherhood. If someone betrayed us, he'll know about you too."

"Let him come, my king. The Mountains fortress is warded against him."

"Where's Ailis?" In the fragile, new light, Roaran's face was drawn, his movements stiff and painful. "She—they—should be back by now."

"If they hit trouble with the Varee, she'll make sure no one follows before she returns," Cadan said. Muscles flexed in his back as he stretched. Kaell knew Torin a little. But this man surely stood straighter, his shoulders wider, his smile warmer and disarming.

Roaran drew Cadan into a fierce embrace. "You know what you must do."

"Find Dace Caelan's king's sword, Aleyn Ail. Find the rest of the brotherhood. Those Archanin did not kill."

# VAL ARQUES

The door, the centre of his existence—a philosophical matter—swung open. Not Griffin with brisk commands or servants with tainted wine. Just Myranthe, her grey man, and her servant-girl smile.

Val sprawled on the bed, plotting. Heath would be pleased. Lazily, he rose to an elbow. *Only the two guards loitering outside?* "No Griffin and his hammer? Shall we sit and talk as equals? Surely not."

"We are not equals," she said. "Given you are surely a prisoner and I am surely not."

Though she was surely something. He just wouldn't say it aloud, especially in polite company. No, wait. There was only Penn. So maybe he should just go ahead.

Penn stomped over with cord to bind his hands. Val was done with restraints, with barred rooms. With Myranthe's games. He considered the open door. No Heath. No Griffin. He shoved Penn back, leapt up, and bolted past an amused Myranthe.

Guards outside whirled. Val grabbed the nearest by the shirt to fling him into the wall. He punched the other in the jaw. That man dropped like a stone, his breath smashed out.

Four more ran up the stairs, their bulk blocking the light. A fist came at his face. He blocked it. Another blow to his head knocked him flat. A boot swung at his belly. Curled, he sucked in air, helpless as they dragged him back into his room.

"Now you've had your romp." Myranthe gestured at the bed. "It's time to be nice."

The guards hauled him past a scowling Penn and threw him on the bed. They backed away.

Val half rose. "I prefer to be stubborn."

"You're beginning to sound like Heath." She sighed impatiently. "Even if you escaped these caverns, where would you go? No boots, no coat. You'd freeze. So just give Penn your wrists like a good boy. This rebellion achieves nothing."

Except a moment's satisfaction at denying her his compliance. Val studied the guards sizing him up like prey. With a resentful huff, he held out his arms. Penn bound his wrists with velvet strips rather than rope.

"Move into the light," she said as Penn departed. "I want to see your face as you answer."

"I'm comfortable as I am."

Myranthe gestured impatiently. "I could have you chained to that bed."

Val stayed put, grasping at prideful resistance. Not that his defiance was really about pride. It was to hide that raw, vulnerable part of him her pitiless gaze exposed.

"I refuse to play your games any longer. You don't play fair. You promised that in return for the truth about Kaell, you'd tell me what a Quisnaf blood sniffer found in a tavern."

"I told you the price of that information was in two parts. Kaell, yes. But you also had to sweeten the pot—agree to see Aric. Now. Move into the light."

Val folded his arms.

"Shackles, then." She rose for the door and knocked.

Penn looked in. "My lady?"

"Settle him down. You know how." Myranthe strode out. She didn't look at him.

Val glared at Penn and the guards. They paid him no heed, only stood around at the door, waiting for Myranthe. Candlelight hit the length of chain fastening his wrist to the bedframe. The light's warmth mocked, a stark contrast to the cold dread webbing him.

She was right. He had no power, certainly not the power to get to Kaell. Whatever game unfolded, she outmatched him, her rules still unknown.

Myranthe returned, nodding at his shackles. She pulled the shutters tight then swept up his candle to fire the others. Their light fell in eerie blotches like dabbed moonbeams.

"So where do you want me?" Val dragged his back up against the headboard. "To establish the disadvantage? You do want me at a disadvantage, don't you?"

Myranthe took the chair. "The bed will do nicely. It did nicely last night."

His stomach turned over. *Oh.*

Penn sniggered as he left. The guards pulled the door closed behind them.

"I was concerned the wine might affect your performance." Myranthe watched his face slyly. "Gladly, no. Your desire was suitably deep… Yes, deep." She laughed.

Val stilled, all but his stirred-up heart. Hazy memories tumbled: a woman's perfume, her naked warmth, a pleasurable blur of wine, caressing fingers, lips, and arousal. "I thought—"

"That dear Judith at last visited your lonely bed? You called her name more than once." Myranthe studied her nails. "I don't stoop to jealousy. Not when I merely claimed what was clearly on offer. You may call out as you choose."

She had drawn him into another game. Except, it was his game to begin with. He had been prepared to do exactly what he had done—apparently. *Use this.*

"So now I am claimed." He patted the bed, summoning a lazy tone. "Will you be claiming me again? No wine will diminish my performance this time."

"Did I say it was diminished?"

From that knowing gleam in her eyes, Myranthe would never let him use one night of desire to his advantage. No, it had been a calculated move on her part. He just didn't understand why—yet.

"Now shall we pick up where we left off?" she said. "And I don't mean from last night."

He forced a disinterested shrug. Until he could get to Kaell, what else was there besides useless questions and answers that were sometimes truth and sometimes something else? Only the door and what came through it. Wine. Sleep. And pleasure… apparently.

"Well, ask away," he said as she took the chair opposite. "Seems I'm not going anywhere. Though surely we've run out of conversation."

"But not out of secrets." She looked pointedly at his scarred wrists.

Val squeezed his eyes closed to shut out her words. Candle flames whisked about him. Their beeswax mingled with crisp, cold scents of autumn. There were beeswax candles, too, in many chambers at Vraymorg, but autumn there was different. Here, the whitewashed stone drained the season of life. How he hated this place.

Myranthe leaned to stroke his arm. "Don't you see yet, Val Arques? Very little of this matters. This is a shadow tournament. Not about you at all. Your defiance has no point."

"If it is a shadow tournament, then why even bother with it?"

"Because I still need something from you." Her fingers traced his scars. "Before my brother sells you on, you will surrender the truth about why you did this."

For a heartbeat, panic swallowed him, a dizzying sense of

plunging into never-ending blackness. *No.* He yanked his hand back.

"These scars go very deep, don't they? They are who you are. Strip away the dutiful Vraymorg, and the man beneath, Val Arques, the one with the scars, is pitiful. He failed. He was weak. He's unworthy of love. He's unworthy of respect. That's what you think."

Val could not trust his voice. His heart, his thoughts were frantic. His skin hot.

Myranthe sat back. "That was cruel. Even for me." Her tone held no remorse. "Let me ask you a simple question then, one that costs you little. Why drink my wine? Surely you don't trust me, Val Arques?"

Val wanted to draw away from her, to hide in the shadows. But as her words maimed him, the light caught his every expression. He dragged in a slow breath.

"Dreams are an escape," he said dully. "Drugged, not drugged." He shrugged. "I might drink regardless. Look around. If a man can die of boredom, I'm dying."

"Because you're the man of action, not reflection? You must be riding horses, fighting battles or tournaments to be content?" Myranthe laughed shrilly. "You delude yourself. No, Val Arques, you can withstand the silence."

"This conversation takes a philosophical turn. In that vein, have I told you of the door?"

"Is that a question?"

"No. And by the way, you asked me two. So I will have two in return."

"So you will. Tell me about the door." She smiled like a mother humouring a precocious child.

"Is that a question? No, unfair. I raised it. So, the door. Shut in as I am—"

"Surely you realise you'll never be free again. Not now you are revealed."

He blocked out those unsettling words. "Shut in, in your care—you must tell me, Myranthe, if last night is to become part of our conversations. I will bathe in anticipation."

"Do I not send hot water for you daily, as befitting an Isles man? However, don't make the mistake of thinking that sort of conversation will be as two-sided as we enjoy with words. If I want something of you, then I will have it of you."

"And shall I expect Venivan wine as payment each time?"

"I will count that as one of your questions. The answer is: If you so desire. Or if you prefer desire to be veiled by wine. As for payment..." She let the words hang then smiled faintly. "Your words, not mine. Now finish this nonsense about the door."

*Payment.* Why had he chosen that word? "Merely an observation. A man shut in craves distraction, but distraction comes only from one source."

"Through the door, I see." Myranthe patted a yawn. "Your life has become the door. It represents survival. Comfort. Danger. I'm sorry I permitted this. I'm bored now."

"I intended to put it more elegantly than that. But I am a little hungover."

"Too much wine." She shook a finger. "When will you learn? You have one question left."

"Was last night about power? Nothing about desire?"

Myranthe tilted her head. With grudging admiration, he watched her keen intelligence click. "If I desired you, it served to satisfy a temporary need. I was restless. I drank a little too."

"I think I am insulted." Val laughed without humour.

"I haven't finished. A few nights ago, Velleran revealed your unpleasant fate. You showed no fear. So I admired you a little. Even wanted you. So I sought to punish you for my desire. So you tell me, Val Arques—is that about desire or power?"

"Ha," Val said. "It's about a complicated answer to a simple question."

A complicated answer offering nothing he could use to get free.

No hint at a softening in her feelings, no sympathy. But friendless, alone in a strange city, he had no other way to escape except manipulate, or even seduce, his captor.

"Enough questions." Myranthe sat beside him. "No. One more." She touched fingertips to his lips. "If I resume our conversation from last night, is that about desire or power?"

If he merely sought to manipulate her, why did his body react to her thigh brushing his? Boredom, perhaps. Or twisted longing. Whatever it was, he had to take control of the game. "It depends where we left off, Myranthe. My memory is a little hazy."

"Let me remind you." She grasped his wrist. Her moist tongue flickered over his skin, leaving a slick, silken trail that kicked his heartbeat up a notch.

"Is that what you did?"

"And this." Her hand in his hair, she pressed her mouth to his, demanding his lips open. Her tongue explored at will, a flood of tastes and sensations, burning away his resistance. This was madness. He didn't even like her.

Through her kiss, Myranthe whispered, "And this."

She untied his pants and closed fingers around his straining erection. Val shifted as she stroked, every muscle tensing. The taste of her, the heat, overwhelmed his senses. In vain, he tried to ignore his arousal. *Why bother?* This could help him escape. Forcing aside the objections of his mind, he let his body take over.

Her mouth plundered his again, her tongue's thrust matching the rhythm of her hand. That fire beneath his skin wanted only to roar up. He reached to touch her, needing to slide his palm over her skin, to cup her breasts.

Myranthe slapped his unfettered hand away. She grabbed his hips to drag him flat, bunching her gown and straddled his thighs. Her probing tongue irritated deliciously. In his mouth. On his neck. Circling a nipple.

Val moaned as she mounted him, shifting, straining, enveloping. He arched his back as sensation flooded. Her nipples pressed through cloth against his breast. The heat of his arousal, its fierce smoulder in his body, swept away rational thought.

Wanting to bring her pleasure, he edged his shackled hand beneath her gown. Myranthe grabbed his wrists and pinned them above his head.

Displeased, he growled. The chain slapped the bed as he half rose, half withdrew.

Myranthe put her weight on his body. Still holding his wrists, she sank down onto him. Her chin tilted up, lips quivering. She rocked hard, moaning with pleasure.

Deep inside her, Val drove his mouth against hers, her lips softening beneath his hard kiss. Her rhythm built to a pounding. As she gasped, whimpered, and shuddered, he lost control of his body.

It was a fierce convulsion of pleasure, more draining than usual, yet it left a hunger for tenderness behind. When she collapsed beside him, panting, he threw an arm about her shoulders to embrace her. Myranthe abruptly pushed him away.

For a moment they lay like that, not touching, not speaking.

"It's about power," he said. "The power to satisfy desire, if nothing else." For her. For him, it was loneliness. A need to feel something. Yes, that. He would not think about her unsettling words about his lack of self-respect. He would not.

Myranthe rose and tugged down her gown. "It's about payment. If you agree to see Aric, relieve his guilt, I'll consider the pot sweetened."

"Why do you care so much about his guilt?"

"I offered him a last request. He asked to see you. I must honour it."

Val turned to stare blankly at the wall. He did not trust himself to talk to Aric without violence. But that was a chance to leave the chamber. To see more of these caverns, perhaps glimpse doors or passages into the city. A way out. A way to Kaell.

He rolled back. "I'll see Aric."

Myranthe smoothed her hair. "Then I shall tell you a strange tale that reached us from the Downs. A Quisnaf blood sniffer hired by the king came upon an Isles man with Caelan blood. She described him to Gendrick as dark-haired with blue eyes."

Val frowned. Blue eyes were almost unheard of in the Isles. As for Caelan blood, he knew few who shared it. Besides his sons, Philip and Alecc, only Gendrick Caelan, the king's uncle Tomasin, and the treacherous Aric were direct descendants of the god-king.

"The man was with a girl. The blood seeker could not swear to it, but she told Gendrick this girl also had Caelan blood."

Val closed his eyes to hide his expression. *Could it be? Could it?*

"The blood seeker says the girl was Varee." Myranthe shrugged. "In any case, she lost both of them. The Varee attacked, killed a lot of soldiers. Gendrick was displeased."

That faint hope died. Kaell would never fight with the Varee.

Myranthe's gaze dwelled on his face. "That news interests you. I wonder why. Never mind. We have time yet to uncover all your secrets, Val Arques."

She turned to leave then paused, hand on the door. "I'll send Penn to take off those chains. Velleran will be displeased at your bruised wrists, as it is. And tomorrow, I'll take you to Aric. You can peer about on the way and plot how to get out of here. It's only fair." She laughed softly. "After all, you earned it."

Compared to Val's room, Aric's prison was lavish. Beeswax candles offered light, a fire warmth, and furs and pillows added to the comfort of a large, curtained bed. Splendid tapestries, pleasing to the eye, covered the walls above numerous chests.

Upon the floor, back to a wall, Aric lifted his head off drawn-up knees at Val's intrusion. Months of imprisonment had refined his Isles cheekbones to sharpness. His warrior's body looked thinner in its fine garments, his eyes huge in a pale face. "You came."

"I came."

"Thank you. I don't deserve it."

*I don't deserve it.* Anger niggled at him. Val concentrated on the rattle of keys as Penn locked them in. He peered about, disappointed there were no windows.

Gruffly, he said, "Say what you will, then I'll go."

Aric made a sound, half a sigh, half a dispirited groan. "I have only words you won't want to hear. That I'm sorry."

There was a silence. "Sorry," Val said in disbelief. "You're sorry."

"I know I can't make amends. Nor do I want to make excuses. But Heath threatened Azenor. I had to think of her. That's why I betrayed you to him." He laughed coldly. "Ironic, but fair, that Heath betrayed me too. I deserve nothing less."

How foul his guilt must taste. Rightly so. Everything had begun with his betrayal. The thought twisted darkly inside, like a gutting knife. Those months in that hole, hungry, dirty, alone. Myranthe's games, his former life ripped away—all because of Aric's betrayal.

But worse, Aric kept him from Kaell, who had surely awoken frightened and confused.

Anger speared him; a bright, hot gash burst from his head to toe. It was irresistible, as though he had unknowingly bottled every resentment, every moment of shattered pride. Every prick of loss. And now they all roared out in uncontrolled rage.

Bellowing, he grabbed Aric and pounded his face. Again and again. Blindly. Heat raced through his body into his fists. Too furious to talk, beyond rational thought, he was capable only of punching. Hurting. Hating.

Aric just let Val hit him. At his refusal to defend himself, to fight back, Val struck him harder, until his knuckles were torn and wet. His tongue loosened to yell sounds, not words. Blood streamed from Aric's nose and his split lips.

The grille slid. A guard cursed. "Do you have a key? Quickly."

"No key," another man said. "We'll have to fetch someone." The grille shut.

As fast as it had poured into him, Val's anger drained. He looked at his bloody hands. He looked at the man he still gripped by the arms. With a shocked sound, he dropped him on the floor. Aric curled on stone, his face ripped, his clothes and hair bloody.

Panting, sweat on his hairline, Val slowly took in the destruction he'd wrought. A speck of pity punctured his resentment. What to say? That he had lost control? Sorry? He wasn't.

He slumped beside Aric. Time moved around them, measured only by Aric's rasped inhalations, by a tread of boots that clapped then faded as someone passed outside, and by that drip, drip of sweat from Val's hair into cracks running red with blood.

Groaning, Aric dragged his back against the wall. "Have you ever thought about what you would have done? If Heath threatened Kaell, you would have betrayed me in a heartbeat."

Val said nothing, only let the silence gather.

Aric sighed. "I thought about you again and again these months, Vraymorg. Wondering what they did to you. Fearing—" He winced. "Fearing you were dead."

"I'm no longer Vraymorg. No longer lord of the Mountains." *Because of you,* he might have said. *Because of Heath.*

"They refused to tell me about you," Aric said. "I hoped you escaped. Why did Heath abduct you?"

"For the same reason as you. Except I'm tainted by other magic. Useless to them."

"As I am not." Aric leaned his head against stone.

"What has she said? Myranthe."

"About what she intends?" Aric's dark eyes flared briefly then flattened to despair. "Don't worry, it doesn't fall to you. Myranthe told me about how I'm precious to her. Precious…" His voice trailed off into bitterness.

"She's going to kill you," Val said bluntly.

Aric shrugged.

"You want to die? You'll just let her throw you onto a stone slab and cut out your heart?"

"What do you care? I didn't care what Heath wanted to do with you." Aric laced his fingers around his knees. "Better this way."

"Better with you dead? Redemption, is it? For the ills you did me?"

"Maybe."

"Fool."

"Maybe. I don't care. Not really."

"A fool. A coward too."

That last word clearly hit its mark. Aric turned to squint. "Why?"

"Because you've given up." Val surged to his feet. "You shame me in that we're both Isles born. You're not worthy to call yourself an Isles warrior."

"Don't say that. Don't you say that." A vein throbbed in Aric's neck. "What do you know about giving up? They're not about to throw you down and tear your heart out."

"You're right. Instead, Heath chained me to a rock in a gloomy hole. The breaking stone."

Aric shifted. "And here you are—broken? You don't look broken, Vraymorg."

"I have no right to that name. Not anymore."

"Then what do I call you?"

"Val. Easy even for you to remember."

"Ha, ha. I see why Heath chained you up. So you could delight him with your wit."

"Hmm." Val scratched his chin.

"Oh gods." Aric's nervous laugh faded to an embarrassed huff of breath. "He *did* chain you up so you could amuse him. Were you… amusing?"

"What an evil mind you have. Heath says I give him tingles, but it's a sort of joke."

"A joke." Aric frowned. "I don't understand."

"Nor do I. Heath is too clever for me. He has a weakness, though. He likes me. Wants us to be friends or to carve me up in a fire hall or something. That's why he chained me to the rock. I had only the rock and Heath. He talked back. The rock didn't."

"Gods, you've lost me again. You really are a strange man."

"We're no different. Both Isles men. Both Serravan trained. If I can hold on, so can you."

"For what? There's no way to escape. I tried. I even got out of this room once, into passages that just led to more passages. They marched me back quick smart." Aric waved a hand. "All this? They fatten up their calf for slaughter. I'm going to end up on an altar as Myranthe cracks my ribs to cut out my heart, and no one can stop it."

At Aric's despair, a bitter taste coated Val's mouth. "There might be a way." A desperate way. He knotted fingers in his hair. Dangerous threads weaved in his mind.

That sunlit room flashed at the back of his eyes, a moment of black terror before his barriers shot up. Bars. A locked door. Cushions on the divan. The fragrance of roses. *No. Shove it down.*

"There's something Myranthe wants. I can use it." Yet even as Val said the words, his mouth filled with saliva, his limbs shivery despite the room's fire. No one could know. No one could see him exposed. But it was all he had to barter with. "When?"

Aric jerked his head up. "You mean when will she kill me? Two nights from now. The next three-moon night. Myranthe told me to give me time to prepare." He shook his head. "Prepare. How do you prepare for a sorceress to take your heart?"

*You don't. Couldn't. No, I have to save him.*

"Just be ready. If I give her what she wants. If I tell her—" His breath cut in panic.

Aric watched him uneasily. "From your face, she wants something bad. Don't do it, Vraymorg—Val. You're only a captive because of me. I don't deserve your compassion."

"Be done with it, Aric. The guilt. Just be ready."

"Ready to fight?"

"No, ready to play the fiddle. Of course fight."

"I never picked you for a sarcastic man." But Aric's expression lightened. He scrambled up. "I know how to fight. Every muscle is trained to do only that."

Val straightened. He appraised the other man. "You're thinner. Weaker, too, I'd guess. Every muscle may need a little reminder."

"A reminder how to kill?" Aric scoffed. "You never forget that."

The door thumped the wall. Heath strode in, immaculate in a silver-clasped cloak and polished boots. "Please tell me you're plotting. I need distraction."

Hatred distorted Aric's handsome face.

"What do you want?" Val asked.

Heath shrugged. No one shrugged like him. Careless but full of intent. "The guards seem to think you're beating my sister's guest to death. If you're done throwing your fists around, I'm to escort you back to your pen, Val. I'll give you a moment, though, to say fond farewells—by that, I mean finish plotting."

"I'm really not in the mood for your company."

"I don't know about that." Heath looked from Val's bloody knuckles to Aric's gashed face. "You're in a delightfully violent mood. I entirely approve of violence. If only I could escort you to a fire hall and let you get all that rage out."

"If only. I'd gladly show you just how violent I can be."

Heath clicked tongue to teeth. "I'm tempted to disobey Myranthe and take you off so we can play with pointy sticks. But Myranthe wants Aric in one piece at least and you locked up safe and sound. And Myranthe always gets what she wants." He turned away. The door banged at his back.

Aric bristled. "I long to wipe that smug smile from his smug face. I can't take this."

"Hold on," Val said. "There's something I can offer Myranthe in return for a chance at getting out of here."

He reached deep for the will to tear down his shields and uncover his shame. To let her see. Know. He was no coward. He could do this. He must.

# HEATH

"**S**omething Myranthe wants... From your face... it's bad." Heath shoved a shoulder into the wall to control a shudder as he pawed over the words he had just overheard.

He did suggest Val plot mischief or mayhem. But nothing as extreme as taking on Myranthe at her own games. Reckless man. He would have to save Val from himself. Not that the proud fool would thank him.

"Ask Val Arques to join me," he said to the guards. "He's had time for tearful goodbyes."

A guard shoved the door open and barked, "You. Out."

Heath shook his head. So impolite. It was more fun to be quietly menacing.

The conspirators exchanged a look. Very meaningful. They weren't cut out for cloak-and-dagger games. It required cunning and a cold heart.

Guards marched Val out and snapped manacles on his wrists. Heath took his arm. "You're not going to run, are you? I just bathed and don't want to get sweaty chasing you."

"No," Val said quietly. "I'm not going to run."

Heath grinned. "At least not today. Or at least when I'm armed and you're hampered by those pretty bracelets."

He fell in beside the man. Their steps echoed on stone. Flames spat from sconces. Wind ground through the passage with cold scents of winter. Bleached sunbeams, stripped of warmth by the season, streaked close walls.

"What does Myranthe want that you're going to give her?"

Val jolted but did not break stride.

"What does Myranthe want?"

"I don't know what you mean." His voice was flat, his eyes dead.

Heath grabbed his arm to stop him. "You know exactly what I mean. Whatever it is, don't do it."

Val swallowed. "You sound very serious—for you."

"I am serious. Don't play with Myranthe, Val. There's a reason for everything she does, and it's never good. We lesser mortals must only try to keep out of the way."

Val shoved off his grip. There was something broken and terrible about his face. "I don't know what you're talking about." He walked on.

Heath's sword arm tingled. *Not now.* Impatiently, he wrung his hand and caught the other man up. "She will destroy you. Listen to me. Don't you see I want to protect you?"

Val rocked to a halt. He turned, his gaze intense. "And why is that? I don't understand you at all. You throw me in some hole, then you say you want to protect me." He flung his arms up. "What do you want from me?"

"Why must I want something?" But he did. Desperately. By all his fiery gods, how had his longing to fight a formidable bladesman become so bewilderingly complicated?

It had started as a need to test his skill against a man who must surely push him to the edge of death and fear. A yearning for that thrill of danger, for the elated release of victory after an intense, dangerous struggle, as heady as lust.

The more he learnt of Val Arques Caelan, the more he understood the contest would be like nothing else before or after.

Val would not surrender. When fire closed at his back and Heath thrust steel to his neck, perhaps he might beg for his life. Perhaps.

If only it were still that simple.

Maybe it had once been about the contest, even a desire to dominate. But he liked this man. If they both weren't born to duty, could there be a meeting of wills, of thought? A friendship?

*Or…* Another darker thought gnawed at him.

Heath didn't want to look at it. But sooner or later, he must bring it out and examine it.

Perhaps it wasn't about friendship but about keeping Val as a solitary possession, unable to be defiled by the world.

*Obsession.*

Val looked away. He muttered, "Everyone wants something of me."

"You've learnt something. You might just survive here."

"What do *you* want, Heath?" he asked, emptiness in his tone. "I can't pretend to understand you, so you'll have to be blunt."

Heath squeezed a fist. His grip weakened. *I want to kill you,* he might have said. *I want to save you.* "You're in too deep if you take on Myranthe." His tone grew urgent. "I don't know what you intend, but please don't do it. My sister's plots dazzle even me."

Val said nothing for a moment. There was a flatness to his eyes, a void. "Protect me?" He laughed softly. The laugh sounded impossibly bitter and crazed. "Even you can't protect me, Heath Damadar. Certainly not from my past."

# KAELL

Shadows lengthened towards dusk. Kaell curled on the bed, fighting panic. He could not forget the horrors of two nights before when a man had choked and died while Archanin laughed beneath the rattling wind.

The man, the seer who had woken the dead, held him prisoner. There was no way out, no one coming to help him.

His head spun. Bile shot up his throat. He dropped to the floor to retch into the bucket.

Nicky let Juliette into the cage. She held his shoulders as he spewed again, then she placed a cool cloth at the back of his neck. "Hush, hush," she said. When he calmed a little, she sat beside him on the floor. "I'm sorry you're so upset. Tell me how I can comfort you."

"Let me go," Kaell said. "Please. You've been kind. Help me."

"Where is your courage?" Juliette stroked his cheek. "Roaran would not ask this if he believed there was another way. He's kneeling to the gods now, though I cannot tell if he believes in them, seeking strength to do what he must."

Kaell dropped his head into his hands. "Or asking the gods for the words to convince me?"

"Kaell." Juliette pulled his hands away to see his face. "Look at me. Roaran will not hurt you. He asks only that you think about what he's said."

A horse snorted. Sharp voices followed by quick steps carried to him.

Ailis burst into the tower. "Where is he?" She dragged fingers through her hair. "I must speak to him. Roaran."

Nicky came forward. "Ailis, where have you been? We expected you back days ago."

"There's been trouble."

"Let me take you to him."

She strode after him, careless of her sword as it thumped her thigh.

When Nicky returned, Juliette bid him unlock the door. Outside the cell, she paused. "This is no easy fight, Kaell. We go up against a fallen god. We all must make sacrifices to beat Archanin. Be brave. I'll have wine sent to settle your belly."

Alone, Kaell hugged his knees. He rocked back and forth, trying to banish shameful self-pity. No one here would help him. No one would take his part against Roaran.

If only his lord had killed him in that prison below the fortress of Vraymorg. Then none of this would have happened. No burden of guilt. No bitter taste on his tongue knowing he'd failed a dead man.

When dew-scented night fell behind the windows, Juliette lit candles. Kaell listened to her footsteps, watching for the first shimmer of moonlight. No longer able to keep still, he strode up and down the cell.

A hooded man pushed a cup through the bars. Voice muffled, he said, "Juliette sent a little wine. For your stomach."

Kaell snatched up the wine and drank. Almost at once, his head roiled. He braced a hand against burning iron. *No, no, no.*

The cup slipped from his fingers. He slumped dizzily to hands and knees, muttering, "Roaran Caelan, you coward. You knew I didn't want this. You knew."

# VAL ARQUES

H is mind detached from what he was about to do. Another man waited in the gathering darkness. Another man watched the door.

Tallow smoked from the passage. A crisp edge sharpened the air. The blue bird pecked at mortar. Dusk. That was when she would come. It was when she always came.

Myranthe burst in with a curt "Leave us" to dismiss the guards.

Val curled his fingers about the chair arms. He did not rise, only lifted his head, his gaze locked on her like an arrow on a target.

"I have run out of time," she said. "You are bought and sold. So what will it take? You must want something. Name it."

Her body was stiff with tension, her mouth set, an unguarded flicker in those dark eyes. Impatience. But there was something else too. Fear.

"For what?"

"Do not be disingenuous." Her perfume wisped as she pressed her palms into the chair's carved wood. "The one thing you hold on to."

"Why?" he muttered, still resisting. "How can it matter so much to you?"

"It matters, Val Arques. Not because of you. Our shadow

tournament, remember? You're…" She paused, considering. "Merely the first step. This is about him."

Dry-mouthed, he croaked, "Who?"

Myranthe seized his face between her hands. "Your shield is still raised. What must I take or give before you lower it?"

Val recoiled, arms crossed at his breast to hold in his dread. Myranthe studied him for a moment then straightened. She stalked the room, lighting candles, just as she had before.

Her movements were mechanical, her expression shuttered. Soon, a suffocating net of lavender and beeswax closed about them. Myranthe shifted a candle to the table so its light fell on him, again, just as she had before. That same soft, enticing setting. Except everything was different. Beneath her every movement, every gesture, urgency coiled. This time, she didn't wish to possess him physically. No, she had to seduce his will, his mind.

Val shifted in the chair. "Who is this really about?"

"Tonight it is only about you. Tell me what I want to know. Name your price."

"There is something." He got the words out even though his heart tore at his ribs and nausea curdled in his belly. *Think about Kaell. Think only about Kaell.*

"Name it."

"Let me go."

A stillness settled. In its cocoon, the whip of flames, Myranthe's slow breaths resounded. Footsteps outside echoed like a partially recovered memory. There was only him, this woman, and the stone-walled room.

"Is that it, Val Arques? The chink in your shield?" She wet her lips. "It seems impossibly simple. A need to be free. Yet it's not simple, is it? Because I cannot free you. My brother, even now, makes final arrangements to pass you on for a lot of gold. There must be something else. Tell me. What else can I offer?"

"Only death," Val said.

Myranthe searched his face. "You're serious."

He watched her uneasily as she tapped fingers on a corded belt, afraid she would refuse but terrified she would agree.

"I'll give you a chance at freedom," she said. "Once I hear this story, I'll walk out and leave the door open, taking the guards with me."

"You'll just let me go? Like that?"

"Not quite. I'll let you run if you choose. I'll let you try to get to Aric. That's what you want, isn't it? To save him from me? Two of you—better odds against the guards too."

"Yes," he said dully. "Yes."

"Maybe two bladesmen as skilled as you and Aric could bring havoc to these caverns and in the chaos, escape. So take this chance. It's all I can give you. If you try to leave, I'll not stand in your way or give the alarm."

"I can't trust you."

Candlelight glittered on her rings as Myranthe spread her arms. "I give my word before the gods, you will have your chance. One chance. Whether you run into guards elsewhere, or even Heath, who restlessly seeks the fire caverns, is not my concern."

Their eyes locked. He sensed her apprehension. The arrogantly confident Myranthe Damadar feared even this offer might not earn the story she desperately wanted.

Val looked at his wrists. Time had stolen so many memories. But never this. This, he couldn't face. But he had to free Aric and find Kaell. Too many times, he'd failed the boy. With deeds. With words he was too afraid to say. Now he must do the right thing for Kaell. He must let her see him naked, the shadow exposed.

"You know what I want," she said.

He touched a white scar. How ugly it was. Angry, knotted, blemished skin.

Myranthe watched him greedily.

"You want to know why I did this," he whispered.

# DANNON

Patrick backhanded Dannon's face then grasped his jaw so the mage could force an acidic draught down his throat. He dumped Dannon on the floor of the mage's hut and kicked his belly. "You had everything. And you didn't want it. Now you have nothing but an inglorious end. Not a warrior's death. A slave's."

How Patrick must loathe him to ridicule a defenceless man. And Dannon had never seen it. Never suspected the man envied and resented him.

As the door banged at his captors' backs, Dannon tried to rise. His useless limbs did not obey. Helpless, he could only lie on the planked floor and wait for the mage's return.

For two nights, they'd drugged him and locked him in this hut, cold and thirsty. Every minute, his imagination stirred up panic.

Now more time passed on into the gathering darkness, though his potion-hazed mind could not grasp its passage beyond dusk's miserable chill seeping through his garments into his bones. Again and again, he submerged into emptiness then resurfaced to blackness. What thoughts he recovered from the wreckage became part of his nightmare.

A key turned. Men charged in. Dannon was too weak to fight

as they hurled him onto a pallet.

The mage pulled back Dannon's eyelid, nodding. "There you are. My draught now saturates every pore, every muscle. You're ready. Trapped on the edge of what's real and what lingers beyond our nightmares."

He ripped a knife across his wrinkled palm, hissing at the pain. Then he seized Dannon's hand. Dannon tried to recoil but could not. He could only manage a murmured protest as the old man cut him. It didn't hurt.

"Leave us," the mage said. "I'll call for you when it's done."

Dannon shut his eyes, only to snap them open at a whiff of stale flesh and rancid breath as the mage stretched out beside him, their bloody hands clenched together. The old man muttered in a strange tongue. The words tingled through Dannon's veins.

Dazed, his body shackled by invisible bonds, unable to resist the spell, he seized upon one thought. *Do not sleep. Do not sleep.*

But at once, he spiralled into darkness and into the familiar dream.

It seemed impossibly clear. Clearer than ever before. He stood in the familiar castle ward, but this time, he could feel wet grass brushing his legs. A bird's shriek carried from a tower.

"Show me, Dannon." The mage was with him in that castle courtyard.

"No."

"Show me."

He could not hold back the dream. It was no longer insubstantial. It was vivid and real. The ward became a stone-walled passage. Smoke from torches was thick enough to make him splutter as he crossed their interlocking circles of yellow light towards a door.

The secret room lay beyond; the one he tried in vain not to enter. For they were there—warriors in archaic armour who turned and called his name, who beckoned. At their backs, stick in hand, the mage watched. Listened. Nodded.

The images shattered. "No," Dannon cried. "Don't go. Tell me what you want. Tell me where to find you." Loneliness infused his body and mind. He'd never felt so wretched.

"Shh. It's over, Dannon. The ordeal is over."

Oddly comforted, Dannon drifted, caged in that hazy layer below the waking world. When someone put a cup to his lips, he drank before his mind caught up.

The mage stroked his hair with gnarled fingers. "How interesting you've become, Cahirean. That the seer should choose you. Why? You're of no particular bloodline. You're no one."

"I don't understand. What do my dreams mean?"

"The brotherhood calls to you. Archanin's enemies. The seer will come for you or again send his vicious servants. They'll slaughter anyone who keeps you from him."

"The seer?" Thoughts lethargic, his weighted body no longer part of him, Dannon struggled to make sense of the odd words. He badly wanted to sleep. Yet in a dim corner of his dull mind, a warning simmered. *Do something. Fight. Lie there, and you die.*

Uneasy, he croaked, "What did you give me?"

A fist hammered at the door. The mage unlocked it to let Patrick and Shahven enter.

"Well?" Patrick dropped a hand to his hip. "Is it true?"

The mage nodded. "Prepare the rack. Every drop of an overlord's blood belongs to our god. We'll drain him at dawn then present his blood to Archanin as a gift."

The rack. They would bleed him out before the entire tribe. A slow, humiliating death. Not the quick, brutal end he'd expected from a thrust of steel either in battle or when a younger rival challenged him.

"Robert," he whispered. "Let me talk to Robert."

"He will not help you." The mage faced Patrick. "Search harder for the girl, his lover, and bring her to me. This Kate must be a Sister of Cyrah. Their spy. No doubt that's how they penetrated our defences."

"I searched everywhere," Patrick said. "There was no sign of her."

"Watch the dead city. Our scouts report strangers coming and going there."

"If you think that's where we'll find her." Patrick cast Dannon a pitiless look. "Should we restrain him?"

"Cord would cut his wrists. The blood of his body belongs to our lord. Do not worry. He is going nowhere. I poisoned him."

With a cruel snigger, Patrick stomped off.

Shahven faced the mage, his face crumpled. "Please, I beg of you, don't do this. You can't kill a man for what he hasn't yet done."

"The boy doesn't need to be here," Dannon murmured. "Spare him this."

The mage touched Shahven's hair. "You have a kind heart. But my duty is to protect our people."

Dannon coughed. "What did you give me?"

The mage considered him mercilessly. "Do not bother fighting my poison. You don't have the strength. Instead, spend your final hours finding a god to believe in." At Dannon's blink, he jeered. "You think I don't know? What a curious creature you are, Cahirean. To believe in no power beyond yourself. Yet *he* chooses you. A godless man."

"No." Dannon shook his head fiercely. "That can't be right. I'm no one. Everyone's made a mistake. Whoever this seer is, he wouldn't want me."

"Your dreams are clear."

"Why are you doing this?" He pushed to his knees. "I came to you for answers. I sought help to understand."

"You came to me because you were afraid," the old man said. "Afraid these dreams meant you did not belong in this life you clung to. Oh yes, I know you, Cahirean." He poked a finger. "I know how desperate you are to never be alone."

"The dreams," Dannon said. "They still make no sense to me."

"You really don't know what they mean? How sad."

Dannon dragged a hand over his sweating brow. "My father once told me a story. He named us legatees of the brotherhood. Promised to explain when I grew older. Only he died." He'd tried to forget his father's words, to forget his old life, to find his place among the Varee. To belong. To survive. "Who is this seer you speak of?" His tongue thickened in his mouth.

"Caelan's descendant returned. The son of that witch, Marginet of Quisnaf."

"Old father"—Shahven tugged at the mage's arm—"please be merciful. This is Dannon. We know him."

"He is destined to turn against us, Shahven," the mage said. "Watch and listen. You must learn what you will need to do to protect our people when I am dead."

Dannon huddled against a wall, grateful he could control his body a little. But he would not recover his strength before dawn. They would strip him, bind him to the rack, and cut his flesh before the entire village. Every one of them would watch him die. Slowly.

"It's not right. Only in challenge can an overlord be killed. It's our law."

"He's not Varee, Shahven. This man is Cahirean. Never one of us." The mage patted the boy's arm. "I know you're fond of him. Stay with him until dawn if you wish. Bring him what comfort you can. He can't hurt you. The poison will subdue him."

"This isn't right," Shahven said. "I won't let you do this." With sudden resolve, he hauled Dannon up and took his weight to half carry, half walk him to the door.

The mage blocked them, waving a knife. "Stop. I am your master, boy."

"He's my friend."

"He's a viper. Why help an outsider, boy? Unless…" His eyes stretched in understanding. "Unless he corrupted you. Ah, you stupid, deluded child. I will stop you." He lunged with the blade.

The boy dropped Dannon and shoved the old man hard. The

mage hurtled back, losing his balance. His head hit the corner of a chest with an awful crack. As he slid down, his necklace rattled. A death rattle indeed.

Shaking, Shahven dragged his hand to his mouth. "Archanin protect me. What did I do?"

"Help me," Dannon murmured, desperate to snap the boy's focus from the dead mage before Shahven fell into shock. "Please. Help me."

Shahven stared at him blankly.

"Help me," Dannon said.

# VAL ARQUES

"You never shared this. Not even once?" Myranthe quivered with thinly contained triumph. Smug. Certain now of his submission.

*It's just words,* Val told himself. *An old story. It can't hurt me.* But he didn't believe it. Not at all. What had happened in that room poisoned him, the guilt and shame a hidden well of sickness oozing within. "I never think about it."

Long ago, he'd shoved this piece of his past down and down. So far down it only leaked out in nightmares that he woke from sobbing, pawing the air. Those few miserable hours in a tower room and what he did to end them had cost him everything—his wife, his son. All stolen from him. Even time. "You've heard of the contest of swords?"

Myranthe pushed a cup of wine towards him. "A dangerous, prestigious tournament. Held once every twelve years. It drew bladesmen from across the world, even beyond the Ice Sea."

In the candlelight, the cup gleamed, just like the gleam of the blade draped over a tasselled cloth on a table made of crystal in the magnificent hall of the Wardorian palace.

"The prize was a blade crafted in Seithin, an offer of a place on the Wardorian emperor's personal guard." Val's words came out flatly, apart from him. "But the stakes were more than that. Honour, glory, a chance to test your skill and courage, all those foolish things warriors crave above gold. The risks—high. At night, carts rumbled along empty streets, carrying broken bodies for sea burial."

A dam of memories broke inside. Every sound, scent, and sight of the city upon the bay was clear in his mind: its watchtowers spiking a cloudless sky; merchants' cries as they enticed buyers in the dusty squares where stray dogs padded, their tongues out in the heat; women's bright taffeta gowns dragging over cobblestones.

The air was filled with the stink of sweat, kelp, and fish. A gull's piercing squawk mingled with waves lapping boards. A ship's rigging creaked as the sea glazed serene.

Butterflies fluttered everywhere. In flower beds. Among the weeds along the shore. Bright blue. Bobbing above fountains. He brushed them from his face as he strode wide streets, breathing in the city's musk from sewers, its spice, as he shouldered through crowds to the palace. There the clangour, clash, and clank of steel drowned the murmur of princes and lords as they watched warriors bleed and die for their pleasure.

Val snatched up his cup and drank. "That last fight. I can't seem to remember—"

Myranthe covered his hand with hers, her touch and her glances solicitous now that she knew he would give her all she sought. "A Wardorian account of that contest is in our library. It is written that a nineteen-year-old traitor's son did what no other Telorian bladesman did in five hundred years. He won."

"Won," Val echoed. "I remember the cheers. I remember wishing my father could see me. My father, the man Wardorians called traitor but Telorians called hero. I wanted to tell him my victory was for him. Because Telorians might be enslaved, but we were better than that."

"Indeed." Myranthe's gaze did not move from his face.

"I cannot recall that final bout in detail. I fought as I always did, with control, the blade an extension of my will. Every thrust and cut so well drilled, they were more than instinctive."

His arm had obeyed every twitch of thought, leaving him free to listen to the intonations in swordplay. To a Serravan bladesman, its secret language had such poisonously sweet rhythms.

"Winning was a blur. Spectators shouted my name, tried to touch me."

The boy, though, Val remembered—a serious child called Alecc who had watched each fight then sought him out with questions. Why that defence? What weakness did his opponent reveal? How did he take advantage of it?

Val answered all with a patient smile. He resisted the urge to ruffle the child's black hair, knowing a fifteen-year-old would find the gesture undignified.

At that final fight, Alecc patiently waited as others milled with congratulations and a robed man, sweat shining upon his thinning hairline, presented Val with a sword. At last, after an eternity of ceremonies, backslapping, and empty talk, as the thick throng of well-wishers faded away to drink in the taverns, Val laughed in surprise.

He'd won. He'd actually won. Surely it must be a dream. He would wake back in the Isles, the memory of Wardour slipping away. Happily dazed, he assembled his belongings, wondering what had become of his father's weapons master. Seeing Alecc, he smiled. "How'd I do?"

"I have no questions." The boy flicked hair from dark eyes more common among Telorians than Wardorians. "I understood it all. Especially the sequence of strokes to wound him."

"That's good, then." Val slid the new sword into his belt beside his old one. Its gleam excited him. Seithin steel. His father carried such a blade, a curious beast—as Val thought of it—called Tearbringer. "Not so many men read the conversation of swords."

"I can."

Again, Val forced down the temptation to muss the boy's hair.

"Then no doubt, we'll meet in the next contest." He laughed. "You studied my technique so closely, you'll have the advantage."

"My father will forbid it. I'm surprised your father let you risk your life so."

"My father could not say no," Val replied tersely.

The emperor's invitation had been carefully worded. The threat implied. His father's council had argued it out for many hours. "Send the boy, or we take him," he'd overheard one Isles lord say. "That's what he means."

"The Mazart fears the prophecy," Val's father had said. "That a swordsman of Caelan blood will kill him in the ruins of Seithin. He wants to test Val. Make certain it's not him."

"At least you have another son," the first lord had said. "If the emperor murders this one."

The Mazart considered Val's father a traitor—a forgiven traitor who reluctantly bent his knee. Traitors could not refuse to send their sons or daughters to Wardour as hostages or to fight in contests for the emperor's diversion.

"But if you win, Alecc"—Val scooped a damp cloth from a bucket to sponge his neck—"you'll bring honour to your father."

Alecc did not reply. He stared over Val's shoulder and muttered, "No, no, no."

Val spun. Wardorian guardsmen approached. "They after you, Alecc? What did you do?"

"You joke a lot." Alecc grasped his arm. "But there's no more time for jokes. They're here for you. I saw him, the Mazart. Watching you. You have to run."

"Why?"

"Val Arques Caelan?" The guardsmen surrounded him.

"Yes."

"Your emperor wishes to express his admiration at your skill. We're to take you to him."

"The ship for Telor sails on the tide. My friend is waiting." *Somewhere.*

"You'll make your ship." The man's fingers brushed his sword hilt. A captain's badge crested one shoulder. "This is your emperor, Telorian. He wishes to reward you."

"I-I do not think I am worthy to meet an emperor."

"No Telorian is worthy. But in his benevolence, he wants to greet you."

"My companion will wonder what has become of me."

"Your lord's sword, Saltman?"

"We call him the Salt Sword." Val's laugh flowed easily. His was a nature to find everything pleasant in life, to think himself fortunate. He was well-liked, a young lord with a pretty wife and infant son. Men called him generous and kind. They didn't call him naïve. But he was. He just didn't know it. Alecc was far worldlier than him.

"He's waiting at the emperor's rooms." The captain's glance fell on Alecc. "You, boy, scamper off. This isn't your business."

"You don't tell me what to do," Alecc said.

The captain shoved him. "Get lost, brat."

Val grabbed the man's shoulder. "Leave him be. He's not causing any trouble."

"That boy is always underfoot. Come. Your emperor grows impatient."

Val rubbed his sword hilt. The man's tense expression, his companions' watchful stances niggled. "I'm not fit to greet the emperor. My clothes, my hair. I need a bath."

A guard sniggered. "You Avanti girls do nothing but bathe."

"Hot in Avanti. Hot here too. Maybe you should bathe more often." Val wrinkled his nose.

The guard's face darkened. "Why you—"

The captain stepped between them. "It's of no concern how you look," he said to Val. "The emperor bid us bring you at once. You cannot refuse him."

For all his growing unease, Val could see no way out of it. "Then lead the way."

As they fell in about him, he looked for Alecc. The boy had disappeared.

"The pretence fell away fast after that." Val blankly watched Myranthe rise to refill his cup. This story felt unreal, as if told by someone else. "But even then, I didn't understand. I didn't know that sort of thing happened—or that it could happen to me."

Myranthe returned to her seat. She sat forward. "Just tell it. Say it."

The guards flanked him through vast halls of gleaming marble, up circular stairwells with polished bannisters, and along rugged passages brightly lit by braziers. The Wardorian palace was a place of sunlight and cavernous, opulent rooms with balconies overlooking a glaringly bright jewel-blue sea.

He didn't see the shadows. He didn't feel that undercurrent of malice or iniquity. Not until one of his escort sniggered. "The emperor appreciates a good swordsman." Not until the others laughed and a guard nudged another, muttering, "Especially sweet, young Telorians."

Only then did his neck prickle. Val drew up hard. "Tell me where you're taking me."

"Fierce, isn't he?" their captain said easily. "To your emperor, boy."

"Why exactly?" Val gripped his hilt.

"Steady. No need for alarm." The captain swept an arm. "Just along this passage. Your emperor, the Mazart, the majestic, gracious ruler of every land, awaits."

Val glanced over his shoulder. He had no clue where he was,

but he could run. He could most certainly fight.

His escort drew their blades. Metal prodded Val's back.

"I don't understand—"

"They're so stupid." The sweating guard tapped his temple. "All that bathing washes their wits away."

"Bring him." The captain no longer masked his dislike.

They did not disarm him but took hold of his arms to march him up winding stairs encased in stone. The captain stood aside as his men shoved him through a doorway.

Val stumbled, found his balance, and turned in time to see the door clank shut. As a key rattled, he hammered a fist against its wood. "What are you doing? Let me out."

A snigger. Laughter. Retreating steps.

Val slammed his shoulder into the door. Then again and again, until he nearly sobbed in frustration. Dread cut along his ribs. *Why lock me in? Where is Saltman?*

He fought his panic. It had to be a mistake. Overzealous guards, that was all. They hadn't stripped his blades from him. So he must not be a captive. The Mazart would apologise for his men's enthusiasm.

Val smoothed his tunic, combed fingers through his damp, tangled hair, and considered the cheerfully bright tower room's divans and couches, high-backed chairs, and tables. Silk cushions, embroidered with gold thread, spilled in careful disarray. Upon an oak corner table, yellow roses filled a china vase painted with violets and tansies.

*Hardly a prison.* Yet his unease did not recede. He trod over patterned rugs to the window. Late-afternoon sunlight, pleasantly warm on his bare arms, glared through bars. A breeze lifted his fringe. More butterflies, beautiful bright-blue marionettes, flitted.

Across tiled roofs, coloured sails rippled against the cloudless sky, either at anchor in the white-capped waters of the bay or docked at long wharves. Any Isles man could name the different vessels. Cogs from Veniva. Warships belonging to princes seeking the Mazart's favours. A sleek Adorean galley perhaps hired by merchants to bring silks or jewellery from the Icelands to the markets thriving alongside the contest.

The ships felt unreachable, as if from a different world. Even sunlight on his face, golden and pure, could not rid him of the coldness etching his spine. Val gripped the smooth, warm bars.

*All a mistake.* He stoked his courage. *It will be all right.*

A key jangled. The door opened. A solidly built man entered. Val recognised him from the hall. He had sat high on a velvet-padded throne, leaning forward to watch a close bout or applaud a deserving swordsman. The sorcerer king who had conquered Telor, who subjugated every land. The emperor who called himself Mazart. Overlord.

"Val Arques Caelan, my guards found you then?" Ordinary words from a man less so.

The emperor wore a linen shirt with pants and boots of soft leather, his garments simple and no better than Val's father owned. A brocade cloak swung from a broad shoulder. A scabbard of worked leather clung to his hip, encasing a long sword with a hilt of patterned silver. His face was too gaunt to be handsome but was as compelling as a bird of prey's. Tattoos swirled up his neck onto a bristled jaw. Jewels glittered from ringed fingers. A gold medallion dangled at his throat, and bracelets snaked about a warrior's upper arms.

"I wished to greet you." His voice was of a moderate timbre, not as deep as Val's father's. "I am in awe of your skill. That last fight—" He came forward, smiling.

"Why am I locked in?"

The Mazart gripped his arms. Val trembled as the emperor studied him. This man was the most powerful prince in all the known lands, perhaps the entire world. Even beyond the Ice Sea. Men whispered of places on the far side, but no one ever returned from there.

"Locked in?" The Mazart's smile disarmed him. "I desired only to say how much I admire you. My men must have misunderstood."

Tension eased from Val's shoulders. *Overzealous guards indeed.* "Then I can leave?"

"Certainly. But first, you'll have something to eat, drink? We'll talk." The Mazart bid Val sit on voluptuous cushions on a couch as he took a high-backed chair.

"Yes, of course. Thank you," Val stammered, awkward and awestruck. The Wardorian stank of power, as ruthless kings and princes often did. Yet for all the stories of the man's cruelty, naked ambition, bloodthirst, and sorcery, the Mazart was not the fire-breathing monster Val had expected.

*Evil.* He heard his father's voice. *Mind how you go, Val. Remember that old saying. You're not in the Isles anymore. You're not among friends.* "My protector. Saltman. I seem to have lost him. Your guards said he would be here."

The Mazart clapped his hands. Servants entered with trays of food, gilded goblets, and carafes of wine. They set them upon the table beside the vase of roses and silently withdrew.

"We shall seek him out. But first, you'll take wine?" He poured for them both.

"Surely I should serve you, Your Grace."

Bright sunlight slanted the emperor's face. At Val's words, he smiled. His smile was sly, almost predatory. Hairs rose along Val's arms. He glanced at the barred windows then at a shackle in the wall, nearly hidden by cushions.

"We shall drink to your talent." The Mazart clashed his goblet against his guest's. "Perhaps I can persuade you to join my personal guard. You are, no doubt, Serravan trained at that ghastly mountains fortress, Vraymorg? A frightening, bleak place, indeed."

Val sipped steadily. "At fourteen, my father sent me to train with the Serravan, yes. Until then, he taught me the language of swords himself."

"Your father—" The Mazart's knuckles whitened as he gripped

his goblet. "A formidable man." He masked a scowl with a warm smile. "You must be uncomfortable. Why not remove your weapons belt? It can rest over there." He waved an arm.

Val preferred to carry a blade. But a warrior should not bring steel into his king's presence. He rose, surprised to find his head spun, unbuckled the belt, and slung it on a chair.

"The new sword pleases you?"

"Very much." He touched the hilt with awe. "I long to blood it. What is known of it? All Seithin blades have a legend."

The emperor shrugged. "If it does, I don't know it. The sword was among spoils from the Seithin temple."

Taken when the Wardorian army burned the desert city the year before Val's birth. Everyone knew the story, how the fall of Seithin had changed the world.

"It is a blade worthy of you," the Mazart said. "You have a swordsman's pure instinct."

"I shall have to name the sword after I blood it." Val slumped onto a couch near the emperor, smiling as he recalled what Avanti warriors called their blades. Dream-maker. Blood-drinker. Crude, but they cut to the truth. A bladesman killed or died. That was all.

"Ah, that smile." The Mazart sat back. "What might a man risk to possess something so sweet? Of course you cannot know what I mean, Val Arques Caelan, all of—what? Eighteen?"

"Nineteen." An uncomfortable sliver of ice juddered down his back.

"The helm hides much. Even so, it could not hide the cut of your cheekbones, that wide, full mouth." The Mazart took the goblet from him. "Enough, I think."

"You're right." His vision blurred. "It must be the heat or exhaustion, but I feel unwell."

"Not exhaustion. The wine is enspelled."

"What?" Fear jagged through him. A cold, hard stab of it, then a slow spread.

"So you don't fight so hard. Though"—the Mazart put a hand

on Val's thigh—"I hope you fight a little."

Val glanced at his hand. He looked up at the emperor's face.

He bolted for the door.

It swung back. A man blocked him.

"Please," Val begged the stranger. "Help me."

The man stared at Val then at the Mazart. "So it's true." He tore ringed fingers through receding brown hair. "My son says you unlawfully hold my nephew. I don't like this."

*Nephew?* Hope flared in him. *This must be Julian, king of Adorean.* The Mazart's closest ally had wed Val's aunt, his father's beloved sister, as part of that peace accord reached years before.

The Mazart shrugged. "To be accurate, he is your wife's nephew and a traitor's whelp. To you, he was nothing when you woke up this morning, and he is still nothing."

"I have vital affairs to concern me beyond who of my kin is at your bloody tournament." Julian's bulk blocked Val's escape. "But this boy is Avanti's son and of my wife's blood."

"A boy she never met."

"She has regular word from her brother. Avanti writes often."

"You allow her his letters?"

"Am I her gaoler? I know too well what this is about. Let him go."

"Do not interfere, Julian. I don't intend to kill the boy."

"No, what you intend is worse. I've seen it before. Only last year, you abducted the daughter of that Cahirean nobleman to punish an insolent lord for his defiance. Next, there was the wife of that Venivan trader who insulted you. You didn't bother to try to seduce her, either. And there have been others. This is about power and vengeance. Nothing else."

"It's about taking what I want. Look at him. Have you seen a more striking creature?"

No guards were on the stairs. Val tried to push past. His uncle shoved him back. The room spun. He groped at air and found himself on his knees.

Julian grabbed Val's arm to steady him. "You look like him." A flicker of sympathy dissolved to a glower of distaste. "Like your father. Like Avanti."

He dropped Val and whirled on the Mazart. "No word must ever reach my wife. He'll have to disappear."

"No," Val gasped. "Please. Don't leave me here." A despairing sob thickened in his throat. He shoved it down. Warriors didn't sob. Not before others. And not from fear.

"He's already disappeared. As far as anyone knows, he left the hall for the docks."

"Please," Val begged his uncle.

Julian threw him a pitiless look. "I'm sorry." He turned away. "I can't help you." The door thumped shut behind him.

FEAR TRAPPED VAL on his hands and knees. He crawled to the closed door and thumped his palms against it. Sunlight billowed through the windows, warm and soft. Children's laughter carried from the streets. The world outside was tantalisingly near. But it lay on the other side of this door.

The Mazart settled back in his chair. "By every god, you're perfect."

Heat flooded his face. Val drew knees to his chest, a barrier against this man's intrusive eyes. He glanced at his swords.

"Your steel can't hurt me. Even Seithin steel." The sorcerer gave him a long look. "The wine, it seems, fails to soften your will. Your Caelan blood, no doubt."

"What do you want with me?" The truth hammered at him, but he couldn't face it.

This wasn't like those summer afternoons after training when he and his cousin, both seventeen, would lie naked on fur bedding in Val's tiny room in the Serravan Mountains fortress. His smile quiet and sleepy, Dace would run his hand over Val's body. When Val kissed his cousin's neck, his skin tasted like cinnamon.

The Mazart didn't intend to seduce him. He wanted to hurt him. To humiliate him. Just like he had hurt the daughters and sons of others who defied him.

"I watched you fight, how that splendid body strained with every stroke," the emperor said. "I imagined the play of those muscles beneath my hands. I desired you. I am emperor of every land. Ruler of your land, your father—of you. What I desire, I take."

Val's spine hit the door hard. He nearly clawed at it. But a Telorian prince showed no fear. His father, the renowned warrior who nearly defeated the Mazart with a daring counterattack through drifting snow and knifing winter winds, had taught him that. "Is this about my father?"

"It certainly makes it sweeter." The emperor's gaze passed over him slowly.

Val braced a palm to wood to straighten. Without steel, he felt naked. Vulnerable. But he had his fists, feet, teeth. He could fight. The Mazart was no taller or broader than he.

But he had guards. Magic. And Val had already disappeared.

Wildly, desperately, he blustered, "I'm Serravan trained. I know the order's every mystery. I know how to unleash that secret rage. I have the words."

To know a spell was one thing. To leap into danger, another. His Serravan masters warned a warrior paid an unspeakable price for resorting to such magic. Val shuddered. That magic might save him, but it would also destroy him.

"You won't. You won't even fight, let alone use such a dangerous incantation."

"You don't know what I'm capable of."

"I have no doubt you're brave enough to risk it. But you have a wife, a father, a younger brother in Telor. A son. Telor belongs to me. All I need do is sign a piece of paper or speak a command, and they're dead."

"No." Val choked on useless anger. He collapsed to his knees once more. What could he do? Disobey, and this monster hurt those he loved.

"Stand up," the Mazart said. "Remove your clothes."

Helpless fury burst through him. Val glared his loathing at the foul creature who calmly watched him, knowing he must obey. He drove his fist into the floor.

The Mazart sipped wine. "Such passion in you. I will take my time taming you. Now obey, or your family dies."

The rage washed away to a despair as tangible as a garrotte about his throat. Useless to resist. Stupid. The Mazart would hurt his wife. His brother. His father. Oh gods, his son. No, this man could do with him as he wished, just so long as he kept them safe.

Val staggered up. Numb with misery, he unfastened his cloak and let it drop. Then he drew his tunic over his head and tossed it to the floor.

The Mazart rose. Slowly he circled, as though savouring the pleasure of one sense at a time. First, he devoured with his eyes. A mortifying, intrusive inspection. Next, he leaned to breathe in the scent of Val's hair. When he touched his captive's shoulder, Val jerked.

"Stay still." The sorcerer's caress roamed down his belly and across his hips.

Val tensed every muscle, wanting to fight. To run. He could do neither. He must take this, accept the repulsive brush of fingertips down his back.

The world shrank to his captor's controlled exhalations, the heat of his body, its odour of sweat and oil. Moist, hot hands prodded, rubbed, caressed. Val closed his eyes against the leering gaze. His every breath snapped out, sharp with humiliation. No one could touch him like that. It wasn't right.

The Mazart stopped in front of him. "Open your eyes."

Reluctantly, he did. The emperor put a hand at the nape of Val's neck to draw his head close. Val pulled back. The Mazart raised a hand to strike him. The blow did not fall. Instead, he held his palm just above Val's face.

Val locked his eyes on that palm, badly wanting its sting on his cheek. That pain, he understood. Like any wound, he could endure it. The rest, he could not.

The Mazart knotted his fingers in Val's hair. "Don't ever do that again."

He pressed a key into Val's hands and nodded at a couch against the sun-bathed wall. Sunlight streaked bright pillows. Mocking ribbons of it.

"There. Shackle your hand."

Dazed, sick, Val stumbled to the couch. He shoved his wrist into a manacle attached by chain to a wall ring. As he turned the key, his tears fell unchecked.

⁓⸖⁓

"You stopped." Myranthe's voice dragged him from the past. "Why have you stopped?"

Val sank his head into his hands. "I can't. Please. I can't."

She studied his face. Then she rose, crossed to the table, poured wine, and brought him another cup. When she pressed it into his fingers, her hands shook. "Find the courage to tell it all, or we have no bargain. I won't leave the door unlocked, and you won't have your chance to escape. Whoever is behind your need to get free, say goodbye to them. You know what happens when Velleran passes you on."

Val drank fast. "You don't know what you're asking. You don't know—"

"Oh, I think I do."

He stared at her glumly. "If you know, then I don't need to say."

"Tell it."

"I can't. I can't… be there again. In that room. I don't want you to know. I don't want anyone to know."

She straightened. "Then our conversation is at an end. You'll never be free."

"No. It doesn't have to be like this."

"I'm offering you a chance to escape. But it's up to you."

Val fought down sickness. Did it matter what happened to him? Saving Aric from her murderous intent mattered. Finding Kaell. That mattered most of all.

He said, "I'll tell it."

A scuffling roused him. Val opened puffy eyes onto darkness. The sound came again. Someone had entered the room. Determined steps crossed the floor.

His silent scream ached in his throat. *No, no. Not him.*

A candle flamed. Alecc peered at him, his face tight with concern.

Val stirred in surprise. Then hot shame flooded his body. He, a warrior, a lord's son, lay chained and naked, his cheeks stained by tears. He sank his face into the pillow. "Don't look at me."

"It's all right," the boy said. "I understand." He moved away, returning with a rug to cover Val. "Don't be ashamed. What could you do?"

"Run. Like you told me. You tried to warn me." Val lifted his head. "How did you know?"

"I've seen it before," Alecc said solemnly. "There was a girl he had guards bring to this room, the daughter of one of his generals the Mazart thought too powerful and too popular. Then there was a Cahirean noblewoman who refused his advances. I didn't like it, but I put it out of my mind. But when it was you—"

"What makes me special?"

"You really don't know who I am? I thought you did and that was why you were kind."

"I don't understand. I don't know who you are. Truly."

"Then you're simply kind." The boy stared into the shadows. "And other things, like my mother said. Brave."

"Not brave," he whimpered. "I've wept."

"That's nothing to do with being brave. My father says all men break."

"I think I'm broken, then."

"Broken things mend. I broke my arm falling off a wall, and it's fine now. Bats fly again when a wing heals. My mother told me stories about you. You fight like the man in those stories should. Fearlessly. More than that—you fight fairly. Of course that makes you a typical Isles fool, according to my father."

"I still don't—"

"Gods, Val Arques Caelan. Are you a fool?"

"I may well be, because—" Then it hit him. Julian had come because of his own son. Val's usual laugh forced its way through his misery. "Are you my cousin? Are you? Why, you must be. My father's beloved sister is your mother. You bid your father help me."

"A fat lot of good that did. I should know he's too cowardly to defy the emperor."

"So you are my cousin."

"One of them," the boy said in that serious tone. "The unimportant one. They all forget about me. Because I'm just a younger son."

"I had an older brother."

"Who died. That made you important. My brother is alive and very, very well. All grown up. A strong, young bull who's worthy of attention now he's old enough to fight for Adorean and give her more heirs and all that. But me? They all forget about me—still think of me as 'the brat.' That's what my father calls me."

"So we are kin. I shouldn't be surprised—"

"Given how I understand the language of swords?" The boy disappeared into the darkness again before returning with a cup of water.

Val took it in his free hand and drank. "Why didn't you say, Alecc?" He returned the cup. "That explains a lot. Like why your hair is so dark for an Adorean."

"I look like my mother. I wonder if my father even believes I'm his."

"Well, Alecc of Adorean," Val said formally, "I am pleased to meet my kinsman."

"So am I." The boy's face clouded. "But I wish the circumstances changed."

Val's throat knotted again. Dismally, he shook the chain. "How did you get in here? I don't suppose you can free me?"

"I brought the guards drugged wine. A gift from my brother, I said. When they fell asleep, I stole the door key." He sank teeth into his lip. "But the Mazart keeps the key to that fetter about his neck. Besides, the lock is probably enspelled."

Val dug fingers into the divan. "Then—" He could not voice his fears.

"He'll come back." Alecc didn't look at him. "I think—" Again, his teeth scraped his bottom lip. He muttered, "No."

"Say it. Don't worry about scaring me. The truth is always better."

The boy darted a look at his face. "He let the general's daughter go at once. But others…" Alecc moistened his lips with his tongue. "He keeps them somewhere. A place only he goes. I think…" His voice faded. "I think he'll take you there."

"And keep me for months? Years?"

Alecc said nothing. He placed a knife on the divan beside Val.

"Alecc of Adorean," Myranthe said. "A rather interesting king in his time. To conquer Cahir then Telor, only to lose them both to Rainer. To have the gods favour him then turn against him because of his pride. He certainly knew the giddy heights of triumph and the depths of despair." She brushed fingertips along Val's arm. "How strange that Rozenn of Cahir should name her son after him. It's tempting fate."

Her words came to Val as though through a fog. The fingers on his skin were the emperor's. Damp. Lecherous.

He clawed back to the present. A metallic taste coated his tongue. Bile shot up. Hot, dizzy, he slumped from the chair to hands and knees, retching into the slop pail. How foolish to imagine he could ever speak of it. That he was strong enough. It wasn't just words, another story. It was part of everything that twisted in him.

Every fear, every nightmare he fled, all lived in that tiny sliver of the past, trapped in a sunlit room where a sorcerer had shamed him.

Myranthe stroked his hair. "It's nearly done. You're nearly done."

"I've said all I can."

"Just a little more, then it's forgotten. I won't ask again. No one will."

Val brushed off her hand, wiped his mouth on his sleeve, pushed to his knees then slumped in the chair. He didn't want her to see him like this.

"Drink." Myranthe offered wine. "Just a little. It will help." She watched him sip. "Then finish it."

"What do you want to know?" Val surrendered to anger. "I've said the worst of it. Things I tried to forget. Things I've not given voice to ever."

She gripped his wrist. "Tell it. About that knife. You picked it up. You cut."

He let out a cry that was half exasperation and half fury.

"Yes, all right. I did pick up that knife. Not at once. Not for a long while. No, I lay there for hours, sobbing or yelling, thinking of my wife, Finya, of my son. All the while, the candle burned low. All the while, I choked on that scent of rose oil. I knew despair that night. Not sadness. I was well beyond that. Hollow. My mind gone. You can't know—"

"You took up the knife."

"Yes. I took up the knife. Why did Alecc leave it? A kindness? Maybe so. Hard to understand Alecc, given all he would become. Even as a child, he was complicated."

Val's anger died as quickly as it flared. The boy had been braver than him. Far, far braver. He had done the only thing he could to help.

"I took up the knife." His voice broke up. "My hand trembled. I wept so hard, I could no longer see. I think I shut my eyes as I cut. How it hurt. I didn't expect it to hurt like that. I thought it would be simple. Once I decided I couldn't face—once I realised what Alecc tried to tell me."

"You took the knife."

"I took up the knife." An odd calm came with the repetition of these words. "I hacked at my wrists. So much blood. Everywhere, blood. Running down my arms, soaking the couch, pooled on the floor. Then he came. Curse him. Why did he come?"

"The Mazart. He cast a spell?"

"Something like that." Weariness pricked his eyelids. Dully, he registered Myranthe whispering in an unfamiliar tongue. But he didn't care. He wanted only to bury his head beneath the pillow and sleep.

"And knowing you were dying, he sacrificed you in your last moments to his god, Aziarr. An act that made you immortal but also a prisoner of that god, kept in his temple deep beneath the earth, unable to ever see your wife and son."

"To the world, I was dead. My brother Karolus became Lord of the Isles. My wife wed my cousin, Dace, only to die in childbirth. The Mazart took my son hostage then later murdered him. I knew none of this. I was Aziarr's slave, bound to him by magic. Until the day he sent me to kill Dace's son Rainer, Khir's grandson, and Rainer bested me with magic."

"But that wasn't the end of your torment, was it?"

"No."

"No," she echoed softly. "This is what I've pieced together from various sources. Rainer shut you away, chained you in a secret room where you suffered alone for nearly two decades. Again and again, you starved to death, your immortality a curse."

Val shuddered at the memory.

"At last, years after Rainer died killing Aziarr, and on the very day a Cahirean king murdered Roaran Caelan, Roaran's ward, Devarsi, heard you weeping and freed you. Grateful, you served her faithfully in the civil war that followed Roaran's death. Until you had Roaran's son Ryol in your power and refused to slaughter him. Devarsi was furious. She banished you to Vraymorg. Out of sight. Out of mind."

How pitiful his life sounded when boiled down to its bones. "Yes, you have it. Now leave me alone."

"Not yet," she said. "I have another spell to cast."

# HEATH

He didn't trust himself to enter. Instead, he thrust a shoulder to the doorframe, saying nothing. Holding in his anger.

Myranthe did not look up from her book. The glow of a single candle carved her face with ridges, hollows, and shadows. Only her back, too stiff, and her jerky flick of hair off her face betrayed her disquiet.

"You heard then." She sounded displeased.

"I heard. Every word the scribe outside the door took down. Even your spell at the last."

Still, she did not lift her head. An eerie torpor shrouded her chamber, as though her spell closed about the caverns. Only a sliver of wind slipped in through the shutters, lifting a wall tapestry. Its wooden frame tapped stone. In the fireplace, logs popped and crackled.

"Why are you pretending everything is normal when you just destroyed a man?" Heath asked. "What are you waiting for?"

With deliberate care, she closed the book. Holding her eyes on the table, she said, "I'm waiting for sounds of alarm. But of course, there is nothing. How can there be?"

"I don't understand."

At last, she looked up. "I promised him a chance to run. But he can't leave. Not now. He's cowering against the wall, trapped by my final spell in the misery of the past, his shame uncovered. When the time comes for Velleran to pass him on, he'll go meekly, still lost and broken."

"No." Heath furiously gripped the door. "No. He's better than that."

She looked at him. "Better than what? I've tolerated your obsession, Heath, because it didn't interfere with my goals. With our family's goals. But this new rebellion of yours ends now. If you get in my way, if you challenge me again, I'll stomp on you. I'll break you down until you're a sobbing wretch."

Confident steps rang in the passage. Velleran paused on the threshold, a brow tilted at Heath. "I didn't expect you." He faced Myranthe. "Does he know then?" At her nod, he moved to the fire to stamp his feet. "I trust you won't interfere, Heath."

"I have been warned," Heath said. "Myranthe will stomp on me until I cry."

Velleran rubbed his hands over the embers. "Myranthe, I commend you. The guards found the door open, just as you left it."

She nodded.

"They found him curled on the floor, just as you left him."

Myranthe nodded again.

"The door wide, no guards, and yet he does not flee. Quite an intriguing spell, to leave someone trapped in their own past. I take it this magic is the first step in subjugating Roaran Caelan?"

Heath grunted in disgust. "An intriguing spell? Do you know what she forced from him?"

"The brother-keeper imparted enough. I suppose it is well he wrote it down. We are preservers of history, after all, and it is our duty to record the truth about this man."

"The truth." Heath couldn't believe such nonsense. "At what cost?" He spun on his sister, poking a finger in accusation. "You didn't need to destroy him."

Myranthe considered him dispassionately. "I needed to practise on a man of Caelan blood to ensure I don't hurt Roaran when I use the same magic on him. That's all."

"An unsettling story," Velleran said. "I admit to a faint stirring of compassion. Faint."

"Disappointing for you, Heath." Myranthe threw back a sneering laugh. "To find this man shattered. You so enjoy your games."

"I'm sure I'll overcome my disappointment," Heath said unpleasantly. "Perhaps by getting drunk on disappointment wine. Or cutting up some fool in a disappointment fire dance."

Velleran turned from the fireplace. "Well, Myranthe, what happens now? My buyers expect the merchandise to be in tolerable condition."

"I could leave him like this." Myranthe tapped fingers against the table.

"What?" Heath burst forward a step, hands raised. "You can't."

Velleran stroked his chin. "That does seem unnecessarily cruel. Our buyers don't wish him broken, only—I cannot quite recall their word."

"Compliant?" Her smile was grim. "Then I shall complete the spell. After all, I must know how it will affect our wayward death rider. So another visit tonight, I think."

# KAELL

Kaell woke beneath an endless, velvet sky bathed in starlight. Hard ground needled his spine. Witch weed prickled his wrists and ankles. Wind stirred branches to a slow creak in a silvery forest all about him. The cool night smelled of grass and fecund earth. Enlivened by the breeze, sparks of a nearby fire jigged.

His back to Kaell, a man crouched to rub his hands over the flames.

"Who are you?" Kaell squirmed, unable to grasp what had happened. "Why am I here?"

The man threw a twig into the blaze. It fizzed as it caught. A log rolled with a thump into crumbling embers. Smoke spiralled towards the sky and the bleak light of a wafer moon.

"Answer me, curse you. What do you want with me?"

With a drawn-out sigh, the man pressed his hands to his thighs and rose. Slowly, he turned. The wind plucked at the edges of his cloak. His leather boots squeaked. A buckle scraped against his scabbard encasing a plain iron-hilted sword for a no-nonsense warrior. Even in the poor light his tight, wary face with its jagged scar was impossibly familiar.

*Arn Tranter.*

Kaell stared. A ghost. A dream. It had to be. Sheer incomprehension stole his breath. Choking, gasping, he could only mouth words.

"Take a breath, Kaell." Arn came towards him. "You're all right."

Kaell released a bestial cry of hurt. He thumped his heels in the dirt and thrashed, desperate to get at Arn. To shake him. To grip his jaw and just scream, "Tell me it's not you! It can't be. Not you."

"But you were my friend," he finally managed. The words sounded pitifully childish, as if his pain had stripped him back to a younger core, as if everything about being a man fell away in the face of it.

Arn said nothing.

"I thought I saw you in that castle where Archanin held me, but I didn't believe it. Even now, I can't believe it."

"You saw me."

"No," Kaell howled. "I didn't. I couldn't. You wouldn't leave me like that. Not if you knew what Archanin intended to do to me."

"What do you want me to say?" Arn said. "That I did nothing? That I left you? Yes. But I was sick with it."

"He tortured me, Arn. He forced his blood on me—other things too." Disgust whipped up, a hot burn beneath his skin. "And you were 'sick with it?'"

"I know you don't understand." Arn clenched his hands. "He won't, either. Roaran. When he finds you gone, he'll think I betrayed him."

"Roaran?" Kaell jammed pieces into place. "You were at the dead city. That was you talking with him. First at the table. Then outside. Then you know—" His voice caught with hope. "Did you bring me here to save me?"

Arn looked at him. In a quiet voice, he said, "No. Not to save you, Kaell."

"Then why?"

"To save him."

The words sluggishly took shape in his mind. Not just what they meant but also what they didn't mean. The man he'd called friend had left him to Archanin. Even now, he didn't help him for his sake but another's.

"I loved him long before I loved you, Kaell," Arn said.

"Love…" Kaell echoed in disbelief. "Love."

"I'm Varee, Kaell. Or I was. My family, we serve Archanin. I did, too, until in a raid on some nameless Downs village, some fool slashed me deep with a knife. The Varee abandoned me, left me lying there in the dirt, wounded." He touched the scar on his jaw. "Roaran healed me. Showed me the truth about Archanin, about the price my people pay in bondage. In blood. I owe him everything."

Kaell said only, "You disgust me."

The words hung in the air, unanswered. Too much sat between them for simple answers, for indifference. Theirs was no longer a bond of friendship, if that was what it had been, but a bond of scorn and pain. Everything soured. Everything lost, and no way back.

Arn drew his knife. Kaell's back bore down hard into the ground.

"At Thom, you knelt to pray, your sword just beyond your reach," Arn said. "How many times did I warn you not to do that? I only needed to cut your throat and end it then. For your sake, I nearly did. But I had to trust Roaran."

"And now? What now, Arn?"

Their eyes locked. Kaell looked away first, afraid the other man might glimpse the need in him. Despite the wrong Arn had done him, Kaell missed his old friend. Oh, how he missed him.

Arn released an uneven breath. He took the knife and cut Kaell free.

# DANNON

In the darkness, Shahven helped him wade the river. He left Dannon in the forest and went for horses. But upon his return, the bridge sentry challenged him.

Dannon's breaths cut his ribs like knives. They were discovered. Oh gods, Shahven would be caught and punished. But the guard waved the boy on.

"I told them the mage wants me to take an extra horse to Patrick and the others," Shahven explained when he joined Dannon in the trees. "So they could bring back Kate."

On horseback, they had a start. But the moment someone found the dead mage, the Varee would come after them. It was hopeless to think he and Shahven could evade Varee trackers. Nowhere was safe. No one could save them.

Dizzy, sick, Dannon struggled to stay in the saddle. Yet an innate stubbornness meant he could not let the reins slip from his fingers or let his heavy, drugged body slide to the ground.

The interminable journey blurred to flickering trees, to clouds shifting against the moons. His stiff fingers grew numb as they gripped worn leather. There were only plodding hooves, the saddle chafing his buttocks, and rain icing his face. On and on. On and on.

Sounds broke through. Voices. Tramping steps. Hands pulled at the horse's bridle. Slumped upon the horse, Dannon vaguely registered figures crowding around Shahven.

"He's dying." Tears glistened on the boy's smooth cheeks. "Save him. Please."

The figures cleared a path for a man. A silver-hilted blade hung at his hip, his hair as dusky as a starless sky. His gaze expressionless, he stared at Dannon.

Blackness edged behind Dannon's eyelids. *Just let go. Let it end.*

He dropped the reins and let his body fall. Men lifted him then carried him through shadows into a tower. They dumped him on a cold, slabbed floor. Dannon was aware of the dark-haired stranger beside him. The man put a hand to the nape of his neck and leaned in. Soft lips brushed his. The world fell away into welcome darkness.

# KAELL

The weight in his limbs bound him to the earth. Numb, bone weary with grief, his mind detached as clouds shifted over the wedged moon until there was only a rolling sea of star-streaked grey. The fire spat. A distant stream trickled over pebbles.

Arn… here. Alive. Another man he thought loved him who had abandoned him. Kaell's ribs contracted hard. That ache snapped him from his inertia. He leapt at the crouched man, knee to his chest, ripped the knife from his hand, and thrust it to his neck.

Arn did not struggle. "I am content, Kaell, if you kill me."

"Content? You don't deserve content." Beneath Kaell's knee, Arn's breaths rose and fell. With one stroke of Kaell's knife, those breaths would stop. The man might gurgle as blood filled his mouth then fall still. His betrayal repaid in full.

He clasped the knife harder. Arn watched him calmly, his eyes empty of condemnation. Kaell choked a sound. So many times those same eyes had fallen on him with warmth or understanding.

All at once, his anger bled out. Kaell tried to snatch it back, but it was gone, leaving only bleak emptiness in its wake. He rolled aside, his back to pine needles. A slow caravan of thunderheads overhead mesmerised him. Nature at least was constant.

Arn rose. Softly, he said, "I wish I could say I freed you to save you pain, Kaell. Or to right the wrongs I've done you. But it's too late."

"But not too late to save Roaran?" Kaell didn't care that he sounded bitter.

For a long moment, Arn's gaze fell into gently soughing trees. "Roaran lost part of himself a long time ago," he said at last. "He can't lose the rest. If he holds you against your will, then he is on a dangerous path. I had to save him from himself."

Kaell let the knife slip from his fingers. "You love him."

No one loved Kaell like that. Not anymore. His lord was dead. He couldn't return to the Varee. He had nothing and no one.

"I don't know what to do." Again, he was a child at Vraymorg. "Arn, what can I do?"

Arn's gaze held unbearable compassion. "I've heard things, Kaell. About you. I understand, but it must stop. Find a way to live without the Varee, without anger, or it will destroy you."

"I can't." Kaell knuckled the ground. "The anger is all I have."

"Roaran took that path too. He's done shameful things. Tried to smother the guilt with duty. It will destroy him in the end, that guilt."

"Roaran this, Roaran that," Kaell muttered. He would not look at Arn. His eyes pricked, his chest so tight, it must burst. "What right does he have to manipulate us?"

"There's a price for destroying Archanin. Roaran is prepared to pay it. He must. It's all he has—duty. He'll come after you because he has to."

"You should have killed me at Thom."

"Yes," Arn said, his voice husky with regret. "I should have killed you. Everything Archanin did, I could have stopped that."

Kaell could not speak. The trees whispered. The night shifted as it lengthened. It was darker, menacing, its moonflower perfume overbearing. Storm clouds banked the moons.

Arn rose as ponderously as an old man. "Find a way to live, Kaell. Without anger. Without guilt. Roaran never has. He holds his self-hatred tight, but it leaks out, and it's ugly."

"For all your fine words about duty, he's not worth your loyalty."

"He's a man who lost his way trying to do the right thing. Archanin must be overcome. Just not like this." Arn began to walk away.

"Please." Kaell rose. "Don't leave me. Not again. I'm always alone."

Arn stopped, turned. "Roaran is my lord. I must return and accept whatever punishment he deems just. You need to find your lord and get to the Icelands. It's the one place Roaran can never go."

"My lord is dead. Why did he have to die? Why did he leave me?"

Arn took a step closer. He lifted his hand as if to touch Kaell then let it drop. Softly, he said, "Who says he's dead, Kaell?"

"What?"

"Who says so? A too-clever Damadar lord with reason to lie, who might hold your lord for some purpose of his own." The second moon broke through clouds. Its flitting beams streaked Arn with shadow and light.

"Is it possible?" Kaell asked almost soundlessly.

"He must be in the Icelands, Kaell. He has to be. Vraymorg is alive."

*Alive.* The blaze of hope nearly overwhelmed him. "I want to believe you. I want him to be alive. Oh gods, let it be true. But if he is—" A knot formed in his throat. "When he learns about the Varee"—*About Philip*—"he'll despise me."

"No. He won't."

"You can't know that."

Arn glanced into the darkness. "When you live a life of deceit, you see into the hearts of men who live the same. Your lord has secrets. Not just who he is but a deep hurt. He's not an easy man. But his mind runs on straight lines, and there's a strange sort of purity there, of action and thought. He'll find a way to forgive you."

"I don't understand. What do you mean *who* he is?"

"You don't know?" Arn frowned. "You don't know about Vraymorg?"

"What?"

Arn looked away. "No. This is not my story to tell."

"Please," Kaell said, ashamed of the childish need in him. "Please. What don't I know?"

The wind scuttled dead leaves into piles at the buttresses of creaking trees. Moonlight edged feathers as black wings glided. A curlew sobbed.

Arn dropped his hand to his sword pommel and rubbed it beneath his palm. "Val," he said quietly. "You and I both heard Ewen call him that. Except Ewen's careful never to add the rest, to call him by his real name. Only Val. Never Val Arques Caelan."

Kaell stumbled a step, not understanding.

"Val Arques Caelan," Arn repeated. His laugh fractured. "I can still hardly believe it. Your lord's true name is Val Arques Caelan. A prince of ancient Avanti. Trained by the Serravan."

"No," Kaell said. "That's impossible."

"It explains why a bladesman with his skill chooses exile in the Mountains. Why he looks like an Isles man. Why whispers spread about Quisnaf warriors hunting him. It even explains why the Damadars might abduct him."

A hard, tight knot of pain stiffened Kaell's shoulders. Incredulous thoughts ground out then jammed together. *My lord a prince of Avanti. Does that mean he's immortal? How?*

Pattering rain fell. It slid down his neck. Kaell didn't care. "He did not even trust me with his name," he muttered when he found his voice. "He kept his name from me, just as he kept everything else." A crazed laugh spilled from him. "It's all been lies. My whole life. Who I am. Where I came from. He knew and never told me. Nor did he tell me who he is. All I get is empty words. Empty promises. Oh gods, I'm so alone."

"But you're not alone, Kate," a mocking voice said.

Five men burst from the trees to ring them.

"You have us," Patrick said. "And we're here to take you back to the warm, loving embrace of the Varee."

# HEATH

Val cowered against the wall, knees to his chest, his stare locked on Heath as he entered. "Don't touch me," he whimpered.

"I won't touch you, Val," Heath said. "I only ever wanted to save you. I told you if it got too much, to say the word, and I'd come."

"I have to find the knife." The man on the floor groped about in a panic. "Alecc left a knife."

"By all that's good, what did she do?" Heath touched his cheek. "Where are you?"

"Don't." Val fended him off. "Don't."

"It's me. It's Heath. I said I'd save you. Why didn't you let me? Why did you play with Myranthe? She's clever, Val. Too clever."

"He's coming." Val's voice rose in terror. "I hear him at the door. Hide. We must hide."

Hide. If only they could. If only Myranthe had delayed a moment longer with Velleran. But her shadow fell on the floor.

"Heath," Myranthe said. "Leave."

"No." He moved between her and Val.

Alabaster moonlight flooded through half-open shutters. Sinuous lamplight etched cascading dark hair, leaving her face in darkness. "Get out of my way."

"No."

She was very still, very composed. Her arm rose. An unseen power tugged at his body then flung him back. He braced as he hit the metal bedframe. Pain shot through his hip, his breath gone. She had never used magic on him before. But their purposes had never diverged. Until now.

"Stop this," he wheezed. "Please. Just leave him be."

She looked at him, her top lip curled back. "Do not get in my way, Heath. I'm warning you now. Enough. Forget him. Very soon, Velleran's buyers will collect this man. Do not waste your time or mine over him."

As if dismissing him, she lit a torch, pulled it from a sconce, and turned to face Val.

He watched her from a corner like a wounded beast. She dangled irons in her fingertips. "Remove your clothes." The Mazart's words. "Then shackle your hand."

"Myranthe," Heath panted. "Don't."

Ignoring him, she chanted. Though not aimed at him, the incantation iced his skin, writhed and rolled within. He realised it didn't matter that Val didn't do as she commanded; her words were intended only to salt his wounds and complete her spell.

Eyes wide and blank, lips parted in horror, Val did not move. Mesmerised, he stared at Myranthe. He cried out. Just once. Then he slumped.

Myranthe crouched to whisper in his ear. Heath caught only stray words.

"You fell. Head wound. I tended to you. You must stay here. So I can help you." Myranthe rose. She cast Val one last, lingering look.

"Our shadow tournament is done," she said softly, stepped over her brother, and left.

DIZZY WITH ANGER, Heath went after her. He seized her arms. "What did you do? Myranthe, what did you do?"

"What I had to." She shrugged. "He's to blame, anyhow. He let this fester. I even warned him. Told him our secrets give others power. If years ago, he had faced what happened to him, it would have rendered my spell useless. Leave it be, Heath. There's nothing you can do." She pulled free and swept down the stairs.

"How can you just walk away?" Heath called after her. "Have you no pity?"

Myranthe paused. Slowly, she turned back. "There is no place in this game for softer feelings, brother. You know this. You've always known this. You know what I must do."

"Oh, I know, Myranthe. And I'm beginning to think I don't like it."

Flickering torchlight caught red strands in her hair. "I don't care what you like. All that matters is Roaran. He's coming. Fate set his path."

"Another man for you to destroy."

"Roaran will not be destroyed. Only controlled." She shivered with pleasure. "How I long to trace his Isles cheekbones, to stare into those eyes the chronicles record as dark blue. To show him how powerless he is."

Anger heated his neck. "Obsession. Isn't that the word you used, Myranthe?"

She shrugged, indifferent as always to criticism. "And what if it is? Yes, I've desired this one man, or the thought of this man, since I was a child. Only him. Your hands are unsteady again, Heath. Do you still insist there's nothing wrong with you?"

"There's nothing wrong." He dropped his fists at his side. "Tell me what you did to Val."

"Why should I? I don't care about Val Arques. This isn't about him. Not any longer."

"But I do care. So tell me what you did."

"You need to forget about him, Heath. You need to remember

your duty, your place in this family. You're an enforcer. Nothing more."

"What if I want to be something more?"

Myranthe studied him. "I used to admire your self-awareness, the way you assessed your every motive. When did you become afraid to look within? At why he fascinates you?"

"I'm not afraid."

"Then let me tell you."

He braced. "Go on then, Myranthe. Tell me. Strip me the way you stripped him."

"Very well." She was watching him intently, even slyly. "You're lonely."

"I have friends," Heath said. "Dillon."

She scoffed. "He's afraid of you. Even Griffin is afraid of you. Unlike nearly everyone you meet, Val Arques isn't. That attracts you. Maybe you've wondered at this attraction, wondered if you should seduce him. But that's not it."

"No. It's not—that."

"It might be less pitiful if it were. But it's simple. You just want him to be your friend. A brother, even. Velleran has never been that. He's too self-absorbed. Griffin doesn't understand you. But Val Arques? Could he? He's a bladesman, after all. You think he might come to really know you. To love you."

"You know what's pitiful, Myranthe? Your attempt to get into my head. 'Shall I tell you?' you said. And here I am, waiting to hear this great insight into my character that wounds me to the core. Instead, all I get is that I'm lonely. Why can't Val and I be friends?"

"It's an illusion, Heath. You haven't looked hard enough at him. His mind forms different angles to yours. He could never be deliberately cruel or manipulative. His anger is pure, shall I say. That means he won't forget what you've done to him. Nor forgive."

"This is nonsense. You think you see into me? You don't."

"He shows you how insignificant you are," Myranthe said abruptly.

Heath's breath died. Pools of light and inky darkness disfigured the walls. The wind carried the chalky scent of old stone up the tower well. He turned his back on her and pressed his palm against grainy, rough stone. He pressed until a drop of blood stained the centuries-old layers of grime.

"I know what you yearn for," Myranthe said. "To feel fear. To find an opponent who tests you in the fire hall. He's a Serravan-trained bladesman who might, just might, be better than you. But then, what else would a killer aspire to? Only to find a man worthy to kill."

"I don't think you should say any more."

"How pathetic. To want him to love you, call you friend when you know you're not the sort of man he ever could care about. But even this isn't why you want to kill him."

She paused, waiting until the silence forced him to face her. "You want to punish him for his disregard. But most of all, you want to kill him because he makes you feel small. And you can't stand that, can you, Heath?"

"You're belittling me to put me in my place," he said. "I've never defied you before, and you don't like it."

"Because next to him"—Myranthe went on as if he had not spoken—"next to this man who helped win kingdoms, thrones, trained warriors to defeat monsters, what are you? Nothing."

"I know who I am," Heath said.

"Something less than him. That's what you think, deep down. He's the one with Caelan blood. He's handsome, a better bladesman than you. A man descended from kings. He withstood months chained to the breaking stone when you know you'd crumple in a day."

"You're cruel when you want to be," Heath said.

She laughed aloud. "I'm truthful. It's only others who fear staring down the truth."

"You taint everything. Strip it down to sound foolish. It's more complicated. You know it, but you want to wound me."

"You should be pleased to see him like this. Lost. Broken. Frightened. Because maybe broken this man could love you, brother."

A stale taste silted Heath's mouth. He couldn't shift the image of Val huddled on the floor. "You made love to this man, and still, you destroyed him."

"Oh, poor Heath." She mocked him with pouted lips. "It's a game. I thought you understood that. I just played out the final moves."

"I don't believe you. You feel something towards him. I know you do."

"Do I?" Briefly, she looked down into the tower's dark well. "Perhaps many years from now, I might sit in my room, my hair grey, listening to winter winds shriek, and think of Val Arques. I might remember how soft his mouth was, how dark his eyes. How I've never seen a man so handsome since. But it will be an idle musing. Only one man enthrals me. Or"—she smiled to herself—"the thought of one man."

"It's too late, Myranthe. I'm not going to fall back in line because you throw hateful words at me."

"I really don't care. But if you're that disturbed by what I did, go and wave your sword around in a fire hall for a bit. After all… you're only good at that brutish sort of thing."

Myranthe picked up her gown and swirled down the stairs, leaving him staring after her. Her footsteps faded. Without their *tap, tap, tap*, the tower's hush unnerved him.

Heath sank onto the steps. Myranthe's vitriol, he understood. She'd warned him not to challenge her. Now she sought to bring him back under her control by demeaning him. Yet… why then did her words disturb him? He never consciously wondered if he hated what he had become. What he, as a second son, was always destined to become.

Maybe he should just get up, dust off his clothes, and walk away. After all, Myranthe served their gods, and he believed in her purpose. Didn't he?

No sound came from the room above. Puzzled, Heath rose and returned to the tower cell, wary of what he would find. But no one cowered in a corner. No one curled on the bed, weeping. Instead, Val gripped the bars at the window, the shutters thrown back despite that knifing chill of early winter. Myranthe's cloak carelessly draped his broad shoulders.

He turned. "Who are you?"

Still shaken by Myranthe's assault, Heath fell back into old patterns. "Your tormenter, sweet boy. Is the light that bad?"

Val just stared. "I don't remember you." He ripped fingers though his tousled hair. Groaned. "I don't remember anything."

Astonished, Heath stiffened. He thought back. Before Myranthe bent to whisper to Val, she had cast a second spell. What if that spell had wiped Val's memory?

"Do you know who you are?"

Val wet his lips. He looked frightened. "I—I don't know."

"Your name is Val Arques."

"Val," the other man repeated blankly. "There's a faint chord, but I don't know why." He banged the heel of his palm into his brow. Then again. "Why don't I know? I have to know."

"What about where you are?"

"The Icelands. A woman told me I got hurt and she tended to me."

"Tended? Is that what she called it?" Heath grabbed Val's arm, angry. Only partly at Myranthe. She'd behaved as she always did. Dutiful to the last. No, he was mad at Val.

"You fool, I warned you. Gods help us, you're handsome, Val, but your mind isn't twisted enough to take on Myranthe. How did she do this? How did she break you down to this?"

"Break?" He edged up a finely shaped brow. "I don't understand. She said I hit my head."

"And you just believed her?" Heath grabbed Val's arm. He wanted to shake him, slap him, snap his wits back. But he had no magic, no way of overturning what Myranthe had done.

Once, he might have turned to Judith, to drink wine as the fire burned low and talk through the problem. She was always there, the one person who took his part.

He looked at his hands clasping Val's forearm. A memory stirred of Velleran's fingers bruising his arm as he hauled him into a dark, cold room and bid the guards leave a twelve-year-old Heath there until dawn, without light, water, or even a blanket. He remembered the awful sounds of the key turning, of Velleran's steps retreating. In the quiet, in utter blackness, his own breaths filled his skull as he drowned in silence.

Then she came. Judith, on tiptoes, trembling as she unlocked the door with the stolen key, knowing she, too, faced punishment if caught bringing him a waterskin, a candle from her room, and the blanket from her own bed. Heath had hugged the blanket that long night. It smelled of her. He could almost imagine she was there, her arms around him, holding him until dawn.

A decade and a half later, no one was coming with a blanket. No one to help him. Just him. A pit opened in his gut.

Heath dropped Val's arm. He took a step back, resisting the selfish desire to take advantage of Val's vulnerability, to once more throw him into that cavern with the breaking stone. Safe from Myranthe but kept for him so Heath could visit whenever he chose and enjoy those barbed words between them.

Heath pressed his palms over his belly. An even darker longing stirred. *What did Myranthe say? This broken man could even love you.*

If he left Val with no memory of his past—of their past—he could tell Val whatever he wanted. That they were friends. Close. Yes, like brothers. He could lie. Deceive this man. He could have all he wanted.

Wind gusted hair about his face. Shame tasted bitter in his mouth. He closed the shutters, surprised only the second moon wedged clouds. Just after midnight, then. The night, which had started with Myranthe drawing a vicious story from Val, felt impossibly long.

"We've going visiting," Heath said.

"She said not to leave."

Hands to his hips, Heath laughed in disbelief. "Now you choose to do as you're told?"

"She told me not to leave."

"I like you better when you're irritably disobedient." He slogged Val in the jaw. The blow knocked the man onto the bed. Heath tore strips from the bottom of his cloak and bound Val's hands at his back. Dazed, he struggled weakly.

Heath waved his knife. "Be a good boy, or I gut you."

A bluff. But no-memory man didn't know that. It would have been safer to knock his captive out, but even he couldn't sling a heavily muscled warrior over his shoulder. No, the obedient-to-Myranthe one had to walk. Quietly.

"I guess this version of you will shout out for help too." He stuffed cloth in Val's mouth then tied a gag. At Val's indignant sounds, Heath patted his head. "Settle down."

Val grunted angrily through the gag.

Oddly content, Heath hummed. This was more like it. Violence, threats, abduction. Plots to outwit Myranthe. He yanked Val up. "Let's go visit the mad mother."

The rectangular passage skirted an inner courtyard. Beyond arched windows, brown leaves piled along walls. Skeleton trees, cutouts against the night, swayed. Clouds sped above, rimmed with pearly moonlight. Through gaps in stone, a moist wind, viciously cold, whipped Heath's skin. Hunched in his cloak, he pushed Val to the tower door.

A guard spun then let his lance tip wilt. "Oh, it's you, my lord."

Heath kept a firm grip on Val's shoulder. "I want to see her."

"I can't let you through, my lord. The lady Myranthe says—"

"Myranthe says, Myranthe says. Myranthe can go shout orders

down a well for all I care. I need to see *her*."

"But my lord—"

Heath grabbed the man's padded surcoat. "Know what happened to the last fool who argued with me? Here's a clue. Something to do with fire."

The guard trembled. When Heath dropped him, he dipped his head. "This way, my lord."

"No silliness, oh disobedient one." Heath shoved Val after the guard, their steps a hollow din within stone encasing stairs so steep, a thick rope on steel brackets corded along the wall.

When Val stumbled, the guard stared openly. "Is she to punish him? He looks dangerous."

The gag hiding Val's lips accented those Isles cheekbones, the intense dark hue of his eyes now slitted in anger.

"This one? He's a kitten."

They reached a bolted door with warding sigils carved in its wood. The guard unlocked it.

Heath's heart crashed into an uneven rhythm. A fire hall held few fears for him. *This room, though*— "I'll call out when we're ready to leave."

The relieved man scuttled off.

Heath prodded Val inside with the knife, grinning at the muffled curse. "Haven't forgotten vulgar insults, then? Though even Griffin can be cruder than that."

After the stairwell's chill, the room's sleepy warmth struck like a furnace. Worn tapestries blotted white walls. Tattered rugs, their burgundy and pale-blue threads faded, covered the slabbed floor between a fur-covered couch and plain, iron-framed bed.

A red-ember fire and a single lamp upon a wooden chest scarcely troubled the gloom. Though comfortable, the chamber succumbed to neglect. A close look, surely, would uncover cobwebs in the corners and grime in the cracks.

Heath shut the door. A woman contemplating what lay beyond the window turned.

*Contemplating. Ha.* That was generous. His mother plotted. She always plotted, usually a cruel death for her enemies. She had a long list. He hoped he wasn't on it tonight at least.

"Is he dead?" The woman was frail and stooped, but her eyes were compellingly alive. They were very dark and very hard, like a neglected sword hilt. Her shock of uncut white hair always reminded Heath of a bird's nest. He could imagine flames taking hold in it, how it might sizzle.

"No, Mother, Velleran is not dead."

"I told you not to return until you killed him, Heath. He won't steal your place as lord."

"I've no intention of killing Velleran. Not tonight, anyway."

"You are a useless son. I only seek your advancement."

He took her hands, her skin as dry and brittle as aged paper. "Yes, yes, I am a useless son who needs your help, Mother. Meddling Myranthe cast a spell—"

The old woman scoffed. "Her magic is crude. It isn't right it should be her who puts that collar of ice about the seer's neck." Her gaze fell on Val. She rose to circle him.

Val turned with her, warily.

"The handsome man I see from my window." She looked gleefully to Heath. "A gift?"

Gods help Val if he were. "Meddling Myranthe hurt him. He can't remember who he is."

The old woman groped Val's arm. He twisted away.

"How Myranthe smooths her hair when she visits him," she said. "How she smiles. She wants to touch him. Don't you want to touch him, Heath?"

*Indeed. With a fist, usually.* "I want to undo Myranthe's spell."

"Oh no. We can't do that."

"Why not?"

Again, she circled behind Val. When she trailed fingers over his back, his shoulders shot up, his eyes sharp with disgust.

"Why not?" Heath said again.

"Because he's coming, you see," his mother said. "The seer. So precious."

"Yes, yes. Roaran Caelan. Collars of ice. But what did Myranthe do to this man?"

A curiously childish smile flitted across her face. "She will take him. Roaran. After so many centuries, Myranthe will imprison our wilful death rider, and he shall obey the gods."

Heath tapped fingers against his hip. "Mother—"

"Why haven't you killed Velleran?" She turned on him. "You're the cleverest of my children. Myranthe's cunning, but you, Heath, should be lord. Not that viper. *Her* son."

"Mother—"

"I'll mix you a potion. You can poison him. No one will know. You'll be as great a Damadar lord as the Ice Rider. With my magic, no one will stand against you."

"My ambitions don't run in that direction. Now about this spell—"

"You're not a weak man, Heath. Not like your father. So pathetic. So afraid to anger the gods. After all I did, he didn't kill me. No, not Rolland. Instead, he threw me in here."

"Well, Mother, you were a bit mischievous," Heath said.

"Rolland the Ridiculous. That's what I call him. How I laughed and laughed. Such a stupid man. He refused to put aside that brat Velleran for you. So I waited. I schemed—"

Heath sighed. He heard the same story every time he came to her tower.

"I took a knife to his rooms. As he slept, I stabbed. But he moved. My blade struck his arm. His guards arrested me. Such nonsense. Rolland the Ridiculous threw me in here."

"Yes, yes, Mother. The Lord of the Ice and too cowardly to kill you. Now can we talk about Myranthe's spell—"

She sniffed in contempt. "Dangerous magic for a clumsy enchantress like Myranthe. That's why she practised on the handsome man with Caelan blood. So she doesn't kill Roaran."

His captive seemed too quiet. Not distracted but concentrating. An up-to-no-good look. Heath spun him. Val had nearly worked the ropes off.

"That's very naughty," Heath said. "Even with no memory for wickedness, you are a thorn in my side, Val. I'm only trying to help you."

The prisoner swore again through the gag.

Heath pushed him into a chair. "Let's settle you down so the grown-ups can talk." He passed his mother his knife. "Hold that to the handsome one's jugular. But don't kill him unless he's very, very wicked."

She poked the tip at Val's throat. "Can I touch him? I want to touch him."

"Do what you want." He tied Val's hands to the chair arms. At his captive's glare, he patted his cheek. "You, thorn in my side, behave. Mother, fix the thorn."

The old woman sifted Val's hair as she might rice. "Pretty. Pretty. I smell Isles blood."

"Yes, he's a pretty Isles thorn. But the spell. Can you reverse it?"

She pouted. "I can undo anything Myranthe does. But I don't want to."

Heath sighed. *It couldn't be easy, could it? A simple, "Of course, Heath. Let me help."* "Mother, play nice. What did meddling Myranthe do?"

"It's nothing to do with you, Heath. Why are you bothering with this nonsense? You have to act before it's too late. *Her* son can't be lord of the Icelands. You must find Velleran and kill him."

"Perhaps later," he said. "When I'm drunker and feeling meaner. For now, indulge me, Mother, and tell me what Myranthe did. You can touch the pretty man again as you tell me."

"Can I?" She fondled Val's breast. "Poor thing. No emotional past."

"What does that mean?"

"It means he'll remember a city, but not whether he likes it. He'll know how to use a sword, but not whether he likes to kill. People, though. He'll never remember them because there's always emotion with people."

Heath frowned. "Why should Myranthe wish to do this to Roaran?"

"A death rider with free will? That will never do. Love. Friendship. Loyalty. He doesn't need such frivolous things. He must be an empty vessel, ready to be filled. Ghani-Jai shall fill him. I am bored now. Go away."

"How do I fix what meddling Myranthe did? Tell me," he said.

"Then you'll leave?"

"Yes."

His mother chewed her lip. "So tiresome. All so, so tiresome. I told Myranthe to seek out a deep pain. A lover's death, perhaps. A child's. A time when he failed. Best of all, a secret shame. Yes, that most of all. She must force him to lay it bare."

Heath fidgeted with his sword. "How can she be certain Roaran has a secret shame?"

"The brother-keepers kept close watch on Roaran over the centuries. Everywhere he went, his every deed since he escaped us, is recorded. Oh, such things he's done." She rubbed her hands in delight. "Wicked things."

"How do I fix Val?"

"Why do you bother me with this?" She flapped a hand. "Just repeat what Myranthe did. Jar that memory, the one he hides from. That will release the rest. Just so long as the spell has not held him for a time. Your hand is shaking. Are you ill?"

Heath trapped his arm at his side. "Not at all. I'm in ravishingly good health."

He glanced at Val. The man was listening keenly, a mix of emotions blazing across his face. Puzzlement. Agitation.

"So to save him, I must make him remember what he wants to forget. I must be cruel."

Months ago, he would have shrugged that off. He wouldn't have cared who he hurt. But something had changed. He was not ready to admit it might be him.

# KAELL

They moved in fast. Tullan shoved Arn down, steel at his neck. Rob and a barrel-chested man called Derry circled Kaell. Derry's brother, Colla, held back, his watchful gaze upon the forest.

Patrick clasped a hand dramatically to his breast. "I'm so alone. Alone." His smile did not match his hard face. "Dear Kate, you had us. Until you ran off. Where have you been?"

"Here and there."

"Time to come home, Kate. The mage wants you."

"Why?" Kaell fisted the knife, uneasy. The rain stopped abruptly. A slit of moonlight breached racing clouds. "Where's Dannon?"

"Dannon's dead."

He staggered. For a moment, he could not take it in. Then a bewildering grief and loss took him over, the world narrowing in. "No," he said. "No."

"Aw, are you sad, Kate? Your lover dead. Actually, I exaggerate. Dannon's not dead yet, but he doesn't have long. Get the horses, Colla. If we hurry, we'll get back in time to watch him die. Maybe Kate can say a fond farewell."

Tullan cackled as he prodded Arn with his sword. The man on

his knees watched his tormentor in a careful way Kaell recognised. Ready to pounce.

He slid Arn a look. The man gave an almost imperceptible nod. "I'm not going back with you. I'm done with the Varee."

"We're not done with you, Kate," Patrick said. "The mage wants you, so that's what he gets. Now drop to your knees, girl. Put your hands behind your back so we can put a bit of rope about those pretty wrists."

Kaell's heart kicked up a notch, his body tensing at the idea of bonds. Despite his ghoul strength, his female body left him vulnerable in unsettling ways.

"Knees, Kate." Patrick sounded impatient. "Be a good girl."

"But I'm not a good girl, Patrick. You know more about being a good girl than me."

Rob laughed. "Ha, she's got you there."

Patrick struck him across the face. Rob went down.

Arn dived at Tullan. The man sprawled with a grunt. His sword spun away. Kaell pounced on it and rose, the blade extended. Arn locked an arm about Tullan's windpipe.

Cursing, Patrick ran at Kaell with a swinging blade. Kaell took the wild stroke with the thick of the sword, locking steel tightly. He smashed his elbow up into the man's chin. Patrick cried out in pain, staggered, then fell. "You'll pay for that."

From nowhere, an image flashed in Kaell's mind. For a sliver of a second, he was lost to it, caught in a vision where he was moving along a charred plank as liquid fire raged in a pit of ash beneath him. A man came at him, his blade raised. Kaell cut him down.

*Gods.* He shook his head to clear it. Not his memory. Roaran's blood still infected him.

Patrick had regained his feet. He lifted his sword. Without thinking, Kaell drove steel through his breast. A cold kill. As cold as the way Roaran had struck down a man in that fire hall. He expected guilt, a voice of conscience about how a bonded warrior only killed ghouls. But there was nothing.

Derry lunged. Kaell edged back. Slashed. Blood splashed as he ripped the man from shoulder to hip. Two men dead. Men, not ghouls. Still, no guilt.

He whipped about as Colla ran in, yelling with vengeful anger and thrusting. Kaell caught the blade, again high on his sword, and forced Colla's weapon down.

Another memory rushed him, a clear picture of performing exactly that action in combat. Only Kaell was on a guard walk, and the man wasn't Colla.

Colla wrenched his weapon free. With no room to manoeuvre a long blade, Kaell bent his sword arm behind his head, creating distance to stab. Steel sliced Colla's arm. He reeled. Kaell punched him. He fell hard and didn't move.

As Kaell turned, looking for Tullan, the vision clung to him: a castle's wall walk. Two men slashing at him with iron. With a quick thrust, he impaled one. The other fled. Kaell let him go. A dark strength was surging through him, a fierce power.

*Curse Roaran. Curse him.* Again, he forced the memories aside.

Tullan was tussling Arn for the knife. Moonlight glinted on its cool metal, but in the tangle of straining bodies, Kaell couldn't tell who held it. Then Arn stiffened. For one awful moment, the two men clung to each other, motionless—until Tullan staggered back, the blade gripped in his bloody fingers.

Kaell looked at his surprised expression.

Then he looked at Arn. Looked as Arn collapsed in a pile, his limbs like a rag doll's, his mouth slack. Slowly, his lifeless body sank to the ground. His back pressed into dewy grass, his face turned towards the starlit sky.

Shock blanked Kaell's mind. His lips formed words that snagged in his throat. A single one escaped with his breath. "No."

Tullan fled into the trees. Kaell's horror exploded to rage. Sword drawn, he plunged after the man. But as he ran, another vision roared up, taking over his mind. In that instant, he had become Roaran, running through the trees, intent on vengeance.

To his ghoul hearing, Tullan's rasped breaths shouted. His rushed steps as he crashed through undergrowth were like a beacon.

Kaell moved swiftly, relentlessly, his mind as cold as Roaran's. Anger enflamed his muscles. He let it smoulder and build, anticipating its violent, bloody release with a sick elation. This man had killed his friend. He could not escape.

Tight-packed trunks cast long, purple-hued shadows. The wind prodded scratching branches. The forest was alive with mewling, creaks, and chirring sounds. Nothing so loud, though, as Tullan's heart.

Kaell slashed at bushes. Yelping, the man shot up. He tried to flee, but Kaell struck him down with one swipe. A crimson ribbon burst upon his back. His body jerked even before he screamed.

Kaell grabbed him. Tullan's eyes bulged. He whimpered. Mercilessly, Kaell pushed his head back. Blinding hatred ignited a frenzied hunger. He thrust his teeth into the tendons in Tullan's throat. Pumping blood shot over his hands, into his mouth.

It tasted good, so good. Warm. Ferrous. Velvet on his tongue. At each gulp, power surged through his body. Tullan quivered then died. Kaell dropped him.

A dizzying euphoria took him over. Then a heady strength. Just like the strength that flowed through Roaran when he killed. That last vision still gripped him, almost as if Roaran had become his shadow, urging Kaell on.

Unease niggled in his mind. Two men dead. No guilt. That wasn't him. That wasn't who a bonded warrior was. Gods help him, what had Roaran done to him?

Kaell stalked back to the clearing, ripping branches aside as though they sought to cage him. Rob was gone. Colla crawled on his hands and knees.

Kaell's conscience pricked him. His lord was alive. How could he face Vraymorg and tell him he'd killed like this? As indifferently, as relentlessly as Roaran.

Once, he might have taken heart from hearing his lord lived. But too much had happened. He was no longer the boy who laughingly chased "pluckers" about the ward at Vraymorg, made up poems about the cook, and dreamt of kissing a girl he'd never met in a ruined castle.

But he was not Roaran, either. Kaell swung a fist to knock Colla out.

Arn huddled, his stare empty. Grass stuck to the toe of one boot. The earth around him was black and moist.

Kaell knelt in that blood. He pushed his friend's shoulder. "Arn, wake up now. This isn't funny." He sat back on his heels. His mind rebelled against the truth. Arn couldn't be dead. Not when he'd just found him again.

Gently, afraid to hurt him, he lifted Arn's head onto his lap. His throat lumped. With trembling fingers, he closed the man's glassy eyes. The lump hardened. Misery prodded him like a blade's edge, a spreading wound that surely must tear his heart within.

"No," Kaell muttered. "He left me to be tortured. I will not shed tears over him." Beneath the turmoil in his breast, he searched for the anger. It must be there. It was his shield, his sword too. He needed his anger.

Yet when he looked at Arn's face, he could not see the man who had betrayed him, only the friend who laughed with him, comforted, and encouraged him.

Memories came fast and hard. Arn's grin as he pulled Kaell up when swordplay put him in the dirt. Arn by his bed, telling a wounded Kaell a story of some fool knight's quest to find a golden frog or peacock so he could kiss a fair maiden. Arn laughing with Olier. Arn's huge hands on his shoulders.

He broke inside. Kaell beat his fists on the ground. His bitter tears splashed into rivulets of blood.

# DANNON

They bound his hands, shoved a hood over his head, and forced him to his knees in a chamber of broken stone.

"Kneel to your new lord," a man commanded. "Kneel to Roaran Caelan."

*Roaran Caelan.* Terror blistered up Dannon's backbone. Not that crawling unease that turned his gut into a battle, but a consuming fear. He wanted to flee, to sob, except he could not breathe.

Footsteps came towards him, unhurried. They stopped. The silence ran into his heartbeats. Dannon knew someone stood close, that everything he believed was about to change... that he wasn't ready.

Desperately, he twisted the ropes. *A dead king here? No, no, no. Impossible. Oh gods, take back time.* To yesterday, even, when he belonged with the Varee. When all he needed to do was fight and die.

"Who are you?" he whispered through sackcloth.

"I am who they say, Dannon." The compelling voice held an Isles intonation. A beautiful voice. A sorcerer's voice. The clear silver tolling of the darkness.

"You're—you're really him. What do you want with me?"

"I've been waiting for you, Dannon. You're the warrior I glimpse at my side at the very end."

Such strange words. Terrifying words. He didn't want to hear them.

"If I release you, will you run?"

Dannon had nowhere to go. His place in the world had become a cliff edge crumbling away. "I won't run."

Roaran untied his wrists. At the touch of his hands, Dannon trembled.

"Calm yourself." The man tore off the hood.

Dannon blinked into torchlight, afraid to look upon the figure crouched beside him. Reluctantly, he lifted his eyes to meet the brilliance of the raven-haired stranger he had glimpsed outside. In the lamplight, Roaran's irises might have been black or purple. Dannon, fancifully, could think only of the vast emptiness of a sea beneath a storm.

"What did you do to me? I don't understand."

"Do you know what I am? I don't mean who I am, but *what* I am."

"I don't know anything," Dannon cried, bewildered. "You put your lips to mine, and my body healed. My strength returned."

"The dreams called to you." Roaran began to pace. "You're meant to be at my side. But you, not another from the past, like the others."

The grim-faced men with iron helms. Dannon had longed to understand what the dreams meant. He'd yearned to believe in something that had meaning. Now he didn't know what to think.

In awe, Dannon watched Roaran stride back and forth. The seer king. Not dead. *Not. Dead.* Roaran's steady steps marked Dannon's past as it slipped away. One life lost to him. Another before him, dazzling but frighteningly unknown.

Yet for all his fear, his shock, something uncomfortable was rising up in him from a great depth. A desire to let go. To believe. To just accept.

"What am I meant to do?"

"Lead." Roaran stopped and faced him. "It's a hard road for you. Harder than it is even for Val, for Cadan, or any of them. You'll know love, Dannon. But also despair. There will be hopelessness and agony when you will think upon death as a saviour. But in the end, in a city of caves far away, you'll find peace." He laughed, an embrace. "You'll even find something to believe in. Beyond me."

"Tell me what to do," Dannon said. "Tell me who I'm meant to be."

Roaran's slow pull of breath, his slow exhalation filled the quiet. "Soon. But once I do," he said, "there's no turning back."

"I know," Dannon said.

⟡

No one forced him into his new prison. A man called Nicky took his boots and, with a flamboyant gesture, invited Dannon to enter a room before locking him in.

They didn't trust him or know what to do with him. What could they do with a man who no longer understood where he belonged or even what he should be?

Dannon wandered about, his thoughts in turmoil. Beneath his bare feet, uneven boards creaked. From the high, unreachable windows, he guessed the room might once have been a child's bedchamber.

It held only a mattress on the floor, a pail, a stool, tallow candles and flint, and a jug of water. Part of the corner roof had collapsed. In a rambling vine, a red-crested, black-winged bird nested. A wooden beam splintered with rot slanted against broken stone. Even without shoes, he could climb through the hole to escape. *But then what?*

Abruptly, Dannon stilled. He passed his hand over his eyes. With a complicated sense of loss, even of sorrow, he knew his life with the Varee was done. He could not turn back.

Since his father's violent, bloody death, that life had been all he knew. But now he did not know where to go, where he belonged. Whether he should flee or take the leap into the unknown with these strangers, with this dead king who had breathed strength into him with just a kiss.

He touched his lips. That kiss. Not erotic. Powerful. Unsettling. It had ignited a need in him he didn't understand.

*Roaran Caelan.* He mouthed the name. *Roaran Caelan.*

A thrill of wonder tore away his unease. The dreams had led to the seer king. Dannon had always wanted something or someone to believe in. Perhaps it was Roaran.

A jangle and squeak of harnesses came through the window, followed by running steps. In the Varee camp, he might expect a rider to burst into his hut with an urgent message. But in the seer king's domain, it was not his concern.

Dannon dropped onto the mattress and stretched out on his back, his arm cushioning his head. Urgent voices swept up the stairwell from the hall. A key rattled. He sat up. At the sight of Juliette, he self-consciously smoothed his hair.

She set a tray down on the stool. "Roaran says you haven't had anything since you got here."

"I… yes," he managed. "Thank you."

Juliette passed him a bowl then poured wine. "To settle your nerves."

"I'm not nervous," Dannon said.

She flashed a disbelieving smile.

"All right. I'm a bit uncertain."

She sat beside him on the mattress. The scent of sunlight and soap in her hair roused pleasurable memories. "It must seem strange. I know."

Dannon sipped wine. "It's… unsettling. I have questions. Lots of questions."

"Roaran will answer them."

"Roaran," he echoed. "That's my first question. How is it possible he's Roaran Caelan? A king thought dead for centuries."

"You've seen him, spoken with him. How can you doubt it?"

Dannon dragged his fingers through bristled hair at the nape of his neck. "I am full of doubts. I don't know who I am anymore. Where I belong."

"You belong here." Juliette squeezed his hand. "Roaran has been waiting for you."

"But why? I'm no one, Juliette. Not a prince. Not a lord. Not wellborn. Just—" He must not speak of his mother. "Just a silver-sword's son who became an outlaw. A killer."

"Why do you do that?" She frowned. "You always do that. Find a word that diminishes who you really are. Not just an outlaw. Not just a killer, Dannon. A seeker."

"A seeker," he tested out the word. "That sounds terribly noble, Juliette. A searcher, perhaps. I searched for so long for something more, just more, without knowing what it was. But I'm afraid to let go of who I am. Varee. Part of them—yet not. I suppose none of that makes sense." He smiled. "The only thing now clear is you."

Juliette lifted a brow. "Oh?"

Dannon touched her arm. "I only mean I understand what changed between us."

"Dannon—"

"Don't worry. This isn't a reproach. I guessed you had a new lover and wished you well. Now I've met him—" Roaran Caelan. A Serravan captain. A young king who married for love. A king murdered for love, in his prime, plunging Telor into war. That was history's account.

But even a few minutes in Roaran's presence revealed a man more complicated than the legend. He clearly drew others to him. However, Dannon sensed a darkness, a frightening resolve beneath his compelling beauty and charm.

Juliette's eyes hazed. "He's everything the poets say, Dannon. Fearless. Powerful. Charismatic." She shook herself. "Sorry."

"No. I understand."

The door swung in. Roaran stood on the threshold. He looked weary.

Juliette rose. She gathered up the tray and carafe and swept past him. Roaran closed the door at his back. He took the stool, his long legs stretched, ankles crossed.

Dannon waited, tension in his spine, still in awe of this man.

Roaran fixed his strange blue gaze on Dannon's face. "Things are moving quickly. Too quickly. First, Archanin uses my spell to try to destroy the brotherhood. Now Kaell is gone."

*Kaell...* A note of recognition rang in Dannon's mind. *Kaell. The last bonded warrior at Vraymorg. Executed outside the walls of Tide's End. Or—not?*

"I need to tell you all of it. It will be a lot to accept, but you must." For all his urgency, Roaran fell quiet. A candle flame slapped air. In rustling branches, an owl hooted. He sighed. "You need to hear it. Then decide if you can accept what I want of you."

"Nothing to say?" Roaran pressed his hands into his thighs, his shoulders sagging with exhaustion.

Dannon's mind whirled in disarray. He didn't know how to start making sense of Roaran's explanations.

"Only the next time I see *Kaell*, I'm going to knock him down hard." Embarrassment heated his neck as he remembered his arousal that night they sat on a hillside.

Kaell had deceived him. Hadn't he? Dannon puzzled over their conversations. No, that wasn't fair. In everything else, Kaell had been honest. It was only in that one thing. And he could not blame a bonded warrior for hiding who he was from a slaver and a killer.

Fast-moving steps echoed in the stairwell. Nicky burst into the room. "Sloana's back. She followed Arn's trail to the forest. There's news. Not good news. Come quickly."

With a weary sigh, Roaran rose. "This night is interminable." He started for the door.

Dannon did not move.

Roaran beckoned. "You're not a prisoner, Dannon. I need you to know everything now."

"Why? For all you just told me, I sense there's something you're not saying."

Roaran paused at the room's threshold. His knuckles whitened on the door handle. "Yes, you're right. I need you to know it all because my visions have changed. There are shadows in the Enarae that weren't there before, as if I've set in motion something I can't control. A choice I'm yet to make that throws me off the old path."

"I still don't understand—"

"I'm no longer sure what's going to happen to me, Dannon," Roaran said, his tone bleak. "If something does, then I need you to lead the brotherhood."

"I'm not ready."

"No one ever is," Roaran said.


IN THE RUINED HALL BELOW, a woman menaced a bound prisoner with a sword. "Brought you a gift, seer."

At the sight of Roaran, Colla's eyes bulged. "You're dead."

"We know that, fool." Nicky pummelled his belly.

The captive collapsed in half. The young woman yanked him straight. "You want to bow to our lord, you do it gracefully."

"Ha." Nicky raised his eyebrows appreciatively. "That's funny, Sloana."

Colla fought for air, his startled look swinging to Dannon. "It's true then." He spat at the ground. "You were a traitor all along. Cahirean dog."

Dannon fidgeted. To see a man he'd fought beside as a prisoner challenged his loyalties. He closed out pity. The Varee had intended to bleed him to death.

Roaran tapped his belt. "What happened?"

Sloana shoved Colla's head down hard. "Found this one knocked out. The rest of his scum companions are dead. Some sort of fight."

"Arn?"

She hesitated. "Dead. I'm sorry, my lord. Too long dead for you to save."

Roaran briefly closed his eyes. "Kaell?"

"No sign of him. Maybe this one can tell us." She kicked Colla's legs.

Roaran gripped the Varee man's hair. "What occurred? How did Arn die?"

"Not telling you anything, dead man."

"That's my name," Nicky said. "You call him 'lord.'"

"This one's a goat." Sloana sniffed her contempt. "My sisters like to cut up goats."

"Sisters." Colla nervously wet his lips. "No one said anything about them."

Roaran dropped him. "If he's got nothing to say, let the Sisters of Cyrah have him." He walked away.

"Wait."

Enough stories about the Sisters of Cyrah swirled at Varee campfires to make any man perspire. And Colla's hairline and the armpits of his tunic were wet with sweat.

Roaran turned back.

"We came after the girl," Colla said grudgingly. "Kate. The mage thinks she's a spy. That she let her sisters know when to attack our village."

"And Kate killed your companions?"

"I guess." His tongue slid over his lips again. "Didn't see. She hit me."

"And Arn? Did this *Kate* kill him too?"

"The man she was with?" Colla lifted his shoulders. "He was about to leave when we closed in. They were friendly enough, I'd say."

Nicky grabbed Roaran's arm. "So where's Kaell gone?"

Dannon shifted uncomfortably, still struggling to accept who Kate was.

Sloana taunted Colla with her sword. "Can I kill him now, lord?"

"No. Bind him."

"Roaran." Again, Nicky caught his elbow. "Why? This one's scum."

Roaran wearily passed a hand over his brow. "It's fortunate Sloana brought him back alive. I need to cast a blood spell."

*I need a sacrifice.* The words were left unsaid, but Dannon knew what a blood spell meant.

"No." Colla jerked up. Sloana thrust him down. He thrashed. "Let me go. I swear I won't say a thing about you, about this dead city."

Nicky's hand fell away. "That's draining magic, Roaran."

"I have no choice." Roaran's face was gaunt. "We have to find Kaell and quickly. I can't trace him through the Enarae without a blood spell. Not when Archanin blocks my visions."

"It's dangerous, Roaran. You just raised the brotherhood. You've never cast two blood spells at once before."

"I have," Roaran said with a hard grin. "I just didn't tell you."

# VAL ARQUES

Beneath his frantic struggles, the chair toppled. He lay cheek to stone in that first tower room, straining at ropes, groaning into the gag. Indignant anger burned through his veins.

Whoever this Heath was, how dare he bind and gag him? Val had to get free. He had to remember. *Why don't I remember?*

The walls closed in. His breath cut. A bolt of fear shut down thought. The sheer terror at the emptiness in his mind threw him onto a precipice. Trapped him on its edge. He couldn't jump. Couldn't back away.

His breath released in a panicked, anguished cry. The humiliating gag muffled the sound. He tried to yell. He drummed his heels and twisted his bruised wrists.

If he could recall just one thing, like who he was or even who Heath was, then he might be rid of this nausea in his belly. But his memories started only hours ago with this room and the woman who had whispered to him.

The night aged interminably slowly. A tall candle in a silver holder burned down to a stub. Two moons ghosted light through chinks in the shutters. A chill rose up through stone into his bones. Val didn't care about the cold. He no longer bothered to struggle.

Even if he got free, he wouldn't know where to go. To take back any control, he had to learn what measure of man he was. His abilities. His place in this frightening new world. And he had no clue where to start to find himself.

Heath returned. Without a word, he righted the chair.

Val watched him warily. Heath moved with a warrior's restlessness, as if a fire kindled within his limbs, while at his core, he remained perfectly still. Aware. On guard. *Dangerous.*

He sat on the edge of the bed, his knee brushing Val's. "I'm sorry to leave you alone, but my brother insisted I soothe a furious queen."

Unable to do anything but make sounds, Val glared.

"I'm even sorrier for what I'm about to do now," Heath said. "It's cruel to make you relive this again. To go back to that tower room with the red, silk cushions, to the man who abused you."

*Abuse?* Val twisted his clenched hands.

Heath sighed heavily. "I have to do this, Val. If I'm to save you, if you're to remember who you are, then you must listen very closely to what I'm about to say." He paused. "Alecc sent me."

*Alecc?* A fragment of memory formed in his clouded mind, a thread that slipped away.

"He sent me with a knife. To save you."

*Why to save me? From what?*

"You're nineteen. You're alone with a monster. The room is bright with sunlight. Pillows spill everywhere, their embroidered strands gold and red. Butterflies, bright blue, bob beyond the window. His hands are damp on your skin. His lips crush yours. It's unbearable."

Val squirmed. Flashes of memory wisped then slipped away, as intangible as a fading nightmare. Sunlight through bars. Waves lapping boards. A distant roar of the tide over reefs. A gull's squawk.

"You're Val Arques Caelan. A bladesman. He brought you to this room to hurt you. You must remember that room, Val. I know you don't want to, but you must. Think about its scents. His skin, the fragrant oil. That, most of all. It's a scent that sickens you, even now."

Sweat broke out at the back of his neck. *Do not remember,* a voice in his head screamed. *Remember, and it becomes real. Don't let it be real.*

He choked. Heath ripped off the gag. Val spat out threads, accepted the cup put to his lips. The wine tasted of berries and cinnamon. Another memory sparked. *Just like the wine in that tower room.*

For a moment, he heard a ship's rigging creak and glimpsed butterflies jigging in sunlight. A perfume lingered. Roses. The present blurred with the past.

"He's coming back." Val's terror-stricken gaze fixed on the door.

"It's all right. Alecc left a knife. To save you."

Hot breath, rancid with lust, fanned his face. Hands gripped his hips then his thighs. Fragrant oil spun his head, its rose perfume overpowering. Sickening. Roses and pain bound together. But then a boy came—his hair dark, his young face earnest. Afraid for him. Val knew that boy, the boy who covered his nakedness with a blanket. The boy from the tournament. Alecc.

Heath leaned to free his wrists. He turned one over. Val stared in surprise at old, knotted scars. *Did I do that? Why? When?*

"Take up the knife, Val. It's the only way to be free of that monster."

"The knife," Val muttered, dazed. "The knife will save me."

That tower room could not be a dream. Not when sunlight warmed his skin. Not when he tasted salt and blood on his lips as a man bruised his mouth. Val thrashed against the memory. "No, get away from me."

Heath held his shoulders. "Stop him hurting you." He pressed the knife into Val's stiff fingers. "Stop him."

"I hear footsteps." Panic tore through him like fire. "It's him."

"You have to be free of him. There's only one way."

Sickly rose. Oil on his thighs. Tears on his cheeks. The sorcerer must not touch him again. The knife's gleam dazzled. Just two quick strokes would end it. He'd never feared death anyway. He was an Isles warrior, the son of a lord.

*No thought. No hesitation. Just slash. Do it. Escape.*

Wheezing, he slid from the chair. The knife slipped from his sticky fingers. Blankly, he stared at the blood streaming down his arm.

Heath knelt to bind his wrist. Val could not grasp if this man was real. Nor could he understand why Heath touched him so tenderly when only a short time ago, he'd bound him and shoved a demeaning gag in his mouth.

"You saved yourself. You're safe."

"I want you to be real, not him," Val whispered. "I don't know why. You tied me up, gagged me. But I can't hold on to my anger at you."

"I'm real. He's been dead for centuries. He can't hurt you now."

*Dead for centuries—*

The past knotted in Val's mind. A festering knot. Engorged, it strained against his skull. Then his memories exploded, ripping and surging against the seams of reality. He screamed. Too much poured into his head all at once.

The sorcerer, the bright-blue butterflies, the nauseating perfume of lust and oil vanished. He was in the Icelands, in a tower cell. And the man who gripped his shoulders was no longer a stranger. "Heath. It hurts. How it hurts. It's too much."

"It won't last. Nothing lasts."

Slowly, his life threaded into place, each memory a jigsaw piece jamming against another. A story knitted into a jumble of faces, sounds, scents, images, snatches of conversation. He winced, laughed, shook his head, smiled as each one formed.

Until… Myranthe. Oh, how he remembered Myranthe. "Tell it," she said.

And he told it. He had unlocked centuries-old fear and shame.

Val wept. Not a tide of tears, but hacking sobs forced out one at a time. He shuddered, aching with humiliation. Between his wretched gasps, sounds scraped.

Heath drew him to his breast, stroking Val's hair as he might comfort a child, whispering, "There now, it's done with."

At last, Val quietened. They sat in silence, his head against Heath's shoulder. There was no longer a need to speak. The wrongs that embittered the past were on hold.

There were words Val might have said. *You're not who I thought. I want to know you, this you. The man who knows I can't bear empty phrases, who knows only to hold me.* But as time passed, there was less and less a reason to say what was already understood.

When he at last stirred, Heath brushed hair from his face. "It's all right. You're all right."

He pressed his lips to Val's brow. Almost sleepily, as though unaware of what he did, his lips moved to Val's mouth. His kiss was hesitant, soft.

Val pulled free. He stared. Puzzled.

Heath turned his head away. He rose, straightened his garments, and scooped up his knife. He walked to the door. He didn't look at Val. His voice awkward, he said, "You need to sleep."

⚜

The candle guttered. Val let the darkness take him, possess him. Flat on his back on the bed, arms beneath his head, he stared up at nothing.

"Tell it," Myranthe had said. "Tell it. You took up the knife…"

He touched his bandaged wrist, remembering her chant, how his thoughts had scattered like smashed glass as the spell soaked into him. His mind blank.

Then Heath was urging him to use the knife. Pain, the storm of his past hurting, invading his mind until it at last settled into place.

Val shifted his hips at confusing memories. Heath's arms, comforting. Heath's lips pressed to his brow. A brotherly kiss. Then not a brotherly kiss. He considered it with only a baffled curiosity. It wasn't what it seemed. Nothing was with Heath Damadar.

This man he'd thought he hated had saved him by forcing him to confront what Myranthe had exposed and laid bare. What a scribe had taken down. What Heath had heard.

Val's knees stole up, his body curling from the truth. Others knew. They would look at him and know. His face burned. He wrapped his arms about his core, the way Heath's embrace sheltered him against the shame Myranthe had wrung out.

*She knows. Heath knows.* He could not stay here. He could not be seen, naked before them.

The door was open. No guards. He'd earned the right to run. He'd played Myranthe's game to its end.

Val rolled to his feet and snatched up his woollen cloak. No shoes. That would make it harder to escape. Not that he cared if he froze outside. He had to get far from Myranthe. Far from Heath, who would look at him with understanding. He didn't want to be understood. Not like that. He certainly didn't want pity.

Val stole down the stairs. *Find Aric. Get to Kaell. Run.* Heath was right. Myranthe was a vicious, clever sorceress who had outmatched him in her shadow tournament. She didn't care about him. Not really. She cared only about binding Roaran Caelan with a collar of ice.

He drew up hard, a hand on the rough wall. Roaran. They all said his name as if they knew he lived. No debate. No maybes. They expected him to come.

Val knuckled stone, unable to take it in. He could only hope Roaran outwitted Myranthe, that he was far cleverer, far stronger than Val had been.

At the bottom of the stairwell, three passages offered three possibilities of escape. Val ran to the right. Two guards patrolled. He retreated fast, only to hit more guards in the left. They shouted and chased him into the third corridor. Metal-caged torchiers splashed a yellow glow on whitewashed walls. Huge brass doors at the end blocked his way.

Val hesitated. The guards tore around the corner. They drew up, grinning, then advanced slowly. Light glinted on their drawn swords.

He backed up to the doors. As he pushed inside, heat hit him, the odour of charcoal and ash as dense as fog. The guards closed in. He braced to fight, but they only dragged the heavy doors shut. The clang echoed like a tolling bell then slowly died away.

Val's spine tingled with alarm. *What just happened? Why herd me in here? Unless—*

Unless they had locked him in with something.

Something dangerous.

Reluctantly, he turned into a wall of battering heat from a pit that took up most of an amphitheatre cut from cavernous rock. Rows of benches led down from the doors towards a flaming abyss of blackened craters and islands of rocks surrounded by a fiery sea.

Over this horror, long planks of wood and steel—some high, some low—were suspended from the roof by chains. Some were burnt or had snapped, their dangling remains charred skeletons dipping towards the chasm with its smoke, charcoal, and deadly tongues of fire.

In awe, Val wandered down through benches to stand as close as he dared to the pit. Level with the bottom row of seats, the lowest beams were at eye level as if to ensure spectators could easily follow warriors as they traded blows from the swinging planks. Or maybe the thrill was watching them chase each other from plank to plank while avoiding the leaping flames.

He peered down into the massive square hole. Val had never seen a volcano erupt, but he imagined the landscape was as nightmarish as this. Rivers of liquid fire ribboned between rocks. Fingers of flame burst up into the air. Ash, smoke, and cinders were everywhere.

*A fire hall.* An arena of death he'd only ever heard stories about.

"You took your time." Heath balanced on a plank on the edge of the spitting inferno. His feet were bare, and he gripped a sword in a gloved hand. Sweat glistened on the finely cut muscles of his naked breast and shoulders. His thighs strained against tight pants.

"I told the guards to watch out for you. Find a sword. Join me."

A tongue of orange ruptured at Heath's back. He swung to another blackened plank then leapt gracefully onto sandy ground beside Val.

For all his shock at finding himself trapped in the vile cavern, Val couldn't think beyond one thing. This man had seen his shame. This man must pity him, find him diminished. Val dropped his head. "You know."

"I know. A keeper took it all down as you told your story to Myranthe."

"You know." Val heard only that. "Don't look at me. Please. I don't want you to know. I don't want you to see me."

Heath touched fingertips to Val's jaw to lift his chin. Those dark-brown eyes, brilliant in firelight, sought and held his. "I see you, Val. You. Not the young man trapped in a tower room. That isn't who you are. You're a bladesman. You need a sword in your hand to remember that. You need to be here."

"I can't be here. I can't even bear to *be*."

Heath spread his arms. "If you were Icelands-born, you, too, would love this arena. Empty now. But the mob strains against the walls during a fire dance. Cheering. Heckling. There's nothing like it, Val. It defines me, the thrill of the challenge. The contest defines you too."

"No. You're wrong. My shame defines me. I can't hide from it anymore."

"Listen to me." Heath's eyes held his. "You're everything you've experienced, everyone you've loved, every moment of joy as well as sorrow. That's who you are. You are not defined by what was done to you."

"I shoved it down," Val whispered. "I shoved it so far down. I wanted it gone. But it's never gone, is it? It just sits there and poisons you. The past." He dragged his hands down his face. "I'm so tired of it. The pain of it. The secret of it."

"And there's the rub. Our secrets give others power over us. Not my words—the infamous Ice Rider's. Very wise for an Ice lord. Buried pain left you vulnerable to Myranthe's spell."

"She said something similar." Val dropped his head. "No. I can't talk about this."

"And there it is again. Stare it down, Val. Accept you could do nothing." He grabbed Val's shoulders as if to shake him. "Do you hear me? You. Could. Not. Do. Anything. Not your fault. Not your weakness. His fault. His weakness."

"I didn't fight. Didn't summon that Serravan rage. If I'd cast that spell, if I'd let it take me, I would have killed him."

"And if you'd failed, this tyrant would have killed your wife. Your child. Your brother. Your father. No, do not blame yourself. You had to submit."

"He didn't put the knife in my hands."

"He robbed you of choices."

"I don't understand you." Val shook his head fiercely. "You chain me up for months. Then you're kind. Then you do something unsettling."

"The kiss," Heath said.

Flames whipped about them. Oppressive heat prickled and roiled.

Heath still held his shoulders. He dropped his hands and took a step back. A deliberate step as if to show he did not want to cause Val unease. "I kissed you because you needed me to."

Flames shot up at their backs, the air alive with cinders and soot.

"It was heady, your vulnerability," Heath said. "It still is heady.

That you—*you*—needed me to save you, to comfort you."

"And what did *you* need, Heath?"

Heath's gaze hung on Val's face. He laughed shortly, surprised. "Maybe I did want something deeper. Maybe I felt close to you and wanted something more."

"I'm sorry," Val said after a long moment. "I don't know how to give you what you want."

Heath's laugh this time held a dark edge. "The problem is I no longer know what I want." He gestured to the cavern. "Once, I felt alive in these halls. Knew that thrill of fighting, killing, surviving. Now a fire dance is empty of all but duty. I never lose, you see."

"That's a dangerous thing to say. A challenge to the gods."

"The gods love me. I feel their pleasure when I dance and when I kill. Though the flames take every fire dancer eventually. When they get old. Slow." He tapped his head. "Dull-witted. Until then, there remains only duty."

"How sad."

"That's better. Sarcasm is more like you."

"Surely you yearn for something?"

"Do I? Velleran wants power. Myranthe wants to control and humble a man she's dreamt of since a child. Judith seeks love. I never sought anything like that."

"I think you want to feel again. Feel something. Anything."

That dark gaze settled on him, a flicker of fire within. Val thought he'd uncovered the real Heath Damadar at the Fern Castle. A man moulded by duty and death who must return to that. Cynical. Ruthless. But even that had proved to be a mask.

"Or perhaps, perhaps," Heath said softly, "it's all very simple after all. What I need. What I need from you." He looked into Val's eyes. "I need to kill you."

THEIR GAZES LOCKED. A silence held between them. Even the sounds of the firepit dimmed, rippling, roaring flames as muted as breath. Then a beam splintered with a violent crack. As if released from a spell, Val swore and ran at the doors. He shook them. Locked.

Palms flat on the curved wood at his back, he faced the other man. "This is beyond belief. Kaell is out there, somewhere. I don't know what's happened to him. I only know I stabbed him with a cursed blade—"

"What are you babbling about?" Heath frowned. "Kaell died. I saw it. You saw it."

"I have to find him, tell him why I did it. If I even understand it myself, that is. But instead, I'm here in some stupid hall of fire." With a man who wanted to kill him for no better reason than he felt empty inside. Or for the simple, heartless thrill of it.

"What do you mean? About Kaell?"

Val slid his back down the door. "I won't fight you, Heath."

"Ah, avoidance. Still you keep secrets, Val. Is this why you fascinate me?"

"Gods, what do you want?"

"That's better. That's the scowling, young lord who sauntered into the king's tent on the edge of a battlefield. I remember that man. A proud man. An angry man. I knew this was the opponent I had searched for."

"You do want to kill me." An ache needled his skull. He had no time for this.

"Kill you. Save you. When did it all become so complicated, Val?"

"It's not complicated. I'm not fighting you, Heath."

Heath rested his sword on his shoulder, tip up. "I imagined this moment. How we fought. How you begged for your life."

"I won't beg for my life," Val said coldly.

"No, I begin to think you won't. I begin to understand I will have to kill you." He twisted a smile. "I think I have to. I didn't realise that until right now."

Val could not look away from the nightmare reflected in

Heath's sword. He wanted to lose himself in that mirror world, that mire of heat and smoke, that he could see in the steel.

"Could we have been friends?" Heath mused. "Could you have understood me?"

"I'll never understand you."

"Perhaps in another life, you might. In this life, you make me question my place. My duty to my ambitious family. You awaken some need in me to immure you from the world, to possess you. I don't trust this feeling. So I think, I think, I might have to kill you."

"Rather than face yourself," Val said.

Heath laughed. It held a wild, crazed undercurrent. "For someone who doesn't understand himself, that was too perceptive. I do enjoy you, you know. From that moment you swaggered—and you do swagger—into Cathmor's tent, I wanted to know you—through the sword." He tossed Val a blade from a rack.

Val caught it. "I'm not fighting you, Heath."

"Of course you are. You need to remember what and who you are now. Not a powerless nineteen-year-old. A bladesman. So you can finally be rid of the past."

"So now you want to save me again? Which is it, Heath? Save me or kill me?"

"Except I can't really kill you, can I? Not with steel. Not unless I push you into the fire."

"I won't fight you," Val said. "I certainly won't kill you."

"Maybe you can't kill me."

"You don't believe that."

"Then do it, Val Arques Caelan." He pulled Val to his feet. "Or take me prisoner. Walk out of here. But…" He paused, his hand on Val's arm. "Walk out truly free, Val. If I could give you that gift, I would. Be free of that sorcerer. Live without that shadow."

"Or I could be stubborn—I know you like that—and refuse." He dropped the blade.

Heath pressed his sword's tip to Val's throat. "Or I could just kill you right now."

Val knocked the sword aside with his hand. "You won't do that."

"No. I won't do that." Heath dragged a gloved finger along his blade's polished surface. "Aren't you curious? No one's defeated me since I was a boy. Surely the man who won that infamous contest so many centuries ago is the one man who can. It should be you."

Heath's expression was neutral. His breaths too steady. Everything controlled.

Val rocked back. "You want me to kill you."

"No," Heath said. "I don't."

"It has to be me. Not the flames, not a stranger. Oh, gods take you. I see it now. You never wanted to kill me. You intend to die at my hands."

Heath kept his eyes upon the firepit. He didn't look at Val. Beneath the whipping fires and the angry creak of timber, silence brooded.

"Heath." Val grasped the other man's shoulder. "Heath."

Still, that intense quiet held. The world shrank in to just this cavern. To just this man. His face was strained, lips compressed, his jaw tight—tiny signs that leached through his iron control. Then he released the tension in his body.

"Maybe I do want it to be you." Heath pulled away, his voice wistful. "I want it to be a bladesman, a true bladesman."

"What are you not telling me?"

"Not a thing. I'm an open book. Terribly shallow, really. You ask Judith."

"No. There's something. You know even if you strike me down with steel, I'll recover. Killing me is a smoke screen. For what? You don't fear death. That's not it. No. No." Val backed up another step, palms raised, unwilling to accept the truth. "You don't want to survive. You're not afraid to die. You're afraid I *won't* kill you. That I'll baulk at the last."

Heath turned with a smile. An odd smile. Not bitter. Sad. "How do you do this? See into me? I always prided myself on my self-knowledge. I've never been afraid to examine my intent or my feelings. Usually without guilt. Yet here you are. The master of denial. One look at my face, and you know."

"I don't know. But I want to."

"I don't want to tell you." Heath laughed shortly. "No one has ever pitied me. No one ever will. I'd kill them right then and there."

"I won't pity you," Val said.

Heath released a long sigh. It disappeared into the flames as though it had never happened. He straightened his hand. "What do you see?"

"A tremor."

"It's a sickness. It killed my uncle. I watched him weaken and die."

Val wet his lips. "How long?"

"Not soon enough. I dropped the sword in my last fight. Next time, some fool with no skill may get lucky and beat me. Not because they're better, but because I can't grip a hilt."

"Then stand down. Stop fighting."

"A fire dancer does not stand down. He gives the gods blood, and in the end, he gives his own. No escape. Only death. I want to die at the hands of someone worthy. Let it be you." He picked up the discarded sword and held it out. "Fight me, Val. I pray my gods are kind and you're better than me. Yet I think they'll prove cruel, and it will be the flames—another day—with some talentless nobody sneering when I drop my blade and he pushes me into the fire."

Val took the sword. Anger beat up. At Heath for demanding this of him. At Heath's ridiculous gods who demanded this man's death in this smoke-filled hall. At fate.

With a frustrated cry, he hurled the weapon away. It clattered against rock, echoing only briefly. He realised he wanted to save Heath as he had saved him. "How can you ask this?"

The mockery was back in Heath's smile. "I threw you in a hole.

Chained you to a rock. Surely, you want revenge. Here's your chance."

"No," Val said. "I don't want revenge. I want to escape. If the only way out of here is to fight you, then I'll fight, curse you. But don't ask me to kill you."

"Beat me, and you can leave. I swear it."

"Your brother won't let me go, I think."

"Neither Velleran nor Myranthe knows we're here. No one will disturb us unless you ring one of the bells upon the ledge around the outside of the pit. This is your chance. But—" Heath pressed his palm to Val's breast. "Leave here free of not just me but the man who hurt you. Be rid of guilt and every burden you carried alone for centuries. Fight me and remember who you are. Though—"

"Though?"

"Though chances are I'll clip your wings. I clip a lot of wings, except none as elegant as yours, Val."

"It's not really arrogance, is it? You're simply stating the truth."

Heath grinned. "No. It's arrogance."

He swung onto a swaying plank on the pit's edge. Sweat glistened on muscles in his warrior's arms. Whatever the sickness, in that moment, he looked like a perfectly formed young god.

"Choose another blade, Val. Carefully. Some are poorly weighted. Others fell into fire, only to be spat out later, their metal weakened."

Val took a sword and cut air. The satisfying swish always lifted a bladesman's heart. But he knew only a flatness, a sadness, as he climbed onto the dangling plank, its charred wood warm beneath his soles. He glanced below, glimpsing a rock ledge a few metres down. He could not imagine any fighter ever reaching it nor the chain fastening a bell to the wall.

Heath waited in the chaotic forest of charcoal and metal. He grinned. "Shall we play?"

# DANNON

Roaran knelt in a circle of candles, his naked body coated with Colla's blood. Arms extended, he chanted. Flames whipped then straightened. A pall of stillness settled.

Upon the stairs, Dannon gripped his knees. He was unable to forget Colla's terror as the seer cut his throat with one slash.

At his side, their shoulders and thighs touching, Juliette grasped his hand. Before the ceremony, Nicky and Sloana had borne Colla away, stripped him, washed him, and bound him. But after they brought him to their lord, both had disappeared.

Roaran broke off his chant. A hush cloaked the chamber. It held for a moment. Then wind swooped and rattled. Roaran screamed. His body convulsed, twisted, contorted. Within the circle, a force flung him back and forth like a leaf slamming against invisible walls.

Juliette covered her face. A shiver tore through Dannon. Not even the mage performed such frightening magic.

Roaran collapsed. He struggled to his knees, his stare on nothing. The wind died. Gloaming light blinked through clouds. Pattering rain spread its scents of stirred dust and sweetness. Minutes stretched into nothing, their passing exposed by the candles' restless flickering.

At last, Roaran rasped a breath. He fell forward. Juliette jumped up and ran to him. Shaken, Dannon stumbled after her. This strange, new world terrified him. He wasn't certain he wanted to embrace it.

What if he ran? Not just from the Varee but from this dead king. But within his doubts, an internal voice nagged, *You searched for this. For him. For meaning.*

Hand braced against a pillar, Roaran rose. Skin damp, hair matted, he wheezed with each breath. Juliette pressed a cup of water into his hands, her eyes wet.

Roaran managed a weak smile. "Did I scare you so much?"

Her look held reproach. Her tone scalding, she asked, "Was it worth it? Tell me?"

Roaran staggered. Dannon rushed to grab him. "I need to wash off the blood," Roaran said then sighed. "As if lukewarm water can wash away anything I've done."

Dannon helped him into the kitchen and into a ready tub. As Juliette sought fresh garments, Roaran sank into the water. "You don't look too shocked, Dannon. Nicky passed out the first time I performed a blood ritual."

"It shocked me a little," Dannon said.

"The violence of that death sickens me," Roaran said. "I am ashamed to be so cold, to be the man who can cut a stranger's throat for a spell."

"You said you didn't have a choice."

Roaran's gaze fixed on Dannon's face. He laughed shortly. "I want to believe that. But I've lost count of those I hurt in this war. For that is what it is. War. The enemy powerful. If not stopped, Archanin will bleed this land."

"In war, not all of us have the luxury of moral choices." Dannon wasn't sure his words were only for Roaran.

Juliette brought a cloth. She dumped it on the bath's edge. "You didn't answer me. Tell me it was worth murder, worth the pain to you."

Roaran cushioned his head on the rim. "What do you want me to say, Juliette? That any spell that takes us closer to defeating Archanin is worth murder and whatever strength it costs me? Then I'll say it. It was worth it. My vision took me to Kaell. I heard their words—Kaell's and Arn's—the pain of it." He closed his eyes. "I know where Kaell will go."

"Where?" She thrust her hands to her hips.

Roaran didn't answer.

"Where?"

He massaged his temples.

"Why won't you tell me?"

In the silence, rain beat upon what remained of the roof. Leaves scuttled across the floor to pile against the ivy-tangled walls. Beneath storm clouds, two moons blinked through crenulations on the dead city's red walls.

Part of one night—that was how long Dannon had spent in his new life. With no understanding of its undercurrents, its patterns, or its rules—anything that would help him grasp what was behind Juliette's unease.

Juliette stared. Just stared. Then emotion built on her face. Shock. Anger.

Roaran must have known what was about to happen. As she yelled and cursed him, he ducked beneath the water, only resurfacing when she stormed out.

He grinned tiredly at Dannon. "She'll be back with reinforcements."

Juliette dragged an impatient Nicky into the kitchen.

"So he's naked," Nicky said. "Frightening sight, I'm sure, especially for a gentle lass."

Juliette called him an offensive name.

Nicky appealed to Roaran. "That's just not nice, is it? Perhaps you can calm her."

The wood witch stabbed a finger at Roaran. "Tell him. Tell him where you're about to go."

"In all fairness," Roaran protested, "I didn't say I would go there."

"Oh gods." Nicky said, his levity gone. "No, Roaran, no."

Dannon looked from one to the other. He was missing something. He didn't yet know enough of the complicated knot of history between them to understand what Nicky and Juliette feared.

Roaran rose from the tub amid a splash of water, snatched up a cloth, and dried off.

"I could throw you in that cage," Nicky muttered. "Until you see sense. A century or two should do it."

Roaran scrunched the cloth and tossed it aside. Exhaustion deepened tiny lines about his eyes, his face drained by hidden pain. "Kaell seeks his lord. I know where he's going and how we can get to him."

"The Icelands?" Nicky dragged knuckles down his face. "You can't follow him. Not there."

Juliette grasped Roaran's hand. "Ro, please. You know what's written. We've lived with those words, worried about them."

"Run from them?" Roaran said softly.

"'Though fled and free, will here be drawn,'" she recited, her lips trembling.

"I've heard this." Dannon remembered Gendrick scoffing at Archanin's warning about the rise of a sword brotherhood. "In Dal-Kanu. It's an old Icelands rhyme."

"Just that. A rhyme," Roaran said. "It doesn't have to come true."

Nicky tugged at his fringe. "They're waiting for you, Roaran. They've waited for centuries. Sons, daughters, sisters. From one to the other, they've passed down the words. They've prepared for the day you return so they can enslave you again."

"I know the danger."

"No, you don't. Or are you so arrogant, you don't fear Myranthe Damadar?" He appealed to Dannon. "You tell him. He seems to think you're important. Tell him what you've heard of her. She's vicious."

The rain drummed harder. Its mist softened the air. "If she's as powerful as reputed, Myranthe will expect you to come," Dannon said carefully. "She'll set a trap."

Roaran threw on a loose tunic over pants. "In all these centuries, I've kept away, Nicky. When I escaped, I vowed never to return." He grimaced as if a memory stung him. "Don't you think I know what awaits me there?"

"You cannot go back."

"If I don't, the boy dies," Roaran said stiffly. "He's going to blunder into Myranthe's poisonous embrace. I have to take the chance. Myranthe might be powerful, but I am too."

Beneath the veneer of confident resolve, Roaran's hand trembled slightly as he smoothed his tunic, his gestures tight. Dannon wondered what could have befallen him in the Icelands. *What could be so horrendous to rouse a death rider's fear?*

"If Kaell dies, it's all been for nothing," Roaran said. "Archanin will take this land."

"And if you die?" Nicky said. "Or if Myranthe Damadar puts that collar of ice about your reckless neck and destroys your mind?"

Roaran bit his bottom lip hard. "If I baulk from fear for myself, then what sort of man am I?" He shook his head. "No, Nicky. I cannot fail at this last hurdle. Otherwise, my life means nothing, the sacrifices I've demanded of others mean nothing, and you may as well walk into that cursed chamber in the Icelands where my heart sits in glass and destroy it."

Dannon frowned. *Heart sits in glass?* Roaran, it seemed, had not told him everything.

"Roaran... Ro..." Nicky could not find words. His hands clenched helplessly at his side.

Roaran walked out.

Juliette wept. Dannon draped an arm about her shoulder.

"I'll not see you die," she shouted through her tears at the door. "I told you that at the start, Roaran. I won't go with you to the Icelands, because I won't see you die."

He found Roaran leaning against the parapet on the roof. Dannon pressed his palms onto grainy, wet stone. Raindrops slid from leaves. The darkness rippled about him with soft chittering, soft murmurs, even the trickle of water over river stones.

He breathed in the perfume of violets, nutmeg soil, and woodsmoke, wondering why his heart must disturb the peace of the moment. But there it was, its ragged beat a primal warning that he might not see too many more nights like this. "Is Nicky right? If you go to the Icelands, Myranthe will destroy you? How?"

His companion did not answer at once. His gaze fell across the red walls into the sheen of moonlight ribboning beneath the retreating squall. "If I fail," Roaran said. "If Myranthe captures me, she may take up four Seithin temple knives and kill me for defying her god. But I fear she won't be that generous. No, she'll take every memory of my past from me so I know only her will and the will of the gods."

"The legends say a death rider has no memory of who he was." Dannon frowned. "Then why—"

"Why do I remember?" Roaran turned to face him. "Because a sorceress corrupted the ceremony so that I forgot nothing, so I would know all I'd lost. Her lover, you see, was my king's sword. A man called Karmarna of the Ice. He died protecting me."

Dannon shivered. "You cannot return. There must be another way."

"There is only one way. Track Kaell to the Icelands. Save him."

"Take me with you. I know Kate—Kaell." Again embarrassment heated his skin.

"I need you safe. If anything happens, you must lead the

brotherhood against Archanin."

"They'll never accept him." Nicky walked onto the roof. "They'll string him up, even."

"They won't."

"How can you trust this man, Roaran?" Nicky flicked Dannon a baleful glance. "He is your enemy. Overlord of the Varee, the servants of the fallen Seithin god, Archanin."

"I have no gods," Dannon said.

"That's worse. A man who believes in nothing."

"A man ready to believe in something," Roaran said gently.

Nicky grabbed his shoulder. Roaran's elbow jarred a sliver of stone. It plunged below.

"Tell me why I should trust him. Make me understand."

Roaran sighed. He turned and pushed his back into the wall. Sorrow clung to him, gossamer thin. "This man was born to lead this fight. And he will lead."

Dannon flushed with faint pride. To bask childishly in this man's approval was ridiculous, but Roaran filled him not with a sense of destiny—that was for seers—but with purpose. It gave him a dawning sense of who he could be, beyond the ruthless Varee captain.

*Oh gods.* The enormity of that rocked him. He had searched for this man without knowing what he sought. Everything he believed had fallen away. Here, at last, he could belong. And yet he wasn't... worthy.

"Why him, Roaran?" Nicky strained the words through clenched teeth. "Tell me."

"Because he's there at the end, Nicky. He's the last one, the final swordsman I see stand with me at the fortress of Vraymorg when Archanin comes for us."

# VAL ARQUES

"You think you can beat me?" Val said quietly.

"Maybe." Heath tapped his tip on metal. "I know you're Val Arques Caelan, Prince of the Isles, Serravan-trained, blah, blah. But I'm a fire dancer." He swept an arm. "There's a mood to the flames, Val. You have to listen, feel. Ready?"

"Oh, I'm ready." He was ready to be rid of this place. Ready to shove every foul thing that had happened to him down and lock it away with everything else he could not look at. Not ready to kill this man but ready to end his games.

Val had always taught Kaell that attack offered better odds than defence. However, in an unfamiliar cavern he needed to understand the rules. The heat beading his skin with grimy sweat, his mouth tasting of smoke, Val edged enticingly, dangerously close.

Heath obliged with a lazy thrust. The plank wobbled as Val blocked.

"Careful. This isn't your usual swordplay. No solid ground to anchor your feet. A heavy parry will put you in the pit if you don't use your weight as a counter—" Mid-sentence, Heath swung at Val's head.

Val dropped fast. Steel swished air just as flames spouted, hot on his back.

Heath advanced, unhurried, light spitting off his jabbing blade. Val backed up, hit the end of the plank, and leapt down onto a mound of earth lapped by molten fire. It shook. He braced.

"Give you a lesson, new boy," Heath said. "When the earth moves, you do too."

"What?"

"Jump."

Val sprang up, snagging the plank with one arm. The mound below crumbled. Flames roared up through a collapsing hole. They licked at his legs.

Heath reached down to help him crawl up and straighten. They faced each other.

"You don't want the fire to take me," Val said. "If you win, it has to be your sword."

"I want an honourable contest. Yes."

Val dragged a hand through his damp fringe. Draining, nerve-racking heat lashed him from all sides. "Has anyone who isn't a fire dancer survived this?"

"One man walked away. But then Roaran did cheat."

Val bounced on his toes, his soles heating up. "How?"

"That would be telling. Let's just say Roaran did something illogical."

A tunnel of flame roared. The plank rocked violently. Val slipped and toppled onto another mound. It shook. Gasping in alarm, he scrambled to a blackened mass of rock. Fire exploded beside him in a torrent of cinders. As it died away, it sucked earth down with it.

*Gods, what is this awful place?*

He edged back to a head-high plank, threw his sword up, and climbed after it. As he straightened, the beam wobbled. Val clutched at a red-hot chain. Pain erupted in his left palm. Shoving it down, he lurched long the plank, the sword slick in his damp right hand, the smell of burnt flesh lost in woodsmoke and ash.

The thick grey curtain blinded him. The inferno heated his feet through the wood. Val could not even say where in the arena Heath was. The dreadful expanse of swinging beams, steel bars, and chains was alien and terrifying.

*Get above him.* Grasping a higher shaft with one hand, sword in the other, he swung his legs up.

"Too slow, Val." Heath stomped on his fingers.

Val fell, clawing air as he plunged towards what could be earth, rock, or the chasm. As he hit ground, it shuddered. Smoke filled his mouth. Through the chaos of spitting flames, beams clanked beneath swift feet. Where, he wasn't sure. This treacherous cavern distorted sounds.

Val shoved his sword into his belt and climbed up into a crisscross sea of charred timber and rattling metal, choosing one of the highest beams. Metal whirred through air. Heath was right beside him, hacking. Val ripped his sword out. The thinnest part of his blade took the thickest part of Heath's. A mistake.

To cover, he swung an arm, catching his opponent's shoulder. Heath fell against a chain. Val tore his weapon free. Billowing smoke blinded him as he backed away fast, coughing up ash as thick as grease, his every step precarious.

A blade thrust at him through the haze, seemingly dismembered from the hand holding it. He blocked. But the sword disappeared.

Val ripped his tunic to pad his burnt palm. Gripping chains for balance, he ran lightly from plank to clanking plank, his steps quick so his soles were not scorched.

"Watch out, sweet boy." Heath appeared in front of him, swiping at his head with iron.

Val ducked. The tip followed him, cutting his upper arm. Blood wet his sleeve. No stranger to the shock of pain, Val ignored it. He threw himself at a lower plank. For an awful moment, he feared he'd misjudged the distance, that he would plunge into the fiery pit.

Then his arm hooked badly charred wood, too brittle to hold for long. His fingers ached with the effort of holding the sword. With straining muscles he dragged himself up—beside Heath.

Val scrambled to his feet and shied back. His heel brushed air. No more wood. Only the furnace's terrifying glow.

Heath closed on him, still unhurried, grinning. "Nowhere to go, Val. Yield."

Flames burst between them. Heath cursed and stumbled. The fiery vortex blistered wood, its force snapping the timber they both stood upon in two.

Val's half dipped. He skidded towards the yawning inferno. Heat tore through the fleshy part of his palm as he snatched at a glowing chain. Unable to save himself, he slid off the plank, the sword clenched in his other fist.

His body was in free fall. No time to think about dying. Then he hit another mound. Winded, in pain, he never wanted to rise again.

From an iron bar above, Heath stretched down a hand. "Here."

Prideful, Val staggered up and crossed cindered earth. He had no clue about his position within this nightmarish firestorm nor even where it ended or began.

Reaching a plank creaking above his head, he flung up his sword and grabbed the charcoal-rimmed edge. A hot breath of fire whipped up. He drew his legs to his chest and clung to the wood.

The blaze died. Val dragged himself onto the beam then to his knees. A blast of air from below knocked him flat. A whirlpool of dirt and dust sucked in earth right beside him. Rock and flames spewed into clouding ash. Through smoke, he glimpsed a man's shape coming at him fast.

Val only just rose in time to block stabbing metal. Heath redoubled his attack. Their blades met in a mighty clash. Blue sparks exploded, vivid against the grey. At each furious stroke, the plank rocked violently. Val glanced nervously at the fires raging near his feet.

Again flames parted them, throwing Val to his knees, knocking his sword from his hand. He snatched at it as it slewed into the pit.

Heath found his balance. Sword in hand, he moved in. Unarmed, Val threw up his hands to protect his face, braced for an agonising final thrust.

It didn't come. And still didn't come. He looked up.

Heath grinned. "Well, you are on your knees. Ask me to spare you, and that's an end to it."

"No."

"You proud fool—" A fiery wall roared up between them. Heath stumbled, dropping his sword. Sparks hit Val's tunic. Ignoring the danger, he grabbed Heath's blade and thrust low into flames, intending to injure, not kill. Not this man.

The haze thinned. The fire died down. Heath knelt, fingers webbed over blood oozing from his thigh. Slowly, he lifted his eyes to Val.

With a thunderous crack, the plank splintered. Val scrabbled uselessly at a chain. But he was already falling. Shooting embers, smoke, darkness all snapped at him as he flailed, his body out of control. He hit rock, his back on fire. Yelling in agony, he rolled back and forth to smother the flames.

A cry pierced the inferno's din. It ripped along Val's spine before he deciphered it. A man's screams.

He crawled towards the dreadful sounds. Heath clung to a dangling beam. It tilted deep into the glowing pit. Flames snapped at the man's toes.

Val dropped to his belly, reaching to pull the other man to safety. Just as he grabbed Heath's shoulders, a tongue of orange engulfed the Ice lord's legs. Heath shrieked.

Desperate, Val tugged, every muscle at breaking point as he dragged the wheezing man up. He hurled his body onto Heath's legs to suffocate the fire.

"Oh gods," he whispered. Heath had blacked out, his breaths shallow. Val collapsed beside him in agony. But he must not lose consciousness. Not until he had saved his companion.

He peered about in panic. They were halfway down the pit. "Help!" he shouted into the smoke-and flame-streaked blackness. "He fell."

The furnace hissed and spat. Swaying planks clunked eerily, like enormous wind chimes in the shadowed cavern. Val groped about, trying to make sense of his surroundings. Was that rock behind him a wall? Could they be on that ledge he'd seen at the pit's sides?

He lugged Heath along the ledge, away from the choking smoke and heat. A blackened chain dangled from above. Val summoned the last of his strength to push to his knees. He tugged at the chain. Somewhere above, a bell pealed.

"Help. Someone, help."

Only the purl and crackle of flames answered.

In unbearable pain, exhausted, he crawled back to Heath.

"Hold on," he whispered, holding Heath tightly to him as if that would keep him alive. "I know you want to die, but don't let the fire beat you. Be the stubborn man I know. Refuse to let go. I don't want you to let go."

A light flared above. "Here," Val yelled. "He needs help."

Footsteps tapped over rock. Torches bobbed. A man's face appeared above.

"He's hurt," Val said. "Please help him."

"Help's coming," the man said. More steps. Muttered voices. A rope dropped.

Val tied it under Heath's arms and chest. "Pull."

As they yanked the young Ice lord up, Val groped for the wall. The intense pain in his burnt back was crippling. Just a bit longer. Then he could pass out.

He waited for the rope to fall again. It did not. *What? Have they gone?*

"You can't leave me here," he shouted. Cold fear dampened his skin. His limbs folded. It hurt to breathe. "Someone? I'm still here."

Still no one replied. Val writhed in torment, his lungs thick with smoke. He was desperate to lose consciousness. He didn't. Pain trapped him on the edge of oblivion. The fires danced behind his closed eyelids, their tremor in his skull. Time passed. It must have.

At last, they came with torches and ropes, their hands hard and faces hostile. He screamed as they hoisted him up and dumped him near the doors.

"By Ghani-Jai, his back," a man said. "Do we move him?"

"Best fetch her."

They left him on his belly on stone, barely conscious.

Myranthe came. Val sighed in relief. She surely had ointments. But her gaze held no pity.

*Oh gods, she won't help me.* More sweat broke out at the nape of his neck.

"Carry him."

"He's burnt bad."

"Bring him. He'll live."

Grunting men heaved him up. In agony, he passed out at last.

Val came to, disoriented and nauseous. He was propped facedown on pillows in a cavernous, windowless room. Torches sputtered from wall brackets doused in cobwebs, throwing pale light on worn rugs and moth-feasted tapestries on grubby walls.

Myranthe knelt at his side. She pressed wet cloth onto his back. His skin surely disintegrated beneath her hands. Moaning softly, Val sank into blissful emptiness again.

When next he woke, he was in the same cavern. The sharper edges of pain had blurred, the raw ache in his back now more akin to the aftermath of a flogging rather than the embrace of fire. An hour might have passed, or a day. He could not tell.

Myranthe wore the same blackwork gown as she peered down at him. "You heal faster than you deserve. Has the poppy juice eased your agony?"

"A little." That explained his clouded mind.

She moved away to light torches, her steps pronounced and ponderous. Soon, a line of flames burned through stale air. The taste of dust coated his tongue.

Within shadows, something stirred. A sinister presence on the edge of his vision waited within the abandoned grotto. Val shivered, his body reacting to what his dulled mind struggled to name.

Her hair tousled and wild, her gown dishevelled, Myranthe paused by a waist-high, carved stone only a sword's length from him. Upon the floor about it, candles in tall holders cast alabaster light upon a shape on the flat surface.

*Altar.* His mind clicked. *Candles.* Another click. *Ceremony. Sacrifice.*

Val struggled to his elbow. A man lay on that altar. His chest was bare, and a blanket covered his hips and legs. A ghastly moan scraped from his lips.

"Heath," Val whispered.

Myranthe whirled. She poked a finger like a dagger. "You did this. You did this to my brother."

"The flames—" His voice shattered. "His legs—"

"He's in agony. It's taking all my skill to keep him alive."

"Can you save him?"

Myranthe dabbed cloth at Heath's brow. She looked weary. "No."

Heath moaned again. "More of the poppy," he breathed. "Myranthe, please."

"Hush. Be strong. This will be over soon."

Heath thumped the stone with his fist. "It hurts. Oh gods, it hurts."

"Give him more," Val said. "Please. Poppy juice. Something."

"I've given what he can take. More, and he'll pass out. My brother can hold on."

"This is cruel. Why keep him here like this?"

Myranthe pressed her palms into the altar. She looked through him into darkness drawing in like a noose. Gooseflesh lifted on his arms. He stared where she did, seeing nothing.

"Do you know what this stone is?"

He forced words out in horror. "An altar."

"Yes. Though not used for centuries. Not since Roaran Caelan escaped the fire hall and crashed a blade of Seithin steel down against this altar in a futile attempt to destroy it." Her hand drifted over chipped stone. "For centuries, we created death riders in this cavern. Until the magic was lost. Forgotten."

Val trembled. Cold sweat salted his burning skin. Even in his fogged mind, a terrible suspicion lurked. *Death riders. She would not, surely. Not her own brother. Unthinkable.*

"Until now." Myranthe's voice rose in triumph. "I have the knowledge to restore our god's servants. When the seer kneels and admits his folly, he shall lead them as it is written."

*You're mad,* Val might have said. *This is barbaric. The world existed without death riders for centuries. We don't need to bring them back.* Except forming words was too hard and arguing with Myranthe pointless. She truly believed she served her gods, that it was right to murder for them.

The tall altar candles flared as the doors swept in. Six robed figures entered. A chill spread with them into the chamber as if an unseen force stalked at their backs.

"Good," Myranthe said. "Good."

Heath again drove his fist into stone.

Myranthe stroked his hair. "Not long."

"It hurts." He wheezed through gritted teeth.

"You're a sorceress. Help him," Val said. "Or don't you care?"

She moved fast—one step, then she kicked him in the face. Val plunged onto his back. Knifing agony hurtled him into emptiness.

A chanting called down to him. Val surfaced into shadowy light. The scent of smoke and death swirled, acrid on his tongue. He did not know how much time had passed.

The robed figures surrounded the altar in a semicircle. At their head, Myranthe stood imperious, her brow streaked with blood. Heath moaned. The sorceress put a cup to his lips.

"Say you're willing. Say it. I won't do this unless you are willing."

Heath's head lolled. From his wretched, torn gasps, he clung to life through sheer will. Val swiped at his gritty eyes. Beneath his wretchedness, a black anger raced in his veins.

"I want to die," Heath rasped. "But not like this. An honourable death in combat. Not butchered on a slab." He clutched at her arm. "You saw this. That's why you delayed and delayed the ceremony. Why didn't you tell me?"

"My poor Heath." She thumbed matted hair off his brow. "You must trust the gods."

His grip tightened, her skin whitening beneath iron fingers. "You let this happen. Why?"

"I saw you fall. I saw you in great pain. I remember thinking, 'He is worthy. The gods choose wisely.' How it made sense they should demand Damadar blood."

"You could have stopped it. Warned me."

"Your fate was set the moment you brought that man here. Val Arques Caelan. That's when the visions changed. Why did you do that? You cursed us by bringing him here, brother."

"No." Heath rocked his head. "No. I didn't."

She leaned. "Say you are willing."

Heath dragged up a breath from dry lungs. "Is he here? Val, are you here?"

"I'm here," Val said. He waited, bleak loss pitting within.

Torches whipped, flattened, and whipped again. Cloth brushed stone as a robed figure fidgeted. Yet there was silence. An undercurrent of it. As if time, like Val, waited.

Heath said, "I didn't want it to be like this. That we must speak when so many others listen. But I must tell you. I have to tell you—" His back arched.

"It's all right. Whatever it is, it doesn't matter."

Heath forced out another ragged breath. "I think you could have understood me. No one else does. We could have been friends."

"Yes," Val said. "We could have been friends. We nearly are friends."

Heath laughed, the sound so thin, Val's breast ached. "Nearly. You're always honest. And it's complicated, friendship. Odd edges to it. Things we want but can't quite name. Val?"

"Yes?"

"Promise me you'll be free of it. Free of that monster. Forgive yourself. That, most of all. Forgive."

Myranthe stroked his wet hair. "Save your strength. Say you are willing. Give your death the meaning you seek."

"It's too hard to care anymore. I want the pain to end."

"So say it." Myranthe's tone grew urgent. "Say it."

"Yes, willing. Let dying mean something at least." His voice fell away to a sigh.

"It's first moonrise," a hooded figure said.

Myranthe nodded. Their chant picked up. She dropped her robe and took up a knife.

Time stalled. Only the lift and plunge of that knife could release it. Val didn't want time to move on. He didn't want that knife to come down.

The doors flew back again. Two guards dragged Aric inside. He was barefoot and naked from the waist up beneath a samite cloak. His hair looked washed, his skin scrubbed.

At the sight of the altar and robed figures, he bucked. "No... No!"

"Keep him quiet," Myranthe said. "I'm not ready for him."

Aric freed an arm and swung at his captors. An impassive guard absorbed the blow. He grabbed Aric's arm again. Their prisoner dug his heels in, writhed, and yelled.

With an impatient sigh, Myranthe turned. She lifted her arm and spoke two words. There was no flash of light or ripple in the air. Just those words. Aric slumped. The guards dragged him to the wall near Val and shackled him to stone.

Val crawled to him. "Aric. Are you hurt?"

The man put his back to the wall. "You said you had a plan. You told me to hold on."

"I was not strong enough." Another man he'd failed. Like Kaell.

"So this is the end, Vraymorg—Val."

"Shut them up." Myranthe leaned against the altar, panting.

Val savoured a useless moment of satisfaction. Even a sorceress paid a price for magic.

A guard stepped in to kick Aric's legs then melted away. Aric's uneasy gaze flickered to the altar. "My gods. There's someone... she's about to—"

"It's Heath." Grief lumped in Val's belly. "He's dying."

"Her own brother?" Aric tipped his head back against stone. "If she can do this to her brother—" He swallowed. "Then I can expect no mercy."

Val had no words. He gripped the man's shoulder.

"Gendrick always said I'd die like this." Aric coughed a sardonic laugh. "In some miserable, dark prison. Do you think he even looked for me?"

"Your brother thinks you're dead. Everyone thinks you're dead."

"You mean to be kind, but I know Gendrick. He didn't look."

Myranthe kicked away her puddled gown. Beads of sweat glistened on her naked back, her skin ivory in the torchlight. Again she lifted the knife.

Her companions' chants built to a crescendo. The torch flames beat heavy air. A haze, red like blood, shimmered. Aric started to turn his head.

"No," Val said. "Do not look."

Too late for him, though. The knife plunged down. Heath jerked once. Blood pooled beneath his body, then streamed to the floor. The robed figures screamed in excitement. Myranthe touched her brother's hair, her expression tender as she reached into shattered ribs and ripped out his heart.

She held it up, grasped in her bloody palm, as if to show the gods. Flames drummed, their rhythm wild in the windless chamber. In a language like a whining song, Myranthe shouted an incantation. Magic ripped through and around her in waves of light. Then she collapsed to her knees in her brother's blood.

With cries of triumph, the robed figures fell upon the body. They stroked and caressed, their sounds sickening. With great care, they lifted Heath above their heads and carried him back into the darkness.

Myranthe braced the altar to rise. Reverently, she put her brother's heart in a glass container. Candlelight softened her face as she placed the glass in a crevice beside an identical receptacle.

She still held the knife, its vicious blade coated in Heath's blood. With stained fingertips she touched its gleaming tip. Slowly, she turned and lifted her head. Her lips parted in a gloating smile as she looked right at Aric.

"Aric—" Val started.

*What to say?* Val could not comfort Kaell, either. Not when the boy had returned to Vraymorg, begging to die. Not at the stake. "Aric, when they free you, fight. Don't let them get you on that stone."

Sweat dampened Aric's hairline. "I never feared death, Val Arques. But I thought I'd die in battle. Not like this. By The Three, not like this."

"You have to fight." Stupid, inadequate words.

"Fight, get free, and go where?" Aric's face was bleak. "My brother is king. If not this dark prison, I'll die in some other dark prison of Gendrick's choosing. He never could tolerate rivals. For power, for love, for anything. But you're right. I can't make it easy for them. I'll fight." He shivered. "Will you take someone a message for me?"

"Yes, if I can."

"His name's Aiden Saltman. Will you tell him—" He shook his head. "Oh gods. I don't have the words. I just want him to know—"

"I'll tell him."

"Bring him," Myranthe said.

The guards freed Aric. The instant the shackles fell off, he exploded. He swung his fists, thrashed, and yelled his defiance. His flailing arms knocked a man back.

"Fools," Myranthe said. "Hold him."

They seized his shoulders and hauled him to her. Restrained, helpless, Aric said, "Don't do this. I'm a warrior. Let me die a warrior's death."

The torches' glow pearled Myranthe's skin as she touched his cheek. "Still, child. Do not be afraid. Hush, hush. Listen to my voice. You will be still."

His eyes flattened. Docilely, he let Myranthe remove his cloak and help him onto the altar.

"No, stop," Val shouted as her faceless companions bound Aric. "He's not willing."

Figures ringed the tethered man. Their chant picked up again. Val wrenched his head aside.

Myranthe stabbed a finger. "He must see. He must know."

A guard locked an arm about his throat, forcing his head around. Val squeezed his eyes shut. But he could not block out Aric's scream.

Myranthe kept him close, chained by wrist and ankle to the wall near the benches in a gloomy, square, stone-walled room. Her lair. The lair of a beast. That's what she was. No woman could turn a knife in her brother's chest.

That made him her prey. As days blurred into a week, Val no longer cared. The poppy juice numbed his pain, but nothing shut out Heath's scream. Whenever he closed his eyes, that was all he heard. Every nightmare took him once more to that glowing cavern with its stone altar and its hearts in glass.

Shelves crowded the lair with vials and pots containing ingredients the beast needed for spells or lotions. Herbs in bunches dried before a smouldering fire. Their earthy, resinous fragrances assaulted him daily. When she left a cauldron bubbling in the fire, other scents like bark or peat, even molasses, layered the air.

Myranthe stirred, mixed, and cut. Sometimes, she chanted. She threw him scraps and plonked clay cups of water or wine diluted with poppy juice near his bare feet.

Occasionally, she shook him awake on his thin pallet, insisting he'd slept for hours when Val guessed it was a few precious minutes. More games. For the most part, though, she ignored him.

As another week passed and his pain retreated, he regretted Aric's senseless death. Heath, he deeply mourned, his grief simple and clean. Val knew loss. An ache of it in his gut. He had spoken the truth in that foul chamber. They could have been friends.

Thinking back, he remembered Heath's nonsense with a smile and wished he would stride in, ready to rile him or frustrate him with that mocking wit. In the end, even in such torment, Heath tried to give him a gift. "Be free," he'd said. "Be free of that monster. Live without guilt. Forgive yourself."

But he could not. Not when Myranthe knew. She looked at him and knew his shame. At every scornful glance, Val's shoulders shrank towards his chest. He wanted to hide, to draw back into the shadows.

As the tangle of weeks became a month, others came and went.

Velleran to ensure Myranthe did not damage his merchandise, servants to summon her to treat illness, messengers delivering requests from nobles or their ladies for tonics or remedies.

"The long freeze sets in soon," Griffin told him one day as he watched his sister grind roots with a mortar and pestle. "We'll be shut in the caverns for months."

Muscles strained in Myranthe's back as she worked. "Yes. With nothing to do but torment our prisoners." She turned, her smile sweetly venomous. "Seems I'm stuck with you until spring. Once it snows heavily, your buyers won't be able to get here."

⁓∙⁓

A boy brought a lidded basket. The sorceress pressed a coin in his hand before he sped off, grinning. Bruised and sore, Val rose to one elbow as she carried the basket to a bench. From her sly glance his way, that basket meant trouble.

Myranthe edged the lid up with a stick. Something rustled inside the basket. A flat, scaly grey head slithered over the rim. At her chant, the snake curled its whiplike body about the stick. She carried it towards Val.

With an Isles man's dislike of snakes, he recoiled. There were too many serpents in too many valleys near Tide's End where only venom hunters dared go. "What are you doing?" His back hit the wall. "That's a jape snake."

"Isn't it pretty? A baby. From the Isles. I hear they grow big enough to swallow a man." She put the stick close to his bare arm. The snake's tongue flickered. "Just be still. Move, and it might bite your face, and Velleran forbids me to scar your face."

The snake coiled. It struck at Val. He jerked back as its fangs pierced his arm. At first, he felt nothing. Then his muscles constricted. A burning tore from his wrist to his shoulder.

With great care, Myranthe returned the snake to the basket. She shut the lid and turned to watch him, her gaze dispassionate.

"Young snakes are immature and release all their venom at once. They kill fast. But I added a serum to your wine these past few days. The bite will hurt but won't kill you."

"Why do this? To torture me? Revenge?" Sweat beaded on his brow. A scorching beneath his skin traced the venom's path, drawn with every breath towards his heart.

"The venom alters blood so I can use it to cure many winter ailments. Until the victim dies. But you." She flashed a radiantly vicious smile. "With your lovely Caelan blood and my serum, you'll survive. The venom will course in your veins for days. Very useful."

"I can't—" Sweat streamed off him. Every laboured gasp hurt.

"Breathe? I know. But you'll pass out fast enough."

His body convulsed. Blackness spread like a net, dragging him down.

Even when the darkness released him, the pain did not. He could not move, could scarcely blink or swallow, but every so often his muscles twitched.

Myranthe cut his arms to milk his blood into a cup. Val murmured a protest. He wondered if she intended to repeat the whole vile procedure when he recovered. The snake and its basket had disappeared, but he suspected they weren't far away.

Over hours of misery as he lay helpless on his pallet, the venom's fire ebbed. Myranthe dripped water down his parched throat. When he could sit up, she fed him odd-smelling pottage. "This certainly clipped your wings," she said.

*Heath's words from the fire hall.* Sadness struck deep, a raw weight on him. If anyone had told him a year ago he would mourn an Ice lord who abducted him and chained him up, he would have laughed aloud.

On the third night after the snake had bit him, she opened a new gash in his thigh. Despondent, Val no longer cared if she bled him or not.

"Does it hurt?" Myranthe twisted the knife in the cut until he groaned. "How sad."

He didn't bother to reply.

"Perhaps I should have scarred you," she mused. "So every time you look at the scar you remember I know the truth and saw you as you really are."

"Myranthe." Velleran stormed in, cape whipped back, head uncovered.

The sorceress straightened with a frown. "It's not good if you need more so soon."

"No, my son is much better. Thanks to your venom."

He drew Myranthe outside. In the stillness of night, their harsh whispers reached Val.

"Now? I thought they'd wait until spring. Did we have warning, brother?"

"I didn't expect them, either. Not with winter setting in. But they're here, demanding to see him."

"I'll have him bathed and dressed."

"Do that," Velleran said.

"No." A woman's curt, accented Telorian drummed with authority. "Don't do that. At least until we see what state you're keeping him in."

"Did you follow me?" Velleran asked. "I suspect you don't trust me."

"It's a matter of urgency, not trust. Take us to him at once."

"You must understand. My sister—my family—has reason to punish him. In the circumstances, he's better kept than he deserves."

"We'll see."

Footsteps trod on stone, some lighter, some heavier. Velleran led two women into the lair. With their pale hair, the empty sheaths for swords in their belts, and their brash confidence, Val could guess who they were.

Quisnaf warriors.

"I've caught up now." Val scowled at Velleran. "How much am I worth?"

"A lot of gold. You should be flattered. The other bids were impressive, too, but the Quisnaf insisted they'd better any offer. Now be still and let them look at you."

"He's like some glorious, untamed beast with all that unruly hair," the younger said.

"But a poorly kept beast." The elder turned on Velleran accusingly. "You kept him chained here? Half naked. Probably half starved. From the blood, the bruises, tortured."

"Any damage to the goods is superficial. He's well enough."

The woman's nostrils flared. "You." She grasped Val's arm. "Turn." She examined his bandaged back. "What's this?"

"He fell into fire." Velleran squirmed. "He and my brother danced in a fire hall."

"Danced?" The woman blinked fast.

"That's what we call it. Swordplay over pits of shooting flames."

"And you allowed this? Knowing he was bought and paid for?"

"Not allowed, no." Myranthe twisted her hands. "The prisoner escaped. My brother Heath tried to stop him. And Heath paid with his life in that fire hall."

Not the way Val remembered it. He closed his eyes against stabbing memory.

Myranthe pressed his bruised shoulder, as if daring him to argue. "Velleran is not to blame. I kept this man here for good reason. Your council suggested tamed was preferable."

"Tame?" The younger scoffed. "An Isles warrior? That would be a waste."

Myranthe flicked her tongue over her lips. "I kept him here while I treated his burns. I thought chains might soften his will— as your council wished."

"Regardless of intent, you used him poorly." The older one tapped her empty scabbard, the rhythm heated. "The burns. Bite marks. Bruises." She confronted Velleran. "You'll accept less gold to compensate us for your neglect."

"We agreed on a price." Velleran shot Myranthe a malicious look.

The Quisnaf woman thrust hands to her hips. "You'll accept less."

Two strong-willed individuals clashed like horned bulls. If the Quisnaf woman gutted Velleran then and there, Val might well cheer.

"We'll accept less," Myranthe said with a sharp nod at her brother. "And we'll do what we can to make up for our neglect now."

Val knew the stories of the Damadar caverns. That they veined like silver in ore into the mountains. Some forgotten. Others lost. Some led to silent, dark pools or into grottos of stalagmites where a single note of music might echo endlessly.

He listened for that music as guards walked him through caves where icicles dripped and the wind scattered snow onto stone, through chambers with white frozen walls and floors.

For all its strange beauty, the city of ice and darkness was repellent for a man raised in the sun-drenched Isles. He longed to see the sky. Longed to feel warm. Longed to shove off hands that pushed and prodded.

What he wouldn't give to know one of those secret ways through the Damadar caverns or to have one ally here. But to get free and find Kaell, he had only his wits. In the face of this city's extremes, against enemies who commanded powerful magic, that wasn't enough.

His will, then. Except Myranthe's game had stripped him naked, exposing a raw wound. He barely held onto himself.

The guards walked him through more whitewashed passages, passing doors of soft brass etched with scenes of tournaments or entrances disguised by hanging rugs with gold tassels.

At first, they met servants lighting torches, scurrying messengers, or noblemen and women who stared after him, curious. Then the passages emptied, and his escort forced him down hewn steps through rock. The air was ripe with the odours of damp soil and chalky stone. Water trickled behind moss-green walls.

The stairs stopped at an open door. Uncertain, Val backed up.

"Inside." A guard shoved him.

Val stumbled into a small rock-walled chamber.

A single brazier revealed low wooden benches and shelves crowded with oils and lotions in glass ampoules. Soap, cassia oil, and bergamot perfumes drenched the suffocating warmth.

A woman brushed through a sheer white curtain at an entrance to a second room. She assessed him with an impersonal gaze.

"No clothes," she said in accented Telorian. The steamy heat plastered strands of chestnut hair onto her cheeks. "Bathe."

Val gladly stripped off pants stiff with dirt and blood.

The woman pushed back the curtain and gestured. "My lord Velleran says be quick." She swept another glance up and down. "An honour for you. His personal baths, this."

Val didn't feel honoured. Only grateful to wash. He padded into a steamy bathhouse carved from rock, its tiles warm beneath his soles. More steam misted, rising off a hot spring converted to a pool.

Faint from the heat, the venom, and Myranthe's bloodletting, Val groped for the edge as he waded down stone steps. The woman splashed in. She pushed him gently. "You go deeper."

Val did. She followed, armed with soap and cloth. When she again reached for him, he flinched away, fed up with strangers' hands on him. "I can do that."

"Please," she said. "My lord will be angry."

He sighed and gestured submission.

The woman nudged him to a rock ledge beneath the water. He

put his weight on it so she could sponge his back. At her first stroke on his naked body, a pang of alarm tore through him, a resistance to anyone's touch. He forced his tensed muscles to relax.

The woman had an instinctive understanding of what to do with him. Her fingers were firm where he was uninjured, as gentle as a dove's wings on burned skin or bruises.

When he ignored her attempt to shove him underwater, she scolded him. He spoke tolerable Venivan, Quisnaf, and even Wardorian, but he didn't recognise her language. Vaguely, he wondered how she had ended up in the ice caverns.

"Wash hair," she said. "Nasty dirty. Then out. Told to hurry."

Val sucked in a breath and ducked. The woman soaped his hair. He rose for air. She pressed him beneath again. When he surfaced, gasping, dirt floated by. *Nasty dirty" indeed.*

"Out. Please."

Val dizzily found the steps. He squeezed his eyes shut. Once the world righted, he followed her to a bench in the outer room. She pushed him down, placed a cool cloth about his neck, and hacked off his hair. Dark locks piled on wood.

"Not all, please," he said when she wet his skin to remove the beard. A tiny vanity.

She nodded. When she was done, he rubbed his chin, satisfied with the stubble.

At the woman's urging, he rolled onto his belly. But once more, when she put a hand on his back to rub ointments into his burns, Val tensed. Lying on his stomach, his body bared, stirred up feelings of vulnerability.

"No hurt," she said. "No hurt to you."

After a moment or two, he sighed deeply. Her strokes soothed, and the bathhouse was luxuriously warm, its bergamot fragrances pleasing. For the moment, his troubles would wait. Right outside the door.

He nearly drifted to sleep until the woman bid him sit up. As she combed out his knotted hair, Val enjoyed the sensations of heat drying his skin and the kneading fingers on his scalp.

When she was done, she laid out clothing. Rising, he stretched and dressed in flannel undergarments, pants, a short woollen tunic, and a belt. He fingered its leather—a weapon if wrapped around a neck. Velleran's neck. Still, he longed for steel.

The fur-lined boots proved a good fit. *All the better for running.* He wanted to run. *No more feints, Heath. Do you hear? I'm fed up with your kin and their games.*

The woman looked him over, turning his jaw this way and that. He wondered if he should twirl and bob.

Velleran fidgeted outside before impassive guards. He inspected Val, too, even flicked a strand of damp hair into place.

"My lord." The woman curtsied nervously.

"It's well enough," Velleran said.

Relieved, she darted back into the bathing chamber.

Velleran gestured at the stairs then fell in beside Val, with the guards a pace behind.

"How much did you get?" Val was genuinely curious. "You said a lot."

The Ice lord's hazel Adorean eyes flared.

*Adorean eyes that promise all*, Telorian poets warned in song and verse. *Trust their glitter, how low you'll fall.* Val hummed the familiar tune.

"You're worth a few ships," Velleran said. "Good gods, are you singing?"

"I feel all clean and nice, thanks to your servant, so I'm humming, yes." He did feel brighter, his spirits revived. "You know that expression, once an Isles man."

"Once an Isles fool, always an Isles fool, yes. Pampered, decadent princesses who adorn their perfumed bodies in silver and silk."

Val hummed louder. "Ships, you say. Glad to be of use. Though, you'll find the price is blood." He cut off his tune to glare.

"You mean you'll make me pay? You deserve worse than this,

Isles man. You killed my brother, or as good as. Fortunate for you, my father is so ill I'm lord in all but name. He'd take off your head."

"Well, it's a scrubbed-up head, now." Heath, it seemed, had rubbed off on him. "It'll come off quicker. Less dirt for the blade to catch on."

"Save your humour," Velleran said. "You'll laugh a lot, I'm sure, when some Quisnaf warrior makes you hers. What a satisfying thought. I might visit Quisnaf. When they've taught you to drop your eyes when you drop your pants."

"I don't think I'll be there long. Don't even think I'll get there." He hummed again.

"There's that sense of humour once more. Heath seemed to enjoy it. I don't."

"Your brother was twice the man you are."

Velleran smiled unpleasantly. "Quisnaf is only a short journey by sea. I might visit. Yes."

⁓⧟⁓

Ribald laughter, along with the tinkle of glass, reached into the passage through a closed door.

"Celebrating." A guard wriggled his brows lewdly at Val. "Wonder if they'll make you part of their celebrations, salt-head."

His stone-faced companion chuckled.

"Your face will crack," Val said.

"The salt-head does speak nonsense," Stone Face said to the brow wriggler.

"He'll soon learn to speak nonsense in the Quisnaf tongue."

"Or just learn about the Quisnaf tongue."

Grinning, they knocked and, at the call of "enter," shoved Val inside. He expected another suffocating, windowless room with stone walls. But this chamber had a long window, shuttered against the cold, but a window, nonetheless.

For one wild moment, he wanted to rush to it, pull back the

shutters, and mutter like a fool, "The sky, the sky." The rest of the room was typical of the Icelands except for the two women sprawled in high-backed chairs, a feast on a table before them.

"Join us." The younger raised a wineglass. Etched glass, not clay. Only the best, it seemed, for those ridding the Damadars of difficult captives and giving them lots of gold.

"No, wait a moment. Stand there." Swaying, she rose and swaggered across the room. "My, my. Is it the same man?" She touched his stubble. When he knocked her hand away, she laughed. "You're all pretty. And you have this Caelan blood thing. I'm seeing it, Matilda, what the fuss is all about." With a cheeky leer, she sauntered back to the table.

"Sit," Matilda said to Val. "Eat." Her look, a cool sweep up and down, assessed, too, as if she wondered whether he would cause trouble.

He intended to do just that. First, learn their plans then willingly leave with them. Once out of the caverns, they would part company—quickly.

Val sat. No knives. He picked at baked pheasant with his fingers and dragged in a slow breath, seeking to control his thoughts. Seeking that warrior core within, to put aside every humiliation, every moment of powerlessness he had endured in this dreadful place.

"You want wine?" the girl asked. She was surely not yet twenty. Dangerous, though, because young warriors were unpredictable. Reckless.

*Unless reckless is predictable. Where is Heath to share this nonsense?*

Without waiting for an answer, she splashed wine into three glasses. She nudged one closer to Val. They drank the same wine, but Val considered it uneasily.

"Not the trusting sort, I see?" The girl swallowed a mouthful from her goblet.

He picked up his glass and swigged.

The girl leaned back, a knee drawn to her chest. "What say you, Matilda? Now he's all cleaned up, shall you let the Damadar boy keep all his gold?"

Delightful to hear Velleran called a boy, especially by a child close to half his age. Val could think of other names for the Icelands heir. In familiar company, he might share them.

"You do look improved," Matilda said carefully to Val. "Younger without the face hair. But there's something old in your eyes."

"Oh, I'm at least twenty," he said, wondering what she knew.

"Centuries? I hear it's closer to six."

*A lot, then.*

Matilda pushed another dish at him. "Eat, eat. You're likely weak, curse that sorceress, and we have a journey before us."

"When?"

"First light."

"Good. I hate this place." Val glanced about at their swords, cloaks, and a leather purse on a table beside three small bags made of a gold-leaf material. "No fetters. How do you intend to make me go with you?"

"Aren't we charming enough?" the girl said then laughed.

"I'm sure you're sweet—"

"Not one bit," Matilda said.

"But if I can be honest, I'm fed up with restraints, of being held. All of it."

Matilda nodded slowly. "So you give us fair warning?"

Val rolled the glass stem in his fingers. "I'm only saying what you're thinking. I'll get away if I can." He kept his voice steady to hide his doubt. Could he, a man broken by every degradation of captivity, find enough of himself to escape?

"Still. No ropes," Matilda said.

The girl laughed.

"No chains."

The girl laughed harder.

Val scowled. "So I'll just walk out with you?"

"What do we call him? This is what—" The girl counted with her fingers. "The seventh we retrieved. So number seven?"

"Morgan, shut up," Matilda said mildly, her gaze on Val's face.

"What then? I know we're instructed to treat him gently—"

"Gently?" Val edged up a brow.

"More gently than the Damadars treated you, I'm thinking." Matilda nodded to herself. "Call him Val Arques if you choose, Morgan, given our instructions."

"I don't do gentle." Morgan reached for the carafe. "That's for healers and the like."

"I thank you for your warning, Val Arques," Matilda said. "It was honest. And I always like to reward same with same. For you, the sorceresses of Quisnaf made something special."

"Magic?" Alarm kicked in his bowels. Again, he controlled the shake in his voice. "Spells sometimes work, and sometimes don't."

Matilda nodded again. "Your Caelan blood? Myranthe tells us of a sleeping draught her brother used to bring you here without protest."

"Without protest." Morgan snorted heartily. "I like that."

"We're not so crude in Quisnaf," Matilda said. "This is more sophisticated."

"Hmm." Val rubbed his chin uneasily. Only one object, he could not explain. The bags.

Matilda smiled faintly. Fine lines etched her eyes. "Yes." She rose.

"You could still try." Morgan sculled wine. "To protest. I'd like that."

Matilda emptied the bags, spilling three silver bracelets onto the table. Morgan slipped one onto her upper arm. Matilda did the same with the second. She put the last in Val's palm and closed his fingers around it.

"On your arm, please." Her steady gaze held his.

Val touched the bracelet's cool engraved metal. Even though he had no magic, the tingle of enchantment burned his fingers.

He put it on the table and sat back. They watched him, unconcerned.

"On your arm, please, Val Arques," Matilda said again. "I've asked twice. There won't be a third time."

He shook his head.

Morgan pounced. Val expected it, but she was quick. In a heartbeat, her arm throttled his windpipe, her knife thrust up into his jaw. "Or I do it for you."

"Make me." The words felt good. Defiance felt good.

Morgan breathed hot air on his ear. "I'm so glad you said that." Her arm tightened.

Val tipped the chair back. With an annoyed cry, she leapt out of the way. He fell with the chair, scrambled up, snapped off a leg, and brandished it like a sword.

"The wine." Morgan moved between Val and their weapons. "Why does it take so long?"

Matilda shrugged and sipped.

"Wine?" Val echoed. Then he shook his head. "No, we all drank the same."

"A potion smeared on the rim of your glass, fool. Matilda, how long?"

"Not long now."

"It's a bluff." He backed towards the door and tried the knob. It only rattled.

"Locked from outside." Morgan sneered. "Just settle down and go to sleep."

"I did worry you'd be tired for our journey," Matilda said. "Given their neglect."

Val slid down the door. His back throbbed. He was so tired of struggle, sick to the teeth of restraints and orders. All he wanted was to find Kaell. He rested the chair leg on his lap. "I'll wait until morning, then."

*Now who's bluffing?* His vision already blurred.

"Did I tell you," he said to Matilda, "of how fed up I am of being

chained to walls and given all sorts of cursed potions and the like?"
His head fell sideways into sleep.

"Up, dopey head."

Val ignored Morgan's grating voice. He was too comfortable
beneath a warm blanket near the hearth, boots off, his head
cushioned on a rolled-up cloak.

"Up." This time Morgan poked him with a sword. Puffy-eyed,
she looked as vicious as an agitated snake.

*Drank too much? Headache? Furry mouth? How sad.* He rolled
to his knees, groaning at a wave of dizziness. *Curse potions and
sorceresses.*

"Do you have snail blood or something? Get up." Morgan
grabbed his arm and gestured to a chamber jutting beyond the
walls. "Use the privy. We've a long way to go."

Val rose and padded off shakily, drawing together scrambled
thoughts. No need to resist yet. They intended to take him through
the locked door and away from the city.

When he returned, Matilda shoved a bowl of porridge at him.
He ate, idly scratching his upper arm. His fingertips brushed metal.
The bracelet. With an incensed cry, he tore at it. The silver band
would not come off.

"You'll need a spell to remove that, Val Arques," the Quisnaf
woman said calmly. "We're assured you have no magic. Apart
from the ability to cast a few old, and useless, Serravan charms,
that is. So please, just accept it, and all will be well."

"You could always gnaw your arm off." Morgan turned to
pound on the door.

Matilda tossed him a fur-lined cloak and hat. "Cold in the
valley."

She waited patiently as he pulled on his new boots.

A key turned. Morgan shouldered past the guard. "Let's go. I've had enough of this place."

Matilda slipped Val an indulgent smile. "She's not good before noon. One for nights is our Morgan. Says the dawn is for roosters and twittering birds and the like."

Morgan waited along the corridor with the guard. "Are we meant to touch our forelocks to Velleran or something?"

"No," Matilda said. "I bid Velleran farewell last night. Assured him once we have this man safely in Quisnaf, the council will send the rest of the gold."

"Good." She spun. "I hate fuss. I just want to be on our way."

Matilda grinned at her hunched shoulders. She ushered Val before her. He was willing enough to be prodded—out of here. But then the prodding stopped. *New captors. Same goal: Get free, find Kaell.*

*How?* The shame of the past, the physical toll of the fire, the ignominy of captivity all shook him. But worst of all was doubt— that after all he had endured, he could never again be the warrior he was.

⁓◦⟜⟞⟠◦⁓

The guard led them through more whitewashed corridors. Only a few servants or slaves were about, lighting fires, dousing torches where early-morning light entered. But for their steps and the sputtering flames, that crisp stillness of dawn dampened sounds.

They entered a long room of gleaming marble with pillars buttressing a vaulted roof. At the far end, beside iron-studded doors, Judith waited.

"Do I have a moment?"

At Matilda's nod, Val went to her. Judith twisted her hands. She did not quite look at him. He bent his head to kiss her tenderly.

"I couldn't come," she murmured. "I want you to know that. Myranthe then Velleran, too, ordered me to keep my distance. But I didn't like to see you a prisoner."

He touched her flushed cheek. "I'm sorry about Heath."

For a moment, she lifted her eyes to his. Then she turned away.

"Judith."

She whirled in surprise. "Matilda. You? Here?"

The Quisnaf warrior drew her into an embrace. "You look well and little changed."

"A reunion. How sickening." Morgan threw back the doors. Sunlight streamed in, bleached by shifting clouds, but sunlight nevertheless. Val wanted to run into its brilliance and spin about like a madman.

"The high priestess Sorcha still talks fondly of you." Matilda squeezed Judith's hand. "You use your gifts wisely?"

"I use them to advance my family's interests." Judith sounded defensive.

"And this man?" Matilda nodded at Val. "What is between you?"

"It is like you to be direct, Matilda. We were intimate for a few nights. But I'd not go against my family and interfere, if that's what you're worried about."

With a flick of long, dark hair, she was gone.

"You should have asked the Ice princess more," Morgan said. "About him. Given they're acquainted in a carnal way. How do you know her?"

"A story for the road." Matilda shuffled the girl out then stepped aside for Val.

He willingly strode into a walled courtyard. Burnt orange and russet leaves flaked at the trunks of naked trees. They were skeletal, robbed of their autumnal plumage but impossibly lovely. So much space. The glorious open skies, the sun too pallid to warm his face, the crisp air nipping his neck, all buoyed his spirits with the prospect of freedom.

Guards let them through a gatehouse onto a road weaving over a bridge spanning a deep ravine. More bony trees fleeced by wind lined its stark banks above a fast-flowing river.

But for a few clumps of foliage, a vast plain stretched beyond fallow fields to snow and pine-crusted mountains. Empty. Yet Matilda shifted her eyes right and left uneasily. Morgan must have sensed her disquiet, for she touched her companion's arm. "Trouble?"

"I don't know." Matilda frowned. "I thought I saw something. Someone. Following us. Probably my imagination."

Morgan laughed. "You're twitchy. This place gets to you like that."

Val paused to stare back at the walled city built into huddled mountains. Its size was astounding. But for all its grandeur, he hoped to never see the hateful place again.

"It's not as large as Quisnaf." Matilda stood beside him. "Though, it is truly a wonder."

"A prison."

"All you see is its surface. A metaphor for the Damadars, this city."

"It would be a hard place to take."

"And you intend to conquer the Damadar twin cities?" Morgan jeered. "You and how many armies?"

Still, he did not move.

"Is this where you run?" Matilda asked quietly. "Now we're beyond the gatehouse? Though, we're still within reach of archers on the walls. If they have archers."

"They have archers," Morgan said. "In the many, many towers."

"Heath took me to a woman imprisoned in one tower. He called her Mother."

"The Mad Mother," Morgan said. "Thought they executed her for treason." She shifted impatiently. "Why are we standing about? Let's find Ross."

"Why is she the Mad Mother? And who's Ross?"

"In the answer to the first: a story for the road," Matilda said. "In answer to the second: never you mind. Now, about your plans to escape."

"And return with an army to take this city." Morgan shoved hands to her hips. "Or maybe Val Arques Caelan, victor of the infamous Contest of Swords, thinks he can do it alone."

"I know what you're thinking, Val Arques. Now we're outside the walls, you'll be plotting your escape. So I want you to try to run. To end your fantasies from the start." Matilda gestured at the plain. "Go on."

The road twisted through windswept fields of turned soil, bare of crops. The valley was flat, bowling against white-capped mountains, with little cover, crisscrossed by streams and more bridges. Withered grass rustled in a swooping wind, its scents dry like potpourri.

"A trick." His skin tingled beneath the bracelet. "It's some sort of trick."

"No doubt. But you'll never know unless you try."

She was right. For Kaell's sake, he had to try.

Val ran. When he glanced over his shoulder, neither woman had moved. Maybe they had horses to ride him down. There was nowhere to hide on the stark plain until the straggling fir trees in the foothills.

Val sprinted onto another bridge. A bolt of pain roared from the bracelet on his upper arm, tearing across his shoulder and up his neck. It flung him, moaning, to his knees.

"Step back towards us." Morgan walked towards him.

Neck ablaze, Val tried to crawl away. He managed an inch or two. The excruciating agony rolled down his back and across his breast, taking over his body.

The women reached him. The pain vanished. Unsteadily, he staggered up. The bracelet hummed. He stared at it. *Did you do that? All that from a little thing like you?*

Morgan shook him. "You kept going. What's wrong with you? The pain only gets worse, you stubborn, stubborn fool."

"The bracelet."

Morgan's sword squeaked against leather as she gleefully

jiggled from foot to foot. "Just smeared a drop or two of your blood upon it last night, said a few words as our sorceresses commanded, and we have ourselves an invisible chain."

"You're enjoying this a little too much," Val said, irritated. "You have a sweet face, but you're not very sweet at all, are you?"

"I'm a specialist. A retriever. We're not sweet. We're efficient—and fast." Her blade creased air as it whipped to his chest. Just as fast, it disappeared back into the sheath.

*Quick as a lightning bolt. And vicious in the mornings. A charming combination.*

Matilda drew Morgan aside. "Trouble, do you think? Should be here."

"Maybe someone did follow us. Though we'd see them, surely, in this denuded valley."

Val leaned his elbows on the bridge's stone, stunned by the setback of his invisible shackle. He shook his arm and its glittering adornment. What if only a sorceress could remove the bracelet?

*Stay calm. Think like Heath. A lot might happen between here and the Icelands port.*

Beneath clouds, the thin breeze nipped at his back. The river's stagnant odour rose like mist. Unlike the deep ice-blue river he had glimpsed from his tower room, a mere trickle of water covered moss-pelted stones. The sun cleared clouds. Metal glimmered.

Val squinted. "Something's there."

The women rushed to him. He pointed.

Cursing, Morgan scrambled down the banks into shallow water, stooping to lift a body by its sodden clothes. Wet hair plastered a young face. Morgan shook her head at Matilda.

"Ross," the older woman said solemnly for Val's sake. "He went into the caverns yesterday to arrange for fresh horses. The plan was to meet here with the horses at first light."

"I thought—"

"That all men are enslaved in Quisnaf? You have a lot to learn, Val Arques."

Morgan climbed back to the bridge, her face grim. "Sword wound. No money. His blade's gone too." She fisted her hands. "I can track whoever did this."

Matilda stood undecided, her body stiff with contained anger. "We keep on."

"I can track them," Morgan said, her hands still stubbornly clenched.

"I know you can. But lose a day, and that Venivan ship sails without us. We'll walk. No time for vengeance or to buy more horses."

Morgan grabbed Val's arm. "You. Help me."

Val followed her to the river. They dragged Ross out and covered his body with stones to deter beasts, at least. The other beasts. Not the cowards who'd killed a lone young man. When it was done, they set out for the distant line of mountains.

"Warriors do not walk." Morgan kicked a pebble. "I want a horse."

"Lady Muck, are you?" Matilda asked mildly.

*A universal expression apparently.* Val tried to hide his grin, but Morgan scowled.

"What are you so happy about?"

The day got no warmer. The sun struggled to pierce clouds shrouding a bleak landscape of stunted bushes and wilted grass. Wind whipped across emptiness and cut about their ears. In late afternoon, a dusting of snow fell.

Val hunched his shoulders, glad to have the fur-lined cloak, hat, and boots. He was glad to rest, too, when Matilda paused to again talk quietly with her companion.

"Are you sure?" Morgan glanced behind.

"It could be nothing. Though I'm almost certain I glimpsed someone."

"I'll scout back to see if anyone is following us."

"No. It will be dark soon." Matilda pulled out a map. "If we had delayed any longer in the Twin Cities, we might have been trapped for winter." In the poor light, she strained to read. "The long freeze, they call it."

"Where the Damadars have nothing to do except torment each other and their prisoners—or so I was told," Val said.

"Torment, huh. That wretched Alana has Damadar blood," Morgan said of some unknown Quisnaf woman. "Explains a lot."

"People think *your* blood explains a lot," Matilda said.

Morgan only grinned. Definitely after noon.

"There's no such thing as Quisnaf blood really, is there," Val said. "You're all mongrels of some sort or other."

"No need to get nasty, Val Arques," Morgan said, still amused. "Though you're right. No Quisnaf blood—only bloodlines. Powerful ones."

"What's yours?"

"Targan-ah on my father's side. He was a warrior on a raiding ship, captured in battle. My mother is a direct descendant to Dekarne. I don't mean Roaran Caelan's Dekarne, but the original member of the first Quisnaf council."

"Impressive."

Morgan's smile this time was superior. "Matilda's got Sorgaine's blood."

"Quiet, girl."

Val scratched his arm beneath the silver. "The first Quisnaf sorceress. Then this bracelet—"

"Can I remove it? That's what you want to know, isn't it? That's behind the questions."

"Not at all. Making conversation."

"Talking of bloodlines," Morgan said. "That boy of yours. The warrior bonded to your gods. What happened to him? There are all sorts of strange rumours."

"A story for the road."

"We're on the road," she snapped, her postnoon humour gone. "You sound like Matilda. She knows all these things and never says."

"Well," Val said, "it's a long walk."

Matilda stabbed a finger at her map. "Caves about two hours off." She looked at the grey sky. "We'll stop for the night."

They trudged on. Val's footsteps dragged as his strength drained. Not just the journey, but the months of confinement, the blasting winds, the chill leaching through his thick coat and fur hat, all took a toll. He fell behind.

Morgan muttered, "He'd walk faster if he got another jolt."

The ring of mountains closed slowly, their bulk no shield against wind that only tunnelled through valleys.

"Beyond"—Matilda took out the map again—"is the harbour they call the Cauldron."

In the foothills, she sent Morgan up ahead.

She returned in a scurry of pebbles. "Found a dry cave. There's peat. It'll burn just fine."

Val struggled after her up to a ledge. A cave mouth gaped at an angle to the scathing wind. With an exhausted sigh, he stumbled inside and slumped, back to a wall. Matilda unloaded a pack. Morgan soon had a fire going.

Val leaned his head against rock and fell asleep at once.

⚜

He woke hungry, his bladder full, still clad in boots and fur hat.

Near a glowing fire, Matilda slept wrapped in her cloak. When he rose, she sat up. "Don't go too far."

Val thrust out his bedecked arm. "You mean this little thing?"

She nodded. "The bracelet has a memory. You strayed once. Stray again, and the pain will be far, far worse."

"How do you know this?"

"Morgan and I both endured a taste of this magic so we'd be careful with you."

"I thank you for the warning."

"There's salted pork if you're hungry." She curled up, head on her hands.

Val lurched to the cave mouth. A sinking moon scratched at the darkness. Frost glistened on dying tufts of grass between rocks. The air was stiff with cold, the wind gone.

An arm snagged his neck. Metal pricked through cloth into his spine.

"Going somewhere?" Morgan asked. "Not learnt your lesson, then?"

Val showed his palms. "Only to relieve myself. I slept forever, I think."

The blade fell away. "You dropped like a farmhand." She gave a soft laugh. "Don't stray, Telorian."

He clambered through gnarled rocks and untied his pants. Done, he climbed back up.

A shape moved.

"Morgan?"

The figure stopped and turned.

Val's neck crept. Not Morgan. Taller. Wearing a hooded cape. Holding gleaming steel.

*Run.* The single thought ignited his limbs too late. The stranger rushed him, a drawn blade cutting off his escape.

"You. Inside." The muffled voice belonged to a woman. "Inside, I said."

Driven at sword point, he stumbled towards the cave.

A pebble rolled. The stranger half turned. "Another step, and he dies."

Morgan's shadow fell on the ground. She raised her arms. "No need to do that."

The stranger stripped Morgan of her knife and sword and hurled them into the darkness. Metal clanked on rock. "Inside."

From Morgan's taut shoulders, she intended to wait for her chance to fight. Should he help? Maybe the stranger had no interest in him, only the Quisnaf pair.

Morgan reached the cave. She started to turn. The woman shoved her. As she sprawled, the stranger pounced on Val, an arm to his breast to hold him against her, sword to his neck. Her shallow breaths warmed his cheek.

He cursed. Maybe he was her target after all.

His captor forced him inside. Matilda groped for her blade.

"Leave it." The woman swung Val to show he was one thrust from death. "Or I drive this blade up into his brain."

Matilda stilled, her face a mask.

Morgan coiled to strike. "Fool," she snarled at Val. "You let her jump you."

"What do you want?" Matilda asked the stranger. Still calm. Still in control.

"Him. I have no dispute with you. Don't interfere, and you don't get hurt."

That voice. He knew it. *Could it be? Could it?* A vivid memory, very clear, formed in his head. The castle at Vraymorg. Trenchers, wineglasses upon a long table. A young woman seated across from him. Monster, she'd called him. Monster.

Recklessly, Val yanked at his captor's hood. He nearly staggered. Even in poor light, even in profile, he recognised her. Azenor. But not Azenor. Kaell in Azenor's skin. Here.

"You. It's you. How are you here?" His heart skidded across his ribs.

"You know her?" Morgan stared. "She's come to rescue you? Some Telorian girl? Ha."

"Not rescue."

Hearing Kaell's Mountains lilt, so familiar, Val was certain. He nearly sobbed in relief. Kaell was alive. *Alive. Thank The Three. Thank every god.*

"He and I are going to talk. If I don't like his answers... I'll kill him."

Val jolted against Kaell's arm. Vertigo shook him. His thoughts froze then released into chaos. *He blames me. Thinks I did this to hurt him. I have to explain.*

"We can't allow that," Matilda said.

"He's ours," Morgan said. Still crouched. Still ready. "Paid for."

"Paid for?" Kaell breathed close to Val's ear. "Is that right?" He laughed mirthlessly. "And what do you intend to do with him?"

They watched him with cool eyes.

"Not talking? No need. You're Quisnaf, so I can guess." Kaell laughed harder.

"If he's your enemy," Morgan said, "leave him to us. If you know anything of the Quisnaf, you'll know he won't be heard of again."

"Name your price to surrender him," Matilda said. "Whoever you are."

"Whoever I am—" Cold metal dented Val's neck. Val had taught him that strong, defensive hold. If the captive squirmed, one thrust skewered the brain. "Ask him who I am."

"A child, I'd say," Morgan taunted. "With a big sword she doesn't know how to use."

"This is… Azenor Caelan." Val's voice faded. He trembled, unable to grasp Kaell's bewildering appearance in the middle of nowhere.

"She's dead," Morgan said. "Ghouls killed her and her brother. Such a waste of rare Caelan blood."

"Name your price," Matilda said.

"My price—" Kaell gave another harsh laugh. "What price betrayal?"

"Betrayal?"

"My lord and I are overdue a long talk. Then he'll pay for what he did to me."

"Your lord?" Matilda echoed, puzzled.

Morgan dived at her companion's blade. Val knocked Kaell's arm away. He weaved clear as the Quisnaf warrior swung at Kaell. Locked blades shrieked. The two combatants sprang apart. They circled, their shadows long on the ground, distorted by the fire's glow on rock walls. Sizing each other up.

Yelling, Morgan broke the impasse with a violent slash. Kaell weaved back. A storm of strokes exploded, each at the other with clanking, ringing steel, their feet dizzyingly fast in the tight space.

Val flattened against a wall as swishing metal carved air. Fear for Kaell turned his gut. For all Kaell's training, he couldn't possibly in Azenor's body hold off a warrior produced by centuries of harsh Quisnaf breeding.

And Morgan was relentless. Her steps were lithe, her bladework swift. But Kaell answered every furious stroke skilfully. He swept iron across then crashed it down, his face a mask of concentration as he countered her speed.

Impossible… unless Kaell had transformed Azenor's body and adapted his style to this new form. Yes, he should have realised at once. Kaell was just as deadly as ever.

They broke apart. Morgan prowled, seeking an opening. Wary, Kaell moved with her. At her simple thrust, he blocked at the last moment, as if expecting a feint, then swung high. The Quisnaf warrior ducked, smirking. He cut at her legs. She jumped. The smirk widened. She didn't see the danger. She didn't know who this really was.

Morgan took up the attack again, stabbing low. Kaell defended then answered with a jab.

"Not bad," Morgan taunted as she skipped clear. "Who'd have thought some Isles princess could riposte—"

Kaell slashed at her calf. She knocked steel aside. Lunged. He took the blow with the thickest part of his sword. Blades caught, Kaell pressed with ghoul strength, forcing her weapon down.

Afraid now for Morgan, Val took a hesitant step. Sweat beaded on her hairline as she strained to break Kaell's hold. He whipped his sword away. Overcommitted, Morgan stumbled. She fell heavily against the wall. Her forehead hit stone. Her knees buckled.

"Morgan!" Matilda dived for a knife in a strewn belt.

Kaell darted in to kick the belt away. Then he turned on Morgan. Dazed, she tried to lift her blade. Kaell stood over her, sword raised.

"No!" Val started forward. "Kaell, no."

Kaell whirled. Disbelief twisted his face. "You'd take her part against me?" His voice broke up. "A stranger's part?"

"No. You don't understand—"

Kaell threw up a palm to stop him. He tossed what looked like vine at Matilda. "Tie her hands. Then yours."

The Quisnaf woman did as he bid. Kaell bent to tighten the vine about her wrists then checked Morgan's bonds.

"Kaell, you can't leave them—"

Kaell thrust the sword against his ribs. "Move. Outside."

Val could not command his legs, could not take this in. Kaell. Here. They were at last together. There was so much to say. But this Kaell he didn't know. Not only did this man wear a different face, but he was ruthless and unfeeling in a way the boy he had raised never was. "I don't understand how you're here. How did you find me?"

"I was watching the city gates. For days. I didn't know where else to look for you. Move, I said."

"I can't. This—" He pushed his cloak back to reveal the bracelet. "Binds me to them. I have to stay close. If this bracelet is too far from the others, the pain cripples me."

"I don't believe you. Outside."

Val studied his pitiless expression.

"Kaell—"

"No. Do not talk. I'm not ready for more of your lies. Just walk."

"Kaell, listen—"

"Are you deaf? I said shut up. One more word, and I knock you out and drag you."

Swallowing hard, Val staggered from the cave. Dawn edged the horizon, a palette of streaming grey and rose. The heavy air was snow scented. The plains stretching back towards the distant walls of the Twin Cities seemed peaceful, at odds with the turmoil in Val's mind.

*This is my fault.* He had stabbed Kaell with that sword, without explanation, without assurances, and left him alone to face what could not make sense. Of course Kaell was angry. Of course he blamed him. He had to put this right.

His boots dislodged pebbles as he stumbled down the slope, braced for the pain. Every nerve pricked, the waiting unbearable. He wanted to yell in frustration.

Then it hit. Worse than before. Val screamed. His knees and hands hit the ground.

"It's a trick." Kaell prodded him with steel. "Get up."

Val nearly wept. Crescendo after crescendo of agony roared through him. "No trick," he breathed. "The bracelets are too far apart."

"Curse it." Kaell stomped off.

His skull imploding, Val could not crawl, could hardly breathe. No one could stand this for long. He willed himself to pass out. He *must* pass out.

Footsteps crunched on shingles. The pain vanished. Kaell leaned over him, staring curiously. He dangled a bracelet in his fingertips.

Drained, Val sprawled as lifeless as a straw doll. Slowly, his battered mind took in what the bracelet meant. Morgan had said they could not be removed. "No. You didn't. Tell me you didn't—"

"How little you think of me. I didn't kill them. The older one took it off her arm. In fact, pleaded with me not to hurt you. Get up."

Val dragged himself awkwardly to his knees.

Kaell dumped a length of a trailing vine beside him. "Tie your hands."

"What is this vine?"

"You mean you don't know?" Kaell considered him pitilessly. "I thought you knew everything."

"Very little, it seems. What happened to you? How are you here?"

"Your hands. Tight. No tricks."

This was his chance. *Resist. Grab the bracelet. Run.*

But he didn't want to run. He had to talk to Kaell. To understand his anger. To explain. If that meant restraints, if that meant Kaell hurt him, then so be it. Reluctantly, he looped the vine about his wrists. Kaell wrenched it tight.

Exhausted, hollowed by shock and pain, Val drew a long breath, summoning every reserve of strength. "What now?"

"Walk."

Val managed to push to his feet and stagger down the uneven slope. Every time he tripped, Kaell rapped an impatient "get up." On level ground, he shoved him. "I said, move."

Val stumbled, fighting for balance. He had no words, let alone the right words, to pierce Kaell's mistrust. "Where are we going?"

"Just walk."

"Kaell—"

"Shut up."

"Listen. Please."

His companion grunted irritably. "Not yet. Later. So take this time to think hard, my lord, about what you intend to say."

Val turned his head to peer at him, to stare into hard eyes he didn't recognise. He had no clue what to say to this stranger.

The sun rose late behind grey clouds. Chill air nipped like teeth. Scents swirled: Azara's faint vanilla. Spidery butterflowers on shrubs smelling of witch hazel. The prick of snow.

They walked in silence. It brimmed with too much to be easily broken. Kaell's anger and hurt. His distance. Val's guilt and shock.

"You can't leave them like that," he blurted at last. "The Kaell I know—"

"The Kaell you know?" A bitter laugh burst from his companion.

Val turned. "What happened to you? Tell me."

"Another word, and I gag you."

Val remembered Azenor's warmth that night they drank wine and argued. Now he looked upon a face as cold as carved stone. There was no compassion there. But no indifference, either. Kaell's fury bound them. A dangerous bond, but something at least.

"Seen enough? This is what you did to me. Before you threw me to *him*. Now move."

*Him. Who was this him?* Val stumbled forward, his mouth stale with thirst. His belly rumbled. *Find a way to uncover Kaell's wounds. Help him.*

He tried again. "What happened to you?"

"Who are you? Lord of questions? Shut up and walk. I need to think."

The day lengthened into a cold, never-ending nightmare. Val lurched on and on, his feet dragging, the chill bleeding through his cloak and tunic into his bones. Near dusk, they reached a gorge shadowed by stark sheets of rock. Swirling wind whistled in the valley between bare mountains, nipping at a cylinder etched against the slate sky. A tower. In the middle of a wasteland.

"What is that?" Val's steps faltered. At this break in his shuffling rhythm, exhaustion hit him.

"Tower tomb."

Val swayed. The horizon blurred. He fell but didn't feel it.

"Get up," Kaell said.

The sky rolled around. Val groaned. "I think… I think I'm going to be sick." He retched bile then collapsed to his belly.

"Good gods." Kaell yanked him up. "Why are you so weak?"

"We don't all have ghoul blood."

"We don't all have Caelan blood, either." At his jolt, Kaell jeered. "Surprised I know that, *Val Arques Caelan*? Of course I had to hear your name from someone else. Now walk on." He shoved.

Val yawed towards the tower tomb. Gaunt, black, with stark,

windowless walls, it looked part of the forbidding, windswept land. "My older brother lies in a tower like this." He had to pierce Kaell's anger. "I remember my mother's tears, how my father rested his calloused hand on his dead son's brow just before they closed the lid."

"Shut up," Kaell said.

"Tower tombs fell out of favour centuries ago. Too easy a target for raiders."

Kaell didn't respond. Why should he? Tombs, raiders didn't matter. Only reaching Kaell mattered. Except he didn't have those words.

A single entrance led into the slender tower of hewn stone. At Kaell's shove, Val reeled through the rectangular doorway and fell to his knees again. "Water, please." The words hurt his throat.

Kaell dumped a bag by a stone-lidded sarcophagus and stepped around him to prowl about the dry stone chamber. Round columns fluted an ornate, carved roof, the sculpted patterns of flowers and vines smoothed by time. Steps spiralled up a corner stairwell.

Val flopped onto his back. The emptiness, the odours of flaked stone and dust—the perfume of every forsaken, deserted shell—seeped into him.

"Here." Kaell shoved a waterskin at him. Val took it then struggled to one elbow to drink.

Kaell watched him, his expression odd. Then he rose to wander again.

Between gulps, Val followed his restless steps. "Kaell."

"What?"

"You need to know—"

"That you gutted me with a sword and I woke up like this?" Kaell brushed his hands down Azenor's body. "I must sleep. I tracked the Quisnaf from the gates through the night."

"Those women. You can't leave them like that. Once the fire burns out, they'll freeze."

"Is that what you think of me?" Kaell asked. He was very still. "That I left them to die?"

"Kaell. No. I—"

"I left a knife." Kaell turned his back. "When I returned for that bracelet."

Val released a relieved breath. Some part of the Kaell he had raised remained. He could reach him. He had to.

"I need to sleep." Kaell spun back to consider him. "But what to do with you? I know your mettle. I can't have you running off."

"Make that crawl off. You can chain me to a rock again, and I'm too tired to care."

A flicker of interest pierced Kaell's cool stare. Then he shrugged.

Val sank to the floor, rested his head on his bound hands, and slept.

⸻✦⸻

Coldness ruptured his dreams. Shivering, Val opened his eyes to grey light.

Kaell sat on the floor near him, his arms around his knees. Watching him. Val couldn't unravel his expression.

"How long was I out?" Using his elbows to rise, Val put his back to a pillar. He stretched his cramped legs.

Kaell passed the waterskin again. Wrists bound, Val clutched it awkwardly, wondering if he might be fed. Probably not. Hungry meant compliant. He'd taught Kaell that.

Uneasy, he glanced about. Sickly dawn stole through cracks. The wind's howl tormented walls. Not a good place to die—if Kaell intended to kill him. Or *try* to kill him.

Kaell had learnt his name. Perhaps he had also learnt weapons brought him only a temporary death.

"It's creepy if you spent the night watching me." Val sought an opening to prod a conversation.

"No, I slept. Once you passed out." Kaell rose to stalk.

With every step, Val sensed his growing indecision. He could reach him. Kaell was angry. So angry. He was trying to be cruel, trying to hurt him but only because he himself was hurting.

"Kaell."

"Val Arques Caelan." He whirled. "What?"

"I wanted to save you. I meant to be with you when you woke. To explain."

Kaell's expression shuttered.

A sharp pull hurt Val's breast. *How alone he must feel. If I had just been there. Curse Heath Damadar. Curse every Damadar.*

"I couldn't get to you." Pitiful, inadequate words. "I was desperate to get to you."

Kaell kicked a piece of broken stone. "I came to… like this. All I remembered was you with the sword. Why did you do this to me? Why do this then abandon me?"

*Abandon.* There it was. The heart of his pain. "That last day in the king's camp, I had one thought only—to save your life. Then a man came to me and told me how it might be done."

"Arn."

Val shifted uncomfortably. "How do you—"

"The question is did you know what they intended? Did you throw me to him?"

*Him?* "I called Arn a traitor." Val thought back to that awful night. "He shot me in the leg—"

"I wondered why you limped."

"So I would at least listen."

"You're not always good at that."

Val arched a brow.

Kaell blew out that bitter laugh. "Not how you think of yourself, Val Arques Caelan? *Val Arques Caelan.*" He shook his head. "You didn't even trust me with your name."

"I couldn't tell you. How could I? You don't know what that name means."

"It means you lied to me. Right from the start. Everything, a lie. When you said those words, when you at last said—" Kaell looked away. He dragged his hand through cropped hair. "Did you try to find me? Did you care enough to even look?"

Val made a sound. Half a moan. Half a rending of breath. "Finding you was all I thought about. Saving you. It isn't fair what happened. It isn't fair that I wasn't there, Kaell."

Kaell spread his arms. "Is this saving me, my lord? Saving me for what? Or who? Better dead, Val Arques Caelan, than what you did to me."

"Not better. You're alive. The rest, we'll figure out."

"There is no *we*. All these months, there's only been me. Where were you? Why weren't you there?" He looked right into Val's eyes. A hard, challenging stare. But Val caught a flicker, just a flicker of something vulnerable and needy beneath.

"I wasn't there because Heath Damadar chained me up in a dark hole."

Kaell stilled. He tongued his lips. "Then… then you were a prisoner."

"Since that battle. Months and months."

"They said you were dead. I mourned you, my lord." Kaell's laugh sounded crazed. "Then when I learnt you knew all about me—"

"Kaell—"

"That you'd always known. Who I was. Where I came from. That you stole me from my mother. My father. When I learnt that, I wanted to hurt you for what you took from me."

"The city burned," Val said slowly. His ribs lassoed his heart. Who had told Kaell about Seithin? No one knew. "The Wardorian army put everyone to the sword. That day I took you would have been your last."

Kaell dug his nails into a pillar's crumbly edge. "And this life you chose for me is better? To grow up so badly wanting your love, but every day, having to fight for it. Wondering if you withheld your affection because I wasn't good enough, strong enough, that I disappointed you."

"Oh gods. Is that what you think?"

"Then at last, you tell me exactly what I want. You tell me you think of me as your son, only to do this to me."

Val dropped his head into his bound hands. "I thought I'd be there. It's all gone wrong, and I don't know how to fix it. To save you." All words that should have been said six months ago. Now his explanations sounded like an excuse because they were too late.

"Stop saying that." Kaell fisted his hands at his side. "About saving me. You didn't. You only threw me to him. You must have known what he wanted."

*Him. Archanin?*

"Kaell, who's this *him?* I don't understand—"

"Is this saved? Look at me, my lord."

How easily Kaell slipped back into old habits of address. And his stance—so familiar. Shoulders up, his back taut, his anger drawn into those clenched hands.

Val's heart splintered. He couldn't bear this.

"Look hard at me," Kaell shouted, his voice echoing about the miserable chamber. "I'm trapped in her body. In the body of the woman who betrayed me."

In the face of such raw, awful pain, Val whispered, "I had to try. I couldn't let you die. I thought I'd be there to explain. But I couldn't get to you." He slammed his head against the pillar. "Curse the Damadars. Curse them."

Kaell still stared. "Why?" he asked, his voice broken. "Why couldn't you let me die?"

He knew what Kaell wanted to hear.

"Why?" Kaell's eyes were too bright.

A silence rose about them. Val should have filled that silence with the truth. He didn't. For he heard an echo of Myranthe's voice, insidious, slyly feeding his self-loathing.

*Perhaps I should have scarred you. So every time you look at the scar, you remember I know the truth and saw you as you really are.*

He wasn't worthy of love. To love. Kaell could not want that from him, the man who cut his wrists to escape what he couldn't face.

Kaell's shoulders fell. "You still have nothing for me. I'm still alone."

"No," Val said.

"You think I'm a monster. You think now I have Archanin's blood, I'm cruel enough to leave two strangers to freeze to death. That's what you think of me."

"No. That's not what I think."

"I know what I want." Kaell folded his arms over his chest, a wall against hurt, against rejection. "I can't have it. It doesn't matter."

"It matters," Val said.

"And yet…" His voice shattered against the walls. "You still don't say it."

The cold imprinted on Val's skin, like the cold stealing through shutters that night Myranthe had destroyed him. The air laden with beeswax. With sandalwood.

Val pressed his roped wrists to his brow, hiding his face. Hiding those white scars. "I have nothing to offer you. Not the protection of my position. Not my strength. How can I, a broken man, dare offer you love? You don't know… if you saw me as I am, it would disgust you to hear those words from me. I'm nothing anymore. No one."

"You're my lord," Kaell cried. "You're the man I think of as a father." The words echoed around stone. A brief ringing. Then they died away.

*I want to immure you from pain,* Val thought. *From everything bad in this world.* He had to tell Kaell the truth, to ignore Myranthe's whisper in his head. Otherwise, he may as well have stayed curled on the floor in that tower cell, his mind emptied of his past.

*Be free of it.* He could hear Heath, too, shouting down his sister's taunts. *Forgive yourself. Be free. If I could give a gift to you—*

"I didn't lie to you," he whispered. "Kaell, I didn't lie. I love you as my son."

Kaell did not answer. His expression closed. A soft moan escaped his parted lips.

"I love you blindly, protectively," Val said. "When someone hurts you, I want to rip them apart with my teeth. If I could offer my life to save you, I would."

A mask crumpled from Kaell's face like dried clay. His breath released in a sob. "I can't hear this. I thought I could, but it's too late."

"I see." Val's mouth tasted stale. "You hate me. I am a coward for not saying this before, and now it's too late. I understand."

The young man dragged his hands down Azenor's cheeks. "No, you don't. I don't deserve these words. Not now. Not after what I've done."

How could Kaell believe that? What had happened to him in these months? Val desperately wanted to pull him against his breast, stroke his hair. "None of it matters, Kaell. Not to me. I'll always be proud of you."

"How can you say that? I was cruel. The way I tied your hands and brought you here. I was trying to punish you. You should hate me."

"You only did that because you're hurting. Let me help you."

"It was my sword, wasn't it?" Kaell turned his back. His shoulders rose. "How can you help me when you don't have it?"

"Heath took it off me, so it must now be in Myranthe Damadar's possession."

"Then I'll get the sword off Myranthe. If it did this to me, it can undo it."

"Kaell, listen to me. I don't know what half-cocked idea you have about this sword, but the spell that changed you was blood magic. Neither of us is a sorcerer."

Kaell swung on him. "First, I'll get the sword. Then I'll worry about that."

"If anyone is going into the Damadar city, it's me. This is my fault. I can't have you risking your life. The moment a bonded warrior steps in those caverns, Myranthe will know. She'll arrest you. Strip away your secrets."

"Did she strip away *your* secrets, my lord? Perhaps in her rooms when you were alone?"

Val winced at the sting of memory. He said nothing.

Kaell watched Val's face for a long moment. "Sorry. She hurt you; I can see it. All the more reason why it has to be me who goes for the sword." He drew down a shuddering breath. His voice was weary. "I couldn't bear it if she hurt you again, my lord."

A bright flare of hope took hold in Val's breast. It would be all right. He and Kaell—they would be all right. "It's too dangerous for you in that awful place. Velleran has no reason to treat you kindly. And Myranthe isn't what you think. She's powerful."

Kaell spluttered a laugh. "I'm not what you think, either."

So much in that laugh. Val knew that a man might let his anger consume all else because it didn't hurt as much as sorrow. "What happened to you? Tell me. Let me help you."

"No. This is my problem. I'll find a way into the Damadar caverns."

Val staggered up. He moved between Kaell and the door. "I can't let you go alone. Even if I have to hit you, I won't let you risk your life."

Kaell sighed. He grabbed Val and dragged him towards a stone casket. Twisting in panic, Val muttered, "No, no, don't."

"I didn't think anything frightened you, my lord. Don't worry, you'll be alone in there. I cleared out the old bones while you slept."

"I don't fear a few bones. I'm afraid for you, Kaell. Let me go in your place."

Kaell dumped him into the casket. "Please understand. As much as you want to save me, I want to keep you safe, my lord."

"Kaell, think this through. It's reckless to go there without a proper plan. Besides, once you have the sword, what then? You keep saying you don't want to be in her body. But if not that body, then whose?"

Kaell partially pulled the lid back. "I'll leave you air, my lord. Oh." He dangled the Quisnaf bracelet in his fingers. "Best give you this. And water." He dropped the bracelet and a waterskin through the gap.

"Kaell, let me come with you. You're walking into danger."

Kaell's gaze dwelled on Val's face. "Don't you see I'm trying to protect you?"

Once, Val would have declared without hesitation that he could protect himself, but the words caught in his throat. He swallowed. "You don't have to do this alone."

"I can't do this at all if I have to worry about you. At least if I leave you in there, I know nothing or no one can steal you away again." He smiled faintly. "Be back soon, my lord."

Light died as the stone lid ground into place. Val beat his lashed wrists against it. "Let me out. Don't do this."

"I'll keep well away from Myranthe, my lord." Kaell's voice sounded close, as though he'd put his lips to a crack. "She won't even know I'm there. No, I've heard enough about Velleran Damadar to get him to invite me in. Then I'll find the sword."

"You don't want him to invite you anywhere, Kaell. Velleran is vain, but he's no fool."

"I'm counting on that."

A sword slid into a scabbard. Footsteps moved towards the door. An abandoned stillness folded about the tower again.

# KAELL

Air thick with cold closed around him. A hush webbed, as if the passage to the Damadar caverns was cut off not only from the city boiling with chaotic life but also from time. The only sound was rain breaking against the mountain, its drum on roofs, its murmur against leaves, its trickle through paved streets.

Kaell paused to listen. Beating rain was a safe sound, one he'd heard from within Vraymorg's thick walls. As it slanted against the wind, driving into stone, he'd often nestle with a book by the fire in his lord's rooms while Vraymorg bent over ordinances. He remembered how scents of burning tallow or beeswax whorled from a candle on the table.

Sometimes, Kaell would watch Vraymorg's expressions, every concentrated grimace, even how he dragged fingers through his hair and muttered. Often, he swept papers from the table, grabbed his sword, and stomped outside to seek physical release from tedium.

For all these memories, he'd never truly known his lord. Not Val Arques Caelan. What had Arn said of him? *"He'll find a way to forgive."*

*Forgive.* The promise in that word shook him. Kaell thrust a hand to the wall. He had the only thing he'd ever wanted. Words he'd waited a lifetime to hear. So many times he had imagined how they might sound. How it might be. He and Vraymorg alone. His lord's look softening. His hand on Kaell's shoulder.

*I'm proud of you. I love you like my son.*

Now those precious words were said. But they'd come too late. He no longer deserved to hear them.

Kaell pushed off the wall, trying to order his thoughts. First, trick Velleran into taking him into his family's quarters. Then find the sword. Be rid of Azenor's body. Be free of Roaran's twisted purpose.

The rain's steady throb was an ominous accompaniment as he walked on to doors flanked by guards. They crossed spears to bar his way.

Kaell said, "I want to talk to Velleran Damadar."

"What business do you have with the young lord, girl?"

He hesitated. It wasn't too late to turn back. He could say he'd made a mistake, return to that tower tomb, and let his lord sort out this mess. How easy it would be to fall back into the patterns of childhood, to place his troubles in his lord's hands.

"Velleran will want to talk to me."

A guard levelled his spear. Kaell did not move as the tip touched his belly.

"Who shall I say wants the young lord?"

"Tell him…" Kaell seized a breath. "Tell him it's Azenor Caelan."

Beneath the rain, leather soles slapped tiles. An immaculate man, his beard trim, his dark-brown hair brushed back and shining, burst through the door. A servant trailed behind, muttering "This way, my lord. This way."

The man swept past the guards to Kaell, his steps haughty, a fur-lined cloak swishing the top of delicately stitched, supple boots. A sword's hilt poked from a scabbard tied to his belt. "What is this nonsense? Who is this imposter?"

The servant bustled at his side. "My lord Velleran, the guards said—they said—"

Velleran whipped up a jewelled hand. "Azenor?" With certainty, he said, "Azenor. Good gods. How? Everyone thinks you're dead."

"Not dead, no. But I need your protection."

No one spoke. The guards and the servant all stared.

Velleran grasped Kaell's waist to pull him into an embrace. Then he kissed him. Kaell had time only to gasp, registering the soapy fragrance of the man's hair and a hint of wine on his breath, before the Ice lord pulled away.

"I remember a hot, still night in the Isles, Azenor. You were so eager, so innocent. So lovely."

"I am no longer so innocent." Kaell glanced behind, wondering if he could flee. The danger in this place didn't lie in discovery but in an Ice lord's desire.

"Perhaps it's best we talk in private." With a beckoning hand, Velleran turned.

Kaell followed him into the Damadar inner chambers, through passages secluded from the world, where shadows careened and torchlight muted like orange fog. Even the rain fell away. There was only this strange domain of whipping flames and hewed stone.

They passed a beautiful woman walking arm in arm with a dark-haired man. At the sight of Kaell, the man rocked to a halt. He opened his mouth to speak, but the woman put a hand on his arm and shook her head.

Kaell hid his disquiet. There was something familiar about the man, though he couldn't place him. He walked on, his steps less certain, aware the man's eyes held on his back as Velleran led him into a pitch-black chamber. Shards of light from the passage died at the threshold. Air sharp with cold clung like a heavy curtain.

Too still. Too dark. He edged back. "Why are we here?"

Velleran moved very close, his breaths uneven. He pushed Kaell against the wall. "Because you're as lovely as I remember."

Beneath the Ice lord's weight, beneath his pressing lips, Kaell fought panic.

"Not here," he whispered. "The stone hurts my back. Take me somewhere more comfortable."

Velleran slid Kaell's arm up the wall. His kiss demanded more, his tongue straining at clenched lips.

Kaell's belly lurched. He wrenched his head aside. "You're hurting me."

Steel snapped about his pinned wrist. For a heartbeat, he didn't understand. Then a whip of fear hit him. Gasping in shock, Kaell wrenched at his manacled hand. Iron chinked against the stone wall, a pathetic echo in the blackness.

Velleran still crushed against him. Mouth close to Kaell's ear, he said, "Do you take me for a fool? Azenor Caelan and I were never lovers. I've never even met the girl."

"Let me go." Kaell yanked at the shackle. With his free hand, he shoved Velleran off him. "You have no right to restrain me."

To Kaell's relief, Velleran moved away. A torch flared. Its gleam fell on cobwebs, on grimy grey-stone walls. Murk stretched into nothing.

"My sister knew you'd come," Velleran said coolly. "She said you'd try to deceive me."

Kaell dropped his head. His lord had been right. Myranthe Damadar was powerful. But she could not know who he really was. With his strength, he would escape her trap.

Velleran brushed the back of his hand down Kaell's cheek. "A pity you're not Azenor. I might take you to my bedchamber, undress you slowly, kiss you softly."

"Let me go," Kaell said, unable to keep his voice steady. "This is a mistake."

"Less a mistake and more a puzzle." Velleran stepped back to consider his captive. "You do look so like Aric. That same shade of hair, the cheekbones, the lips. Of course if you were indeed Azenor, this might be a touching reunion."

"What do you mean?"

Velleran walked away. At the door, he paused. "I mean, I've brought you to him. Aric Caelan lies in a casket at the back of this room. For now, at least, he's dead."

Swooping panic turned Kaell's stomach, his breaths thin gasps. Minutes measured in the whip of torch flames. Too few flickers, a mere handful, passed before the door opened. A woman entered.

She was dressed splendidly in a woollen gown and cloak, her slender neck adorned with a necklace of turquoise stones glistening in light that also caught strands of red in her hair. Bracelets curled about her wrists.

She was also splendidly arrogant. It was there in the tilt of her head, the frozen, condescending smile. This woman expected to get exactly what she wanted.

No one needed to tell him her name. Myranthe Damadar.

Kaell slammed a fist into the wall. The sorceress was wasting his time. He had to find the sword then return to the man he had left with only a single waterskin. His lord depended on him to keep him alive. Needed him. *Him.*

At the power he held over his lord, a dark satisfaction rose in him. At once, Kaell was ashamed. It wasn't right to take pleasure in that.

Myranthe leaned towards him, her sandalwood perfume out of place in this abhorrent, dark cavity.

Kaell was too aware of her nearness, not sexually, but with a prey's awareness of a circling hunter. He shoved his back into the wall, wanting a barrier between them. Chained, he couldn't hide, only endure her searching look. It was impersonal. Predatory.

"I've been waiting for you." She paused until he lifted his eyes to hers. When a shiver of premonition tore down his spine, only then did she add, "Kaell."

Kaell heard his name. He saw her gloating smile. But he could not take it in.

Torchlight lit the top of her head, the thrum of flames part of his heartbeat as his trembling body recognised the danger before his mind did.

She knew who he was. She'd known he would come. She had merely waited for a foolish, overconfident young man to stroll into her caverns, thinking to deceive a sorceress.

Myranthe raised her eyebrows. "What, no protests? No denials?"

Kaell forced words out through his fear. "Is there a point?"

"No. But a bit of bluster is expected. It might be amusing to listen to your feeble attempts to persuade me I'm mistaken."

"How?" he stammered. "How did you know?"

"Oh, Kaell." Menace crept beneath her patronising tone. "I'm the most powerful sorceress this side of Quisnaf. Did you think you could come here, to my home, and I wouldn't know? Did you think you could remain hidden when I glimpsed you in every fire vision I conjured?"

"How—" He wet his lips nervously. "How did you know to look for me?"

"Because of something in *his* manner when he spoke of you. I guessed he didn't believe you were dead and asked the gods to reveal you to me in visions. I knew you'd come for him. Your lord."

Kaell could not speak. Wretched, he sagged against the wall. He was in trouble. And he had trapped the one man who could help him.

Light spilled through the open door. Velleran returned, not a hair out of place. The cloak sat well too. All very lordly. This pair made Kaell sick. They had no right to look pristinely groomed, comfortable, and calm when nausea soured his throat.

"He looks like Aric." Velleran waved a hand. "Are you sure this isn't Azenor?"

"Azenor Caelan was a spoilt princess who cared only about fluttering her eyelids at whichever handsome warrior caught her fancy. This young man is something else entirely."

"What do you want?" Kaell uselessly jerked his wrist against thick metal.

"A Mountains accent." Velleran nodded. "Why does he look like this?"

"A spell." Myranthe's gaze did not leave Kaell. "I'm beginning to suspect who's behind this. Only I don't see the point of it. It makes this boy very interesting. And also very useful."

Kaell seethed. "What do you want?"

Myranthe slid his hair between her fingers in wonder. "Why did he do this to you, bonded warrior? Roaran's plots go deep, and I think you know why."

"You don't need me anymore, do you?" Velleran yawned. "My captains gather to plan our invasion of Adorean."

"Go," Myranthe said, distracted. "I wish to talk to him. Alone."

The door clanged. The walls closed in, their dark, cheerless stone threatening.

"So you were his?" Her voice was breathy, her touch on his cheek tender. "The son Val Arques did not have."

"He said that?" At once, Kaell realised what he had given away.

Her look sharpened. "Oh." The single word stripped him bare. Myranthe laughed. There was no merriment in it, only cruel fascination. "You love him. Is that why you're here? To save this man you love?"

"That's nothing to do with you."

"Oh, Kaell. I understand now. How magnificent Val must have seemed to a child. So powerful. A formidable warrior. Master of all you could see. And there you were, following him about, seeking any kind of attention. A smile. Praise. A fond word."

"You know nothing of me or him."

Her malicious smile taunted. "What sort of father was he? A distant one, I'd guess. Holding part of himself separate and hidden. And that only made you want his love more."

"Shut up," Kaell said. Her words struck too deep. His lord was right. She unmasked not only his yearning but his pain. What a fool he'd been to come here.

"Such a shame I don't have the time to sift you like I sifted him. I should like to draw out every bit of your longing. Paw it. Dissect it. Show you how pitiful and pathetic it is. If only you knew how broken that man is. Then you would never expect what he cannot give."

Kaell tilted his chin. "Broken? No one can break him."

"Dear boy," she mocked, "I've seen him cowering in a corner. Curled, knees to his belly, weeping. He's not what you think, Kaell. He's not even *who* you think."

"I know who he is."

"Do you?" She stroked his hair. "If he let you into that secret, then you mean even more to him than I imagined. If only I had you in my power when he was here. What games we could have played. How I might have used you to manipulate him. Bend him."

"I would never let you use me to hurt him. I'd kill myself first."

Myranthe studied him intently. Torchlight glistened on beads of sweat on her hairline. Beneath the cold, a metallic bite to the air reminded him of the mordant scent of battlefields.

"How you love him," she said. "My brother loved him too. I understand Heath's fascination. A curious man, Val Arques. A man who withstood the darkness by ignoring it. But the darkness does not go away just because we pretend it is not there. It waits. It festers. It grows stronger. Forces us to look at it. Then it reflects back every weakness, every fear."

"What did you do to him?" Kaell whispered.

How could he have thought he had wanted to punish Vraymorg for lying to him? He ached at even the idea of this sorceress hurting his lord.

"I broke him, Kaell," she said. "I uncovered his secrets, as I always do. And this man you love had one secret he held too close. He is gone from here, but he is not the same man. He will always know I saw his shame."

The shock of her words struck him hard. His lord—broken. Because of some hidden shame. "Are you proud of this? Proud you destroyed this man? Is that what makes your blood run hot, sorceress? The pain of others?"

Myranthe pressed her palm into stone near his shoulder. Her stare held on his face, her perfume as tenuous as lambent torchlight in the oppressive, joyless blackness. "Let's talk about *your* pain, Kaell. Your need for his love, his attention. Poor child. You didn't know how damaged he is, what he's done."

"I don't care what he's done. Broke him? Destroyed him? You did not. There's a purity in him even a vile creature like you cannot stain." Arn's words. He realised he believed them.

The torch spluttered and died, throwing her into darkness. The quiet exposed the drag of her breath. Slow. Steady. Her gown rustled against stone as she struck a flint. When new light flared, her expression seemed altered. Thoughtful. "Pure. Can there be purity and shame and guilt together?"

"Yes," Kaell said.

Myranthe brought the torch close to his face. "And yet… did you ever wonder about his wrists? How old were you when you first asked why your lord, one of Telor's most powerful men, took up a knife and did that?"

"I didn't wonder," Kaell said.

"You were never curious about what happened to him, what could be so horrific that he wanted to end his life?"

"I didn't wonder."

"I can tell you if you like. About what took place in a tower room, bright with sunlight."

"No," Kaell said.

"I can tell you why he picked up that knife, why he sought

death, an ending, rather than endure what was unendurable. He was nineteen. Younger than you. Will I tell you?"

"No."

As if absorbing how her barbs went in, her gaze did not move from him. She shrugged. "So be it. Hold onto your illusions about him. But know this: Your beloved lord's shame is no longer buried. He carries it with him. And because he cannot forgive himself for not only what he submitted to but what he didn't do, the past, not me, will destroy him."

With that, she left him.

Silence closed about Kaell. Angry at himself, he strained against iron until his wrist bled.

So stupid. To end up a prisoner. He had to find the sword and get back to Vraymorg. Whatever sat between them, there was more to be said. More to be understood. Myranthe had uncovered that, at least.

Kaell dropped his head against the wall. He closed his eyes, imagining the tomb in that bleak, colourless desert of wind and frost, hearing again those simple words. *I love you as my son.*

To think he believed he could hurt his lord. Khir help him, he'd been so cruel. Because he had been angry. Where was that stupid anger now?

He could have told his lord the truth. That for all Vraymorg's secrets, he would never think less of him. That this man might not be his father by blood, but he wished it was so.

Light briefly pooled at the door. Careful footsteps closed.

Kaell braced. He was not ready for Myranthe to bloodlessly batter him again.

"Azenor." The man from the passage waved a torch in his face. "By The Three, it is you."

Kaell cursed inwardly. He didn't need another complication.

"How are you alive? Why are you a prisoner?" The man waited, then cried, "Answer me. Tell me what happened to you. To Aric."

"Aric's in a coffin at the back of the room," Kaell said. "Murdered, probably."

The stranger reeled as though struck. "No. That's impossible."

The door flung open. Guards rushed in. The man's torch spilled as they grabbed him. He did not bother to struggle, only boldly faced whoever entered after them.

"What does she mean? She says Aric's here. Dead."

"You, dear sister," Myranthe spoke to someone behind, "forgot to mention your bed warmer called Aric Caelan his close friend. You didn't think that made him dangerous?"

The beautiful woman from the passage took a hesitant step towards the man as though jerked by a cord. "I said he was an Isles captain."

Isles captain. Another link clicked in Kaell's mind.

"Is it true, Judith?" The man pulled free of the guards. "You told me Aric died in a fire."

"I took his heart out on an altar," Myranthe said dispassionately.

"Myranthe!" Judith cried.

"No." The man recoiled against the guards. "Judith, tell me she's lying."

Judith said nothing. At her anguished expression, at the man's distress, Kaell winced. *What have I done?*

"Judith, why? Why lie?"

"To save you pain." She snatched at the edge of his tunic. "So you wouldn't try to free him and get killed in the attempt. To save you sorrow, Pairas. I thought it a kindness."

*Pairas.* At last Kaell remembered a tournament on the Downs and the Isles man who had argued with his lord. Kaell could picture the tents, the spectators, the two women with the Isles captain who had kept their faces hidden.

Pairas shuddered in disgust. "Free him. So all this time, all the while I took pleasure with you, my lord and friend was held captive perhaps only a room away?"

Judith lifted a hand to his face. She traced his cheekbones, the shape of his jaw, the outline of his lips as though committing his features to memory. "It's broken now, isn't it?" She spoke so softly,

Kaell wondered if the words were to herself.

"Your sister murdered my lord, and you said nothing. Of course it's broken."

"Very dramatic," Myranthe said. "Should I applaud?"

"Don't you see, my love?" Judith touched his hair. "We searched for the right warrior for months. That's why my brother questioned you in that tavern."

"So even then, you intended to murder my lord."

"To restore death riders. On the next three-moon night, Aric will be reborn, Pairas. He'll serve our gods. Tell me you understand."

"Reborn, but not as he was. He will no longer be Aric."

"No," she said. "He will no longer remember who he was."

Kaell frowned. A flash of Roaran's memories tore through his mind. Ice upon stone walls, an altar, candles in tall holders. A woman holding a knife. Is that what had also happened to Aric? But Roaran still knew who he was. What was different about him?

"Aric was here, captive. And I… I…" Pairas wet his lips. "I was in your bed."

Judith reached for him. Pairas flinched. She let her hand fall to her side.

"It's a dangerous thing—vengeance," Myranthe said. "It will not be swayed or softened."

Judith swung on her. "I can fix this. In time, his anger will fade."

Myranthe beckoned the guards. "Imprison him here. Let him have tonight to find peace with his heathen gods. Tomorrow, hang him."

"Heathen or not, he is wellborn. So it must be the ice. His father is lord of—"

"Nothing." Pairas stopped her, his tone bitter. "Do with me as you like. Just so long as I am free of this nest of vipers."

"Look at you," Myranthe mocked. "So unafraid. How glorious you must have been when you were—whole. I did wonder idly what Judith saw in a cripple. It's not like her to fall only for a handsome face."

Even Kaell felt the force of those few words, how they stripped and demeaned. He looked at Pairas's mortified expression, and he hated Myranthe Damadar.

"Myranthe," Judith said. "He is held and unable to strike back. It is not fair."

"I can be merciful, Judith. Surrender him to the slave masters to sell. Away from here, he is no threat. Call it a kindness on my part."

"That is no kindness," Judith said.

Myranthe shrugged. "Very well. The ice. At dawn tomorrow."

They tramped out. Myranthe was last to leave. She cast Kaell a long, cool look. "I'll be back for you soon."

"Why?" He kicked the wall in frustration. "What do you want of me?"

"You're bait." Myranthe did not bother to douse the flame before she left.

PAIRAS HUDDLED WHERE the guards had dropped him.

"Pairas, listen to me," Kaell said. "Find something to use on this manacle."

"Why are you speaking like that? With that Mountains lilt."

"Because I'm not her. We're not friends or whatever you think."

Pairas laughed cynically. "I know Isles princesses are not for penniless warriors with drunken, useless fathers, no matter how quick a warrior might dance or how ready his smile, but surely you haven't forgotten what once was between us?"

"You're not chained," Kaell said. "Don't they fear you'll escape?"

"No one fears a broken warrior. Even sea roaches could catch me if I ran."

"What's a sea roach?"

He blinked in surprise. "You used to hide them under Gendrick's pillow."

"I have no time for this." Kaell thumped a fist into the wall.

"Listen hard. I'm not her. Just find me a piece of metal so we can get out of here."

"I never reproached you, Azenor, when things ended. Was it him? The man who brought you back from that snake valley? Aric and I sat up late, talking about how you changed after that. One of those breathless, heavy nights when it's too hot to sleep."

Pieces of Roaran's memory slotted in Kaell's mind. "How strange. I can guess what happened in that snake valley. I think she met *him* there. That's where it started. Her betrayal. All of it."

"What?"

"Just find me something metal."

"I don't understand any of this. Not the way you speak. Nor how you can see again. Or even why you're here." Pairas rose. "Will my knife do?"

Kaell bit off an exasperated curse. "You had a knife all this time? Give it to me."

Pairas put the blade in his hand. Kaell jiggled the lock with the tip until the manacle sprang open. He rubbed his wrist. There would be guards at the door. He must deal with them then find the sword and get back to Vraymorg.

"By The Three." Pairas caught his arm. "Azenor, where did you learn to do that?"

"For Khir's sake, I'm not her."

"I don't understand. If you're not Azenor, why do you look like her?"

"It's a long story. Once we're free, I promise I'll explain." He slid his tongue over dry lips. "What I blurted before—about Aric. I didn't know they'd kill you if you found out."

"They think I'll seek vengeance."

"Will you?"

"Yes," Pairas said.

"What did she mean about the ice?"

"It's how they execute those highborn. Tie them down in the snow. An offering to their gods. Of course, if I were still a warrior, they'd let me die in combat in the fire halls."

"Then you'd best run."

"I'm not going to run," Pairas said. "I'm going to tear out Myranthe's throat."

"No. You're not. Neither am I, at least not tonight. You'll have vengeance but not yet."

"I begin to think their hateful god indeed protects them. No ill seems to touch them."

"Or the gods merely bide their time to punish their arrogance." Kaell started for the door. He paused then turned back. "I don't know you, Pairas. But I must ask something of you."

"What?"

"I left a man trapped in a tower tomb half a day south of here. On the road to the sea. If something happens to me, I don't want him to die of thirst."

"Judith says there are tombs scattered through the valley but only one that close." Pairas frowned. "But we're going to escape. Both of us. Aren't we?"

"I must recover a sword. Do you know where Myranthe's rooms are?"

Guards spun as he kicked down the door. Kaell sprang at the first. The man fell hard beneath him, his half-drawn blade clattering on stone.

Kaell rose fast as a second thrust with steel. He weaved aside, caught the man's wrist to force the sword down, and kneed his belly. The guard's breath whooshed out. Kaell fisted his hair to yank his head up then slogged him. The man dropped.

The other crawled for his blade. Kaell kicked him in the jaw.

"By The Three." Pairas whistled. "Maybe you aren't Azenor after all."

"Myranthe's rooms?"

He pointed down a corridor. "That way. The door is carved with symbols."

Kaell grabbed a sword. "Then you go the other way. Get out of this city. Find my lord."

"Your lord? Who is this lord? Who are you?"

"Another time, Pairas. We'll sit about a fire, drink Cahirean wine, and talk it all out."

"If I get out of here. I'm not what I was."

Kaell clasped his shoulder. "My lord always told me a good warrior uses his weaknesses."

Pairas smiled faintly as if a memory sparked. He touched his brow. Kaell listened to his steps fade then followed the passage to a door covered in sigils.

No guards prowled outside. The door, surprisingly, opened at his touch. Cautiously, he pushed inside. From the benches crowded with bottles, jars, roots, even bones, the herbs strung from rafters—the manacles struck in stone—a witch's lair indeed.

Bedsprings creaked. He whipped about. Myranthe appeared on the threshold to an inner room, a candleholder in her hand. She wore a long woollen shift, her feet bare.

Kaell levelled the sword. "Don't move. I want something, and once I have it, I'll go. There need not be more trouble between us."

"What do you seek, Kaell?" Myranthe showed no alarm, only curiosity. "Is this why you came to these caverns? To find something? Tell me what it is, and I may give it to you."

"It must be here." Kaell whirled. "Where would you hide it?"

"Something big? Something small? Shall I guess? So much simpler if you tell me."

"A sword. My lord's sword."

Her candle's flame caught the glitter in her hard, dark eyes. "Val Arques asked about that sword too. More than once."

"Where is it?"

Myranthe nodded behind her. "In there. I promise I won't move."

Kaell edged past into a suffocatingly warm bedchamber. Embers glowed in a hearth. Their light licked at chests, tables, a mirror, at an enormous rug covering slabs of grey stone.

At the sword. His sword. Laid out upon the undisturbed bed.

A flicker of alarm killed his breath. She hadn't been asleep. She had been… waiting for him.

Kaell dumped the guard's weapon and shoved the Seithin blade into his belt. For a moment, his fingers lingered on its cool, pale steel. So exquisitely dangerous. Yet its weight was familiar and comforting against his body.

He returned quickly to the outer chamber, expecting Myranthe to be gone. She wasn't. But she stood between him and the door.

"I thought you'd come for this," Myranthe said, her smile sly. "The sword that changed you. Such perilous blood magic. Only one man could master such a spell. At last, I understand what will draw him back to the Icelands after all these centuries. It's you, Kaell."

"Get out of my way."

"I can't let you leave. You're the final piece in fate's puzzle. My visions show *he's* coming for you."

"Move aside."

"Where do you think you might go? You don't just get to walk out of these caverns."

"I'm going to find my lord."

"He's on a ship a long way from here. Probably in chains. Beyond your reach, Kaell."

Kaell relished a moment of pleasure at outwitting her, in this at least.

"No. He's not. I freed him from the Quisnaf."

Something flickered in her eyes—alarm? Surprise?—and was quickly concealed.

"Velleran will be displeased." She pressed a finger to her lips. "Val Arques will no doubt seek to rescue you. I'll deal with him once I've dealt with you."

Her hand shot out. Kaell's strength leached away. All of it, at once. He crumpled.

Myranthe bent over him. "You didn't wonder why I left my door open, Kaell? I needed to be sure about that sword. Thank you for confirming what it is."

Unable to move, he could only watch as she dug fingers into his skin. Through his ribs. To squeeze his heart. Kaell jerked in agony. Then he spiralled into blackness.

Guards hauled him by the arms up a tower stairwell. He could not control his limbs or even shape a thought. His bruised knees scraped over stone.

Myranthe waited at the top. At her gesture, the guards carried Kaell through a doorway and dumped him like a discarded robe in a dark, circular room. Light from a single candle fell on grimy stone walls, tattered rugs, and cobwebs.

A chair creaked as an old woman leaned forward, wrinkled hands spread upon her knees. She looked as shabby as the room, with a tangle of white hair, a stained gown, and dirty feet. "At last," she said, her smile childish. "The Seithin boy trapped in a woman's form. He shall satisfy my appetite."

*Appetite?* "Who—" Kaell's voice was barely a whisper. "Who are you?"

Myranthe waved a hand. "*What* she is would be a better question. Kaell, meet my mother."

Mother. Another witch. Or a sorceress. Kaell desperately struggled to his hands and knees. He tried to crawl.

Myranthe snapped a command. As if lifted by wind, he slammed against a wall. A force pinned him to stone. Helpless.

Myranthe staggered, her face drawn with pain. She thrust a hand to the door.

The old woman jeered, "You're weak. Even simple spells hurt you."

"I had to use powerful enchantments to find him. Roaran."

That was who she'd meant before. He was bait for Roaran.

"He's near." Myranthe's voice dropped to a satisfied growl. "Soon, the gods will have their due—their wayward death rider returned. Enslaved. Obedient. How I long to place that collar around his lovely neck. To see those bladesman's shoulders stooped in defeat."

"It should have been me," the old woman muttered. "You don't deserve it."

Myranthe smiled in contempt. "The gods did not judge you worthy, old woman. You're good only for one thing. To keep this one safe. Roaran is coming for him."

"No need to be nasty." The old woman stretched a gnarled hand towards Kaell. "Child, come to me."

Kaell fell forward onto his elbows. An insidious murmur picked up in his head. It compelled him to move. Desperately, he dug his knees into the floor.

"I like him, Myranthe," the woman said. "So stubborn. He'll survive longer than the others." She uncurled a hand. "Come here, child."

Kaell could no longer resist that voice, its urging. With a frustrated cry, he crawled to the witch and collapsed at her unwashed feet, choking on the doughy stench of her soiled gown.

Myranthe sighed. "Such a waste. Seithin blood. If the Quisnaf consider Val's Caelan blood valuable, what might they pay for this remarkable boy?"

Her mother paid no heed. She seized Kaell's head between her palms and pressed fingers along his temples, her skin as dry as a clay pot, dirt beneath her stained, broken nails.

She squeezed. Pain spiked his skull. Kaell screamed. He uselessly tried to jerk back. The woman dropped him. Kaell slumped against her knees, his will and strength drained.

"Such a precious thing." She patted his damp hair. "Ghoul and Seithin blood."

"Be careful with him," Myranthe said. "Do not take too much at once. I need him alive until Roaran is drawn into my trap. After that, I do not care."

"With his ghoul blood, he'll last many days." The witch still fondled Kaell's hair. "When I am sated, I'll give you what you want, Myranthe. Enough power to awaken our death riders."

"What did she do to me?" Kaell lifted his head to Myranthe. "I can hardly move."

"She's taking your strength to feed her magic. Don't be afraid. It's unpleasant, but you won't suffer for long. No one lasts more than a few days."

"I'm not afraid."

Myranthe slid hands to hips, her smile savage. "Oh, Kaell, of course you are."

# VAL ARQUES

Val heaved against the stone keeping him from Kaell. He shoved and thumped his fists until his knuckles bled, shouting to summon every ounce of strength. But no matter how hard he struggled, no matter how much sweat ribboned off his face, the lid stayed put.

Exhausted, he sprawled on his back, still trapped. Kaell had been gone a day and a night. If he'd fallen into Myranthe's clutches, then even the gods could not help him.

A boot scuffed stone. *Kaell? Let it be Kaell.*

"Hello?" a man called out.

Val didn't have the luxury of caring if whoever was there might not be friendly. "I'm here," he yelled. "Help."

The lid scraped an inch. With a crash, it toppled to the floor. A man peered in. Val stared at him with complete astonishment. Flashes of memory came to him: dull sunlight on steel, the odours of charred meat and stale wine at that Downs tournament where Rozenn sent three assassins after Kaell. How could the Isles captain who'd aided them be in a tower tomb in the Icelands?

"By The Three." Pairas blenched. "I know you. You're Vraymorg."

Val clambered out. "Get these cursed ropes off me." Once

Pairas freed him, he stretched stiff muscles. "I have to go."

"Hold up a bit, Vraymorg." Pairas blocked him.

"It's not Vraymorg," Val said irritably. "I'm no longer Lord of the Mountains." He heaved a breath. "Look, Pairas. I don't know how it's possible you're here, but I have no time for explanations. Please get out of my way. I've got to get to the Damadar cities quickly."

Pairas didn't move. "To find a girl who looks like Azenor but says she's not?"

"What do you know about this girl?" Val grabbed Pairas's arm. "Is she safe? Tell me she's safe."

"She went in search of a sword in Myranthe Damadar's rooms. In case something happened there, she wanted me to find you so you didn't die of thirst. That's why I'm here."

*In case something happened…* "Explain," Val demanded.

Pairas passed him a new waterskin. "First, drink so you don't actually die of thirst. Second, *you* have some explaining to do, too, Vraymorg. Judith said Velleran sold you. Now you're in this place, entombed in the middle of nowhere."

"Judith?"

The Isles man looked at his boots. "She owns me, apparently. Or she did. Now they intend to execute me because I learnt they murdered Aric."

"I can't do this now," Val said. "I have to go back."

"To get this girl? Who is she? Why does she look like Azenor?"

"Kaell," Val said abruptly. "It's Kaell."

"What?"

"It's Kaell."

The man spluttered, aghast. He entwined his fingers on the crown of his head. "What are you saying? This doesn't make any sense."

"Maybe not, but it's true. He looks like Azenor, but it's Kaell."

Pairas made a confused sound.

Val swigged from the skin. From the light, he would have to

walk through the night, in the cold, to get to Kaell. A miserable journey.

"This can't be right." Pairas spread his arms. "I mean—she—he—certainly didn't fight like any woman I've met who wasn't Quisnaf, but what you're saying is—" He stopped, frowning. "How?"

"It's a long story. All to do with magic. I'd like to tell it, but I have to get to him."

"How am I supposed to believe this? It's incredible."

"Believe what you like," Val said. "I'm speaking the truth."

"For how long?" Pairas shook his head, bewildered. "What sort of magic?"

"I have to go. If you're here, and he's not, the fool boy is in trouble."

Pairas grasped his elbow. "Judith told me a little of what they did to you. About her sister's cruel games. You can't go back to the Damadar caverns, Vraymorg."

"It's Val Arques." Val pushed off his grip. "And I must. Kaell is all that matters."

Pairas rubbed a bristled chin. "It's madness. By some good fortune, we're both free. That sort of luck doesn't hit twice. Go back, and Myranthe will take you prisoner."

"Maybe. Maybe not." He started for the door then stopped. He passed a hand over his brow, sighing. "I'm grateful you freed me. At daybreak tomorrow, head southeast, towards the Cauldron. With luck, you'll find a ship to take you back to the Isles." Val walked to the doors and flung them open. The cold air knifed his scalp.

The light had dimmed to washed-out grey. The air even smelled grey. He pulled his cloak tight, steeling his will to return to the prison he swore only two days ago never to think upon again.

"Wait." Pairas started after him. "Kaell helped me escape. I owe him my life."

"You're not coming if that's what you're leading up to."

"I don't want to go back." Pairas trailed Val outside. "But I think I have to. They murdered my lord. I can't just get on a ship for the Isles if Kaell's in Myranthe's clutches. Not after he saved me. Don't ask me to just do nothing."

"You don't understand. We're pawns, you and I, in a deadly tussle of gods and power and magic. Myranthe will sweep us aside without a thought. She cares only for the real game. The one that begins when Roaran Caelan returns to the Icelands for the first time in centuries."

"Stop." Pairas threw up his hand. "Did you say Roaran Caelan? But that's impossible. What is going on here?"

"A bloody game to seize all of Telor."

"Oh, is that all?" Pairas laughed shortly as he fell in beside Val. "Nothing important then. You'd best explain. We've a long walk ahead."

"A story for the road," Val said without smiling, repeating Matilda's words. The Quisnaf warriors were still hunting him. *One problem at a time.*

❧

Slanted sheets of rain iced his skin as he trudged towards the walls. It pattered against the city's imposing towers and upon the drawbridge slowly juddering and clanking into place. The wind blistered across the ice-blue moat, singing a desolate dawn song.

Hat pulled down, damp wool chafing his neck, Val crossed a few steps ahead of Pairas in the tangle of farmers and merchants with their trundling, rattling carts and wagons.

The barbican barely threw a shadow in ashen light as he stepped off the bridge and walked across frozen ground towards iron gates. Ahead, vanishing into the looming mountain, the city's stone and timber buildings clustered, a bustle of people already upon the paved streets, despite the cold.

A farmer leading an ox pulling a wooden-wheeled cart bumped into him with a muttered apology. Val nodded distantly and moved around two riders.

As the crowd parted, his breath cut. Soldiers at the gates were searching drays and questioning those seeking entry. Crossbowmen lined the walls, bolts nocked.

His steps faltered, his heart loud in his rib cage. Too late to run. The bowmen would take him out on the exposed land beyond the moat.

He drew down a breath. *Do not panic. Think it through.* The Damadars weren't after him. They believed him to be on a ship for Quisnaf. *But… what if they're hunting Pairas?*

He glanced over his shoulder at his companion. Pairas caught his eye and nodded grimly towards more soldiers inside the gates, their watchful gazes passing over the flow of people. Val's heart kicked up another notch.

"Halt."

He could only walk on, head down, hoping the command was for another.

"I said, halt." A guardsman blocked him.

Blood pulsing in his skull, Val peered up beneath his hat. "Me?"

"Yes you, you deaf fool. What's your business?"

"Commerce," Val said. "I've a commission to buy slaves. For the Lord of Batan." The lord was an infirm peer of a northern Icelands fortress these men were unlikely to have met.

The guard's stare bore into him. "Move on." The man confronted a trader behind.

Val expelled a relieved breath as he stepped around. It would be all right. Now they were safely inside the city, he could work out a way into the Damadar caverns.

"Stop that man." The shout from the wall ruptured the racket of squeaking carts, mewling animals, and strident voices. Val froze in shock. Turning, he looked up towards the voice.

Griffin Damadar rushed down stairs, men-at-arms at his back.

Griffin pointed right at him. "That man," he said. "Arrest him."

Val's locked-up muscles released. He turned to flee. But the gate guards were already upon him. They grabbed his shoulders.

"Don't let him get away," Griffin said. "Or we'll all face my brother's wrath."

Val struggled, writhed, and cursed them. More men-at-arms moved in, blocking escape, driving their fists into his belly, until at last he gave up his useless resistance.

Doubled over and gasping for air, he cautiously sought Pairas, hoping he had stolen away in the confusion.

Griffin put his sword tip to Val's throat to force his head up. "You fool, Val Arques. Why come back?"

"I missed your humour, Griffin."

The young man's face darkened. "I see Heath rubbed off on you." He glanced nervously at the gathering mob. "Bring him. No fuss."

Clucking hens flapped into the air as a merchant violently fell against splintering cages. Pairas shoved a second man into a cart. Pans clattered upon flagstones. Traders in fleecy hats, farmers, wives in woollen caps, servants with pails all jostled to look.

"Val Arques," Pairas shouted. "Run."

In the chaos, Val broke free of the soldiers. He sprang at Griffin, knocked the young Ice lord down into the slush, lifted him by the tunic, and beat his face with a closed fist. "That's for that unprovoked blow in your father's rooms."

Men grappled at him. He jerked an elbow up. One tipped into his companions. They sprawled in a heap. Val scrambled clear of stacked guards. More ringed him. On the edge of his vision, he glimpsed others holding Pairas on his knees.

*No. Help him!* With a wild roar, Val slammed shoulder first into the nearest men. Two reeled back. The rest fell on him, thrust him into the ground, his cheek squashed against wet grass. Winded, Val protected his head against swinging fists, boots, and a press of bodies. He stilled so they thought him subdued. The instant they rose, he thrashed off the last few hands then lurched to his feet.

Guards surrounded him, swords drawn. Val whirled within a snare of armed figures. He yelled in frustration.

"Don't be stupid," Pairas cried. "Get away. Just—" A grunt cut short his words.

Val tackled a random guard to the ground. He leapt up, seeking a way to get to Pairas. Too many men surrounded the other man, with reinforcements on the way from the wall.

Griffin staggered into view, holding his jaw. "Take him. What are you waiting for?"

Val ran. Startled onlookers parted. The braver clutched at his sleeves. He weaved clear.

"No swords," Griffin ordered. "My brother needs him alive. Put him down but aim low."

Val glanced behind. An archer had a bowstring drawn back. Val yawed. A shaft whirred, clunking into dirt. With gasps, with startled cries, the crowd scattered.

A storm of arrows nipped about his feet as Val sprinted to the gloom beneath the city wall. One whooshed by his hip and clattered into stone. Too close.

He broke cover to dash for a crooked alley between steep-roofed shops across the street. Halfway across, he slipped on slush, fought for balance, then ducked behind a bricked well.

"There." Griffin waved his arms. "Stop him."

Keeping low, Val bolted to the shadowy laneway. More arrows zipped. One skimmed his sleeve. He hit the alley, nearly stumbling over piles of dumped ashes. Another step, and they would have no line of sight.

A whirring parted air. Pain exploded in his hamstring. The shock of it drew him up hard, his body clenched in rebellion, his mind briefly paralysed.

Blindly, Val groped at the wound. Sticky blood but no shaft. The arrow had grazed muscle. Running was too painful, but he managed a fast limp.

With a vague plan of hiding in the caverns, Val stumbled across a square into another slitted opening between closely built shops, their awnings dripping with water. Putrid scents rose off piles of rotting garbage. Charred animal bones were scattered along its length.

A dead end. Cursing, he retreated as guards burst into the square, shouting as they spied him.

Val veered right and ploughed through bald bushes into a narrow street where the wind rattled signs proclaiming merchants' names. Grunting pigs blocked his way. He waded through the herd into another muddy alley stinking of urine. Slipping again, he scrambled to his feet.

Someone grabbed his elbow. Val wheeled, arms flung up defensively.

"I'm a friend," a hooded figure said quickly. A man's voice. Low. "This way."

The guards reached the alley.

"Come with me." The stranger took off.

No time to think. Val hobbled after him. The opening narrowed so they had to turn sideways to squeeze through. The guards pursued.

The stranger pulled Val into an even tighter passageway with grimy walls, where even the dreary light faded. They were beneath rock. In the caverns.

Val drew up, hands on knees, scraping air into his burning lungs.

"We can't stop here," the man said. "They're close."

"Who are you?"

"A friend."

"I don't have friends here."

"You'd be surprised." The stranger strode on.

Val hesitated then followed. Alone, lost, he had little choice.

The passage ran parallel to busy markets. Through cuttings in the rock, canvas stalls and tents filled high-roofed caverns.

Merchants and buyers haggled. A cow bellowed. Chimes tinkled in air dense with smoke and incense from braziers. A myriad of scents flared. Spices. Spilled milk. Roasting meat. Cabbage. Tallow. Sweat.

The merchants' shouts hid the noise of their pursuers as Val limped after his rescuer deeper into the mountain. Guilty, dismayed thoughts whirled in his head. Pairas had distracted the guards so he could escape. Now the Damadars had him. He must free both Kaell and Pairas.

The stranger led him from the clamour of commerce into even gloomier tunnels. Stale air thickened. Fetid odours greased his skin.

"This way." His companion snatched up a fiery brand.

Half hidden by overhanging roof, a door broke the rock surface. At the stranger's raps, one sharp and six long, it inched open. The man beckoned to Val. "There's someone inside who'll help you save the boy."

The boy. Saving the boy was worth the risk.

Almost afraid to hope, Val followed the stranger into a stone atrium. Heat from a grated fire hit him at once. Candles churned out yellow light and the scent of beeswax. More flames burned in braziers about a large chamber, opulent even for the Icelands.

A long table with high-backed, regal chairs dominated one end, a hearth the other. For all its size, the room was bloated with dyed rugs, plump couches, lattice screens, scrolled tables, and silk wall hangings, their intricate threads like golden spiderwebs.

Men slouched on cushions before the crackling fire, some with shaped, clipped beards. They looked up. Ice men. All had the soft brown eyes and chestnut hair that betrayed centuries of blended Adorean and Icelands blood. At any other time, in any other room, Val might study their faces, wonder at their stories or whether they posed a threat.

But he at once forgot them, for a man turned from the fire. A striking man, perhaps closer to forty than thirty, a nonchalance to his stance. His raven hair fell in waves about an elegantly boned face. He lifted eyes of an indeterminate colour to Val.

A current hit him, a trembling awareness of something otherworldly.

Beside him, his rescuer pushed his hood back. Candlelight fell on dark curly hair and an unshaven face. "I watched the gates as you said," he told the raven-haired man. "Scooped this one up."

The stranger nodded. "Thank you, Nicky."

Nicky waved a hand at Val, his smile disarming. "Sit."

Val didn't. He wanted to know why he was here and who the man by the fire was.

"Sit," Nicky repeated, his smile turning harder. His fingers stole to his sword, its crested hilt naggingly familiar.

"You're wounded." The raven-haired man spoke with an Isles intonation.

Throat dry, pulse shaky, Val mumbled, "It's nothing."

The stranger leaned a shoulder to the hearth. He was long limbed, but his bulk was proportionate. Back. Breast. Arms. Thighs. All taut with muscle. Barefoot, he wore only pants and an ivory tunic, carelessly laced. Its embroidered emblem, a crown and blindfolded man, stirred a flutter of memories Val couldn't hold on to.

"Please." The Isles man gestured at cushions. "We'll talk."

He was harder to refuse. Val sat.

The stranger dropped beside him, knees drawn up. "You're not only wounded but bleeding."

"A scratch," Val said distantly. This close the man's eyes were a strange hue of blue. Nearly black. Darkness and light together. "Why am I here?"

The man poked a tong at the fire. "I'll do my best to answer not only that question but all your questions. In a way, these words should have been said centuries ago."

Unease crept at Val's neck. "Centuries?"

"You're going to do the roundabout thing again, aren't you?"

Nicky reproached the raven-haired man with a fond glance.

"I think Val Arques Caelan is a man who deserves a truth that is simple, Nicky."

"Then be direct. You said time is short. Your creature is in danger."

*Creature?* And they knew his name. "I don't understand. Any of this."

The stranger locked those blue eyes on his. "You must hear what I say, Val Arques, and accept it. We have no time for you to come slowly to the truth through debate."

Val tried to swallow, but his mouth was dry. He managed, "What truth?"

Still, the man's eyes held his, unnerving but compelling.

"I'm going to give you my name. You won't believe it. You won't want to believe it. But you simply have to because too much is at stake." The stranger dragged ringed fingers through his tousled hair. "There's no easy way to reveal this except to say it straight."

He paused. Took a breath. "I am Roaran Caelan."

Silence. A silence formed within Val too. A place where the words sat, meaningless in that void of shock. He peered into the fire, hypnotised by the flames. His thoughts dammed up then spilled in a torrent as the name and all it meant hit him.

*So it's true. The rumours. Myranthe's insistence Roaran would return.* He hadn't believed her. Not really.

*Roaran Caelan.* He repeated the name, trying to take it in. *Roaran Caelan. The seer king lives. Where has he been? Has he come to destroy Archanin?*

Nicky snorted. "He's got that dazed look, Roaran."

"It's impossible," Val muttered, afraid to accept it. "A trick."

Roaran sighed. He stretched out his arm as if to touch Val.

The world shrank to the two of them. Fire popped. Sparks scattered as a burning log rolled. A thin, cold draught slid through a crack. It nipped at Val's neck as he stared at Roaran's hand suspended between them.

The man wore a simple but exquisite silver ring engraved with whorling sigils. Val could not look away from that ring. He could not move, only watch as Roaran brought his hand closer, until he pressed calloused fingertips to the bridge of Val's nose.

His skin tingled then heated. In vain, Val tried to take control of his muscles and pull away. An intense, uncomfortable presence filled him. As if this man had taken over his thoughts, an image flashed of the towers at Tide's End, shrouded in mist. Briny wind lifted his hair as it brawled with white-capped waves and tall grass upon the headlands.

Men armed with swords or bows were with him on the cliff. He adjusted the helm covering his face, his gaze upon Wardorian ships sailing into the bay, the pennants and flags fluttering from masts the heraldry of Deminar I.

A young woman stood at his side, her eyebrows dark, her black hair knotted beneath a helmet. With a laugh, its brittle, mocking edge familiar and dear to him, she said, "Well, husband, shall we have at them? Shall we show this foul king our defiance?"

Roaran dropped his hand. Val slumped, panting. Indignant at the invasion, he snapped, "What was that? What did you do to me?"

Breath sharp, skin ashen, the other man did not reply.

Nicky frowned. "My lord?"

Roaran flicked his wrist. "Don't fuss. I'm all right." His unsettling gaze shifted once more to Val. "I'm sorry for what I just did."

Val rubbed his eyes. "I saw… ships belonging to Deminar of Wardour, Deminar the Destroyer. Then there was a woman. A stranger, but she called me husband. And I knew her. Knew."

"My queen." Roaran's voice was flat. "I took you back to a single moment in my past, to let you feel it as I did. I had to show you who I am. So you believe. At once. Kaell is in danger. I need to find him."

"Why?" Val pushed to his feet, still bewildered. "What do you want of him?"

"It's complicated."

*Complicated.* An evasive word. "That's not an answer."

Roaran shrugged. "It starts with a prophecy then becomes tangled up with who Kaell is, with his sword, and what it can do."

*Prophecy.* An unnerving, dangerous idea formed in Val's mind. *Kaell's sword…* He followed the thread back to Arn coming to his tent in the king's camp.

"Arn told me he served a prince of light with a heart as dark as Archanin's. Strange words, I'd thought. But what if Arn came to me, bid me use the sword, because *you* told him to. His lord. But that means…" He lifted his eyes to Roaran.

Roaran said nothing. He met Val's gaze unblinking.

"Oh gods." Val stepped back, resisting the thought. Resisting the ice-cold shard it drove into his breast. "That means you wanted Kaell in Azenor's body."

"Yes," Roaran said. "It was the only way. It's still the only way."

Val pressed his fists into his thighs. Anger, fear, and confusion coiled within him. "For what reason? What do you want of him?"

"Right now, I want only to save his life. Myranthe Damadar knew the moment he walked into those caverns. She threw Kaell to her mother. Her mother is deadly."

A laugh rattled loose from Val. Uncontrolled. Crazed. "And you're not?"

Too much filled his head. Too many questions. But one thing he understood clearly. Everything he had done was because Roaran had manipulated him. Manipulated Kaell. "Because of you, I struck Kaell down. Condemned him to be as he is now."

"Ever heard a man scream as the fire takes hold?" Nicky asked. "Steel is a quick end. The stake is not. You saved him that. You did the right thing."

"The right thing?" Val turned on him. "None of this is right."

"What isn't right is a fallen god returned. Or are you too thick-witted to see that?"

"There's no time for this." Roaran stepped between them.

"There's not even time for you and I to talk about the bond of family between us, Val. What matters is Kaell. I swear to you, Val Arques, I swear to you, *uncle,* once he's safe, I'll tell you everything."

Anger lumped in Val's gut. "You used me. You want Kaell for some purpose I don't yet understand. How can I trust you?"

Roaran's sigh was drawn out. "Then trust I want Kaell safe."

Val stared at him, suspicious. Uncertain about what to do, he dragged in a breath. Exhaled. Inhaled again. He wasn't ready to trust Roaran, but only Kaell mattered. Until the young man was free, he would put aside his misgivings. "How do we get to him?"

"We walk into the Damadar lair," Roaran said. "And take him."

With Roaran's words, the atmosphere changed. Men shifted uncomfortably. Some muttered.

"Roaran." Nicky's hand upon his sword hilt trembled slightly. "The prophecy. A collar of ice. I'll go for the boy. But you cannot enter those caverns."

*Prophecy. Collars of ice. What did Myranthe say? They played out a tournament of shadows. The real game was Roaran.*

He still struggled to accept that the seer king was close enough to touch. The rest—that Roaran was his brother's son—he had always accepted dispassionately, but he could never relate the Roaran of legend to the motherless boy Karolus had raised alone. By the time Roaran was born, Val had been thought dead for many years.

"Myranthe's waiting for you," Val said. "She'll enslave you. If she can."

"If she can." Roaran's smile was edged with sadness. "We go tonight. I'm counting you among our numbers, Val Arques."

"You're a seer," he said rudely. "You know my answer already."

"You're hidden from me in the Enarae, Val Arques. No seer can find the dead among the living. But I don't need a vision to know you'd give your life for Kaell. So you'll come. You'll overlook your doubts about me until we have him back."

"You're right. But it's not only Kaell I must save. There's another man."

"We're not meant to help Pairas."

Val's hands curled. "We can't just let them execute him."

"You have to trust me, Val Arques. Certain events must happen."

Val shook his head violently. "If you mean this man has to die, I don't accept it."

"That's not what I mean. Please trust me."

Trust? Not at all. If he could get to Pairas, he would. "When do we breach the witch's lair?"

"Between the second and third moon." Roaran swiped at unlikely sweat on his hairline. "Myranthe knows I'm close. But I cannot hold back because of fear for myself."

At his detached tone, Val looked harder at him. Was that a flicker of dread—quickly hidden—in Roaran's eyes? Was it possible Roaran *expected* Myranthe to take him, that he'd seen it?

He glanced at Nicky. Roaran surely hadn't told his friend the reckless path he'd chosen.

"Roaran." Nicky swung his foot back and forth into the wall. "A sorceress waits for you in those caverns. She expects you to come. If Myranthe Damadar gets that collar on your neck, there'll be no escape. Not ever. The risk is too great."

"Isn't that why they call it risk?" Roaran asked.

They called themselves a sword brotherhood—so the strangers told him in those few hours before midnight while they waited in the secret chamber. Val learnt a few names, even how this curious group had formed.

"The signal for the brotherhood's rise," said a young bearded Icelands man called Aodhan as he bandaged Val's thigh, "is a true Caelan king once more upon the throne."

He settled beside Val, keen to talk during hours empty of all but anxious anticipation.

"What do you know of him?" Val nodded at Nicky, seated near the fire.

His new companion laughed. "An Isles man from the swagger. He's closest to Roaran. Fiercely loyal. But as to who he really is?" Aodhan shrugged.

Nicky broke into song. His lusty voice and Isles accent peeled back the centuries. Val was once more in the hall at Tide's End, listening to his father's warriors boast of bloody deeds.

"When slumbering men whose dreams are sweet," Nicky sang as he polished his sword. "Fail to stir as the enemy creeps. In night's emptiness on restless seas, the gods send death with a rising breeze."

"Oh for the Isles," Val picked up the tune. "We'll dance with steel, and every enemy we'll bring to heel."

Nicky paused, hand on his blade. Even Roaran, head bent close to talk with two men, looked up. He grinned. A surprisingly unaffected grin.

Val shivered in awe. He might not trust this man's intentions, but in that moment, he wished he'd known Roaran when he ruled Telor. That he'd ridden to war beside him. That he'd heard him shout defiance at invading Wardorians.

Roaran would take up the struggle against Archanin… wouldn't he? Val could surrender the burden he'd borne for centuries and let this king lead the fight. Let *Roaran Caelan* lead the fight.

*Roaran Caelan.* A Serravan captain, trusted by his men. A king who had found his queen while a prisoner in Quisnaf, where a sorceress taught him to harness the Enarae. A king murdered by a man who had called him friend. A father torn from his son, from his foster daughter. He considered that last—Roaran as not only a king but a father.

"I forgot that version," Roaran said, his face shadowed.

"I've never heard it." Nicky turned to Val. "You have a pleasant voice. Did you sing often at Tide's End? In the old days?"

"What exactly do you mean by 'old days'? Anyway, when I was a young man in the Isles, everyone sang." Unlike in the Mountains, where warriors thought singing was unmanly. Like bathing.

"Takes offence easily, doesn't he?" Nicky resumed polishing.

Aodhan brought Val food and sat beside him.

"Tell me more of the brotherhood," Val requested between mouthfuls.

"They're scattered across Telor," the man said. "Descendants of warriors chosen by the seer king. From father to son or daughter, the word is passed down: Be ready to rise up."

"Rise up and…?"

The man shrugged. "Serve Roaran upon his return. Offer up our bodies if need be. Help him defeat this ghoul god."

They slept a little until the first moon. Not asked to take a turn at watch, Val rested his head on clasped hands, staring up at the rock ceiling. Strangeness clung to him, as if he'd left the world and wandered into a dream. There was so much to accept: the sworn brothers of a sword cell, a returned prince of Caelan.

But for all Roaran's allure, that sense of terrible purpose upon him, if this man sought to hurt Kaell, he would stop him. With that thought, he shut his eyes and fell asleep.

Aodhan shook him. "It's time."

Men roused and slid weapons into belts. Nicky handed Val a sword. He wore a new tunic but with the same insignia upon it.

"I know that badge," Val said.

"So you should." Nicky's expression shuttered. "It's the Saltman shield of arms."

"Saltman." Val shifted uncomfortably. "My protector was called Saltman. He was with me in Wardour. He—"

"Fled? It's an old story in my family. One of shame. About how this man centuries ago failed to protect his lord's son."

"He didn't abandon me. I'm sure of it. They killed him. The Mazart and his soldiers."

"Maybe." Nicky turned away.

Men grouped near the fire. Roaran stooped over a rough drawing. "This route takes us deep into the Damadar caverns." He nodded to a cowled stranger standing a little apart. "We know this, thanks to the keeper who brought us this map."

*Keeper.* Val had heard the term while a prisoner. He wondered why the man hid his face.

Roaran outlined his plan—where to expect guards, the tower where he glimpsed Kaell. "If all goes well, we'll be in and out quickly, without raising alarm."

"What have you seen?" Nicky asked quietly.

"Nothing. The Damadar caverns are shrouded. Myranthe expects me. But she won't know exactly when we're coming."

"So if the caverns are shrouded, how did you find Kaell?" Val asked.

Roaran did not look at him.

"How? If Myranthe blocks your visions, then how do you know where Kaell is?"

"You won't like this, Val Arques."

"There are a lot of things I don't like. I still need to hear them."

"All right." Pressing his palms hard into the table, Roaran sighed. "I bound Kaell to me with my blood. Not even Myranthe can stop me tracing him."

Val blinked slowly, biting down on smouldering anger. "You're right. I don't like it. Nor do I understand it, but I can't afford to care. At least not yet."

He would save Kaell. The rest must wait.

The keeper's torch bobbed at the front of the column of armed men. He led them into the mountain, through bricked passages stripped by cold of every scent. Only that single flame with its thin trail of smoke broke up turgid darkness.

"Keep close," someone said.

"Any closer, and I'll smell your armpits," a man grumbled, drawing relieved laughter.

Val squeezed past Nicky to Roaran. Torchlight gleamed on the seer king's thick, black hair. With that hair, his warrior's poise, his contained assurance, Roaran was the epitome of an Isles prince. Val badly wanted to trust the man, to believe in him. But the further they stole into the mountain and the more he turned over what he now knew, the greater his disquiet.

"Roaran—" *Your Grace? Nephew?* What should he call this man?

"I know what you want to ask, but this isn't the time, Val Arques."

"Tell me why Kaell is so important to you. You're risking a lot for one boy."

"You won't like this answer, either." Roaran didn't look at him.

"Try me."

"When Kaell's safe, I'll tell you. You have my word."

"Tell me now."

Roaran turned his head. A faint smile curved his lips. "You're hot-tempered by all accounts, Val Arques. What I say will shock you. I'll have to brace for your blow."

"Maybe I should just hit you now," Val muttered. He dropped back. Unsettled. He shoved his growing unease down. Roaran might be the only man with magic to rival Myranthe's. He needed the man's help to get to Kaell.

Nicky appeared at his shoulder. "I know what you're thinking, Val Arques."

"Is this where you warn me you'll kill me if I hurt him?"

"Anyone who wishes ill to my lord must contend with me. That's all I'll say."

Val shrugged. "My only concern is Kaell."

They left the bricked tunnels behind as their hooded guide led them into larger caverns layered in dust, where cobwebs stuck to hair and cloaks. A rat chittered in the murk. When a man screamed, Val rocked to a stop, teeth on edge, hand on his sword hilt. The sound cut off.

"Thank the gods for that," Aodhan muttered. Others laughed nervously.

"Poor creature, whoever it is," Nicky said. "Must be close to the slave caverns."

They walked on, seeing no one.

When rock closed in, men clasped sheaths against their thighs so metal didn't scrape the walls. The only sounds were their muffled steps, hushed breaths, and rustle of cloth.

At a door, their guide paused to whisper to Roaran. The seer nodded. He pressed his palm to iron and spoke what sounded like a spell. The door squeaked open.

The cowled man shone his torch into another passage. The walls were dank with age, the moist air surprisingly hot. Water burbled nearby.

"We're near the fire caves," the man said.

Val shivered. In his nightmares, he heard Heath's cry as he fell. He squeezed his eyes shut. His foot slipped on mustard-coloured lichen.

Nicky caught his arm. "Careful, old man."

A door of carved wood blocked their way. The bulkiest of the brotherhood shoved his shoulder into it. The wood splintered. They all froze, expecting a raised alarm. But the layers of stillness remained unbroken.

Steps cut into rock, slimy with moss, led up into more darkness filled with the pungent odour of damp earth and wet stone. Men groped at the walls as they crept higher, the sound of their footsteps drowned by rushing water.

The heated springs? Val's skin prickled in anticipation. They drew closer and closer to Kaell. But also closer to Myranthe.

The stairs stopped at a sheer wall of rock. Their guide walked right at it. He flattened his body sideways and slid into a hidden opening. The others followed. Val's shoulders rubbed on stone as he squeezed through the crevice.

In the cavern beyond, pools of water glistened beneath flaming torches. "I think I know where this is," Val whispered to Nicky. "We're near baths that are right below the Damadar caverns."

"Good." Nicky turned to Roaran and spoke softly. The seer nodded.

They passed through an iron door into a corridor of stone washed white by torchiers. Val shakily clutched at a wall. He didn't want to be back in these foul caverns.

A hand fell on his shoulder. Roaran slipped him that half smile. "I understand what you're feeling. I, too, hoped never to see this place again. In and out, fast. Come on."

He went ahead to speak to the torchbearer. Val's feet dragged as he followed. He almost expected to see Velleran appear or to hear Myranthe's silky voice.

"No talking," Nicky said. "Swords ready. The tower is just beyond."

The passage opened into a high, wide chamber. Just one torchier sputtered light and heat on melting ice walls. Beneath the drip, drip, metal scraped. *A blade drawn from its scabbard?*

"Someone's here," Val hissed.

Men snatched at hilts then stilled, listening. Nothing. No sound except a whisk of a solitary flame and that miserable dribble of water.

A shadow changed shape. A line of torches flared as figures

spilled into the cavern. Val had time to draw in just one breath, to brace, before armed men rushed them in a chaos of swinging blades, battle cries, and trampling feet.

Roaran put down two men, his sword a flash of bright steel. "Don't do this," he shouted. "I don't want to kill—" More came at him.

Enraged, Nicky yelled as he hacked and cut. Men shrieked in pain. Torchlight, too bright after the gloom, splashed on blades as carelessly as blood splashed on stone. Val dropped to one knee to thrust at a surging figure. The skewered man screamed. Val flung the body off his sword and sprang up in time to block a hefty blow.

As his riposte speared ribs, their guide abandoned his torch and threw off his cowled cloak. His tunic blazed with a Damadar badge, his face familiar from the king's camp. Dillon. Heath's cousin. If the man was pretending to be one of the brotherhood, that meant—

His breath stalled.

Val had scarcely recovered from that shock when Aodhan slashed at Nicky. His thoughts slammed to desperate claps.

*Betrayal.*

*Trap.*

*Outnumbered.*

"She wants them unhurt," Dillon yelled. "Ring them. Herd them to the back."

Val stabbed at an Icelands guard. Slick black blood sprayed. The crumpled man looked so broken, so pitiful that a pang of regret tightened Val's throat. Every death here was senseless, Telorians against Telorians. Not Telorians against invaders or against ghouls.

"Ring him," Dillon ordered. "Force him down."

A line of guards, shoulder to shoulder, shields jammed together, moved in.

Cold dread spiked Val's breast. He charged into the barrier of wood and rimmed iron. Guards fell on him. As a weight of shields pressed him down, Val wedged his sword above his head.

Then the pile of men on top of him broke apart. Bodies gyrated or spun away. Roaran appeared. His sword sang a merciless melody as it ripped apart flesh and bone, corpses strewn in his wake. A shadow moved with him. Grotesque. Big.

Val blinked. The light played tricks.

Roaran pulled him up. "Quick, through those far doors. I sense Kaell. He's close."

Yet more guards closed in. An endless tide of them. Fear kicked up Val's heart. The Three help them, they surely must be overwhelmed.

"You're outnumbered," Dillon yelled. "Drop your swords. Get on your knees."

Roaran lacerated another man, that same shadow at his back. For a heartbeat, no more, torchlight etched wings on walls.

Val gaped. His sword arm wilted as he paused, not understanding. Surely he glimpsed a shape extended from Roaran, part of him. But not the shape of a man. No, not at all.

He dodged a stabbing blade and careened towards the far doors as Roaran shredded a guard's belly. Fingers spread, the dying man groped at spilled entrails.

Roaran turned. The shadow moved with him. "Nicky," he shouted. "This way."

Another of the brotherhood leapt at Roaran, bellowing. The seer whipped up his blade. Torchlight flashed on iron as his riposte pierced his attacker's throat. The man gurgled an awful sound and dropped in a bloody heap.

Others scrambled over his corpse to get at Roaran as he backed up fast to join Val at the doors. Nicky fought his way to them. They hit a passage, guards on their heels.

"Tower," Roaran panted. Men charged after them. At the bottom of a staircase, a sentry baulked in terror. Nicky clouted him in the head with his hilt. He dropped.

Val followed Roaran and Nicky up the winding stairs.

Footsteps thumped behind. Shouts carried up the well. "Up here. They're trapped."

Nicky crashed through a door at the top. A rocking chair creaked as a white-haired woman rose. Hands raised, she moved between them and a figure slouched in a corner.

*Kaell.*

Val pushed her aside and ran to Kaell. "Thank The Three." He dropped to embrace him.

Kaell blinked at him in astonishment. "My lord. You? Here?" The words came out in barely a whisper, his voice too thin. "I dreamt you came for me."

"Of course I would come for you. I'll always come for you." Val held back the fear-fuelled rebuke. *I told you this place was dangerous. Why didn't you listen?*

"Get away from him." The white-haired woman clawed at Val. "He's mine. Mine."

Val poked his sword. "Back." He drew Kaell to his breast. "What did she do to you?"

"My lord." Kaell's stare fell over his shoulder. Val swivelled his head. Arm extended, the old woman chanted.

*Another cursed witch.* Val braced for pain. It didn't come. Instead, she shrieked and skidded across the floor into the rocking chair.

Hands on hips, Roaran laughed savagely. "Two can play at that sort of nonsense."

Voices swelled outside. Boots pounded stone. Nicky dragged the woman's bed across filthy slabs to wedge the door. Blood pooled on his tunic.

Aching with exhaustion and helplessness, Val held Kaell to his breast. Three against too many. Trapped.

"How is he?" Roaran set a lamp from the table down on the floor beside Val.

"Weak. Passed out just now. A blessing, probably. What has she done to him?"

"The witch is draining his life force." Roaran wrapped cloth about a gashed arm. "It's a particularly unpleasant way to fire up magic. I should have killed her."

Nicky looked through a gap in the ruined door then recoiled from a thrust blade.

A woman said, "I wish to talk to him. I wish to talk to Roaran Caelan."

*Myranthe.* Val's jolt of distaste sparked to fury, to a senseless urge to kick down the door and confront her. As if that could kill his shame.

Roaran drew very still. "What do you want, Myranthe Damadar?"

At his words, Val imagined her smug triumph, that sickening gleam in her eyes.

"I've been waiting for you." Her voice was dark and low with satisfaction. "Seer."

An axe crashed into wood. Guards tore away splintered timber.

Myranthe stood framed in what was left of the door. Her gaze passed over each of them then stopped on Roaran. The silence exposed her quick, uneven breaths.

Lips slightly parted, the faintest tremor in the hand clasping her gown, she studied him as she might assess an intricate jewel of inestimable value. Then, as though deciding to put aside what could be properly enjoyed later—alone—when there was infinite time, she moved on to Val.

"Val, dear, my brother will be glad you're unharmed. He has no wish to part with that Quisnaf gold." Myranthe tilted her head to consider Nicky. "You, I don't know."

"I'm the dead man," Nicky said.

"Oh yes, you are. Mother, can you hear me? You're a sorceress. A little help."

The witch pouted. "He hurt me. He wants to take the boy. You promised me the boy."

"I want you to have him. But if you want him, you have to stop these men."

The old woman glared at Val. Her hand shot up. For a single, stunned moment, he was weightless. Then he hit an iron-studded chest. Hard. Pain jagged in his scarring back.

She turned on Nicky.

Roaran stepped between them. "Nicky, watch the door," he said, his gaze boring into the old woman's. When he whispered, Val was not sure he even spoke aloud. It could have been a murmur beneath the wind. A breath in a void.

The witch blinked, surprised. Then she blenched in terror. "No, no," she cried. "Stop."

Sweat beaded on Roaran's brow. Still, he mouthed words.

The woman shrieked, "Make him stop." She dropped to the floor, writhing. Then with a final agonised cry, she fell still.

Eyes wide, cheeks flushed, Myranthe stared at Roaran. "It is you," she breathed. "I wasn't sure until this moment."

Roaran straightened his shoulders, his face hard. "What do you want?"

Mesmerised, she could not look away.

"What do you want?"

"You." She did not smile. "I want the son of Marginet of Quisnaf. I want the son of Karolus of Telor. Surrender. Or we'll overwhelm you."

"You can try," Nicky said.

Myranthe laughed. "Oh, I like you, salt-head. Who are you, I wonder? What stone shall we put at your head when we bury you on a slope of ice?"

"A slope of ice awaits us all, witch," Nicky said, his tone careless. "When you're dead, nothing will mark your grave, and no one will care."

Roaran turned his back on her. At the window, he gripped the bars, his knuckles white.

Val staggered to Kaell. He sank to his knees and drew the young man's head onto his lap.

"My lady." Dillon hovered at Myranthe's shoulder. "We can rush them."

She threw up a hand. "I prefer not to hurt him. Be patient. He knows he's trapped."

Roaran returned to the room's centre. He sat cross-legged on the floor, sword on his thighs. His gaze fell on nothing. But his eyes were incandescent, huge, his stare frightening.

Val watched him. He could not help but watch.

"Your salt-head friend is wounded, seer." Myranthe licked her lips, her leer never moving from Roaran. "Kaell won't last until dawn. Surrender, and I will help them both."

Val fearfully touched Kaell's hair, his face. The young man's breaths wheezed. "Or maybe the three of us can fight our way out," he said.

"Val, Val, Val. You're very capable, I know that. In and out of bed." At her salacious laugh, Nicky shot him a startled look.

Val winced. How easily she needled him.

"Yet even with your skill, with the seer's death rider strength, there's no way out."

Val's breath choked. Death rider? Did that explain the black shadow and those wings? Was this the final truth about what had happened to Roaran Caelan all those centuries ago?

Impossible. Yet, it explained everything. Roaran's immortality. Myranthe's insistence she must return him to her god. Why she'd sacrificed only two warriors, not three, on that altar.

A bolt of hope tore through him. Did that mean Aric and Heath, when she woke them from death, would be like Roaran? Oh, thank the gods. Heath might be as he was.

"There is no way out." The sorceress looked at Roaran. "You, seer, know this is true."

Only broken wood separated them. But even across a vast chasm, Val would always feel her menace.

Roaran stirred. "You prepared your trap well."

"I shrouded these caverns as soon as the omens revealed you were near." Her tone was smug.

"And the brotherhood? They're sworn to me. How did you corrupt them?"

"Heath's work. He uncovered them. Arrested them. Replaced each one with guards loyal to our family. I guessed you wouldn't risk enfeebling yourself by casting your blood spell again to draw the dead into their bodies. Not when you first had to find Kaell."

Val stared at Roaran in surprise. *Draw the dead into their bodies?*

"Heath Damadar," Roaran said. "I didn't take him into account. A mistake."

"This is the end, Roaran," Myranthe said. "It is fitting, surely, that it ends where it began."

Roaran's shoulders bowed, his bunched tunic almost shredded in his closed grip. "It seems my fate has swept me up," he said quietly.

"It was always your fate to become mine."

Roaran looked at her. In that same soft tone, he said, "And if I give myself to you?"

Nicky wheeled. "Roaran, no."

"If I surrender myself? Nicky, Val Arques, Kaell—"

"I want only you, seer." Myranthe's voice rasped with elation. Her covetous gaze never moved from him. "Submit to me, and I will spare them."

"Roaran," Nicky said. "Don't do this."

Val scrambled up. "We can fight our way out of here."

Roaran dragged a hand over his eyes. "No," he said, his voice toneless. "We can't. I just let the Enarae show me what happens if we fight. Nicky dies first. You take a lot of them out, but then they have you, Val Arques." He shuddered. "I saw what she does to you—before she passes you to her brother."

"It's better to go down hard."

"You're not hearing me. You don't die. It's far worse than that."

"Then what?" Val threw up his arms. "You just submit to her? Don't do this. You have a purpose. You're the only one powerful enough to defeat Archanin."

Roaran rose. A look passed between him and Nicky. So much

in that look, yet Val could not understand it at all. Nicky nodded, his face hard.

"I will have your word, sorceress," Roaran said. "If I surrender, Val Arques Caelan, born of Tide's End in the Isles, Nicholas Saltman, also of the Isles, and Kaell, born of Seithin, once of Vraymorg, can leave the Icelands unhindered."

Myranthe watched him with undisguised glee, as if unable to believe it could be so easy. That she was about to get all she wanted.

*She should tremble,* Val thought. *She's foolish, too confident. She should fear him.*

He did. His mouth dry, his belly pitching, he could not forget the shadow at Roaran's back as the man fought. For all his glamour, the seer king was dangerous.

"Your word."

"You have my word, seer."

"Swear it," he said. "Swear it before your gods."

"I swear it before the gods of the Icelands. I swear it once, twice, thrice as one creature of magic to another. If I should break my word, the gods will punish me. So I swear it."

"How can I trust you?"

"Trust that I have no interest in them. Only you."

"No." Roaran shook his head. "It's not enough."

"Dillon." Myranthe snapped her fingers at the armed man at her side. "Your knife."

He passed it to her. The sorceress faced Roaran. She held up the blade. With two quick flicks, she cut her arms. Myranthe staggered, her face drawn with pain as blood streamed down her arms.

"You have my blood oath," she said. "The three you named and named properly before the gods"—she gave an approving nod— "will walk unhindered from here."

"Roaran, don't do this," Val said. "I know what she's capable of."

"It's the only way to save you all. She's left me no other option. Bring me Kaell."

Val sheathed his sword and carried the young man to the seer. Roaran stroked Kaell's hair. When he leaned to press his lips to Kaell's, a hush enfolded the tower. Guards watched in fascination, their restless trail of fingers over hilts, their shuffles all halted.

And Myranthe. Motionless. Never once looking away from Roaran.

Roaran straightened. "He'll recover, Val Arques."

He turned and faced her. For all his apparent calm, his dread leaked out in a single clenched fist and the tight line of his mouth.

The sorceress tongued her lips. "We are agreed."

"We are agreed," he said.


STILLNESS GATHERED IN THE TOWER. Tiers of stillness. Time paused. Waited.

Nicky tilted his sword down then stepped aside.

Nothing blocked Myranthe from her prize. Unable to speak, she gestured. Men broke apart the door. They advanced on Roaran then hesitated nervously.

Unhurried, with studied nonchalance, Roaran placed his sword on the floor. Still, they didn't move.

"He will not do anything," Myranthe cried. "Take him."

The emboldened guardsmen pounced, grabbing Roaran's arms. Val hugged Kaell as others surrounded him and Nicky. They threatened them with naked blades, but Val didn't really see them. He could feel nothing for himself in that moment. Only terror for Roaran.

"Let them go," Roaran said quietly.

Myranthe stepped through the wrecked door. She trembled with dark satisfaction.

"Let them go," he said again.

"First." Her smile was vicious. "They shall witness your humiliation."

Val shuddered. He knew how Myranthe could belittle and demean someone she had in her power, how she caught them in her snares and destroyed them.

Guards pressed Roaran to his knees. Restrained, defeated, he held his head unbowed as Dillon brought Myranthe a jewelled casket. Torchlight struck its silver.

Val shrank away. Nicky recoiled a step.

Dillon offered the casket to the sorceress. Back to Roaran, Myranthe opened the lid. She turned, ecstatic, holding a collar like those the Varee fashioned of iron for slaves. But instead of iron, Myranthe held a smooth ring of ice.

Only then did Roaran's composure fail. He bucked against imprisoning hands, a reflex.

At Roaran's panic, too much swelled in Val. Sick dread. A need for violence. And compassion. Not for a seer king with all his magic and death rider power, but for a too-human man, afraid at how he could be hurt. Afraid at what was to come.

His chest hot and tight, Val gripped Kaell hard. Roaran was about to pay an awful price for their freedom. But in some small corner of his mind, he guiltily realised he would choose to let Roaran suffer if it bought Kaell's release.

"You know what this is?" Myranthe watched his face, savouring his rising fear.

Roaran's voice caught. "I know."

She gestured. "Strip him."

Guards pulled their captive to his feet. They tore off his clothes, then forced him, naked, to kneel once more.

Kaell groaned. Val lowered him to the floor, whispering, "Hush, all is well."

"This day was written, death rider," Myranthe said. "Look at me."

Roaran lifted his eyes. His breaths were sharp and broken, his knuckles white where his fist pressed into his thigh, his nails bruising his skin. But even stripped, humbled, afraid, Roaran Caelan still looked like a king.

Myranthe wore the guise of righteous priestess, of dutiful

servant to her god. As she held the collar high, uneasy men fidgeted or stepped back.

"Welcome home, Roaran Caelan," she said. "Welcome back to your god." She placed the collar of ice about his neck.

The tower rumbled. Wind rattled through the window, a cold blast that died away at once. Air thickened like a glove, enclosing, suffocating. Stiff with menace.

Panicked guardsmen muttered and carved the air with warding sigils. Something otherworldly was rising up, rushing like a roaring tidal wave towards them. Then it hit, an anarchy of shrill sounds, acrid odours, and light-fractured darkness.

Myranthe staggered. She braced a hand against a wall. "At last… At last."

Unnaturally bright moonlight flared. The collar at Roaran's neck transformed. Pellucid ice darkened to pewter. Its brittle, frosted lacquer hardened to steel. Barbed steel.

As its hooks ripped into his throat, as his blood pulsed out, Roaran screamed, clawing at the collar. He tore at it until his fingers bled. Then his hands fell away. He sagged.

Val knew what had changed in him. For the first time, Roaran doubted himself. He'd lost hope. Despairingly, Val looked from the man kneeling in defeat to Myranthe, with her gloating smile. He could not hate her more than he did in that moment.

"My lady, what's happening?" Dillon groped for comforting steel. Even Val shivered. Only Nicky stood unmoved, his expression unknowable.

"A shifting," Myranthe said as the magic settled amidst the return of the chill scent of winter. "An acknowledgement from the gods."

"Myranthe." The old woman spluttered awake. She crawled to grab her daughter's leg. "Please. Give me what you promised. Then I'll help you revive those who sleep."

"Get off me, you old hag." Myranthe kicked her away. "I no longer need you. My precious captive will give me the strength to rouse our sleeping death riders." She snapped her fingers. "Guards, get rid of her."

They carried the old woman off.

Myranthe swept the room with a haughty gaze. It stopped on Val.

"Take your would-be son, Val," she said, her tone imperious. "Go. You, too, dead man. I swore to let you leave. But I give you fair warning: away from this city, my guards will track you down and bring you back."

"You can't." Roaran jolted against hands clamping his shoulders. "It was a blood oath sworn before the gods. Even you would not risk breaking that."

"No," she said, an odd gleam in her eyes. "I would not risk that."

Nicky nodded at Val. "Quick."

Val took Kaell's weight to support him to the door. Guards parted, their stares hostile.

Nicky paused before Myranthe. "What will you do to my lord?"

"You fear for him, dead man?" She studied his face. "You should."

"What will you do?"

"He defied the gods. They wish him disciplined then returned to them, his will surrendered. I know his mettle. It shall not be easy. But once he's in a more compliant mood, he'll tell me a story."

"The spell you used on me." Val's mouth tasted rancid. "Perhaps there's nothing shameful in his past to give you power over him."

"You don't really believe that, do you, Val Arques?" she said.

"Didn't your ancestor do enough," Nicky said. "She stole everything from him. His throne. His queen. His son. Even the peace of death. Then she corrupted the magic so that he did not forget who he was, so he was aware of what he had lost. Now you want to take more. More. Whatever he's done in the past, he doesn't deserve that."

"Yet my ancestor could not control him," Myranthe said. "He

escaped. Through the fire halls, through fire itself, according to legend. And ran. Beyond the Ice Sea, it is said."

"I know this story," Nicky said.

"I served him. Ghani-Jai," Roaran said quietly. "Every death my blade delivered is his. And he rejoiced in my skill."

Myranthe knelt. She touched fingertips to Roaran's lips as tenderly as she might a lover's. "He wants more than service. My god. Your god. He wants you, Roaran. I feel his anticipation, his hunger for your surrendered will, just as I feel your power, even bound by this collar. I shall taste that power. As my reward."

"You won't have anything of me," Roaran said.

Myranthe dropped her hand and rose. "Release him," she told the guards.

They stepped away.

"The collar enslaves your body," she said. "Let me show you. Embrace me, kiss me."

Roaran hesitated long enough to cry out in pain. Panting, he staggered up and slid his hands to the nape of her neck to draw her head close. When he kissed her, Myranthe closed her eyes, her mouth moving softly against his.

Their hips, their thighs touched. His fingers tangled in her hair. Yet Roaran's back was rigid with repugnance. Then he gasped, pulling away. He touched his bleeding lip.

"One kiss to take a little of your strength," Myranthe said. "I shall have your blood, Roaran, and its power, and how I take it can be intimate. Ahead is both pleasure and pain."

Nicky turned away. "I cannot see this."

"Run," Myranthe said. "I find you insignificant now." To her guardsmen, she ordered, "Let them pass. Do not stop them until they leave this city, then hunt them down."

Nicky shouldered through. He didn't look at Roaran.

Val lifted Kaell and helped him into the stairwell. His thoughts tumbled in a despairing mess. They couldn't leave Roaran to an unspeakable fate. But he had to get Kaell far from Myranthe.

Nicky waited at the bottom. He grasped Val's arm. "Take me to the chamber with the altar. Roaran says you know where it is."

"No. We have to get away from her."

"Don't be a fool. Myranthe Damadar is not going to let us go. She's just pulled her guards back. But the moment we leave this tower, she'll send one hundred, maybe two hundred, men after us."

"She swore a blood oath we could leave."

"By The Three, are you really that naïve, Val Arques? She lied. Of course she lied. Do you think Myranthe Damadar, drunk on my lord's power, is frightened of the gods?" Nicky seized a calming breath. "You have to take me to that chamber. You've seen it?"

A dull pulse of dread drummed between Val's ears. A portent of what? He remembered the look Nicky and Roaran exchanged, then Nicky's almost imperceptible nod.

"I've seen it."

"It's important. Take me there."

"But Kaell. Roaran—"

"Take me."

Nicky smeared liquid from a vial on the door lock.

"What are you doing?"

"Only way into this chamber is a sorceress or sorcerer's blood," Nicky said, his face grim. "I'm using Roaran's blood. Unless you prefer to go back and ask Myranthe for hers?"

The door swung in. Val went cold. Surely a presence stirred.

Reluctantly, he helped Kaell inside and lowered him to the floor.

Nicky lit one torch after the other, as if delaying an act he did not want to do.

The cavern blazed with senseless light. It fell upon the stone altar and upon the silent caskets at the back where Aric lay. Where Heath lay entombed in stone, sword at his side. Not dead. Not sleeping. Waiting. Val would not look. He would not.

Nicky stood before a rock ledge with three glass containers upon it. "His heart. I have to destroy it."

Val's scalp crawled. "No. Don't."

"You would see him kept by her? Used by her? And not just by Myranthe, but a hundred others like her, over a hundred centuries?"

Val caught his arm. "So you'll destroy them all to make sure? I knew them. Aric, a little. Heath Damadar, more so. From what you said about how Roaran kept his memories only because of corrupted magic, I know it won't be them when they wake, not really, but don't do this."

"Get your hands off me."

"Wait." Kaell pushed to his feet. For a single moment, Val's thoughts splintered, time rolled back, and he thought it was Azenor standing there.

"Hello, dread creature," Nicky chirped without humour. "I think it best you keep your pretty but precious nose out of this."

Kaell stumbled to him. "I'll know his heart. He bound me to him by blood."

Nicky paused to consider. Then, nodding, he brought the first container to Kaell. He sniffed and shook his head. With the second, he bit his lip. Slowly he lifted his eyes to Nicky.

The Isles man held the glass to his breast. A turmoil of emotion flitted across his face. Despair. Anger, sorrow.

Val looked away. Even a glance intruded on a private, naked grief.

Boots scuffed stone slabs in the passage. Val edged the door open. Armed men stormed by.

"Find them," someone said. "They came down here. Search every room."

"Well, sweetness," Nicky said to Kaell. "Is there a song for the occasion? Our enemy about to break down the door. Our lord captured."

"Perhaps the one that goes, 'oh for the Isles.'"

Nicky managed a bitter grin. "You know, dread creature, for all your anger at what he intended, for all the wrong you think he did you, Roaran only wanted to save this land."

Kaell flushed. He nodded curtly. Val wondered what had passed between them. Another story he must get from Kaell. Later.

Nicky smashed the container on the ground. Then he did nothing; only stared as if stuck in that moment, unable to go on. Yet Val knew the world tilted. That it was about to become impossibly wretched.

Knife in hand, Nicky crouched. As his tears hit the slabbed floor, he stabbed the heart. Then again. And again. With each blow, he moaned, a sound so miserable, so bestial, Val wanted to clamp fists to his ears, to turn away. Instead, he forced himself to watch as Nicholas Saltman wept for a friend.

That brief hope that had flared when he first met Roaran faded. Now no one could stop Archanin. One by one, each region of Telor would fall.

Val threw an arm about Kaell's shoulders. There was no point to anything. Not now. Except getting Kaell to safety. Finding time to be honest with each other. Painfully, vulnerably honest. "It's all right," he said. "We'll be—"

Beneath running steps, beneath the guards' shouts, another sound drove through the whitewashed passage. It crushed every sound beneath it.

At first, Val didn't recognise it. Then he did.

A woman's scream.

Nicky gasped. He slumped near the torn heart.

"Saltman." Val knelt beside him.

Nicky was very still, his eyes closed. Val pressed fingers to his throat and found a pulse. An awful, paralysing thought took hold of him. How exactly did Roaran's blood bind the seer to Nicky? To Kaell? If Roaran died, did Kaell die too?

He whirled. Kaell had fallen to one knee, his face ashen.

"Oh gods, Kaell. What's wrong?"

Kaell swayed. Sweat broke out at his hairline. He flattened a palm against the floor to steady himself. "I felt him die. Just like I felt him die on a stone altar centuries—" He broke off, his eyes wide and staring. "My lord, there's something there."

Val peered into the gloom. At first, he wasn't aware of anything. Then a shiver tore down his back. A shape shimmered on the edge of his vision, moving towards him like a shadow. It passed through him, cold, tangible, drifting towards Nicky. It hovered over the unconscious man. Val trembled, his breath caged in his lungs.

The door crashed inward. Guards streamed in.

"Take them," Dillon said.

Icemen disarmed Val. Two went for Kaell. As they pulled him off his knees, he struggled. A guard hit him hard in the jaw. He fell back. His head hit the wall with a sharp crack.

"Kaell!" Val tried to get to him, but others seized him. They held him as he bucked and twisted.

"Bring them all," Dillon ordered.

Guards carried Nicky into the passage. Others lifted Kaell off the floor and bore him outside. The rest fell in around Val, prodding him back towards the tower. His legs moved without conscious thought, his fearful gaze upon Kaell, limp and unmoving in his captors' grips.

Their one chance to escape was gone. He didn't know how to stop what happened now. Everything was lost. That old witch would drain Kaell's life. Myranthe would torture Val until the Quisnaf retrieved their property.

A knot of men outside the top chamber, their stares spooked, broke apart to let them pass. Even Dillon's face was tight as he pushed Val through the door.

Lamplight still lit the tower room. In its centre, Myranthe knelt beside Roaran's body. An ever-spreading pool of his blood soaked the rim of her gown.

Val fixed his eyes upon blood seeping into cracks between stone so he didn't look at Roaran, at his naked, ruined body.

"They were in the forbidden chamber," Dillon said. "Just as you thought."

"He had no time to scream." Myranthe didn't seem to hear. "His chest just ripped open. Like an invisible hand drove through his spine. He gasped. Died. I need my brother." Myranthe smacked the floor with her palm. "Get him here."

Dillon barked a command. A guard took off.

"Good gods." Griffin cast Val only a cursory glance as he rushed in a few minutes later.

"Velleran," Myranthe muttered as he dropped beside her. "Where's Velleran?"

"Not back from the border," Griffin said. "I'm sorry, Myranthe. There's only me."

"Griffin. Help me, Griffin." She flung her arms about him, whimpering.

He held her. A prick of dawn skirted peaks beyond the window, clear and crisp and sharp with blustery wind. Griffin freed himself from her embrace. He rose to close the shutters.

"What will you do with us?" Val asked.

Myranthe lifted her head. She frowned as if surprised he was there.

"Please. Let Kaell go. I'll do anything you want."

Myranthe sneered. "What do I care about you or him?" She gestured to the guards. "Keep them back there. I'll settle with them soon."

The guards shoved him into a corner. Others dumped Nicky and Kaell beside him. Val pulled Kaell to his breast, holding him tight. He would not let her hurt him.

Myranthe crawled to Roaran. A first, fragile slither of sunlight crept across boards and fell upon the seer's body. Only a red ring at his neck hinted the collar had ever bound him.

"So precious." She touched his hair. "Even in death."

"How is he dead?" Griffin asked. "Your trap was perfect."

"A perfect trap," she repeated. "Yes. Perfect." Her face changed. "Oh. Oh." Fists knuckled, she surged to her feet. "I'm a fool. That look between this man"—she kicked Nicky's legs—"and Roaran. A command. Then his nod. Roaran sent him to destroy his heart. He knew I'd take him. Roaran knew."

"Yes," Val said. "I think he knew."

Her chest heaved. "Does he think he has defeated me? Me?"

"No one has won," Val said. "Only Archanin."

Myranthe's hem smeared blood as she knelt again beside Roaran. "I was so clever, seer." She brushed a tender hand down his body. "I trapped you. Do you think you've outwitted me? Not even your death will strip me of victory." For a long moment, she studied his face. Then she rose and smoothed her sodden gown. "Griffin, bring him to the window."

Her brother heaved Roaran's body onto the window ledge. He looked at her, frowning.

Myranthe said, "Throw him out."

Val knew what was below. So many times, he had peered from his prison at that ice-blue river. "No…"

"Are you certain?" Griffin's eyes rounded with horror. "This is—was a king of Telor."

"Do it. One last humiliation. Even in death, I can humble him."

"No!" Arms raised, Val lurched to the window as Griffin shoved.

The body plunged straight down into the river. A glacial tomb. Myranthe Damadar's final revenge. Roaran Caelan would lie frozen in ice, unclaimed, in an unknown grave for eternity.

Slumped beside Kaell, Val covered his eyes with his hands. Again and again, he saw Roaran fall. Heard that crack as his body hit ice. Glimpsed waves surge as the river took him.

*A petty, childish show of contempt. She didn't have to do that.*

"Oh gods, what's happened?" Nicky was groping at the wall to push himself onto his knees. His eyes were blurry. Strange. Almost different.

Val shook his head to clear it. His exhaustion and the early-morning light played tricks with his vision.

"You." Myranthe stabbed a finger at Nicky. Her hair sprayed untidily. Her eyes were puffed, her crimson-soaked gown dishevelled. "You robbed me of what was mine. Your death will be slow. I'll make your agony last months. And you, Val Arques. You'll suffer as never before."

"Myranthe." Griffin clutched at her arm. "The Quisnaf. Velleran must keep his end of the bargain. You have to surrender this man to them."

She wrenched free. "They can have him when I'm done. What's left of him."

Exhausted, Val hugged Kaell to him and surrendered to despair. He no longer cared what she did to him. He regretted only that he had nothing to bargain with to save Kaell. No plan. No hope.

Myranthe paused beside him. She brushed a hand over Kaell's hair, her smile spiteful. "Not only you but the young man you love in my power, Val. What games we can play, the three of us."

Val fiercely shook his head. "He's done nothing to you."

"I'll start with why you cut your wrists. I'll tell him your words. 'I took up the knife,' you said. 'All the while, I choked on the scent of rose oil. My mind gone.'"

"Shut up."

"I'll tell him how you offered yourself to me. About the nights I came to your bed. How you were willing. More than willing."

"Don't do this."

"What will he think of you then? The lord of the Mountains who cowered in a corner and sobbed. An Isles prince who let his captor—"

"Stop," he said, unable to take any more. "Please."

Myranthe fondled a strand of his hair between her fingers. "So pretty and so broken. Perhaps he won't think less of you. Or… perhaps he'll despise you."

*Not your weakness.* Heath's words echoed in his mind. *His weakness. Be free of it, Val.* But for all Heath's gift of words, he was not free. His shame defined him.

She would tell Kaell that he'd cut his wrists because he didn't have the courage to face what a sorcerer had done to him. Maybe Kaell would understand. Or maybe he would think less of him.

Either way, Myranthe would hurt Kaell to punish Val.

The wind bawled. It had not been so loud before, he was sure of it. Now it rattled shutters, shrill with cold. Dawn crept from the window. But it did not vanquish shadows.

Val's neck prickled. At a whisper in his ear, he jolted. A pang of horror and fear cut his breath. He knew what it must be. Except it was impossible. Unthinkable.

Like ghouls drawn to blood, his misery had drawn the spirits of the dead. The Serravan dead who came to a warrior when he fell into an abyss so dismal, his spirit so wretched that he no longer cared about right or wrong, honour or duty, or other such nonsense.

Val gripped Kaell tighter, his tether to who he was. He fought the urge to listen, refusing to let the whisper comfort and seduce him.

In the darkness, chained like a beast, he had held on to himself. When Myranthe humiliated him, when she bared his shame, still he held on. Because Kaell needed him to.

Now Roaran was dead. Icelands guards blocked any escape. Even if Myranthe surrendered him once more to the Quisnaf, she had no reason to spare Kaell or Nicky.

"I can feel them." Nicky put a hand on his arm. "The Serravan dead. Let it happen."

Val jerked his head up. Nicky's face was half in shadow. But Val's scalp tingled. Something was different about this man. His gestures, his posture, even the rhythm of Nicky's words weren't the same.

"You know?" Coldness crept down his spine. "How can you know?"

As if choosing his words carefully, Nicky hesitated before answering. "Roaran was a Serravan captain. Once, he nearly gave himself over to that rage."

Val dragged a hand through his lank hair. Something unseen brushed his skin. A breath, a murmur, warmed his neck. The spirits of the dead pressed about him, invisible but as tangible as the wind, leeching off his pain. They wanted to consume and control him, to free him from the unbearable.

How he yearned for that release, to surrender his misery. He could be their instrument, the deadly instrument that would save Kaell. All it took was a simple, muttered yes.

No! He snatched at control. Even in that crucible of self-loathing when the Mazart had broken him, even then, he had not surrendered to this darkness.

*You could have saved yourself.* Rozenn's taunt echoed in his mind. *You could have used that Serravan magic to kill him. If only you weren't afraid of its power.* Except the price of this Serravan magic was too high. Then. Now.

*Hold on. Just hold on… For what?*

"You're Serravan-trained." Nicky's manner was sombre, his mocking tone gone. "You know the power that waits just beneath this veil of what we think is real. Let the dead have you."

"You don't understand what you're asking."

"Let every dead Serravan warrior come upon you. Use their power."

"I can't give myself over to them. I can't lose control."

"Then you'll watch Kaell die."

The truth in that hit Val like a slap.

Yet even in that moment, he could have chosen a different path and beaten back the voices. He did not need to do what he did.

If only he didn't hear an echo of Heath's scream as he died on a slab. If only he didn't remember Roaran, stripped and humbled on his knees. If he didn't think of Kaell and how he had to save him. In the end, he always had to save him.

A quickening snatched at him. An offer. A promise. He no longer had defences against the summoning. No, a lie. He no longer wanted to fight it.

Myranthe whirled to face him, frowning. "What's there? There's someone there." Her surprise fell away to pure terror. "No. No." She whipped up her arms. "You cannot. You wouldn't dare use that Serravan spell."

Val hardly heard her. He concentrated only on one word he'd sworn he would never say. Willingly, he embraced darkness that must scar and destroy him.

"Yes."

Nothing. Just a murmur within the cadences of silence. As insubstantial as distant leaves scuttling in wind.

Then an exquisite pain exploded in him. A fierce joy. The dead poured into him, spirit into flesh. Banishing his weariness, his doubt and despair.

"Look after Kaell," he bid Nicky, knowing in a few heartbeats, he would be unable to speak.

"No!" Palms raised as if to fend him off, Myranthe took a step back. "You fool. Oh, you fool." Then she whirled and ran.

Val did not want to let her go, but too much was changing inside him. A haze misted behind his eyes. His flesh burned with terrible purpose. Invincibility.

*What am I doing? Stop this.* He struggled against the building rage.

Too late. The need for violence was rising in him. Then he was lost to it, his body and mind craving only bloodthirsty release. Thought blurred to pulses only. His anger. His body. Their strength. The strength of the dead. A need to kill. To protect. A need for vengeance.

He pushed to his feet. Nicky pulled Kaell towards the door, out of his way. Griffin stepped into Val's path, jabbing. Steel pierced Val's shoulder. He laughed coldly. There was no pain. No fear. Only rage. He tore the blade from Griffin's hand then drove his elbow up into the man's face. Griffin went down hard. That Val didn't kill him was his last act of control.

Guardsmen ran at him. His new sword rose and fell, rose and fell. Light splashed off iron. Blood splattered his clothes. He walked through the doorway, the blade a scythe in a field of flesh. Men on the stairs fell, whimpering and pleading.

Nicky trailed behind, supporting Kaell with one hand, carrying naked steel in the other. Both of them were fragments on the rim of Val's reality. Not part of him. He belonged to something much darker, his frightening skill harnessed and targeted. Shaped.

Guards died in cascading blood, in chards of bone and mashed innards. A wounded man sobbed for a sweetheart. It should have moved Val to pity. But the warrior who had tethered his body to the dead felt no compassion or softness. Val cut off the man's head. A black splash tarred the walls.

A shape crawled from his path. Val plunged steel into a spine, impaling a man to stone. He tore out the blade, swiped his eyes, shook sweat from hair, and killed again.

No need to think of his sword. It would do its work, shrieking, whistling, crunching, relentlessly cutting through whatever—whoever—was in his path. He could no longer stop. He didn't want to. Nor did he scream. That was what others did.

A thought flashed. *Did Roaran feel like this when he killed for his god? Was it as heady? As dreadful?* Then he thought only of how many more he could slaughter.

Still guards flooded up the stairs. Val bunted them aside, reaping death with a cold, remorseless brutality. His fury bore him into a passage. A man begged for his life. Val struck him down. Iceland guards came at him. They crumpled in gruesome heaps, limbs twitching as they died.

In his wake, Nicky laughed, the sound scornful. For an instant, Val knew a strange bond with this man who had been forced to kill his lord, how guilt and that burning need for vengeance narrowed to simple urges. *Strike out. Repay. Kill.*

Onwards, he swept through caverns like a firestorm, delivering blows that dropped men heartlessly. All his helplessness, his locked-up wrath at what he had suffered behind these whitewashed walls, roared out of him in this bloody tidal wave of death.

Yet there was a part of him locked away within that the Serravan dead could not claim, a part that shuddered at what he did, that wanted to take back his body and will and weep at how he so coldly, viciously slaughtered men.

A man came at Val, yelling with hatred. Another figure to be hewed down. He stabbed. The man parried, a heartbeat's delay in a maelstrom of butchery. Val knocked a blade aside, gripping a windpipe in the crook of his arm, ready to rip steel across the tendrils of a throat.

Griffin's frightened eyes swivelled towards him. Val hesitated. That was all it was. A break in the rhythm of killing, the feather-breath pause in his rage, and a fragment of humanity wormed into his mind.

"No," he whispered. "No more."

Shouting voices of the dead hammered at him, trying to pull him back. He struggled against them, searching his mind for memories, anything that reminded him of who he was without the rage. Val grasped at them like a drowning man desperate for air, beating back the anger.

It was no good. He could not stop himself. His sword drew back then drove forward. As steel cleaved his ribs, Griffin jerked then collapsed. His blood puddled like melted snow.

Val looked at him. His eyes, the same brown as Heath's, stared sightlessly. His hair, the same colour as Heath's, fell over his face.

"No!" The word caught in Val's lungs. The dead and their battle fever poured out like arterial spray. The haze cleared. There was only blood, soaking his clothes, his skin, his hair. Torches whipped in air clotted with terror and the stench of death.

His knees gave way. The weight of killing piled into him, all of it at once, its sickness in his gut.

More guards spilled into the chamber. Val staggered up, struggling to lift his sword. He had nothing left.

But then she came. Judith Damadar.

Impossibly weary, guilt-ridden, horrified by his callous rampage, Val wanted to fall at her feet, offer his blade, and beg her to strike him down. But some speck of innate pride propelled him to stand his ground as she waved guards back. He said, "Is Pairas dead?"

"No," she said. "Nor will I let Myranthe kill him. I've had enough. I'm going to take Pairas, and we're going to leave this place."

"We're leaving too."

Judith looked from his bloodied sword, to Kaell, to Nicky, and then to Val's face. "You should," she said. "And never come back."

⁓⁑⁓

They reached the tower tomb at dusk.

"They'll hunt us," Nicky said. He hadn't said much else. His hood up, his movements awkward, he seemed lost in thought. "*She'll* hunt us."

Val wasn't so sure. They had left behind misery and disorder in the Icelands cavern.

He sank down inside the stone tower, his head in cradled hands. Emptied. That vengeful rage had drained, scarred, and broken him in ways he could not fathom.

Val's Serravan weapons masters long ago had warned those who surrendered to this darkness that it was a deception. Not a gift from the battle god Khir. A curse.

He kneaded his temples, wondering what to do now. Roaran

was dead. Who could stand against Archanin? Telor would be enslaved, its people mesmerised by their new god, with no one to take up the fight or reveal the truth about Archanin until it was too late.

Kaell dropped at his side, back to a stone wall. Neither spoke.

"We still don't have the sword," Val said finally. "Without it, I don't know how to change things, fix what I've done to you." Helplessness bowed his shoulders. So much had been lost. He didn't know how to go forward. Or even where.

Take Kaell and sail beyond the Ice Sea? Run from Archanin, from Myranthe. Or stay and fight a war he no longer understood how to win.

He threw an arm about Kaell's shoulders. They were together. He would sort it out. *Except…* Val bit his bottom lip. *What if the rage takes over again? If I hurt Kaell?*

"What happened back there?" Kaell asked. "To you."

"Something bad." Val himself wasn't sure what he was now. A killer. There was no honour about what he'd done. Nothing brave. "I don't know if it's safe to be around me."

"What?"

"What I did, it wasn't right. I was like a beast. You can't be around me, Kaell."

"Don't," Kaell said. "Don't do that. Please."

"Kaell, I—"

The young man clasped his knees tightly. "You're pushing me away. Why?"

"Kaell—"

"No." Kaell's face crumpled. "You don't do that, my lord. You don't get to push me away."

"He's right, you know." Nicky shoved a shoulder to the doorframe. He held a knife with a curved ivory handle. There was something in the way he handled it, lovingly, carefully, his fingers lightly brushing its hilt, that stirred a memory in Val. But he could not follow its trail. "Why do you push him away? Because you're afraid?"

*Afraid to love? Yes.* The terror of it simmered. Always there. But that terrible day when Kaell was to die, he had laid himself open. It was too late to guard his heart again.

"I just released a blood rage I swore I'd never surrender to. I don't know what it means, Nicholas Saltman. I feel different, but how?"

"You did what you had to." Nicky slapped the flat of the knife against his palm.

"But what if it comes upon me, and I can't clamp it down?" What if he lost control and hurt Kaell?

"You're in control, Val Arques. My father always said you were the most controlled man he ever knew. Even as a boy, you were in complete command of yourself."

Val glanced up quickly. He began to shake. "What did you say?"

"I think you heard."

It couldn't be true. It just couldn't. He jammed together what had bothered him for the past few hours. Nicky's ungainly walk—as if he were unfamiliar with his own body. The absence of Nicky's customary caustic humour. The way he kept his face shadowed as if to hide something he wasn't yet ready to reveal…

Like dark-blue eyes. The blue of a man half of the Isles, half of Quisnaf. The blue of a king, a seer, his brother Karolus's son.

Val pushed to his feet and stood staring in shock at the other man. "You're not Nicky Saltman."

"No."

"You're Roaran Caelan."

Roaran did not look away. "Yes."

Val recoiled, hands raised as if to push the truth away. Impossible.

"It *is* you," Kaell breathed, his expression not of fear, but of wonder. "Roaran. You tricked her."

"I tricked her." Roaran nodded. "It was a desperate risk. Nicky didn't know. Not at first. He had to be genuinely afraid for me, or she would have guessed I had something planned. Something desperate and dangerous."

"Where's Nicky?" Val demanded. He'd killed those men for nothing. Roaran wasn't dead. The seer could have used magic to get them out of the caverns.

"You're angry. Don't be," Roaran said. "Nicky's here. It's like he's sleeping. It's only until we retrieve my body from the river."

That did nothing to appease Val's disquiet. Roaran had no right to just possess another's body. "I just did something horrendous because I thought you were dead. Because I thought I had no other way to save Kaell."

"You did save Kaell," Roaran said. "I couldn't do it. Myranthe took too much from me for powerful magic. If you hadn't done what you did, we'd all be at her mercy still."

"All that death. Oh, gods help me. That rage possessed me, took me over. I wasn't human."

"Hold on to that rage," Roaran said. "Use it. Turn that rage towards destroying Archanin."

"What?" Coldness wormed its way down Val's spine. He stared at Roaran with growing horror. "You let me do that deliberately. You wanted me to give in to the darkness. Maybe you even cast a spell to *make* it happen."

Roaran's face was hard and unwavering. "The rage was already there, Val Arques. It's been there for centuries. That magic just gave it a release. A focus."

"What have you done to me?" Val cried. "What have you made me?"

"I did nothing to you. That anger was always part of you. Admit it, Val Arques. Part of you liked the killing. Liked the brutality of it all."

"You don't care about anyone, do you?" Val said. "We're just here to be manipulated and used up by you. Whatever it takes, Roaran, is that it? You'll sacrifice whatever or whoever you have to for the sake of your nebulous duty."

"You think stopping Archanin is nebulous? Yes, you're right,

Val Arques. I'm prepared to let a few suffer to save the many. To save thousands. To save a kingdom."

"All this deception." Val dragged his hands down his face. "For what? What happens now?"

Roaran glanced at Kaell. "That depends on Kaell."

"Keep Kaell out of your plots."

"My lord, it's all right." Kaell scrambled up. He touched Val's arm.

"What's all right?"

"I can't grasp all it will mean." Kaell was looking at Roaran. "Afterwards. About my role, what you'll expect of me. But I think I understand now why it has to happen."

Val spun him by the shoulder. "Understand what? What's he want from you?"

"I'll be upstairs, Kaell," Roaran said. "Come to me when you're ready."

He walked away. In the emptiness, Val's heaved breaths hammered. Maybe Roaran was right; that anger had been with him a long while. He just hadn't wanted to look at it, to look inside at who he was.

Kaell sat again. "Can we talk? I mean really talk?"

At his bleak expression, sweat moistened Val's armpits. He dropped beside him. "I want us to talk too. There's been too much hidden between us. Too little said. Or too much, but the wrong words. I want to fix that."

Kaell stared into the murk. Moonlight shaded pillars, its pallor the hue of a starless, winter night. "I need to tell you about Roaran," he said. "About what he wants."

"Wants?" Sharp fear speared Val within.

"It was too hard to accept, too strange. Even when part of me, deep down, recognised Roaran was right, I just couldn't." Kaell took a swig from a water bottle. "But in the tower as Myranthe Damadar put that ice collar about Roaran's neck, I railed against my powerlessness. When that witch, Myranthe's mother, drained my life, I wanted to hurt her. To hurt them all. Witches, ghouls. Anything or anyone who abuses their power to take from us what they have no right to." He shrugged. "It's how you trained me, my lord. No. It's how you raised me."

Val nodded slowly. His father had taught him a good warrior did not desire to kill but desired justice, driven by outrage to do what was right.

Kaell looked him in the face. "It will be magic, only. He promises he won't touch me. But he's going to take a piece of my soul and a piece of his and—" He swallowed. "And make a child."

"What?" A tremor of shock ran through him.

"Three impossible bloodlines," Kaell said. "It had to be me. It had to be Azenor. This has to happen, my lord. Roaran intended this from the start. I must play my part."

Val surged to his feet. "No. You don't know what you're saying."

It had been right there in Rozenn's cursed book. Again and again, he had read that prophecy, afraid Kaell might be the bonded warrior who served Archanin. Yet he'd never pondered the rest, because it was impossible. Archanin must have thought the same. Or he would have killed Kaell.

"You know." Kaell rose. "You know about this prophecy."

Val groped for the wall. "I didn't see," he whispered. "I drove that sword into your breast, and I put you in Roaran's path. I believed the lie that it would save you. Instead, I threw you to him."

"It's not like that."

"You don't have to do this." He clasped Kaell's shoulders. "Magic or not, what he's asking of you is too much. If you're doing this to punish yourself for something you think you've done—"

"If I don't do what Roaran wants, Archanin will destroy us all. The prophecy says a child born of these bloodlines can stop him. I can bear that child."

"I'll take you somewhere away from him. So he can't hurt you."

Kaell pulled away. "What if I don't want to be safe? What if I want to do everything I can to defeat Archanin? I'm going to walk up those stairs, my lord."

A pounding picked up behind Val's eye sockets. The walls were closing in. If only he were back in that stone sarcophagus, unable to hear or see. Unable to breathe. All of this never said.

"You haven't thought it through," he said. "It means carrying a child, having that child. Then what? You raise that child as their *mother?* It's too strange. There has to be another way."

"This must happen," Kaell said patiently. "Otherwise, all that befell me, all I suffered is for nothing. My life means nothing."

Val shook him by the arms. "Don't you say that. Your life means everything."

"Then let me make that so," Kaell said. "If you do really love me, if it isn't just words, then say you understand."

Val's hands fell to his side. He did not look at Kaell. He walked outside.

"You abandoned me once," Kaell called after him. "Don't abandon me again, my lord. Help me get through this. Help me find the strength to do this and save Telor."

# KAELL

There was a moment when he wanted to go after his lord. To wrap his arms around the man's knees and be a child again. To let this man sort out everything Kaell couldn't understand.

"Please," he would say, without knowing what he really wanted. "Please tell me it's all right. That I will be all right."

But he wasn't a boy anymore, hugging his lord's legs to stop him leaving for battle. He would do what he thought was right. What was necessary.

Kaell ran up crumbling steps to an empty room, its walls and the roof hewed stone. Pausing at a grimy window, he flattened his palm against a ledge. Distant wind shrieked through the valley. He had made his decision. There would be no going back.

At a sound, he turned his head sharply. Roaran stood in the doorway. He didn't speak.

Kaell wet his lips. "I'm ready to destroy Archanin."

Roaran searched Kaell's face with his eyes. Then he nodded.

# DANNON

Unable to sleep, Dannon wandered along the guard walk. Pearled light bloomed between distant peaks amid the whistle and trill of birdsong. But it was yet to stretch across the empty plain towards the dead city's red stone.

It was not the first dawn he'd found himself on the walls, restless, struggling to accept how fate had swept him up and brought him to this. *This.*

Dannon passed a hand over his eyes. He could now draw back and look at his life as a whole, at how each step, unclear at the time, had led here. But he had also stepped into a chasm, with what came before and what lay ahead, sheer, impassable slopes.

A light blinked in a tower. Dannon stopped. He squinted into the darkness. A flash came again. Someone was there with a lantern.

With stealthy steps, he rounded the walk to the tower. A figure stood against the balustrade, slowly swinging a lantern both up and down and across.

At his footsteps, the figure spun. Sloana's breath caught in a small gasp.

"Who are you signalling?" Dannon said.

She didn't answer at once, only stared at him unashamedly.

He slipped his hand to the knife in his belt. "Who are you signalling?"

Sloana slowly put the lantern on the ground. "My sisters."

"Why?" Dannon growled. "To tell them to attack us?"

"No." Firmly, she shook her head. "Not us."

Air swooped in his gut as her meaning became clear. For a moment, he could not speak. Then he managed, "Why? Why now?"

Even in that blackness, he knew her eyes held on him. He could feel the intent in her watchful appraisal, as if she took pleasure in his shock.

"Because you're here. Because there were dead Varee warriors in that forest. Because they're vulnerable." She turned her head to spit. "Varee scum."

*Robert. Shahven.* Alarm pulsed through him. "I'll warn them."

Sloana's lips thinned to a sneer. "So you are Varee still."

"No," Dannon said. "No." His hand fell away from his knife hilt. He swallowed thickly. "No." This time, the word was weary. A sigh.

Sloana still watched him. "My sisters are going to finish what they started. They're going to raid that village. You can warn them if you like. Or you can do nothing."

Dannon groped at a wall. Everything was very still. The cold brushed his cheeks, but not a whisper of air stirred.

"It's time to decide, Varee Host Captain," she said. "It's time to choose a side."

# VAL ARQUES

Wind blistered his cheeks as Val drew his knees to his chest. Rain struck the tower tomb's stone below this mound. It melted his hair to his brow and chafed skin at his neck beneath damp cloth.

*My life means nothing. Help me. Make it all mean something.* He wanted to shove those words away at once, to dismiss them. Not dwell on them. Not give them power or let them worm their way into him.

But he could only think about all that had befallen Kaell. How Archanin had tortured him and hurt him in ways he did not speak of. He tried to imagine the young man's loneliness these past months, trapped in a stranger's body as a dangerously powerful man hunted him.

He thought about Roaran, too, wanting to hate him. Instead, he remembered watching Roaran in that chamber deep in the caverns, the man's gaze distant and troubled. Once more a lord, a king contemplating the unquiet seas. Doubting the future. Questioning himself.

So flawed this elegant prince of the night. This death rider. So humanly flawed.

Some drew others with their warmth. Roaran wasn't that. If

warmth was golden, then he was silver. Molten silver in moonlight. Bright. Shining. Cool.

*You abandoned me once. Don't abandon me again.*

He rose. He walked down and into the tower tomb.

Kaell leaned against a stone sarcophagus, arms folded.

Val stood helpless. "Kaell, I—"

Kaell closed the distance. He grasped Val's arms. His grip was firm, firmer than Azenor's.

"It's done." Kaell smoothed his tunic. The gesture was tiny, but something was not right about it. Nor about his steady gaze.

A chill tore through Val's body. He looked quickly to Nicky. His shoulder to the doorframe, his ankles crossed, Nicky lifted his dark eyes to meet Val's.

*Not Roaran. No longer Roaran. Then…*

He stepped closer, peering hard at Kaell. A bolt of anger and shock rocked him to the core. Blue eyes. Kaell had blue eyes.

"What have you done?" he demanded. "Wasn't stealing one body good enough for you? You dare take his? *His*?"

Roaran regarded him unblinkingly. "I would have killed Nicky if I stayed in his body much longer. Kaell has Seithin and ghoul blood. There's no risk to him. It also gives me the chance to start training this child even while in the womb."

"So you shifted bodies again? Curse you. You have no right." Senseless fury beat up in him. "Did Kaell agree to this?"

"No."

Val fisted his hands. "Where is Kaell?"

"He's in a dream, Val. He's in no pain. When the time comes, when we've recovered my body from the ice, I'll release him from this peaceful sleep."

Val turned away, stiff with rage. How dare Roaran play with others like this? Just how ruthless and dangerous was this man? How easily he sacrificed others if it served his purpose.

"This isn't right, Roaran," he fumed. "No matter the cause, we do not use others, dismiss their pain as of no consequence. Duty is no excuse for hurting others."

"All that matters, Val Arques, is defeating Archanin. I will do whatever it takes to bring him down."

"No," Val said. "You cannot defeat a tyrant by becoming tyrannical. You cannot bring down a killer if you kill unjustly. There is a right way to do things. Otherwise, victory is worthless. If you don't see that, something is wrong with you."

"There's nothing wrong with me." Roaran's voice was cold. "I see things very clearly. What it will take. The sacrifice needed to bring down a god."

Anger caught up the rest of Val's words. He turned his back, his hands curling.

Kaell's life counted. It wasn't Roaran's to toy with.

It didn't matter if Roaran had once been king of this land. It didn't matter if his magic rivalled Myranthe's, if he was the only one who could destroy Archanin.

Roaran Caelan was a ruthless man who cared only about power, who would sweep others aside without a second thought.

That made him dangerous. That made him as vile as any despot.

That made him Val's enemy.

# THE ISLES

**KING HATTON,** Lord of the Isles. His children, Gendrick, Aric and Azenor. His brother, Tomasin.

**GENDRICK CAELAN,** Hatton's eldest son and heir.

**ARIC CAELAN,** Hatton's second son and Commander of the Isles.

**AZENOR CAELAN,** Hatton's daughter, once betrothed to the Lord of the Henge, SHERRIN CROSS, and later betrothed to KING CATHMOR.

**PAIRAS MORGAN,** Aric's captain and heir to The Rock.

**AIDEN SALTMAN,** Aric's second captain.

**AINGEAR,** High Priestess to The Three, the Isles gods.

**ETHNE,** a young sorceress in service to the gods of the Isles.

# THE MOUNTAINS

**VAL ARQUES CAELAN,** the second son of Rhoslyn and Teynan Caelan. Teynan was Lord of the Isles when it was called Avanti. Val Arques became Lord of the Mountains. As custodian of the Mountains fortress Vraymorg, he is addressed as Vraymorg.

**KAELL,** the 19th warrior bonded to the ancient gods. His duty is to take up the sword against the inhuman followers of a bloodthirsty god.

**ARN TRANTER,** Kaell's captain and friend.

**OLIER,** Kaell's second captain

**EWEN,** Vraymorg's trusted servant.

**FELIX HILLBORN,** a noble of the Mountains, his brother **AALART,** a new captain at the fortress of Vraymorg.

## THE ICELANDS

**ROLLAND DAMADAR,** Lord of the Icelands.

**VELLERAN,** the son of Lord Rolland and Vivianna, princess of Adorean. Velleran is heir to the Icelands.

**HEATH,** Lord Rolland and the Mad Mother's eldest son. The Damadar enforcer, Heath is also a fire dancer whose duty is to fight in the Icelands' notorious fire halls and kill opponents as sacrifices for the gods.

**MYRANTHE,** eldest daughter of Lord Rolland and the Mad Mother.

**GRIFFIN,** younger son of Lord Rolland and the Mad Mother.

**JUDITH,** younger daughter of Lord Rolland and the Mad Mother. The Quisnaf trained Judith in the art of seduction.

## THE DOWNS

**NATE CAELMARSH,** Lord of the Downs. His daughter **ANNATISE,** his lord's sword, **PAULIN.**

# THE FALLS

**MAGLO,** Lord of The Falls.
**YVONNE,** his wife.

# THE VAREE AND THOSE WHO LIVE ACROSS THE GORGE

**DANNON BLOODTAKER,** Varee battle (or host) captain who becomes overlord.
**CONROY,** overlord of the Varee.
**THE MAGE,** the magic man and priest of the Varee.
**SHAHVEN,** a Varee boy apprenticed to the mage.
**NATASHA,** sister to Shahven and Dannon's some-time lover.
**JULIETTE,** a wood witch and healer, now an ally to Roaran Caelan.
**ROBERT,** a Varee council member who took an orphaned Dannon in.
**ELOISE,** Robert's daughter and Dannon's wife (deceased).
**SLOANA,** a warrior of the Sisters of Cyrah.
**PATRICK, TULLAN, DERRY, COLLA, ROB**, warriors of the Varee.

# CAHIR

**ROZENN,** Queen of Cahir.
**ALECC,** her son and heir.
**TARVAN BLACKSTONE,** Rozenn's captain.

# DAL-KANU

**CATHMOR,** King of Telor, once wed to **ANNATISE** of the Downs, then betrothed to **AZENOR** of the Isles.
**CAEL-CARREN,** Cathmor's uncle.
**JANAK,** Cathmor's king's sword.
**GOFFREN,** Once the king's sword, now disgraced and executed.
**BELLICENT BLACKSTONE,** the king's interrogator.

# KINGS AND WARRIORS OF OLD

**KAROLUS,** Val's younger brother who became Lord of the Isles because Val had been declared dead.
**ROARAN CAELAN,** son of Karolus of the Isles and Marginet of Quisnaf. Known as the seer king. He came to the throne upon the death of Rainer Caelan, the son of Dace Caelan.

**DEKARNE CAELAN,** a warrior of Quisnaf, Dace Caelan's daughter and Roaran's queen.

**RYOL CAELAN,** Dekarne and Roaran's son, who became Lord of the Isles after the civil war that followed Roaran's murder.

**DEVARSI CAELAN,** Rainer Caelan's daughter who became Roaran's ward when her father died in distant Quisnaf. In return for freeing Archanin from his otherworldly prison, the ghoul god helped Devarsi seize the Telorian throne from Ryol after Roaran's death.

**THE MAZART,** the Wardorian sorcerer, emperor, and tyrant who destroyed Seithin and ruled the known world until killed by Dace Caelan in the ruins of the desert city.

**DACE CAELAN,** a legendary king and bladesman, and Val's beloved cousin.

**NICKY SALTMAN,** once a warrior of the Isles, restored to life by Roaran Caelan after Nicky died saving Ryol from an assassin sent by Devarsi. He served as lord's sword to **MORGAN THE DAMNED,** ruler of The Rock, and Dekarne Caelan's bastard son.

**SABIN THE REBUILDER,** the warrior who restored Quisnaf after an earthquake nearly destroyed it when the God of Fire escaped his prison centuries ago.

**CAELAN,** the son of a Cahirean princess and the god Ghani-Jai, who established the kingdom of Telor. Known as the gormel slayer.

# THE GODS

**ARCHANIN,** God of Seithin, banished centuries ago, along with those of the Seithin who chose to follow him into exile. The other gods condemned his followers to become like him, drinkers of blood. Members of Archanin's council, called the Nobles of the Night, include **LASTENARRON, RAGGAMIRRON** and **TARTHALLON,** and the **LADY YAMA.**

**KHIR,** the god of battles. An old god of Telor.

**CYRAH,** a goddess of war worshipped by the Quisnaf and the outcast Sisters of Cyrah.

**KUTRON,** Telorian and Cahirean god of the wind and sky.

**AZAIRR,** a god of fire imprisoned deep in the earth beneath Quisnaf. With Roaran's help, Rainer Caelan killed Azairr with an arrow made of ice, only to die moments later.

**THE THREE**, the old gods of Avanti, as the Isles was once known.

# THE SWORD BROTHERHOOD

**CADAN TIERNAN**, Roaran Caelan's captain.

**GETHIN MAELSTROM**, a legendary warrior of the past.

**NEIL CULLY,** the warrior-priest who served King Rollo.

**ALEYN AIL,** the king's shield to Dashel the second.

If you love Kaell, Val, Heath, and Dannon...

If you enjoyed this book, please consider leaving a review on Amazon or Goodreads or both! I'm a new author and reviews help other readers discover the Shadow Sword series. Thank you! And watch out for the third book in the series, *The Sword Brotherhood* coming out in the first quarter of 2020.

Thank you so much to everyone who dropped me an email after reading *The 19th Bladesman*. I seriously love hearing from you, even if it's to tell me I'm really cruel to Kaell. Feel free to drop me a line at writersjhartland@gmail.com.au, on Facebook at www.facebook.com/the19thbladesman/, or at my website www.sjhartland.com. There's nothing better than talking characters!

Warm regards, Susan.

# ABOUT THE AUTHOR

S. J. Hartland is an emerging author of epic fantasy who calls the Darling Downs, Queensland, home.

She is an Australian journalist, and a former fencer, who watches too much TV, spent too many holidays wandering around obscure castles, and is obsessed with anything medieval.

*The 19th Bladesman (2018)* was her first published novel. The *Last Seer King* is the second in the Shadow Sword series, with the third, *The Sword Brotherhood,* to be released early in 2020.

Find out more about the series and the characters at www.sjhartland.com, or drop her an email at writersjhartland@gmail.com.

# ACKNOWLEDGEMENTS

Kaell, Val, and co had lots of help coming to life on the page.

To Dad, who taught me what fatherhood is all about.

Thank you to Annie, David, Annette, and Kate, who only ever encouraged me. Jenna – I hope the fire dance was what you imagined. (PS. I can't wait to introduce you to the "evil" Jenna in the fourth book.)

Thank you to my amazing, wonderful mentor Dr Kathryn Heyman of the Australian Writers Mentoring Program who taught me so much about writing and gave me the confidence to publish the series.

Many thanks to Sasha and Eleanora who patiently put up with talk about characters and publishing every Saturday.

Dear Meghan H. Thank you for reading 1800 pages, and then willingly taking on more when I shoved the first 100 pages of a new series at you. I'm so glad you didn't defriend me over Kaell.

Dear Jo, thank you for always being so ready to sort out all the dumb things I muck up on the computer.

Thank you to the wonderful team from Red Adept Editing. Your professionalism really helps take books to the next level.

And thank you to Jason and Marina from Polgarus Studio, who make everything look amazing on the page.

Printed in Great Britain
by Amazon